judy's 377?

W9-BLC-678

THE BOOK THAT EVERYONE'S TALKING ABOUT . . .

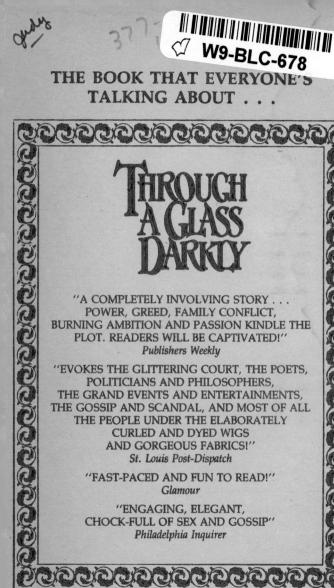

THROUGH A GLASS DARKLY

"A COMPLETELY INVOLVING STORY . . .
POWER, GREED, FAMILY CONFLICT,
BURNING AMBITION AND PASSION KINDLE THE
PLOT. READERS WILL BE CAPTIVATED!"
Publishers Weekly

"EVOKES THE GLITTERING COURT, THE POETS,
POLITICIANS AND PHILOSOPHERS,
THE GRAND EVENTS AND ENTERTAINMENTS,
THE GOSSIP AND SCANDAL, AND MOST OF ALL
THE PEOPLE UNDER THE ELABORATELY
CURLED AND DYED WIGS
AND GORGEOUS FABRICS!"
St. Louis Post-Dispatch

"FAST-PACED AND FUN TO READ!"
Glamour

"ENGAGING, ELEGANT,
CHOCK-FULL OF SEX AND GOSSIP"
Philadelphia Inquirer

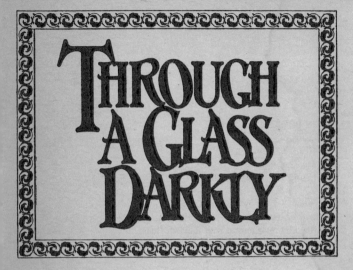

THROUGH A GLASS DARKLY

KARLEEN KOEN

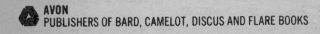

AVON
PUBLISHERS OF BARD, CAMELOT, DISCUS AND FLARE BOOKS

AVON BOOKS
A division of
The Hearst Corporation
105 Madison Avenue
New York, New York 10016

Copyright © 1986 by Karleen Koen
Front cover illustration by Teresa Fasolino
Published by arrangement with Random House, Inc.
Library of Congress Catalog Card Number: 86-422
ISBN: 0-380-70416-1

The Random House edition contains the following Library of Congress Cataloging
in Publication Data:

Koen, Karleen.
  Through a glass darkly.

  I. Title.
PS3561.O334T47   1986   813'.54   86-422

First Avon Printing: September 1987

First and foremost, to my husband, Edward,
who insisted I could write and then
supported and encouraged me.
And to my children, Blake and Samantha.
And to my stepchildren, Eddy and Scott.

ACKNOWLEDGMENTS

To Randall M. Stewart
for his professional word processing of the manuscript
and for his continuing encouragement.

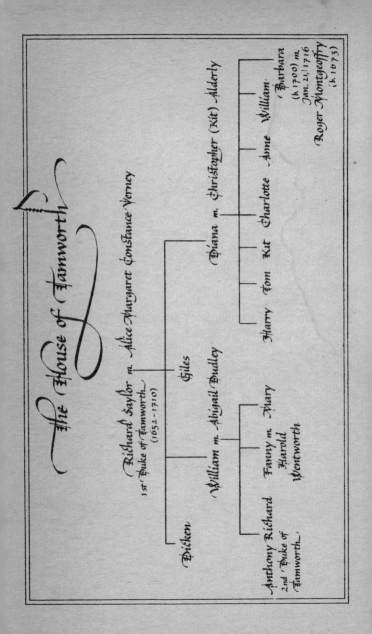

The House of Tamworth

Richard Saylor m. Alice Margaret Constance Verney
1st Duke of Tamworth
(1652–1710)

Dicken

Giles

William m. Abigail Dudley

Diana m. Christopher (Kit) Alderly

Anthony Richard
2nd Duke of
Tamworth

Fanny m. Mary
Harold
Wentworth

Harry Tom Kit Charlotte Anne William

Barbara
(b. 1700) m.
Jan. 21, 1716
Roger Montgeoffry
(b. 1673)

When I was a child, I spake as a child, I understood as a child, I thought as a child: but when I became a man, I put away childish things.

For now we see through a glass, darkly; but then face to face: now I know in part; but then shall I know even as also I am known.

And now abideth faith, hope, charity, these three; but the greatest of these is charity.

I CORINTHIANS 13:11–13

PART I

*B*EGINNINGS

ENGLAND
AND
FRANCE
1715–1716

CHAPTER ONE

*T*wo voices, raised in anger, carried through the half-opened window of the library. Recognizing them, Barbara stopped and looked for a place to hide, a place where she might listen but not be seen. Seconds later she was burrowing into the ancient ivy that crisscrossed the mellowed red-pink brick of the house. Entangled, dense, persistent, its vines as thick as her wrists in places, the ivy released the house reluctantly. Each spring it sent cunning, thin green fingers curling under the window frames and into the rooms, and each spring her grandmother calmly snipped the fingers to bits with a pair of sewing scissors and ordered the gardeners to trim it down to size. Now, in November, it clung to the house stubbornly. Already many of its glossy dark green leaves were dulled yellow-brown with cold.

"Fool! Impudent young fool!"

Her mother's voice carried clearly from the library.

"Did you imagine I would approve it? Were you going to come crawling like a whipped dog for my blessing? Blessing! I could kill you. Do you realize what you have almost done? Did you think—or has all feeling ceased, save for that hard prick between your legs?"

It was impossible to describe the effect of her mother's voice. Its usual tone was low and husky, and when anger and scorn were added, the result was numbing.

Harry muttered something, and Barbara tried to move closer to the window so that she could hear better, but the ivy

3

was tenacious. It had been there first, being as old as the house, which had been built well over a hundred years ago in the time of Elizabeth I. The house sprawled over several stories, its once modern features now considered quaint and old-fashioned: twisted chimney stacks of brick, no two of them alike; sharp, pointed gables all across the roofline; windows with many small panes of blown glass; dark, cold rooms with uneven floors; and outside, arbors of wych elm, a bowling green, fish ponds, an old garden maze. Barbara loved it, for it was both her birthplace and her home. She knew every path and pond and orchard and creaky place on the stairs. She felt safe and beloved here . . . except when her mother visited, which was fortunately not often. It was Harry who must have brought her down from London, she thought. How could she have found out? She envisioned her mother's beautiful, white face and felt foreboding for her brother.

"You are such a fool," said her mother, and her voice paralyzed with its scorn. "The match is totally unsuitable. Now more than ever. John Ashford was appalled when I told him." Harry must have made some movement—she could picture him, crouched in a chair, his face as hard and cold as their mother's, his hands clenched with the effort to hold his temper—because her mother's voice changed.

"Yes, I told him! With his daughter standing beside him to hear me. If she had not cried, like the weak, mewling child she is, her father would have beaten her. Something I would have done, at any rate. God, I wanted to strike her! As for you, your conduct is unforgivable. Any alliance we form now is crucial—as you should know better than anyone!"

Each word had the clear, harsh sound of finality. Barbara knew that Harry, always thoughtless about the future, must be stunned by their mother's sudden appearance from London, by her quick, sure, numbing action.

"Damn the family!" Harry said. "And damn you. I love her. What does it matter whom I marry? There is no scandal I could create to equal what you and my father have already begun—"

The crack of a palm sounded against flesh. Barbara's body jerked as if it were she, and not Harry, who had just been slapped.

"Do not say your father's name in my presence again."

What venom there was in those words.

"He is out of my life. As Jane is out of yours. She is to marry her cousin within a few months; already the Ashfords are packing her off to London to stay with a relative. And you are going away also, Harry. Tomorrow. A few months' stay in Italy, a visit to France, should add the polish and patience necessary to a youth of your . . . what? Impulsive? Yes. Impulsive nature. I prefer impulsive to stupid. Your face, Harry! I wish you could see it. The mention of Italy calms the ardent lover within you somewhat, does it not?" She laughed. "I thought it might."

It was always fatal to show emotion to her mother; she pounced on it and turned it against you. Her voice was fainter now; she must have moved from her position in the room. Barbara had to stand on tiptoe, straining, the ivy around her uncooperative, to hear.

"You will obey me in this. Meres will be with you until you sail, so there can be no final, romantic farewells between you and your little sweetheart. And no final surprises nine months from now, either! It is over. Accept that. It was calf love, a brief spark, the first of many, I trust. I leave you to your thoughts, my dear Harry. If you are capable of summoning any."

There was silence. Barbara wanted to go to her brother, but she knew better. He had been humiliated, quickly, ruthlessly, thoroughly, and he would not want her witnessing the aftermath. She wedged her foot on a thick ivy vine; she would climb up slightly, just enough so that she could look in the window and see him—

"Mistress Barbara!"

She jumped. Without a doubt, it was one of the serving girls calling to tell her her mother was home. Well, with any luck, she could miss her mother's visit entirely. Or, at worst, see her for a few moments tomorrow before she returned to London. She backed off the ivy, still torn between her instinct to escape and Harry.

"Mistress Barbara!"

The voice of the serving girl was closer now. Escape won hands down. She ran across the wide flagstone steps of the library terrace. She ran past her grandmother's faded rose garden, the bushes bare now, ugly with their thorns and fat

hip pods, the lush petals of summer all gone into her grandmother's potpourris and brandies and wines and remedies. She
ran past the clipped yew hedges whose dense evergreen shapes
would hide her. The woods bordered the yews; once there it
would be easy to spend the afternoon in the warm kitchen of
one of her grandmother's tenant farms, sipping tea, eating
blackberries or walnuts while the housewife baked a winter
wildplum pie and talked of the corn and barley harvest, of
recipes and children.

"Mistress Barbara!"

She doubled her speed, her cloak billowing out behind her
like a dark sail. The woods loomed ahead. She ran toward
them as if her grandfather's hunting dogs were at her heels.
It did not matter that now no one could see her from the
house. Her mother was home.

In the withdrawing chamber of the Duchess of Tamworth,
Diana, Viscountess Alderley, sank into an armchair and lifted
her feet to an old-fashioned, embroidered, silver-fringed stool
with heavy, dark, twisted legs. She was a beautiful woman
with dark hair and violet eyes and a white complexion and
sweet, red lips, all of which she emphasized to the fullest with
paint and powder and dye pot. Her looks were deceiving. She
had the stamina (and sensitivity) of a horse. All that giving
birth to eleven children had done was take away her waist,
which her stays disguised, and make deeper a hard line on
each side of her face from nose to mouth. A young girl fluttered beside her to arrange pillows behind her back, her gown
into more graceful folds. Diana waved the girl away, taking
no more notice of the maidservant than she would of an
annoying fly. She surveyed a dish of comfits (small, fat plums
preserved in sugar) on the table beside the armchair, selected
one and bit into it slowly. Some of the sticky plum juice ran
down the corners of her mouth and stained the bodice of her
gown.

Seated in a straight-backed chair, her mother, the Dowager
Duchess of Tamworth, waited impatiently. Her wrinkled
hands were folded over her cane, her eyes fixed on Diana, and
a muscle clenched now and again in her jaw. Unlike her
daughter, the Duchess had never been beautiful. Once it had
mattered, but it did no longer. Time had taken care of such

things, peeling away her youth and flesh until she was almost nothing, but in the process highlighting the strong, clean bones of her face, the sharp intelligence and will of her eyes so that now, in her sixties, she had a presence—made up of character and age and strength—that Diana, in spite of her violet eyes and beautiful face, would never know (but then character was not something Diana worried about). The Duchess watched her daughter select another comfit and eat it slowly.

"Enough, Diana," the Duchess said. She knew her daughter as she knew her own heart, and she would stand for so much, for Richard's sake, bless his departed soul, and then no more. "Send the girl from the room," she said in her gruff way.

The heavy doors creaked closed behind the girl.

"Harry." The Duchess spoke his name abruptly.

Diana licked her fingers, taking her own time with each one. The Duchess knew the action was deliberate, and so she remained impassively in her chair, even though her hand itched to pick up her cane and beat her daughter across the back with it. She and Diana had been in a struggle of wills most of their lives, and she had no intention of allowing Diana a victory at this late date. She had not expected Diana to come from London when she had written her of her suspicions about Harry and Jane. She had expected to handle it herself. So Diana's sudden appearance today had been as surprising, and as heartrending, to her as it had been to Harry. Because she knew how her daughter had handled the situation. Ruthlessly, going straight for the jugular, without one thought to anyone's feelings or needs.

"He was angry," Diana drawled. (Her voice was low and husky, as distinctive, as famous as her eyes. When she had first gone to London, years ago, as a young wife on Kit's arm, men could talk of nothing else but her beauty and her voice.) "Angry and defiant. The defiance was not difficult to handle. Now, if it had been Barbara . . ." But she veered away from where that thought would take her. "And he went from defiance to . . . acceptance. Like his father, he has no backbone."

The Duchess rose stiffly and limped to one of the leaded windows overlooking a parterre, which was a garden of box shrubs kept rigidly pruned to create an overall design. Richard had worked for over a year on that garden, laying out its pattern, an **A** surrounded on each side by an **S**, choosing the gravel, planting shrubs, directing the gardeners on how closely to clip them, interweaving masses of flowers into their pattern. It was looking unkempt. She must see to it . . . but not now. Now she must deal with Diana and this mess of Harry's—like his father perhaps, but only in some ways, and her grandson nonetheless. And Diana had a few messes of her own which must be cleaned up. Her hands clutched the intricate, golden handle of her cane.

"You hurt him," she said. It was not a question.

"Of course I hurt him! What else was I to do after you wrote me the news? Send the pair of them my compliments?" Diana did not notice the spasm of pain that crossed the Duchess's thin face, but was diverted by another thought, like the heedless, selfish person she was.

"I must say, Mother, I was surprised by Jane. To my mind, there is nothing there to catch any man, even if she and Harry have grown up together. She is quiet. And not pretty. Especially when she cries. Of course, Harry was thinking with what was between his legs. Anything could have caught him. Well, he leaves tomorrow; Meres is packing a trunk right now. I have written to Caroline Layton in Italy. Do you remember her?"

The Duchess nodded grimly.

"Harry will stay with the Laytons. They owe me a favor. And knowing Caroline as I do—she has such a weakness for young men—she will be certain to further Harry's knowledge of women." Diana laughed wickedly, her sharp little teeth glinting. "And then there will be France. Between France and Caroline, poor Jane will be nothing but a faint memory by the time six months have passed."

"You have been thorough," the Duchess said from the window. Her words were not a compliment, but Diana did not notice.

"I am always thorough. In my position, one learns to be." Her tone was bitter.

The Duchess smiled sardonically. For once Diana, clever Diana, beautiful Diana, was caught in a web she had not devised, and if the Duchess had been less personally involved, she would almost have enjoyed watching her daughter's desperate twists and turns. But she was involved—the merciful

Lord above damn Diana and Kit to the hell they both deserved. They had been foolish and reckless all their lives. Kit drank; they both gambled and lost money neither possessed; Diana went from bed to bed like a cheap Southwark whore. All of which paled beside the fact that five months ago, two steps ahead of the bailiffs sent to arrest him, Kit had fled to France. He stood accused of supporting the Stuart Pretender to the throne against England's newly crowned King George I of Hanover. Diana was liable not only for the enormous debts he left behind but also for his treasonous conduct, and she, without asking anyone, had petitioned Parliament for a divorce. It was almost unheard of; marriage was, after all, a sacred sacrament, forever binding, and people made the best of what they had. Oh, there were unofficial separations, sometimes nasty court wrangling over finances and dowers, but divorce itself was so rare, so contrary to the Lord's word, so much trouble and scandal (too much family dirt aired on both sides) that it was seldom tried. The entire family, including the young present duke, the Duchess's least favorite grandchild, "that fat, idiot spawn of Abigail's," as she referred to him, was in an uproar, tarred by his actions and divided over hers.

It galled the Duchess almost beyond bearing to think that a daughter and son-in-law of hers should so threaten the family. All those years that she and Richard had spent in loyal service—the money, the lands they had amassed—to be threatened by the whims of a feckless gambler, who could hold neither his liquor nor his mouth, and by a woman who did not know the meaning of the word "loyalty." Thank God, Richard was dead. At one time, she would have written letters to all she knew, somehow made things right with her own sheer persistence and political skill. But time and age and events (all the deaths—tearing out her heart) had left her too easily tired, too easily disgusted with the machinations of those about her. Thus, she only said bitterly, as bitterly as Diana, "The Alderleys were always fools for the Stuarts—"

She was stopped by a knock on the door. Hannah Henley, a distant cousin, entered the room. She was one of those women who are poor relations, there not having been enough money or property in her family to make her a good marriage. She lived on the Duchess's charity, repaying her by tutoring Diana's children and serving as their nursery governess. She belonged neither with the immediate family itself nor the servants, and the dependency of her position had etched bitter lines in her face. She made curtsies to both women, saying as she did so, "I am sorry, Cousin Diana, but Barbara cannot be located." She refused to call Diana anything but cousin, clinging stubbornly to the tie that they both hated.

Diana stared at her. Cousin Henley, as she was called, said quickly, "They have been looking for over an hour, but no one knows where she has gone to."

There was silence. Cousin Henley hurried into more speech. "Barbara is most difficult. She will listen to no one and runs wild half the time. I do my duty, as best I can, but—"

"Obviously your best is not good enough. You were to teach my daughter French, geography and proper deportment. You have failed in deportment, I see. Let us hope she can speak decent French." Abruptly, Diana dropped the subject of her eldest daughter. "And how do my other children do?"

Cousin Henley reported on her other charges: Harry was down from school for dueling, as Cousin Diana already knew; Tom was at Eton; little Kit had enough Latin to be ready next year; Charlotte had stitched a sampler for her mother; Anne was learning her prayers; and Baby had a cough.

Diana dismissed her, whatever motherly feelings she might possess now satisfied.

"Tell me of Barbara, Mother."

Her words caught the Duchess off guard. Her daughter had no regard for her children; she had borne them as thoughtlessly as a cat and left them as soon as she could. If anything, Barbara was the true mother of Diana's brood, in spirit, if not in body, and the Duchess herself had raised all of them here at Tamworth. This sudden interest in Barbara, her pet, boded no good. What more was there in Diana's visit than Harry?

"She has grown since last you saw her—"

"Not taller?"

"Yes, taller. She looks more like your father than ever."

"Well, perhaps it will not matter."

Diana said the words as if she were not listening to what her mother was saying, but was rapidly refiguring a balance sheet in her mind. "Is she still thin as a rail?"

The Duchess pursed her lips. Of course. Diana must be on the scent of a husband for the girl. Well, pray God the man was not blind or crippled. She put nothing past Diana when she was this desperate.

"Her bosom will fill out. She's a late bloomer, as I was. She is not yet sixteen. She will fatten up."

"Is she pretty?"

"She is not the beauty you were, Diana, but yes, she will do." Privately, she considered her granddaughter beautiful. Not with Diana's rich, dark, florid beauty but with Richard's—light, fair, angelic. His blue eyes. His red-gold hair. His sweet, heart-shaped face crowned with a smile so charming that it made you forget what you were thinking . . . ah, Richard. . . . Of course, there was also Barbara's stubbornness and pride. And her impulsiveness. And her temper. . . . She did not have her grandfather's angelic nature, only his face.

"Mother, you are not listening. I asked if she spoke French well."

"Of course she does," the Duchess said irritably. "I taught her myself. I may be buried in the country, but I can still remember the needs of a young woman of good family. So, you are planning a marriage for her, are you?" She pretended that Diana had not taken her by surprise, pretended that it was only natural that Barbara be married. As it was. The girl was fifteen. Diana had been married and with a first child on the way at sixteen. (Of course it had been against her and Richard's wishes.)

"I have an earl on the hook. Wriggling, straining against my line, but hooked, just the same. He travels to France often. And until children or boredom sets in, he would naturally want his young wife to travel with him."

The Duchess waited breathlessly. Damn Diana. This sudden announcement of marriage plans for Barbara caught her unprepared. And she did not want Diana to see it. She had thought to begin handling it herself, next year perhaps, when some of the scandal had died down. Now, with the surprise of Diana's visit, the worry over Harry and this new piece of news, her legs were aching. She could feel the ache spreading up to her hipbones. She tried to hold on to herself. It would take more than any of these irritations to make her lose her composure. She was the widow of a soldier—England's finest soldier. Her sons were dead. And in the last year, her son-in-law had proclaimed himself a traitor and her only daughter had petitioned for a divorce. What was a marriage proposal after those? Nothing. Nothing. Except that she loved Barbara. And Diana did not. Diana loved no one but herself.

"It is Roger Montgeoffry," Diana said, watching her mother to see her reaction.

Roger, thought the Duchess, surprise filling her, as his handsome face formed itself in her mind. He was an old, dear friend; he had been Richard's military aide for years, had visited whenever he could to see the dying Duke . . . even though he was dividing his time between England and Hanover, a fact that had not endeared him to the late queen, but which had paid off handsomely with a Hanoverian on the throne. An earl . . . yes, she knew Roger had been given an earldom, though she could at this moment remember none of the details. But this . . . Sweet Jesus! She was getting old to let Diana surprise her with such news. Why had no one written her? Was Diana so clever that none knew? Bah! Diana would never be cleverer than she. No matter how old and forgetful she became. Roger. A memory nudged at her mind. Something faintly disturbing. She felt unease prickle itself along the corners of her memory, but then Roger's face was before her again, smiling as only he could, and the unease evaporated. Roger was the essence of all that was charming and gallant in a man, and he knew it; he was the clever one. He was far too old, however, for Barbara . . . and yet . . . Roger smiled at her in her mind's eye . . . and yet . . .

Diana laughed, pleased with the effect of the news.

"Bah!" said the Duchess, moving to summon her tirewoman to help her to her bedchamber. "How like you to drop this on me. We will speak later. After I rest. I am tired. Too tired to think. What is Roger's title? I forget."

"He is styled the Earl Devane."

"The Earl Devane. Yes, I remember now. Well, Roger Montgeoffry has come a long way to think he can ally himself with our family. But it is interesting . . . interesting. I make you my compliments, Diana. Disgrace always brings out the survivor in you."

* * *

The dark bulk of the house, with its steep gabled roof and tall, twisted, brick chimney stacks loomed ahead in the twilight as Barbara made her way back. The wind whipped at her gown and cloak so wildly that she could scarcely walk. Candles glimmered in one of the two-story octagonal bays that decorated each side of the house, but the rest of it was dark. Supper had been eaten, and her grandmother was most likely in her bedchamber reading a book of sermons. Her mother would be in her rooms, ready for bed. With any luck, she should gain her own room in the upper stories without being seen. At the most, her grandmother would lecture her for missing supper and evening prayers, but she would tell her she had been visiting with the tenants, which would please her grandmother because seeing after one's dependents and those less fortunate was one of the duties of a gentlewoman. She laughed to herself at her cleverness in bypassing her mother today. It was more than possible she would return to London tomorrow without bothering to send for her. She had done it before. Harry had been her mission. And she had accomplished it with her usual ruthless skill. There could be nothing she would want her daughter for. She paused near a hedge, then darted down the path that crisscrossed the kitchen garden, her feet crushing some of the rosemary and chamomile and marigold that edged the paving stones. Swirling leaves, and the pungent scent of the herbs she had stepped on, followed her inside. Carefully, she crossed the hall, then ran up the back stairs to her room. Hands trembling with chill, she struck the flint and breathlessly tried to light her candle.

"Barbara . . . how enchanting to see you again."

Her mother's voice paralyzed her for a moment. She stood motionless, still holding the unlit candle. She could just make out her mother in the shadows.

"I wish to speak with you. Wash your hands, then come to my bedchamber."

Her gown whispering against the floor, Diana left the room. A serving girl immediately entered and set a bowl of water and some cloths on a table. Barbara strode over to the girl, who had been training as her personal maid and did not raise her eyes.

"You tattling slut," Barbara said coldly, her voice low and husky, unnervingly like her mother's. "You might have at least warned me. Bring some cheese and bread. I will not face my mother on an empty stomach." She shed her cloak and began to wash her face. Her hands were shaking. Her mother was cleverer, after all.

She walked slowly down the gallery. The portraits stared at her, their eyes dark and furtive, like rats', or wide and fixed, like idiots', depending on the artist's skill and his subject's expression. Diana's bedchamber lay near this long, echoing corridor, once so integral to the life of the house, but now simply another space sharing time with the spiders and mice. This wing, this very gallery she was now walking through had been especially created for laughter, dancing, games, for the many guests his grace, the first Duke of Tamworth, had once housed. Her grandfather's importance, his position, was emphasized by some of the portraits: Charles II was there, and his brother, James II, and two of James's wives, the English one and the Italian one. King William and Queen Mary were there, and Queen Anne smiling like a fat, broody hen. All staring mutely at her, their expressions somehow all the same. Put not your trust in princes. These were all dead. Like her grandfather. She could still remember a time when the warrens of bedchambers were all filled, and she could peek into them and see the heavy brocades, the ornate tapestries, the dark furniture; when servants bustled throughout the day to satisfy any whim of a guest; when family and friends dined in state each afternoon in the great hall with her grandfather like a king presiding at the head of the table. And she also remembered the time when all the rooms were closed, draped in black for the death of her uncle, the oldest son. Her grandfather had changed after that; so had this house. It had become a sadder, quieter place.

She entered her mother's bedchamber to find her sitting like an empress in a small straight-backed chair placed at the foot of the bed. The room smelled musty, seldom used. It was one of the state bedrooms, added to the house years ago when her grandfather had been alive and vigorous and laughing. Its walls were covered with rich, red damask, and the same damask covered the chairs in the room and the bed cover and curtains. On the hand-painted ceiling, a bevy of nymphs in flowing, sheer gowns trailed ropes of flowers as they ran nimbly toward a center blue-and-golden oval in which sat Zeus himself, his wife, Hera, at his side. The painter had made the features of the god and his consort resemble the Duke and Duchess. As if stunned by their elevation to Olympus, the pair stared off into the distance, at some corner of the room divorced from Diana and Barbara. Barbara did not like this room. It had none of the dark, shabby, cramped comfort of the rest of the house. It was always cold. Her mother used it whenever she visited. Red was her favorite color. Even now she had on a red dressing gown that made her blend into the chair she sat on.

Diana motioned her daughter to a heavy, armless chair nearby. So I am to sit, am I? thought Barbara. Why has she summoned me? She searched her mind to think of what she might have done, but there was nothing, except for missing supper and prayers, and she was ready for that. Besides, such things did not interest her mother; it was her grandmother who had raised and trained them all. She would be surprised if her mother knew everyone's name correctly. Barbara, stop that immediately, she heard her grandmother say in her mind. Her grandmother's lectures were always popping into her head to remind her of her duty, her obligations. Honour thy father and thy mother, her grandmother's voice was saying this time, which is the first commandment with promise; that it may be well with thee, and thou mayest live long on earth. Honour. Do it, Barbara.

Skillfully—it was years of practice (and it did not always succeed)—she ignored the voice because it was more important to concentrate on her mother; she had been the victim of her temper too'many times not to have learned she must study her face and gestures as carefully as her grandfather had his campaign maps. She noticed there were lines of fatigue about her mother's mouth, and her hands twisted nervously. Was it Harry? Was she going to question her about Harry? Diana frowned, and Barbara realized her mother expected her to greet her. I will not, she thought, her chin lifting, ignoring the immediate start-up of her grandmother's voice again. For Harry's sake, I will not.

As if she divined Barbara's thoughts, Diana smiled.

Barbara could not repress a shudder that her mother could read her so easily. She would have to do better.

"My dear girl," Diana said caressingly (under the caress was a sarcasm that made Barbara clench her teeth), "how are you?"

"Very well, Mother."

"Very well? I should think it dull in this old house. Do you not want to escape? I always do when I visit. You should, too."

She considered her mother carefully. What was behind that white mask of a face, that smiling red mouth? Surely not some invitation. Diana never hinted that her children would be expected, much less welcome, to return with her to London. She came down once, perhaps twice a year, and stayed for less than a week. Her children were brought to her for an hour each day, and if they bothered or fretted her in any manner, she slapped their faces and called a servant. The only time Barbara saw her mother for any length of time was during her lyings-in for childbirth. Diana would sit faint and fragrant afterward and wait for visitors to call.

When Barbara was small she would be dressed up to visit her mother and her guests.

"Here she is," her mother would say. "Give me a kiss . . . oh, do not squeeze so hard. You crease my gown. Take her away." And she would be carried away until the next day, unless she was bad, as she'd taken to being the older she became (screaming and stamping her feet, to the delight of her younger brothers and sisters), and was banished to her room altogether. It did not matter; Diana was soon gone anyway, and the latest addition to the nursery joined the others, perhaps making it safely into childhood or—sometimes— dying. She could remember each of the four little deaths she had witnessed as clearly as if she had borne the babies herself. Each death made surviving children more precious; it made each day of life more precious. She loved her brothers and sisters with all her heart. It was as if she, and not Diana, were their mother. And they loved her in return, for her bravery, and high spirits and care. She looked at her mother's waistline. It had been nearly three years since a baby. Nothing showed. Red blended into red.

"You are—is it fifteen? Yes, fifteen. Near to sixteen. Time to think of putting up your hair and meeting the world."

"Meeting the world?" She knew better than to venture any curiosity, any small piece of herself that might be hurt.

"Perhaps not the world, but a few friends, surely. It is time you learned some manners if this afternoon is any example of your conduct. This running about the estate as if you were a boy—"

"It matters little here, Mother. Everyone knows me. And I was visiting tenants, not running—"

"It matters in other places . . . such as London."

London! All the world, her future, was in that word. Diana laughed to see her daughter's careful facade crack. "London, indeed, my girl. New clothes, new friends, dancing, the court, a husband . . ."

Of course, Barbara thought. A husband. It was time. She knew that. Whom had her mother unearthed? And why approach the subject in such a roundabout way? Why not present it in her usual forthright fashion . . . unless he—she bit her lip. Harry had once told her and Jane the story of a French girl being dragged to the altar by her brothers while her bridegroom drooled and trembled and pawed at her, so ancient, so senile was he. I'll drag you willingly, Harry had teased, pulling on her. She had laughed, and Jane had cried. But behind her laughter was the knowledge that the same fate could happen to her, though not likely because her grandmother loved her so much. It was her duty to marry obediently, as her parents decided. She was not afraid of duty, and she looked forward to her own home, to children. But she had not expected to face it all today . . . and without the presence of her grandmother. That alone made a sudden fear pierce through her. She could feel it course from her head all the way to her toes. She tried to disguise it by lifting her chin and saying, "A husband? You have someone in mind?" Unfortunately, her voice shook.

"Yes, I do. Someone interested in you. The Earl Devane."

Her hands tightened in her lap. "I do not know him. . . ."

At this, Diana laughed again, and Barbara willed herself not to show any emotion. How like her mother to taunt her this way. As she had done Harry earlier. She would not give her the satisfaction, she would not . . . she would not. . . .

"It is Roger Montgeoffry."

She sat stunned, and she did not care if her mother saw. Roger, beautiful Roger, who used to come to visit Grandfather, who always had a kind word for her. A present. He was the handsomest man in the world. He was charming. He was everything. She had always loved him, always, and to think that her mother was arranging a marriage with him . . . it was like a holy miracle . . . it was too wonderful to be borne. She rose impulsively and hugged her mother.

"Thank you! Thank you!" she babbled.

Diana stared at her, nonplussed, then said slowly, "It is not final yet . . . only something he and I have discussed. He must see you, and—there are a thousand details."

"I will charm him, Mother. You will see." Her face was radiant in its happiness.

"I had no idea you would be so . . . pleased," Diana said.

Barbara kissed her mother's hand and ran from the room. She felt she would burst with happiness. She wanted to run through the halls screaming his name. She could not believe her good fortune. Roger . . . Roger . . . Roger . . .

She burst into her grandmother's chambers without knocking. Her grandmother was already in bed, but not sleeping. Warmth, familiarity touched her cheeks like soothing hands. This room never changed. Dark paneling encasing the walls as closely as smooth leather gloves. Portraits of family members in heavy gilt frames hanging from faded velvet ribbons on every inch of wall space. Her grandfather's portrait above the fireplace. Enormous. His face young and smiling, dogs curled at his feet. Small, mismatched tables everywhere, littered with books and papers and bowls of late yellow autumn chrysanthemums and holly. Her grandmother's bed taking up half the room, its bed curtains woven by her grandmother's mother when she had been a girl. A curious, fanciful pattern of flowers and birds. Yellow, green, red. Petals and feathers picked out in embroidery with painstaking care so many years ago.

Her grandfather's dogs lifted their heads from their place near the blazing fire, sniffed once or twice at her, then settled back onto their paws. Her grandmother's tirewoman, Annie, seated in a chair near the bed, frowned at her, as she always did. Dulcinea, her grandmother's cat, a fluffy, silver-white

vision of pride and enormous condescension, raised her head
from under her grandmother's hand and stared at her.

"Oh, Grandmama . . ." She began to cry. She could not
help it. She despised crying, but she had expected—she did
not know what—and this . . . this was a dream come true.

The Duchess of Tamworth, looking like a child's mummy
in her layers of shawls, her lace nightcap covering her head
like a limp pancake, struggled to sit up and motioned for
Annie to light more candles.

"Child! Child! What is it? Come here, here beside me.
Move, Dulcinea. Move! Damned cat. She thinks she owns this
bed! There, there, my pet, my little Richard. What is it? Tell
your grandmother, and she shall try to help you out of trouble."

Barbara smiled and wiped her eyes. It was a standing joke
between them that she was always in trouble. Usually, of
course, it was true. She snuggled against her grandmother's
thin body. It felt like bones and nothing more were encased
in the nightgown. Dulcinea, who had grudgingly moved to the
foot of the bed, yawned and then began to clean her private
parts with great delicacy.

"You have spoken to your mother? And the news has made
you sad? My darling girl, we both know it is time. I blame
myself for putting it off. Roger is much older, I realize, but
do not say no just yet. At least let us see what he has to offer.
Of course, if you truly dislike the idea, there will be no marriage—not to him. Bab, what is it? Tell me."

Barbara caught her breath. She was suddenly exhausted.
"You do not understand, Grandmama. It is that I am so
happy!"

"Happy, my pet?" The shadows on her grandmother's face
changed position.

"Oh, yes. I have always loved Roger."

What was this? the Duchess thought, startled. Love? She
tried to see the girl's face in the dimness. Only its sweet shape
showed clearly. There were depths here apparently even she
knew nothing of.

"I did not know."

"No," Barbara said. "No one did. What use was it to tell
anyone?"

The Duchess felt agitated. "You know it is not final? I understand your mother owes Roger much money. And there are dowry arrangements to be made." She had already been gathering information. To make Diana prove this marriage would benefit all concerned.

"I know he does not love me, Grandmama. It does not matter. I will make him love me." Barbara spoke with the clear confidence of someone nearly sixteen.

"He is older than you, child. At least forty-two. There will have been other loves . . . things you cannot know about."

"I do not care. I will make it happen."

Seeing the sudden, hard, clean line of her jaw, which changed the sweetness to something else, the Duchess believed her. Like Richard. He never knew when to quit, and it finally broke him. The Duchess felt a kind of premonition clutch her heart.

"Love is not always important, girl. There are other things . . . duty, devotion, children . . . between a man and a woman. Mutual love is so rare—" She broke off. The girl beside her was asleep, smiling even in her sleep. She pursed her lips. Dulcinea came to lie beneath her hand again. Annie snuffed out all but one candle.

Tomorrow she would talk with Diana, find out why Roger would marry the daughter of a traitorous fool. And she would talk to Barbara. The girl could not go into any marriage with such a starry-eyed attitude. Not if she wished it—and herself—to survive. She began to pray, her greatest source of comfort. Dearest Father, protect this child beside me. Lead her not into temptation, but deliver her from evil. Let your light be about her always. Let your love, your teachings, be her guide. She glanced over at the portrait of Richard, knowing even in the dark exactly where it was. And bless the soul of my dearly beloved husband, Richard. . . . Oh, Richard, there are times when I still miss you, still need you so.

CHAPTER TWO

When Barbara awakened a few hours later, she found she had been put into her own bed, and she lay there waiting for Harry. He would come; she had no doubt of that. There had been no chance to talk since his expulsion from Oxford; he had appeared at Tamworth, shamefaced, sulky, only to be followed almost immediately by Diana, whose bloodred lips had shaped sentences that changed both their lives forever. Outside, she could hear the night wind rustling dryly through dead leaves, invisible fingers searching, scrabbling, for what? Her mind lay floating gently, probing the bits and pieces of thought that had bobbed to its top while she slept.

". . . match is totally unsuitable . . . now more than ever. . . ." Her mother's words to Harry echoed in her mind. Why? Because Father had fled to France during the summer's investigation conducted by Parliament? "Hens' scratching!" her grandmother had snorted about the investigation, then . . . before Father had run away. "Digging in the dirt to see what they can turn up!" He never even said goodbye. Sir John Ashford's voice had carried clearly the day he had ridden over during summer's hottest hour. His face flushed and sweating. He found her grandmother in the stillroom. She stood silent while he shouted. "Like a rat!" Her father had run like a rat, he said. Lost his nerve.

Words clashed together and fell apart in her mind. Tory, Jacobite, treason. Her grandmother's abrupt questions. The

21

shade of the stillroom. The coolness. The smell of drying herbs. Sir John's face. Veins standing out on his forehead. The sun shone jewellike through the jars of red and orange and plum jellies. Father had never said goodbye. Just disappeared in the dead of one night. They sent her away. Harry, home for the summer, had explained.

"He is not a traitor, Bab." His darkly handsome face, Diana's face, was strained, pinched at the nostrils. They had sat under the shade of one of the great oak trees. He kept jabbing at the smooth green lawn with a stick as he talked.

"Politics. It is all politics, my little innocent sister. Hanover or James III. King or Pretender. But who is the Pretender? One is a Protestant; one is a Catholic. One is supported by a majority of the powerful men in this country. One is not. It is so simple, Bab. Not the divine right of kings, but the divine right of power. He who has promised and can uphold those promises wins. Father backed the loser. He always has!"

His face was bitter. She stared at him. Poor Harry. He was too young, too handsome for bitterness, and yet there it was, the black slimy worm in the glistening red apple. Their father had gambled away his inheritance. Everyone knew it. Harry's school was paid for by their grandmother, who also gave him a small allowance. But not enough for him to live in London like other young men his age. And now Father had risked the last bit left to him—his title. She reached out her hand to him. He turned away from it, his face bleak. She could be content with the obscurity of disgrace; after all, what had she ever known but Tamworth? She had never been farther than Maidstone for the fair. But Harry. Harry had been to Oxford. To London. He had seen what life offered. He hungered after its treats and could not have them. No wine. No women. No song . . . and no Jane. Strange that one man's actions could touch so many other people, like a single thoughtless breath of wind coming in an open window and blowing the playing cards every which way. "Any alliance we form now is crucial." Ah, Roger. She shivered and sat up in the bed. Somehow her father's act had reached out and brought Roger within her grasp. The thought whirled around in her head just as the leaves did outside in the dark night.

She threw back the bed covers and swung her feet over the edge. Legs dangling, she sat there, her hair hanging down, thick, curling, falling about her shoulders like a lion's mane. She felt she could jump out of her skin. Her chamber, her very life, seemed suddenly too small for her. She understood now how Harry must feel. She looked around her, knowing even in the darkness where every item, no matter how small, was located. This was her refuge, her nest. How she had resisted her grandmother's suggestion that she move down to the next floor and enjoy a larger apartment. No. She would stay in the nursery wing. She had lived here all her life. Everything was to her liking: the small, cramped sizes of the rooms, the way they ambled about with no rhyme or reason, some feeding into others, some being approached only through odd little halls and narrow little stairs. During the day, she could hear her brothers and sisters reciting their lessons. She was nearby when they cried at night. Nearby to comfort, to scold, to love, for she had always taken care of them. Always.

She was queen of this small kingdom; her dearest subjects slept in adjoining rooms; her bedchamber held her kingdom's treasures. Bird's nests she had lovingly saved. (You had to be so careful; harming a robin was bad luck. If you took their eggs, your legs would break. If you were holding one when it died, your hands would always shake. . . . Annie said so.) And in them, not eggs, for she could not have borne to keep the young from their mother, but instead a potpourri of herbs and flowers she made herself every autumn. A small French box of fragrant, inlaid wood holding her hair ribbons curled into obedient circles, her few jewels. The toilette set her grandmother had given her for her thirteenth birthday, composed of ivory and silver, the comb, brush, mirror and matching candlesticks laid out carefully and with great pride on a small table. An old Dutch chest, inside of which lay some of her mother's ball gowns, lavender sprinkled among their folds.

She would brush her hair until it crackled with life and then try on those gowns. Anne and Charlotte hung on her every movement as she swayed about the room in an old pair of high-heeled shoes she had stolen from her grandmother's wardrobe. "Oh, Bab, you are so beautiful!" The gowns rustled; they shimmered. They were the symbol of all she would one day possess—when she became a woman. How carefully she would fold them away (Anne and Charlotte begging to help), caressing the velvet, the lace, and then closing the lid, somehow secure that one day the secret they represented would be known to her. This chamber was her cocoon; she was the chrysalis, encased, content, putting away bright gowns as she put away dreams. But tonight she felt that her wings had unfolded and were as shimmering with magic as those gowns. This room was suddenly too small. Tamworth was too small. The world was too small to hold her soaring spirit—

"Bab!"

Harry's white face was floating in her doorway. She scrambled across the covers and lit a candle before he could run into anything. The smell of brandy burned her nostrils at the same time as the smell of smoking wick. She felt her wings fold back into themselves. He had been drinking. He would be difficult, ready to quarrel. He would not be able to share her joy.

And then she saw his face as he sat down on the edge of the bed. Its handsome darkness was marred. His beautiful, violet eyes ("I want your eyes!" she always told him. "I have more need of them than you do!") were swollen with weeping. His mouth, with its full lips, was grim and unnaturally thin. And she remembered that while she had gained her heart's desire this day, he had lost his. He sat down heavily on the bed, and she pulled the covers up to her shoulders and rubbed her feet against the sheet for warmth, her own joy forgotten.

"Harry . . . I am so sorry. . . . " The words fell between them softly like the faded petals of a summer flower. He put his hands to his face. She saw his shoulders heave, but he made no sound. She sat quiet and still, awed by the emotion radiating from him. This, too, was love, she thought, the words slipping through her mind quicksilver slick, dropping into the well that was her feeling for Roger. This pain, this desperation. I will know it. I will know it all. The good with the bad . . . oh, Roger. She felt rich, powerful, blessed. The wings on her back gave a strong flutter.

"Did she tell you?" His hands were away from his face now, the words quick and harsh. She breathed in the brandy. The shadows of the room hid his feelings, but his voice did not. It betrayed him. She shivered.

"I . . . she . . . I overheard."

He made a bitter sound, half laugh, half cry. "Ah! You 'overheard.' Bad Bab! Someday you are going to overhear something that will singe your pretty little ears!"

She said nothing. What was there to say?

"Well, tell me, my dearest sister"—the sarcasm in his voice hurt even though she knew it was not meant for her—"how did you like my part in the comedy Mother and I played this afternoon? Was I not heroic? Did you note how gallantly, how firmly I defended my love? How cleverly I argued? I was a man. But not the man our mother is."

"Harry," she said breathlessly, the violence under his words frightening her. "She—you were not ready for her—"

He laughed softly. "No. I was not. I walked into that room like a cock on a dungheap, ready to fling her words back into her painted face. I thought she had come down to skewer me for being expelled." He laughed again, a grating, unpleasant sound. "And I was ready for that. Oh, I was ready. Of course I was in a duel, I was going to tell her. When a man calls your mother a whore who would sell her soul for a guinea, it is your duty to defend her honor. Even if such a quality does not exist in her."

"Who said that!" She grabbed his arm and tried to see his face more clearly.

"I should have killed him. I misjudged my aim. Or perhaps my heart was not truly in it, knowing that what he said was true."

"Harry! Who would say such a thing to you?"

The candlelight threw odd shadows on his face. "It little matters whom I dueled with," he said softly. "A friend . . . or so I thought. Our lady mother in her wisdom and avarice has petitioned Parliament for a divorce. The news of it has for the moment eclipsed even the pitiful, half-baked rebellion brewing in Scotland."

She lay back on the bed, stunned. "Sweet Jesus in his heaven above," she whispered. "A divorce . . . " No wonder Harry could not have Jane.

"Yes," he said, mocking her tone. "Father's flight left her reeling, but she has landed nimbly. She has become the most fervent Whig of all, and begs the Parliament, humbly, to sever her ties with a treasonous Jacobite who has besmirched her lineage. She is, after all, the only daughter of the great Duke of Tamworth, the hero of Lille, the defender of England's foes at home and abroad—do not look at me so! I am quoting you directly from the pamphlet she has had distributed to plead her cause. 'She only wishes to live her life quietly in the king's service'—which caused my friend to utter the words which I fought him over. Though God knows he is correct."

"When did this happen?" she demanded.

The tone of her voice made him focus on her. She lifted her chin.

"Are you angry—"

"No one told me!" she cried out. "I have a right to know!"

He tried to take her hand but she pulled it out of his grasp.

"I am not a child," she said. "Why does everyone treat me so!"

But Harry's attention had drifted from her. He was staring into the darkness over her shoulder, darkness the light of her solitary candle could not penetrate.

"She thinks if she is divorced from Father she may be able to save some of the properties. Some . . . I missay her, Bab. All of them. She will have them taken from Father and given to me. I will be the new viscount, and Father will be banished forever—erased. A mistake the Lady Alderley made in her wild youth. I will inherit his debts, his title, his estate, and more than likely I will go to debtors' prison before I am twenty trying to salvage the mess. All hail the new regime, Bab. Those who do not will be crushed." He quoted softly into the dark:

"Farewell Old Year, for thou with Broomstick Hard
Had drove poor Tory from St. James's Yard.
Farewell Old Year, Old Monarch, and Old Tory.
Farewell Old England, thou has lost thy Glory."

His words, faintly treasonous, froze her heart and overlaid the anger she felt. Oxford and London had already seen the flashes of unrest. Men were massed in Scotland waiting for the Pretender to sail across the sea to march at their head toward London. Sweet Jesus, Sir John had been shouting about it to her grandmother only the other day. "Hang them all, now! Every suspected Jacobite among the Tory scum!" "Nonsense!" her grandmother had snapped. "It is a tempest in a teapot!"

"It is rebellion, woman, pure and simple!" And on and on they went. They loved to argue with each other. Sir John would ride over with the latest news from court. (More than likely her grandmother knew it already. Someone in her wide circle of friends would have written.) And they would begin their debate. Her grandmother liked to switch sides; one day she would argue the Tory position, the next day the Whig. The point was not to be consistent; it was to win the day's argument. "I do believe that man has kept me alive longer," her grandmother would say, as she watched Sir John ride off in a fit of temper, knowing full well he would return as soon as he had fresh powder in his own guns. But then, her grandmother's loyalty was above question, unlike . . . ? Her thoughts ran and leapt and fell over themselves.

When she married Roger, she would be wealthy. That was why her mother wanted the match. She would be wealthy and surely she could persuade Roger to give Harry money, to find him a position in the government, something with a handsome salary. If Jane would wait. Would refuse to marry her cousin. If Harry did nothing rash, like proclaiming himself for the Pretender and joining their father in France.

"I will talk to Grandmama," she said, her words spilling out into the silence. "I have news of my own, Harry—"

"Who do you think wrote to Mother?"

She blinked rapidly in the darkness. "I—I do not understand," she whispered.

"I should have seen it coming. God! What a fool I am!" He slammed his fist on the bedside table, and the burning candle fell over onto the bed. With a cry, Barbara slapped at it before it could set the bed covers alight. You drunken fool, she wanted to say, angry as much over what he implied as she was over his carelessness. How like Harry, upsetting things and leaving others to deal with them. Well, the candle was out, her hands were smarting, and he went on talking in the darkness as if nothing had happened.

"Jane and I were too open this summer. I saw Grandmama's face. But I was not going to press Jane for a vow yet. I thought—perhaps in a few years—I might have something more to offer her. I should have known Grandmama—Mother—would have other plans."

"What do you mean?" She felt like crying. Betrayal. By Grandmama of all people.

"This rotting branch of the Tamworths must be saved. Mother has plans . . . witness the petition, the stamping out of any hope between Jane and me. If I were destined to be a poor relation, happy on my mortgaged property or some piece of land a rich relative might rent me, worrying over my harvests, excited with my yearly trip to London, Jane would be a good helpmeet. But a future viscount—particularly an impoverished one—must look higher or at least at someone with some real money"

She flinched at the tone in his voice. He had minded the disgrace, the lack of money, so much more than she had imagined.

"And do you know what makes it all so much more amusing—or do I mean sad? Underneath my grief"—how self-mocking his words were!—"I feel a faint sense of relief. They say Italy is beautiful beyond words."

There was nothing to reply. The bitterness, the yearning, the self-disgust in his words were more than she could understand. She felt exhausted suddenly, unable to form the simplest response to him. As if he felt her withdrawal from him, he said, "Do you know what it is like to go to London and see my cousins living like kings, and know that—that we—have nothing because of someone else's stupidity! I would be as stupid as he if I insisted on marrying Jane. Do you understand that!" She refused to speak.

Groping in the darkness, his hand found her hair. He smoothed a long curl.

"Poor baby," he said softly. "Still believing in dreams—"

She pulled away from his hand. Yes, she believed. And she always would. She was not some weak, cynical human being to allow others to dictate to her. She had her own thoughts and feelings and no one, no one could change them!

"You despise me," he said.

She sighed. Poor Harry, he was drunk. Half of what he said was the brandy. She crawled over and sat close to him. They put their arms about each other and she leaned her cheek against his. It was wet. He did care; he did love Jane; his heart was broken.

"I love you, Harry."

They were silent for a long time, content to sit together closely in the darkness, weakness and temper forgiven, as they always were. She must have dozed a little because she thought she was somehow standing in front of Annie, trying to explain away the burned hole in her sheet. "It just fell," she kept trying to say but Annie was shaking her . . . and shaking her. . . .

"Bab! Wake up!" Harry's sour breath was in her face. She was lying down. "I must leave."

"Not yet!" she said, still confused. "There was something I had to tell you—"

"Later!" He squeezed her hands. "Write to me—promise." She was pulled roughly into his arms. "I love you," he whispered. "Tell Jane . . ." but she never knew what he meant her to say because he did not finish. Instead, he kissed her hair, and pulled the covers up over her and she heard his boots against the floor and the door shutting with a final sound. I will get up, she thought, and go to him and tell him . . . but the bed was so warm and soft and she felt so very tired. Too much . . . Harry, Jane, divorce, Grandmama . . . the hole in the sheet . . . Annie would be so angry . . . she would pray for Harry and then get up. . . . Dear Lord . . . patch the hole in the sheet . . . No! . . . that was not what she meant to say . . . but before she could straighten out her thoughts, she was asleep.

They gathered in the courtyard to say goodbye to Harry: Barbara, her grandmother, Diana, Kit, Charlotte, Anne. The morning around them was bright and clear, shattering in its coldness. The wind rustled through the lime trees that stood like sentinels on each side of the avenue that led to the road away from Tamworth, through the village, past the town of Maidstone, up toward London, to the banks of the Thames, where Harry would catch a ship somewhere along its marshy, salt-kissed banks.

Harry, his face set and still, took cold, formal leave of his grandmother, who had tears in her eyes. He said nothing at all to Diana, only nodded his head shortly to her. Diana was shivering, impatient to go back inside and stand by a fire. When he embraced Barbara, she felt his body trembling, and in spite of herself, she began to cry. Little Anne, who was four and had a fat, rosy face and loved Harry best of all after Barbara, kept saying, "But why is Harry going away again? Why is he going again?" until Barbara thought she would scream, and Diana sharply ordered for the child to be taken away. Even normally brash Kit, who was ten and considered himself almost grown, was subdued. He had his more than likely dirty hands shoved into the pockets of his coat, and his face, which was fair like Barbara's, had the set, still look of Harry's. Charlotte, who was seven and thin and serious, cried quietly. She had been crying since they had assembled in the forecourt, and her face was swollen. Barbara took her in her arms to shush her before Diana became even more irritated.

"Is Harry going? You will not go, too, will you? I love Harry!"

The impatient horses' hooves pawed the gravel. Each time they snorted, their breath rose in cool, gray vapors. At a nod from Diana, Meres opened the coach door for Harry, who climbed inside silently, his face averted.

"Hush, darling," Barbara whispered, her eyes on her brother. "You make Harry's leaving harder. He is going on a journey, a wonderful journey. There is no reason to be sad."

"That is a lie!" said Charlotte. "You are sad! Why is everyone lying?"

The coach lumbered off with a jerk, and Charlotte sobbed. "Everything is different, Bab. I do not like it."

Barbara waited for Jane in the apple orchard. The apples were picked. She and her brothers and sisters had been in the midst of the harvest. She could climb a tree as nimbly as any boy in the village, better even than Kit. She loved to scramble as high as she could among the branches and feel the sun shining on her through the leaves. All the bad apples lay rotting on the ground, food for the squirrels and birds and small animals in the woods. The good ones had been set carefully on marble shelves built especially for their keeping so that they should not touch one another. Or they now resided in dry glazed jars whose bottoms were covered in stones. The village carpenter each year carved new tops of wood that fit each jar exactly. When the jar was filled with apples the wooden lid was inserted and fresh mortar spread over it. What a pleasure it was to watch cook wedge open the top and shake the apples and stones out and know that soon an apple tart would be cooking, filling the house with its warmth and smell of cinnamon and sugar, while outside, wind and snow beat against the windows. She and Jane had walked through the orchard during harvest, laughing and whispering. All around them, men and women and children gathered apples into big baskets. She picked the juiciest off the top and sat under a tree with Jane. She carefully peeled Jane's apple with a sharp knife. Jane clutched the dangling peel to her heart, closed her eyes, then threw it over her shoulder. The letter the peel formed was supposed to be the initial of her future husband. Barbara ran to it. It had made no letter she could recognize, but she told Jane it was an **H** and then laughed at her friend's blushes. If you stuck two apple seeds to your cheeks, and named two suitors, the seed that stuck the longest was the suitor that loved you the most. But Jane refused to play that game, and Barbara had no suitors, so they were content to eat their apples and talk. She knew Jane would come here, if she could get away. This spot had been their meeting place as children and had become the trysting spot for Harry and Jane as they began to care for each other. Poor Jane. She would run all the way expecting to see Harry. Barbara stamped her feet to dissipate some of the afternoon's bone-chilling cold.

Yes, there was Jane now, running breathlessly through the evenly spaced rows of trees, her breath coming out in little puffs of white. She looked wretched, her face swollen from crying, her nose red. She had never been pretty anyway; her lashes and brows were so light they faded into nothing; her hair was wispy; her nose snub. But she had a lovely smile that radiated the beauty she possessed inside. She was loyal and resourceful, and in her own timid way, brave. Before Jane and Harry had fallen in love, when the three of them were still running wild together, Jane had always been the one to think of the most convincing lie after they had done something bad. She and Harry had grown to rely on Jane's creative mind even though they could not always rely on her joining them in their misdeeds. And she never tattled on them. Never.

Jane stopped, her slight breasts heaving under her cloak, and looked around. She bit her lip and glanced at Barbara with red-rimmed eyes. He has not come, she thought, the fact taking her heart and squeezing it. It is truly over.

Abruptly, as if something inside had broken, she sat down on the ground, her arms clasped around her legs. "Oh, Bab!" she croaked. "I have cried so hard, so long, that I did not think I had any tears left. But I do!" She rocked to and fro, oblivious of dignity in her grief. Barbara knelt down and put her arms around her and rocked with her. When Jane finally quieted, she gasped out, "Thank you for c-coming. Harry is—"

"Gone. Mother sent him off this morning. He is to go to Italy for a while."

"Oh, God," Jane sobbed. "I cannot bear it!" She lay back against the ground and covered her face with her arms. Except for the sound of the wind stirring the branches of the trees, only her sobs broke the silence. Dusk was coming. Some of the day's bright sun had lessened. Barbara felt it, through the increased cold, rather than actually saw it. Today had been glorious. Clear, cold sunny. One of the most beautiful days of the entire autumn. A leaf detached itself from a tree and slowly drifted down. Barbara opened her hand and caught it. Annie said catching a falling leaf meant a day of good luck. Did it still mean luck when it fell into your hand of its own volition or did you have to grab for it? Bah! Annie was a bag of old woman's nonsense. She also said blackberries were poison on Michaelmas Day because the Devil put his foot on them the night before. But when Barbara dared to eat every blackberry she could find two years ago on Michaelmas Day, she had gotten nothing more than a tonguelashing from her grandmother for being greedy.

Jane's sobs settled into tiny whimpers, and without looking at her, Barbara leaned her head back against the trunk of the tree and looked up into the sky, as Jane was doing. What dreams did Jane see in those fleecy, starched white clouds? For a moment, their two profiles were etched against the sky; one, swollen, disfigured from grief, the other, sharp, strong, untouched.

"I never imagined he would love me," Jane said. "I loved him so amazingly for years. Ever since we were children. I cannot believe it is finished."

"What will you do?"

Her mouth was grim. "I shall marry Augustus Cromwell, of course, as I always knew I would. And I shall try to be a good wife to him. I shall even try to love him."

"Do not do it!" Barbara said quickly. "Tell your parents no. Wait. Wait, and perhaps things will change."

"How can they change? Harry is gone. I do not know for how long. I am contracted to my cousin. They are crying the banns this Sunday! I should have been stronger, my mother told me. I was wrong to sneak and promise myself to someone else. I looked at her and said, 'Did you never love, Mother? Have you no heart at all?' And she began to cry with me. Imagine my being so brave! Of course, I have no real courage, not like you, Bab. I always do my duty. Do you think— in the end—everyone does so? Forgets the loves, the passions of his youth and does his duty? My mother says so, but I can hardly believe it's true." Her face was bleak, her tone bitter and discouraged. As Harry's had been last night. How easily they gave up, Barbara thought. I would fight—and then she remembered her fear before her mother the night before, the power and tradition her mother represented, power and tradition which commanded that a well-bred girl do as her parents proposed in all things.

I would have married whomever she chose, she thought defiantly, but if I did not love him, one day I would have had Roger as my lover. Even if it were only for one hour, I swear I would have had him for my lover. And to Jane, she said, knowing her words would shock and horrify her friend, but feeling angry at the sense of hopelessness she had encountered in both Harry and Jane, "I would have had his baby . . . so we would have to marry . . . if I loved someone so much."

Jane was too distraught even to gasp. "You might," she said wearily. "But I have not the courage." She looked up at Barbara. At the clean strong bones of her face, such a lovely face with its heart shape and the fine, wide blue eyes. And the beautiful, abundant hair, red-gold, curling, thick. She was a duke's granddaughter. Yes, thought Jane, without bitterness. You might, as your mother did before you. But I am a country knight's daughter, and such ways are not for me.

Barbara shivered from the cold and from pity for her friend. The afternoon was now twilight. In a far-off field, a tenant farmer unhitched his oxen and began the walk home. Cattle, grazing in the fields, lowed to one another. Children ran to them herding them toward the warmth of barns and stalls.

"I am to go to London," she told Jane. At the last minute, she could not tell her the whole of her joy, just as she had been unable to tell Harry. But she said, "My mother is taking me there to see if I can catch a husband. Jane, do not marry this Augustus. Wait. And if I marry well enough, my husband will find Harry a position, money somewhere. And then you may marry. Wait and see. Please." She said this in spite of Harry's words of the night before, some stubbornness in her insisting it was the brandy that had spoken longingly of Italy.

Jane sat up and pulled leaves and twigs from her cloak. She opened her mouth and then closed it again. Finally she said, slowly, choosing her words with care, "Thank you for the offer, my dear, dear Bab . . . but what if your mother cannot—I mean, my father says that—forgive me, Bab, but he says no decent person would associate with her. There might not be a husband as easily found as—" She looked at Barbara's face, and what she saw there made her say quickly, "Though, of course, I know you will find one with your beauty. I know that, Bab. I do. But I cannot wait. I am afraid. And it is promised, already binding me. If I were to wait, as you suggest . . . and then something went wrong— why, I would be without a husband at all. Who would have a woman who had broken her vow to marry? And if I do not marry, I will have nothing—no children, no home of my own—"

"But I thought you loved Harry!"

"I do! Oh, I do! But . . . Harry was a dream, Bab. Something I hoped for. Something I think I knew in my heart I would never have. He is a duke's grandson! And now, with your father and all, he must marry someone who can help him rebuild; someone with a name and fortune. Oh, I know you despise me. I despise myself. But please try to understand . . . please."

She touched Barbara's cloak with her hand. Barbara stood up abruptly, and Jane did, too.

"I must leave," Jane said, her eyes glancing off the stony expression of Barbara's face. "They think I am in my room, and Father most likely will beat me when I return. But it does not matter. Thank you for coming here, for telling me about

Harry. Bab—" Her voice cracked, and she swallowed. She hugged Barbara in a light, quick, darting motion and then said, "I wish you happy husband hunting." Turning, she ran back through the row of trees. Barbara watched her. Jane had made her realize for the first time that marrying Roger might not be as easy as she had imagined.

The Duchess climbed the last step of the center staircase and paused to rest a moment, her hand on the horn of the carved unicorn that decorated the end support of the stair railing. She was searching for Diana, and she was tired. Harry's leave-taking this morning had exhausted her, wringing her feelings the way a quarrel with Richard always had. Arrogant young hound! So he blamed her, did he? Odd, how for a moment he looked so much like Richard. He had none of his grandfather's fairness, but something about the set of his face . . . it had cut through her heart like a knife. Ah, her joints ached! She should be in her bed, strips of hot linen wrapped around her legs, sipping her special wine while Annie read to her from the Song of Solomon. I am too old for this folderol, she told herself, but she held tightly to her cane and limped over to the set of doors leading to Diana's chambers. She must do her duty by Barbara. Diana was not going to carry the child off to London and marry her willy-nilly until the Duchess had confirmed and augmented the bits of detail Annie had ferreted out of Diana's servants. Her foreboding of the night before had faded with the dark, but some scrap of gossip about Roger eluded her, and it bothered her. Most likely it is nothing, she told herself. People always gossiped of Roger. It was Barbara's feeling for the man that vexed at her like the humming of an insect. The girl was too impetuous, claiming she loved Roger. What the devil could she know of love! Or of Roger, for that matter!

She rapped impatiently on the door with her cane. One dark half of it opened, and she hobbled in to see Diana, as naked as a Rubens nude, lying sprawled across huge white sheets that protected the damask covers on the bed. The maid Diana had brought down with her from London was kneading glistening oil into her body. For a moment, the Duchess could only stand there, staring, her eyes outraged. She jabbed her cane toward one of the red damask chairs that lined the wall like soldiers on duty, and another maid, one of her own household servants, who was serving as an appendage to the pagan ritual, scurried to pull the chair from the wall to the spot the Duchess indicated with her cane. The servant dropped a quick curtsy to her mistress, her pale eyes blinking rapidly. She reminded the Duchess of a terrified rabbit. The maidservant glanced toward Diana, lolling on the bed, and her eyes began to blink even more rapidly. The Duchess barked out an order to keep from suddenly laughing.

"Leave the room! Both of you!" She sat down in the chair, her back straight. "Cover yourself, Diana. You are going to give my maids apoplexy."

Diana sat up and lazily pulled a sheet about herself. "It is the latest fashion from France," she said, as she knotted the sheet at her breast. "The Duchesse d'Orléans has her body massaged three times daily. It keeps one young and supple."

"Call the maid back, then! You have no time to lose!" She moved irritably in the chair, trying and failing to find a comfortable spot. She glared at her daughter as if her aching bones were her daughter's fault. Damn Diana. Pickling herself in oil like a French whore. She would not be put off by it.

Diana glanced at her mother's face. What she saw made her grit her teeth, but she picked up a nearby hand mirror of pale ivory and began casually to examine her face, as if she had all the time in the world.

"This business with Roger," the Duchess said, not bothering to pretend she had come for anything else. She stamped her cane on the word "Roger." "It bothers me."

"What can bother you?" Diana snapped. "You know of his family. It was always good enough; he just never had any inheritance to speak of. But the time in Hanover has served him well. He possesses the gift of Midas these days. Whatever he touches turns to gold. Why, his original investment in the South Sea Company has made him rich twice over, and his earldom is as much a reward for helping King George's skinny mistress make money on the exchange as it is for past services rendered to the House of Hanover. He is a powerful personage in court circles, and I—we—are fortunate to have him."

"Why do you *have* him, Diana? A rich earl like Roger has no need of the Alderley branch of the Tamworths. Your husband is a traitor, run away to France. You are left with debts and an encumbered estate. Your petition for divorce has scandalized everyone. Why—I repeat—do you have him?" That has her, she thought with a satisfied nod. She could almost enjoy these bouts with Diana, except they tired her so, and she was already weary from the worry of Harry and Jane. And then Diana had dropped the news about Roger, about Barbara, like a cannonball in their midst. She was too old for such bother. She tried to rub her legs so that Diana would not notice. The pain, the tiredness, were making it difficult for her to concentrate.

Diana took a deep breath and spoke lightly. If her mother had not known her so well, she would have been fooled by her apparent casualness.

"We are old friends. You know how fond he was of Father." She put down the mirror and smiled winningly. "He is proud to ally himself with the Tamworth family—any branch of it."

"Surely you can do better than that, Diana."

Diana frowned. The Duchess sat impassively, never taking her eyes off her daughter. Diana retied the knot at her breast. She held the mirror back to her face and smoothed her dark brows. She examined her teeth. Her eyes fell away to her mother and then back to the mirror again. The Duchess knew she was trying to think of a lie that she would believe, and she also knew Diana could not fool her and was slowly, angrily, unwillingly coming to the core of the matter. The truth would emerge sooner or later in the whole business. With Diana, it would be later, and so overset with lies and halftruths that it would be hard to recognize. This way, straightforwardly and at the beginning of whatever was happening, was not the way Diana would have wished to approach her goal. But it was the way the Duchess wished to. And that was all that mattered.

Diana put down the mirror and threw the words at her mother.

"He wants the Bentwoodes lands."

The Duchess was taken aback. "My mother's London properties—"

"Promised to me when I wed, only you thought Kit too reckless and never deeded them! How I hated you at the time. And how I blessed you since. For Bentwoodes, Roger would see my divorce through Parliament, settle South Sea stock upon me and upon Harry, and marry Barbara in the bargain." She looked at her mother triumphantly.

The Duchess's legs ached abominably. Diana's words faded in and out of the sensation of pain as she tried to think clearly. It was not a bad settlement—ah, God curse these aching bones—it was an excellent one, in fact. Diana drove a shrewd bargain.

Sensing her approval, Diana leaned forward, her lovely violet eyes shining, words spilling out of her lips in exultant self-congratulation.

"He wants Bentwoodes badly now that he fancies himself the great nobleman. Our Roger! He aches to have a fine London mansion and square named after himself. And not only do I hold the key to the property he desires, but I offer him the chance to play savior to me, the disgraced daughter of a national hero, a man he served under and adored." She smiled to herself. "Not that I am so blind that I believe he would save me for Father's sake alone, Mother, but my divorce petition has become quite a cause for those Whigs trying to crush all the breath out of the Tories. Roger sees political gain in helping me, in establishing himself as my champion. And our new earl, determined to become a duke before all is said and done, has begun to think of an heir. I hold another trump. I possess the granddaughter of that same adored man—a girl of fine family, tarred now by her father's action, but one whom he may rescue by marrying, thus raising her back to the level she was born to. And that girl is young enough to be molded as he chooses. Roger would be a fool to refuse, when all is said and done!"

Trust Diana to know her prey, thought the Duchess, trying to concentrate over the pain in her legs. . . . Mold as he chose. . . . Roger could charm the birds from the trees. . . . The molding would not be difficult. . . . He always had women about him. Following him. Sending him love notes. Lending him money. Barbara would have her work cut out for her. Barbara . . .

"I will sell him Bentwoodes for your divorce," she said, leaning down to rub her legs, damn what Diana thought. "But leave Barbara out of it. I had a bad feeling last night—"

"You are senile!" Diana cried, her heavy breasts almost spilling out of the knotted sheet in her agitation. "How else will I marry her! You know as well as I what happens to girls who have no inheritance! And Kit has spent it all! Every last penny! Hers and all the children's. There is nothing left! Nothing!"

The Duchess had a vision of Henley's tired, bitter mouth. "I will take care of her. I will—"

"When? Next year? The year after that? I have a chance to marry her now! A chance to obtain something for Harry to inherit other than his father's debts. A chance to see my own way clear."

Their eyes locked. The Duchess no longer paid Diana and Kit's debts. She had stopped five years ago. Go to hell in a basket, she had told them one night, not long after Richard's death, when her grief for him was as raw as bleeding meat, and they had come to Tamworth not to see her, nor to visit Richard's tomb, but to ask for money. Always money. And without her, they had dug themselves deeper and deeper into debt. . . .

"I need this marriage," Diana said, her strength, her will at this moment as powerful as her mother's. "I will have it. Do not oppose me in this, Mother. I will do it despite you."

The pain in her legs consumed her. It was such that she almost did not care what Diana did. It was time for Barbara to marry. And it was Diana's duty to find a husband. Not hers. Roger was an old friend. He had loved Richard as much as any man could. She would not always be here to protect her granddaughter, and the girl must never, never go the way of the Henleys of this world. A countess. It was as much as— or more than—the Duchess could do for her. Between the two of them, she and Barbara could provide for the other children, if Harry and Diana did not, as likely they would not.

"I will not oppose you," she said slowly, the pain making her clench her teeth, "since Barbara wishes it. But he is too old. And there is his reputation."

"Better an old man's fancy than a young man's slave," Diana said flippantly, rising to ring for a servant. "He has settled down, Mother. You would scarcely know him, and no one reaches forty without past mistakes. Not you. Not I. Not even Father."

"Is he still as handsome as the Devil?" She just managed to rasp the words out, her curiosity for the moment overwhelming even her great pain.

"Handsomer. I have rung for your woman, Mother. Go and rest now. I am glad we had this discussion."

"Where were you all afternoon, Barbara?" Diana asked idly. They sat in the small winter parlor. Not only was it near the kitchen, but it had two corner fireplaces which her father had added to the room. They joined the older, Jacobean paneling on each of their side walls snugly, but showed their modernity by their simple marble surrounds. The area above each surround rose smooth and straight for perhaps two feet, then it ended to form a shelf with the adjoining right-angled walls. A bronze bust of her grandfather sat on one of the shelves. A yellow-and-blue Chinese jar stood atop the other. A handsome cabinet of burled walnut with glass doors held more of the Chinese jars and bowls. Several small tables, a harpsichord and armchairs jostled for space. Window seats were recessed into the large windows that had a fine view of the formal gardens, but it was too cold for them to be of use now; their yellow velvet draperies were closed and tied against the chill. This room joined a larger parlor, and instead of a door, more yellow draperies hung across what would have been the door's opening. These, too, were pulled closed to protect against the winter drafts that penetrated through every crack and joint of the older part of the house.

A footman was removing the remains of their supper, while Perryman, her grandmother's butler, directed another to move the gateleg table they used for dining back to its place against the wall. Barbara sat on a fringed stool near one of the fireplaces furiously poking her needle into the embroidery attached to her embroidery frame, while Cousin Henley sat on another, mending napkins. The fire crackled and spit behind the firescreen pulled in front of it so that no sparks should burn their gowns or set the room burning. Harry's leaving and Jane's heartbreak and other things raged inside Barbara.

The Duchess sat in a chair with arms, her legs across a stool that had been put against the chair to support them. Dulcinea lay in her lap, and she stroked the cat's fur slowly. The candles in the wall sconces highlighted the strong bones of her thin face, and the pain that pinched her mouth and shadowed her eyes. Her legs were wrapped with linen strips covered with liniment, and she had taken dandelion wine laced with poppies—not enough to sleep, but enough to dull the pain, enough to let her rest. Her mind floated above her body, free from it for a bit, and she watched Diana and Barbara with dispassionate interest. Barbara had not answered her mother, and Diana looked annoyed. As much as the Duchess's sentiments were with her granddaughter, it was no way for the girl to treat her mother. She waited until Perryman and the footmen left the room.

"Mind your manners, Barbara!" she said sharply. "Your mother spoke to you."

Barbara's chin lifted a fraction, but she said politely, "I was about, seeing people, saying goodbye."

"Well, enjoy your freedom while you may," Diana said. "In London, a young lady never goes out unescorted by family or servants."

Dulcinea yawned and then with a quick, unexpected, graceful leap jumped into Diana's lap. Diana hated cats, and Dulcinea knew it, purring and stretching out her claws so that they caught in the fabric of Diana's gown. Diana picked her up to throw her off her lap, and one small, hard, ivory claw caught in the lace on her sleeves and tore it.

"Damn it!" Diana pushed the cat to the floor with a shove and inspected her sleeve. "She has torn my lace, and it is expensive!"

"When do you leave?" the Duchess asked, as Dulcinea leapt up and back under her mistress's hand, to purr once more and regard Diana with slitted, steady green eyes. The Duchess had begun to reconcile herself to the marriage. What better could she do for Barbara? And if Barbara found that, after all, she did not care for Roger, why, she could stop the negotiations. In spite of Diana. She could. And she would. The wine she had drunk gave her a feeling of wellbeing and made her fears and forebodings seem the crotchets of an apprehensive old woman. Roger was an experienced man, and he would be kind. Kindness went a long way.

"I would like to leave as soon as possible," Diana was saying. Barbara did not speak, but her chest rose and fell a little faster. The Duchess gazed at her fondly. Dear pet. She would be married soon and have children of her own. I would like to live to see Barbara's children, the Duchess thought. She listened to Diana talk about what Barbara would need for London, and they discussed the cost of a court gown, and whether it should be made in London or here by Annie and the village seamstresses. Barbara never said a word. They might not have been discussing her at all, but the Duchess did not notice; she was too amused by Diana's sharp reactions to the new Hanover court. The king had a very long, pointed nose, clear blue eyes and the social grace of a turnip. His mistress Melusine von Schulenberg looked like a maypole because she was so tall and thin, unlike his other mistress, Charlotte Kielmansegge, who was fat. She spoke English, but the king communicated with his courtiers through French and Latin. And he kept to himself. Why, his bedchamber was guarded from unwanted visitors by two Turkish soldiers he had captured. The Prince of Wales was handsomer than his father, but that was not saying much. His wife, Princess Caroline, was plump and fair—all the Hanoverian women wore their hair in the most ridiculous style, built up on pads from temple to temple, looking like a row of hot-cross buns covered with hair! And on this concoction, they put gauze and ribbon and huge hairpins covered with jewels. The ugliest thing ever seen! Oh, and she had seen the Hanover pearls. Magnificent! The Princess of Wales had worn them outlining the bodice of her coronation gown and set in hoops at the shoulders. They were everything rumor had said, but she had not yet seen the incredible necklace and pearl drop earrings said to be part of the set. The coronation itself had been a disappointment; the Hanovers had no style, unlike the Stuarts.

"It will be a dull court, that I prophesy." Diana sighed. "But then Queen Anne's was hardly lively."

The fires in the two fireplaces snapped and crackled and filled the room with drowsy warmth. Cousin Henley rose and excused herself, taking her basket of mending with her. Diana yawned, raised her full, white arms overhead in a graceful stretch and rose from the stool she had been sitting on.

"If you will forgive me, I am going off to bed. The country air tires me so. Good night, Mother . . . Barbara."

The draperies lifted and drifted closed behind her. The log on the fire fell apart with flying, sizzling red-orange sparks. Barbara's needle jerked in and out. The Duchess lay almost dozing in the warmth . . . the peace. . . .

"You wrote to Mother of Harry and Jane!" Barbara accused, her voice low and furious. The Duchess sat up abruptly, startled, to focus her eyes on her granddaughter, hand poised above the embroidery frame, the firelight highlighting her red-gold hair, a seeming tableau of domestic contentment, now seething with anger.

"I never believed you would betray them, Grandmama! What did it matter if they married? The Ashfords are a fine family! I have heard you say a hundred times that their kind makes up the backbone of England. They love each other!" Her needle had been flying in and out of the linen faster and faster with each word she spoke. Now it knotted, and she threw it down in disgust, staring coldly at her grandmother.

"Do not take that tone with me, missy!" the Duchess snapped automatically, stalling to gain time, so surprised was she by Barbara's attack. How like the chit to burst out in such a way. Impetuous. She was never one to hide emotion. Dulcinea leapt down and stalked from the room, her fluffy white tail up in the air, a signal flag which said I am bored with your petty human concerns.

"I betrayed no one!" the Duchess said. "I did my duty! Do not clench that jaw at me, Bab Alderley! I will slap it off! I did my duty, pure and simple, and I care little whether you like it, or Harry, or Jane! I did what I had to!"

Barbara's steady, contemptuous stare goaded her into more speech. "Harry must make a proper marriage. The circumstances demand it. And never forget he is the grandson of Richard Saylor, first Duke of Tamworth! The daughters of country knights are not for such as we! We do better!"

Barbara tossed her head. The firelight glittered through it. Like Richard's.

"Do you think I do not love Harry, child?" she continued in softer tones. "Do you think I want him hurt? Bloody hands of Jesus! You children are my heart. But duty comes before love. Harry will heal, as will Jane. First love seldom lasts, seldom endures. Only one thing does—"

"If you parrot 'duty' once more, I shall scream!" Barbara flashed.

"Do so!" her grandmother flashed back. "And I will strike you with my cane!"

"Impossible! You do not have it with you!"

The Duchess glanced about her. The child was right. She looked back to Barbara. They glared at each other, both jaws set, both pairs of eyes hard.

"Shall I fetch it for you, Grandmama?"

She meant her words to be contemptuous, but the idea of fetching her grandmother's cane so that she might then be beaten with it made her bite her lip not to smile, which took a little of the edge off her anger. The Duchess saw it at once and pressed her advantage

"Impudent chit! If I could move, Bab, I would beat you." She sighed. "As I cannot, take your punishment by coming here. Sit by me. Let us try to understand each other." She moved her legs so that Barbara could sit on the edge of the stool they rested upon. Barbara pushed her embroidery stand aside. I will never understand a duty that hurts others, she thought stubbornly. She sat down haughtily on the spot the Duchess had indicated and stared at her grandmother, her face closed and mutinous.

Where on earth does she inherit that stubbornness? the Duchess thought. Yes, Richard had been stubborn, but not with this locked-in setness, that could not be moved, except perhaps by reasonable argument, and not even then if the girl decided she was right. I have been too easy on her, the Duchess thought. I should have beaten her more often. She is not docile and quiet enough. I would never have dared look at my grandmother so. Ah, the young today do not know what manners, what duty are. She leaned her head against the tall back of the chair. The wine had given her a pretense of strength, but underneath its false sweetness crouched her age, her fatigue, always ready to pounce, to drag her down and shake her lifeless. She closed her eyes and spoke softly, to spare herself as much as possible.

"Likely neither Harry nor Jane will remember the intensity, the pain, two years from now, Bab. Two years is such a long time when you are young. Harry will find an amusing mistress. Jane will marry and have a baby. Life goes on . . . our duties to it go on . . . I hardly knew your grandfather until the contracts were signed." What liars we become with age, she thought. Tell the girl how you followed Richard Saylor with your eyes and heart long before he ever spoke to you. Tell her that. "But I knew my duty. I knew what I owed my family. And I did it." She paused, her face soft with memories, and Barbara, staring at her, caught a sudden, unexpected glimpse of how she must have looked years ago. She listened, in spite of herself, intrigued by the idea of her grandmother's youth.

"Ah, Bab . . . he was the handsomest man in four counties, besides being the best! At first I loved him because it was duty. But then I loved him because I could no more help myself than the sun can help rising in the morning." That is how I feel about Roger, Barbara thought. "And he learned to love me—a sharp-tongued, skinny stick like myself. And we worked together to build our fortune. . . ." What a brave, handsome soldier he was, the Duchess thought to herself, picturing him in his scarlet general's uniform, the medals pinned to his coat glinting in the sun. Second only to Marlborough, and in the Duchess's eyes, not even second. Ah, those were good years. Three strong sons survived all the other dead babes, the estate rebuilt, added to, a daughter coming like a lovely bloom of love—a girl as beautiful as her father was handsome. Life seemed so rich, so easy. Nothing could stop them; they would rival anyone in power and land and wealth. They did. And then, the wheel of fate shifted: one son dead in a battle in that years-old French war, the other two dying unexpectedly of smallpox, a demon from the Devil himself, finding and also killing their oldest and dearest grandson—the heir since his own dear father had died. The dukedom went to Abigail's son. Sweet Jesus. She had always disliked Abigail, wondering how her funny, charming William, William who was never jealous of his older brother's inheritance, William always with a joke and a smile, William dying like a dog in a faraway land—they never found all of his body—could have married her. So in five years, after twenty years of good fortune and prosperity, all that was left of their children was Diana. It was far too late to bear anymore. Three fine sons—strong men to continue the family name, the family honor, to care for them in their old age—gone. And with them, Richard's heart. He, too, dying. Widows and children left. Gone. Ashes to ashes. Dust to dust.

"Grandmama? Are you well? Shall I call for Annie?" The look on her face stabbed Barbara's heart. Betrayal or not, this old woman was her rock, her touchstone for life.

The Duchess shook her head wearily, her face once more thin, old, sad.

"I love Roger, Grandmama," Barbara said slowly. "The way you loved Grandfather."

The simple, startling truth of Barbara's statement hit the Duchess between the eyes. Yes . . . perhaps she did. But Roger was forty-two, and Richard had been two years younger than she when they married. Roger was a man, established in his ways . . . his faults as well as his graces. Richard and she had grown old together, twining around each other like two young greening vines until you could hardly tell one from the other. And even then, they had had their share of quarrels and troubles. Roger was not the man Richard was. Once more a feeling of foreboding clutched at her. "You are fifteen!" she said more harshly than she meant because she was afraid. "What do you know of love? It comes from being with someone, from facing life together! Life in its awfulness, as well as its joy! You love a handsome face. Nothing more!"

Barbara shook her head, her face stubborn and mutinous once more.

"Listen to me, chit! I will tell you of love . . . the kind of love you feel. Your mother fell in love with Kit Alderley, a handsome, worthless devil, even then—may God forgive me for speaking so of your father—and we let her marry him because he came from a good family, and because we had three boys to inherit. Diana could do as she pleased; your grandfather was always too soft with her! I begged her to wait. I begged him. She was fifteen at the time, mad for Kit. Yes! Stare, chit! You cannot think that your mother was ever fifteen." She moved impatiently. She was expending too much energy on this, but she was beyond stopping herself.

"Well, she was! And a wild, willful piece if ever there was one! Worse than you could ever be! So we let her have Kit. And one morning, Diana woke up with seven children to feed, a traitor for a husband, and no more money left. No! And no love, either! It had dribbled away in fits and starts for years! So do not speak of love, missy! Even the greatest love will fly out the window without truth, honor and duty to anchor it down!"

Barbara was silent. Am I wasting my breath, the Duchess thought, staring at her, trying to fathom what lay behind that smooth, young, untouched skin on her forehead. Does she understand? Can one understand at fifteen? A Bible verse sprang into her mind: "When I was a child, I spake as a child, I understood as a child, I thought as a child: but when I became a man, I put away childish things."

"Make your mother tell you why she wants this marriage," she said harshly. "Make her tell you why Roger Montgeoffry considers you at all. It is for land, for property, and not for your pretty self! Make no mistake about that!"

"Your love came later," Barbara said softly. "His will, too."

"And what if it does not?"

Barbara smiled a slow, seductive smile, one the Duchess had never seen on her face before. "I shall make him love me, Grandmama. I can do it."

Sweet Jesus! Had not Richard often said the same thing, smiled the same way, thinking to charm someone into doing what he wished—and succeeding! Except for death. He could not charm death from his sons or from himself.

"Your love for Roger may change after you marry, Bab," she said, exhausted now by the futility of this talk, by the girl's stubbornness, by her own, old woman's fears. "You may not find him to be all you want him to be. That is when you need to remember your duty. It is all that lasts." These last words were faint; the color of her face looked like putty. Barbara rose quickly to ring for her grandmother's tirewoman, thinking, as she did so, Grandmama is old, she does not understand, does not remember. Of course she would do her duty; after all, she was a Tamworth as well as an Alderley. But she would also follow her heart.

* * *

There were no more lectures on duty in the days that followed. Trunks had to be dragged down from the attics and aired and then packed. Then, more often than not, they would have to be repacked, according to her grandmother's latest dictate. The Duchess had taken to her bed, cold and emotion having taken their toll on her legs. She ran the household as forcefully as ever and oversaw every detail of Barbara's leaving. A hundred times during the course of a day Barbara would be summoned to her grandmother's chambers. She would find her propped up in bed, pillows behind her back and all around her to support the wooden trays that held her paper and pens and ink pots and empty teacups. She wore at least three Spanish shawls, her huge lace cap and mittens, these in spite of the roaring fire in the fireplace. Dulcinea stayed nearby, dozing, or if she was in a playful mood, slapping at the feather in the Duchess's pen as she checked yet another item off her ink-stained lists. All the clothes must be checked, laces resewn, ribbons cleaned, dried lavender, mint and rose petals sprinkled carefully in their folds.

"Mother! I will have gowns made in London! These are old-fashioned!" Diana cried in exasperation, but the Duchess paid no attention because she was arguing with Annie on how best to clean the stained silk ribbons.

"You pare four or five good-sized potatoes, being careful to slice them very thin. You lay them in a quart of cold water for a few hours. Then you sponge the silk with the water and iron it dry!"

Annie folded her arms stubbornly. "Spirits of wine, powdered French chalk, and pipe clay is what my mother always used—"

"Your mother was an idiot, then! Check my receipt books! It is my grandmother's recipe! Are you missaying my grandmother, God rest her soul, you stubborn old stick!"

Then Annie must find the milk of roses—made from sweet almonds beaten to a paste with drops of oil of lavender and rose water added—and carefully measure out a portion for Barbara to take with her. It would protect her complexion and keep it smooth and white.

"It is already smooth and white, Mother!"

"This will make it smoother and whiter still! She is after a husband, and a good complexion helps! And you, chit! If you do marry Roger, and I am not saying you will, but if you do, be sure you take care not to wear pearls at your wedding. They are a symbol for tears, you know!"

"She is driving me mad!" cried Diana. But Barbara said nothing. She knew this briskness and bustle covered softer feelings, and was her grandmother's way of blessing her venture not with holy water, but with the more intimate, homier ingredients of lavender and rose milk and clean silk ribbons.

"Will she need candles? There are some freshly made—"

"Good God, Mother! Candles may be bought in London!"

"Do not take the Lord's name in vain, Diana. It is a sin—run along, Bab. You will never get to London and that fine husband you covet if you dawdle in my chambers all the day!"

She slipped out of the room, away from the beginning of a rousing quarrel between her mother and grandmother. She would be summoned again in a few hours with fierce demands as to why she was never around when she was needed, but for now, while she was free, she would go up to the schoolroom and hear the children at their lessons. Her one grief in all of this was leaving them and her grandmother. But Roger was rich now, they said. And he was kind. She knew that. Someday soon her brothers and sisters would come to live with her. And Roger. She would provide for them. It was one of the duties of a gentlewoman, to provide for family. She opened the door quietly and sat down at her scarred wooden desk-table, folding her hands to listen. They were reciting their Bible verses and the sound of their clear, high young voices soothed her.

"'Blessed are the meek: for they shall inherit the earth.'

"'Blessed are they which do hunger and thirst after righteousness: for they shall be filled—' "

She closed her eyes. Kit and Charlotte recited smoothly, while Anne stayed just a word behind. She had not learned her verses and was trying to fool Cousin Henley.

Bless me, dearest Lord, she thought, on this, the most important venture of my life. I promise I will be good; I promise, if you will make Roger marry me . . .

The day had arrived. She stood in the middle of her chamber, her woolen cloak lined with fur tied securely, her traveling gown laced and hooked in place, her hair combed neatly, her heart beating like a drum. Everything that had made this chamber hers was gone, packed in those trunks tied to the luggage cart that would follow the carriage. She had given her birds' nests to Kit. Her mattress had been rolled up, taken outside to air before servants replaced it on her bed. She touched the edge of one of her bed curtains, her fingers on the raised pattern of the crewelwork. Her heart was beating so hard that she thought it would explode from her chest. Her childhood was over. The next time she returned to Tamworth, she would return as a wife, possibly as a mother, God willing, as He must be willing. She felt dizzy with the emotion swirling inside her.

"Your lady mother says to hurry." Her maidservant spoke sullenly. Barbara was not taking her servant to London with her—her retaliation for the betrayal that first evening to Diana. If she could not be loyal here in Tamworth, what would be her worth in London? Besides, she would hire a French maid as her personal attendant. She was going to be fashionable and elegant, as Roger was. He would be proud of her.

"Tell her I will be only a few moments longer." She had to say one last goodbye to her brothers and sisters, a task as heartrending as that of leaving her grandmother. She had spent all morning in her grandmother's chambers. Together they had said prayers, and her grandmother had read to her from the Bible.

"'Keep thy heart with all diligence,'" the Duchess had recited, "'for out of it are the issues of life.'" She had sat holding her grandmother's hand while Annie brushed her hair and tied ribbons in it. She promised that she would remember to say her prayers, to attend church services, to mind her manners, to watch her temper, to be polite and respectful to her elders, to listen to all that was told her, to speak quietly and seldom, as became a modest young woman of good family.

And take this, her grandmother said gruffly, at the last minute, thrusting a bag of coins into her hands.

"I gave your mother money, but I have no doubt it will fall through her hands like water. It always has. It always will. This is a secret between you and me, mind. Now, go and say your farewells to those brothers and sisters of yours."

Kit, Charlotte and Anne were lined up like a row of bowling pins in the nursery. Only the baby was missing, asleep in
his cradle, and Tom away at school, and—of course—Harry.
She came forward with a smile, holding out her arms to them.
They ran to her, even Kit, who usually felt that he was too
old a man to show emotion. She sat down on the floor, heedless of her gown, and pulled Charlotte, who was already
crying, into her lap. Anne clutched a fold of her sister's traveling cloak in one tight little fist and said nothing.

"Do not leave me, Bab!" Charlotte sobbed. "Please! You are
the only one I can talk to. Grandmama is so old!"

From her corner by the window Cousin Henley frowned,
and Barbara saw it. Anne began to cry. Even Kit made a
furious wipe at his eyes. Cousin Henley rose, and Barbara
shook her head at her.

"Leave it be, Cousin," she said. "They may cry. Listen to
me. Listen!" she soothed. "When I am married, I will send
for you, all of you, and if Henley is not kind, I shall hire a
new governess to care for you, and we shall live in a big,
grand house. And you will be aunts and uncles to my babies."

In her corner, Cousin Henley shook her head.

"Really, Bab?" said Kit.

"R-really?" hiccoughed Charlotte. Anne kept her head fastened to Barbara's cloak, but she stopped crying. A footman
peeped around the doorway. "Mistress Barbara, your mother
says come."

Charlotte began to wail again. Barbara crushed the three of
them in her arms.

"Hush, my darlings," she said. "I am going to London for
a great adventure, and you must wait here until I write for
you. But I will send dolls, sweets, soldiers, and even something for Cousin Henley, if she is very nice. Think of those
things! Think of what I will be sending!"

"You will not forget, Bab?" said Kit. She took his face in
her hands.

"You are the oldest until Tom comes home from school, Kit.
You must look after the little ones. In my place. Protect
them."

Kit glanced toward Cousin Henley and squared his jaw.
Barbara stood up, and with Anne still clinging to her cloak,
went over to the baby's cradle. The last Alderley lay sleeping

like an angel. She touched a curled-up, plump fist. Goodbye,
little William, she said silently. She closed her eyes a moment.
It was so hard to leave them. Gently, she disentangled Anne
from her cloak and put the child's hand into Kit's. Charlotte
continued to cry. Barbara spoke hard and clearly to her cousin. "Be kind to them, or by God, when I am a countess, I
will have you sent packing to someone else!"

"Bab!" Charlotte cried out, but Barbara ran from the room
and down the series of staircases and out the great hall before
the children could see her weep. She ran past a startled and
disapproving Perryman and, her heels crunching the gravel of
the courtyard, she jumped into the carriage without waiting
for a footman to assist her.

"You are crushing my gown!" Diana exclaimed, pulling
away irritably. The carriage lumbered away. Barbara hung
her head out the window, ignoring Diana's protests. She
thought she caught a last glimpse of a limp lace cap on a thin
face in one of the bay windows. They lurched past the out-
buildings, the dovecote, the dairy and the stables. She saw the
kitchen maids carrying in pails of water. A stableboy trotted
down a path leading one of the horses. Then they were on the
avenue of limes, and then turning sharply out of the entrance
gates, on the road to London.

There was a spreading ache in the center of her chest, and
a burning in her eyes, but she would not allow herself any
indulgence, not with her mother and her mother's maid in the
carriage with her. She set her jaw and rolled down the window's leather shade. She focused on the only thing that could
soothe the pain she felt . . . Roger.

"Did Mother give you any money?" Diana said, breaking
into her thoughts. Barbara stared at her mother, not knowing
what to answer. Diana held out her hand. "I thought so. Give
it to me at once."

The Duchess sat upright in her bed, her heart pounding.
She stared into the dark, remembering now what had eluded
her. That scrap of gossip about Roger. In one of her letters.
Not even written out plainly. Hinting of Roger and the French
vice. She had laughed out loud when she read it. And wished
Richard were alive so she could tell him. He would have
laughed louder than she. The two men had once been as close

as brothers. As father and son. Why, she could still remember the expression on Roger's face at the funeral. . . . Something long buried turned over and showed her its face in her mind. She cried out.

"Annie!" she said, her voice rising. "My candle! Hurry!"

There were scuffling sounds in the dark, and then the scratch of steel striking flint and Annie's grumbling. She saw tiny sparks catch the cotton rag shreds in the tinder box and smelled the pungent sulfur as Annie touched a stick dipped in it to the burning shreds, and it caught fire, and she lit the candle with it. The Duchess's eyes fastened on the flame. In the shadows, Annie stared at her, her features frowning, sharpening into worry. She opened her mouth to speak.

"Go away!" the Duchess said harshly. "Leave the candle."

The flame. She would stare at the flame and cleanse her mind with it. It would catch hold of her thought, igniting it as the sparks had the cotton shreds. Before she had the chance to think on it more. Oh, dear God, why should she have suddenly thought what she had? As if a piece of puzzle were about to be fitted into place, but she did not want its fit. Why, she knew Richard as she knew her own heart. There had been no vice in him, no darkness. And none in Roger . . . no . . . none. . . . She began to breathe a little more easily. The thing was going. Slipping back into its hole with all else that was unspeakable. Unthinkable.

"Bah!" she said out loud, not meaning to. Meaning only to hurry it away.

Annie started up from her chair and was at her bedside in seconds.

"My legs," the Duchess said gruffly. Annie gave a satisfied nod. The Duchess allowed her to rub them, to bring her a cup of wine, which she drank down gratefully.

"Extinguish that candle and go to bed," she said after a while. And at Annie's look, "I am better."

And so she was. There was no need to write Diana. What could she say? I remembered some gossip. People always gossiped. I had a fear. She always had fears. No. She would leave it be. She knew both men. She would tarnish neither with her foolishness. She turned over to sleep, comforted now by her decision.

Unbidden, familiar words came to her as she lay there: "For now we see through a glass, darkly; but then face to face; now I know in part; but then shall I know even as also I am known."

"Go away," she said loudly, not caring what Annie might think. "I will not hear you."

CHAPTER THREE

*T*he first Earl Devane, or Roger, as his friends called him, turned to better view himself in the long, gilt mirror of Venetian glass held by his valet. A wig maker and tailor hovered like shadows in the mirror's murky backgound. It was late morning; not a morning on which Roger received visitors, but a few friends had called, and since he never liked to be alone for long, he allowed them in. He stood staring at himself seriously, the eyes of everyone else in the room riveted on him, as if the cut of his coat or the style of his wig were the most important thing in the world. And, at this moment, both were. He struck another pose before the mirror in a room that was one of the most luxurious in London.

Ten years ago, he had lived in rented lodgings and on the largess of his latest mistress. Now, in his bedchamber alone, expensive silk imported from Lyons, the shade of a new daffodil stalk, lined the walls and the inside of heavy, oyster-colored draperies. Green and silver-threaded tassels tied back the draperies, which edged tall windows overlooking the most fashionable square in London, in which Roger had leased the largest house. Silver fringe hung like moss from the edges of all his chairs and stools. His writing cabinet, veneered in elm and ebony, boasted silver mounts, silver drawer pulls, and a silver ink pot. Even the fireplace tongs and shovels were of silver. Various opulent Italian landscape paintings, their colors dark and moody, hung from the walls on long, velvet ties. Only three of the paintings were of people. One was a small portrait of King George; another was a portrait of Madame, Princess Elisabeth-Charlotte of Bavaria, sister-in-law of the dead French king, Louis XIV; and one was a portrait of his grace, Richard, first Duke of Tamworth.

A loud belch broke the silence. Everyone's eyes shifted to Robert Walpole, sitting on a fringed, green velvet stool near the fireplace, wiping the last bits of a currant bun from his fingers onto his coat. Glazed sugar clung to his fat, cherublike face, a face punctuated by two heavy, dark eyebrows over intelligent eyes. At thirty-nine, Robert was leader in the House of Commons and first lord of the Treasury.

"Was that an opinion?" asked Roger.

Robert shook his head. Near him, in a chair with arms, dozed his brother Horatio, just as fat, but not as talented. Horatio was serving as minister to the United Netherlands because of his brother's influence. He opened one eye to look at Roger, then closed it again. Roger frowned at himself in the mirror. Both the wig maker and the tailor held their breaths, each hoping it was the other's merchandise he might be displeased with. Lord Devane was a style setter, and if he was satisfied, he would not only buy at least five wigs and order who knew how many coats, but everyone else in polite society would copy him.

"Do not buy the wig," said John, Duke of Montagu, wearily. He was a tall man with drooping eyelids, and he stood on the other side of a shining walnut table that held silver trays of food: currant buns white with sugar; fluffy scones so fat they looked like sponges; and plump cheeses like castles surrounded by moats of hothouse grapes and oranges. Silver bowls held yellow-white butter, thick, fresh cream, shimmering strawberry and plum and apple jellies. Three silver urns served coffee, tea and hot chocolate. But, unlike Robert Walpole, Montagu had not touched a bite. He and Roger had been up most of the night gambling in one of the private rooms at Pontac's, a fashionable tavern. Roger never drank heavily when he gambled, but Montagu did, and this morning he was paying for it. He was in Roger's town house because he had passed out in the middle of the last game, falling over on the table with a dead man's thud, and Roger had decided to bring him home to sleep in one of his spare bedchambers, rather than send him off at dawn to face his wife.

"Do not buy it," he repeated. "If you do, I must purchase one like it, and the style will not flatter me the way it does you."

"My lord," the wig maker squeaked hurriedly, "I assure you it is the latest style from France. You are the first I have shown it to."

"I know it is the latest style," Roger murmured. "But is it becoming?"

"My dear one, you look wonderful, as you well know," drawled Tommy Carlyle, a rawboned, hulking man with rouged cheeks and lips and a face powdered stark white. He sat in a chair pulled away from the others, his big hands folded on top of his cane, his eyes following every move Roger made. In his left ear was a large diamond earring. It was an affectation of his, and only one of the reasons that the other men in the room despised him. But Roger was amused by him and allowed him free access, almost like a lapdog, except that Carlyle was far too big and apt to bite.

"God's wounds!" Robert Walpole muttered. "He looks as if he could eat Roger whole!" Without opening his eyes, his brother grunted.

Roger turned back to face the mirror, smiling at what he saw. Reflected was a man in his early forties, who passed for thirty-five, or, on a good day, even less, when he had had plenty of rest the night before. This morning, his face was puffy; the small sags along his jawline, the tiny wrinkles around his eyes, were there in full force, but he was still an extraordinarily handsome man, his looks more striking, more refined than any of the other men in the room, even those who were far younger. Shorter than average, he was lean and spare—some might say slight—like a boy, and his face was tanned and thin, with the high, pronounced cheekbones of an Italian Renaissance angel. His smile was unexpected, charming and wistful, possessing a quality that made women think he had suffered a tragedy they alone might be able to heal. That smile and his face had always been his life's good luck charms, charms he needed, for he was the younger son in a family that had lost everything in the civil wars, as had so many families. But while his older brothers were content to farm the land and marry in obscurity, he had more ambition. He somehow cajoled the money from them to buy a position in the army, and once there, his smile, his face, a very definite grace of manner and his bravery had done the rest. He always knew the right thing to do, whether it was to lead a surprise attack against an enemy's flank or charm the wife of a general at a tea party.

Attached to the staff of the Duke of Tamworth, he might have been content to remain there forever, except that his thirties crept up on him, and in the mirror were lines that would only deepen, and in his heart were things he could not explain, and so he left Queen Anne's England and the constant bickering between the men surrounding the ill queen, men jockeying for power and using the army and war in Europe as their battlefield. He went across the sea to Hanover. Proximity to the next heirs to the English throne might provide him opportunities that England itself could not. The duke had written letters of recommendation. His charm and face and personal courage did the rest. And his luck. When he heard of Robert Harley's idea to create the South Sea Company in 1710, a firm to be allowed the monopoly of South Seas trade in exchange for taking over part of the public debt, he immediately sold or pawned everything he owned or could borrow from friends, relatives, acquaintances and willing women, sailed to London and invested every penny into that stock—every penny and every prayer to God that it would succeed.

His hunch paid off a thousandfold (he was one of the first on the huge, speculative wave of credit foaming over England and Europe). It paid off just as his leaving England for Hanover had a few years before. Money seemed to fall into the very pockets that had once been empty, for his relationship to the future king broadened all his horizons. Now he was considered a fortunate man; no one remembered those years when he had simply been another young officer living off his face and wits. Everyone wanted some of that good fortune. Merchants, tailors government officials, petitioners, impoverished poets, poor relations, gossipmongers and friends crowded his downstairs hall every Thursday when he held his official morning reception, each hoping to be bid past the ornate public rooms into his even more ornate private rooms, until finally, like pilgrims reaching their shrine, they entered his bedchamber, a paean to his taste and power and ability to indulge both.

Among them was Diana, lovely, drooping, an old friend in need, an instinctive judge of people whom she could use. The idea of developing Bentwoodes, first seen on a morning horseback ride with Diana, who had been weeping with fear because Kit had just fled the country, at first intrigued him, then began slowly to obsess him. He would found a great family, symbolized by a house and square that would astonish London with its beauty (his years in Europe and particularly in France had heightened a natural eye for beauty of form and line). And the idea of a young, fecund wife who could give him sons to carry on his wealth and title did not displease him. It was time he married, and a young wife would not expect him to remold himself for her benefit; rather she would change for his.

He remembered Barbara only as an engaging, talkative, long-legged ragtail of a girl, with glorious red-gold hair rioting all over her head, her blue eyes—her grandfather's eyes—following him whenever he moved. She had had a fondness for him. He knew that, and it had both amused and touched him. The last time he had seen her was some five years ago at Richard's funeral, not that he could remember her. He remembered only the black, terrible grief that had consumed him, lingering for too long afterward, a darkness coloring all he said and did and achieved. It was as if he had seen the burial of his youth, his ideals, with Richard's body, and he had begun an affair out of that feeling—and the darkness— an affair that opened depths within that exhilarated him beyond all he had known but the immediacy of the battlefield, when all issues in life crystallize to one point, that of survival. He felt destroyed inside when the affair ended, felt burned to ashes, felt for the first time . . . old. More than old. He needed Bentwoodes, its concept, its symbolism, its connection to Richard and to his young self, to fill the empty places inside.

Ironically he was at the apex of his life, rich beyond what he had ever imagined; courted by one and all; handsomer for all his wrinkles than when he had been a fresh-faced youth. Diana did not know all of his feelings; she did know that in spite of his wealth and power, he was vulnerable. And she intended to use him. And, for his own reasons, he intended to let her.

"Are you going to buy it?" repeated Montagu.

Roger's smile faded to a frown. The wig maker began to murmur to himself, almost as if he were praying.

"I am afraid," Roger said slowly, pausing for dramatic effect—small beads of sweat broke out on the wig maker's forehead—"I shall have to take it." The relief on the wig maker's face was so obvious that Robert Walpole choked on a biscuit, and even Carlyle allowed himself a pointed smile. Montagu walked around the table and pounded Robert on the back. Walpole's choking laughter woke his brother up.

"What did he buy now?" Horatio asked immediately, his wig slipping off to one side. Robert went off into another bellow, unencumbered this time by the biscuit.

"You need not worry about it, Horatio," Carlyle answered in his biting, effeminate way. "Nothing you wear can help."

"I shall order four more," said Roger. "Two of brown, one of black and one of blond."

"You will look superb in blond," drawled Carlyle, holding up an eyepiece connected to his smooth, swansdown waistcoat by a twisted gold chain. "Yes, I see you in blond."

Montagu groaned out loud. Carlyle turned the eyepiece toward him slowly, like a bear who had been diverted from the catch in hand to another more tempting.

"You must buy one, too, Monty," he said. "It will make you look more—how should I express it—theatrical, perhaps? A good thing, too." He touched his red lips with a filmy handkerchief.

Montagu flushed. Robert Walpole put down the jam scone he had begun. Roger bit his lip. Everyone knew Montagu's latest mistress, an opera dancer, had run off with an actor from the Haymarket Theatre, but no one, except Carlyle, had the impoliteness to refer to it. Horatio, who did most things slowly, stepped into the awkwardness of the moment with a sudden loud question about Montagu's father-in-law, the Duke of Marlborough, who was ill. Montagu slowly unlocked his eyes from Carlyle to answer the question, and conversation turned naturally to the duke's illness and to his quarrelsome wife's arguments with her daughters. Carlyle sat back, quiet for the moment, content with the tension he had been able to create. Roger took no part in the conversation, which ambled from the Duchess's quarreling ways to the duke's winning ones, for Marlborough was one of England's great military heroes. He pulled the new wig from his head and ran his fingers through his own short-cropped silver-blond hair. He consulted with his valet about which wig he would wear today, and once or twice his eyes strayed to the portrait of the Duke of Tamworth. But no one, except Carlyle, noticed. They were too interested in Montagu's family gossip.

A door set in the far wall opened, and two young men walked over to Roger, who was intently watching his valet adjust on his head a short wig tied with a black ribbon at the back. Both men waited quietly and respectfully. One of them was Francis Montrose, who served as Roger's secretary. He was neat and slim with an earnest, round face. The other was Caesar White, an ordinary-looking man except that his left arm was deformed. It stopped just below the elbow, from which grew a tiny, useless hand. White was a poet, serving as Roger's clerk of the library so that he would not starve to death before he finished his third volume of poems (which would, naturally, be dedicated to Roger). Carlyle's gaze ran over both men, and then returned to Montrose.

"Where do you find them?" he murmured. Both the young men ignored him. They were accustomed to Carlyle; they were accustomed to the way Carlyle looked at Roger, and other men. If Roger did not mind, why should they?

"The Duke of Bedford and Sir Christopher Wren are both here, sir," Montrose said.

Roger clapped his hand to his head. "I completely forgot about Bedford. We will have to delay him, Francis. Tell him . . ." He paused, tapping a finger against his lips. He grinned suddenly, and Montrose, a serious-minded young man, could not help grinning back. "Tell him I am undecided—it is true, Francis, I swear it—and that I have stupidly made another appointment, which I will cut short for his convenience. Meanwhile, send Sir Christopher to the red withdrawing room, and have him wait for me. Give him some wine—women, whatever he wishes. I will see him immediately and change our expedition to another day. Then, if these gentlemen will go home, where they belong"—he bowed to

his friends, who had stopped talking to listen to his business—
"you may allow Bedford in here to wait for me. He can view
the painting again; it will whet his appetite, not that I intend
to sell. I will join him as soon as I can politely leave Sir
Christopher. There, Francis. I have solved all your problems.
Whatever do I pay you for?"

"What painting?" Robert asked Montagu.

"A Rubens," answered Carlyle before Montagu could open
his mouth. He pointed with his cane. "That wall. Fourth from
the right." Roger was already shrugging out of the tight coat.

"My lord—" began the tailor.

"Not now!" Roger said impatiently. "Attend me next Thursday morning. Francis, write it down." The wig maker, packing away his samples with much rustling of tissue paper,
smiled complacently from his corner. The tailor looked as if
someone had just hit him in the stomach.

"The volumes of Plutarch you had rebound have arrived,
sir," said White, who had been standing behind Montrose
patiently waiting his turn. "As has the new book on architecture by Giacomo Leoni. I put them both on the table in the
library so that you might view them before I shelve them. And
I have finished a third canto you might want to read—"

"Sir, you are scheduled to sit for your portrait this afternoon," interrupted Montrose, with an impatient look for
White. "Sir Godfrey Kneller sent a note around this morning
to remind you. And you are to have supper tonight with Sir
Josiah Child after the Princess of Wales's reception. And there
is another note arrived from Lady Alderley—" Roger held out
his hand, and Montrose shuffled among his packet of papers
and handed him a folded and sealed note on dark red paper.
For a moment, the scent of musky, strong perfume invaded
the room. Every man's nostrils quivered, and Carlyle suddenly looked very satisfied with something. Roger whisked the
note into a pocket of his waistcoat and then let his valet finish
pulling the tailor's coat from his shoulders and help him into
one of pale blue satin trimmed with lace along its front opening. Everyone watched, feeling free to make various comments,

"I like the coat."

"Blue is not my color."

"What is your color?"

"Is that wig new?"

"I see you are wearing covered buttons now—"

"Go home," repeated Roger. He walked over to the three by the fireplace. "Monty, you look terrible. You must rest, and I am sure it is safe to return home now. Mary will be out shopping. Robert, will I see you at the Princess of Wales's drawing room tonight—what have you spilled on your coat? It looks like jam. Horatio, remind me that there are some books I wish you to send me when you return to Amsterdam."

A footman entered bringing tricorne hats, cloaks and gloves and began to distribute them. Robert wiped at the stain on his coat. Montagu handed him a linen napkin. He blew his nose in it. Carlyle, standing some distance away, shuddered. Roger laughed and walked to White, who had gone to stand by the windows, the sheaf of papers containing his poetry bundled in his good hand.

"Caesar," he said, "I promise I will find time to look at your verses today. Leave them on the table by my bed. 'Many brave men lived before Agamemnon,' " he quoted softly, " 'but all unwept and unknown they sleep in endless night, for they had no poets to sound their praises.' " He turned immediately to say goodbye to Carlyle, and White watched him, a combination of fond respect and admiration in his eyes.

"Is it true, then, Roger—what I have heard? That there is a bridal in the air?" Carlyle spoke loudly, suddenly, and his voice startled everyone.

For a moment, motion in the room stopped. Montrose coughed and kept his eyes carefully lowered. Montagu and the Walpoles hung suspended, in and out of their cloaks. White glanced at Roger's face, and then out the window. Roger flushed, looking stunned. It was a coup for Carlyle, for Roger was almost never caught off guard.

"I have no idea, Tommy," he said. "Unlike you, I never indulge in malicious gossip. That is why I keep my friends." He turned on his heel and left the room, Montrose following like a shadow. Two spots of natural color appeared under the rouge on Carlyle's cheeks. Immediately, the others, the Walpoles and Montagu, surrounded Carlyle.

"What bridal?" asked Robert.

"Not Roger's?" said Montagu.

"The Alderley chit," snapped Carlyle.

"Nonsense!" said Montagu.

"Roger was devoted to the duke," ventured Horatio.

"Has she some fortune no one else knows of?" asked Robert. "Why else would he do it?"

Carlyle took a small muff of silver fox from the footman. "Use your eyes and ears," he told them wearily, while the three of them stared at him with the concentration of fascinated schoolboys. "Giacomo Leoni's new book on architecture. Sir Christopher Wren—our premier architect—waiting. I daresay if we searched the library we would find Colin Campbell's new book on architecture as well as a copy of Palladio's." He waited for their response.

"Roger wants to build something," Horatio said hesitantly.

"Excellent!" spat Carlyle sarcastically. "How well you must serve us abroad, Horatio, with your keen mind. Of course Roger 'wants to build something'! And who owns a prime piece of property called Bentwoodes?"

The three stared at him.

"Exactly," he said, and sauntered from the room, pleased with himself. The other three remained huddled.

"I know Diana—" said Montagu.

"Who is Diana?" interrupted Robert.

"—and she will want everything but the moon in return. Damn! I refuse to help Roger sponsor her divorce. You can be sure that will be one of her conditions. Of course"—he smiled slowly—"no one can perform fellatio like Diana. It might be worth the price of a divorce."

At that moment, the Duke of Bedford strolled into the room. The three nodded to him, and he returned their nod, but walked over to a painting on the wall and stood staring at it.

"The Rubens," said Robert. "Roger is spending money like Midas. I wish I knew where he finds it."

"If it is a misalliance, Roger will never do it," said Horatio.

"If you think Diana Alderley will let him slip through her fingers once she has him entangled you are a bigger fool than I am!" said Montagu irritably. "I may as well face the fact of Roger's marriage and see what I can gain from it!" He crushed his hat under his arm and headed for the door. The other two followed him.

"What I want to know," said Robert, "is why I have never met Diana."

"But you have," argued his brother. "Last summer when you were conducting that investigation she was in and out of Westminster bothering everyone. Think. Dark hair, beautiful eyes, huge, white tits. 'I would like to jump her,' you told me. Your exact words—" The door closed behind them.

The Duke of Bedford was still examining the Rubens.

"I do not know how Roger managed to outbid me," he said. "I was assured I made the highest offer. Just look at those flesh tones."

"Lord Devane has excellent taste," ventured White, not quite sure whether he was included in this conversation or not.

"Yes," snapped the Duke. "So we all know."

Barbara sat staring at the fog, terrible impatience filling her as surely as the fog filled the square of Covent Garden below her with its thick, gray, rolling mists. I want something to happen, anything, she was thinking, as the flower and vegetable and herb vendors packed away their goods, putting a child or two in among their baskets of walnuts or onions, to carry them both under the vaulted arcades of the stuccoed houses on the other side. They would gather there in groups to gossip, smoke their pipes, and nurse their babies until the fog lifted. Then great carriages, pulled by four or six horses, would lumber up again, their occupants spilling like melons from a box to shop the market. Housekeepers, cooks, maidservants and merchants' wives would wander among the heaped baskets, pinching at the produce, haggling with the vendors. Noise and confusion would begin anew, just beneath her window.

She was unbelievably homesick for Tamworth, its gardens and woods and familiar comfort, for her grandmother's gruffness and for her brothers and sisters. From the moment the carriage had squeezed across London Bridge, nothing had gone the way she expected. The carriage had lurched to a stop just off the bridge, and her mother pushed the French maid she had brought with her from Tamworth out the door, tossed a handful of coins after her and told the coachman to drive on. The woman ran after them, screaming French obscenities.

"I cannot afford her!" Diana snapped to her wide-eyed look, and Barbara had known from that moment that nothing

would be as she had been led to believe. She was correct.
Instead of pulling up before the house she knew her parents
owned in Westminster, the carriage had rattled through narrow, twisted streets filled with shops until it had pulled into
the piazza of Covent Garden. They stepped out in front of one
of the four-story brick buildings with curving Dutch roofs. She
followed Diana up the flights of stairs—Clemmie, her mother's serving woman, stood smiling gap-toothed at the top—to
dark, small, smelly rooms consisting of a parlor and hall, two
bedchambers and a tiny adjoining room. The rooms smelled
of other tenants and dirt and had only the barest essentials of
furniture. Meres reappeared like a stray dog to sleep under a
table in the parlor, during the day lounging on the stairs until
Diana should have an errand for him to run. Barbara had
thought to go shopping for gloves and fans and ribbons. She
had thought to visit her cousins at Saylor House, the mansion
her grandfather had built in London. She had thought to see
Westminster Abbey and St. James's Palace and the Tower of
London. She had thought to see Roger, not to be cooped up
in these rooms as day led into day, while her mother sat by
the hour in the parlor, at the same table, slowly emptying a
bottle or two of wine, as she dashed off note after note in
sprawling, blotted handwriting. Why? she asked her mother,
daring her slaps—which she received. Because, her mother
answered, swaying a little with the wine she had drunk, I
have debts. Many debts. And no one can find me here. Once
the marriage is announced, it will change. She stared at Barbara, who was rubbing her cheek, and who had not cried,
but stood looking at her mother with blue eyes Diana read too
clearly. Never mind thinking you can write to your grandmother, Diana said coldly, because Clemmie is watching you
every second I am not.

Clemmie. Her jailer and savior, for when her mother left,
on some errand, Barbara would cajole Clemmie into taking
her along as she shopped. It was the only way she could leave
the lodgings. She had been no farther than a few surrounding
streets, though Clemmie had once taken her across the busy,
wide thoroughfare of the Strand so that she might see the
Thames River, where she could have stayed for hours watching the river craft: the slender, quick wherries, the barges
painted all the colors of the rainbow, the sailing ships with

their great, billowing white sails and their many little colored signal flags. But Clemmie was old and wished to rest her feet. "You cannot trust this river. Sometimes dead rats and babies float by," she told Barbara, her face as shapeless under its layers of fat as her body was. "It is the time of floods. Come away." And so back they had walked, Barbara soaking in everything she could: shops with brightly colored signs hanging above the doors. Gloves, books, jewels, old clothing, soft, glowing fabrics, cheeses, fat, dressed geese displayed in the windows while the owners' wives followed her halfway down the street entreating her to come inside. Women, their rich, heavy skirts held up out of the street mud, walking on elaborate leather clogs to protect their cloth shoes. Gangs of apprentice boys, their hair cut short, running through the streets snatching at pretty girls' cloaks and old men's wigs. Street vendors, their wares strapped to them, calling out to the passing carriages and up to the closed windows and doors of the houses around them. "Pancakes! Piping hot!" Or, "Rare holland socks, four pairs a shilling!" Or, "Knives and scissors to grind!" "Death to rats!" "Hot baked warden pears and pippins!" "Brooms! Buy my brooms!"

The bells in the church of St. Paul's of Covent Garden began to ring. Barbara listened to their clear sound, pressing her cheek against the window. How long? How long must she wait?

The window vibrated beneath her cheek. That was not church bells. That was a rapping at the front door. It was so unexpected that she sat up, startled, then thought of Roger and nearly tripped over her skirts rushing to the hall. Her mother stood framed in the parlor opening, staring at the door. If Barbara could have believed her mother capable of fear, she would have believed it at that moment. Clemmie was frozen in the hall, lumplike, staring at Diana. A long look passed between them. Rap! Rap! Rap! went the door, again.

"Meres," said Clemmie. "Meres would have warned us."

After a moment, Diana nodded her head, and cautiously Clemmie opened the door, her mouth a fat O of surprise at who stood there. Barbara's aunt, Lady Abigail Saylor, sailed in like a ship of state, flags flying in the size of her pearl earrings and brooch, the rich look of her brown striped gown, the soft fur lining her yellow cloak and muff, the gray lace on her widow's cap, topped by a stylish velvet hat. Abigail was in her late thirties, still attractive in a harsh, pug-nosed, fading blond manner. ("Women like Abigail," her grandmother had sniffed, "are pretty in a pert way when they are young, but as they age, they resemble nothing so much as the pigs in my pens!") It had been several years since Barbara had seen her aunt, but from her aunt's first words, she knew there had been no changes.

"It took you long enough," Abigail said to Clemmie. "Did you think I was a bill collector?"

She saw Barbara, smiled with her mouth but not with her eyes, offered her a powdered cheek to kiss and said, "My, you have grown. You are prettier than I expected. Go away to play, like a good girl. Diana, you are looking thin. And I must say it becomes you. You were getting as fat as a pig. Come, we must talk." Abigail never asked; she always commanded.

Dismissed as if she were a small child, Barbara did as she was told. She sat back down in her chair by the window, but the fog was complete now. She could see nothing. Her glance went to the Advent wreath lying on the table by the bed. She had fashioned it herself from sweet evergreen bought at the market below. It was the season of Advent. If she had been at Tamworth, she would be walking in woods and gardens gathering mistletoe and holly and evergreen and rosemary, which she and her sisters would weave into garlands and wreaths to decorate the village church, her grandfather's private chapel, and the great hall at Tamworth. She would be supervising the packing of baskets of food for the tenants and the poor, her task since she was ten: "Time enough to learn one of a gentlewoman's duties, the succor of those less privileged," her grandmother had said then. . . .

She heard the raised voices of her mother and Aunt Abigail. Already they were quarreling. They always quarreled. Why was her aunt here? To take her and her mother to Saylor House? She would not wait to be told. She would find out . . . just as she always had.

She crept into the hall to listen. Clemmie was already there, her ear against the parlor door. Graciously, she moved over for Barbara.

"—do not like it! None of us do! I thought it my duty to tell you so. I have only your welfare at heart!" her aunt was saying.

"It is none of your affair!" shouted Diana.

"Bentwoodes belongs in the family—"

"I am family, and Bentwoodes belongs to me! Yes, stare, Abigail, you greedy bitch! It is mine, promised to me when I was born, and I may sell it to the Devil if I so please!"

"Roger Montgeoffry has no right to it! He is an upstart! A nobody!" Her aunt's voice trembled with rage.

"A very wealthy and powerful nobody! And how did your grandfather earn his earldom, my dear? I always heard it was from service in the right bedchambers!"

"How dare you! You are trash, Diana! You always have been! You always will be! Stealing off like a thief in the night, leaving your house in Westminster empty, your servants wageless, while you conspire in Tamworth and hide here to escape the horde of creditors and tradesmen trying to catch you! Why, they are sleeping seven deep on your front steps— it is the scandal of the street! When I drove up to find you, they descended on my carriage like a plague of locusts! And then I heard you are selling your daughter like a whore in Covent Garden to the highest bidder! Without even one word to us! Tony is the head of the family! He should have been informed—"

"Tony is a blockhead!"

Barbara and Clemmie looked at each other. Barbara covered her mouth to giggle. Tony, her aunt's oldest son and the present Duke of Tamworth, was indeed a blockhead.

"How dare you! Tony is the kindest, the dearest—"

"He is a fool! And you know it!"

"Well," her aunt said, "no bigger a fool than you to marry your young daughter to one of London's biggest libertines. I wish her the joy of him! He will make her unhappy! That I prophesy!"

"What husband does not? She can do as the rest of us and be unfaithful—"

"Speak for yourself!"

"Ah, yes, I forgot. It was my brother who was unfaithful in your marriage, was it not?"

Clemmie rolled her eyes at Barbara.

"You go too far, Diana! I came here in loving kinship to keep you from making a terrible mistake. You must know Roger's reputation! I could wish better for my niece—"

"Do not bleat 'my niece' to me! It is the dower you are concerned for! Bentwoodes! I see it in your face! Barbara could marry the Devil as long as Tony got Bentwoodes!"

There was a long silence. Barbara held her breath. Her aunt began to speak again, in a calmer voice.

"Let us not argue, Diana. I came here to help you. I have talked it over with some of the family, and we feel that it might be better to dower Barbara with money, rather than lands—lands that belong in the family. In exchange for Bentwoodes I might be able to come up with a significant cash settlement."

"Not three months ago, I went to you begging for money, and you refused to loan me so much as a penny." Diana's voice was deadly quiet.

"I was upset, distraught over Kit and your petition for divorce. Everyone in the family was aghast. Those dreadful street pamphlets, calling you every sort of harlot. Our name bandied in Parliament as if we were common criminals. The suspicion, the distrust stirred up. I could not forgive you for your part in it all. Now, I am more myself, and I want to do my duty to you, and to my dear niece. If you must marry her, good. There are any number of young men I can recommend. But listen to reason; leave Bentwoodes out of it—"

"You are too late, Abigail! I intend to marry my daughter to England's newest earl, upstart that he is, and enjoy a considerable amount of money for myself as part of the bargain! I will never need you or anyone in the family again, and nothing you can say or do will stop me!"

"Stop you!" her aunt spat out, all pretense of family feeling forgotten. "You fool! It is all over London that you plan to marry your daughter to Roger Montgeoffry. I may not know Roger well, but I know men. They never do what you want them to when they think they are being forced. Ah, now it is your turn to stare, Diana! You have overplayed your hand!"

"Who gossips so?"

"Tommy Carlyle, among others. You know how he is—"

"And who told Tommy?" Diana interrupted.

"How should I know!" her aunt snapped. "But the bucks at White's coffeehouse are betting as to whether you will pull off the marriage or not. It is vulgar and common, Diana! I expect such of you, but Roger, upstart though he is, has more taste. He will not be pleased to have his name, or his bride's, a byword in the streets and taverns. You should see your face. Yes, you are going to lose! And when you do, I will still be here, at Saylor House, to bail you out. But I promise you, I will not forget what you have said to me, and I will not be as generous as I planned to be today. You will regret to your dying day that you ever spoke so to me, Diana Alderley! Now, good day! And good fortune! For the Lord above knows you will need plenty of it!"

The parlor door opened, and Barbara and Clemmie fell back. Her aunt stopped short, raking them both with her eyes, her bosom (a bosom she was fond of displaying) heaving with anger.

"You are more like your mother than I imagined!" she said.

Barbara raised her chin.

"Yes," her aunt said, "be proud. 'Pride goeth before destruction, and a haughty spirit before a fall.' And you have a long, long fall, my poor girl."

She reached into her muff and pulled out a bag of coins, obviously struggling with her temper. "Here," she said. "I meant to give your mother this. At least move to a better section of town!"

Barbara would not take the bag, but Clemmie had no such scruples. She curtsied and smiled her gap-toothed smile and thanked Abigail profusely as she scuttled to open the front door. With a great, final swish of hoop and petticoat, Aunt Abigail was gone. Barbara ran into the parlor. Diana stood by her table, draining a glass of wine. She turned on Barbara like a tigress.

"If you say one word to me—just one—I shall beat you until my arm drops off! Now get out of my sight! I have to think!"

Behind Barbara, Clemmie waved the bag of coins.

"Thank God," Diana said. "Bring that here. I will get my jewels out of pawn—"

Lying on her bed, Barbara tossed and turned. The quarrel meant she was not going to Saylor House. That she must stay here. They were hiding, hiding from creditors, from family, from disgrace. Her mother would not move them to better lodgings. Her mother did not care how they lived. She had not realized what her father's flight, her mother's action, the debts, meant, not really. None of it mattered at Tamworth. With her grandmother and her brothers and sisters. But here, it was different. She was ashamed, and shame was a new emotion to her—scalding and corrosive, like wormwood. Please come soon, she prayed, her thoughts going out the window, into the square, past the cobbled, dirty, busy streets, somewhere into the great, throbbing city she had yet to see. Please, Roger, come for me. I know as soon as I see you everything will be fine again.

Roger mounted a restless Spanish stallion and nodded for the groom to loosen his hold on the bridle. He was to meet Sir Christopher Wren at one. The horse beneath him reared and pawed at the cobblestones, but Roger held him back as he trotted past the fountain railed off in the center of St. James's Square. He moved into Pall Mall Street, his horse pulling for his head and prancing sideways. Fingers of sunlight had managed to poke holes into the day's grayness. It was slow progress, weaving his way with a restless horse through pedestrians, sedan chairs, other riders and carriages with footmen running beside them. He lived near the royal palace of St. James, near Westminster Abbey and Parliament, and traffic was always terrible. On St. James's Street he managed to avoid trampling some government clerks coming out of White's, so intent were they on their conversation that they did not notice him until he pulled his horse up to keep from riding over them. At the corner of St. James's Street and Piccadilly, he pulled short and sat gazing at the walls of the Earl of Burlington's house to his left. He had heard rumors that Burlington was going to redo it, and sure enough, from where he sat, he could see piles of brick inside the gates. The house itself was modest, red brick, two stories, but its gardens were magnificent, extending far out until their walls stopped amid undeveloped land and fields at their rear. But not undeveloped for long. He had also heard that Burlington intended to convert those fields to the north of his gardens into streets and houses. Restive, the stallion struggled to have his head, and

Roger spurred him into Old Bond Street. There was less traffic now, and he let the horse trot smartly. So Burlington was going to build. And the Earl of Scarborough was said to be planning to develop land farther north of Burlington's. And to his right, where there were now small rolling hills and a sprinkling of farms, Richard Grosvenor had started two roads that were to give access to a square he was planning. Already in his lifetime, he had seen open fields across from the palace of St. James become bustling, cobbled streets crammed with town homes and shops. The city was growing this way.

He was now on New Bond Road; Tyburn Road was ahead. He let his impatient horse find his own stride. At Tyburn Road he reined him in and, trotting the animal up and down, allowed him to cool down. To his northwest rose the spires of the church in the village of Marylebone. To the southwest lay the broad, green acres of Hyde Park. To his west were more fields. To the east was the Tottenham Court Road, the way to the village of Hampstead.

Between Tottenham Court Road and the boundary of Hyde Park lay smooth, fertile fields that were leased in small farms. An old country lane led to a crumbling manor house, built in the time of Henry VIII, and lived in by the Duchess of Tamworth's great-great-great-grandfather, Baron Bentwoodes. A rambling stream coursed through fields until it reached Tyburn Brook. Part of the land near Hyde Park was still dense woods where deer and hare could be hunted. The Bentwoodes and then the Duke of Tamworth had always allowed their sovereigns full use of it, as Roger intended to do when it belonged to him. He glanced to his left. Sir Christopher was arriving. Ahead pitched a coach pulled by four horses, the coachman pulling them to a stop in front of Roger.

A leather shade at one of the windows rolled up, and Sir Christopher Wren put out his head. An old man now—he was in his eighties—with staring, lashless eyes, a domineering nose and a genius for building, one of his most magnificent creations being St. Paul's Cathedral in London. He wore a heavy, black wig that ridiculed the lines in his face.

"Can the coach go in?" Sir Christopher asked.

"I will show you a road. Have your coachman follow me."

The coach lurched dangerously over the deep, muddy ruts, but Roger did not stop until he was in front of the crumbling

manor house and the remains of its courtyard. The manor
house had once been **U**-shaped, but a fire had gutted one of
its arms to make it a leaning **L** of singed and darkened red
brick, intersected every foot with dark wood, a Tudor carpenter's trademark, as were the old-fashioned windows, with
their many small diamond-shaped panes of broken glass. A
sagging porch shaded the front of the ground story, and Roger
tied his horse to a porch support and watched the coachman
spring down to pull at the coach steps. Wren, leaning on a
cane, stepped down carefully. All around them was silence,
broken only by the occasional lowing of a cow. Roger offered
Wren his arm, and the two of them wandered out of the
courtyard and into the overgrown gardens, where they talked
for a long time, one or the other of them pointing to different
views of the property. The stallion grazed on the grass growing between the bricks. The coachman settled under the safest
part of the porch to smoke a pipe. He was lighting his third
one when Roger and Wren returned.

"See if there is any furniture inside—a chair or stool for
your master," Roger told him.

The man hesitated. "Will the door not be locked and
barred?"

"And rotted. Never mind it, just push it in. I know the
owners."

The coachman shrugged and pushed at one of the half-tim-
bered doors. To his surprise, it gave almost at once. He went
inside. Wren leaned against one of the stronger porch sup-
ports and rubbed his gloved hands together for warmth.

"You are correct, sir," he told Roger. "It is a fine property—the finest in one complete piece that I have seen in
many a year. I will have it surveyed for you. Happily. But I
am too old, Lord Devane, for all else you suggest. I would die
long before you were finished, and I do not like to see things
left uncompleted."

"What if I told you the property could be mine by spring?"

Wren shook his head regretfully. "Even so, there are plans
to be drawn up, permits to be granted, roads to be made. It
would be a year before building could begin, and you want
such a grand scale. You speak of a church, a playhouse, town
houses, shops, a square, a mansion for yourself, a market, the
surrounding streets necessary for access. I could not do it."

"If I have it by spring, you could build me a church," Roger said persuasively, smiling into the eyes of the older man. Churches were Wren's weakness. "You could do that, could you not? Within three or four years—"

"A church—"

"Just a small one. Like the one you built for Henry Jermyn at St. James's. I am inspired whenever I am in it. It is small enough to allow worshipers to see and hear all, yet lovely and spacious enough for them to think themselves truly in paradise."

"You flatter me."

"On the contrary, I cannot flatter you enough."

Wren was visibly softened. He looked past Roger to the fields that lay all around them. "It will be very beautiful here when you are finished," he said softly. "Done on a grand, unified scale. I like that. After the great fire, we tried to rebuild the city according to a model plan, but it never quite worked out; business interests and politics interfered. This"— he spread his arms, cane and all, wide—"would last long after you are dead and buried. Bentwoodes House—"

"Devane House." The words were quiet, but firm. "How well you put things, Sir Christopher. Nothing can so symbolize a man as what he leaves after him—as well you know, having left so many beautiful things to survive after you. I had hoped, had dreamed really, of having one of your churches. I saw it as a rare jewel, perhaps the last achievement of your brilliant career. No politics, no business interests, just your own free will and imagination combined with your long years of experience."

"Free will, you say."

"I would not consider interfering in any way, except to provide money, of course. It would be sacrilege. But I see that you know best. A man knows when a project is too much for him. I forget your years—you act so much younger."

The coachman appeared in the doorway, his hat and coat covered with dust and spiderwebs, a smear of dirt across his left cheek, but triumphantly, a chair, its back nearly broken off, in his hands.

"I had to look everywhere, your lordship. All over this great barn of a place. I nearly broke my leg on those stairs. They are rotten, you know. But I found one—"

Roger gave Wren his arm. The older man leaned on it as they walked toward the coach. The coachman might never have existed. He sighed and dropped the chair and followed them to the coach.

"I might do a church," Wren was saying. "Just a small one, mind you. And look over your plans for the rest when they are done. Offer suggestions. Nothing else."

"You are kindness itself, Sir Christopher. I cannot tell you what an honor you do me. But men will see how I have been honored, each time they worship their Lord. Tell me, sir, since you refuse my whole project, what do you think of Colin Campbell or even William Kent as architect?"

Wren pursed his lips. "What you desire calls for a man of extraordinary talent—"

"But you said you would not do it!"

Wren smiled sourly at him. "Extraordinary talent and patience." Roger helped him inside the coach. Wren shook his cane at him. "One church now. No more. And perhaps a few sketches to give you an idea of how it all could look. But no more."

Roger smiled at him. "It is entirely more than I expected. You are graciousness itself."

Wren looked around him. From where he sat, he could see a line of great oak trees following the curves of the hidden stream. "I congratulate you. This will be the finest property in London in ten years' time."

"So I hope, Sir Christopher. So I hope."

That evening, after several hours' sleep, Roger made an appearance at the Princess of Wales's drawing room in St. James's Palace. The chamber was crowded with people, rich in their velvet and damask and satin, jewels glinting under the candlelight of the chandeliers. A massive allegorical painting covered every square inch of the ceiling. Gods and goddesses lolled on clouds or posed in chariots; from their hands ropes of roses trailed through blue sky and legions of cherubs. The faces remained plump and forever serene, unlike those of the humans who strolled beneath them. Except, of course, for Roger, who had rested and therefore looked handsome and unbelievably young—and distinguished. He wore a silver-blond wig on his head, a black velvet coat trimmed in silver lace and silver braid, with matching black velvet breeches, a few tiny black silk patches on his face, black leather shoes with huge velvet bows and diamonds in the heels. People could not help but look at him as he walked by, bowing and smiling in every direction. It was as if everyone wanted a moment of his attention, for he was golden, blessed, untouched, unlike the rest of them with their liver spots and missing teeth and fat hanging over their breeches. It was as if his age underlined his continued beauty in a way the smooth roundness of youth could not.

King George stood at one end of the room. Near him was his thin, ugly mistress, Countess Melusine von Schulenburg. A semicircle of courtiers had formed about them, most being content to be seen by the king, make their bows and curtsies, then leave discreetly. King George did not speak English, only German, French, and Latin, and even if he had, he did not have the magnetism of his Stuart predecessors. Nodding to the right and left at friends and acquaintances, Roger went first to the Princess of Wales, Caroline, a plump, blond woman with a pretty, round face and shrewd blue eyes. He bowed over her hand and kissed it, smiling charmingly at her young maids of honor, who surrounded Caroline's chair like luscious flowers. They fluttered their fans at him.

"The king seems in good humor tonight," said Roger.

"George is behaving himself," she said, rolling her eyes at Roger, who laughed. She was referring to her husband, George Augustus, the Prince of Wales, a slightly stupid and very impatient man, busy flirting with his mistress.

"I let him amuse himself," the princess said. "It keeps him out of trouble."

"You are very adroit." Roger smiled down at her. His eyes crinkled in the corners, and he looked as if he, too, understood disillusion in love.

"One learns," she said more softly, his charm having disarmed her. "Dear Roger, you are always so kind. My Aunt Liselotte asks of you in her latest letter." Liselotte was Princess Elisabeth-Charlotte of France and Bavaria, the same Elisabeth-Charlotte whose portrait was in Roger's bedchamber. She was cousin to King George and widow of Monsieur, brother of France's Louis XIV.

"Write her that I kiss her hand a thousand times, and that I am coming to France very soon, where I shall most certainly visit her for all the latest gossip."

Caroline smiled. "She will be delighted to hear that. Go. His majesty sees you. We will talk later."

He made his way, smiling and bowing, toward the King of England, a plain man of fifty-five with a very long, pointed nose. The courtiers moved for him, many noticing King George's smile of genuine pleasure as Roger walked toward him. Few Englishmen brought it to his face. The king was a private man, dining alone, keeping to himself. But Roger walked in the palace gardens with him and hosted him in his own home and was welcome at any time behind those palace doors closed to so many others.

"Just look at the two of them. He looks like a king. The king looks like his groom," said Robert Walpole, looking like a fat brown bear in his brown velvet suit and striped waistcoat. He stood with his brother and brother-in-law, Viscount Charles Townshend, one of the king's secretaries of state, not far from Roger and the king.

"Handsome is as handsome does. Is it true he is going to marry Kit Alderley's girl?" asked Townshend, watching Roger bow and smile and begin to talk as naturally with the king as if he had known him all his life. The king laughed at something he was saying, and Countess von Schulenburg smiled, too.

"Where did you hear that?" asked Robert.

"You told me. But everyone is talking of it anyway. It seems the girl is bringing some vast pieces of property to the marriage. For Roger's sake, I am glad. But I hate to see Diana pulling herself out so well."

"Diana," repeated Walpole. "I keep hearing her name. Where is she? Is she here tonight? Point her out to me."

Townshend and Horatio exchanged a look.

"Over there is a faction of the Tamworths, but I doubt Diana will be with them. She is up to her neck in creditors and hiding out."

Robert looked to where Townshend indicated. Lady Abigail Saylor sat with her family. She looked worn and irritated tonight as she watched Roger and the king talk, her mouth pinched in, her fan snapping open and shut. She wore a blue velvet gown which squeezed her breasts up like melons. Her breasts were smooth and full; it was a shock to look upward and encounter her aging, determined face. Her son, Anthony Richard, second Duke of Tamworth, sat beside her. He was seventeen, plump and vacant-looking in a pink satin suit and a blond frizzy wig. Her eldest daughter, Lady Fanny Wentworth, and her husband were sitting with them. Lady Fanny was a prettier, softer version of her mother. And two of the late duke's sisters, Lady Elizabeth Cranbourne and Lady Louisa Shrewsborough, both magnificent in the amount of wrinkles, jewels and haughtiness they displayed, also sat with them. The women were focused on Roger while Tony and Lord Wentworth watched the musicians at the other end of the room.

Horatio shuddered. "Tony Saylor did not inherit his grandfather's looks—"

"Or his mind," cut in Townshend.

"I would hate to be caught in a dark alley with that group tonight. Lord, look at Lady Saylor's face. She looks fit to be tied."

"She is opposed to the marriage. Roger will be lucky if he obtains one acre of property from them," said Townshend.

"Diana sounds like a spirited woman," said Robert. It was obvious he had been paying no attention to them.

Horatio and Townshend exchanged another glance.

"Diana Alderley will have nothing to do with you, Robert. You do not have enough money," said Horatio.

"And you are too ugly," said Townshend.

"And too fat," said Horatio.

"Those are my plans, your majesty," Roger told the king in flawless French. "I would like to be in France in time for carnival. There are estates I wish to see, and old friends. I thought to summer in Italy and"—he smiled at the king and bowed—"Hanover."

"There is a Scotchman in France, a John Law," King George said. "Have you heard of him?"

Roger winked at Melusine, who smiled back at him. "Certainly, sir. He has some theories about credit which are said to be revolutionary. I thought I might look into them."

"I thought you might do so also, Roger. And you might take some private messages to the regent, nothing official, that anyone need know of, just some personal notes to him from me."

Roger bowed.

"You turn his pleasure trip into one of business," said Melusine. "He works too hard and will have you do also, Roger."

"I owe him too much to refuse him. He would put me in the Tower and cut off my head. Has he been ignoring you, Melusine? You could always leave and run away with me."

"You mock me, Roger. I hear you are promised to another. Do send him to the Tower, your majesty, for trifling with me. But do not cut off his head. It is far too handsome."

Roger stared at her, openly annoyed. "Who says I am promised?"

She pointed with her diamond-studded fan to Tommy Carlyle, obvious in very high, very red heels that made him tower over almost every man in the room. Carlyle looked toward them, and seeing them staring at him, blew Roger a kiss. In spite of his annoyance, Roger had to bite his lip not to smile. The king snorted in disgust.

"Why do you have anything to do with him, Roger! He is an unnatural, an aberration of nature!"

"He is a friend, your majesty. I am loyal to my friends. And he can be very amusing, as you have just seen."

"Even when spreading gossip about you?" asked Melusine.

"A man such as that knows no loyalty," said King George. "He is ruled by his unnatural passions. How it used to sicken me to watch Monsieur mince about! How cruel he was to my cousin Liselotte with his pretty boys and handsome lovers!"

"Perhaps such people are to be pitied, rather than abhorred, sir—"

"Do not keep talking of Carlyle," interrupted Melusine impatiently. "Is it true you are to marry that traitor Alderley's daughter?"

"Melusine!" said the king.

"There was no man more loyal than her grandfather," Roger said. "Her mother has the same blood in her veins. And you know you may count on the Tamworths, sir." He nodded toward the group of them sitting against the wall, the young duke, his mother and sister and aunts. Lady Saylor saw them looking and said something to her daughter. They stood up and shook out their gowns.

"I can do better for you," said King George. "The branch you choose is on the brink of ruin. Let me find you a German heiress."

Roger bowed. "No, thank you. It might be amusing to bring them back from the brink. And in any case, it is my own affair. Your majesty . . . Melusine . . ." Backing away, he joined the Walpole brothers and Townshend.

"You offended him," the king said.

"How romantic," said Melusine. "And how English. And how foolish."

"Bah!" said the king. "Now I know why Lady Alderley requested an audience with me. She is burning her bridges behind her."

"What does that mean?" demanded Melusine.

He smiled at her. "It is a military term, my cabbage. I think the lady has Roger outflanked."

"Pooh!" she said. "Oh, dear, do smile, George. Here comes that haughty Lady Saylor and her daughter."

"Let us leave at once, Robert," Roger said, glancing at the two bearing down on the king. "Abigail Saylor has me in her sights, and I am in no mood to be polite."

Clemmie brought the note in, holding it as if it burned her fingers. Diana snatched at it and tore it open. She read it once, then once again. Barbara, watching her, thought, The note is from Roger. I know it. I feel it. Why does Mother stare so? He is dead. Yes, that is it. He has died, and it is all over. Or worse. He has changed his mind. He never wants to see me—

"He is coming tomorrow," Diana said slowly. Barbara could not move; her limbs were turned to stone. She stared at her mother like an idiot.

"He is coming tomorrow," Diana repeated, half shouting the words. Clemmie threw her apron over her head and began to dance a jig. Diana laughed and tossed the note up in the air. It fluttered to the ground like a white bird. Barbara's heart was beating so fast she thought she might be dying. She tried to speak, but when she opened her mouth, no words came out. Diana pointed at her and began to laugh harder. Barbara felt bubbles of hysterical laughter floating up inside. Clemmie whirled around the room like a fat, brown jug come to life. She whirled into a table and went crashing to the floor. The apron was still on her head. Diana screamed with laughter.

Clemmie pulled the apron off her head. "I fell," she explained to them unnecessarily.

Barbara looked at her mother. "S-she f-fell," she repeated. Then she exploded with laughter. Clemmie's face rearranged itself into folds of disapproving, hurt fat. Diana shrieked with laughter; so did Barbara.

"I may have broken my leg," Clemmie told them.

"Her l-leg," howled Diana, bending over and holding her sides. Barbara stamped her feet and fell back against the chair. The room echoed with their baying laughter.

Clemmie slowly heaved herself up. She looked at Barbara. She looked at Diana. She sniffed. Their laughter doubled. She shuffled from the room in a dignified waddle.

Barbara held her sides. They ached. Diana wiped at her eyes. They were both breathing as hard as if they had been running, and every now and again, one or the other would break into fresh laughter. Barbara smiled at her mother. Diana smiled back. For a moment, she looked as if she loved Barbara.

Barbara stood up and took a step toward her. "Mother—"

Diana turned away. She sat down at her table and picked up her quill pen. "Leave me be. Tell Clemmie to send for Meres. We have work to do before Roger arrives."

She sent them all out scurrying to find items carefully noted on ink-stained lists. Doling out coins, she warned them to obtain the best bargains for their money or she would beat them all. Meres must fetch water, buckets of it, and buy sand and potash and scrub brushes and a soup pot and cups and plates and spoons and pewter. Clemmie and Barbara must go to the baker's and order food for the tea they would serve Roger tomorrow. And they must find Turkey carpets, pictures and lace curtains in the secondhand shops. And flowers. Clemmie and Barbara were to wait until the market was closing and then buy as cheaply as possible.

"Do not pay where you do not have to; insist on a down payment rather than the full amount; and give a false name and address," she told them. It was after dark when they had everything Diana wanted. Barbara was sent to bed, but she heard her mother and Meres and Clemmie in the parlor working for what seemed like a long time. She rubbed milk of roses in her cheeks and said her prayers. Tomorrow. Her life began tomorrow.

The next morning, she leapt out of bed and ran into the parlor. Clemmie and Diana had been up before her, and they had wrought a miracle. Gone was the threadbare, dirty room. In its place was a warm, cozy, almost charming one. Tables and chairs had been polished with beeswax. Fresh, white, starched lace curtains hung at the windows and red-orange geraniums and white hyacinths bloomed in pots on top of the sills. The fire was burning brightly, and soup (bought in the shop last night) bubbled in a soup pot and filled the room with its delicious smell. Turkey carpets, bright blue and green and gold, spread across the tops of the scarred, mismatched tables. Shining pewter peeked out from the cupboard shelves. Pictures hung on the walls. Rugs were scattered on the floor. A table was set for tea. There was even a Christmas wreath over the fireplace.

"It is almost beautiful," breathed Barbara.

"I am glad you approve!" Diana snapped.

Barbara knew that tone. Her mother was running on nerves alone and the least thing would set her off into a rage. The lines on each side of her mouth were deep and hard. Though it was hours before Roger would arrive, Diana marched Barbara into her bedchamber. She was to bathe all over. The water was icy cold, and she gasped like a fish when Clemmie lathered her hair with a mixture of ale and egg and herbs and rinsed it with two buckets of water. By the time they were finished, Barbara's teeth were chattering so hard she thought she might bite her tongue. Clemmie wrapped her in a blanket and set her on a stool in front of the fire. She and Diana began the business of pulling together Barbara's toilette. Barbara shivered and sat as close to the fire as she dared. She felt scraped raw inside and out. Once her hair was dry they began to dress her. She stepped into a delicate lawn chemise of her mother's, and pulled on her own white stockings and tied them about her thighs. Clemmie helped her step into Diana's stays, and Barbara gripped the bedpost while Diana pulled the laces so tight that tears came to Barbara's eyes.

"I cannot breathe!" she cried out.

"Be quiet!" hissed Diana, and Barbara, hearing the barely controlled tone of her voice, was silent. Next they tried one of Diana's hoops and a petticoat of quilted, white satin. Both were too large, but Clemmie, who had lived with the ups and downs of Diana's life too long not to be versatile, produced needle and thread and went to work. The needle flew like the wind and within an hour, both were tucked to fit. Barbara held up her arms as Clemmie and Diana slipped a gown over her. It was her own, her best one, of pale blue velvet with elbow sleeves set in foaming lace the color of cream. Her white neck rose out of the gown's front like a delicate flower stem. Diana motioned for Barbara to sit and began to brush her hair. But she jerked the brush so brutally that Barbara cried out, and Clemmie took the brush without a word and began gently to pull her thick hair up into a knot of curls. Diana paced back and forth like a lioness. Barbara bit her lip, all her joy at seeing Roger dissipating. If I fail, she will kill me, she thought. If I fail, I will kill myself. She half smiled at her gallows humor, but the stays were pulled too tight. Clemmie calmly threaded ribbons of pale blue and green and silver and pink into the red-gold topknot of curls on her head. Diana looked her up and down.

"Go to your room and stay there," she commanded.

"Keep thy heart with all diligence," Barbara repeated to herself as she obeyed her mother, "for out of it are the issues of life." She said the phrase over and over as a litany against panic. Some calmness returned to her. And confidence. There was no reason Roger should not marry her. He wanted Bentwoodes, and she came with it. That was all. That she should love him was a dividend he would not be expecting. A sweet dividend. She would not let her mother's impatience and bad temper sway her. Roger. She must concentrate on Roger. This was their first meeting in five years, and though it might not mean much to him, her whole future was in it. Calm. Calm yourself. Think of Tamworth, of the woods and gardens. Think of summer and cool, green things. Think of bees humming over red and white rambler roses. Grandmama strolling on the lawn with Anne and Charlotte toddling after her. Yes . . . yes . . . calm, peace, serenity—

A knock sounded at the door. She jumped. Her heart began beat so loudly that it was all she could hear. Now. She sat on the bed and waited for her mother to summon her. The roaring in her head quieted. Her heart slowed down. Her mother's summons did not come. She waited a few minutes more. I will not go and see what is wrong. I will wait, she told herself sternly. One of her vows to God had been that she would stop eavesdropping if God would make Roger marry her. But perhaps her mother had called and she had been so upset, so excited, she had not heard. She would go into the hall only. No farther. She crept there, skirts lifted. Clemmie sat in a chair. When she saw Barbara, she rolled her eyes and pointed toward the parlor. Barbara crept closer. Clemmie shook her head at her, but she ignored her. Just once more, she thought. Then I will stop. I swear it. She put her ear against the door.

"I do not like having my hand forced, Diana." It was his voice. Surely it was his voice. Her heart thumped violently. Clemmie pulled at her arm. Come away, she mouthed. Barbara snatched her arm back and shook her head.

"I do not understand you," her mother said.

"You understand me perfectly. It is all over London that I shall marry your daughter. I do not like to be anticipated."

"Roger!" her mother said. "You know it was not my doing. I would never be so foolish."

Aunt Abigail's words bubbled up suddenly in Barbara's mind like witch's brew. She could no more have moved from where she was than she could have stopped breathing.

"I hold you to nothing." Diana's voice continued, calm, but with a note in it that Barbara knew well. She will beat me tonight, she thought. And I do not care. "Someone will marry Barbara for Bentwoodes—though Father would have been so pleased—but that is neither here nor there. If you are no longer interested, I am free to pursue other offers. I am sure you will understand—"

"Do not play games with me, Diana. There are no other offers. No one yet realizes what Bentwoodes can be. The stink of your scandal clouds their foresight—for God's sake, why are you crying?"

"If you only knew what I have been through, Roger," her mother said in low, throbbing tones, her voice raw with emotion. "I had such hopes for this marriage. It would help us both, I thought. I could begin anew; put the past behind me;

lift my children out of the mire their father has thrown them into. And you, a young wife, children, land. . . . Oh, well, I shall manage yet. I cannot pay back the money you have lent me, but I shall. I am hiding here from bill collectors and creditors, but you will be the first I pay!"

"Diana, I did not mean—"

"No! You have been more than kind! Here, take your handkerchief. What a weak, silly woman I am. You have been a good friend to me, always. I will not forget it. When I make other arrangements for Barbara, I will pay you back. I swear it."

"Other arrangements?"

"Abigail has been here. Yes, just the other day. She is displeased beyond words at our proposed alliance. She said she would arrange for a cash settlement in exchange for Bentwoodes and—oh, I really do not know what else. I will go to Abigail and beg her pardon. Yes, I see that is what I must do."

"Abigail was here?"

"Out of a sense of duty, she said. She felt you were not— forgive me, Roger, for being so frank, but then, we are such old friends—not good enough to marry into the family. Of course, I told her it was no such thing—"

"My family is as old as hers! I would match pedigrees any day!"

"Now, Roger. Do not be angry. I did not mean to upset you. I should never have said anything; I can see that now. Come. Stop pacing like a tiger. Sit down and we will share a glass of wine for old time's sake. Let me have your handkerchief back. Perhaps you might suggest some suitors for Barbara's hand—"

"I will suggest no such thing! I came here to give you a deserved tongue-lashing for allowing gossip to spread, and end by losing Bentwoodes to Abigail! Abigail! She would turn it into a rabbit warren of narrow streets, shops and taverns. In five years, it would be a slum."

"Then you are still considering my offer—"

"Go and fetch your miserable girl while I still have the wits about me to think!"

"Of course. Have some wine while I am gone. Remember, for my sake, that Barbara is young and has grown up in the country—"

"Enough, Diana!"

"Yes, I will say no more. She has been dying to see you. You were always a favorite of hers—"

Barbara backed away from the door and rushed into her bedchamber. She was sitting on the bed when her mother came in, shut the door carefully, then whirled around.

"Bloody hands of Jesus, but I need a glass of brandy! Carlyle has done his work well! Roger is as skittish as an old woman!" She clenched her hand into a fist and shook it at the heavens. "If I survive this . . ."

Barbara looked at her mother's face. There was nothing there to show that moments before she had been weeping. Everything she had overheard whirled around in her head. "Someday you are going to overhear something that will singe your pretty little ears!" Harry's words were haunting her now. She needed more time, just a few moments more to compose herself. But she found she could not ask her mother for them. She could only sit there staring at her, looking the Lord above only knew what kind of fool. She lifted her chin.

"What is the matter with you!" hissed Diana. "He is waiting!" For the first time, she noticed the expression on Barbara's face. Instantly she was at her side, one white hand digging fiercely into her arm. Barbara had to struggle not to cry out.

"He is waiting." Diana spoke slowly, deliberately, through clenched teeth, her red nails digging deeper into her arm with each word, so that Barbara could almost not understand her for the pain. "And he is uncertain. If you spoil this now with your foolishness, I swear I will beat you until I drop, and you die from it!" She gave a final twist to Barbara's arm. Barbara did not cry out, but her face whitened. Satisfied, Diana let go.

"Bite your lips to redden them," she said contemptuously, walking out the door and not bothering to see if Barbara followed. Barbara rose slowly off the bed and took a ragged breath. Her arm was throbbing. I will not cry, she told herself as she walked out the door. She will not make me cry.

She concentrated on that thought as she entered the parlor and saw Roger Montgeoffry for the first time in five years. He was sipping a glass of wine, but he set it on the windowsill at once, and came toward her, smiling.

She had an immediate impression of overwhelming richness, from the great ruffles of heavy lace cascading down the front of his shirt to the diamonds on his hands, to the soft, cut velvet of his coat. He exuded an aura of wealth, power and fashion as distinct as the jasmine scent he wore, the black patch at the corner of his smiling mouth, the dark curls of the wig framing his thin, dear, beloved face. Her last memory of him had been his terrible weeping at her grandfather's funeral. He had not seemed so distant, so grand then, only frailly human—like everyone else. She struggled to impose his real features atop the blurred, remembered ones. How was it possible that he was handsomer than she remembered! How could she have forgotten how sweet his smile was! She caught her breath. A rush of love shook her. It was too much emotion—too suddenly. Her eyes filled with tears that had been building for days, since they had crossed London Bridge and she had realized her mother's lies. She slowly sank into a curtsy.

"God save me, Barbara," he said in a voice that was trembling slightly, "but you are the image of your grandfather!"

His words warmed her, but they also weakened the command she had left, and her mouth, which had begun to answer his smile, went awry. I am going to disgrace myself and cry, she thought wildly. As if he divined what she felt, he turned from her and said to Diana, "She has grown into a lovely young woman. I make you my compliments."

Barbara still struggled not to cry. She could barely see where Diana was indicating that she should sit, but she sat down anyway. Roger ignored her, talking all the while to Diana, his voice filling the room with a steady, comforting stream of words that allowed her to find her way back to calmness. She concentrated on making her breathing even, on swallowing back tears. Diana coughed. Startled, Barbara stared at her. She nodded toward the tea table beside Barbara, while Roger talked of Hanover, of her grandmother's health, of some act before Parliament. There was a pause in the conversation. Barbara took a deep breath. She was ready to try once more.

"My lord," she said in her low, husky, throaty voice, not daring to look at him, "may I offer you a cup of tea?"

Roger stared at her. She allowed herself to look up. She did not yet know it, but her voice made her immediately sensual. Roger looked stunned, and Diana saw it. As inexperienced as she was, so did Barbara. The sudden admiration in his eyes was different from that of a few moments ago, when it had been man to child. His look now was man to woman, acknowledging a part of herself she did not yet know she possessed. And she smiled tenderly at him, her love openly on her face, because he was the first man to look at her so, and because he had been kind to her when she came in, and because she loved him, as she always had. And this time it was he who caught his breath, for when Barbara truly smiled, eyes were dazzled. It was part of her legacy from her grandfather.

"You have grown up," he said to her slowly. "A monstrous thing to do in my absence. You make me feel ancient."

"You could never be ancient," Barbara said softly. She had to lower her eyes before the glow in his. There was an awkward pause.

"I will have some tea, Barbara."

Her mother's words reminded her of her duty, and she busied herself pouring tea and arranging ginger cakes and sweet scones and clotted cream on plates. She was able to hand Roger his tea without her hands trembling, though she did not dare look at him again. She smiled to herself at the thought of the way he had stared at her. Self-confidence returned. She tossed her head. Roger said nothing, sipping his tea, his eyes on her. Diana said nothing, sipping her tea, her eyes on him.

"When did I last see you, Barbara?" he asked her.

She lifted her eyes, no more the shy violet, but rather a sunflower unfurling itself in the warmth of the beloved sun.

"At Grandfather's funeral. You gave me a gilt ribbon box you had brought with you from France and held me in your arms, and said that I must not cry too long, for my grandfather would not like it."

"I am amazed that you remember!"

"I remember everything that you have ever told me," she said.

He smiled. The warmth of it burned her. How can I love him more than I already do? she thought. He is all I remember and more. She searched her mind for anything that would keep him talking to her, staring at her with those eyes that made her feel so beautiful.

"Do you know the king? I mean, my mother tells me you are friends with his majesty."

"I am as friendly as one can be with a king," he told her. "They are dangerous to know. People envy you when you have their friendship and scorn you when you do not. When I went to Hanover, I served his mother as a secretary and messenger and sometimes spy, and through her, he and I became friends. People say he is stupid. They are wrong; he is merely deliberate."

"I have not yet taken Barbara to court," Diana said. "As you can see, we are living in reduced circumstances just now. Perhaps, one day soon, she will meet his majesty."

"He will be charmed," Roger told Diana. "He was a great admirer of your father."

"How does he know my grandfather?" Barbara asked.

"When Marlborough was leading the allies against Louis XIV, your grandfather and the king worked together on several campaigns."

"Do you still have William the Conquerer?"

"What an amazing memory you have! No, I sold him with my commission. He was a magnificent horse, wasn't he? I tried to find him later and never could. Do you remember how I used to let you and Harry ride atop him?"

"Yes, and do you remember how you and Grandfather used to play at bowling pins for hours? And how angry he would be because you always beat him. When you were gone, he made Harry and me play with him so that he could practice. Grandmama always told him she was ashamed he could not take defeat any better than he did. He was sad when you resigned from the army. He said England lost a fine soldier. You never came to see us after he died. Why was that?"

"I could not, Barbara. Your grandfather was very dear to me, and I could not bear to be around places or people that reminded me too much of him. He was the most honorable man I ever knew, and you should be proud that you are his granddaughter."

She lifted her chin. "I am."

"We all are," Diana said. "I cherish my father's memory. I am hoping that one of my sons, Tom or Kit perhaps, will find a career in the army."

"It will have to be Kit," Barbara interrupted, in her element now that Roger had mentioned her brothers and sisters. "He is mad for soldiers and horses and military campaigns. Last year, he wanted to study Caesar's *Commentaries*, but Vicar Latchrod felt he was too young. I think it was because the vicar's Latin is weak."

Roger looked amused. "Which one is Kit?"

"There is Harry, me, Tom, then Kit. He was just a little boy last time you saw him. After Kit comes Charlotte, Anne and William. Except that we never call him William. We always call him 'Baby.' He is a darling and so bright for his age—"

"Barbara," Diana interrupted. "Roger will be bored with all this talk of family. Serve him more tea. Forgive her, Roger. She is not used to city ways and does not realize people are not interested in every detail of domestic life."

As Barbara held out her hand for his cup, the lace on her sleeve fell back and exposed the place where Diana's nails had dug into her arm. A piece of lace was sticking to the blood that had dried.

"You have hurt yourself!" Roger exclaimed, taking her arm and examining it. "How did it happen?"

She did not answer, nor did she look at her mother. She was very conscious of his hand on her arm. He watched her face carefully, and when she raised her eyes to his, a long look passed between them.

Gently, he let go of her arm. "Put something on that," he said, "or it may leave a scar."

"She is young," Diana said. "She heals quickly."

Roger compressed his lips and leaned back in his chair, his hands folded under his chin. Barbara could not look at him.

"You should take better care of her, Diana," he said, gravely. "I would hate for that arm to become infected."

There was a short silence.

"Tell me what you have seen of London." He spoke to Barbara. The incident about her arm was ended, but she had a sudden sense of having been drawn under the cloak of Roger's protection. She gave her mother a quick glance and told Roger of seeing the Thames.

"You have not seen the lions at the Tower or the tombs at Westminster?"

She shook her head.

"You must. They are among the sights of London—and the mad folk at Bedlam."

"I do not think I wish to see that—"

"It is quite amusing," Diana interrupted. "They dribble and slobber on themselves and howl and scream. Some of them are tied by a rope at the neck like dogs." Diana laughed, a delicious, tingling sound.

There was another silence. Roger stood up. He smiled down at Barbara. "Thank you for the tea. And for the memories. If I may, I will send my carriage round so that you may see the sights."

Barbara held out her hand, and he bent over it, and to everyone's surprise, he lightly kissed it. It was a breach of etiquette, but Diana said nothing, and Barbara would not. She felt she would never wash that hand again. With a glance at Barbara that told her to stay where she was, Diana followed him from the room. In the hall, Clemmie was handing him his cane and gloves and cloak.

"Have you been flirting with my coachman?" Roger was saying. Clemmie giggled. Roger poked her in the side with his cane. Clemmie winked at him. Diana took a deep breath. She had to hold herself back not to grab his arm.

"What did you think of Barbara?"

"I am most pleasantly surprised, Diana. She is a charming girl."

"Then—"

"Then our lawyers may meet and begin on the contract. We seem to have agreed among ourselves on all points. I leave for France at the end of January, and I would like the matter settled one way or another before then. I will be away for months."

"Of course," Diana said graciously. "Whatever you say. Have a pleasant evening. Good day, Roger."

As soon as the door closed behind him, she lifted her skirts and ran into the parlor, Clemmie behind her. Barbara was at the window, trying to obtain a last glance of Roger. Clemmie, grinning, poured Diana a glass of wine. Then she poured herself one. The two of them clinked glasses and drained them in one gulp, as adroit in their neatness as any tavern regular. Barbara looked away from the window.

"What is it?"

"He has indicated interest. We are going to begin to negotiate the contracts—"

Barbara clapped her hands together. She danced around the room, twirling her long skirts and clicking her heels together. Clemmie watched her fondly and sneaked another glass of wine. Before I know it, Barbara sang to herself, I shall be married . . . married . . . married. . . .

"I wonder if he will notice if I add a settlement for myself," Diana said.

Roger sat in a half-hidden alcove just off the crowded public room of Pontac's tavern. It was after midnight. Respectable citizens were snug in bed with their wives, doors bolted against the realities or imagined terrors of the night. For over twenty years rumors had come and gone of gangs of drunken, abusive young men (belonging to the best families), who called themselves names like Scourers and Mohocks and terrorized London at night. They began by brawling in the taverns, breaking the furniture, windows and heads of waiters unlucky enough to be in their path; they progressed to the streets, throwing rocks at windows and street lamps, erasing the chalk marks left for the milkmaids. But it was the violence to people met randomly on the dark, night streets that had established their reputation—there was always some talk of noses being split, backs of legs being slashed like so much meat hanging in the butcher's window; talk of maiming, blinding, beating, robbing, rape. The last outbreak had been in 1712, when Queen Anne had issued a proclamation against the barbarities committed in the nighttime in the open streets. Since then, although the streets were quieter, and some people believed the mischief was made up or exaggerated, others still crept through the dark streets certain at any moment they would be seized and slashed.

Inside Pontac's, no one was worrying about the night outside. Serious drinking, gambling and discreet whoring had begun at the wooden tables crowded with laughing, singing men and women. Already, several young men had leapt to their feet, their hands on the swords tied about their waists. Their quarrels, over everything from imagined cheating at cards to the insulting way someone had spoken, would be settled in the early morning hours in Hyde Park or Lincoln's Inn Fields, when one or the other or both would die from sword cuts or pistol shots. Roger sat contemplatively in an alcove curtained with looped draperies, sipping at a brandy and watching the other tables. He had eaten a late supper— ragout, calf's head, goose, Cheshire cheese. Pontac's was famous for its food and claret—and now he was alone. He could have joined any of the several groups laughing and singing, but he chose to sit in solitary majesty, surveying the crowd, speaking now and then with those who came up to talk with him. Later he would gamble in an upstairs room or walk to White's and gamble there. Near dawn, he would hire a sedan chair to carry him home, alone. There was no woman he wished to share the quiet, lovely hours of dawn with.

There was a sudden stir at the entrance. Tommy Carlyle stood poised inside the doorway. As usual, he was outrageously dressed. He wore a flaming-red wig topped by an enormous hat. His suit was a bilious, shining green; his waistcoat boasted yellow stripes; his white stockings were embroidered with gold clocks—the latest fad. Two young, slim, painted men hung on each arm. Roger smiled, watching Carlyle languidly survey the room and then begin his progress— there was nothing else it could be called—across the main floor until a place to his liking could be found. He stopped at nearly every table, since there was nobody in London he did not know. Roger made no effort to let Carlyle see where he was; if Tommy was looking for him, he would find him.

Carlyle chose a table and ordered the waiter to make up a bowl of punch to his specific recipe: hot wine, rum and sugar, plenty of lemon juice. The two young men with him simpered at his severity with the waiter. Carlyle rapped out one more question to the man. In answer, the waiter pointed toward the curtained alcove where Roger sat. Carlyle rose from his chair and touched the curls of his red wig. The diamond in his ear glittered.

"I must attend to some business," he told his companions. "Behave yourselves while I am gone."

He walked toward the alcove. It was a show simply to watch him. A big, hulking man, he always wore very high heels on his shoes so that he towered above the men around him. Added to his height was a tiptoeing, swiveling, mincing kind of walk that was amazing to see, as if an effeminate bear were walking carefully, but sociably, through thorns. Carlyle pushed back one of the loops of the draperies at the alcove and stood staring at Roger. His glance took in the fact that Roger was, indeed, quite alone, and that the brandy bottle Roger was pouring from was almost empty. His glance fell on a stain in the front of Roger's coat. He blinked once or twice. Roger indicated the empty chair.

"So here you are, my angel," he said as he sat down. "You completely disappeared after the princess's drawing room. Robert said you didn't come to the hazard game at his house. I called in at yours, but Cradock said you were not expected until quite late. So I began a tour of the taverns—and found those two yonder almost as a reward for my perseverance! The brothels were my next stage. Thank God, Roger, you did not force me to that! Can you imagine their faces when I entered and announced I was looking for a man! Your reputation would be quite ruined. But you and I are both saved. Here you are!"

"Yes. Here I am."

There was a silence. Carlyle pulled at the diamond in his ear.

"Oh, very well," he said, pursing his lips and sighing. "I have been bad. I admit it. Tell me I am an atrocious, meddling gossip and be done with it."

"You are an atrocious, meddling gossip."

"Very good, Roger! You almost hurt me! Well, what have I done? Are the proceedings with the Lady Diana quite, quite ruined?"

Roger smiled and sipped his brandy. Eyes narrowed, Carlyle watched him.

"You have been drinking alone," he said slowly. "You are . . . sad? Disillusioned? No? It must be Diana. Rumor has it you saw her today—that is it! You saw her and met the daughter and now you must drink alone tonight to solace yourself. No! Do not speak! Let me finish my scene—I am enjoying it so! The girl is a horror—buck-toothed, sway-backed, spavined. And you, my fastidious one, are comforting yourself tonight only with the thought of all that lovely land she brings as her dowry. Never mind. Marry her. Bed her once—twice if you must—then lock her away and do as you please! It is what most married men do anyway!" Smirking at his own wit, he summoned a waiter to bring him a glass.

"I am going to marry the girl, Tommy," Roger said. He spoke quickly, softly, maliciously. "And I am drinking tonight—alone—because when I first saw her today, it was as if Richard himself were walking toward me in all his youth and glory. For a moment, I found myself struck to the heart . . . in truth I did, Tommy. Even tonight I am affected by it." And he raised his hands above the table and held them out. They trembled slightly. He put them back on the table.

Carlyle stared at him, his rouged mouth open, his face sagging with surprise. Roger laughed aloud at his expression. The sound of his laughter floated above the roar of songs and other laughter. Several groups of people glanced toward the alcove, smiling to themselves at its sound.

"Good God! Are you in love?"

Roger shrugged, his handsome face grimacing. "The girl has the look of her grandfather. I admired him more than any man I have ever known. I loved him, as everyone did who knew him. If we marry, I shall have children of Richard's to comfort me in my approaching old age . . . no more. No less."

"Not to mention two hundred acres of the best land left in London!"

"Not to mention that."

"There is more," Carlyle said dramatically, putting one of his huge, clumsy hands over his heart. "I feel it. No! Do not deny it, Roger. Tell me you have fallen madly in love."

Roger shook his head, amused rather than irritated by Carlyle's theatrics. Tomorrow, he knew, various rounds of this conversation would be repeated in the coffeehouses, and by evening, in the drawing rooms. It was inevitable.

"All I know," Carlyle was saying, "is that I must see this vision for myself. Not that I will. Diana despises me. When is the happy bridal?"

"I leave that to the lawyers and my prospective bride's family. I simply want the affair settled before I go to France so that I may leave some instructions with my bankers. I would like to start building roads by spring—"

"France! Roads! Spring! Do stop and explain yourself, dear boy. You will leave this treasure behind? A honeymoon in France would be quite romantic."

"I am too old for romance. And she is only a child. She can wait. The regent has invited me to carnival, and I find myself yearning to see Paris, and to visit the homes of my friends there. And Italy beckons. Burlington has just come from there. He says the villas are magnificent. I want to build the most beautiful house London has ever seen. Before Burlington does."

"Then you ought to know that one hears Lady Saylor has had the land surveyed."

Roger had been relaxed in his chair. Now he straightened up. Several different emotions chased themselves quickly across his face. Carlyle waited with interest; he loved to watch Roger's face.

Finally Roger said slowly, choosing his words with care, "Lady Saylor, no doubt, interests herself in her family's welfare. It is certainly too bad that her interest does not spread itself to opening her home to her sister-in-law and niece when they are in reduced circumstances."

"Very well put! I could not have phrased it better myself—"

"But you will!"

"Of course, dear one—"

"Why does he not call on me!" Barbara cried for the tenth time to her mother. Diana was sitting near the window to catch some unexpected morning sun. Her store of money was far too small. Abigail's generosity made no mark against her press of debts. Her creditors were like hounds on the scent of blood, and she paid them just enough to hold the most vicious of them at bay. Yet when her lawyers brought the marriage proposals, she rejected them as though she had all the time in

the world. She was haggling over every penny in every portion and jointure with the desperation of someone who knows
this may be her last chance. Just now, she was totaling again
what amount would keep her in the style to which she was
accustomed. She looked up from those figures to Barbara's
dancing, impatient one.

"Take a piece of advice from me," she said coldly. "Learn
to wait. It is a woman's lot. You are the furthest thing in the
world from his mind at this moment. You may always be. If
you learn that now, you will save yourself much grief later
on."

Barbara tossed her head. She would not listen to her
mother. Outside the window, Covent Garden was readying
itself for the coming twelve days of Christmas, England's
greatest holiday other than Easter. The market baskets were
filled with Christmas greenery, with yellow pears and red
apples and different kinds of nuts (to be given to guests and
carolers and as presents to children), with logs (called Christmas blocks or yule logs, to burn in fireplaces on Christmas Eve
and turn the night into day as a celebration of the Lord Jesus'
birth). At Tamworth, the church choir would be practicing
carols. Vicar Latchrod would be a sight, pursing his lips and
waving his arms and finally pulling off his wig and stamping
on it if the choir should sing too off-key (as it usually did).
Grandmama, thought Barbara, staring out the window.
Grandmama and Harry and Tom and Kit and Anne and
Charlotte and Baby. . . . The names were a litany against
homesickness and her mother's miserliness and her own impatience and the fact that Roger had not called again. . . .

But he did call on them unexpectedly, and Barbara was
beside herself with happiness. Diana, watching her scamper
about the parlor, frowned. The parlor was cold. She was cold.
The words flung at Abigail were coming back to haunt her.
She did need her family, their support . . . their money. For
all Roger's generosity in the settlements, she would still not
have enough money to live on. The debts on Kit's estate were
too enormous; they ate into the income she had expected to
give to herself. Roger had agreed to pay off these debts, but
neither he nor Diana had realized their total. He was settling
stock on Diana and Harry, as well as giving Barbara a quar-
terly allowance and jointure at his death. It was more than

generous. And it was not enough. Her own allowance and jointure were long ago spent. It would take Harry years of careful management to re-create it out of the estate. And the other children must be provided for. She was going to have to live with relatives or remarry or find a rich patron. Of the three, only remarriage offered any security. But it would be the hardest to achieve. She could only do it if her divorce were granted. But then she would have to surmount the obstacle of the divorce and having no money to bring to the marriage. She needed this proposed marriage of Barbara and Roger's to make her every extra penny she could squeeze out of Roger's lawyers.

Roger settled the fur rags about their legs. There were warm bricks to put their feet upon and extra cushions to lean against. He had thought of all the comforts. Barbara watched every move he made: the quick, sure, lean grace of his movements, the way his eyes crinkled at the corners when he smiled, the way he cocked his head as he listened. She did not know when she might see him again. They rattled through the narrow, crooked streets; she with her window shade rolled up, Roger beside her, pointing out the sights, the Guild Hall here, the Royal Exchange there, all rebuilt since the great fire of 1666. Diana shivered under the fur throw and yawned.

"This is my favorite building in London, St. Paul's Cathedral," said Roger, smiling at Barbara, who was watching him with her heart in her eyes. The carriage stopped, and Barbara stepped out to see sweeping steps leading up to enormous white pillars that crowned the classical portico on the western front of the cathedral. Atop this portico, magnificent in its height and depth and carving, was a smaller portico, no less magnificent for its smaller size. Each end of this front was flanked with columned towers. Everything was of white Portland stone, already graying from London's ever-present coal smoke. She walked into the deep porch. A vast door creaked open on one side, and a priest of the Church of England bowed them inside. She blinked suddenly at the dimness, then began to blink again at the magnificence of marble, wood, gold and space all about her. Roger introduced himself to the priest, and the man said he would send at once for the dean.

"No," said Roger. "I want my young friend to see this cathedral as anyone else would. Would you have the kindness and the time to show her some of it?" The priest, whose name was Father James, blushed and led them forward into the great, echoing vastness of the nave. Diana looked around her once, then sighed. Her glance flicked over Father James, then away.

"The original church was almost completely destroyed in the great fire," Father James told Barbara. "As were three hundred ninety-five acres of the surrounding city." It had taken Sir Christopher Wren and his workmen thirty-five years—from 1675 to 1710—to finish this cathedral. Being as slow as a St. Paul's workman had become part of the vocabulary. But the slowness had been worth it, for now the cathedral was the most beautiful sight in the landscape, its landmark the huge central dome topped with a forty-foot lantern and cross of gold that towered over all other buildings and church spires.

Barbara drank in the dark, silent beauty of the church. Roger, watching her, smiled. Everything, the choir, the altar, the great soaring arches and huge columns, the intricate wood carvings of angels and fruit and flowers, the gilding, had only one purpose, to draw one's mind to an almighty and all-powerful God. She stood in the very center of the cathedral, while Father James recited statistics: overall length, 513 feet; diameter of dome, 112 feet; height of dome to top of the cross, 365 feet; weight of lantern and cross, 700 tons. His words meant nothing; all that mattered were her feelings as she stared up, up, up into the center of the dome. Far above her was a gallery circling the bottom rim of the dome, then great windows, then a mural, then, at the dome's center, a small opening that led up into the lantern. On a sunny day, the light must pour in like God's divine blessing. Leaving her mother and Roger, she followed the priest through a doorway and then up and around a twisted and seemingly endless flight of steps, through a narrow, dark hallway and out onto the gallery circling the widest part of the dome. She looked down, down to the marble floor below her, to her mother and Roger, then up, past the tall windows, past the muted colors to the mural, up to the windows circling the topmost part of the lantern.

"Stay where you are," Father James told her. "I will show you something special. Put your ear to the wall."

She did as she was told. He walked around the gallery to a point directly opposite her. He put his lips against the wall and spoke quietly. She heard his every word: "O God the Father, creator of heaven and earth; have mercy upon us."

He walked around to her again. "This is called the Whispering Gallery. Now you see why. Sound carries only in that way. If I had faced you from the other side and said the words, you would not have heard me."

"Well, Roger," said Diana below them, "we have come to a pretty pass when you take me to see a cathedral!"

He laughed, and for a moment sunlight filtered in from the windows above and highlighted his face, with its striking cheekbones. He took Diana by the arm and led her toward one of the side chapels. They sat down in a wooden pew. After a moment, he reached into a pocket and pulled out some gold coins.

"Out of funds, again?" he said, an ironic look on his face. "Barbara ought not to be living so."

"I will be the judge of that!" Diana snapped, taking the coins from him.

"Go and stay with Abigail awhile—"

"She and I have quarreled."

"When do you not? I understand there are some problems with the marriage contracts, Diana. Craven tells me that my terms, terms I thought you and I had both agreed to, keep coming back to him with new demands. And he, knowing I want Bentwoodes, agrees to each demand, only to have another one attached when the papers are sent to you." He looked at her. His face was hard. "I want Bentwoodes, Diana. But I will not be made a fool of. I have been more than generous with you—"

"It is not my doing," Diana exclaimed. She looked at Roger, her lovely violet eyes wide and sincere. "Truly, you must believe me, Roger. But Wilcoxen and Blight have been with my family for years. And they advise me not to give in too easily, to realize the potential value of the land, to—"

"Realize the potential value of the land!" Roger cut in. "Phrases like that make me nervous. Who have you been talking to? Do you not understand that I will have to invest thousands before I 'realize' a penny from that land? That I am looking at ten years' work—perhaps twenty—can you wait twenty years, Diana?"

She looked away from him, looked at the lovely, drooping marble angel standing with folded wings above a tomb, the tomb of the person for whom the chapel had been built. She closed her eyes.

"I want this settled before I leave for France, or I do not want it at all," Roger said, trying to see her face.

She opened her eyes to the marble wreath of bay and rosemary that the angel was holding in her hands. "It will be," she said. "I promise."

Barbara and Father James were climbing up more dark, twisting stairs, much narrower than the others. Her side was beginning to hurt from the climbing and the tightness of her stays. Father James unlocked a door, and gestured for her to precede him. She stepped outside onto an intricately railed gallery circling the base of the lantern. She caught her breath, put both hands on the railing and leaned forward. She was high, high above the city, up in the sky like a bird. The wind snatched at her cloak and hair and chilled her through to her bones, but she did not care. London spread before her in every direction she looked, a patchwork of tiled roofs, church spires, chimney stacks, narrow lanes, broad roads, the shining ribbon of the Thames and finally fields and pastures merging into the overcast sky at its border.

"It is not a day for it," said Father James beside her, "but to my mind, it is the finest view in the world. I have never been anywhere else; yet all our foreign visitors say so. And I cannot but think that God in His beauty could not have created anything finer."

When they were back inside, as soon as Roger and her mother walked up to her, even as she was breathing heavily, trying to get her breath back from all those stairs, she was aware that something had happened. It was in both their faces. Roger, who had wanted her to see the cathedral, now seemed anxious to leave. Father James took them to the effigy of John Donne, standing straight and tall in his niche, his marble eyes closed, his body encased in a marble shroud.

"He was a dean of St. Paul's," Father James said to Barbara. "This statue is the only one from the old church to survive the fire intact."

She stared up at Donne's severe, bearded face. "He posed for his effigy during his last illness, clothing himself in a shroud, and then keeping the portrait of his effigy by his bedside as a reminder of man's mortality."

At that moment a clerk approached them and said that Dean Sherlock, hearing that they were in the church, wished them to take tea with him. Diana sighed and Roger started to make an excuse, but seeing Barbara's face, seeing that she had correctly read his impatience to leave, agreed. They followed the clerk through a doorway and down a hall and up a flight of stairs, to a room lined with books, its tables littered with papers. An old man, with dark, piercing eyes stood before the fire. Another, much younger man, sat beside a tea table piled with food: scones, biscuits, crumbling cake, and bread and butter. Diana opened her eyes wider at the sight of the young man; he was in his mid-twenties and handsome in a beefy, overfed way. Both men wore black, flowing gowns over their clothes and short, full wigs. Roger took Barbara's hand and led her to the man before the fire.

"Dean Sherlock," he said, "this is a young friend of mine, Mistress Barbara Alderley. You know her grandmother, the Duchess of Tamworth. And Lady Alderley you know, I believe."

Dean Sherlock nodded frostily in Diana's direction. She lifted one dark brow and curtsied.

"I know your grandmother," Sherlock said to Barbara. "She argues as precisely as a fifth-year student at university, and did so anytime my sermons did not please her. I miss her astringent presence. She kept me on my toes. You have the look of your grandfather, a fine man and a good Christian. Your grandmother does well, I hope?"

Before Barbara could answer, Diana said, "My mother does beautifully, thank you."

Sherlock pursed his lips. It was obvious he did not approve of Diana, and just as obvious that she did not care.

"I thought you lured us here for tea," Roger said.

"Tea . . . ah yes. Come, let us sit here, where Julian—he is my secretary—will serve us. Lady Alderley, Lord Devane, Mistress Alderley, my secretary, Julian Weathersby."

They all nodded to one another, and Diana smiled slowly, brilliantly, with a great show of small, white teeth to Weath-

ersby, who blinked. Diana sat down gracefully and batted her
eyes at him.

"The tea, Julian," said Sherlock.

Weathersby started. Then he began to pour tea and pass
around plates of food.

"We were just admiring John Donne's effigy," Roger said to
Sherlock. "An admirable man. I maintain his best writing was
temporal, rather than spiritual."

"And I maintain that it was a combination of both," said
Sherlock.

"You straddle the fence—"

"Not at all, my dear boy. But come, we bore your young
friend."

Everyone's eyes focused on Barbara, who was just taking a
sip of tea. She choked. "No! Not at all. Please! Please do go
on!"

Sherlock nodded his head approvingly. He held up a finger,
as if he were ready to begin a lecture. "A short background
might be in order. Would you care to hear it, Mistress Alderley?"

"Oh—yes."

"And I will have more tea," Diana said in her low, husky
voice to Weathersby. He poured it at once, and she sipped it
slowly, her violet eyes on him. Every now and again he
glanced at her and then quickly away.

Dean Sherlock settled more comfortably in his seat. He
sniffed, then began to talk in a dry, lecturing tone. "He was
a great man, Mistress Alderley, an unusual man, a sinner who
found God's way. In his youth, he loved wine, women and
poetry—"

"As who does not?" Roger smiled.

Sherlock ignored him. "He was the son of an ironmonger, of
Roman Catholics. He went to both Oxford and Cambridge,
taking his degree at neither. He was admitted to Lincoln's Inn
as a law student, but he never finished. He served as a gentleman volunteer in the Earl of Essex's expeditions at Cádiz and
Azores, which seems to have partially quenched his taste for
adventure. For when he returned home, he became secretary
to Egerton, the lord keeper, and even sat as a member of Parliament. But fate—in the guise of love—interfered—"

"How poetically you put it," said Roger.

Sherlock sniffed. "He fell in love with his master's niece, Anne More, and married her. Her father was furious and had him thrown into prison and dismissed from his post as secretary. Her father even brought a lawsuit to test the marriage—"

"Donne is said to have signed his letters to friends at this time as John Donne, Anne Donne, Undone." Roger smiled at Barbara, his eyes crinkling in the corners. She smiled back.

"Oh, dear," Diana said softly, "I have spilled my tea." She looked at Weathersby, who immediately handed her his handkerchief. The stain was on the bodice of her gown, just above and around where her nipple would be. She rubbed at it with the handkerchief. Her nipple grew stiff and pointed through the fabric of her gown. He could not take his eyes from it. She looked at him.

"I need your help," she said. "Will you try to see if you can remove it?"

He swallowed and glanced at Roger and Sherlock, but they were deep in their discussion. He leaned forward and took the handkerchief. It hovered just above her breast.

"Perhaps we had better move here, near the window, where the light is better and we can see what we are doing," said Diana. Weathersby nodded.

"After his dismissal," Sherlock was saying, "it took him some thirteen years before he finally found his true vocation—the church. From then on his rise was rapid. Preaching was his forte, Mistress Alderley, not poetry, as Lord Devane insists, though I concede he was a good poet. St. Paul's—the old St. Paul's—was completely crowded on the days he preached, and he left us the legacy of his thoughts in his *Devotions*, written when he was ill."

"The world lost a fine poet to the church," said Roger. "Listen to this, Barbara. It is from a poem to his mistress.

"License my roving hands, and let them go,
Before, behind, between, above, below.
O my America! My new-found-land,
My kingdom, safeliest when with one man manned,
My mine of precious stones, my emperie,
How blest am I in this discovering thee!
To enter in these bonds, is to be free;
Then where my hand is set, my seal shall be. . . .

"There are other lines I could recite, but will not, for your innocence," Roger said.

Someday, Barbara thought, I will ask you about those lines, Roger, and you will tell me.

Sherlock held up a finger. "That same man wrote, 'No man is an island, entire of itself; every man is a piece of the continent, a part of the main; if a clod be washed away by the sea, Europe is the less, as well as if a promontory were, as well as if a manor of thy friends or of thine own were; any man's death diminishes me, because I am involved in mankind; and therefore never send to know for whom the bell tolls; it tolls for thee.'"

They were silent. Sherlock sniffed. "I rest my case. That was from his 'Devotions upon Emergent Occasions.'" No one spoke. Sherlock leaned over and smiled at Barbara. His teeth were brown with tobacco stains.

"You have been a good, patient child to put up with an old man's prattling. How old are you, dear?"

"Nearly sixteen, sir."

"Time to be thinking of a husband and family. Lady Alderley."

From the window, Diana looked over at him. She had been enjoying herself with Weathersby.

"It is time this girl was married," he said.

"The thought has crossed my mind."

"Julian!"

Weathersby jumped and moved back instinctively from the dangerous Diana.

"Find *The Lady's New-Year Gift.* It is there on the fourth shelf by the Greek testaments. I will give it to you, young Mistress Alderley. It was written by Lord Halifax to his daughter."

Sherlock took the slim volume handed him, pursed his lips, sniffed and opened the book. Its thin pages rustled in his hands. He ran his finger down the pages.

"Religion . . . husbands . . . Here. Listen, young lady. 'It is one of the disadvantages belonging to your sex, that young women are seldom permitted to make their own choice; their friends' care and experience are thought safer guides to them, than their own fancies; and their modesty often forbiddeth them to refuse when their parents recommend, though their inward consent may not entirely go along with it. In this case, there remaineth nothing for them to do, but to endeavor to make that easy which falleth to their lot, and by a wise use of every thing they may dislike in a husband, turn that by degrees to be very supportable, which if neglected, might in time beget an aversion.'"

Barbara did not know how to reply. She had no aversion to her parent's choice. Sherlock handed her the book.

"You keep it. Study it. It will make you a better daughter, and God willing, a better wife."

Roger stood up. "She must read it, then, by all means. See that you do so, Barbara. Dean Sherlock, you have more than entertained us with your interesting conversation, you have edified us. But I must see this young lady and her mother home before dark—"

Weathersby offered to walk with them to the carriage. He tucked the fur throws carefully about Diana and Barbara's legs. Diana, watching him, smiled. As the carriage lurched away, Roger said, "Do you always find someone to flirt with?"

Diana tossed her head. "If I can. It helps to pass the time. What a pompous old windbag Sherlock is! He hates me. He always has! Old ass!"

Embarrassed, Barbara glanced at Roger, but he was knocking his cane against the ceiling of the carriage, which obediently lurched to a stop.

"I want Barbara to see the monument commemorating the great fire," he said. It was now so cold that his breath made little puffs of smoke with each word.

"Do hurry!" Diana called after them. "I am ready to go home!"

It was dusk, but not so dark that Barbara could not see a Doric column rising up into the sky, higher than the buildings around it.

"Charles II had this built to commemorate the great fire, the one that destroyed St. Paul's and the surrounding acres," Roger explained. They walked around its square base. Two sides held Latin inscriptions relating a history of the fire and what had been done to rebuild the city. Roger helped Barbara translate them. A fourth side was an English inscription accusing Roman Catholics of being the authors of the fire in hope of destroying the Protestant religion.

"Is that true?" she asked.

"Some people believe the fire was a warning from God, against man's ungodliness. Others, as you see, think it a plot. When James II was king, a Catholic king, mind you, he had the inscription erased. When he was overthrown by William III, a Protestant king, the inscription was cut deeper. I think it a symbol of man's ignorance.

Something in his face made her say quickly, "Do you not believe in God?"

It was obvious her question surprised him. "When I am in St. Paul's I believe with all my heart. But when I am anywhere else, I confess I doubt He exists!"

"But that is heresy!"

He laughed and she felt foolish. Back in the carriage, she thought, He is the first person I have ever known who does not believe in God. She had been raised with God as one of the cornerstones of her life. It had never occurred to her to question His existence. That Roger did so was upsetting. Her mother's next words put the subject completely out of her head.

"When do you leave for France, Roger?"

"Around the twenty-third of January. I am anxious to leave. They will still be celebrating carnival. Then I shall summer in Hanover if the king goes there and also stop in Italy. So you can see why I wish our affair settled."

"Yes, I can see."

Barbara had become as still as one of the statues they had just seen in St. Paul's. She was doing some rapid figuring. In a little over six weeks Roger would be gone. And it sounded as if he would not be back for months! Her mother had not said one word to her. She had thought they might be married by spring. Now it looked as if it would be almost a year. A year was forever.

The carriage stopped. A ragged child ran forward with a basket in which bunches of winter violets and holly were tied together. Roger bought two and gave one to Barbara and one to Diana. He walked with them up to their lodging, chucked Barbara under the chin and told her to be sure to read Sherlock's book, but he declined to stay, and he did not say when he would call again. Barbara stood staring out the parlor window after his carriage. She had not taken off her cloak;

the slim volume Sherlock had given her was still in one gloved hand. She turned around. Diana sat at a table working on a column of figures. Her face was absorbed. She had already poured herself a glass of wine. Clemmie was back in a chair in front of the one fire they were allowed a day. Her slippers were off, and her feet were dirty. She picked at her teeth—what few she had left—with a whittled piece of wood. The room was shabby again. Here and there, pieces of its borrowed finery were missing. Returned, no doubt, before the rental could add up. Barbara looked down at the violets in her hand. They were already wilting. She unfastened her cloak and took off her gloves. She poured some water from a pitcher into a cup and put the violets and holly into the water. Balancing an unlit candle and the book in one hand and the violets in the other, she went into her room and shut the door. She lit the candle and then sat on her bed to read. She opened the book, smoothing back the title page until she came to the first page of text. She began to read the tiny, cramped words: "Dear Daughter, I find, that even our most pleasing thoughts will be unquiet; they will be in motion; and the mind can have no rest whilst it is possessed by a daring passion. You are at the present chief object of my care. . . ."

Roger leaned his head back against the soft leather of his carriage seat, thinking of Diana. She had seemed subdued. Did this mean she would be reasonable or was it a new trick? He knocked on his carriage roof. A small door opened above him.

"Drive down Oxford Street," he told the coachman. Even though he would not be able to see the fields of Bentwoodes, he wanted to know he was driving past them, wanted to envision his dream, feel it enfold him before he returned home and began an evening surrounded by people who had no idea what his dream meant to him. He never once thought of Barbara, sitting alone in Diana's Covent Garden lodgings, plodding through Lord Halifax's advice to his daughter because he had mentioned it in jest, at the mercy of her mother's whim and his, like a bird in a cage that must wait for others to open the door.

CHAPTER FOUR

he same morning of the afternoon that Roger was taking
Barbara and Diana out, Lady Abigail Saylor sat in the
great parlor of Saylor House. It was a large room, with windows overlooking the gardens, famous for the twisted, wooden
chains of fruit, foliage and birds, carved by the master Grin-
ling Gibbons, around the ceiling and the chimneypiece. An
extravagant mural of the first duke's victories in the Netherlands hung in panels on the walls. The furniture was French
and Dutch, made with precision and care, the fruitwood and
beech blending together as delicate patterns of birds and flowers on the tops of tables or the front pieces of cabinet and desk
drawers. In each corner was a huge Dutch cabinet that held
the duke's collection of Chinese porcelain. All the rooms in
Saylor House were on the scale of this one, their intricate
moldings and paneling done by the finest craftsmen, the furniture in the best and most expensive of taste, the rooms filled
with collections that were now priceless—collections of furniture, medals, coins, porcelain, plate, paintings. It was a
public house built to represent what the first duke had
become; it had been finished in the 1690s when he was at the
peak of his life.

The house sprawled along one side of Pall Mall Street, near
St. James's Palace, one of the busiest and most fashionable of
streets in London. There were several acres of gardens on each
side and to the rear of the house, and they balanced its massive rectangular bulk. A brick wall separated the entrance

courtyard from the street, with a gate tower on each side of wrought-iron entrance gates, decorated with the Tamworth crest picked out in gold paint. The house was cushioned from the urban sprawl around it by the blooming trees and flowers and well-kept lawns that formed its gardens. Though adjoining landowners were selling their lots to be profitably divided into smaller ones so that two- and three-story buildings crowded against the garden walls, the Tamworths refused to part with one inch of ground. Let the others bawl greedily over money. The Tamworths bawled quietly.

Abigail, sitting in the parlor of this house that was a symbol of all she had ever desired, had a full, square face, fresh and pretty when she was younger, but now settling into the placid, fleshy lines of middle age. She carried herself regally, always dressed expensively, never appeared without her makeup, and comforted herself that what she was losing in youth she was making up for in character. She sat with her eldest daughter, Fanny, and with her aunt by marriage, Louisa Shrewsborough. It was a family meeting, summoned to discuss family policy. Abigail considered herself a fair woman. She considered herself an outstanding woman. She was the daughter of an earl; not the only daughter, nor the prettiest, nor the sweetest. It had been upsetting to her to see her sisters, older and younger, being married all around her while she stayed at home. She could not understand it. She was competent, attractive, well mannered, amply dowered and intelligent. She knew exactly what was the right thing for everyone to do, and she gladly shared her knowledge. She had always known that she was the most suited of all her sisters to marry an oldest son, the one that would inherit the estates and titles. Therefore it was a shock when her younger and older sisters had done so, while she was left still sitting at her mother's side, doing yards and yards of exquisite, useless needlepoint to pass the time.

She would never know what had possessed her to accept the offer of William Saylor, second son of the Duke of Tamworth, and a soldier to boot. The truth was she was a little in love with him, though she considered passion an unnecessary ingredient to a good marriage. She was also feeling more than a little desperate. Some people said William was in love with her younger sister, Kitty, who married William's older brother. Abigail did not believe that. She had never allowed herself to believe that. And whatever she had felt for William had soon faded against the irritations of his personality. Everything was humorous to him, particularly her own ambition and drive. She wanted him to earn his own title, to step out from under the shadow of his father, his indomitable mother and his older brother. She wanted him to use his family's influence to feather his own nest, their nest. But not William. He was satisfied with the second-best house, the smallest estate, with simply being a soldier. Abigail fretted and fumed and planned and plotted, and watched her sisters live on a scale she deserved far more than they. To her credit, however, she never envisioned what the Lord above had seen fit to grant her. She had been as grieved as anyone when her sister Kitty had died in childbirth. But she had thought nothing of it. Kitty's husband would marry again; the churchyards were littered with the second and third and fourth wives of men. Childbirth was the great reaper.

Therefore she had been truly unprepared for the death of her brother-in-law . . . and, more important, for the death of his young son and heir. Suddenly, without warning, William, her William, feckless, irritating William, was heir to the dukedom of Tamworth. For once in her life, she had been speechless, paralyzed for days with the shock of it all. Her life, so bounded and still, had opened up to unlimited horizons. And all her ambition, all her intelligence, characteristics she had had to keep trammeled down, were now suddenly necessary. For Tony, her only son, was also an heir, the most important heir after his father. If Abigail prided herself on one thing, and she prided herself on several, she was proud of her maternal instincts. She knew exactly what was right for each of her three children (born with bone-grinding, gasping, raw, naked pain; she could not think of it even now without shuddering). And she insisted that they do what was right for themselves, whether it suited their personalities or not. Then, again, as if the Lord above were testing her, the unthinkable had happened. William had died, died in a ridiculous battle he did not have to fight in. She had known then that finally destiny had caught up with her. Trailing her yards of widow's veils, she had paced up and down, thinking, planning, listening to lawyers as the estates of the Duke of Tamworth were explained to her. She hoped, of course, that the present duke, her kind father-in-law, would live for many, many more years. But she believed in being prepared. And she was. She knew every acre, every plow, every township the great duke owned, and at his death, she stepped naturally into the vacuum of power (To her surprise, the Duchess did not oppose her. I am finished with all that, she told Abigail, it is dead and buried with Richard). Her son, Tony, the second Duke of Tamworth, was only twelve years old. She was there, ready, able, willing to guide the boy's every decision, every footstep.

She felt her sense of duty and conduct set an example for the entire family. She kept track of different family members and spent hours composing letters to them which suggested conduct that was more becoming to the family in general. She considered herself the spiritual guide of the entire family. Which was why she now sat in the parlor with Fanny and with her Aunt Shrewsborough. She gazed fondly at Fanny, who was recovering from childbirth a month ago. Fanny looked much as she had when she was young, the same blond hair, same fresh, smooth face. Fanny did not have her character, but that was just as well because Fanny always did as she was told, and this pleased Abigail immensely. Aunt Shrewsborough was another matter. She had not been asked; she had simply shown up, and Abigail had had to receive her because she knew her tiny but indomitable aunt would have simply swept by the butler's excuses and come into the parlor anyway. Aunt Shrewsborough represented another age, another set of manners, those of Charles II. She said exactly what she pleased, and did exactly what she wanted. She and her sister, Lady Cranbourne, were a great trial to Abigail. But she did her duty; she prayed for them; she made suggestions as to how they should act. If they ignored her, it was not her fault.

At any rate, Aunt Shrewsborough, who always knew everything that was going on, had called about the same thing that Abigail had summoned Fanny for—Diana. The only time Abigail ever lost her temper was when it concerned Diana. Somehow, Diana always managed to penetrate through her painstaking facade of intelligent reason. She had quarreled with Diana from the moment she had met her years ago when she was considering William's marriage proposal. In fact, Diana's name led the negatives on the list she had carefully written out when she was deciding whether or not to accept William's offer. Diana was quite simply bad. She was immoral, ruthless and selfish. Her conduct had embarrassed Abigail for years. She was surprised she could have any feelings of shame left when it came to Diana. But she did. Both Aunt Shrewsborough and Fanny were now confirming what she herself had just heard—from Tony, no less. Merciful heavens, if Tony was reporting it to her, the rumors must be far worse. Abigail sighed secretly at the thought of Tony, her only, her dearest son. He was a disappointment. He was not bright. There was no other way to put it. Abigail schemed and planned and did as much thinking as possible for him, but when she looked at him, she always had a secret desire to take him apart and reassemble him along better lines. She cosseted him, she petted him, she planned his every move. But he was still not bright. Only to herself would Abigail admit that fact. She hid her feelings from even Fanny. But that was neither here nor there. What was here and there was Diana. People were saying that Diana and her young daughter were starving and that Tony, pushed by Abigail, refused to help them. People were saying that Abigail had always hated Diana, and that this was her way of paying back old scores. People were saying that it was disgraceful that anyone as rich as the Duke of Tamworth would not support a relative in a time of need. People were once more bringing up the dreadful scandal of the past summer, Kit's flight, those pamphlets about him and Diana, her divorce action. People were saying that Abigail hoped Diana would starve to death; that she wanted to upset marriage negotiations between Diana and the Earl Devane; that she wanted Bentwoodes for Tony. It was infuriating, especially since so much of it was true.

Aunt Shrewsborough had heard the gossip from her lady's maid, who had heard it from the butler. Fanny's husband, Harold, had told her the news. He had been at a meeting of the Royal Society, and Roger's plans for Bentwoodes (both Roger and Sir Christopher Wren were members) had come up. Everyone was curious; some people were even driving out to Bentwoodes in their carriages to see it. Roger's plans were said to be grandiose. Gossip about Bentwoodes had led naturally to Diana, and then to the way she was currently living. No one said anything directly. How could they with Harold right there? It was more by silences, and bits of sentences and significant lifts of eyebrows that he had pieced together his information. Fanny had been impressed. If Harold went to the trouble of telling her, it meant he took the rumor seriously. Usually one could explode a firecracker in front of his face, and he would not notice.

"There is more," Aunt Shrewsborough told Abigail. She reached into her pocket and pulled out a letter. She handed it to Abigail, who read it quickly. A spasm of irritation crossed her face. The letter was from the Duchess. She asked her sister-in-law to send her news of Diana and Barbara. She had not heard a word from either of them since they had left Tamworth Hall a month ago.

Abigail smoothed the front of her loose, gray morning gown that contrived somehow to display an inordinate amount of full bosom. Aunt Shrewsborough, who was tiny and frail and wrinkled, wore a brown curling wig and a jaunty hat that would have suited a woman far younger and far, far less wrinkled. Two huge spots of rouge were centered on what used to be full cheeks, but was now sagging flesh. Dark red edged over the border of each thin lip. A black, star-shaped patch winked in and out of the wrinkles by her left eye. She waited for Abigail to say something. Fanny, caught between the two of them, bit her lip nervously.

"Well?" said Aunt Shrewsborough. "Well? Do I write Alice that her daughter is the talk of the town! Do I write that her own relatives are accused of letting a family member starve in the streets! Do I write her that no one in the family knows what the devil is going on!"

Abigail's handsome bosom heaved.

"You should have offered your home immediately! I cannot understand what possessed you to behave otherwise. In my day, we knew how to treat our own, even when they had disgraced us. I will not have my great-niece living like a beggar in a garret. The child is not even sixteen! What must she think of us!"

"I had every intention of opening my home—" Abigail began, but Aunt Shrewsborough swept past her, her wig and hat trembling with temper.

"Hah! You let Diana make you angry! She always has! She always will! Now she has managed to drag Tony's name down in the mud with hers. To think that I should live to see my brother's heir spoken of in such a way. Richard was the kindest, the fairest man on earth, and he would be appalled to see the way this town is talking about his family. It is shameful! Shameful!" The feather in her hat quivered with outrage.

Abigail took a deep breath. "If you feel so strongly, why did you not offer your own home—"

"I am not the head of the family! Tony is. And as Tony's hostess, you should have done what was necessary. I do not care if Diana dances in the street in her chemise, she is still the only daughter of the first Duke of Tamworth. She is my niece! And that child with her has no right to be punished for her mother's sins! What on earth am I to write to Alice! She will come up here herself if she does not hear something soon. Then we will all be in a fine fix!"

Abigail shuddered at the thought of her mother-in-law descending on Saylor House.

Fanny said, "I am afraid I must agree with Aunt, Mama. I know you do not like to hear it. I know you and Aunt Diana have quarreled, and I know—we all know—what Aunt Diana is. But there is no reason Barbara should suffer. Particularly when Aunt Diana is trying to provide for her. It will look very odd when her engagement to Lord Devane is announced, and the address for the bride-to-be is a hovel somewhere in Covent Garden."

"And that is another thing," interrupted Aunt Shrewsborough. "I had no idea of Diana's plans for this marriage. Everyone is asking me about it, and I do not know what to say. Things have come to a pretty pass when my niece has a marriage planned under my nose, and I know nothing of it!"

"I am completely against this marriage," Abigail said. "Diana never even offered to discuss it with Tony, and we all know how Tony worries about the family. Roger Montgeoffry is too old, and he is far too licentious. His companions—that odious Carlyle man, that Walpole person—" She wrinkled her nose.

"You forgot the King of England!" snapped Aunt Shrewsborough. There was a silence. Aunt Shrewsborough had made her point. "If Diana wants to marry that child to a blind, deaf and dumb cripple, as long as the man has the money, and the insanity, to restore some of their fortune, I say more power to her! Ye gods, Abigail, have you lost your reason! Diana is ruined! Ruined! There is not a penny anywhere that is not mortgaged or owed to someone. Kit has left her in a fix I would not wish on my worst enemy. Think of Harry! At this point in his life, he faces debts he could never repay, not unless I left him my fortune—which I ought to do!"

Abigail was silent. She wanted everything for Tony, for Tony's heirs. She wanted to build the richest, the largest dukedom in the kingdom for her son. Even the thought of a penny going to someone else, deserved or not, hurt her. Bentwoodes belonged to Tony, not some other grandchild. To Tony.

"I am against her choice for marriage—not the reasons behind it," she said. "Tony echoes my sentiments. If we offer our home, it will look like surrender—"

"It will look like good manners! Use your brain, woman! You can do more to influence the marriage negotiations if the principals are under your own roof than you can by exclaiming against it from a distance of several miles!"

There was an arrested expression on Abigail's face. Aunt Shrewsborough saw it, and nodded, as if satisfied.

"A word here, a suggestion there, and the negotiations are bogged down. Time passes; Diana, secure here with you, does not have to accept the first thing he offers. She has time to think, and therefore time to want more."

"She said she was going to marry Barbara to him, and nothing we could do would stop her."

"My dear Abigail," Aunt Shrewsborough said with a sigh, "Diana has always been able to twist you inside out. She is the greediest member of this family, which says a lot, I should think, considering the family. I would wager my best diamond that she is haggling even now to increase her own share. She will push Montgeoffry just as far as she can. She always has done so to people. You get her here; offer a few suggestions yourself, and I will eat this hat I am wearing if the whole thing is not called off. Montgeoffry may look like an angel, but I doubt he has the patience of one." She stood up and shook out her gown. "I know you see the sense of what I am saying. You can always be depended on for sense.

Fanny, give your aunt a kiss, and bring that new baby to visit."

Abigail rose to walk her to the door and their arms linked. "You know what to do," Aunt Shrewsborough said softly. "Thank God you have the sense to listen to me. I despise family scandal, and we certainly need no more about Diana. I do not like that rouge color you are using, Abigail. It is too harsh. It does not do for a woman to try too hard, and I never knew a blonde that took aging well. Lighten the color. You lighten the years. I will go with you to talk to Diana, if need be. Lizzie too. We are agreed on this—Diana must come here. You will handle it? Good girl!"

Abigail kissed her aunt's wrinkled cheek and promised she would do the right thing. She smiled until the door closed. The smile faded from her face. She went back to Fanny, who was leaning against the chair she was sitting in. Fanny's face was pale.

"What do you think of my rouge, Fanny?"

Fanny opened her eyes. "Your rouge? It is fine. Why, Mama?"

"Never mind. Your aunt wears a wig fit only for a sixteen-year-old trollop, and then tells me—never mind! Fanny, was I wrong?"

Fanny did not answer. Abigail paced up and down in front of the huge fireplace centered in the north wall. "It will never do for Tony to get a reputation for smallness of character." Neither of them mentioned his reputation for a small mind. Abigail shook her head.

"It is my own fault. I ought not to have let my temper run away with me. Temper is the flaw of the Saylor side of the family, not mine. Oh, dear, how will I ever convince Diana to come here? You know how she is! She would starve to spite me—"

Fanny shook her head and smiled. "Not Aunt Diana, Mother."

Abigail stared at her daughter. "You are correct, Fanny. Diana always does what is best and most convenient for herself. All we have to do is convince her that it is best she be here—"

"Well, it would certainly look more impressive to Lord Devane."

"So it would. . . . I wonder whom I could offer in his place . . . Wharton. . . ."

"In whose place, Mama? Wharton married in March."

"Carr Hervey has a younger brother. . . ."

"What are you thinking about, Mama? Are you really going to try to stop the marriage? Aunt Diana would never give Bentwoodes to Tony, not unless he married Barbara himself—"

"Bite your tongue, Fanny! I would sooner see Tony married to the Devil than to anything of Diana's!" Abigail gathered her thoughts together. "She might be amenable to certain arrangements, if they are presented properly. I think a group of us ought to see her, not just me. I seem to bring out her worst . . . not that she has a best. . . . Hervey. . . ."

"Why not Carr himself, Mama? He is due to inherit an earldom."

"Nonsense! A second son will do quite adequately for Barbara. The Alderleys are not what they once were. Cash . . . or an allowance . . . a yearly allowance against the property. . . . The Newcastles might have a cousin hidden away in a village somewhere. . . ."

"Mama, whatever are you planning?"

"Tony and Harold could sponsor the divorce. . . . I wonder exactly what Roger is offering her. . . . It must be a pretty penny. . . . Fanny, you look pale. Have you been resting as you should?"

Fanny sighed. "Yes, Mama. But somehow, this time, I cannot seem to regain my strength—"

"Three babies in three years would make anyone tired!" Abigail spoke sharply. The square, stubborn line of her jaw, hidden by youth when she was a girl, and by flesh, now that she was a woman, was apparent at this moment to anyone who might look at her. She loved her children, and she worried about them all. But only Fanny had to face death each year. Tony would never have to, and Mary was years away from marriage. She remembered the pain of her childbirths. Time blurred some of it but enough remained seared on her mind, a throbbing cord that only had to be touched to vibrate.

"I hope Harold understands your tiredness."

Fanny looked away. This was not a subject she and her mother agreed on, but she did not have the strength to argue.

"He should have more regard for you," Abigail was saying, her mind now completely off Diana and the marriage. "You cannot, you must not go on having a baby every year. It will ruin your health, your looks—it has already begun to ruin your figure. Has your maid been making the green tea caudle recipe your grandmother sent?" (The Duchess had recommended a quart of strong green tea poured into a skillet set over a fire. Added to this were four beaten egg yolks mixed with a pint of white wine, grated nutmeg and sugar. The mixture was stirred over the fire until very hot, then drunk out of a china cup.)

"Yes, Mama."

"Do as I did, and make him understand that his attentions are not welcome—for your own sake, Fanny."

"Mama, please."

Abigail looked at her daughter. Fanny reminded her so much of herself, except that she had never been that gentle. "I do not want you to die," she said softly.

Fanny smiled at her. "I will not die, Mama. You did not."

"A part of me did," Abigail said. Fanny reached out and took her mother's hand and pressed it against her cheek. Abigail was silent. All her planning, all her plotting would not protect her daughter from death. She had to leave that to the Lord. And she did not trust Him. "I will greatly multiply thy sorrow," He had told Eve, "and thy conception; in sorrow thou shalt bring forth children; and thy desire shall be to thy husband, and he shall rule over thee." A poor way to handle things, Abigail had always thought, particularly for Eve.

It took Abigail only a few days to construct her strategy, days which she knew worked to her advantage. It had been easy to learn that Diana was living on the last of her resources, that she had not yet signed the marriage contracts, but was holding out for more money. Nor will she, thought Abigail, confidently. She had already instructed Tony and Harold to begin a counterrumor that the Tamworths were distraught over Diana's sense of false pride, that they had offered their home and been refused. Tony and Harold were to talk about it at the various coffee shops: Tom's, Will's, Button's, White's, St. James's. They were to mention it on their club nights, casually, to a friend or two, in between eating their beef steaks and drinking their ale and singing their club songs. Enough people would overhear and repeat it. Aunt Shrewsborough and Lady Cranbourne were to shake their heads regretfully and talk of it in front of their servants. They were to mention it to various friends—in strictest confidence. This meant so many different versions of the same rumor would meet and collide that no one would know what the truth was.

She also decided that Aunt Shrewsborough was right: There was strength in numbers—and in surprise. As her famous father-in-law had always believed, attack the enemy before he can attack you. That way you choose the time of battle and the place.

Four days later, Abigail's troops were assembled in her blue drawing room, drinking tea, eating toast and biscuits, and arguing among themselves: the aunts, Tony, Fanny and Harold. The braver members of the family bolstered the faint of heart.

It took two carriages to settle everyone comfortably. There was much running to and fro by the footmen for hot bricks and more fur throws. The aunts were argumentative and kept ordering everyone about, so that people were colliding with each other and undoing what the others had done. And it had begun to snow. But, nevertheless, Abigail kept calm and managed to coax everyone in. The carriages started with a lurch. They would not stop until they reached Covent Garden.

Barbara and her mother were playing cards when the knock sounded at the door. It was Aunt Shrewsborough, rapping at it firmly with the handle of her cane. She and her sister, Elizabeth, had been frail, pale, porcelainlike beauties in their youth. Now, they were tiny, wrinkled women fond of wearing too much makeup and too many jewels, and they were as delicate as iron hitching posts. Both had buried several sets of husbands and birthed numerous children, and were as strong as oxen, in spite of it all. They wore their rouge and black patches as boldly as they had done twenty years ago, oblivious of the fact that they were like caricatures of themselves. The rouge might crust inside the wrinkles, the powder might cake. They did not care. In their own minds, they were still twenty and beautiful.

All of the women had on cloaks or tippets trimmed with soft furs. Pearls peeked from their ears, around their necks, around the fingers of their soft, fragrant, crushed leather, fur-lined gloves. There was enough money represented in jewels and lace and furs to support several families for a year. Harold and Tony were dressed more quietly, though both of them wore new wigs under black hats with broad brims and gold lace hatbands. Each of them had the fashionable snuffbox (a picture of a popular actress painted on the inside lid of Tony's, while Harold's had a mirror) inside a pocket. And each of them had an expensive gold watch, with its seal and watch key and handsome outer ornamental case attached to their breeches with gold chains. Everyone looked sleek and prosperous and powerful. Abigail had almost dressed Tony herself. And she had carefully coached him on what he was to say. (Sometimes—not often, but sometimes—he surprised her. This morning he had said, "Always thought Aunt Diana should be here with us." "Why did you not tell me?" demanded Abigail. He shrugged. "Thought you would be angry.")

At the sound of the knock, Diana had become perfectly still. She and Clemmie exchanged a long look. Barbara knew what this all meant now. Diana lived in fear that her numerous creditors would finally track her down, like hounds running the fox to earth. She expected no visitors, received no one but the lawyers, and their visits were never unannounced. But then again, there was Meres. It was his job to skulk around outside and keep an eye out. If someone was knocking at the door, it was because Meres thought it safe—or because he was down the street, drinking in a tavern. Diana nodded abruptly. Clemmie went into the hall and opened the door, and when she saw the crowd of relatives before her, her mouth hung open.

"Announce us, you fat slug!" snapped Aunt Shrewsborough, moving past her.

Clemmie came to the parlor door. "It is your family," she got out, before they began to spill around her into the room. The family stood clustered at the parlor door, their eyes taking in the condition of the room, which was once more bare. Barbara felt herself blushing.

Diana stood up. "My trick. You owe me five shillings," she said softly to Barbara. "Stand up and smooth out your gown. And for God's sake, smile."

"I do not have any money—"

"I will take it out of your dowry. Aunt Lizzie . . . Tony . . . Harold . . . Fanny . . . Abigail." Her husky voice grew flatter and flatter as she enumerated the names. She made an ironic curtsy. Aunt Shrewsborough held a handkerchief scented with orange water up to her nose and looked around the room again. It was worse than she had imagined.

"To what do I owe this visit?" asked Diana, still standing by the table. No one had yet moved to close the space separating them. Clemmie stood off to one side, her eyes, barely visible inside the fat of her cheeks, moving back and forth between the two groups. "Surely it is not a welcome to London, for I have been here nearly a month. Will you not all sit down—no, I do not have enough chairs. We burned them to keep warm. I will not offer you refreshments. As you see, my facilities to entertain are quite limited."

"Diana," said Aunt Shrewsborough, walking across the space and embracing her niece. At first, Diana was stiff in her arms, but then suddenly, she melted and hugged her aunt. Aunt Shrewsborough stepped back, her hands still on Diana's shoulders, and looked her over. She sniffed.

"It is all right now, girl," she said roughly. "The family is here."

Behind her Aunt Cranbourne followed and she, too, embraced Diana. Harold and Tony and Fanny came forward. The two men bowed. Fanny kissed Diana's cheek. Only Abigail remained by the door. She watched the scene being played before her without any expression. Diana smiled across at her. It was a pointed, cat's smile.

Now the two aunts and Fanny were clustered around Barbara. Fanny kissed Barbara's cheek and said, "I am your cousin Fanny. Do you remember me?"

Barbara smiled at the pretty woman whose cheek was so soft and fragrant. She had seldom seen these people since her grandfather's funeral but none had changed so much that she did not recognize them. Of them all, she herself was the most changed. She had been a thin, coltish ten-year-old. Now she was on the verge of young womanhood. The ten-year-old was still there—behind her eyes, in the impatient, long-legged way she moved, in the way her hair still rioted out of place. But her body and face were poised on the brink of adulthood, and she was both familiar and unfamiliar to all of them.

"Of course she does not!" snapped Aunt Shrewsborough, pushing Fanny aside with her cane. "Move over, girl. Let me look at this child! Ye gods, kiss your great-aunt, Barbara! Look, Lizzie, she looks like Brother!"

Her Aunt Cranbourne enfolded Barbara into her furs and laces. Her thin, old shoulders were bony and she smelled of stale perfume and snuff. The two old women were looking her up and down as if she were a horse they were about to purchase. Aunt Shrewsborough poked at her with her cane, and Barbara obediently turned around for her.

"God bless me," said Aunt Cranbourne, "but she will be a beauty! She is too thin now, but put some flesh on her, and I swear she reminds me of myself forty years ago! Look at that hair!"

Barbara, caught between them, smiled. She vaguely remembered these two old women. They were tinier and more wrinkled than her memory of them, and they looked distinctly odd with their big bright spots of rouge on their sagging cheeks and the red drawn crookedly around their lips. But they were family. They poked and prodded at her like family. There was something in them that reminded her of her grandmother. She felt suddenly enfolded in safety, the safety of family, which might criticize you and speak about you for all the world as if you could not hear, but still accepted you. It was something she never felt with her mother. With Diana, there was nothing but coldness.

"I am so glad to see you," she said, impulsively throwing her arms around them and hugging them. She kissed their cheeks with a hearty smack.

"That voice," cried Aunt Shrewsborough. "Say something else!"

Barbara blushed.

"I am Tony—"

Barbara looked at the plump, grave, tall young man before her. Yes, of course, it was Tony. The face might be older, the form taller, but those pale, shy blue eyes still belonged to the same fat boy she and Harry used to tease so. And beat upon.

Except that now, it seemed he had forgiven her her childhood excesses, for he was staring at her with something like admiration and surprise in his eyes and saying, "Awful of me not to have called sooner, Bab. You—you are looking very well."

Diana had been watching the cluster around Barbara with narrowed eyes. She looked as if she might be amused. Actually she was relieved. She felt like a cat that has been rescued from a tree it thought it could climb only to find the limbs too high, the drop below too far. And like a cat, though she was glad to be rescued, she had no intention of making any of it easy on her rescuers.

Abigail cleared her throat and looked across the room at Tony. He was staring at Barbara. She cleared her throat again. Harold nudged Tony in the ribs. He started and turned to Diana.

"Aunt Diana. Offer you the hospitality of my home, and beg that you and my cousin make it your own—" He paused and glanced toward his mother. Abigail mouthed the word "duty." Tony bit his lip.

"Duty!" said Harold and Aunt Shrewsborough and Abigail at the same time. Barbara laughed. Diana did not. She stood there, staring haughtily at each of them in turn, her beautiful face stern and, without its usual allotment of rouge, pale. She might have been a queen receiving penitents, rather than a desperate woman in a stained gown and no stockings.

"Been remiss in my family duty, Aunt Diana," Tony said quickly, trying to spit the words out while he still remembered them. "Ask your forgiveness. As does my mother."

"It is true, Diana," said Abigail, choosing now to sweep forward and join the others. "I allowed my temper to overcome my sense of responsibility, and I heartily regret it. From the bottom of my heart, I ask you to forgive me, and I join Tony in welcoming you and Barbara to my home."

The speech was well done. There was just the proper amount of sincerity in it, but no warmth. Warmth would not have been Abigail. Everyone looked hopefully at Diana.

"You may all of you just turn yourselves around and go home—" Diana began coldly.

"Oh, no," Barbara said to herself. She was standing next to Tony, and somehow his hand found hers and he squeezed it. She felt like crying.

"I have no need of your charity—not at this late date. Where were you months ago when I was almost begging in the streets? Where were you when the bill collectors chased me out of my own home? You have been waiting to see if I would fail or succeed before you chanced having anything to do with me. Well, I am going to succeed, and I have no need of any of you now."

There was a silence. Fanny was staring at Diana, her soft mouth a trembling O. No one ever spoke so to her mother. Harold looked embarrassed. Tony stared down at the buckles on his shoes. Aunt Shrewsborough raised one eyebrow. She sniffed. She looked at her sister.

"I read no mention of a marriage in any of the papers," she said to everyone in general. "Did you, Lizzie?"

"I did not," said Aunt Cranbourne.

"Which means," continued Aunt Shrewsborough, in a hard voice, "that your negotiations are not final. I would not look a gift horse in the mouth if I were you, niece. From the sight of you and this place, Roger Montgeoffry can have you for a song if he waits long enough. Is that what you want, Diana? Because if it is, we will all walk back out that door! You can bargain from a position of power—at Saylor House—with the family firmly behind you. Or you can take your pride and stay here with it. It will not keep you warm at night. Accept Abigail's offer. Overlook its tardiness. Think with your brain, not your temper, girl!"

Diana looked around her. Not a muscle in her face moved to give any indication of what she was feeling.

"Think of Barbara, Aunt," Tony said suddenly into the silence. His speech had not been rehearsed, and Abigail turned to look at him, her face relaying her surprise. "Granddaughter of a duke. Lived all her life at Tamworth Hall. To come to London to—to this! Not used to it. Can see it by looking at her. Let her come to Saylor House, Aunt Diana, please!"

"Well said, boy!" exclaimed Aunt Shrewsborough, rapping him on the arm with her cane. Barbara smiled up at him, her gratefulness in her eyes. Tony was beginning to act like a friend. She had a feeling that she could count on him to help her. Suddenly, she felt ashamed for all those times she and Harry had tormented him. He had just been slow. He could not help that his mind did not match theirs in the speed of

their thinking and their speech. And they had made him pay
for it. How they had made him pay. She linked her arm
through his and squeezed it.

"Thank you," she whispered.

Aunt Shrewsborough was not finished. Like the expert card
player she was, she had saved an extra trump.

"I have had a letter from your mother," she said, shaking
her cane in Diana's face. Again, Diana did not move, but this
time her face changed slightly, and Aunt Shrewsborough nodded, satisfied with the reaction, minute though it was. "She
wrote me over a week ago wanting to know what the devil
was going on here, Diana. She says she has not heard a word
from you. She asked about Barbara—about the marriage. She
said she would come up here herself if she did not hear from
me. Now, I wrote her back that everything was under control, but I can just as easily post a special messenger and tell
her to pack her bags and bring herself up here. And if I do,
Diana, I do not have to tell you what will happen, do I?"

Diana was silent. She bit her lip. No one said a word. No
one had to. Each of them had dealt, at one time or another,
with the Duchess when she was angry. No more needed to be
said.

"Perhaps . . . you are right," she said slowly. "Perhaps we
might come to some accommodation."

Barbara hugged everyone around her. After she hugged
Tony, he stared after her with a dazed expression on his face.
Abigail walked forward calmly into that last bit of space left
between her and Diana. Their cheeks touched. With the edge
of her apron, Clemmie wiped the perspiration that had gathered on her upper lip in spite of the cold. For a moment, she
thought Diana had overplayed her hand, but Diana had been
born under a lucky star. She always landed on her feet,
always. Even now, she was allowing the men to kiss her hand
and the women to hug her as if she were conferring a personal favor on them, when Clemmie alone knew that last
night she had come close to sending a letter to Aunt Shrewsborough begging for money. Clemmie had been all set to send
Meres to deliver it. Diana had not done it at the last minute,
just as she had not given in on the negotiations, trusting
somehow that her luck would change.

Amid the hugging and kissing, Abigail was informing Diana that she would send footmen and a carriage tomorrow. Aunt Shrewsborough and Aunt Cranbourne were arguing over which of them Barbara had gotten her white complexion from.

"You just see you protect it, young lady!" Aunt Shrewsborough said. "There is not a mark on it, and a white complexion is a lady's first beauty. Balm of Mecca. I use balm of Mecca nightly."

"Grandmama gave me her milk of roses—"

"What!" cried Aunt Cranbourne, her tiny body quivering with outrage. "I have begged Alice for years to give that recipe, and she always refused. What is in it, Bab? What!"

"We must go," Harold said to them, coming up to them.

Both of them turned on him like tiny, vicious harpies. He backed off. They turned back to Barbara.

"You be sure you come to see us," Aunt Shrewsborough told her sternly. "I will tell you a thing or two about handling this Lord Devane of yours—"

"A handsome man!" said Aunt Cranbourne. "If I were ten years younger, I would give you a run for your money, Bab. Come along, Louisa, they are waiting for us. Diana, you did the right thing. I want that recipe now! Do not forget it!" There was more kissing and hugging and talk, and then the room was bare and empty again: the babble of talk, the scent of powder and snuff and perfume, the swish of heavy skirts and petticoats, starched linen gone. They might never have been there, except that Barbara felt so relieved inside.

In the silence Diana sat down suddenly as if she had lost strength in her legs. She looked at Clemmie, still against one wall, shapeless as a huge, silent leech, and began to laugh. Clemmie shook her head and grinned, the gaps in her teeth black as night.

Outside, Tony said, almost to himself, "Barbara has grown up." Behind him, Harold winked at Fanny, who giggled. Behind them, Abigail said nothing. She had not heard.

Saylor House was all Barbara had expected and more. From the moment the carriage Abigail had sent wheeled them between the gate towers and into the courtyard, Barbara's heart swelled with pride. The house was massive, symmetrical, solid, rising three stories to a hipped roof, punctuated at regular intervals with dormer windows and massive chimney stacks. In the center of the roof was a marble cupola used by the family in the hot summer for al fresco dining and entertaining. Behind the chimney stacks a white stone balustrade ran along the roof's perimeters to protect anyone who might wish to stroll on the roof and enjoy the view, still a lovely one—even though the surrounding property was rapidly filling with buildings. It was possible to see St. James's Square to the west and across the Marlborough House gardens to St. James's Park on the south. There were stone benches carved into the balustrade so that guests might sit down, and when the Duchess had lived there, she had huge pots of blooming flowers and shrubs placed all about so that the roof was like another garden, but closer to the sky. The front of the house had matched windows blinking evenly across each story. A simple outside stair curved upward to the double doors of the entrance, encased in marble and topped by a pediment.

Two footmen ran down the stairs to open the carriage doors. A butler, short and plump, with a pouter-pigeon-like chest and stomach, stood majestically before that half of the entrance doors opened to welcome them. Barbara followed her mother up the stairs.

"Lady Saylor awaits you in the great parlor," the butler said.

"Thank you, Bates," said Diana. "Bates, this is my oldest daughter, Mistress Barbara Alderley. Barbara, this is Bates. You have been with Saylor House since its beginnings, have you not, Bates?"

"I certainly have, Lady Alderley. I am happy to make your acquaintance, Mistress Alderley. May I say that you have the look of your grandfather, and may I say how pleased we are at Saylor House to welcome you."

Barbara smiled at him, but all her attention was on the great hall she now was standing in. It was the most beautiful room she had ever seen; all its proportions were perfectly equal. The floor was cut into great, even, alternating squares of black and white marble. The hall itself rose up into two stories, and the tall windows cut across the front of the house kept it from being dark or closed in. An intricately carved wooden staircase rose along each far side of the wall to meet directly ahead of her, on the second floor, as a spacious landing. Each arm of the staircase balustrade was carved in the shape of a pineapple, the fruit being the base, the leaves flowing upward to join the top railing. The carver had captured every seam, every crevice of the fruit. Barbara walked farther into the hall. In front of her was a great central door cut into the wall, its position exactly matching the entrance doors behind her. And above her, on the second level, was a door that exactly matched the one on this floor. The frames of all the doors were surrounded with marble columns that met above the doors to form pediments. Into the walls on this and the floor above were cut evenly spaced ovals, outlined with laurel wreaths, in which sat marble busts. Barbara did not yet know it, but they were busts of the most famous men in Queen Anne's reign: Marlborough, Godolphin, Prince Eugene, Prince George, Sunderland, Somers and Cowper. To know who they were was to begin to realize the extent of her grandfather's power. Two huge portraits hung on the side walls, in the shadows created by the staircase. The portraits faced each other across the room. Walking forward to look at the busts, Barbara noticed them. She went to the one of a woman.

"This is Mother," said Diana, coming to stand beside Barbara.

"Grandmama?" breathed Barbara, looking up at a slim, young woman with dark, glowing eyes and hair and a masterful nose. Her face was not pretty in any usual context, but so lively, laughing and intelligent that the viewer was intrigued. She stood in a garden near a marble fountain. She wore a dark green velvet gown, and puppies and three children played at her feet. "Dicken, Will and Giles, my brothers," said Diana. One hand in the painting rested on her hip, the other held a bouquet of roses, fat and full, their petals falling softly onto the ground, among the animals and children.

"She was lovely!" said Barbara, enchanted at this unexpected vision of her grandmother when she was young.

"Her nose was always too big," Diana said. "Here, this portrait is Father."

Barbara walked across the marble floor to the other side, where the portrait of her grandfather hung. It seemed fitting that he and Grandmother should stare into eternity at each other, captured forever in their youth. The man before her was handsome and smiling, his wide blue eyes gazing at the viewer serenely. He wore a great, full, old-fashioned periwig and a military uniform of red and white, and leaned against the side of a black stallion, fully saddled and bridled. Behind him were trees and blue, blue sky, but no bluer than his calm eyes.

Bates was holding open the door to the great parlor. Diana and Barbara walked in. Abigail, sitting in a chair near the massive marble fireplace, rose and came forward. Tony, staring pensively out the windows into the wintry, bare gardens, pulled his hands out of his pockets and followed his mother. Mary, Tony's younger sister, sitting on a stool, remained where she was. Barbara had a confused impression of men charging toward each other, their mouths forever open in silent cries to victory and death on the walls around her dwarfing all else in the room, from the huge cabinets filled with red and blue and yellow china to many small tables and chairs. Above the fireplace was a portrait of Abigail and her children, gazing serenely toward the opposite panels of charging horses, their mouths pulled against bridles, and torn flags and men fighting.

"There used to be a portrait of me," Diana said to Barbara. "I wonder where Abigail hid it—ah, Abigail—" She and Abigail coldly touched cheeks. Barbara kissed her aunt.

"Stayed to greet you," Tony told her, pumping her hand up and down. Barbara smiled at him, and then reached upward and quickly kissed his cheek.

"We are cousins, Tony. It is allowed," she teased. His plump face turned red.

"Mary!" called Abigail. "You remember your cousin Barbara and your Aunt Diana." Mary stood up quickly and made a fluttering little curtsy. She smiled timidly at Barbara. Her eyes were pale blue, as pale as her brother's, and she looked as if the slightest word would send her scurrying for cover. Barbara smiled back, calculating that she must be ten or eleven, older than Charlotte, but if Barbara was any judge, as serious and shy. Oh, I am glad to be here, she thought, not only because the house was all she had imagined and more, but because of Mary, who was someone she could care for, just as she had always cared for her brothers and sisters. Someone to ease the ache she felt in missing them. Yes, she understood shy, serious little girls, and she would understand Mary. And love her.

"Mary, take your cousin to her rooms," Abigail said. "Barbara, I have allotted you a suite of rooms on this side, which overlooks the gardens, so much more cheerful than the street in winter. I hope you find them comfortable." She smiled coldly at Barbara, not really seeing her.

Barbara followed Mary's solid little body out of the room. Tony watched her until the door closed behind her. Even after the door closed, he stared at it, as if she might once more materialize before him.

"What are you looking at!" his mother said irritably.

He started, and turned back to his mother and aunt.

"Only stayed to welcome you, Aunt Diana. Pressing business elsewhere, you know. Treat this house as your own."

"Since it once was, I certainly shall," Diana drawled. "Of course, I can make myself at home anywhere. Father used to say I would have made a perfect soldier's wife." She smiled at Abigail. "But then you were a soldier's wife, were you not, Abigail? Though hardly perfect—"

Tony coughed and glanced at his mother and left the room. Diana sat down in an armchair near the fire. She stretched her hands to the fire. Abigail, watching her, bit her lip. She closed her eyes for a moment and prayed for patience.

"I have every intention of going and coming as I please, Abigail," Diana said. "Do not think you can rule my activities because I sleep under your roof. And I may not always choose to sleep under your roof. I have no intention of offering you any explanation when I do not do so."

"None will be needed," Abigail snapped, forgetting for the moment her good intentions.

Diana, pleased to have drawn blood, sat back in the chair and relaxed, for all the world like a sleek, overfed cat. She held her shoes to the fire, turning her ankles around and around to admire their trimness. "I love this house," she said. "I was a girl here. I danced many a dance, kissed many a beau. One of the Cavendish boys proposed to me right in this very room. Where did you put my portrait?"

Abigail was irritably noting how smooth Diana's skin still was, and so did not hear the question. Diana, only five years younger than she, was still a beautiful woman. Abigail had been pretty, but she had known her limits, known that with her fortune and family name she could have been as ugly as a stone and still married well. But Diana had been beautiful, beautiful in an amazing, rare way. Men had instantly fallen in love with her. One look was enough. It did not matter how she acted, who she was inside. Her beauty changed her in their eyes into something so desirable that they had to have her. What power she had had—the young Diana—a power not of her own creation, not because she was good or kind or intelligent, but because of an accident of nature. She could have married anyone in the kingdom; yet she had married Kit. Here she sat, at thirty-four, her fortune lost, her reputation something Abigail would have died rather than borne, at an age when most women had gone to fat, lost some of their teeth, been disfigured by smallpox, illness, continual pregnancies, and she was still beautiful. Not the perfect, innocent dewiness of her youth, but even more sensual with the lines of experience marking her eyes and mouth and figure. Would she always be beautiful? Would nature never demand its due—

"I asked where you put my portrait."

"What portrait?"

Abigail knew exactly the one Diana meant. It had been the first thing she had moved when she and her children had come into this house. Diana had looked like a goddess in that portrait. Of course she had moved it.

"The one of me in my wine-colored gown, the one by Lely. I wore diamonds in my hair, around my neck and arms, sewn to the lace at the sleeves and throat of my gown. Lely said I reminded him of a bloodred rose, rich and beautiful and fragrant—he was in love with me—"

"One only wonders how he knew how you smelled!"

Diana laughed.

"I moved it into another room; it did not seem to fit this one." In spite of herself, Abigail sounded defensive.

Diana looked upward at the portrait above the fireplace. In it, Abigail sat smiling, plump and fair in a blue gown and pearls, her children beside her. She in no way resembled a bloodred rose.

"And yours fits better, I suppose. But, you live here now—where shall you go when Tony marries, I wonder? You will miss this house, its grandeur, all it stands for. The new Duchess will then take down your picture and put up her own—and thus life goes on."

Tony marry . . . Abigail had not even thought of it. No, that was not true. She thought of it often, weighing this girl against that one, wanting Tony to have only the best, a sweet girl bringing much property with her, but she had never really thought about the fact that she would have to leave Saylor House, that it would belong to Tony and his wife. Diana was smiling at her, that nasty, pointed, cat's smile. How like her to drag her completely away from the topic she wished to discuss—Tony marry! Well, of course he would. And she would be the one who chose his bride. And Abigail would be a welcome guest in their home, an honored guest.

"I want some of my own things," said Diana.

"I beg your pardon—"

"Some things from my house, some furniture and a portrait or two. My clothes. Do you think you can send a footman around to gather them without attracting attention? Just a few things, Abigail, to make me feel more at home—here in this house I was raised in."

"And I thought you were at home anywhere!" Abigail snapped before she could help herself. Once again, as if she knew exactly what she was doing, Diana laughed. Abigail had the most terrible urge to cram her fist into that open mouth, break out all those sharp, little white teeth. But above and beyond all of that, she wanted Bentwoodes for Tony. For that, she could be patient. Let Diana play with her like a cat does a half-dead mouse. She was neither half-dead nor a mouse, as Diana would well know.

"My—Tony's house is at your disposal, Diana. If you require some things from your home, I am sure we can handle that, which brings me to something which I have been wanting to say to you. I know, of course, that you are already in the midst of your negotiations with Roger Montgeoffry. I have told you how I feel about the marriage, so I will not repeat myself. But I have had my bankers do some preliminary figures, purely speculative, of course, on what Roger stands to earn on the long term from Bentwoodes. And I thought you ought to know—"

"Ought I?"

"Of course you should. I realize your immediate need is for cash, but you need not sacrifice something that could pay handsomely in the future—with a little patience and time—"

"I have no time, Abigail. I have no holdings, no securities, no cash, nothing, other than the Alderley estate, which is entailed to Harry, and mortgaged to the limit. I cannot even enter the door of my own house in Westminster for the bill collectors wanting their money. Patience is a virtue I have no time for."

"If someone were to lend you the money to tide you over, give you breathing space . . ."

Diana allowed none of the triumph she must be feeling to show on her face.

"Roger has already lent me money."

The words took Abigail's breath away. Rapidly, she refigured the amount of cash she had been going to suggest to Diana. She felt sick.

"Of course, it was not enough. Nothing is enough to fill the hole I am in. Damn Kit to hell and back—how I hope he is dying from the pox in Lorraine!" She glanced quickly at her sister-in-law. Abigail was thinking about money and did not see her look. Diana looked back at the fire. Her husky voice was pensive, soft.

"Roger offers me nearly everything I need. He is willing to pay my current bills, pay off the mortgages on the estate and settle stock on Harry and myself. But I have no allowance. Even selling the stock will help me only for a short time. I need that allowance, something to tide me over until I remarry—"

"Remarry! But you are not even divorced!" It was all Abigail could do to bring herself to say the word, though it got easier each time she said Bentwoodes to herself along with it.

"The next time I marry," Diana said, as if she had not heard Abigail, "it will be for something other than what he can do under the covers. That can be found anywhere. Security cannot."

Abigail averted her face. Diana was so vulgar. Everyone knew she had had to marry Kit. There was no need to advertise the fact. One needed to set an example to one's children.

"Why do you not simply marry Roger yourself?" The question popped out. Abigail cursed herself. She was a stupid fool cutting off her nose to spite her face, but there was a certain look of surprise and respect in Diana's violet eyes, as she stared at her sister-in-law.

"Two reasons. My mother would never give me the land. And because, dear, dear Abigail, he has not asked me."

If Abigail had not known Diana better, she would have thought her embarrassed. As it was, she hardly knew what to say or think. Except perhaps that life might be fair after all; to think that Diana Alderley could no longer snap her fingers and have a man run to her. Of course, marriage was a different thing. Abigail could have told her that. Diana's reputation was too soiled, too ugly. She would have had to have an enormous fortune to overcome it. Naturally, Roger preferred her daughter, young, innocent, untouched . . . and possessing Bentwoodes. Apparently, Roger, for all his good looks, was no fool, either. Too bad. It would be easier to get the land if he were a fool. And she was going to have that land for Tony, who deserved it as head of the family. Tony would not always have to stand in the shadow of his famous grandfather. No, he would take the land and fortune and treble it, if Abigail had to show him every step of the way. Diana could be bought—at a higher price than she had bargained for, but the land was worth it. She glanced over at Diana's almost perfect profile, marred only by a slight fullness under her chin. Diana had been remarkably honest. A bad sign. But they understood each other.

"Tomorrow, Diana, I will show you those figures."

Diana turned her lovely eyes to Abigail; they were like limpid pools of violet-blue water.

"Yes, you do that."

Like an overgrown duckling, Mary padded silently in front of Barbara. She offered no chatter about herself or the house they were passing through. They were walking down a corridor off the landing on the second floor. Ahead Barbara could see a huge window and window seat. On each side of her were closed doors. Midway, at some point only Mary recognized, for Barbara could see no difference in these doors from the others along this hall, Mary opened one of the sets of narrow double doors that intersected this corridor at regular intervals. Barbara walked into a bedchamber that was as lovely in its own way as the great hall downstairs.

Light, honey-colored oak paneling covered the walls, and the bed hangings, bed cover and chair covers and draperies were of sunny yellow damask. Mary showed her two adjoining small rooms, rooms in which she could read or do needlepoint or receive visitors. A door in the farther led back to the corridor, meaning she could receive her callers without first marching them through her bedchamber. In one of the rooms, a huge portrait of Diana, blazingly beautiful in a wine-colored gown and diamonds, was hanging in the darkest corner. She went back into her bedchamber, and leaned forward to smell the potted daffodils blooming on a small table. Everything around her was rich and comfortable like Tamworth, only lacking the still, shuttered, unused look and smell so many of Tamworth's rooms had. Mary stood silently near the door. She put her hand on the latch.

"Wait a moment," said Barbara. "I will not bite. How old are you?"

Mary swallowed. "Eleven."

Barbara smiled at her. "I have a brother, Kit, who is ten. Only he is not silent as you are. He chatters like a blue jay. Are you always so quiet? You remind me of my sister Charlotte. She is my favorite sister."

Mary said nothing. She had inherited her mother's square face, but not the beauty which softened it.

"Where are your rooms?"

"Up-upstairs."

"Just you?"

Mary nodded. "And my nurse, Mrs. Mentibilly."

Barbara touched the bright yellow trumpet of one of the daffodils. "This is lovely. And very thoughtful of your mother. My grandmama always has our house—Tamworth Hall—filled with flowers. In the rooms that we use, that is. All is almost never open because Grandmama never sees anyone anymore.

Other than the vicar and squire and neighbors and tenants, which, when I name them, make up a lot of people. What I mean is that she has retired from the social world, the world this house represents. How old were you when your father died?"

The pupils in Mary's eyes dilated. "Two." Then she said abruptly, "I do not remember him."

Barbara smiled. "Oh, I do. He was tall and fair and always laughing, always. He used to bring me oranges in his pockets, and I would have to guess which pocket, and if I did not guess correctly he would swear he was going to give them to Dulcinea. As if cats ate oranges! Dulcinea is Grandmama's cat. Actually it was not the same Dulcinea that your father knew. Grandmama always names her cats Dulcinea."

"Mother does not like cats." Mary blurted the words out quickly as if she were a miser and words were gold and too much had fallen from her pocket before she could stop it.

"No," Barbara said. "She would not. Do you have any pets?"

Mary shook her head.

"A dog? Not even a bird? Really, Mary! What a shame! You must get lonely in this big old house."

Mary did not say anything. She lowered her head and looked at the floor. But she was not sulking. I begin to understand you, thought Barbara. You are lonely, and you notice many things, but you do not tell them. And you have learned not to trust people. But you can trust me. I know how to keep secrets. You are so much like Charlotte. I will write and tell her. Come, Mary, trust me, be my friend. To see if she would follow, Barbara walked back into one of the smaller, adjoining rooms. Mary followed, slowly, safely, from a distance. Barbara smiled to herself. It was like luring a bird. Mary stood at the doorway, watching Barbara with big eyes.

"Where do my clothes go?" asked Barbara. Silently, Mary pointed to a door set so skillfully into the paneling that at first glance it was unnoticeable. Barbara opened it. The room was small and narrow, with an oak press at one end and pegs on the wall. Nearby was another door just like it. There was nothing in it but a narrow cot, for Barbara's maid. Barbara closed the door. She looked around her. It was perfect, but for that picture of her mother. She would have that moved if there was any discreet way to do it.

"I think I will have tea in my small parlor," Barbara said, as if to herself. She turned suddenly and caught Mary watching. "Will you join me, Mary?"

Mary nodded her head. A knock sounded. Barbara ran into her bedchamber and opened the door to two footmen who carried in her trunks and set them on the floor.

"Where is your maid?" whispered Mary. She had followed Barbara in like a shadow.

Barbara was kneeling down and unlocking one of the trunks. "I do not have one. I left her at Tamworth because she was bad. Surely your mama will have a chambermaid I can borrow. Look, Mary, in here."

Barbara was lifting out a shallow tray that fitted across the top of the inside of the trunk. The tray had different-sized compartments with lids. Fascinated, but wary, Mary hovered over her shoulder. Barbara opened one of the lids. Bright ribbons were curled inside each other. Mary sighed. Barbara took a red one from the bunch and held it out to Mary. Slowly, Mary took it. Barbara lifted up a piece of lace nestled in the center of the ribbons' curl.

"This is from the sleeve of the man I love, Mary. He is the most handsome, the kindest man in the world, and I am going to marry him and have lots of babies. You will have to be godmother to one of my babies. Somewhere in here is a music box he gave me. I will show it to you later—but first—" She put the lace back carefully into its nest, and opened another compartment. It held her jewelry, her pearls, a few necklaces and earrings, and a miniature of her grandmother. She patted the floor beside her.

"Sit down, Mary. I will show you a portrait of Grandmama. And I will tell you about my brothers and sisters, Harry, Tom, Kit, Charlotte, Anne and Baby. You remind me of Charlotte. I would like to pretend you were my sister. If you do not mind. I feel so lonely here in London without them all. See, this is Grandmama. She looks very old and very stern, here, and she is. She is very strict about manners. At Tamworth, I have to practice once a week with a carving master so that I shall know how to carve and serve fish and fowl and beef properly. And I have to practice my music and my French—"

Mary was nestled beside her, listening. Tentatively she put her hand out and touched the edge of Barbara's skirt; then she drew it back quickly. But Barbara was satisfied. She felt a powerful, protective urge toward this small girl—it was a maternal streak within her toward all beings smaller and weaker than herself. And they loved her back for it. They could not help it.

"My mama does not like yours." Mary stammered the words, and once they were out, she sat staring at Barbara in horror, as if she could not imagine how such a thing had happened. Her life lay in Barbara's hands, but Barbara gave her a quick hug.

"I know," she said. "Not many people like my mother. Look, these are my first pearls. Grandmama gave them to me when I was thirteen. When you have tea with me today, I will let you wear them, and we can pretend you are a duchess, and I shall practice my manners on you. I have to have perfect manners. I am going to be a famous countess after I am married."

"Oh, Barbara," sighed Mary, happier than she had been in her life. She listened to every word her older cousin had to say, storing it away to take out later and repeat inside her head. No one had paid such attention to her for as long as she could remember. Barbara had told her about her father. She had given her a red ribbon. She had many brothers and sisters, and one of them was like Mary. She was going to wear Barbara's pearls. She had told Barbara a terrible thing, and Barbara was not going to tattle on her. She began to love Barbara a little, with her small, lonely heart.

Later, after a chambermaid arrived to unpack her trunks, and Mary had to go away to her lessons, Barbara sat in one of the window seats, the fat yellow cushions piled behind her back. She looked out on the rear gardens, the trees waving bare branches over graveled paths. Away from the trees were rows of pruned rosebushes, their brown arms ugly and stubby. They will be lovely in the spring, she thought, leaning her head against the chill of a windowpane. It was good to be here. It brought her closer to Roger. Surely if she were here, it meant the contracts were to be signed. He must be closer.

Surely he would come to visit her here. There had to be a way she could find out what was happening. No one bothered to tell her anything, and they became angry at her if she asked. Not that they had to tell her, she was only a girl, and she knew her grandmama had spoiled her, always treating her as if her opinion were important, always letting her know what her future held. She was more fortunate than many girls. But it was hard to wait, hard to be patient, when others were deciding your future. She was not a patient person; it was her worst fault, her grandmother told her, that and her impulsiveness and her temper. She sighed for her grandmother, and for Roger, her prince, her dream. To her, he was always that handsome, tanned man sitting way, way up on a horse and laughing down at her and reaching forward to pull her up in the saddle before him. He was the man who had picked her up in his arms at her grandfather's funeral and hugged her and told her not to cry, when he was crying himself. She loved him with all her heart. She always, always would.

Roger sat near the roaring fire that kept the water hot for the coffee and tea served at the St. James's coffeehouse. Rather than sitting at one of the long, wooden trestle tables, along with other customers, who were talking and gambling and smoking pipes, he had pulled his chair close to the iron rack holding the coffeepots and teapots; the rack was positioned in front of the fire so the pots would stay warm. A few feet from him, the cashier, Mrs. Blow, stood behind a waist-high counter. Patrons paid their penny to her and then were free to spend as much time as they liked drinking tea or coffee (or something stronger for extra). Some coffeehouses lured in customers with a beautiful cashier and pretty barmaids, but the St. James's attracted its customers because of its proximity to the palace and, therefore, its access to foreign and domestic news. Roger came in to read its newsletters and pick up court gossip, just as he went to Lloyd's coffeehouse because Lloyd's specialized in news of shipping, to Jonathan's because it was frequented by London merchants and bankers and he could always find out the latest gossip about the stock market, to Garraway's because it sold the finest wines when it held its auctions, to Child's because it had a reputation for being patronized by London's most learned men, just as Will's had a reputation for having poets and wits as its prime customers.

The first coffeehouse in London opened in 1650, sixty-five years ago, and now they were an institution in every man's life. All neighborhoods had one or two just around the corner (near the law courts, the students started their mornings, still in their nightclothes, at the Grecian and Squire's and Searle's, and stayed there until noon, when they went home to change and go to court). A man went to read the latest news in the letters or journals and in the advertisements pinned to the walls; he went to idle away time; he went to smoke his pipe or dip his snuff in peace; he went to meet a friend or business associate; he went to pick up messages and letters he did not want to have delivered at home; he went because all men went and, eventually, he would run across friends and acquaintances and hear the gossip of city and court and abroad.

In the St. James's coffeehouse, as in most coffeehouses, the smoke from pipes created a fog that hung suspended and visible in the air. Walpole and his brother and two other men were playing cards at a round table near the windows that overlooked the street. Roger had played for a while, but he had lost consistently, and eventually quit. Now he sat reading a letter about news of the French court that Elliot, the proprietor, had given him. Elliot knew Roger was leaving for France in January and thought he might like to know the latest news. The letter really did not contain anything Roger did not already know: The regent was quarreling with his nephew, the King of Spain; the regent's daughter had disgraced herself by passing out into her brandied cream dessert at a dinner for the Prince of Venice; there were rumors circulating that the regent was dabbling in black magic in an effort to conjure up the Devil and have him kill the young king, Louis XV, under the regent's protection; the Scotsman, John Law, was the toast of the city, Parisians were falling over themselves to give him luncheons and entertainments and listen to his every word as if it were an oracle from God; he and the regent were said to be planning a grand financial scheme that would pull France out of its perpetual near-bankruptcy. Roger refolded the letter and gave it back to a waiter. He was thinking about Law and how he must be sure to meet him when he was in France when Carlyle strolled in, spotted Roger immediately through the tobacco smoke, laid his pennies before Mrs. Blow, called to a waiter for a glass of wine, another to pull up a chair near Roger, and with greetings throughout the room, finally settled himself by Roger.

Roger, feeling bored, was glad to see him. Carlyle would have all the latest gossip, and had, in fact, just come from Button's, where he had listened to the poet, Alexander Pope, read a few stanzas from his latest poem. There was talk that Addison and Steele might start another newsletter. Hearing Robert Walpole belch loudly from his table, Carlyle said Walpole's wife was rumored to be sleeping with Lord Hervey. Roger smiled. Walpole's wife was sleeping with him. It was accidental; too much wine and ennui; before, her snapping black eyes had seemed intriguing, after, they merely seemed the result of a bad temper. He was already tired of her, just as he was tired of everything these days. If she was interested in Hervey, he would gently prod her in that direction. She would remain a friend if it were she, rather than he, that ended it. He cared for Walpole too much to want his wife to come between them. Carlyle mentioned Walpole's debts; he was desperately short of money. Roger made a mental note to lend him several hundred pounds, it was the least he could do.

Carlyle read Elliot's letter. To his disappointment, Roger said the black magic story was just that, a story spread by the regent's illegitimate cousins to discredit him. The regent did practice black magic; Roger had seen him do it in his basements in his palace, the Palais Royal, but he practiced it because he did not believe in God, and he was trying to test him by raising the Devil. If the Devil existed, said the regent, then so did God. His loyalty to the young king was absolute. Carlyle wanted to know more about the black magic. They talked about an old woman who had been burned at the stake for witchcraft in Chelsea. They talked of a new shop opening in the New Exchange and whether they would go at once or wait until the curious crowds left, of whether they would go to the theater that night; of the rumor that the Pretender, James III, was off the coast of Scotland. They talked of the news that Lady Diana Alderley was now living with her nephew, the young Duke of Tamworth.

Carlyle relayed this news (which Roger already knew) with special glee; he felt his gossip had been responsible for the move. After all, it was the least he could do for his dear friend, Roger, and that young child he was planning to marry. Had the contracts been signed yet? Carlyle wanted to know. He was as interested in this marriage as if it were his own. Roger told him no; they argued whether it would be proper for Roger to send New Year's presents to Barbara if she was not yet formally engaged to him; Carlyle saying no, Roger saying they had already been purchased. They talked of Roger's coming trip, and of the several huge receptions he was holding for the coming Christmas season. Carlyle mentioned that he had seen Diana going into Child's Bank, the bank Lady Abigail Saylor patronized. Roger said that was indeed interesting and asked Carlyle what color he ought to redo the rooms in his town house that would be allotted to Barbara as her bedroom and withdrawing chambers. They could not agree on a color. They decided to go to Button's and see if Pope was still there; Roger wanted to hear the poem. How long was she in Child's Bank? Roger asked. Really, Carlyle said, he did not know.

"Exactly what do you mean?" Roger was frowning, a thing he seldom did, and there was a bite in his voice. Craven, his solicitor, of the firm Craven, Waddill and Civins, shifted in his seat. He was a fat, short man with permanent snuff stains on his yellowed teeth. He cleared his throat.

"Ah . . . well, sir, it seems that Lady Diana suddenly thinks the terms too, ah . . . hem . . . too small, sir."

"I know there was some slight disagreement on a cash settlement, but surely not enough for us to quibble about, Craven."

"Twenty thousand pounds, sir."

Roger opened, then closed, his mouth. He seemed, for the moment, unable to speak. Craven nodded his head in sympathy.

"Yes, sir, quite understandable. It came as quite a shock to us when Lady Alderley's lawyers mentioned the amount. It seems that Lady Alderley feels that she should have something for the long term—"

"The long term?"

"Their words, sir, not mine. If you are not willing to give her a percentage of the fees from the rental of buildings and homes, sir, she wants cash instead."

"There was no settlement ever planned for her, other than stock, and there are no buildings and homes, Craven. I must expend a great deal of money to build them!"

"Yes, sir. Of course, sir. Ah . . . however, Lady Alderley seems to feel that either a cash settlement or a percentage is in order."

"Abigail!" said Roger softly. He slammed an open palm on his desk.

"Excuse me, sir?"

"Nothing! I was thinking aloud. I understand you clearly, I think. This money is not toward Mistress Barbara's settlements. It is above and beyond the money I have already lent Lady Alderley, in addition to the debts and mortgages I would pay off?"

Craven nodded his head. Roger looked at the litter of papers on his desk. Many of them were drawings and sketches of buildings, and among them were cost estimates and construction schedules. He had already spent a great deal of money and time on Bentwoodes. It seemed impossible that now he might not have it after all.

"Shall I, ah . . . break off negotiations, sir?"

"No! No, Craven. Do not allow them to upset you. Anger and business do not mix."

He took a deep breath, his eyes bright blue with anger. He waved the lawyer away and went to stand by the window that overlooked St. James's Square. Outside, the lightest of snows was beginning to fall. The lamplighters had already lit the lanterns that towered every few feet above the iron railing that surrounded the fountain at the center of the square. The lights twinkled in the soft dusk. Below him, a wagon filled with greenery, wreaths of holly and bay, loop after loop of laurel and box, was being unloaded. He could see White and Montrose arguing with each other. They were like two schoolboys. He had put them in charge of decorating the house for Christmas. He intended to entertain royally—there were dinners and musical receptions and card parties planned. He wanted his tables groaning with food and wine, his house shining with Christmas candles and greenery. He had thought to celebrate his leaving for France and his coming marriage and Bentwoodes during the holidays. Wren had two assistants even now creating a plaster facsimile of his master plan that he was going to display atop a table for his guests to see. And now it might all go up in smoke because of a woman's greed. He drew his brows together.

Below him, White and Montrose noticed him standing in the window and waved. But he did not wave back. Bentwoodes was his dream, the chance to put himself among the truly great families, to create something that would forever be a memorial to himself, to what he had achieved. To build it the way he wished to, he was going to have to sell many of his bonds and stock and slowly liquidate the assets his bankers had painstakingly stockpiled for him. He was going against their advice. It was going to be enormously expensive. But his children, his grandchildren, would reap the benefits from the prestige, the rentals, the business, that would be created. In one way, Diana was adroit to want something of that future. But she was risking no investment of her own. She was not creating the dream; he was. Somehow, there had to be a way to make her understand. Somehow, there had to be a way to achieve his dream. He would hang on to his temper; he would be reasonable. He would take the figures to his business manager again and rework them; there might be some percentage they could accord Diana. He would see. He closed his eyes and breathed deeply, trying not to let the anger building inside him overwhelm him. Abigail and Diana and his own rage would not outwit him . . . he would not let them. A chance like Bentwoodes would not come his way again. He felt it in his bones.

Barbara sat at an elegant writing table in one of the rooms adjoining her bedchamber. The table had graceful, curved legs and a top that curled down and locked. Inside was a flat writing surface and many little cubbyholes in which to put papers and letters. A fat letter to her grandmother lay folded, needing only Tony's seal and signature to send it on its way. She wrote her grandmother about Roger; told her that from this very roof she could look over to St James's Square, where Roger lived. With Christmas coming, each day was busy, she wrote. (And Roger did not call, she did not write.) Many friends of her aunt's visited, and she had to be introduced, and often her aunt had her stay and pour tea. She had seen Fanny's home and Fanny's dear little baby and two small children. She was taking watercolor and dancing lessons with Mary. In the afternoons, if there was no company, Tony took Mary and her for a drive. Grandmama would be happy to know that Aunt Saylor ran her life according to a strict schedule. Barbara might eat a late supper with the adults, if they were not engaged to dine out, but then she must work on her needlepoint and go to bed. The mornings were assigned tasks: writing letters, reading from approved books, lessons (watercolor, geography, dance, French, spinet); afternoons were for visiting or receiving guests.

Barbara took out a fresh sheet of paper. She was going to write to Jane, who should be in London by now, and invite her to tea. In the bedchamber, Martha, the maid her aunt had assigned to her, moved into her line of vision. Barbara stuck her tongue out at the maid's back. Martha was a heavy, stern woman with dark eyebrows that met over her nose. Martha had thwarted her plan to write to Roger. In order to write clandestinely to a gentleman, a girl needed a maid who could be trusted to deliver messages. One look at Martha had convinced her the woman would go straight to her aunt. Somehow, though, she was going to see Roger. She lifted her chin; her grandmother would have recognized her determination immediately, but her aunt did not know her well enough, and her mother paid no attention.

"I really do not see that this entire evening is necessary," Abigail said to Tony. They were both waiting in the great parlor for Diana and Barbara to come downstairs. Tony wore a new wig, a silver brocade coat and a white dimity embroidered waistcoat with black velvet breeches. He looked like a pale pear. Abigail was pulling on the lace at his sleeves as she spoke.

"After all, Diana has been to the theater any number of times, and Barbara is far too young, in my opinion, to go. Theatergoing has a bad reputation, Tony, a reputation you might not wish put on your young cousin."

"Will protect her, Mother."

Abigail did not like the way he said that.

"Pooh! She needs no protection. Let her be, Tony. Enjoy yourself. Do not spend your evening watching over a country cousin. See them into your box and leave at the first interval to visit your own friends. Barbara will not be expecting you to hang over her all night—"

She did not finish her sentence because Barbara came dancing into the room. Even Abigail had to admit she looked very pretty in a primrose-colored gown and a white petticoat, pearls around her neck and in her ears. She looked young and fresh and virginal.

"Tony, I am so excited!" she said, clapping her hands. "Tell me again what we are going to see!"

"A farce called *The Cheats of Scapin*. A comedy of two acts called *The Comical Rivals* with Italian sonatas by Signor Gasperini. The Devonshire Girl will dance. Two French girls will walk across the rope. Their father will present the 'Newest Humors of Harlequin' as performed before the young King of France, and Mr. Evans of Vienna will show astonishing tricks performed by his wonder horse, Hercules."

Tony had carefully, painstakingly memorized the program. Abigail stared at him, a suspicion forming in her mind that was so preposterous it died before she could fully formulate it.

"I cannot wait; I have never seen anyone walk across a rope! Aunt, Tony says it is suspended high above the stage! And the Devonshire Girl is supposed to be so graceful! And Tony says he will take us to supper afterward at Pontac's, which is famous for its food!"

Barbara's gushing enthusiasm was irritating. "Supper?" Abigail said coolly. "It will be quite late—"

"Only nine, Aunt. The entertainment is concluded at nine. We should be home by eleven, not late at all! Tony, help me fasten my glove! It has come undone."

Abigail watched her son obediently bend over the wrist Barbara held so imperiously out to him. He seemed to take longer than necessary fumbling with the tiny pearl buttons. Abigail watched his plump face closely. She pursed her lips. He looked far too happy, but before she could think of something to make him unhappy, Diana glided into the room. She wore a gown of royal blue satin that pushed up her breasts provocatively. In her hair were diamonds and sapphires; they matched the necklace about her throat. Where on earth had they come from? thought Abigail, quickly assessing their value. They must have been in the trunks they had gotten for her. She had only to pawn those jewels to have money for half a year.

All Barbara could think of, seeing the way her mother was dressed, the way she had a patch at the corner of her left eye and at the corner of her mouth, was how much she wanted to be grown up, to wear powder and patches and rouge. She had tried to bully Martha tonight into letting her wear just a touch of rouge on her cheeks and lips, but Martha had shaken her head no. "Lady Saylor would not like it, miss. It is not seemly." Barbara did not want a maid who told her what was seemly. She wanted a maid who knew all the latest fashions and so made her fashionable, and desirable, like her mother. If she were allowed to display more breast (not that she had much, but corsets worked wonders with what little there was if they were tied properly), if she wore paint and powder, Roger would fall at her feet. As it was, she had to do her best in primrose and pearls.

"When will I see Lord Devane?" she asked her mother, saying the words that were always on her mind. Diana looked at Abigail. Abigail looked at one of the war murals.

"Soon," Diana said carelessly.

Barbara did not answer; she was thinking about the look she had seen pass between her mother and her aunt and her feeling that it boded no good.

Signor Gasperini was already in the midst of one of his ringing arias when they arrived at the Theatre Royal on Drury Lane. A porter showed them to their box; it was situated with others under a wooden gallery. In front of the boxes was the pit, a large space facing the stage in which benches covered in green matting were placed. The pit was seething with people, people who were paying little attention to Signor Gasperini. Both men and women sat there; but mostly men, men who were talking, playing cards, flirting with the women present, and some who were standing up and leisurely surveying who was in the boxes. It was easy to see who might be there because the stage was brightly lit from candles hanging in large chandeliers stage left and stage right and by candles placed along the edge of the stage. Contributing to the noise were porters busily collecting tickets. Young women carrying baskets of oranges tied round their necks with a ribbon sold the fruit for refreshment.

Robert Walpole and Tommy Carlyle were both in the pit, though not together. Carlyle was one of those standing, and since he was tall and hulking, he obscured the view of those on the benches behind him. There was much hissing and booing for him to sit down, but he ignored it, as did Signor Gasperini, on the stage. Carlyle continued languidly to survey the boxes. He saw Tony enter with Diana and Barbara, and he saw the Duke and Duchess of Montagu in the next box. He waved his hand until the Duchess of Montagu noticed him. She was a dark-haired woman with a sulky mouth. She waved her fan at him. He pointed to the next box, where Tony was helping Diana and Barbara with their cloaks. By now, their entrance had attracted the attention of others in the pit. It was Diana's first recent appearance in public, and since few people had seen Barbara, although much had been said about her, everyone was curious to see how she looked. Three or four other people were standing up in the pit, pointing to Tony's box and discussing it.

Charles Townshend punched Walpole in the side. Walpole, trying to find the freshest, juiciest orange from among those clustered in the orange girl's basket, looked up toward the boxes where Townshend was pointing. There with the young Duke of Tamworth was a dark-haired woman in a low-cut royal blue dress that showed most of her huge white breasts. She was an amazingly beautiful woman, with dark brows and hair and a perfectly shaped face with just a hint of too much flesh under the chin. Beside her was a young girl, pretty, but without the dark, spectacular looks of the older woman. He had no interest in the girl. She might not have existed. The woman was fanning herself and slowly surveying the people in the pit.

"Diana . . ." breathed Walpole. As he saw her eyes move to where he was sitting he stood up and made her a bow. She stared coldly at him, no expression on her face, and her eyes moved on. He sat down and began to peel the orange, and in the process, spilled its juice over the legs of his breeches. Beside him, his brother-in-law said, "She does not look interested, Robert."

"She will be," he said.

In the box next to Tony's, the Duke of Montagu pulled on his wife's sleeve. She looked at him irritably.

"Lord Tamworth is in the next box. I think I ought to say hello." He did not bother to whisper. No one did. The show was as much in the boxes and in the pit as it was on the stage.

"Do whatever you like."

He stood up, leaned over the railing and hissed Tony's name. "Join us in our box at the interval," he said, his eyes on Diana. She looked at him once, smiling slightly so that he saw her teeth, white, even.

At the interval, with Tony dropping cloaks and gloves and fans and muffs, they went to the Montagus' box. Montagu bustled to pull out Diana's chair, to help her settle her long skirts. She paid little attention to him.

"It has been a long time," he said to her.

She looked up at him casually. "Has it?"

"Mary," Montagu said to his wife, who had glanced once at them as they entered the box, then turned her attention back to waving at her friends in the pit and the other boxes, "you know Tamworth, of course, and Lady Alderley. This is her oldest daughter . . . ah . . ."

"Barbara," prompted Tony.

"Mistress Barbara Alderley."

She and Diana exchanged short, hostile nods, then Mary Montagu held out two fingers to Barbara, looking back toward the pit even as Barbara came forward to shake them. She was some years, but not many, younger than Diana, dressed in dark velvet, wearing a rich concoction of jewels in her hair and ears and about her throat and arms. Barbara stood beside her awkwardly, until Tony took her by the arm and led her to her seat.

Montagu sat down slightly behind Diana. He had a good view of her white back and shoulders and neck. Her dark hair, pulled up, made short tendrils that curled against the soft white of her neck. She settled back into her chair, and now he could clearly see down the front of her gown to where her white breasts rose from dark nipples. His breathing quickened.

"We met several years ago," he said, "at Windmere's summer place."

"Did we?"

"Do stop chattering!" Mary Montagu said. "The second comic scene is beginning."

They watched the remainder of *The Comical Rivals* in silence.

Montagu moved his head next to Diana's ear. He was so close that his breath warmed her shoulder.

"Think," he whispered softly. "About four years ago, a hot July, the summer house at Windmere's, you were thirsty, you said. I brought you more wine, even though you had had more than enough. We were alone. We . . . became . . . intimate. Think."

Diana opened her fan and held it in front of her mouth. "Was that you? I had no idea."

She turned her wide, violet eyes to Montagu's and slowly licked her lips with the tip of her pointed, red tongue. He stared at her, fascinated.

"Do you think such conduct could be repeated?" he whispered. She had turned her head back to the play.

"Doubtless I was drunk," she said.

"It might be better sober."

"It might . . . at that." And she suddenly laughed deep in her throat, and he laughed with her. On the stage, nothing amusing was happening. The laughter rose into the silence. It was clearly the laughter of two people who have shared something intimate. Mary Montagu looked over at her husband, whose head was almost resting on one of Diana's bare shoulders. Without any change in her expression, she turned away. Barbara turned pink. In the pit, Robert Walpole heard the laughter and stood up. He could see Diana and Montagu sitting close together. His heavy, black brows drew together, and he sat back down heavily. Carlyle, sitting on a bench closer to the stage, also heard. He, too, stood up to look.

"Diana and Monty," he said to his companions. "Well, well, well. I must, I positively must, investigate. They are having far too good a time for it to be this tired old play." He made his way out of the pit.

The workers were clearing the stage because the Devonshire Girl was going to dance. Diana and Montagu were whispering. Everyone else in the box with them was silent, an awkward, strained silence. There was a sharp rap on the door; it opened, and Carlyle sauntered in, saying, "Mary, my pre-

cious, you must save me. I am far too close to the stage in
the pit, and, therefore, hear every word. Let me stay here and
visit with you—oh, but you have company. I interrupt. I positively do." He positively did, but he made no move to go.
The men stood up. For the first time that evening, Mary
Montagu smiled. Her teeth were rotting; there were brown
spots at their top edges where the teeth met gum.

"But, of course, you must stay, Tommy, if only to keep me
company. You know everyone, I believe, Tamworth, Lady
Alderley."

Carlyle bowed over Diana's hand. She stared up at him
coldly. "I do, I do. Lady Alderley, you look ravishing tonight.
Does she not, Monty? But then the beautiful Lady Alderley is
always ravishing. You are enjoying your new lodgings, I hope,
Lady Alderley. So much more comfortable than Covent Garden, and so much more convenient—but who is this child!
Surely not the mysterious Barbara! Introduce me. Introduce
me at once! I bow before you, my dear."

Barbara found herself looking up, up into eyes that did not
smile as the rouged red mouth did. She had never seen a man
before that wore that much powder and rouge and patches.
A huge diamond winked in his left ear. The curls on his black,
frizzy wig brushed her hand as he held it. She did not know
what to think.

"Where have you been hiding this treasure?" he was saying.
"Lovely, lovely. Has it a tongue? Say something to Carlyle,
child."

"How—how do you do?" stammered Barbara.

Carlyle let go of her hand and pretended to stagger back,
one huge hand over his heart. He had the attention of everyone in the box and quite a few people in the surrounding
boxes as well. The pit, too, was fascinated.

"What a voice!" he cried. "It is wonderful. Wonderful! I
lay myself before your feet as your first conquest!"

"Some conquest," Diana said. Her eyes on Carlyle were
cold.

"But I interrupt. I do!" Carlyle was saying. "You must
watch the Devonshire Girl, child. She is amazing. The grace
of a goddess. Oh, but her dance is finished. I have made you
miss it. Ah, well, the tightrope walkers are something to see.
Mary, my pet, shall I leave? Am I interrupting?"

"Yes," said Diana.

"You sit right here beside me," said Mary Montagu, patting the empty chair by her side, the chair in which her husband had been sitting at one time. "I am confoundedly bored."

"But where is Roger?" Carlyle said as he sat down. "I thought he was engaged to come here with you."

"He was, but he sent a note round at the last minute canceling."

"That woman," Carlyle said, crossing his long legs and sighing. "I hear he is involved with—" and he leaned forward and whispered into Mary Montagu's ear.

"No," she said. She threw back her head and laughed.

"Barbara," said Tony. "Going to walk in the corridor for a while. Keep me company?"

Barbara, who had been sitting as still as a statue, leapt up. "Yes," she stammered. The two of them left the box.

"That was bad of you, Tommy," Mary Montagu said. "The child heard you."

"Oh, no! How thoughtless of me!"

"What a delicious liar you are, Tommy. Do you intend to gossip over the way my husband is making an ass of himself over that titled whore behind us?"

"Of course I do."

"Good. Be sure to bring up every dirty thing about her that you can remember."

"Mary, my pet, do I detect jealousy in that voice of yours?"

"You detect boredom, Tommy, excruciating boredom. She is welcome to him. God only knows I tired of him years ago."

Carlyle pursed his lips. "Tsk! Tsk! It is a good thing the bride has left and cannot hear you talk. You would disillusion her."

"The bride? Oh, you mean the Alderley chit. I did not know the contracts were signed."

Carlyle leaned forward and whispered, "They are not." He jerked his head toward Diana, who was allowing Montagu to fan her while she languidly surveyed the tightrope act. "Diana is holding out for more money. I think she is a fool. She is going to push Roger too far."

"She always was a greedy bitch."

"What did you think of the girl?"

Mary Montagu shrugged. "Young, thin, pretty in a pale way. Not the woman her mother is. Boring. All young girls are boring. What did you think of her?"

"The voice is heaven. But I was disappointed. Our Roger deserves something better, something more dramatic. She is, after all, only a child."

"Poor thing," Mary Montagu said to herself.

"Do not turn around, dear. Your husband is practically slobbering over Diana."

"Ass."

Outside in the corridor, Tony was rubbing one of Barbara's hands between his own. She was leaning against a wall, as if she felt faint. Her eyes were closed.

"Bab. Are you all right?"

Barbara struggled not to cry.

"Sorry you heard that, Bab. But pay no attention to it. Men like Roger always have—that is—it means nothing. Please, Bab, say you are all right."

She swallowed and opened her eyes. Tony's plump, pasty-looking face stared at her with worried, kind, pale blue eyes. He had nice eyes, almost gray. He was a dear to take her from the box, from those dreadful people.

"Take me home, Tony," she whispered. "I feel sick."

"But supper? Surely you will feel better if you eat."

The thought of having to go through two hours at Pontac's pretending nothing was wrong made her feel ill enough to vomit. And what if the duke and duchess came with them, the duchess with her cold, proud face and the duke—and her mother. And that Carlyle man, what if he came! No, no, she had to go home, to her bed.

"Please," she whispered.

"Whatever you say, Bab. You know I would do anything for you."

He left her leaning against the wall and went back for her cloak, whispering to Diana that Barbara was ill, and that he was going to take her home. Montagu assured him that he would see Diana home safely. Carlyle snickered, watching Tony blunder into chairs and drop cloaks and finally leave.

"The bride is ill," Carlyle whispered to Mary Montagu. "Could it have been something I said?"

"Bitch!" she whispered back. "Roger would kill you."

"Roger does not know."

In his haste to return to Barbara, Tony ran into Robert Walpole, who was just outside the door to the Montagus' box. The cloaks fell to the ground. Walpole bent over at the same time as Tony. They bumped heads, but were saved from really hurting each other by their wigs.

"Stay put, Tamworth!" Walpole said. He leaned over again and picked up the cloaks and gave them to Tony.

"My cousin," Tony said, already starting toward Barbara, who was still slumped against the wall. "Ill, you know. Must leave."

Walpole walked in the box rubbing his head. On the stage, Mr. Evans's wonder horse, Hercules, was jumping through a hoop of fire. There were boos and catcalls from the footmen's gallery. Mary Montagu and Carlyle, sitting at the front of the box, waved Walpole forward. Diana and Montagu, sitting over to one side, farther to the back, hardly even glanced his way. He blew a kiss to Mary, but went to where Montagu and Diana were sitting.

"Introduce me, Monty," he said.

"Lady Diana Alderley, Robert Walpole, first lord of the treasury."

At the word "treasury," Diana looked up and smiled, giving Walpole the benefit of her white, even teeth. "Mr. Walton, I am delighted to meet you."

"Walpole," Montagu said. "And do not waste your time on him. He has no money."

"Oh," said Diana.

"I thought I saw him waffling in the pit like a beached whale," Carlyle whispered to Mary Montagu. "I had no idea it was for Diana's benefit. Yet another conquest for our fair, soiled one. The plot thickens."

"If one more man walks in here and goes straight over to her, I shall scream. I have a headache, Tommy, and you are going to take me home. Monty, I have a headache, and Tommy is taking me home."

Montagu nodded absently in the direction of his wife. On the stage, Mr. Evans was trying to lead the wonder horse from the stage, but first, the wonder horse insisted on depositing a pile of dark manure stage left. There were claps and whistles from the footmen's gallery.

"Best thing we have seen all night!" someone yelled.

"Apropos," said Carlyle.

Montagu did not notice. His eye was on Walpole, obviously moving in on territory he had already staked out. His wife slammed the door of the box shut behind her.

"You should remember Mr. Walpole, Diana," he said. "He led the investigation against your husband in Parliament last summer."

Diana's beautiful, white bosom heaved.

"It was my duty, nothing more," Walpole began to stammer, to Montagu's intense amusement. For once, the great man seemed short of words. "Nothing personal, Lady Alderley, I do assure you."

"Tell that to my fatherless children. Go away, Mr. Walton."

"Walpole," Walpole said, to nobody in particular. Mary Montagu and Carlyle had already left, and Montagu was helping Diana fasten her cloak.

The approach of Christmas kept Barbara busy. As it did Tony. He took her to St. James's Park so that she could feed the deer, who trotted up, their hooves touching the wet, brown ground delicately, and ate out of her hand as tamely as any household pet. Mary, who accompanied them, excitedly explained that in the spring, the milkmaids with their cows gathered near Rosamond's Pond and you could buy a cup of fresh milk to drink as you wandered in the park. Barbara had convinced her aunt to release Mary from her rigid schedule of lessons for the holidays. Abigail considered it a small sacrifice if it kept Barbara from asking too many questions.

Barbara had told Mary every detail she could remember about the theater, from the orange girls to the tightrope walkers, but not what Carlyle had said about Roger. She had cried for hours that night, and she thought about it all the time. She had too much pride to go to her mother or her aunt or even Fanny and ask about it. All she could do was wait and suffer silently. Meanwhile she saw the horse guards parade, the king in his carriage, London's fine spacious squares of Soho, Leicester Fields and St. James's (where Roger lived). She saw the city mansions of the Duke of Ancaster, the Duke of Newcastle, the Duke of Bedford and the Duke of Buck-

ingham. She and Mary spent a delightful afternoon with their
Great-Aunt Shrewsborough, who served them tea in a grand
style, with ornate silver teapots and two footmen to wait on
them. Afterward, she took the two girls upstairs and let them
play in her jewelry and fuss with her pots of face paint. She
allowed them to powder, rouge and patch to their hearts'
content, and even if her maid had to scrub their faces until
their cheeks burned, to the girls it was worth it. Barbara put
feathers in her hair and strutted up and down in front of her
aunt's mirror, and pretended she was Roger's countess, while
Mary had so many black silk patches on her face it looked as
if she had the smallpox. It was quite their favorite afternoon
in a series of good afternoons.

Barbara even saw Roger once. Fanny had taken her and
Mary shopping at the New Exchange, a long, sleek building
with small shops lining its corridors. Barbara had some
money, and she wished to buy New Year's presents for her
brothers and sisters. Mary was enchanted with the idea that
she could help choose toys for Tom and Kit and Anne and
Charlotte and Baby, whom, by now, through Barbara, she
felt she knew as well as if she had grown up with them. They
had agreed at once on lead soldiers—bright with red and
white paint—for Kit. They argued over Tom, Mary wanting
a hoop and stick, but Barbara thinking Tom's dignity too old
now. They compromised on a history book that had intricate,
cardboard pages that popped up, to make a scene. Barbara
allowed Mary to choose the dolls for Anne and Charlotte, and
they finished up with a tiny wagon for the baby. Barbara was
giving the man her grandmother's address—for a few extra
shillings, he would wrap them and have them delivered—
when she saw Roger across the corridor in front of a book-
shop. He stood outside, sifting through loose sheets that lay on
a table so the prospective purchaser might read the book if he
were not sure he wished to buy it. Once sure, the buyer then
selected the color and style of the leather binding. That man,
the strange, odious Tommy Carlyle, was with him.

She ran across to them. Roger smiled at her, and she for-
gave him everything. He bowed over her hand with the grace
of a young god. How could he be so beautiful? Fanny and
Mary joined them. "Ah, a nursery party," Carlyle said. They
talked of shopping, of Christmas plans, of his trip to France.

Nothing was said of Diana. Nothing was said of the negotiations. Fanny spoke in a high, strained voice that Barbara knew meant she was nervous. Afterward, in the carriage, Barbara said, "Fanny, what is happening? You must tell me!" But Fanny would only look away and say, "Hush. Hush." Barbara felt a foreboding building inside her. She made a plan. She would be good and meek and patient for Christmas. Surely, sooner or later, it was inevitable that she would see Roger again. And this time, no matter who was with him or her, she was going to ask him straightforwardly about their marriage.

Something was happening. Mary, her ally now, had told her that several invitations had come to her and her mother from Roger, and that her aunt had put them away. She knew better than to bother asking her mother or her aunt about it. They were up to some game of their own, some game that had her heart involved in it, no more important to them than a beggar's off the street. But they had bargained wrongly if they thought her docility covered docility, which was fine for a girl who did not know what she wanted. Barbara did know. And she was going to have it.

With her plan to sustain her, she took over the decorating of the house. She could not believe that Aunt Saylor left it to the servants, that Tony and Mary had never made Christmas wreaths or looped staircases with greenery. She ordered Tony about as if he were Bates or one of the servants. He straddled the hall's balustrades, painstakingly looping holly garlands around the railings, while Mary sat in the middle of the black and white squares of the floor, making laurel wreaths. When they were finished, Tony declared the hall had never looked so beautiful, and it never had. Loop after loop of dark green holly, christened with shining bunches of bright red berries cascaded down each balustrade of the double staircase and met on the second-floor landing's balustrade to form a huge wreath. Each of the busts in the wall ovals wore a necklace of box and holly. Candles were set on the tables, and holly and rosemary crowned their bases. Every picture, every door frame in the hall and the public rooms had its garland of green. Ivy and rosemary and holly peeked from the cupboards, the mantels, around china bowls. Barbara had the kitchen maids pierce oranges and lemons with cloves, and she filled those bowls with these, mixing in crushed cinnamon and rosemary. She imperiously directed Bates to set white Christmas candles on every surface that could hold them. She wanted the house to glow for Jane, who was coming to tea with her aunt, and for Roger, if he should happen to visit. ('She reminds me of her grandmother," Bates told the housekeeper. "The house looks as it used to.")

"My . . . God . . . !" the Duke of Montagu moaned. He lay naked in a bed in rooms he rented for just this purpose. Closing his eyes he moaned again. The woman with him, her mouth sucking his life's juices from his body, impatiently pulled back the covers that were over her. She glanced at him. His head was back against the cover, the muscles in his neck were rigid, his hands were gripping the sweaty sheets. She moved her mouth on his penis in a rhythm she had learned years ago. He groaned and clutched at the sheets. "God . . . !" he cried again, and his body jerked, once, twice, three times. She sat up. She was as naked as he was, and her body was magnificent, huge white breasts with dark nipples, wide hips that curved out from a small waist. Only her belly had lost its shape and sagged from repeated pregnancies. She leaned back on her elbows, her legs open, the dark hair surrounding her sex open to him. He half sat up.

"Diana," he said, his eyes still closed, "you were wonderful—" He opened his eyes and now he leaned on one elbow, amazed and excited at the way she sprawled so openly before him. Not even the whores he bought did so. Watching him, her lovely face pouting, sensual, she closed her eyes and began to caress herself. He could not take his eyes from her. She played with her breasts, pinching the nipples until they stood out. She kneaded the soft, full flesh of her belly and finally, slowly, her hand went between her legs. Her pink tongue licked her lips. To his amazement, he felt himself growing excited, growing hard again. He moved so that he was lying beside her. She had her eyes closed and had begun to move her body in a rhythm as old as time, as old as men and women and pleasure. He grabbed her hair and pulled it. She opened her eyes.

"Wait for me," he said. "I will service you—"

He leaned over to kiss her mouth. She bit him—which excited him even more. Grabbing her arms roughly, he pinned them down and moved on top of her. Her head was rolling from side to side. He plunged into her, and she moved against him and cursed him and called him names that made him rigid with desire. She bit him and scratched his back, and he bucked against her like a madman, until his orgasm came with what was now painful intensity. He lay exhausted on top of her, but she was still moving under him.

"More," she said fiercely. "More!"

"Diana, I—"

She jerked so that he fell off her, and he watched as she put one hand to her sex and one to her breast and then moved, her head lolling from side to side until she began to gasp over and over, while both her hands moved faster and faster. It took a long time. Finally she moaned and then was still. She opened her eyes. He watched to see if she would be ashamed. She sat up.

"I really don't need anyone," she said, shaking her hair out of her face.

"I believe it," he whispered, almost in awe of her sensuality, so openly exposed to him. He felt intrigued and more than a little frightened. She traced the line of his lips with her finger.

"Say you will help me," she said. "Say you will sponsor my divorce—" She stopped. He moved away from her, to the edge of the bed. Something behind her eyes flickered as she stared at his naked, now unyielding back.

"I have told you over and over that I cannot. What would people say? What would they think? How can I justify it—"

"To protect a fellow noblewoman, the daughter of a great hero, who has been taken advantage of. To protect a fellow Whig, who has been cheated, lied to, betrayed by her Tory husband, who is not a husband, who has deserted her." There was not much emotion in her voice. She had said the words so many times that they meant nothing to her, if they ever had.

Montagu sighed. He still had his back to her. "Diana, what can I say to you. I cannot—"

"A diamond necklace."

He turned to stare at her. "What?"

"Give me a diamond necklace—"

"And you will not bother me about the divorce anymore?"

"Give me the necklace and see. . . ."

Jane Ashford was at her Aunt Maude's house in London. Her aunt, who was her mother's sister, lived in King Street in a narrow three-story town house with a Dutch roof. Her husband was a minor official in the navy department, and her aunt lived for the two official court functions they attended each year. She filled in the rest of the year with collecting as much gossip as she could about the court and those people who graced it, such as Roger Montgeoffry, the Earl Devane, the king's favorite English friend. "The king keeps himself surrounded by Hanoverians, you know," she told Jane, as they were out riding in her carriage (of which she was extremely proud, for it was very expensive and put her a step above other wives). "That von Bothmer and Bernstorff are all he ever sees, other than Lord Devane—and you grew up with the girl he is said to be marrying—Jane, you sly puss! She will be so rich and influential! You must ask her about a living for Augustus. Do not look that way, Jane, dear, you will put wrinkles on your face—a wife must do what she can to advance her husband's career. Why, I am always on the lookout for Edgemont—" (Edgemont was her husband, a quiet man who rarely spoke except when paying bills—then he and Maude quarreled as loudly and abusively as Jane had ever seen. She thought that he was silent because he knew his silence maddened her aunt—and made her talk even more, a clear example of cutting off one's nose to spite one's face.)

Jane sighed and looked out of the carriage, while her aunt's voice clacked on and on. Everything about her aunt was thin, even her voice. She was tall and thin, her face was long and thin, her hair was black and thin, her nose was pointed and thin. Every morning she sat at a table positioned in front of her parlor windows and dipped pieces of toasted bread in her tea and wagged her thin leg back and forth while her thin slipper hung on the edge of her thin foot. She watched the men going in and out of the coffeehouses, she read the news sheets bought for a halfpenny from the street boys. She rattled and rustled and talked until Jane thought she would go mad.

She poked and prodded at her—not physically, but verbally. Jane had no idea what her mother and father had written to Aunt Maude, but it must have been something, for her aunt watched her like a hawk, except when Augustus visited. Augustus Cromwell was plain and tall and yes—thin! His nose was too long and he had bad teeth. At twenty-four he was just finishing his studies at Oxford, and he rode down every Saturday to see her. Closing her eyes, she leaned her head back against the leather of the carriage seat.

"Look, Jane, this is Whitehall and there is the Admiralty—Edgemont is there—in the room at that window there—see, Jane—and now we are going to Charing Cross. That statue is of King Charles I, the one that was beheaded—do look, Jane—"

Do look, Jane, do see, Jane, do listen, Jane. Her whole life lay ahead of her, obedience to others, including Augustus, Gussy, as he was called, as her husband and master. She had not minded obedience to Harry; she would have walked on hot coals for him. But Gussy—he talked a great deal about his work—he was beginning a study on the papacy during the Reformation. Excited about it, his brown eyes would actually glow as he went on and on, and she smiled and nodded and her thoughts were so far away—oh, Harry, how will I ever get through this. Harry, so dark and handsome and passionate. At night, she dreamed of his kisses. Yes, she had let him kiss her. Thank Jesus in his heaven above that her parents had no idea. But she had, and they had been so good, making her tingle inside, in her abdomen and in her breasts. Yes, it was true! And now, now all she had were memories. She dreaded to think of the day when Gussy would kiss her. Harry's teeth had been even and white. How could she stand it!

Dear Lord, every day she watched and waited and hoped against hope for a letter. She ran to the door whenever she heard the door knocker sound—"How sweet you are, Jane, what a help you are, Jane. Edgemont, I tell you, this girl is a treasure," her aunt would say, never knowing that she was always hoping that a postboy would be there with a letter and she would slip it in the pocket of her apron and run up to her small room and read it, read his words of love, of assurance and be better, be stronger, be able to face what she had to do. They all thought she was such a good girl, never knowing the perfidy in her heart, never knowing what she really thought—the look on her father's face when she left—she had cried for miles and miles. He had looked as if his dreams or faith in life were gone because of her, because of her wildness. She knew he could not afford to be sending her to London. He was always working, always, and there were so many of them to feed, and there were her brothers to educate, and she had to be sent to London. She was bad, bad.

Why did Harry not write? . . . She knew why. Because he was bold and restless and impatient, and he had found someone else. Oh, she knew it. She knew Harry. He had had a mistress at school; she knew that, but when he whispered to her under the apple trees and held her in his arms, it did not matter. He was so handsome. How could women not love him? Sometimes, she thought her heart would shrivel up and die. She really did. Dear Lord in His heaven above, would her aunt never stop talking? She talked all day. And shopped. And visited friends. Or had them over to visit, drink tea, play cards and talk, talk, talk! Sometimes Jane thought she would scream at the clacking, clacking, clacking sound of her voice— "Jane, dear, do fetch Mrs. Maple some more tea." "Jane, dear, do look at those green gloves. I must have them." "Jane, dear, do not tell your Uncle Edgemont. He would never understand."

Here in London, her aunt looked for ways to fill the days. At Jane's home, Ladybeth Farm, her days were spent helping her mother. There was the dairy to oversee and the alehouse. There were cream and cheeses and butter to make. There was game to cure and beef and pork. There was bread to bake and clothes to sew and mend and clean. Hens and pigs had to be fed, there were younger brothers and sisters to see after. Jane's day had been spent doing tasks that made the household run efficiently. Now, at Ladybeth, they would be in the woods near Tamworth, gathering greenery. The Duchess always allowed neighbors and tenants to gather the bay and holly and ivy from her woods at Christmastime, and Jane's family was the most important after the Duchess's and Squire Dinwitty's. She and her sisters would make wreaths. She would help her mother and the servants in the kitchen, for there was an enormous amount of baking to do—pies, cakes, biscuits, puddings. She and her brothers would go out and find a yule log, the biggest log in the forest, and they would harness the horse to drag it home. Everyone would be laughing and cold, cheeks and noses red with cold, fingers and toes burning with cold. Mother would have hot, spiced ale ready and yule sweets. The log would be placed in the fireplace, waiting for Christmas Eve, when they would light it with the burning remainder of last year's log. It was good luck if it burned through the night. The house would be shining with candles, and Father would lead them in a Christmas prayer, and later, some of the villagers would be by to carol. She and Harry and Barbara would meet—except that this year Harry was in Italy and Barbara was in London, like herself, ready to be married. Her aunt would spend the holidays playing cards with her friends. She would lose too much money and Uncle Edgemont would argue with her, compliments of the season.

The carriage stopped. Jane looked out. They were home. She followed slowly, like an old woman, as her aunt ran up the narrow, steep steps to the front door, talking all the while to the coachman, who doubled as one of their house servants. The other was Betty, the kitchen maid.

"Now, Thomas, you take those horses right back to the stable. I do not want Mr. Lewis charging me for another hour. And see the carriage is stored properly." (Her aunt rented horses; it was beyond their means to keep a permanent pair stabled and fed. The stable owner allowed them to store their carriage for a fee.) "Thomas, be sure the carriage is pulled inside. I do not want rot and mildew on it."

It was the same thing she always said. The carriage was a source of enormous pride, her friends did not see how her husband managed it; and Aunt Maude smiled and bridled and never told them that she paid for it out of her settlement money or that she and Uncle Edgemont quarreled about it at least twice a week, he claiming it was too expensive to rent a stable and horses, and she saying it was her money and she would do as she pleased. And she did. Every other day they went out. She took her friends shopping—the carriage crammed with petticoats and ribbons and clacking chatter while Jane sat squashed in a corner.

Her aunt was stripping off her gloves and going through the letters Betty had left on the table. Jane untied her cloak and hung it up. She sat down.

"Merciful gods!" her aunt shrieked, waving a piece of paper about. "Jane! Jane, dearest! This is for you—" For a moment, Jane's heart beat so fast she thought she would faint, but then her aunt said, "It's an invitation. Just listen, child. Mistress Barbara Alderley invites Mistress Jane Ashford and Mistress Maude Berkley—I am invited, too, Jane, dear. Now whatever will I wear—to take tea at four Thursday—I will go out tomorrow and buy a new gown. I have nothing but rags to wear—Maria will eat her heart out—Jane! Saylor House!" Her aunt clutched the paper to her bosom. "Merciful gods! It is just down the street from the palace! It is one of the most magnificent houses in London. Edgemont went to a function there—the present duke, you know—and talked about it for weeks—actually talked, Jane, about something other than my bills! I was floored, as you can quite imagine. And to think you and I are going to tea there!" She hugged Jane excitedly and danced about the room.

"Jane, you and Augustus are going to go far. I predict it! I do! I do! Lady Saylor is the daughter of the Earl of Bristil. Her wedding to Lord William was brilliant! Absolutely brilliant! Of course, I was just a child, but I remember it, I do! Lord Bristil opened his house to hundreds of people, and there were balls and parties for weeks before she married. You could have knocked me over with a feather when Lord William died. I was devastated. And before that his older brother and little son. I cried. I did. Life is cruel, Jane. Taking all the Duke and Duchess's sons like that. And their precious little grandson. I remember your mother wrote me that the duke looked like death himself. He was a great man, a great man! Why, after the battle of Lille, we were dancing in the streets and lighting bonfires and shouting his name. He rode in the queen's carriage. I saw it. I stood in a great throng of people all day to see him—and someone stole my gray shawl, the one with gold thread in it—but then you would not know about that, would you! Well! Tea at Saylor House. I wonder if Lady Diana will be there? She is so beautiful. I was quite upset with her petition for divorce. I feel it is a woman's place to endure whatever God so ordains. I know I have with Edgemont! Ah, well, the great, you know, Jane, they think they can do as they please—now whatever will I wear. . . ."

Harry was never going to write, Jane thought, not ever.

* * *

Barbara and Mary sat in the conservatory. Their drawing master had them doing botanical studies, and they were industriously trying to copy the lines of a white, lush camellia.

"Something is happening," Mary said softly, glancing back to see if her governess were close enough to hear. The woman, however, was talking to the drawing master.

"What is it?" Barbara said out of the side of her mouth. By now, she knew the signs. Mary was quivering with news. She had seen or heard something, she was always seeing or hearing something. But only Barbara paid any attention to her.

"There was a note delivered from Lord Devane—"

"For me!"

"Hush! No, it was to Aunt Diana, I think. Anyway, Mother laughed about it and said, 'It is his last-ditch stand, Diana. All his personal charm is going to be arrayed against you.' "

"What did my mother say?" Barbara asked.

Mary shrugged. "I did not hear. They sent me away."

Barbara looked at the fat blooms of the camellia, but all she saw was Roger's face. Today was the tea with Jane. And today Roger must be coming. She was going to grab fate by the horns and speak to Roger herself. She was going to say—

"Is your attention wandering, Mistress Alderley?" the drawing master asked her.

She bent her head over the sketch pad. Bah! He could take his camellia and eat it!

She found her aunt in one of the kitchen pantries, inspecting the silver. It was laid out—plate, platters, forks, knives, spoons, teapots, soup tureens, butter dishes, trays—on soft felt on trestle tables. It was polished every other day (one of the duties of the underfootman), but Abigail always inspected it on Thursday and woe to the butler and footman if there was a speck of dark on any of the shining surfaces.

"What have you planned this afternoon, Aunt?" Barbara said it with all the innocence of which she was capable, which was considerable.

Abigail, her square, fleshy face suddenly suspicious, swiveled around. "Why?"

"I wanted to remind you that I have invited Jane Ashford and her aunt for tea, and I very much want you to meet them."

"Impossible."

Barbara's heart gave a sudden leap. Surely, her aunt was going to tell her that she must be free this afternoon to sign marriage contracts because Roger was coming—

"Your mother and I are already engaged at four. I doubt I will have time to meet your friends. Write Fanny to come and be hostess in my place. Now do go away, dear. I am busy."

"Aunt, I would like very much to see Lord Devane this afternoon when he comes."

Abigail stared at her with open dislike. How did she know! She was a headstrong, impatient girl who did not know her place. She was not docile or meek or quiet, as she should be. She had shown entirely too much interest in this whole affair. It was none of her business; she was to do as she was told. She needed a firm hand. As soon as this unpleasantness with Montgeoffry was ended, Abigail was going personally to find the sternest man she could to marry Barbara. Someone with a firm hand. Why, the girl had this household stirred up from one end to the other. Look at the fuss she had made about Christmas. (It was irritating beyond endurance to Abigail that the older servants were comparing Barbara with the Duchess.) And her influence was spreading. Mary had dared express an opinion contrary to Abigail's just the other morning, and Tony no longer seemed to feel that he must verify his every move with her. He seemed to feel affection for this red-haired child staring at her with those wide, blue eyes, eyes that seemed to be pleading, but really covered a brain as tough and durable as Abigail's own. Oh, her face might look sweet, she might have a voice that would melt butter, but behind those eyes was a will every bit as strong as Abigail's. Yes. It was unthinkable in a child of fifteen.

"No!" she said more coldly than she meant because all of those thoughts were flying through her head, and because this morning she had overheard Bates say, "She has her grandmother's touch, bless her. Ah, those were the days, not like now—"

"Please, Aunt. It is so very important to me! Roger—Lord Devane—is very special to me. I have loved him since I was a child! Please let me—"

"What on earth do you think you know of love, and how dare you speak so to me! No!"

It was as if red-black gunpowder exploded in Barbara's head. It was more than just this moment; it was all the moments of having to wait, of not knowing. Her face went rigid, anger on it so intense that Abigail felt it, saw it, and involuntarily stepped backward.

"Leave at once!" she said, pointing to the door. To her surprise, Barbara picked up her skirts and ran like a boy out of the room.

Barbara sat in her chamber, holding her shaking hands together. The worst of the rage had passed; she could think more clearly again. She had been capable of striking her aunt; she knew it, and it frightened her, to know that her temper could be so fierce. Her grandmama would be so ashamed. Thank the dear Lord she would not know of it. Above all things, her grandmother had always stressed, a gentlewoman was just that, gentle, kind, courteous. But all the black anger would not go from her. I am going to see him, she told herself. I am. No one can stop me.

She was waiting under one of the staircases, in its shadows. She was praying that Jane and her aunt would be late, that she would have a moment, only a moment, to speak with him. Her hands were sweating. She heard the door knocker sound, and her heart began to thud. What she was doing was so bold, so unbecoming, so impetuous—yes, she could just hear her grandmother say the word—that she could hardly stand it. But she was going to do it anyway.

There was Roger! He had followed Bates into the hall and stood waiting while the butler went into the great parlor to announce him. He was staring up at her grandfather's portrait. She crept from her place under the staircase.

"Roger . . ." she said.

He turned, startled, looking tired and older, not quite the handsome prince she kept in her mind.

"I-I had to see you." The words fell from her mouth every which way as thoughts tumbled over themselves in her mind: if someone should see her, if Jane and her aunt should arrive; if her mother and aunt should come out the door—

"Barbara," he said. "You look so like your grandfather—"

"Please, Roger, listen to me. I have to know. No one will tell me. What is happening? Are we—are we to marry? Please tell me—" The words died on her lips at the change that came across his face. A coldness. An anger. She put her hands up to her cheeks.

"Oh, no," she said.

"Your mother—" he began, but at that moment the door opened, and Barbara leapt back into the shadows of the staircase near Roger. She watched him walk into the great parlor as if he were walking toward his own execution. Nothing was explained, and she had this sick, sinking, heavy feeling in her stomach. Something bad was happening. It was. Her legs were shaking so that she could barely walk to the small side parlor where they would receive Jane. She looked across to the picture of her grandmother. "Grandmama," she whispered. If only she were here. . . .

A carriage rolled into the Saylor House courtyard. Inside, Jane's Aunt Maude clutched at her hat, a huge concoction of feathers and lace and pearls dripping across its high brim, and cried, "Magnificent! Did I not tell you it was magnificent? Look at those gardens—they stretch forever. Two footmen are coming down the stairs, two! I should have worn my striped tobine. I know it! I feel it! Jane, tell Thomas to turn us around—"

"We are here, Aunt Maude, and we are late. We cannot be so rude."

The carriage lurched to a stop. Maude caught herself from falling into Jane's lap opposite her. She ripped apart the sides of her cloak and straightened her gown, a cherry-colored affair with green striped sleeves. Her thin bosom was covered with a handkerchief of black silk. She resembled nothing so much as a badly dressed maypole.

"It is fashionable to be late," she assured Jane. "I am certain Lady Alderley is never on time." Maude was excited almost beyond bearing that she was to meet the notorious Lady Alderley. She had followed Diana's exploits for years in the veiled references the cheap news sheets printed: "Lady D-A seen in Lord F-R-'s carriage late Thursday night after the Queen's assembly. . . ." Diana was a disgrace to her name, to her dead father, to her noble mother, and Maude was dying to meet her.

Inside, she was made almost speechless by the grandeur and symmetry of the hall, but she pulled herself together and shook out her gown and patted at her curls and grandly handed her cloak to the waiting footman. Her eyes fell on the matching side tables against the walls.

"One hundred guineas if they are a penny!" she hissed to Jane.

She frowned at Jane and her long arms came out like those of a crab and pinched Jane's pale cheeks. "Honestly," she had told her husband just the other night, "I do not know what we are going to do with that girl! It is a good thing she is already engaged. I should never be able to interest a young man in her. She has no life, no spirit, no dash. You can say what you want, Edgemont, but I had dash!" Craning her neck upward to the spacious landing, with its loop after loop of holly, she and Jane passed by the portraits of the Duke and Duchess. "Ancestors," Maude whispered to Jane. Jane hardly even looked.

They followed Bates to a side door in the hall. Maude immediately searched for the breathtakingly beautiful, bad Lady A, but saw only a pretty, blond young woman and a girl about Jane's age. The girl had an odd look on her face, as if she were about to be sick.

Barbara ran forward to hug Jane. Jane seemed a piece of home, a piece of Tamworth. Holding her hand, she introduced her to Fanny, smiling, but her mind kept going to Roger's face, and she had no idea what she was saying. Her face began to feel stiff. She felt sick.

Jane blinked back unexpected tears. Barbara and Harry had the same smile, overwhelming, lighting up their faces and the recipient's heart. Oh, Harry. She was so glad to see Barbara, but in the corner of her heart, like a worm, was envy. Jane tried to ignore it, but Barbara looked so fashionable in her gown and new hairstyle. She seemed so at home in this huge, magnificent house. At Tamworth, the Saylors' great wealth and influence was forgotten. Here it was evident in every fold of the draperies, in every gesture Fanny made as she welcomed them. And Barbara was to marry an earl, while Jane had Gussy. Of course, their stations in life were different, always had been. Jane's father was a prosperous farmer and knight, while Barbara's was a viscount and her grandfather was a duke. But it had been forgotten at Tamworth, not emphasized. She was a fool to have ever thought of Harry! A fool! Her heart hurt worse than ever. She should not have come.

Fanny, her eyes fastened to Maude's hat, gestured toward a small, oval table surrounded by four armchairs. Maude swept toward the table.

"Is this not quaint! It is so tiny! Designed specifically for tea!"

With difficulty, she restrained herself from turning over a teacup and looking at the signature of the manufacturer. She would do it later, when no one was looking. She asked about Lady Alderley and was disappointed to hear she was busy. She contented herself with noting every detail of Fanny's hairstyle and gown and with memorizing the room. The velvet draperies were held back with tassels of thick silver thread; they had a patterned paper on the walls; there was a piece of furniture she had never seen, that looked like a series of armchairs linked together with a common cushion; two people could easily sit on it. She determined to buy herself a tea table.

Jane and Barbara were whispering as Fanny began to pour tea. Maude had warned Jane that Barbara might be changed, might be less friendly, but to Jane, Barbara only seemed nervous and unusually pale. She kept glancing toward the door, as if she expected someone else to enter.

"Have you heard from Harry?" Jane whispered.

Barbara shook her head no, and Jane felt better. Will this never end? Barbara was thinking. I cannot endure it.

"—Lord Devane, you naughty puss," Maude was saying to Barbara. She had missed the first part. "You are a lucky girl! He is the handsomest man I have ever seen. He is! When is the wedding?"

Fanny choked on her tea. Maude leaned over and slapped her several times on the back. When she could speak, she quickly asked Maude where she had bought her hat.

"Oh, you like it!" cried Maude, touching its drooping brim. "I knew you would! I have an eye for things, for fashion especially! It is a gift, you know. Jane has not an ounce of taste. But I help her—"

Barbara stood up. She could not stand it. The three women stared at her. "Excuse me," she choked. "I—I must leave."

"Barbara!" cried Fanny, but she ran out the door. Maude stared after her, her astonishment obvious.

"Is she ill? How very odd!"

Fanny put down her tea. "Do excuse me. I shall be right back."

In the hallway, Bates was handing Roger his hat and cane. Barbara called his name. He turned to her. His eyes were like sapphires. His face was pinched about the nostrils.

"Roger, what is it!"

She was used to people who raged when they were angry; this quiet anger was something that frightened her. He reached out and touched her cheek. Like a kitten, she nuzzled her cheek against his hand, but he shook his head, dropped his hand, and walked away toward the door, which Bates was holding open. Bates was carefully not looking at either of them.

"What is it?" she repeated.

But he never turned around. She followed him all the way to the door, and he never turned around. Bates closed the door and he was gone. Her mother and aunt stood in the doorway of the great parlor, watching. She could feel the tension radiating from them as she ran over to them. Fanny stood in the side door, her mouth a round **O**. Behind her shoulder was Maude.

"What happened!"

Barbara shrieked the words at her mother. She was past caring what anyone thought. "What did you do! I hate you!"

"Go to your room at once!" said her aunt.

"It is over," said her mother.

Barbara felt something crashing inside her.

"Oh, no, oh, no, oh, no!" she cried. Fanny was at her side, holding her. Be quiet, her aunt was saying. Hush now, hush, darling, Fanny was saying. But she could not be quiet. She could not hush. Her heart was breaking. Could they not hear it? She had lost Roger, her beautiful Roger, before she had

ever really had him. It was not fair. It was not fair to have
offered him and then taken him away. It was better to have
never had the chance than this.

Without a word, Fanny led her sobbing up the stairs.
Below, Abigail, Maude, Jane, Diana, Bates, and the two hall
footmen watched until Barbara and Fanny finally disappeared down a corridor off the landing. Barbara's sobs were
the only sound.

"Who is that woman?" Diana suddenly said.

Maude, who was staring at her with avid eyes now the
scene with Barbara was over, blinked.

Abigail stared. She had completely forgotten about Maude
and Jane, and there they were, in the middle of the hallway,
witnesses to the appalling thing that had just occurred. She
closed her eyes for a moment, then straightened her shoulders
and swept forward.

"I am Lady Saylor," she said in her grandest, mother-of-a-
duke voice. "You must be Mrs. Berkley. And you, dear, must
be Jane. Barbara has told us so much about you. Diana, come
here. Surely you know Jane—"

Jane shuddered as Diana came forward, her mouth smiling
in that cruel way she had. Beside her, her aunt was practically quivering with her effort to take in as much detail about
Diana as she could.

"Know her," said Diana. "I know her intimately. She tried
to marry my Harry."

Maude gasped. Jane turned white, then flushed a dark red
that stained her neck as well as her face. Her embarrassment
was painful to see. Abigail sighed. How like Diana to do this.
Now, when she needed help. When these two women were
gone, she was going to tell Diana exactly what she thought of
her—except that that might risk Bentwoodes. Well, she was
going to tell her what she thought of Barbara. Acting in such
a way! In front of everyone! Shocking! Appalling! Oh, dear,
the girl Jane looked as if she were going to cry at any minute.

"Forgive me, Mrs. Berkley, but this is a bad time for all of
us. May I suggest that you take Jane home. She does not look
well."

"What!" Maude started and tore her gaze from the unscrupulous Diana. "Jane, are you ill? Come, pet, come right now
and Aunt Maudie will make you one of her special headache

cordials. Good day to you, Lady Saylor. Lady Alderley."
Maude and Diana exchanged stiff nods like two men do before
they fall on each other, fighting.

"Thank goodness they have left," Maude heard Diana say
just as the door was closing behind her. Her thin bosom
heaved. In their carriage, Jane burst into tears.

"Well!" said Maude. "Can you imagine! Such rudeness! She
is all they said she was! How dare she speak to you so—beautiful, though. And older than I. I wonder how—Jane, do not
snivel! Did you see Lord Devane? I caught just a glimpse of
him! A handsome man! Barbara is a lucky girl—here, take my
handkerchief—was a lucky girl. Poor thing! What manners! I
would never have dared speak to my mother so! But he is too
old for her. A man such as he needs a mature woman, a
woman my age, to hold his interest—"

Jane leaned her head back against the seat and closed her
eyes. She gave her aunt her handkerchief. The way Diana had
looked at her. What she had said. She shuddered. She had a
terrible headache. But at least she had never acted like Barbara. She remembered the way she had cried and begged her
parents' forgiveness. Her one act of rebellion had been to try
to meet Harry. She was a good girl, an obedient girl. Now
Barbara was the same as she was. It did no good to be headstrong. She should feel sorry, but deep down she was glad,
glad that Barbara would experience some of the pain she felt.
Barbara sitting in that beautiful room in that beautiful house
in her beautiful gown with her cousin so well mannered and
polite. Now Barbara would know how it felt to cry every day,
until it seemed there were no more tears left—only there were
and they would be back again. Her face would feel dry and
stretched and empty from them. And the person she loved
would wear a groove into her mind until she thought she
would drop from the exhaustion of thinking about him. Yes,
Barbara, strong Barbara, lovely Barbara would now see how
everyone else felt. Unexpectedly, she began to cry again.
Without a pause in her monologue against the manners of the
children of this generation, interspersed with various comments about the house and the gowns Fanny and Abigail and
Diana had worn, her aunt handed her back the handkerchief.

CHAPTER FIVE

*B*arbara lay on her bed, exhausted. Abigail and Diana stood looking down at her, furious with her, with her stubbornness. They had been talking to her for a long time, and she was so tired. She knew she was rebelling against everything she had been taught; she knew that she had made a public scene, yet the will inside her would not allow her to bend. The more they pleaded, argued and threatened, the more set she became, even though she knew she could not win.

"Be reasonable. He is too old. I will find you someone younger. I know any number of young men," her aunt said.

"I want Roger," Barbara flung at her.

"I will beat you until you cannot walk," Diana said. Although Abigail stood by Barbara's bed, Diana kept farther back. She spoke to Barbara from a distance, as she always had.

"And I will still want Roger!" Barbara screamed the words at Diana.

"He is too dissolute," said her aunt. "His friends are among the most notorious in London. He would never make a good husband."

"I love him."

"Love!" snorted Abigail, who secretly wished Diana would beat her, beat her until she finally closed her mouth, could no longer set that chin and argue like a female devil. Where was the obedience, the docility a young woman her age should have, if not naturally, then through rigorous training? It was obvious that Diana had neglected her duties as a mother, and just as obvious that the Duchess was going soft in her old age. If any daughter of Abigail's had ever dared talk to her so, she would have locked her away until she came to her senses, which is exactly what needed to be done to Barbara. Her impudence was unbearable.

"You are fifteen," she said. "You know nothing of love! You have seen Roger Montgeoffry a bare handful of times—"

"Less than that," interrupted Diana. "He has hardly been ardent in his visiting." Barbara bit her lip. But the stubborn set to her chin did not change. Her face was swollen from crying, and everything they were saying made her cry more, but she would not, could not, give up.

"Heaven help me if my parents had allowed me to marry the boy I thought I loved at fifteen!" said Abigail.

"My parents did allow me," said Diana. "And you see what a wise choice I made. We are doing this for your own good."

"You made a promise! You broke your promise to me and to Roger!"

Diana's face became even colder. "The choice has been made. You have to submit. And you will . . . sooner or later." Her low voice was soft, chilling. Barbara shuddered, but set her chin even harder. She would not show her mother she was afraid; she would not.

Abigail took a deep breath. "A girl must marry as her parents decide. We are older and wiser and know more about life—"

"You are not my parent!" Tears were streaming down Barbara's face. "You want Bentwoodes! You—you do not care what happens to me! You just want Bentwoodes!"

"You need to be beaten," Abigail said in a shaking voice. "If you were mine, I would beat you until you screamed for mercy! You are rebellious, rude, ill-mannered, thoughtless and selfish! As far as I am concerned, you may rot in this room! I shall be damned if I will help you!"

The door slammed behind them. Barbara felt as if any moment her head would burst open it ached so. Every part of her ached.

"Bread and water tonight, nothing more," she heard her mother say. "—door locked, at all times," she heard her aunt say.

She turned her head in the pillow and sobbed.

Outside, Abigail leaned against the wall of the corridor, upset over her outburst to Barbara. It seemed that Barbara had the same effect on her as Diana did; both could make her angry; both could make her say things she regretted.

"I do not think Barbara will accept another marriage offer now," Diana said, with wonderful perceptiveness.

"We will send her back to Tamworth in a week or so," Abigail said. She was exhausted from it all, the scene with Roger, Barbara's hysterics, Maude and Jane being there, Barbara's further hysterics and tears. She had not had a moment's peace since Diana had come back to London. "A year or so alone in the country with only an old woman for company will quiet her down. She will be glad by then to take any offer suggested to her."

"And Bentwoodes?"

Diana had no subtlety. "It would look odd for us to transfer it right away, Diana. Let all this settle. Roger will be gone in less than a month. We will do it then." And meanwhile, she would have to watch Diana like a hawk, or she would sell the land out from under her. And she would have to be careful with Tony, who had not been himself lately. Nothing was going quite as she had planned, but somehow they all had to get through the next few days, when London would be whispering the gossip. Christmas was around the corner; there were card parties and dinners planned here at Saylor House. There must be no behavior from Barbara that fed the gossip. She must behave herself, or she would, literally, stay in her room on bread and water until Abigail determined it was time to send her to Tamworth. It was the Duchess's fault as much as anyone's that the girl knew nothing about obedience, about filial duty. Let the Duchess deal with her! Meanwhile, she would send Fanny—dear Fanny, upset by all the emotion, so softhearted—to talk some sense into that mule-headed child.

At a knock on the door, Barbara sat up and rubbed at her eyes. She must have fallen asleep, her head felt as if it were stuffed with flannel; she felt ill. She heard a key being turned—already her door was locked. Fanny walked in.

"Oh, my dear," said Fanny, running to her and kissing her. Barbara began to cry again. Fanny rocked her back and forth in her arms until she was able to stop. She stroked her hair and began to talk softly of marriage and its responsibilities. Of its not being up to a woman, who was weaker and lesser in the eyes of God, to decide whom she could marry. Of the strength and Christian love there was in accepting whatever God willed and making the best of it. She spoke of the responsibility a parent had to make the best marriage possible, of there being things other than love upon which to base a marriage, things such as background, comfort, compatibility. To all of this, Barbara shook her head while tears streamed down her swollen face.

"I love him, Fanny."

Fanny sighed and went to the water basin and wrung out a rag, made Barbara lie down and patted her face. The rag was cool and soothing, like Fanny's carefully chosen words.

"We were created from man's rib; were we not told to be in subjugation to our husbands? And to our parents? It is our duty to do as our parents so desire. It is God's will. I know you know this, Barbara, in your heart. I cannot believe Grandmama has brought you up in any other way."

Barbara gulped and turned her head away. It was true. Her grandmother had brought her up to do her duty, to be aware of her weaknesses and her duties as a woman. Yet somehow, her grandmother had always seemed to respect her feelings, had treated them as if they were as important as Harry's. She knew she was being rebellious and awful, but she could not help herself. Finally, Fanny went away. In a little while, the door opened again. She heard the sound of someone setting something down. The door closed. The key turned. She sat up, but it was difficult for her to see. Martha had not lit the candles, and her eyes were hurting. She walked dizzily into the little room that connected to the corridor. There on a table was a silver tray with a jug of water and a plate holding a few slices of white bread. Barbara climbed back into her bed. It did not matter; she felt too sick to eat.

By the next morning, her stomach ached for food. She had not eaten since luncheon the day before, having been far too upset to eat any of the delicious, creamy cakes made for tea. Last night she had been unable to do more than sip at the water and nibble on the bread before she began retching. This morning she felt ravenous, but Martha had come in during the night while she was asleep and removed the tray. Martha was too hard-hearted even to leave her the dry crusts. How long were they going to keep her on bread and water? How long could she last? And what was the point? They were correct; all of them. A girl did as her parents wished; she knew that; she had been raised on it. It was just that she had become so excited at the thought of having Roger she had allowed herself to build a hazy, light-filled dream in which he was her husband and they lived happily ever after. If her mother had never mentioned Roger, she would not have dreamed the dream, except sometimes. She would have done her duty. She had behaved badly; it shamed her so that she writhed at the thought of it; the words of apology to her aunt and her mother would choke her. How she hated to be wrong! For now, until she could not stand it any longer, she wanted to be alone. She could take another day or two of bread and water. Then apologize. She sat down in the window seat and stared out at the gardens. Bare and brown and cold like her heart. Oh, Roger, I will always love you. They cannot take that from me. From somewhere, tears seeped up and filled her eyes and fell with fat plops onto her gown. The key turned. She did not even bother to look. She would never look at that sullen Martha again. She wanted her grandmother. She wanted her grandmother to come and make everything better.

"Bab! You—you look awful!"

It was Tony, leaning over her and patting one of her hands, but above and beyond Tony was the smell of food, the smell of fried bacon and coffee! She leapt off the window seat and ran to the tray of food he had brought. She pushed crisp bacon and chunks of buttered, soft bread in her mouth. She dipped her finger in the jam and sucked it greedily. Food! Tony was an angel. She gorged herself, wiping greasy fingers on her gown like a peasant. It filled her stomach; it fed her courage. Each mouthful seemed to make the day brighter, her future less bleak. Suddenly, the food stuck in her throat, and her stomach heaved. She was going to be sick—she ran for her chamber pot and leaned over and everything she had eaten came up in chewed, smelly pieces. She retched and retched until she thought she would faint. The final bitter, yellow bile that came up burned her throat.

When she had finished she made her way, holding on to the wall, to a basin and rinsed out her mouth. Tony, who had been hovering helplessly near her, took her by the arm and led her to a chair. He knelt in front of her.

"Bab. You are sick. Let me call Mother!"

"No!"

"You look terrible. What can I do?"

"I am in disgrace, Tony."

"I know. Everyone does. Heard you all over the house. You—you love him very much, do you not, Bab?"

The tears were there again, closing her throat. She looked away and nodded her head. He clumsily patted her hand.

"You are very kind." She wiped at her eyes. The heartache was as fresh as if a day had not already gone by. It hurt even more. How was she ever going to endure it. Her body was vibrating with it; the smell of the food made her sick. Dear sweet Jesus, help me. Oh, Grandmama. She looked at Tony.

"What, Bab? Anything, short of abducting Roger. Told Mother not to keep you locked up. She is a good girl, I said. Headstrong. But good. Told her it was my house. Brought you food. Did not mean to make you sick."

She laughed feebly. His big, round, placid, white face was so earnest and serious. He was a big love.

"How brave of you, Tony."

"Mother is angry at me. Do not like it."

"Tony, listen. I want to write a letter to Grandmama, and I want you to post it for me. It must be a secret, Tony, because Aunt Abigail would never let me send it. All I am going to do is ask her to come and take me home. I will let you read it. Will you do it for me, please, Tony?"

He took awhile to think about it. Then he nodded his head.

"Oh, Tony." She leaned forward and kissed him on the lips. Then she got up, walking slowly, like an invalid, into the next room to her little writing desk. Tony touched his fingers to his lips, a delicate, tender gesture.

Her hands were shaking so that she spilled ink and blotted her letters, but she managed to write, "Come to London, Grandmama. I am in desperate trouble. I have been bad.

Please, please come. Your loving granddaughter, Barbara Alice Constance Alderley."

She scattered sand everywhere drying the ink. She needed her grandmother. She could endure anything if her grandmother were with her. She would make it better. Oh, she needed her. The pain was so bad.

Tony took the letter, folded it and put it inside his pocket. He took Barbara's hands in his.

"Told Mother you would behave yourself. Will you, Bab?"

"I will try, Tony. It just—hurts so."

Somehow, she was in his arms. He was tall, and she only came to his shoulders, but they were nice shoulders, comforting shoulders, and he did not seem to mind that she was crying on his good coat. He was so dear.

Her door remained unlocked, and Martha brought her trays of food, food she could do little but pick at. She had no interest in it, and too much made her sick. She stayed another day in her room, then straightened her shoulders and went to apologize to her aunt and her mother, both of whom she found in her aunt's withdrawing chamber. Diana sat at a card table playing solitaire. The tables had been designed during the reign of the late Queen Anne when card playing had become so popular. They seated four people, and each corner of the table featured a sconce in which to hold a candle. Diana barely looked up from the cards that were lying across the parquet squares of the tabletop. The deck she was playing with had drawings on one side of King George landing on the shores of England, saluting the English flag, being met by important members of Parliament. Once there had been a deck of cards that celebrated her father's victory at Lille.

Seething inside, Abigail listened to Barbara's mumbled apologies. That Tony should have countermanded her orders was beyond belief. She did not know what was happening to the boy; she only knew this girl had something to do with it. Abigail indulged in a long lecture on Barbara's behavior, a lecture Barbara found very hard to bear. It had taken all her will to make herself apologize. Her pride was bruised, throbbing, and her aunt's words were like salt. She gritted her teeth and tried to concentrate on home, on Tamworth, on her grandmother and her brothers and sisters. Her aunt was saying something about confining her to the house throughout the

Christmas season, about having her stay in her rooms during the festivities, as Mary had to, since Barbara had the manners of a nursery child anyway. That was fine. She had no wish to celebate this season. Diana never said a word; she only continued idly slapping the cards against the table.

It was the day of Christmas Eve. Saylor House was bustling with servants cleaning floors, polishing furniture and silver, with delicious smells of roasting capon and goose and turkey from the kitchen. Various sets of small tables were being moved into the great parlor and the hall and laid with heavy damask trimmed in lace and china plates and silver forks and spoons and knives and cups and saltcellars. It would be a late supper, at eight, and then the adults would stay up toasting the evening and watching the yule log burn. Barbara and Mary were to retire early. Barbara sat now in the conservatory. It comforted her some to be among her aunt's many blooming plants, the small, miniature orange trees, the lemon trees, the lilies and roses. They were kept blooming by many little charcoal braziers the gardeners fueled constantly. It was an example of the abundant wealth of the Tamworths, that they could keep a room at summer's heat in the dead of winter, when outside, people too poor to afford shelter froze to death from the cold. Passing days had not diminished her heartache. It was a constant in her life, the one thing that she could count on. The pain was there before she finally, after tossing and turning and crying, fell asleep, and in the morning, as soon as she opened her eyes, she could feel it fall on her heart. It was a heavy thing, like a cannonball. It made her heart flutter irregularly, so that she always felt breathless. She wished she could go back to those days—they now seemed so far away—when she had lived happily at Tamworth, Roger no more than a golden dream that had nothing whatsoever to do with her real life. How amazing that a few sentences by her mother had started her on a path to such pain.

She wandered to the glass doors which overlooked the back gardens. Today, no gardeners were visible. She could see no one raking leaves and debris from the gravel paths, no one tilling the flower beds, eternally mixing the soil so that it might be moist and open for spring seeding. Suddenly, she wanted to walk in the garden, feel the cold air on her cheeks, breathe something other than the air of Saylor House. She was confined to the house, but surely she could sneak a few moments in the garden.

Furtively, she glanced around her, but there was no one in this room, or in the garden. Everyone was busy preparing for this evening. She fastened one of the cloaks kept hanging on pegs and opened the door and stepped outside and took a breath of crisp, clear, cold air. It hurt her lungs. And it felt good, except it made her a little dizzy. She had no energy, no spirit these last days. She felt empty, listless, tired. She was always crying or sleeping. She still could not eat much. Everything churned inside her. She had managed two cups of tea and toast this morning, but it was not enough; she had already lost several pounds.

She walked a little more briskly down the gravel paths. Ah, fresh air, like freedom. It gave her a new strength. She felt she could walk all the way to Tamworth. How she longed for it, for her grandmother and those she loved. She was walking along a path that paralleled the garden wall. On the other side she could hear sounds from the street, a street vendor calling, "Buy my ropes of hard onions," and the wagons and carts going by, the drivers urging their horses on with Ha!'s and curses. On her side were evenly spaced holly shrubs, painstakingly clipped and trained to resemble candelabra. Their dark, shiny, green leaves were heavy with bright red Christmas berries. She walked by the gate, her thoughts on Roger, on her pain. She stopped. In her mind now was the gate she had just passed. There was no lock on it. Usually all the gates to the gardens were locked, so that passersby on the street could not come in. During spring, when the gardens were glorious with lilac and tulip trees blooming, with apple and pear trees blossoming, with daffodils and tulips and hyacinths, with rows of tender, spring roses, the gardens were open to the public on select afternoons. They were allowed to stroll through them until dusk, when the gatekeepers rang a bell to warn that the gates would soon be locked. It had been her grandfather's way of sharing some of his wealth with the people of London, and the tradition had been carried on by Abigail and Tony.

Barbara found herself standing at the gate. She had an impulse to open it and go out. Before the thought was complete in her head, before she could list the reasons why she had to stay in the garden, she was on the other side, standing on the cobbles of the street, separated from oncoming wagons and carriages by the wooden stiles sticking up out of the pavement. The stiles made a barrier against the street traffic behind which a pedestrian might walk. Ahead of her was a tavern; its sign hung suspended over the street by several branches of iron. There was no wording on the sign, just a painting of a king in a red coat with gold buttons and a golden crown. The name of the tavern was The George. The shops were open, though they would close early. She could see gloves and ribbons mixed with Christmas ivy and holly in a shop window. A young apprentice boy stood near the entrance calling for passing people to come inside and buy his master's superior product. She started walking; she had a confused idea of where she was; she had never been out alone, and never on foot. But it was good to walk up and down the streets, to look into the shops, to smell baking bread and roasting meat, to look up at the huge signs hanging overhead, the painting on them bold and colorful to attract the eye, to listen to the street vendors. "Buy a new almanac." "A brass pot, an iron pot to mend." "New river water." To watch the sedan chairs and carriages coming by. To see other young girls like herself, obviously maidservants, bustling by on errands. Everyone smiled and called out, "Compliments of the season!" Several apprentices offered her free merchandise from their master's shop for a Christmas kiss. She had not felt so carefree since coming to London. She would just walk a little farther, then turn around, go back, slip through the garden gate. No one would ever have to know.

She realized she had walked into one of London's squares, those fine, open spaces surrounded by handsome town homes. They had begun to be developed in the reign of James I, when many noblemen, and a few London bankers with connections to the court, saw a profit in developing the fields around London and Westminster. Each one in its time drew tenants and surrounding shops and buildings, and as time passed, grew slightly unfashionable as another one took its place, all moving steadily out of the City of London and into Westminster, where the monarch lived. Now she was standing in the most fashionable, St. James's. She recognized it immediately, by its central fountain. She walked across the cobbles to number seventeen, Roger's town house. I shall simply wish him a happy Christmas, one part of her was saying, while another part cried, What are you doing? But she knew. She knew what she was doing.

She lifted up the heavy brass door knocker with its lion's head and pounded it confidently against the door, which opened. In front of her stood a stately man with a neatly tied black wig. A crest was embroidered on his dark coat. What have I done? she thought wildly.

She lifted her chin and said, "Lord Devane, please. Tell him it is Mistress Barbara Alderley." (To her dying day, she would never know what possessed her that fatal Christmas Eve; what made her ignore every rule of her upbringing and of society to call, without a chaperone, on a single man.)

Cradock, Roger's majordomo, pursed his lips. He was too experienced not to know that she was who she said she was, but he was distressed by the lack of a maid or relative with her, and even if she were not who she said she was, Lord Devane would be angry with him for leaving her outside on the step. Lord Devane was noted for his courtesy and his hospitality, and as his most important servant, Cradock had a duty to represent those qualities.

He bowed to her. "Come in at once, ma'am," and she followed him inside, into a narrow hallway with a staircase ascending on the left-hand side, and two sets of doors on each side. Through the doorway to her right, she could see servants smoothing white damask tablecloths across tables. The chimney, which was in direct line of vision with the door, was wreathed with holly and ivy and had fat white candles set amid the greenery. It was Christmas Eve and he was giving a reception, and here she was. She was a fool, but she followed Cradock's gesture toward a door on the left.

"If you will wait here, Mistress Alderley, I will inform Lord Devane. May I offer you refreshment?"

"No," she whispered. The enormity of what she was doing made her feel faint. She was in a small parlor that reflected Roger's wealth and taste. It was called the Neptune Room because the patterned paper on the wall featured Neptune, his beard crusted with starfish and sea horses, rising from a cresting blue-green wave and blowing a golden horn while dark dolphins rose out of the waves. Every few feet of the wall was broken up by intricate, tiny fish and shells forever twisting in ribbons of wood. Armchairs of different sizes, their arms and legs carved in the shape of twisting, snakelike dolphins, were pulled up to five small card tables set about the room. In the center of each card table was a white candle surrounded with a rosemary and ivy wreath. Barbara sat down on the edge of a chair and tried to catch her breath. Her heart was beating so fast that she felt dizzy. What on earth was she expecting Roger to do—elope with her? Out of the question for her and for him. An elopement brought scandal and disgrace. Of course here she sat, doing something only slightly less scandalous. Please, please, please, she thought and did not know what she was pleading for.

Cradock knocked on the library door.

"Come in," called Montrose, who sat at his desk rechecking the seating arrangements for dinner. White lounged in a chair near the fire rereading Alexander Pope's *Iliad*, the literary rage of the year.

Montrose made a hissing sound as Cradock whispered to him, and White looked up from his book to watch his friend return to his desk, frown and shift a stack of invitations from one corner to another—an unnecessary gesture and one that gave him away.

Cradock left the room.

"What is it, Francis? Tell me. I know you. You are bursting with news." (If anything, for all his stuffiness, Montrose was a bigger gossip than White.)

Montrose could not contain himself. "There is a young woman downstairs." He paused a moment for dramatic effect. "A young woman without a chaperone who says her name is Barbara Alderley."

White's mouth fell open.

Everyone in the household, from the kitchen maid to Cradock, knew that Lord Devane's marriage plans had soured. And White and Montrose both knew he had invested quite a bit of money in plans, surveys, permits and in loans to Lady Alderley. Even his renowned charm could not hide the fact that he was tired and shorter-tempered these days.

"But why did Cradock come to you instead of—"

"Responsibility."

White understood at once. Great houses, staffed by many servants, were hotbeds of dodging responsibility.

"Carlyle!" he exclaimed after a moment. "It has to be one of his tricks! Think, Francis. Remember when he paid two whores from Shoreditch to call and insist they were ladies-in-waiting to the princess with a personal message to Lord Devane? We lost him for days." He jumped up and grinned at Montrose, like a mischievous boy. "Let us both go downstairs and examine her. If she is genuine—which is impossible—I will tell him for you. I take full responsibility." He darted from the room.

With a sigh, Montrose followed him.

At the light, neat sound of a knock on the door, Barbara jumped up, her heart choking her. She was having trouble catching her breath. The sight of two strange young men, both now staring at her as if she were a freak at a country fair, made her feel faint. The room was too hot, she was going to fall—

White caught her just before she toppled to the floor. Neither he nor Montrose thought it a joke anymore. It was obvious that this thin, pretty girl was someone respectable. What she was doing here without a chaperone—and looking like death—was something neither man wished to know. Everyone was in trouble. Lord Devane should have been summoned at once. White helped her sit down and patted her hand. She put the other one to her head.

"Who are you?" she said.

White bit his lip. "Go upstairs at once and fetch Lord Devane," he ordered Montrose, who was rooted to the floor. The urgency in his voice propelled Montrose out the door. It was only as he was knocking on the door to Lord Devane's bedchamber that he remembered that White had said he would be the one to tell Lord Devane, that he would be the one to take full responsibility. Before he could run back down the stairs, Justin, Roger's valet, opened the door. Like a man going to his doom, Montrose went in.

"I am Caesar White, Lord Devane's clerk," White said to Barbara. "And that was Francis Montrose, his secretary. Forgive me, Mistress Alderley, but you look ill. Is there something I can get for you—"

Barbara pulled her hand out of his. "Go away," she said. She felt so ashamed she thought she would die of it. She was in Roger's town house, and she had no business being there, and now two young men besides the majordomo had seen her, and she was in the worst trouble she had ever been in in her life.

"It is private, sir."

Roger signaled for Justin to leave the room. He had been dressing for the reception he was to hold this evening, and he wore a pale blue satin coat that matched his eyes. He looked extraordinarily handsome.

"Well?"

"Mistress Barbara Alderley is in the Neptune Room, sir. Caesar is with her."

Roger's eyes widened. He stepped closer to Montrose. "What do you mean, Mistress Alderley is in the Neptune Room? Is this someone's idea of a joke? Carlyle—"

"I wish it were, sir. There is more, sir." Montrose swallowed. "She is alone, sir."

"Alone!"

Never, in all the years that Montrose had worked for Lord Devane, had he shouted at him. He shouted now. "Why was I not informed immediately!"

"Cradock came to me, sir, not knowing what to do, seeing as the young lady seemed to be without an escort!"

"Then, why, in God's name, is Caesar downstairs with her! Who else have you told! Jesus Christ, man, I could kill you both! Get out of my way!"

Roger walked swiftly from the room. Montrose wiped at his perspiring face with his handkerchief. He made no move to follow. Lord Devane would find him later.

White was patting Barbara's hand when Roger burst into the room. At the sight of him, White quickly stood up. Barbara said faintly, "Roger, I am so sorry. Please forgive me—" Roger jerked his head at White. "Tell Mrs. Bridgewater to join us immediately and"—he looked at Barbara, drooping in the chair—"tell Cradock, no one but Cradock, to bring some brandy and food immediately." His words were clipped and short, as if White were a soldier under his command. And like a soldier, White ran to do as he was told, relieved to give responsibility to someone who seemed to know what to do.

Barbara was crying. "I do not know how this happened," she was saying. "I was walking, and then I was here. Please do not hate me, Roger. Please!"

The angry expression on his face faded. Whatever he must have felt at seeing a sobbing fifteen-year-old, unchaperoned, in his house, paled beside her tears. She looked pitiful, and he had always had a soft spot for her, ever since she was a little girl.

"Y-you are a-angry with me, and I do not blame you. It was a stupid, wild thing to do! Now I have disgraced my-myself in your e-e-eyes!"

The last word turned into a wail. She covered her face with her hands. Roger, accustomed to years of women's tears, knew exactly what to do. He knelt down in front of her and held her. She gripped the lapels of his coat and sobbed against his shoulder. Part of him now wanted to laugh; the situation was really amusing. Justin would die when he saw what she was doing to his coat, yet she was crying so hard, and he would never hurt her feelings. He comforted her as expertly as he had comforted many a woman before her, thinking that with all that had been going on between Diana and him, they had completely forgotten the feelings of this child.

"Hush, now," he comforted. "Hush now, my sweet girl."

He felt tender toward her, an emotion that caught him off guard. It was a foolish, stupid, impetuous thing she had done, and she had his household in an uproar, and as he knelt there letting her pucker the satin on his coat—he had guests arriving in an hour—he had never felt more like laughing in his life. For the first time in weeks. But, of course, he could not. She hiccuped against his shoulder. He bit his lip and stroked her back. Through her cloak she was skin and bones. Were they starving her over there at Saylor House? Once again, he was struck by the realization that there was someone else besides himself involved in the marriage negotiations. That she might have been punished by her mother or her aunt; that he had never given it another thought as he walked out the door that afternoon at Saylor House. His selfishness appalled him.

A cough sounded behind him. Mrs. Bridgewater, his house-keeper, stood a few feet away, taking in the fact that her employer knelt on the floor holding a weeping girl in his arms. Behind her, Cradock, his face perfectly expressionless, held a tray with brandy and food. Roger stood up, but he still held

Barbara's hand. She was mortified at the way Mrs. Bridge-water was looking at her.

"Mrs. Bridgewater," Roger said smoothly, "this is the daughter of a friend of mine, and she became lost on her walk. Luckily she recognized my house—her father and I are old friends—and knocked on my door. As you can see, the experience frightened her. I depend on your kindness to help me." He had neatly skipped over why Barbara should be tak-ing a walk without her maid. "There is an adjoining room just here, Mrs. Bridgewater. Will you wait for me while I calm my young friend?"

Mrs. Bridgewater did as she was told. Cradock had already laid down the tray and left the room. He had been a major-domo for too many years not to know when a crisis was at hand. He would pay for his part soon enough.

Roger poured Barbara a little brandy. She managed to choke some down. He made her eat a little baked chicken. She ate it, and it stayed down. He pulled a chair beside her and watched her eat. If they spoke softly, Mrs. Bridgewater would not be able to hear every word. He had the feeling Barbara was about to say many foolish things. It came from years of experience. He wished to spare her as much humiliation as possible. Barbara had finished the chicken leg and ate another one. She felt better, if that were possible. She was in total dis-grace and had made a complete fool of herself, but she felt better. Roger was amazingly kind.

"You—you are leaving soon," she said.

"Yes, Barbara, I am. Did you come to say goodbye?"

She blushed at the irony in his voice, but it also made her laugh a little. She looked around for something to wipe her hands on. Roger handed her his handkerchief. After she had wiped her hands and mouth, she blew her nose in it. He watched her without a word, but declined to take the hand-kerchief back. She wadded it into a ball in her hand.

"I know you would like to kill me for coming here—"

"You exaggerate, my dear."

"But not any more than I would like to kill myself. I-I should not have come alone. I-I know that. I really do not know how I got here—"

"But here you are."

"Yes." There seemed nothing more to say.

"May I take you home?" he asked gently.

She nodded her head. The tears were welling up again. "You are not going to marry me, are you?"

"No, it is not possible now. And may I say, that after today, I think I regret it very much."

She smiled at him. Her face was swollen and her nose was red, but it was still the Saylor smile. He was touched again as he had been that first time he had seen her and she had reminded him so of her grandfather.

"You are very kind, Roger. And—and I know you do not mean a word of it. You might have someday. I thought I would make you fall in love with me if I had the chance. But now—well, since I am here, and it is Christmas Eve, and when I go home, I will most likely be killed—"

He laughed, but she plunged on.

"I have something I want to say." She looked down at the crumpled handkerchief in her hands. "I love you. I always have. I hope that your life is long and happy. That—that your future w-wife brings you joy and happiness, as I wished to. Please do not despise me for coming here today, and please do not despise me for what I am saying. I may never again have the chance, and I-I just wanted you to know." Tears were rolling down her cheeks. They fell with fat plops onto her hands.

He could not speak. Of the many things that had been said to him, he could think of none that made him feel the way he felt at this moment—wistful, poignant, very, very old. He leaned forward and took one of her hands and gently unfolded the fist she had made in her earnestness and fear and held the palm to his mouth. Like a lover would, he kissed her palm tenderly, and then held it against his cheek. They looked at each other, and for that moment they were close. (All her life, no matter what happened, she would always remember that moment.)

"I must take you home, my dear."

She nodded her head, and he released her hand. It tingled. She stood up, obedient, quiet, the hood from her cloak hanging down her back like a little girl's.

He called for Mrs. Bridgewater and gave Barbara his hand. They walked out into the hallway, Mrs. Bridgewater following. White and Montrose and Cradock were huddled at the front of the stairs. At the sight of Roger, they broke apart like guilty children. He strolled over to them. Montrose could not help backing away slightly.

"I want to present my dear friend, Mistress Barbara Alderley. All of you met her earlier under distressful circumstances. Mistress Alderley lost her way walking, and recognized my house. I am taking her home. Cradock, send for my carriage and fetch my cloak, and one for Mrs. Bridgewater, who will accompany us. White, tell Justin I have ruined his coat. I spilled water on it. I shall need another when I return. I leave you and White to entertain any guests who might show up in my absence. I need not remind any of you that Mistress Alderley is quite embarrassed and does not want to be reminded of what has happened today."

"My lips are sealed!"

"Not a word will be mentioned."

"Your cloak, sir. Mrs. Bridgewater."

"Excellent. Gentlemen . . ."

Cradock opened the door and walked them down the steps. One look passed between White and Montrose, then they broke into a run and headed for the Neptune Room, which had a clear view of the street.

"They are getting into the carriage," White said. He was leaning against the pane of the window, his nose pressed against the glass. Montrose was two panes over. Roger had only to look up to see them, but luckily he did not do so.

"Mrs. Bridgewater looks as if she has eaten a prune," said Montrose.

"Lord, I would give a million pounds to know what he is thinking. He looked . . . tender, I thought."

"I cannot see his face!" complained Montrose. There was an aggrieved tone in his voice. White smiled to himself.

"I would love to be a fly on the wall at Saylor House when they arrive there," he said.

"Or when he returns home. I have the feeling that he is not finished with us, Caesar, and I must say, I think it is entirely your fault—"

The carriage pulled into Saylor House courtyard. Barbara shuddered. Next to her, Roger patted her hand and said, "You could not help becoming lost, Bab. Remember that." It was as if he was warning her not to tell the truth, but she needed no warning. It was wonderful of him to help her this way, to escort her home. She would never forget it. If she lived.

"Mrs. Bridgewater, you wait here," Roger told her as the carriage stopped. An expression of intense disappointment crossed the woman's face, but Roger did not want her in the house, talking to any of the Saylor servants. This story had to be stopped, now.

"Mistress Barbara!" cried Bates as he opened the door. "We were so worried."

"Tell Lady Saylor that Lord Devane is here, and wishes to speak with her at once," said Roger.

Beside him, Barbara was having difficulty breathing. She was afraid, far more afraid than when she stood waiting in her grandmother's withdrawing room while Annie tattled on her. She hated to face her grandmother's anger, but she hated to face her aunt's and mother's more. Behind her grandmother's anger was love. Behind her mother's and aunt's was nothing. And what she had done was nothing so simple as stealing Vicar Latchrod's church key and locking pigs in his study or riding off by herself without a groom to escort her. Her grandmother understood such things. This she would not understand. Her legs felt weak. Roger caught her arm at the elbow.

"Courage," said Roger. "Remember our story. Stick to it, no matter what."

She wanted to cry, but she had done enough of that for one day, and she hated to cry in front of other people, though you would never know it, the way she had been acting today.

Bates opened the door to the great parlor. Never had the walk across the hallway and into that room seemed so long. It was as if her perspective of distances had become distorted. Abigail and her mother and Tony, all grouped near the fireplace, seemed far, far away. The figures in the war murals, the horses with their mouths open, the men shouting in silent screams, seemed to be closing in on her. Abigail stood with one hand on the mantelpiece. Diana sat in an armchair nearby. Tony stood by his mother. Like Roger, Abigail was expecting guests, and both she and Diana were dressed in velvet gowns and jewels. It was a question as to which one of them showed the most bosom. Abigail's was pushed up high and full, while Diana's lay more naturally. Abigail wore a turban and feathers in her hair. It was an unfortunate choice for her face looked fat and square. Diana had on a beautiful diamond necklace. The biggest diamond fell into the valley made by her breasts. Even Tony looked splendid, in a velvet coat and a blue sash and a full, fuzzy blond wig. He watched Barbara gravely as she came forward, her hand on Roger's arm. Abigail's hand tightened on the mantel as she watched them walk forward. Diana's eyes flicked from Barbara's face to Roger's and then back again.

Ignoring Abigail, Roger led Barbara to Diana.

"I return your daughter, Diana. It seems she went for a walk and lost her way. Luckily I found her. Here she is, unharmed, untouched, but extremely upset, though I have assured her you will deal kindly with her."

"Have you, indeed?" Diana's eyes flicked over Barbara. What Barbara saw in them made her hold on to herself not to cry, at least until Roger was gone.

"Thank you, Lord Devane. Indebted to you. Worried. Thought Bab had done something crazy. Mother upset, you know. Christmas Eve and all. Something to drink?" Tony had come forward and was speaking earnestly to Roger.

Abigail closed her eyes. Roger was their mortal enemy and Tony was offering him something to drink. Roger saw her look and had the audacity to grin at her when she opened her eyes. She scowled at him. He made a sweeping, graceful bow. Even Abigail had to admit he looked magnificent.

"Thank you, no. I, too, have guests expected. I only wanted to ensure that Barbara got home safely." He picked up Barbara's limp hand, but this time he did not kiss it.

"Courage, little one," he said softly, but Barbara was not looking at him; she was looking at her mother.

With another ironic bow, he walked from the room, with Tony escorting him.

The door closed behind them. The silence in the great parlor could be cut with a knife. Barbara shivered. The room was cold, as cold as her mother's heart. She waited. No one said a word. She swallowed and began.

"It—it is true." Her normally low voice came out high and strained. "I saw the gate open. I-I only wanted to take a little walk. I—"

"Did you sleep with him?"

Barbara stared at her mother. "I would never—" she began, but Abigail interrupted her.

"Diana, she was only gone for an hour! Heaven knows I am as angry and upset as you. Barbara Alderley, young ladies do not wander about London unescorted, as you well know! Your reputation will be ruined if anyone finds out! When Martha told me you were missing, I thought I would die on the spot—what with twenty people invited tonight, and half of them here in ten minutes—"

"Do not tell me what can be accomplished in an hour. I, of all people, know. And, after all, she is my daughter."

Diana's voice cut through Abigail's words like a knife. She sat in her chair, dressed in her favorite color, deep red, her necklace glittering around her neck, and to Barbara, she was the personification of evil and malice. Slowly, deliberately, she stood up. Both Abigail and Barbara watched her, fascinated.

"Tell me once more what happened, O daughter of mine. Have you spoiled it all for me?" Her low voice was beautiful, like honey, like velvet.

"I-I told you. I wanted to take a walk, and I became lost and—"

The force of her mother's fist sent her crashing to the floor. Pain exploded in her head, red, orange, yellow. Everywhere. She was sick with it. Slowly it began to concentrate itself on the left side of her face. She tried to understand what had happened.

"Merciful heavens!" cried Abigail, running to Barbara and kneeling beside her.

"Barbara! Barbara! Are you all right! Tony! For God's sake, help me!"

Tony, returning, came at a run. There was a metallic taste in Barbara's mouth . . . blood. Before she could help herself, she spit it onto the yellow crushed velvet skirt of her aunt.

"Dear God!" shrieked Abigail. In her haste to stand up, she somehow unbalanced the turban on her head and it fell off, and went rolling under a corner china cabinet. Abigail's hair was dirty and flattened by the turban. She put her hands to it. "Oh, no!" she said.

The left side of Barbara's face had become one throbbing bloodred pain. She did not think she could stand up without falling. She looked up at Diana.

"I hate you," she said wearily.

Diana made a movement toward her, but Tony put himself in front of her. His pale, plump face was angry. Angry and disgusted.

"Stay away from her, Aunt Diana! I mean it! Mother, I hold you responsible for this entire scene!" It was the first time in years that he had spoken in complete sentences, but everyone was too upset to notice. He turned back to Barbara and helped her up. She leaned against him, thanking God that he was there.

"Me!" shrieked Abigail, who was on her hands and knees trying to fish her turban from under the cabinet. She pulled herself upright. The sound of ripping material filled her ears. Somehow, her heel had caught the edge of her skirt and she had ripped part of the waist away from the gown.

"It is Diana!" she shrieked. "Diana!" It seemed to be the only word she could manage. The blood Barbara had spit on her was centered, large and red, directly on her lower abdomen.

"Tony! Tony!" she cried, but he did not answer. He led Barbara away. In the hallway, Barbara began to cry, and it made her face hurt even more.

"Bab, do not cry. I will protect you. I promise."

"Oh, Tony," she sobbed.

Bates waited until they were on their way up the stairs. Quickly, he wiped perspiration from his upper lip. He had had the presence of mind to put the guests in an adjoining parlor. Then he opened the door to the great parlor. Abigail, her dirty hair plastered to her head, was on her hands and knees in front of a china cabinet. Diana stood by the fireplace, not a hair out of place, beautiful, serene. Bates spoke to the portrait above the fireplace.

"Your guests, madam, have arrived."

Barbara lay on her bed. The left side of her face was swollen, the side of her tongue was swollen and raw where the force of Diana's blow had caused her to bite it, her head ached, and her eye was turning black. No ice or any kind of poultice had been brought to her. Martha was nowhere to be found. Tony had put her to bed himself. She hated Martha, but it was a feeble thing compared to how she hated her mother. Grandmama, she whispered into the darkness. She held the thought that her grandmother would be coming soon, around her like a warm cloak. She did not even have the strength left to cry.

The Duchess was resting. Tonight she must sit for several hours downstairs in the servants' hall and watch the annual Christmas Eve play they would present in her honor. It was always written and directed by Perryman, who also acted the chief part, a parody of herself. Perryman would be dressed in an old gown and wear a badly fitted wig and would scream at servants and limp about, and the younger servants, who were not allowed in the play, would giggle and laugh, as would the children, as would she, though Perryman produced basically the same production every year. There was a lord of misrule running in and out of the plot; he turned her household upside down; she was hunting for him everywhere, under cushions, in the soup pot; somehow St. George and his dragon made an appearance, one of the footman showed off fancy footwork in a sword dance, and various other odds and ends were thrown in for good measure. She would laugh and nod, as she must. Their hearts would be broken if she were not delighted. Vicar would come with Sir John Ashford and his wife to watch it with her.

It had become an annual tradition, Sir John always declaring that they had not made her mean and stubborn enough, and that Perryman was too fat to do the part justice. Vicar would give a small speech afterward, something about her generosity and Christian charity; all the servants, still in their costumes made of bits and pieces of old dresses and rags, as well as those in the audience, would cheer. The whole household would then troop into the great hall, where her grandson Tom would light the Christmas log and everyone would toast it with a glass of ale. The servants would leave to make sure everything was ready for tomorrow, when she gave a great feast in the hall, to which every servant and tenant came, as well as friends. All along a wooden trestle table, a table far older than she, a table that had been used in her father's time, and great-grandfather's time, a table that had been used back in the times when Henry VIII sat on the throne. Faces would glow up and down its long sides, waiting for the crowning glory, the boar's head, borne in on a tray as long as and wider than Anne, an apple in his mouth, surrounded with a wreath of apples and rosemary. It was an old tradition, one that many households no longer celebrated, but boar's head at Christmas was one of Tamworth's traditions. Then in would come the Christmas pies and the puddings, roast goose, turkey, quail, mincemeat pies, apple tarts, nuts and cheese. All afternoon they would feast. There would be church in the morning, carolers tonight. Christmas box—tips to servants—throughout the next twelve days.

She must attend a supper at Squire's, and a dinner at Vicar's and a card party at Sir John's. The children would be going here and there to different parties held throughout the county. And so would she. But, oh, it was all different this year without Barbara. How she missed her Barbara. She had half a mind to bundle up the children and herself and descend on Abigail for the New Year, just to see that child with her own eyes. It was Barbara who ramrodded the finding of the yule log and the wreathing of the evergreens. It was Barbara who had somehow weasled herself into the Christmas play since she was eleven, and convulsed the servants with laughter each year playing a lazy, dirty, insubordinate maid to Perryman's Duchess. It was Barbara who sang the clearest as they sang the old Christmas carols and drank their Christmas wassail of ale and nutmeg and sugar and roasted apples floating in the great silver bowl. It was Barbara who brought life into this old house, and she had never realized it as much as she had realized it this month or so that the girl had been gone.

She found herself listening for her footsteps around every corner; found herself straining to hear Barbara's voice among the children. When she looked out her window, and saw her grandchildren playing in the snow, her eyes instinctively looked for Barbara, no longer there. And it was not just she who missed the girl. The children moped and whined and cried and misbehaved worse than they ever had. Poor Henley was going out of her mind. Even Annie, who had a longstanding feud with Barbara, who considered her impetuous and headstrong (true), who considered it her sacred duty to turn Barbara into a docile lady, missed the girl. Each day, since she had left, the Duchess had expected a letter. She knew Diana too well not to worry. That was why she had written her sister-in-law, Louisa. But Louisa's reply had been unsatisfactory. There was only one long letter from Barbara, written just two weeks ago from Saylor House. The Duchess had read it and reread it until she had it memorized. She had then had to read it to the children and to Annie and to Perryman, and the housekeeper, and the cook, who passed along the news to the lesser servants. Drat that girl, they all missed her. . . .

Strange were the ways of the Lord that one of Diana's children (Diana, her failure) should have come to mean so much to her, as her life entered its cycle of grief. . . . Her sons dying one by one, and Richard changing. . . . That fine, clear, dear mind of his going. . . . Grief . . . yes, that was grief . . . and the further he moved from her, the more she had come to need the child Barbara, who looked much as she imagined Richard must have looked as a child, who became the daughter Diana should have been. And was not. With Barbara's presence, she could accept Richard's death, accept the gaping, dark hole it tore into her life, for he had been the center of her world, well or ill, the center. At the last, though her heart broke with what he had become, she still must plot with Annie over what would tempt him to eat, save bits and pieces of village gossip for him to laugh at, worry over his health, fuss over this and that. Her center . . . yes, Barbara had given her a reason to go on with life, for she must see this girl grown, and grow she had, into a woman, making her own life now, and the Duchess felt as if she had another hole in her heart. She had not realized she would miss the chit so.

When Barbara married Roger, she would send for the other children; the Duchess knew it. Barbara was their real mother, not Diana, who had spit them loveless from her body and left them. And then who would the Duchess have? She pursed her lips. She was old, too old now for the turmoil of young children, and yet . . . perhaps she would move near to Barbara. Yes. Live near enough to watch her grandchildren and her great-grandchildren grow up. Abigail was always panting to add to Tony's legacy. Let him have this dower house in exchange for a London property. Where she might see them all whenever she wished. Ah, there was Annie, cross old stick. Annie missed Barbara almost as much as the Duchess and the children did. She sat up straighter. Annie was bringing letters. The Duchess enjoyed her letters; friends and relatives kept her informed of gossip and family business. An hour or more each afternoon was spent dictating replies to Annie, so voluminous was her correspondence. She might no longer want to rule the family, but she still enjoyed knowing what was going on and commenting upon it. Annie was almost smiling. What was this?

The Duchess accepted a letter and recognized at once Barbara's sprawling handwriting. She ripped open the seal and then read the four sentences: "Come to London, Grandmama. I am in desperate trouble. I have been bad. Please, please come."

"What is it, madam?"

The sharpness in Annie's voice jerked her back to herself. Her girl was in trouble! The Duchess did not stop to think why or how. She only knew that this child, the child of her heart, needed her. It felt good to be needed. She stood up.

"We are going to London, Annie," she said fiercely. Vigor and purpose flooded her tired, old bones. "Our girl needs us, Annie." No more need be said.

It was only two days before New Year's Day. Festivities at Saylor House had proceeded as usual; Abigail held card parties and dinners, teas and suppers, but Barbara's presence hung over the holiday gaiety like a pall. She stayed in her room; there was no need to lock her in; she refused to leave. She was not eating; the trays sent up kept being returned with hardly anything touched. The servants were talking about it; everyone knew Diana had slapped her though no one quite knew why. Abigail, playing cards, entertaining guests, had to pretend that everything was normal, when it was far from being so. The immediate family knew, of course. Barbara had poured her heart out to Fanny the next day. And though Fanny said nothing, Abigail had the strangest feeling that somehow she was considered to be to blame. And what had she done, but prevent her niece from making a serious mistake? Mary moped about the house like a beggar's child. Every time Abigail looked up, those pale blue eyes of her younger daughter would be staring at her with blame in them. She had not slapped Barbara! Diana had!

She sat now in the great parlor, sipping tea. Fanny and Harold were here and Tony and Diana and Mary. At the sight of Diana, greedily licking crumbling cake from her fingers—

and outrageously flirting with Harold—Abigail's blood began
to boil. Tony, her Tony, without half a brain in his head, the
boy she had schemed and planned and thought about for
years, had come to her bedchamber late last night to tell her
he thought that when Barbara had had time to heal from her
attachment to Lord Devane, that he would like to court her.
Abigail had sat on her bed, night cream plastered on her face,
a rag tied around her head and under her chin to stop its sagging, and literally been unable to speak. Barbara and Tony.
It was beyond bearing. And the irony was that Tony could
have Bentwoodes anyway. Diana was going to sell it to him.
(Abigail had somehow not explained all this yet to Tony.)
Dear God, could there be a God, when he sent this kind of
news for a mother to bear? Tony and Barbara. The thought
made Abigail shudder. How Diana would laugh if she knew.

Merciful heavens, sitting here now, with that child upstairs
pacing up and down, growing thinner by the day, a pall over
every holiday joy, seeing Diana across from her eating her
food, sleeping on her bed, borrowing her money, and then
looking at Tony and knowing that he was in love with a
headstrong, impetuous hoyden, well, it was literally more than
Abigail could bear. She had thought she could bear no more
the afternoon that awful Maude Berkley had been witness to
as appalling a scene as any on the stage. She had thought she
could bear no more when her gown was bloodstained and torn
and her turban was beyond reach and five guests out of the
twenty invited were already there. She had thought she could
bear no more when Roger Montgeoffry had strolled in with
Barbara on his arm and Abigail had no idea what he was
going to say or what had occurred. Well, it was nothing compared to Tony's declaration last night. She had simply been
bereft of speech. And Tony, mindless idiot that he was, had
taken her silence for acquiescence and had kissed her and said
that he was glad she did not oppose his choice. Abigail's cup
of gall was full. There was nothing else that could happen to
her.

Bates came into the room. Abigail noticed that his face was
red with excitement. As she struggled to take in the awful,
terrible words that he was saying, she realized that her cup
was not full. The Lord had more for her. She could not
believe this was happening to her. It was all a horrid night-

mare, and she was going to wake up, and it would be two weeks before Christmas and Diana still in Covent Garden. And she was going to leave her there.

"Madam!" Bates repeated. "The Duchess is here. It is her carriage in the drive. I would know it anywhere."

Diana, who had been smiling at Harold, to Fanny's annoyance, stood up slowly, her smile fading. There was no expression on her face, but underneath the rouge, her face paled. Tony had jumped up and was already out of the room, followed by Fanny and Harold and Mary, while Abigail struggled to comprehend what was happening.

She stood up, and like a prisoner in a dream, walked slowly into the hallway. Diana, even more slowly, followed her. Barbara appeared at the top of the landing and flew down the stairs. How did she know? thought Abigail. Was she a witch? Had she put a curse on them? Barbara ran past Tony and Fanny and Harold, past Bates, past the footmen waiting on the steps. An ancient carriage stood in the drive. The coachman leaned into its opened door talking to someone. Behind the carriage was a cart piled to the brim with furniture. Barbara could recognize the posts from her grandmother's bed. There were other large, rectangular bundles covered with layers of soft leather that would prove to be a selection of the Duchess's favorite small tables from Tamworth, and a portrait of the Duke, all items the Duchess considered necessary to her comfort when she traveled.

"Hurry it up, man! These children are half dead with cold, and so am I!"

It was her grandmother's voice, made even gruffer by the journey. Barbara pushed past the coachman and Abigail's footman, who had arrived behind her and were trying to unload the occupants from the carriage. Crowded inside the dark interior were her grandmother, Annie, Dulcinea, whom Annie was holding on to with a firm grip, Anne, who was crying, and Charlotte, who was about to.

"Grandmama!" Barbara cried, scrambling into the carriage in spite of the fact that the coachman was half in and half out of the vehicle himself. She threw herself into her grandmother's arms, hugging and crying and kissing her face. Anne and Charlotte, sitting across with Annie, flung themselves on Barbara, and the Duchess was covered with crying, twisting, squirming grandchildren. She did not say a word, but her face softened and she patted and hugged whatever body she could grasp.

"Anne, Charlotte," Barbara sobbed. "I am so g-glad to see you!"

"I love you, Bab. I am never leaving you again," Anne said. "Move, Charlotte! You are squishing me!"

"Am not!"

"Are, too! Grandmama! Charlotte is—"

"Let us all get out of this carriage immediately! Anne, Charlotte, let John help you down. Barbara—" Here the Duchess, with a quick movement, patted Barbara's face lovingly. She had been about to tell her to move, but she did not. She wanted to keep the girl by her. What had they been doing to her? She was as thin as a stick, and that was an ugly bruise fading from her face, a bruise that had caused a black eye, now also fading. By God in His heaven above, there were some heads that would roll for it!

Somehow, they all tumbled out. Anne and Charlotte were each carried in a footman's arms. Annie walked ahead of the procession like an irritable handmaiden to the Queen of Egypt. (Bates had been unable to take his eyes from her. She was as irritable, as proud, as wonderful as ever. He worshiped her with his eyes. She gave him one sweeping glance to note whether or not he was still her slave, saw that he was, and jerked her head for him to see about her duty in life, the Duchess.) One of Annie's hands grasped the Duchess's faded, leather jewel case, the other a struggling Dulcinea. Finally came the Duchess, leaning on Bates and Barbara.

"Where are the boys?" asked Barbara.

"There was not room for them in the carriage. I left them at home to oversee the Christmas celebrations, though doubtless I will return to find my house burned to the ground. I promised them I would send for them for your wedding."

"There is no wedding, Grandmama."

"Madam," Bates was saying, his joy at having his Annie here making him fulsome and talkative, "I am inexpressibly delighted to see you. You are looking well."

"Be quiet, Bates," rapped out the Duchess. "You are talking too much. Save it for Annie. As if she would have anything to do with you."

"Yes, madam. Oh, madam, it is so good to have you here—watch your step."

"I can still see, man! You watch your step, Bates. My Annie will have you cut down to size before this day is done."

"Yes, madam," Bates agreed joyfully.

"Grandmama," said Tony at the doorway. "Welcome. To my home. To your home, Grandmama."

The Duchess felt tears start, tears that she should be entering this house after five years, this house where she and Richard had lived and loved and been at their zenith. This house, where Richard had lain dead in the great parlor, while all London walked by for one last view of him. She had allowed London its view. Then she had taken him to Tamworth to be buried. The queen had wanted Westminster Abbey, but Tamworth, his favorite residence, was good enough for the first duke. And there she would lie beside him in their eternal tomb when her turn came.

They led her into the hall, where the rest of the family stood waiting, assembled at one end of the black and white marble floor like soldiers waiting for the drums to sound their march into battle. Yes, thought the Duchess, wiping fiercely at her eyes, this house brings too many memories back, but I am here now, and you will all of you pay for your unkindness to my girl.

Fanny crossed the space first, with Harold following. She kissed her grandmother softly on each cheek.

"Fanny, you pretty thing," said the Duchess. Out of the corner of her eye, she could see that Abigail and Diana still had not moved. She poked Tony in the ribs.

"You are still too fat, boy. Your mother feeds you too much. Remind me to give you my recipe for elderberry tea. It will curb that appetite."

"Yes, Grandmama." It did not hurt Tony that his grandmother's first words to him were criticism. They always had been; they always would be. He had accepted his inferiority long ago. Mary moved from behind the skirts of her mother, closer and closer to the two girls hiding behind Annie. She was drawn like a magnet to them. The Duchess, her grandmother, glared at her with bright, dark eyes, but said nothing.

Abigail, who had been standing with the stunned stillness of someone who has had a great shock—she was looking at the two young girls half hiding behind Annie, at the restless, impatient, huge, white cat in Annie's arms, at the baggage the footmen kept unloading in her hall—suddenly jerked forward like someone pulled by unseen strings.

She swept forward grandly and touched the Duchess's cheeks with her own. "Mother Saylor, what a pleasant surprise. I—"

"I am cold, Abigail, and I am tired. See that these two minx here are fed at once and put to bed. Anne, Charlotte, come forward and make your greetings to your aunt . . . and to your mother. Well, Diana, am I not even to have a greeting from you?"

There was a silence in the hallway. Very slowly, Diana glided forward. She had a sensual, swaying walk that made her skirts swirl softly, when she chose to use it. Harold could not take his eyes from her hips, but Diana's eyes were on her mother as she walked forward. They shifted once to Barbara, who was looking at her grandmother, and did not see her.

"Mother," she said, when she finally reached the Duchess. "This is a surprise." She leaned forward and kissed the Duchess's cheek.

"Yes," snapped the Duchess, "I imagine it is."

Anne and Charlotte made quick curtsies to Diana, who never even looked at them. They scuttled back behind Annie's skirts, and their movement startled Dulcinea, who leapt from Annie's arms straight toward Diana. She landed on Diana's shoulder, clawed downward until she reached her skirts. Beads of bright blood popped up on Diana's forearm as Dulcinea skittered downward.

"My arm!" she cried, trying to shake the cat from her skirts.

Dulcinea ran around and around the hallway, searching. Finally, she stood still, appealed to the Duchess for understanding by meowing once, and daintily but thoroughly relieved herself on the white of a marble square. The sharp odor of cat urine and feces filled the hall. Aware that everyone's eyes were on her, Dulcinea stalked over to the Duchess and mewed complainingly. The Duchess scooped her up.

"Abigail," she said. "I am going to my rooms now. See that my bed is set up immediately. It is among those bundles. The

marble in this hallway is dull, Abigail. I will give your housekeeper a recipe to restore it to its proper shine. Tony, give me
your arm. I must have a rest. Barbara, I shall want to talk
to you after my nap. Give me another kiss, child, so that I
may sleep well."

People began to disperse right and left. Footmen were carrying in trunks and wrapped furniture from the luggage cart.
Mary had finally made her move and was smiling shyly at
Anne and Charlotte, who smiled back. The two of them followed her up the stairs behind the Duchess. Annie barked
orders right and left to the footmen. Bates stood nearby, staring at Annie, with what could only be called an adoring
expression on his face. Abigail watched the controlled pandemonium of her house. Fanny and Harold were whispering
to each other, Fanny's whispers sounded like the sharp hisses
of an irate goose. Barbara started up the stairs, but Diana
caught her by the arm. She swung around to meet the lovely,
violet, cold eyes of her mother.

"You are cleverer than I gave you credit for," said Diana.

Barbara said nothing, but ran up the stairs after her sisters
and Mary.

CHAPTER SIX

he Duchess lay now in her bed, the bed she had brought
from Tamworth, which had been assembled in one of the
huge state apartments, a series of three rooms, all connected,
once used for visits from royalty. The bedchamber had been
cleared of most of its usual furniture and replaced with that
brought by the Duchess. A portrait of the duke, *the* portrait
of the duke, was now hanging in a spot where she could see
it at all times. She had hobbled about the rooms—the long,
uncomfortable, cold journey had started her legs aching
again—inspecting every corner and muttering to herself as
footmen carried in trunks and assembled furniture and carried out other furniture and as chambermaids lit the fire and
smoothed fresh sheets on the bed and unpacked trunks. She
opened one of the intricately carved bookcase doors and ran
her fingers along the spines of the books inside. No dust
appeared on her finger, but there were several spots of mildew on the book spines.

"Book mold!" she said aloud.

She went to the windows to look outside; a drop of candle
wax on the velvet draperies caught her eye. She touched it
with a bony finger. "They are letting this house rot to pieces,"
she said to the window.

At long last, her bed was together and made, and she lay
in it. Servants still scurried in and out, one to make sure
Charlotte and Anne had hot soup—she had a recipe which the
cook could make up on the spot—another to make her special

tea to soothe her nerves, another to tell Abigail and Diana that she was too tired to see them tonight, but that she would speak with them tomorrow, one to tell the housekeeper that she wished to tour the house, from top to bottom, in the morning. Annie had dressed her in her nightgown, unpacked her jewel case and was downstairs in the servants' hall. By tomorrow morning, she would have all the gossip.

Late evening tea was being drunk when Bates ushered Annie into the hall. Bates, his pouter-pigeon chest thrust out even farther than normal, if such a thing was possible, led her to his chair, the best chair, by the fire. It was obvious to all the servants that this thin, ugly woman was important. The housekeeper immediately poured a cup of tea; the cook begged that she try some of his special lemon tea cakes, kept in a tin and reserved for special occasions, such as this one. Annie accepted all the homage as if it were her due, as it was. She was the personal dresser, reader, soother and confidante of the great Duchess of Tamworth. She had been with the family for years, knew its secrets, good and bad, and kept them. The younger servants were each introduced, then sent back to their corners while the older servants gathered around Annie. To them, she was a symbol of those years when the duke was alive, and this had been his chief residence, filled with the most important people in London. When the duke died, and the Duchess packed her personal possessions and turned the house over to her grandson and his mother, it had been the end of an era.

Once tea was drunk, a few of the chosen settled themselves about the fire, about Annie. Bates brought in a bottle of wine from the cellar. It was opened. Reminiscences began. Younger servants crept closer to listen, to listen to those times when this had been the most famous house in London. King William and Queen Mary had visited it on Sundays for tea and games of cards. How exciting it had been when their coach, preceded by a few Dutch and English guardsmen in their dashing scarlet uniforms, pulled into the courtyard. The people of London had regularly lined up outside in the street to cheer or boo the coach as it passed, depending on the latest news of the war in Europe. And Princess Anne always called on the Duchess's reception day with her favorite lady-in-waiting, Sarah Churchill. She was still calling when she became queen.

When Dicken had died, for weeks afterward, the porters found bunches of rosemary tied in black crepe on the outside gates. It was the same for William's death a year later. The duke, campaigning with General Marlborough in Europe, had come home with those pieces of his son's body which could be found. He was changing; it was the Duchess who was the strong one; each death bent her body, but not her spirit. It was she who encouraged the duke not to retire, to keep soldiering. He was needed in the war against that great tyrant, the French King Louis XIV.

And two years later, the people of London surrounded the outside gates, this time wreathing them in flowers, crying and cheering the Duchess as she appeared at an upstairs window to wave at them after the news of the great battle of Lille and the duke's part in it. Queen Anne and the Duchess had ridden through the streets in the queen's carriage, while crowds tossed flowers and cheered. The house was filled with visitors from morning until night as the Duchess held court in her husband's place. But then Giles died, and the duke had come home. Everyone could see he was ill. And the Duchess had taken him to Tamworth Hall. The great house in Pall Mall was now empty most of the time. The servants waited, lived for those days when the Duchess, alone, would come up from Tamworth. The duke never came back, not until the Duchess brought his body to lie in state at Saylor House for three days so that hundreds of people might file past it, paying their last respects to England's most beloved hero, a man known for his kindness, his honesty, his fairness, his generosity. The servants had worked themselves to the bone, a last gesture toward their beloved master. Every china plate sparkled, every piece of silver shone. The house was at its most magnificent. The tables groaned with roasted meats, with stews and ragouts, with pies and jellies and tarts. Every room, every window, every door was draped with black crepe. Every important guest was offered food, rest, and asked to sign the mourning book. The house ran effortlessly, efficiently, as the Duchess had always wished it.

She assembled them afterward, when the last guest was gone, and the duke's body was in a waiting hearse pulled by six horses, wearing black feathers in their harness. She thanked them for their service and loyalty. She shook each of their hands, gave them money from her own purse, remembered everyone's name. She said she would understand if any of them wished to leave, even though she hoped they would give the same loyalty and service to the new young duke. And they had stayed. Their loyalty was to the house, as well as to the family. Saylor House was as much theirs as it was the Tamworths'. They loved it. It was home.

The hall was quiet now. Annie had grown soft with the wine and memories. The housekeeper wiped at her eyes. They all shook their heads for the good old days, while those younger servants who had stayed to listen stood up, yawned, rolled their eyes at such open sentimentality, and went to bed. Annie promised the housekeeper she would give her the Duchess's treasured recipes for washing white lace and mending china. The housekeeper nodded. Soon, in return, she would tell Annie all she knew of the present crisis with Mistress Barbara and Lady Diana, as would Bates and the senior footman and cook. It was not something to discuss in front of the younger, newer servants, who had not the old loyalties. But among the few who cared, the family upstairs was their family also. And Mistress Barbara had won hearts with her lively spirits and kindness to little Mary.

The Duchess lay thinking in her bed, the pillows all packed behind her and her huge, favorite lace nightcap, the one that resembled a limp pancake, on her head. One hand stroked Dulcinea, who was tired after her confinement in the carriage with two noisy children and after the humiliation of having to perform natural functions in a marble hallway. The other hand stroked Barbara's red-gold hair, brushed to shining vitality by Annie herself. The girl was asleep in her white, virginal nightgown, her hair spread out over the pillow, one hand clutching the edge of her grandmother's gown. The first sight of Barbara's thin, bruised face had been almost more than the Duchess could bear. She had had to hold on to herself with all her control not to tear Diana and Abigail to pieces then and there. But that would come later, when she knew more of the story than Barbara's version, told to her tonight in sobs.

"Well, young lady!" she had snapped, irritation covering her love and worry and aided by the pain in her legs. "I understand you have been conducting yourself in a thoroughly unbecoming manner!" Thinking to herself, as she watched Barbara's face, Did I give the chit too much freedom? Did I not train her properly? Sweet Jesus, is this yet another mistake I have made?

Bits and pieces of the story tumbled from Barbara's lips; she spared no one, least of all herself. "There I was, Grandmama! At—at his door. And I w-w-went inside. Oh, I know I should have been beaten, more so than M-M-Mother did, but oh, Grandm-m-mama, I love him so-o-o. He is s-so kind. Please make it right! I k-know you can!"

The Duchess had never seen her granddaughter so distraught, so unlike herself, as she sobbed helplessly into her thin hands. Gone was the happy, confident child she had given to Diana, and in its place was this.

"I-I do not know what is the matter with me," Barbara was saying. She tried to wipe away the tears that kept streaming down her face. "I will do what you s-say of course, Grandmama." And she had lain sobbing against the Duchess's chest while the Duchess stroked her hair and thought. So the financial arrangements had gone awry, had they? So Barbara had gone to see Roger on her own, had she? A shocking thing to do.

If she had not looked so pitiful and been crying so hard, the Duchess would have caned her for it herself. But, instead, she found herself only sighing inside, at the heat and impulsiveness of youth. At Barbara's naiveté. At her own lack of moral fiber. Tomorrow she would summon the cook and prepare a special menu for Barbara. Some flesh had to go back on that child's bones. She would tour the house. And she would hear what the others involved had to say for themselves. She would even go see Roger—though not tomorrow. No. Not yet. She smiled at the thought of that, at the surprise and dismay of the others . . . Abigail, Diana, possibly Tony, if he had the brains to be part of it all. If it were not for Barbara's heartbreak, she would have enjoyed watching them squirm before her. Sweet Jesus, how she hated double dealing. It was something she had learned from Richard, who had despised lying and deceit. She had adopted his standards as her own, but she had not his inherent sweetness, his love of his fellowman, to temper her. She was like an avenging goddess, without mercy. She knew it, and did not care.

The only one person who mattered in this entire mess was Barbara, her most beloved, her most dear granddaughter. It did not matter what Diana or Abigail or even Roger thought. Dear Lord above, it did not even matter that Barbara had gone to see Roger without a chaperone. I am old, thought the Duchess, that I should no longer care for society's standards, standards I raised my own children on. But she did not. She loved Barbara with all her heart. Barbara was a gift the sweet Lord above had given her to help her mend over Richard. And she was going to do whatever she had to to make sure her granddaughter was happy. And woe to the man, woman or child who tried to stop her. She felt better immediately, acknowledging that so clearly in her mind. It made her ruthlessness easier. Her mind relaxed somewhat, as she lay between her sleeping cat and her sleeping grandchild. Sleep was hovering, its great, black, soft cape extended, on the edge of her mind. She was dropping off, and it seemed to her that Richard—not the kind, gentle stranger who had lived with her the last four years of his life—but Richard the man, Richard her lover, young, handsome, ardent, was in the room with her, sitting on the bed, watching over her as she drifted off. It is this house, she thought on the edge of sleep. Our house of glory. And she fell asleep with a smile on her face.

By the next morning, long before Diana and Abigail were even stirring in their beds, she had been on a secret inspection of the house (Abigail was not the manager she had been, servants were getting slothful, her visit would do them good) and had Annie carefully writing notes, notes that would be delivered throughout London this afternoon by several of Abigail's underfootmen, telling friends and acquaintances that the Duchess of Tamworth was in town and would be receiving visitors. By tomorrow, the door would be sounding constantly with messages, flowers and invitations, all for her. She might be retired, but she was a retired somebody. And it was time Abigail was reminded of that. This afternoon, she was going to round up her young granddaughters, Barbara, Mary, Anne and Charlotte, and go over to St. James's Palace. She had a feeling that his majesty, even though busy, would take time to see her, and she was furious that Barbara had not yet been formally presented at court. This would be no formal presentation, but it would be a reminder of whom Barbara was related to. After that, they would stop at the New Exchange and buy New Year's gifts. Tomorrow was New Year's Day, and the Duchess had no gifts for family and friends. Except for the one or two that she would be giving Diana and Abigail over the next few days. Now she waited for Tony. She had a few words she wished to say to him.

"Grandmama," he said hesitantly, as he crossed the room to her chair.

She sighed as she watched him. He had none of his father's or his grandfather's handsomeness. This was the second Duke of Tamworth, heir to all she and Richard had amassed. This boy had taken Dicken's inheritance, had taken Dicken's baby son's inheritance. Abigail's fair, stupid boy, the least of her grandchildren. The race is not to the swift, nor the battle to the strong, she thought to herself, looking at Tony. Neither yet bread to the wise, nor yet riches to men of understanding, nor yet favor to men of skill; but time and chance happeneth to them all. . . . I have not been kind to him, she thought. Richard would have been kind. . . .

"Grandmama. Are you well?"

"Of course I am well. Do not just stand there staring at me. Give me a kiss. Here!"

She touched her lips imperiously with her fingers. Gravely, Tony leaned forward and kissed her. Then he stepped back quickly, as if he expected to be caned for it.

"Sit down," she snapped. "Barbara told me what you did for her, boy. I am grateful. Grateful and touched. And surprised. Is there more to you than I thought?"

"No, Grandmama. I am sure there is not." His surprise betrayed him into complete sentences.

"Nonsense. There must be. You are Richard Saylor's grandson. The least of them, perhaps, but his grandson, nonetheless. I want to thank you for your care of Barbara. I would have thought you so under your mother's thumb that you would not say boo to a goose. I was wrong about you, boy. I freely admit it. I am proud of you, Tony. You acted like a gentleman. You acted like the best of Richard Saylor's grandsons!"

Tony's face had gotten redder and redder with each word. He mumbled something, out of which the Duchess understood only "Did what I should" and "Love Barbara, also."

She stared at him with narrowed eyes. What did he mean? Could he . . . had he . . . had her Barbara captured Tony's heart, the heart his mother kept in safekeeping, under lock and key?

"Speak up, boy," she snapped. "Spit it out."

"Love Barbara, Grandmama," he got out. "Have for weeks. Almost since I first saw her. Would marry her if Devane will not. Damn fool if he does not."

Sweet Jesus in his heaven above, thought the Duchess, what have we here! Tony and Barbara. They were cousins, but it was legal. And it would make Barbara the Duchess of Tamworth. But then, there was Tony as the duke.

"How does your mother feel about this?"

Tony looked down at the buckles on his shoes.

"I see," said the Duchess. "You know Barbara has deep . . . feelings for Lord Devane, do you not?"

Tony nodded his head and in a surprising burst of eloquence said, "It does not matter. I do not blame her. He is a handsome man. Elegant. Everything I am not. But I love her, Grandmama, and I could take care of her. I would."

"Tony." The Duchess smiled at him. "Give me another kiss. You are your father's son after all. No, I will not give you permission to court her yet. It is too soon. But I love you for it. Now go away."

Abigail wiped at the perspiration on her palms once again. In one hour, she had fifteen guests arriving to celebrate the arrival of the New Year. Since six this evening, the knocking at her door had not stopped. And each time it was something for the Duchess: flowers, presents, invitations, red roses from the king himself. How did they know she was in town when she had only arrived day before yesterday? And she had had to spend thirty minutes this afternoon listening to her housekeeper explain that she did the best she could and that if the Duchess of Tamworth was not satisfied she would, of course, resign. This, before an evening party! And it seemed that Anne and Charlotte and Mary (Mary!) had gotten into the kitchen and eaten most of the candied fruit prepared for this evening, and the cook had taken twenty minutes of her time swearing that he would not work in such a disorganized household and moaning that his supper buffet was ruined.

She had soothed the housekeeper and the cook. She had sent for the three little girls and talked severely to them, spasms she could not control crossing her face each time she looked at Anne and Charlotte. When she had rung for her footman to deliver a message, she had found that he was busy delivering for the Duchess—again. The Duchess had been gone all yesterday afternoon with Barbara and the girls without a word as to where she was going. But she had found time to reduce her housekeeper to jelly and to talk with Tony. And now Abigail was summoned, an hour before her first guest. She wiped at her hands again and surveyed herself in the mirror. She looked regal, majestic, mature. She wore a dark blue velvet gown, with white lace at the neck and sleeves. Her bosom swelled up satisfactorily, and her sapphires glittered handsomely there. She had done what she thought was correct, done the best for all concerned. She had merely suggested that Roger's terms might not be fair. Nothing more, nothing less. She had offered to find a younger, better husband. She had been—quite naturally—offended by Barbara's conduct. But she had never raised a hand against her. She had nothing to blame herself for. Nothing. Surely, Tony's feelings for Barbara were the result of proximity. They would fade when the girl returned to Tamworth with her grandmother. Thank God the Duchess knew nothing about it. Abigail wiped again at the perspiration on her hands. She had nothing to blame herself for. She had done the best for all concerned, as she always did.

"I only did what I thought was best, Mother Saylor," she said, standing before the Duchess, regal and calm in her blue gown, her soft, fleshy face betraying nothing of what she was feeling. It irked her that the Duchess should be seated like a queen, that she should have to walk across the room and wait until the Duchess spoke to her, for all the world as if she were a schoolgirl. But she betrayed none of her irritation. That would be playing into the Duchess's hand. She explained her position calmy and rationally. Montgeoffry was so much older. His reputation was dissolute. She felt that Barbara would be overwhelmed by his way of life, that she might be corrupted.

"And Bentwoodes!" snapped the Duchess.

"Bentwoodes?" echoed Abigail, not by so much as a blink indicating the sinking feeling in the pit of her stomach.

"You had no interest in Bentwoodes, then?" asked the
Duchess, her dark, snapping eyes on Abigail like two small
searching beacons. Abigail tried to ignore the feeling that they
could see to the bottom of her soul. She carefully explained
that she had merely made a suggestion that Diana do a little
more research, that she not undersell the land. Nothing more,
nothing less. She had no personal interest in the land. None
at all. She had tried to do her duty toward her niece. Sur-
reptitiously, she wiped her hands on the sides of her gown,
still managing to look at her mother-in-law serenely.

"What will happen to Bentwoodes now, do you think, Abigail?"

She shrugged. It was, of course, none of her affair. The land
was worthless undeveloped. Diana ought to sell it and use the
cash to finance Barbara's—

"If the land is worthless, why did you not encourage Diana
to snap at Roger's offer?"

She wanted Diana to get the most for the land, knowing as
she did Diana's financial situation. She never meant for the
negotiations to falter. But again, she was not too upset,
because she had never felt Roger Montgeoffry was a man her
niece ought to marry. He was too—

"Thank you, Abigail," the Duchess interrupted. "Inform
Diana I am too tired to see her tonight. Give your guests my
regards and tell them I wish them a prosperous New Year. I
will not come downstairs tonight."

The Duchess sat back. Abigail, for all her greedy, managing ways, had a sense of duty. Roger might not be the husband for Barbara, whatever his riches. That snippet of gossip
had come to her mind again. Ridiculous, but in the old days,
he had gone from one woman to the next, kind, laughing,
charming, but unfaithful nonetheless. Diana said he had settled. Who knew? It might be better for Barbara that she not
marry the man. He was too old for her. Too old to change.
Now that the marriage seemed to be botched, perhaps, after
all, it was the Lord's will. Perhaps she ought to take Barbara
back to Tamworth with her and live with her tears and sulks
for a year.

There was a scratching at the door. Annie, glancing at the
Duchess, who looked tired, shook her head, but the Duchess
gestured that she should open it. Barbara came in, a tissue-

wrapped package in her hand. Already, today, to the Duchess's eye she looked better. Still thin, but more light to her face, though, when she did not realize her grandmother was watching, the Duchess had seen such a stricken look in her eyes that it had pierced her to the heart. She opened her arms, and Barbara ran and hugged her.

"Do you go to Abigail's party?" She patted Barbara's thin face fondly.

Barbara shook her head. "I am still in disgrace in Aunt's eyes, and, in truth, Grandmama, I do not feel much like celebrating. I will make my curtsies to the guests, and retire with Mary and Anne and Charlotte. I came here to give you your gift early. Already, gifts are piled up for you, and I knew mine would be lost in all the others. Here, Grandmama. Happy New Year."

The Duchess opened the rustling tissue. Inside was a pair of gloves, so soft they felt like rose petals, dyed a dark, forest green.

"Smell them, Grandmama."

The Duchess held them to her nose. They were scented with essence of jasmine.

"It is Roger's favorite scent, Grandmama."

Roger. The Duchess laid down the gloves. She gestured for Barbara to lean forward and held her face in her hands, kissing each cheek and staring into the girl's eyes before she released her.

"Your grandmother is tired," Annie grumbled from her chair nearby.

"Go away, Annie," said the Duchess. "I must speak privately with Barbara." They waited until Annie closed the door behind her. Then Barbara turned, eyes shining with such expectation in them that the Duchess was taken aback.

"What if I told you, Barbara, that I thought it best to leave everything as it is . . ." Before she could finish her sentence, Barbara went down on her knees before her.

"No, Grandmama! I love him so. I will die without him! I will!"

"You do not know him, child!" she said, taking Barbara's hands in hers. Great tears were welling up in the corners of Barbara's eyes. She shook her head stubbornly.

"Let him go to France," the Duchess urged. "You come back to Tamworth with me. I will arrange for an exchange of letters between you. That will give you time to know if—"

"If he goes away, I will lose him, Grandmama! I know that in my deepest heart. And if I lose him, I think I will die."

She was silent. This girl before her was someone she did not know anymore. Once, she had known every corner of her heart. Or had she? It frightened her, to see the depth, the sincerity of Barbara's emotion. There was obviously only one solution Barbara wanted. Last night, it had seemed easy. Tonight, Abigail's objections raised doubts. A woman belonged to her husband, body, soul, property, once they married. If he was a drunkard, a sadistic madman, a lecher, a brute, a wife bore her lot as best she could. Caring parents tried to choose a sane, sensible man who would be good to their daughters in the long term. Many, however, simply sold their girls to the highest bidder, the one with the fanciest title and the most money. It was a contest the parents waged, seeing who could make the best bargain for their time and money. Staring at Barbara's tearstained face, the Duchess was reminded unpleasantly of the young Diana, so many years ago, pleading for her Kit.

"Please, Grandmama! Please! I know you can fix it."

"Bah! Go away, Bab. You have made me tired with all your tears."

Tired and frightened. She had come here to do the best for her girl, but now she was not sure what was the best. Obviously only seeing Roger himself could decide her. She was tired, and her legs, those traitors, those constant reminders of her age and frailty, were beginning to ache. She had been too active today, hopping about as if she were a young girl. She would pay for it tonight and tomorrow. She would have to remain in bed nearly all day. But that was good. She needed the respite.

All across the City of London and Westminster, church bells began to ring out the news of the approaching new year of Our Lord, 1716. The bells would ring tonight at midnight, and tomorrow, to celebrate New Year's Day. Everyone who could afford it would be wearing new clothes, as they attended the king's reception or visited friends and relatives to play cards and deliver New Year's gifts. When the hour of

midnight struck, doors throughout the city would swing open
as people unbarred them to let out the old and bring in the
new. Everyone would watch for signs of the new year's luck:
the first person to enter a house on the new year was a sign,
good luck if it was a dark-haired man, bad luck if it was a
woman. Bibles would be dragged from their boxes, as family
members dipped, an old-fashioned custom of randomly picking a verse from the Bible to indicate the year's luck.

Roger and his friends were gathered about a huge, silver
wassail bowl. In it was the traditional "lamb's wool": ale,
nutmeg, sugar, toast and roasted apples. A garland of rosemary and bay and blue and gold ribbons was twisted around
its base. Walpole and Carlyle, White and Montrose, Townshend and his wife, Catherine Walpole, the Duke and Duchess
of Montagu, and Carr Hervey lifted up cups of the steaming
ale and cried, "Wass hael," ancient Saxon for "To your
health." The meaning was forgotten, but the gesture was part
of heritage. Everyone was already a little drunk, and by midnight they would be drunker still. Catherine Walpole tried to
catch Roger's eye, but he was talking to her husband. She
turned to Carr Hervey, who was smiling at her, and lifted her
cup. Silently, they toasted a new year to each other. No one
mentioned Roger's failed plans. He seemed not to care at all.
Bentwoodes might never have existed. All his talk was of
France.

"I might be gone for years," Roger told his friends. "I might
explore the whole world."

"That is the lamb's wool talking," said Walpole.

"That is disappointment," said Carlyle, but no one was listening to him.

Barbara sat on her bed. The bells were ringing. Her Bible,
especially made for her at her confirmation, lay open on the
bed. It was covered with soft, scrolled, embossed leather, and
the arms of Tamworth and Alderley were engraved on the
front and back covers, and in gold on the front pages. Mary,
Charlotte and Anne, all wide-eyed, sat on her bed. She had
promised them, in her happiness of the afternoon, that tonight
at midnight, they would dip. Now she felt like doing nothing,
except lying on her bed. There was such a weight on her heart
that it hurt each time it beat. If she lived through this, she

would never, never love again. It was too painful. If she lived through this, it did not matter whom they married her to. It would be years and years before she recovered.

"Bab, it is Mary's turn," Charlotte said.

Barbara handed the Bible to Mary, who shut her eyes tightly, fumbled with the pages and finally jabbed her finger down.

" 'Blessed are the meek,'" Barbara read for her, " 'for they shall inherit the earth.'"

Mary looked disappointed. Anne's verse had had the word "whore" in it, which had shocked and titillated everyone. Charlotte's had mentioned "fire and snakes," which they found fascinating.

"You now, Bab. You," said Charlotte.

Barbara closed her eyes and fumbled with the pages and jabbed her finger down.

"'Vanity of vanities, saith the preacher; all is vanity.'"

She could barely finish reading out the words. Her throat closed. She could not help it. She did not want to disappoint them in their New Year's fun, but she lay back on the bed and put her arm over her eyes. The three other girls looked at one another. Roger, Mary mouthed silently. The other two nodded. The three of them were half in love with Roger themselves simply because their Barbara was. Anne crawled over and pulled Barbara's head into her lap.

"I love you, Bab," she said softly. She wiped the tears from Barbara's cheeks.

Mary and Charlotte each took a hand and patted it. Barbara felt the tears trickling down the corners of her eyes into Anne's lap. How could anything hurt the way this did? Just a few months ago, she had watched Jane cry and not understood it. She had been a child then. And now she was not. Oh, Roger, she thought. It is going to take me so long not to love you anymore.

The Duchess lay in her bed, Dulcinea, as usual, curled beside her. Every now and then she could hear laughter and shrieks. Abigail's party guests must be into their third bowl of lamb's wool. The New Year, 1716. Memories filled her the way the lamb's wool filled Abigail's guests. Over five years now that Richard was gone. Barbara had been a little girl.

Now she was a woman. With a woman's heart and a woman's needs. Children, a home—if she were fortunate, a husband she could love. But that happened to so few people. She and Richard had been special. Dear sweet Jesus, how special. Lying here tonight in this bed, she could see the young Richard in her mind's eye the first time she had ever seen him. What had she been doing? She was at court, yes, and she was in a walled courtyard. It must have been spring. Blue sky, and birds singing and green trees were there in her memory. She was eighteen. Unmarried. Comforting a child. Yes, that was it. Some boys had been picking on a younger boy, and she had seen it, and with a sudden fierce surge of temper (she had been a fierce girl—prickly, bad-tempered, angry—because her mirror had showed a plain woman, when her heart longed to be beautiful, as her mother had been) she had chased away the boys, and was kneeling down, comforting the child, almost crying herself, so in sympathy did she feel, and she sensed someone was staring at her. She looked up, her head jerking, to see from one of the buildings around the courtyard a young man looking down at her. He was smiling, and his smile was beautiful, kind . . . tender. She had leapt up and walked away, taking a confused impression of a handsome mouth, a wide nose, full cheeks, a man any woman would look twice at.

It was her first sight of him. And his first of her. Two years later, she would marry him. He was a fortune hunter, relatives warned. She was a fool. They laughed and whispered and talked behind her back. She was marrying beneath her, said others. Her father had been astounded. And angry. And finally agreeable. Her father, who trusted no one, had grown to love Richard as if he were his own son. Her father said that he would rebuild their fortune and power and she . . . what? She saw ambition and honesty combined, but the truth was she was already half in love. Her girlfriends had been married for five and six years and were mothers of children. The truth was she longed to bed him. The first time he kissed her, his mouth on hers was fire and honey. She had known from that moment that she must be careful. She must not let him have too much power over her. But he had loved her. That was his power. . . .

And what did her Barbara want? A man, just as she had wanted Richard. But by the time she married him, she had begun to know what he was: fine, honest, loyal. Barbara knew no such thing of Roger. Yet her heart longed for him. And perhaps the Duchess should trust that heart. Time would tell. She wished that Barbara were older, that Roger were younger, that Richard were here to talk to. But Richard would be old, old now. The man she had buried talked of his roses and his shrubs. He visited his sons' tombs daily, and he cried. How many times had Perryman had to go and find him and gently lead him home? That man could not have helped her. No one could. She would have to trust in herself, and in the Lord. There was nothing else left.

She had asked the key members to assemble in the library. It was the afternoon of New Year's Day. She had made her decision. Or, at least part of it. The rest depended on Roger. Whose turn was next. She sat waiting for them, one hand stroking Dulcinea, who was content for the moment to lie in her lap. The library was a small room off the huge gallery that crossed the entire north front of the third floor of the house. Row upon row of small, leather-bound books marched in straight lines across the shelves. Richard had taken great pride in assembling his books. In one corner was a built-in set of drawers with a flap that let down, turning it into a writing desk. Now, hardly anyone used this room. Tony was not the reader and collector that his grandfather had been, and Abigail had other interests. The fire burning in the charcoal brazier that had been brought in to warm the room up could not disguise its musty smell. The Duchess sat near the built-in set of drawers. She had unfastened the flap and was running her hand over and over her own name, Alice, that Richard had carved into the desk flap with his penknife. A stupid, foolish, schoolboy thing for a man in his forties to do. . . .

Someone coughed nervously. Dulcinea jumped from her lap and walked over to Sir Percy Wilcoxen, senior member of a firm that had served the Saylors for years. Sir Percy had a wart on the end of his nose and a dry, pinched face. Dulcinea wound herself around his legs. He coughed again. The Duchess motioned for him to sit down. He did so, and Dulcinea jumped into his lap. He patted her perfunctorily, then pushed her down, but she jumped back. Abigail, Tony and Diana appeared, all looking heavy-eyed. Too much lamb's wool. The Duchess, however, felt well, fit. She had stayed in bed all day, opening her letters. Everyone wanted to see her: Louisa, Lizzie, Sarah Churchill, Lady Chesterfield, Mrs. Clayton. And there were presents: fans, rouge boxes, packages of pins, bouquets of flowers, perfume, ribbons. She had quite enjoyed herself.

The Duchess waited until bows and handshakes and greetings were finished. Everyone was seated, watching her. Sensing where all eyes would be focused, Dulcinea went to the Duchess.

"You have the document, Diana?" the Duchess asked. An air of expectancy filled the room.

Diana nodded. She made no move to give the paper, a piece of folded, yellowish parchment she was holding in her hand, to her mother. Abigail was watching the Duchess with a paralyzed fascination.

The Duchess held out her hand. Diana stared at that hand. Then she leaned forward slowly and put the paper in it. It was clear to everyone in the room that she had no wish to do so. The Duchess handed the paper to Wilcoxen, who glanced at it, coughed, and then read it aloud.

"'I, Alice Margaret Constance Verney Saylor, Baroness Verney, Countess of Peshall, and Duchess of Tamworth, do hereby give the land called Bentwoodes to my granddaughter, Barbara Alice Constance Alderley, to be used as dower to her marriage. Signed this seventh day of November, 1715, in the presence of Annie Smith and James Perryman.'" He coughed again and stopped. The Duchess held out her hand, and after a moment, in which Abigail and Diana both held their respective breaths, he handed it to her. Dulcinea turned over on her back and batted at the paper.

"The land," the Duchess said clearly, "belongs to Barbara. Not to you, Diana, nor to you, Abigail, nor to you, Tony."

"G-Grandmama," stammered Tony, "I have no interest in it!"

Abigail closed her eyes a moment, as if praying for patience. There was a soft knock on the door, and at the Duchess's command, Barbara entered the room. She went at once to stand behind her grandmother. Now everyone's eyes were on her. Interest in the paper faded.

"Bab," the Duchess said in softer tones, "I have just been saying that this piece of paper"—she waved the piece of parchment—"deeds Bentwoodes to you. Is that not so, Wilcoxen?"

"Ah, yes. Yes, indeed." Wilcoxen stopped, clearly unable by nature and profession to commit himself further.

"Do you wish to sell this land . . . to, say, your aunt, Barbara?" the Duchess asked. Abigail bit her lip. Tony watched his mother with puzzled eyes.

"No," Barbara said, "I do not."

"Do you wish to give the land back to me? I am within my legal rights, am I not, Wilcoxen? I deeded the land to Barbara as a dower; it has not been used so."

Wilcoxen cleared his throat. All four women were staring at him. He had the look of a man set unexpectedly amid a group of lionesses—just as the ones that were at the Tower in the zoo, lean, spare, cruel beasts that could tear out a man's heart with one swift bite—lionesses staring at him with steady eyes, each one ready, willing, capable of devouring him. But of them all, the Duchess herself was the most formidable. He cleared his throat.

"Ah. Yes. Well, your grace, as to that—"

"As to that," interrupted Abigail, "Barbara is under age—"

"No," the Duchess snapped. "She is fifteen. The age of consent is twelve for a girl."

"For marriage only, Mother Saylor, is she a woman," Abigail said. "She can have no say as to where that land goes. Diana, as her guardian, must decide."

"Which of us is correct, Wilcoxen?"

"Ah, yes, well. Both of you have made salient points, your grace. There is precedence on both sides. Mistress Alderley being female . . . of course, that is . . ."

With one swift movement, the Duchess tore the paper in half, then into fourths, then into eighths. Abigail gasped. Wilcoxen coughed. Tony stared. Barbara put her hand to her mouth. Dulcinea batted wildly at the pieces drifting to the floor. Only Diana was cool and motionless, watching her mother without a single movement.

"I take back my gift," the Duchess said. "If you want it now, you will have to sue me for it."

"Never do that, Grandmama," Tony said quickly. Abigail bit her lip.

"What—what does that mean?" Barbara said in an unsteady voice.

"That Bentwoodes is no longer yours, my sweet, but mine, to do with as I see fit. You come home with me, Bab, and we will decide—"

Barbara ran from the room. Tony jumped up and ran after her. Abigail stood up. The Duchess pushed Dulcinea from her lap and reached for her cane.

"Stay here!" she hissed to Abigail, who was already at the door.

She hobbled out into the gallery. At one end, far down, she could see Barbara leaning over, holding her stomach, as if she were retching. Tony was standing behind her. He was talking to her. The Duchess pursed her lips. She went back into the library, walking slowly, as if her legs were paining her. Abigail was whispering furiously to Wilcoxen. The two of them looked up as the Duchess entered.

"Go away," said the Duchess. "Now. Except you, Diana. You stay."

Wilcoxen bowed rapidly, right and left, without looking at any of the three women he was left with. He could not get out of the door fast enough.

Diana's hands opened and closed methodically against the arms of the chair upon which she was sitting. It was the only movement she had made since the Duchess had torn up the paper.

"Your theatrics were uncalled for, Mother," Abigail said, her full, fleshy face showing its stubborn jaw. "And I would appreciate it if you would treat me with a little more courtesy! I am not your tirewoman, to be snapped at like a dog. Now, I am going to my rooms. Not because you order it. But because I wish it! I have a headache!"

The Duchess said nothing. But when the door closed behind Abigail, she sat down and looked at her daugher.

"I am ruined. You know that?" said Diana. The words were without emotion, but the emotion was there.

"Why did you not tell me the extent of your debts? I thought Roger's terms more than generous."

Diana stared down at her gown. "They are. But they are not enough."

"Enough? What is enough?"

"An allowance, Mother. Some money of my own so that I can buy a gown now and then. The estate is ruined. It will take Harry years to earn my jointure back out of it. I needed better terms. I thought Roger would offer them. I thought I could play him against Abigail and come up the winner either way. And I would have."

"And Barbara? What of her?"

"Abigail promised to find her a husband as part of the bargain."

"The bargain."

Diana leaned forward. Her face was cold and white and hard. "I would have had money now, and future money against Bentwoodes' development. I would have been secure."

"Why did you not ask me for an allowance when you were at Tamworth?"

"I thought you would say no."

"And so I would have."

Diana laughed. There was no mirth in the sound.

"A child's spirit is a special thing, Diana. And to have abused it the way you have . . . I would not think of casting my pearls before swine, and yet I gave you my granddaughter—"

"My daughter, Mother—"

"No, my daughter! I raised her. She is more mine than you ever were."

"Have you always hated me?"

The Duchess closed her eyes. That Diana could ask her such a question, and ask in such a level tone, made her heart feel like a stone inside her breast.

"I do not hate you, Diana." For the first time, her voice trembled.

"But you do not love me—"

The Duchess dug her fingers into Dulcinea's fur, felt the warmth of the animal, a warmth that was entirely missing in the voice, in the spirit of her only, her beautiful daughter.

"You are my child. I do not think any woman hates a child that has grown under her heart. But children leave your body.

They grow up and away. You never needed my love, Diana. You never wanted it. And yet I do love you. I know you to the core of your heart; not a pretty thing, like your face, Diana, and I still love you. You lack feelings for anyone other than yourself. You were always so beautiful, and I was glad. I thought that you, with your beauty, the delight that others had in simply looking at you, would use it as a good thing, as a blessing. To be loved and admired as you always were—but then, perhaps we cannot be thankful for what we have never missed. You were selfish and cruel, Diana. Always. Since you were small. And I could not forgive you that selfishness. And I cannot to this day."

"What a long speech, Mother. But it will not keep me warm in winter. Or put food on my table."

"I will give you an allowance, Diana. For the rest of your life."

Diana stared at her mother. It was clearly the last thing she expected to hear. The Duchess kept her eyes closed, one hand on Dulcinea, who had more kindness in her cruel cat's heart than Diana had in her human one. But like Diana, she was a beautiful creature, and so could get away with cruelty. For a while. Until the beauty faded. It was a small satisfaction, but a satisfaction nonetheless.

"Why? Mother, why?"

The Duchess stood up, dropping Dulcinea to the floor. She felt very old, and very tired. And her legs hurt. It was a long way to her rooms, to her bed. And she still had Roger to deal with.

"If you do not know, Diana, I can never explain it to you. Good night. Sleep well, my child."

Her ancient, rattling carriage pulled in front of Roger's town home. She had sent the note over last night asking if she might call in the morning, and Roger had written back that he would be pleased and charmed to receive her. Charmed. His charm. She remembered that. And his thin, handsome, tanned face laughing as he ate at their table many a night in London, when he had no money and was days from being paid. Though he had visited Richard several times in the last years, she had been busy managing their affairs, busy grieving over Richard's change and her sons' deaths. Was he different?

She was immediately ushered into the Neptune Room and offered refreshment, which she declined. She inspected the carvings of fish and shells while she waited. The door opened. She turned, but it was not Roger at all, but a plain young man with a withered left arm. He came forward smiling. His smile made him much more attractive. She recognized him at once.

"White! Caesar White! Come here at once and kiss me!"

"With pleasure, your grace." He kissed each of her wrinkled cheeks. She put her hand in his good one, and he helped her to a chair.

"I thought you had starved to death," she told him.

"I almost did. But as you can see, I landed on my feet." He waved his good hand to indicate the beautiful room around them. "I am serving Lord Devane as a clerk of the library now."

"And your writing?"

"I have not given it up. This feeds me. And well, too, I might add. When I heard you were coming today, I wanted to see you. I never thanked you properly for the money you sent me. It saved me from starving in the street, and I mean that literally."

"It was a lovely poem," the Duchess said softly. "You captured Richard's true spirit. I used some of the lines you wrote on his tomb."

"I am honored and humbled."

"Nonsense. A true poet is never humble. How did you come to be with Roger?"

"It seems he, too, read the poem, and he contacted me when he was next in England purchasing the library from the old Arundel estate and asked me to catalog it. As I was between poems, and had spent your money, I accepted. One thing led to another, and I am still here. But I must leave you. Lord Devane will be here at any moment. He is late because he could not decide which coat he should wear this morning. Your visit means a great deal to him."

"I see he is still vain."

White laughed. He bowed over the hand. She held his and made him look into her eyes.

"Did you see my granddaughter the other day?" She spoke the words fiercely. "Do not look at me so! I know big households. Nothing happens in them that everyone does not know. Did she disgrace herself beyond repair? Was Roger furious?"

White squeezed her hand before he released it.

"I do not think he was angry," he said kindly. "More dismayed, for her sake, than anything else. I think, and I am presuming greatly, that he has some feeling for her and does not wish her hurt further."

"Well put!" the Duchess snorted. "I can see I will obtain no gossip from you. The girl is an impudent, impulsive baggage, and Roger is well rid of her!"

White smiled. "I think you must love her very much. And from what I saw, I do not blame you." Bowing again, he left the room.

So White had met her, she thought, sagging in her chair with dismay. Sweet bloody Jesus, what had Barbara done—assembled the entire staff while she made a scene! The makings of a scandal were here. How would Roger feel about still marrying a girl who had the brashness to visit him on her own?

The door opened again, and this time, Roger came in. His face broke into a smile the moment his eyes met hers, and she could not help smiling back, thinking, Dear Lord, he is as handsome as ever. No, Diana was correct. More handsome! He has not aged a day. She had forgotten that trait of Roger's—his ability to come into a room and mesmerize it, his ability to make whomever he concentrated on feel he or she was the most important, exciting, beautiful person in the world. No wonder my granddaughter is crazy for him, she thought.

"Alice . . . Alice," he said, coming forward and pulling her up into his arms. "You look beautiful," he whispered into her ear, and she could hear the emotion in his voice, and she was touched almost to tears. Memories flooded her mind, memories of all the times she and Richard had shared with him; watching him manipulate his latest mistresses, fend off the women who were always trying to bed him; watching him shake his handsome head and declare he was in love at last, only to change his mind yet once again; watching him try to make his pay stretch and never being able to. He had been eternally in debt but would never let Richard lend him money. "I care about you too much to lie and say I will pay you back," he always said. "Do not worry over me. There is some woman out there, her pockets full, her husband dull, just waiting for me."

He stepped back, and they stood staring at each other, tears in their eyes. She whipped a handkerchief from inside her skirt pocket and blew her nose.

"Sentimental old fool!" she snapped.

"Me or you, Alice?"

"Both of us!"

He laughed.

"I have come to apologize, Roger, for my entire family. From my unscrupulous daughter to my greedy daughter-in-law to my willful little granddaughter." The words came easily to her lips. Seeing him made her feel younger, full of spirit. If he had that effect on her, at her age, with her aches and pains, his effect upon Barbara was understandable. Any other man paled beside him. Well, if this is what Barbara wanted, this is what she would get. That snippet of gossip, lying quiescent at the back of her mind, was discarded once and for all. To see Roger in person made it ridiculous.

He was at the bell pull saying, "Since they have all behaved scandalously, your apology will take some time. I propose we ease it with some wine, or do you prefer sherry?"

"Port," she said, enjoying herself.

"Port. Ah, Alice, you always were a woman after my own heart. Port it is."

"Lord Carlyle is downstairs, desiring to see Lord Devane, and he insists on waiting until his lordship is free." Cradock smiled sourly at the expression on the faces of White and Montrose. "He is in the library."

"No," said Montrose, as Cradock quickly closed the door behind himself.

"We have to," said White, standing up. "Come on."

"I refuse to tell him whom Lord Devane is entertaining," Montrose said, following him out.

"You will not have to," White answered.

Carlyle, immense, hulking, wearing a suit of bilious green and stockings with clocks on them, sat in a chair sipping wine.

"Who is with Roger?" he asked at once.

Montrose closed his eyes for a brief second, then looked at White with an "I told you so" expression.

"Some old friend, I believe," White said airily.

"Which old friend?"

"Lord Devane does not inform us as to the identity of his visitors," Montrose said stiffly.

"You would be adorable if you would just let go," Carlyle told him, batting his eyes. Montrose puffed up like an outraged pigeon.

"I have heard," Carlyle said, tapping his wineglass with a long fingernail (he was letting his fingernails grow in imitation of the Chinese mandarins depicted on the porcelain everyone collected), "that Roger had an unexpected visitor last week. And that Lady Saylor had one this week. Come, boys, you may as well tell me. Is that or is that not the Duchess of Tamworth's dilapidated carriage waiting out front? Only a duchess would dare ride in such a ruin. Is she downstairs with Roger? And why?"

"Really, Lord Carlyle," snapped Montrose, "I have no idea to what you are referring. And if I did, I certainly would not betray the confidence of Lord Devane. When Lord Devane is finished with his present company, you may ask him all of these questions yourself."

"Is he always this stuffy?" Carlyle asked White.

"Yes," said White.

"How boring for you. You have my sympathies. You, Montrose. Pour me another glass of wine." Carlyle settled back more comfortably in his chair, and crossed his legs.

"What do you think of my stockings, heh? Clocks, I ask you! Is it a fad? Oh, well, I must be current. More wine than that, boy. If I am to be incarcerated with you two while I wait on Roger, I may as well enjoy myself. You are to be congratulated, you know. My staff tells everything. I have no secrets. It is shocking. How long do you think Roger will be—never mind. I can see your lips are sealed. You, White, give me a copy of that last canto you have written. Roger told me the other day that it is the best thing you have done."

Roger and the Duchess finished their second glass of port. They were on excellent terms with each other. They had damned Abigail's interference and drunk to that, they had damned Diana's greed and drunk to that. Neither of them had mentioned Barbara. The Duchess fanned herself with her hand. Roger was talking. He had been telling her the whole story. He stood in front of the marble chimneypiece calm, urbane, self-mocking.

"She made a complete fool of me, Alice," he finished. "I lent her money; I made sure that she was not harassed by the investigation. In short, I trusted her." He clicked his heels and bowed sardonically at the idea of trust.

The Duchess set down her empty glass. She pulled a piece of folded paper from her pocket and put it on top of the small, inlaid table beside the glass. Roger watched her, a small, curious smile on his face. She tapped the paper with her finger.

"Bentwoodes," she said. "Yours if you still want it."

The smile on Roger's face faded.

"I tore up the previous deed to Barbara last night. You should have seen Abigail's face. But there was nothing she could do. It is mine. Yours if you want it. But understand this: It is my granddaughter's dower. She comes with it. There are no other circumstances under which I will let the land go. Tony has asked permission to court her. I have told him no for now. The girl fancies herself in love with you, Roger. And I fancy to give her her heart's desire. Bentwoodes is hers. I have half a mind to develop it for her myself if you refuse it."

Roger's breathing quickened. He stared at her as if he could not believe his ears, his blue eyes suddenly as blue and clear as the summer sky. He strode over to her, to the table, and picked up the paper and opened it. His eyes flashed over the few words written.

"How badly do you want Bentwoodes, my lord?"

He took a deep breath. "More than I have ever wanted anything in my life."

"Well, there it is."

"As simple as that?"

"As simple as that."

He looked down at the paper in his hand. An exultant smile was spreading across his face.

"Richard always said you were a woman to have on one's side."

He laughed and waved the paper jubilantly. He picked up one of her hands and kissed it, smiling at her. It was a pleasure simply to sit and watch him. His beauty made every gesture seem more significant than it was.

"There is one thing, Roger."

The laughter on his face, so near hers, completely faded. She said sharply, "I am not Diana! You will get no tricks from me. It is about Barbara." She watched his face as she said the name, but there was nothing she could read.

"Would you marry her before you go to France?"

He was clearly astonished at her request, she could see that. She wished she had another glass of port.

"She thinks if you go to France, you will change your mind. And she does not trust her mother."

"And the marriage terms themselves?" He spoke rapidly. She could see he was weighing the issue in his mind.

"The same as those you settled with Diana, before Abigail's interference."

Roger looked at the paper, a paper he had accidentally crumpled, first in his exuberance, then in his distrust.

"Why not?" he said to himself softly. "Why not settle it all in one fell swoop?" He looked at the Duchess. "I will marry your impulsive, willful little granddaughter, Alice. And I will take her with me. And when we return, may she be carrying a son of mine and a great grandson of yours!"

"Well said, Roger. May she indeed!"

He sat down in a chair opposite her, his legs sprawled out, staring at her. She stared back.

"I am exhausted," he said. The two of them burst out laughing.

"Bentwoodes!" he crowed.

The Duchess sighed. Now that it was over, she felt let down. She looked at the handsome man she had just given her granddaughter to. His thin face was alive with zest and ambition.

"She is very young," she said to him. "She expects much out of life, out of you. I worry about her, Roger. She is my heart."

He was out of his chair and kneeling before hers, like a lover. Once more she felt the charm that he possessed in such magnitude bathing over her, subduing fear. He took her chin in his hand.

"I will take good care of her, Alice. I promise that." He laughed at the expression on her face. "I love you, Alice. Marry me instead."

She smiled at his foolish words, his flattery.

"Nonsense," she said, pushing at him. "It was Richard you always loved."

For a fraction of a second, something flickered behind his eyes, but she did not see it. In a flash, he was up, laughing, pulling at the bell rope.

"More port, Alice!" he was saying. "I intend to send you home drunk as a barrel! We will drink to Bentwoodes, Alice. And to Barbara!"

CHAPTER SEVEN

His face flushed with wine and triumph, Roger walked into the private study adjoining his bedchamber and took a key from a tiny, buttoned pocket sewn inside his waistcoat. He fumbled at the lock of his writing cabinet, which sat solidly on a matching wooden stand with twisting legs, and pulled down the front flap. The inside was littered with papers and sketches, all having to do with Bentwoodes, or Devane House, as he thought of it. The evening of his final talk with Diana and Abigail, he had come straight home, walked in here, and locked the writing cabinet, not bothering to straighten or file the papers strewn about. He could not bear to touch them. He had overreached himself, gambled and lost. So be it. He subdued the anger and disappointment threatening to boil over with drink. The persona he had created these last few years did not allow disruptive emotions; the persona he had created was urbane and content, strolling through life with a charming smile. He glossed over the loss of Bentwoodes to those who mentioned it; another day, another property, he said, reaching for more wine. But he had wanted Bentwoodes more than he had wanted anything in a long time.

The idea of it when Diana had first mentioned it had struck him like a lightning bolt inside his mind. It was an idea whose time had come—a dream. And the dream had become more real than his own life of visiting the coffee shops and smiling his way through the princess's drawing rooms and listening to

Walpole and Stanhope argue state policy. He had deliberately not involved himself in the politics swirling about the king: European policy versus English, Whig versus Tory. His policy was an easy friendship with the king in which he did whatever was asked of him and requested nothing in return. The king granted him more for not asking than he would ever have received if he had asked. Yet for Bentwoodes he had taken sides. He had championed the cause of a Jacobite traitor's wife—when was a man a traitor? When the prince he backed could not summon the money and troops to remount a throne that was morally his? If James III, now in Scotland watching his invasion fall to pieces, watching six thousand fresh Dutch troops mass against his two thousand, had been able to consolidate the very real support of his followers in England, he would now be marching triumphantly toward London, and Kit Alderley would be a hero, and Diana would be scrambling like a rat to prove she meant nothing by her divorce action and petition to have the land and titles transferred to Harry. The only man he had ever known who had been loyal in his politics had been Richard Saylor.

He ran his finger across a pen-and-ink drawing of the temple of arts Wren had sketched. It was an ebullient, baroque design, rising in splendor before a huge, rectangular landscape pool. He wanted something simpler, something more classical, but this design was a beginning. There were elements of it that were good: the dome, the front portico and columns. The temple was going to house his art, it would be a gallery in which he could display his books and paintings and sculpture, a place where friends could walk and dine and talk surrounded by all that was beautiful. He wished it built even before the great house that would adjoin it in the vast gardens he planned. He riffled through more of the drawings Wren had made: a central square surrounded by town houses; a fountain at the entrance to the grounds of his home; follies (small buildings of different architectural styles used for dining or reading) for his personal gardens; the first tentative sketches of the exterior of a small, exquisite church that would link the square to his gardens. He smiled to himself. Devane House. It was going to be known throughout England.

All that he had thought lost had been restored through an hour with Richard's widow. When she had sent round the note last night, he had not been able to sleep. He drank, but the more he drank, the more sober he felt. His excitement was far greater than that he had ever felt for a woman. And when she asked him to marry Barbara now, instead of waiting, he could have laughed at the irony of those three Fates, weaving their webs. For he desired the very same thing; the idea of going abroad and leaving Diana and Abigail, together or in opposition, with Bentwoodes, made him sick with anxiety. He would have married a monkey to obtain Bentwoodes. To marry sweet little Barbara was the easiest thing imaginable. And he was grateful to her. It was she who had somehow made the Duchess the deus ex machina, as the ancient Greek playwrights had called their god who intervened and saved the hero. He would make her happy. She was the instrument by which he could achieve his last dream. Bentwoodes was doubly precious now because he had thought not to achieve it.

Restless with his news, his rediscovered energy surging through him, he found White and Montrose with Tommy Carlyle in the library. He stood there in the doorway, grinning at them.

Carlyle saw him first. He put down the copy of the poem he was reading.

"What is it? You look positively triumphant!" he said with that wonderful discernment of his that Roger found so amusing and irritating and useful. The two other men stared at him, their young faces questioning; his moods of late had been uncertain, and therefore not like him.

"Congratulate me, gentlemen," he announced, coming into the room. "Once again, I am to be married!"

"Married?" Montrose said incredulously from his desk, holding his pen suspended in midair. "But to whom?"

White strode across the room and shook Roger's hand vigorously with his good one. There was a broad smile on his plain face.

"Congratulations indeed, sir! She is a wonderful girl."

"I do not believe it," Carlyle said, exploding the words out. He stared at Roger. "Surely you do not mean—"

"I do." Roger grinned at Carlyle.

Carlyle stood up. "I knew it! I told these creatures it was the Duchess's carriage! This calls for wine! Montrose, where is that decanter? Roger, you have me on my heels! I never thought you would pull it off once Abigail got her hooks into that property. She must be ill with anger! I love it! When is the wedding, dear boy?"

"Not Barbara Alderley?" Montrose whispered to White.

"Yes, Barbara Alderley," White whispered back.

"A calendar, if you please, Francis," said Roger.

Montrose, in his confusion, could not find one. His hands skittered through the neat stacks of letters on his desk. His pen fell on the invitation he was answering and a huge spot of ink slowly spread. White reached down and deftly pulled out the calendar book. He handed it to Roger. Carlyle was looking over Roger's shoulder and trying to pour wine at the same time.

"Here," Roger said. "January twenty-first. That way we can leave for Paris almost immediately."

"This month!" cried Carlyle. "You work quickly! Poor Abigail!"

"So-so soon?" Montrose said breathlessly. "How will we have time to get ready?"

"It will be very small, Francis. Only her family and a few of my friends. By the way, I want the reception held here. Arrange that. Will there be time to finish those rooms Giorgini started on—no? Well, she will have to sleep in my rooms. And I thought we could marry in St. James's Church. It is so close. I leave it to you, Francis. I will invite his majesty to come to the wedding, though not the reception. Start a guest list, now, but keep it small. And I need a special license; there will not be time to cry the banns. Procure it, Francis."

"Roger, you are amazing! Let me buy you dinner, and you may hold me in thrall as you relate every detail of how this came to be! I want to know every syllable the Duchess uttered! Every one! The Alderley chit! Again! I cannot believe it!"

"Did I show you the sketches Wren did for a temple of the arts, Tommy? They are not quite what I want, but he has the central concept. Come with me and give me your opinion." He turned around in the doorway. White and Montrose were both staring at him, their mouths open.

"Take care of the ring and the posies and all that," he said to them. "I leave it to your discretion." He walked out the door, saying to Carlyle, "He has given me a baroque design, Tommy, and I wanted something less—"

Montrose sat stunned. "A wedding," he said to himself. "I have not the least idea where to begin."

White pulled up another chair to Montrose's desk. He blotted the ruined invitation and took out a fresh sheet of paper.

"Well, I have. Both my sisters are married. Let me see, we need a ring, and the colors for the ribbon favors, and food and musicians and—"

"Favors?" echoed Montrose. He took the pen White was waving around from him.

"We have to give out favors to Lord Devane's friends." White spoke with great authority. "And the colors are most important. No yellow—that signifies jealousy. How do you like carnation and silver?"

"Food . . . musicians . . ." Montrose was making a list, a task that would soon soothe and orient him. "Favors . . . I like blue for constancy and green for youth. The bride-to-be is what? Twelve?" He spoke acidly. Surprise always made him irritable.

"She is fifteen," White said. "And her grandmother is the most wonderful woman in the world. I will compose the inscription for the inside of the ring myself. And perhaps a small poem to be read at the reception. What do you think of 'God decreed our unity' for the ring?"

But Montrose was bent over his list. "Lord Townshend, Lord Stanhope, Lord Devonshire," he was saying to himself as he wrote down each name.

"In three weeks?" Abigail stared incredulously at the Duchess lying in her nest of pillows, a shawl about her shoulders, one wrinkled, spotted hand caressing her huge, white cat. "You cannot be serious."

The Duchess pursed her lips stubbornly. She was tired. Her legs ached. She had already had to deal with Barbara's happy hysterics and Tony's disappointment. If Diana and Abigail had not botched the whole thing from beginning to end she could be in her bed at Tamworth, abstractly deciding which gown she would wear to a wedding that she would not have to bother with, rather than here in bed at Saylor House after almost having dragged the groom-to-be into marriage.

"Three weeks!" she snapped. "And if you argue with me, I will tell Tony he has my permission to marry Barbara, and I will tell Barbara she must accept him. For that is the only way you will get your hands on Bentwoodes, Abigail. Make up your mind to it!"

Abigail sat down. Her legs were weak. How long had the Duchess known about Tony's feelings for Barbara? And not to say one word. Not give one hint. It surpassed even her performance in the library the other day. Dear God, give her the patience to handle this irritable, impossible, interfering old woman. Dear God, give her the patience to endure the loss of all those acres of land, ripe for development. Give her the patience to endure having a dolt for a son who fell in love with the first impossible candidate who crossed his path. Give her the patience to endure being outwitted by a fifteen-year-old child. Who had been abetted by her own son. Dear God, what was this world coming to when you could not trust your own children not to stab you in the back? She clasped her hands together and prayed for calm. The thought of Bentwoodes going to Roger Montgeoffry was almost more than she was able to bear. She had been so close, so close. Diana had been putty in her hands, her greed outstripping even her own. Except it was not greed when it was done for one's children. Well, she had tried her best. Done her duty as she saw it— meddling, nosy old woman! She ought to have been in her grave years ago. No! She was not going to brood about this. She had prayed for guidance. Vengeance is mine, the Lord said. There was nothing she had to blame herself for, except for not watching Tony more sharply. Idiot! Dolt! To think that he had actually told his grandmother about his feelings for Barbara. She felt faint, as she had felt in the library when she watched the Duchess tear up that precious piece of paper. Of course, she would never sue a member of her own family . . . especially when she knew that for once in her life, Tony would not support her. She must remain calm. The Duchess, God curse her, had closed her eyes, as if she were asleep. Abigail stared at her, imagining her slowly dying of a terrible, lingering disease. After a bit, she felt better.

"There is bound to be talk about why she is married in such a hasty fashion," she said with credible calm.

"People can count. Even if she should conceive the first time Roger unbuttons his breeches, it will still take nine months." The Duchess kept her eyes closed.

"She has no bride's clothes, and there are hundreds of details—"

"Any competent dressmaker can have her outfitted in three weeks. And the wedding will be small, both Roger and I want it that way. And the reception will be at his home."

"But we are the bride's family—"

"He insists, and I agree. There is no sense turning this into a public festival. There will be talk enough, as it is. And there is no sense spending more than we have to. I will have to foot most of the bill, though Tony has offered to pay for everything. Most generous of him, I thought." She opened one eye to see what effect her last words had on Abigail. She allowed herself a small smile and closed her eye again.

Abigail sat rigidly, struggling with her better self. Tony pay! Three weeks! Bentwoodes was truly lost. Well, she had done her best. If there was any comfort to be taken in any of this, it was in the fact that in three weeks Diana and the Duchess would both be leaving, and that Barbara would be beyond Tony's reach. She would have to remember those things in the next weeks, to be able to act with her usual grace. If she was not going to disgrace herself completely and physically attack her mother-in-law or the bridegroom. She at least would lend a note of decorum to the ceremonies. Three weeks indeed. Roger Montgeoffry was wasting no time getting his land, land that ought to have been in Tony's inheritance from the beginning, land that—but that was neither here nor there. She was not one to hold a grudge. In the bed near her, the Duchess began to snore. Abigail looked at her . . . meddling, interfering, tiresome old woman. . . .

Barbara sat on a whitewashed bench in the garden. It was now late afternoon, clear and cold, the sky above as blue as Roger's eyes. She was so happy she thought she would die from it. She had had to come outside, sit underneath the bare branched trees and let the cold soften some of the excitement churning inside her. It was done, finally. In three weeks, she would be his wife. The dream was coming true. She had already told Anne and Mary and Charlotte, who had jumped up and down and screamed with her. And she had told them she wished them to be her bridesmaids, and they had started screaming again. Dear things. Now Kit and Tom and Baby would come for her wedding, and Roger could see all of her brothers and sisters, except Harry. Harry was going to be so surprised. She a countess, with her own home and servants and husband. When Roger was more used to her, she would have her brothers and sisters come to live with her, or rather her sisters, for her brothers would be at school. But she would have her sisters, and they would be her family, until her babies came. It was all going to be so happy.

Someone's shoes crunched on the gravel, and she turned, expecting to see Martha, telling her it was time to come in. But it was Tony, his nose already red with cold, his hands stuffed into the pockets of his cloak. He smiled at her hesitantly. She smiled back and patted the empty space beside her. When he sat down, she put her arm through his and leaned her head against him. His big, bulky body was warm. She snuggled against it and rubbed her cheek against the rough material of his cloak.

"Tony, I am so happy. Thank you for sending that note to Grandmama."

He did not say anything. They both watched gardeners down at a far corner mulching flower beds. They worked with smooth precision. One would lift a shovelful of mulch and drop it; one would spread it; one would move the wheelbarrow. As the mulch spread, another shovelful was ready to be dropped. Their movements were as precise and unvaried as the workings of a clock.

"Bab."

She looked up at him. His plump face was unusually serious, and it was blotchy, almost as if he had been crying. Poor Tony. Whoever married him would have to be content with his title and fortune.

"Happy for you, Bab. . . . If you should ever need me . . ."

She was touched by his words. His wife would also obtain devotion, if she were lucky. Not that devotion was what Barbara wanted. But then, she had everything she wanted. Devotion was for lesser mortals. She had the stars. They sat together silently, companionably, watching the gardeners until dark came.

She slept late the next morning. And when Martha brought in hot chocolate for her to drink, she sent her back for more food. She was going to have to put some weight on; Roger should not have to spend his wedding night with a skinny stick. Back with the bacon and buttered bread Martha brought came her aunt, carrying in two boxes tied with soft velvet ribbons. She laid them silently on Barbara's blankets. Barbara opened the tiny, scented note half hidden under one of the ribbons.

"Belated New Year's gifts—with fond regards, Roger."

She kissed the note. Her aunt arched her brows and held out her hand. Barbara refolded the note and put it in the neck of her gown. She felt very safe with her grandmother in the house. Her dignity then abandoned, she fell on the largest box, pushing aside the rustling tissue paper to find a tippet, or shoulder cape, of dark green velvet with long trailing ends of black sable. Nestled beside the tippet, like a small dark animal, was a matching sable muff, dark green velvet ribbons attached on each side. Barbara draped the tippet about her shoulders and put her hands into the soft muff. The sable was the softest, most luxurious thing she had ever felt.

Inside the much smaller, narrower box was a fan, its end sticks frosted with tiny diamonds. It opened to reveal a pastoral scene, frolicking nymphs, blue water, green trees, fat clouds. A faint fragrance rose from it. Jasmine. The scent Roger wore. Barbara held the fan to her nose and breathed deeply.

"Oh! I am so happy!" she cried. "How can I ever be happier than this?"

"Roses, pansies, violets," said Montrose to White. They were both huddled at Montrose's desk, a desk that was littered with papers. The fact that they were not in neat stacks showed how busy Montrose was.

"Add gilded rosemary," suggested White. "That will make her posy perfect. Is this the guest list?"

"Yes. Look how many people he has crossed off—" Montrose slapped his forehead suddenly. "The gifts! Her New Year's gifts—"

"Sent yesterday. It is all taken care of. Settle down, Francis."

"I do not see how I can have everything ready."

"You will do it. I will help you. By the way, does he want the drums and fiddles or not?" It was the custom for the bride and groom to be greeted with music at daybreak on the morning after their marriage unless the musicians were tipped not to do so. Butchers made their own serenade by striking their cleavers against marrow bones on the wedding evening to salute the bride.

"Are you mad? Absolutely not! I will take the money to the Marrow Bones and Cleavers Society and to the Fiddles and Drums the day before the wedding and make sure they understand they are not to follow the procession or stand outside the windows."

Roger's favors, knots of gold, silver, blue and green ribbons, began to appear pinned to hats and sleeves. Even though the wedding was to be small, people were talking of it. The news that James III was going to be crowned King of England in the Scotch palace of Scone added relish. That Roger could so coolly marry a known Jacobite's daughter showed his power. Or his stupidity. It was whispered that he had withdrawn his petition sponsoring Lady Alderley's divorce. Barbara made her first appearance at court amid rumors that the Pretender was already on the march to London. She walked proudly between her grandmother and Roger, and bestowed her famed grandfather's smile on the king, who talked with her in French for several minutes. The Prince of Wales danced with her three times and was seen watching her wherever she moved.

The Duchess worked her way slowly through the crowd in the drawing room. She wore a black gown of satin (she always wore mourning for the duke) and rubies everywhere, in her hair, around her neck, on her bony fingers. Walking slowly, one hand on her cane, she had a word for everyone she knew, reminding them of old times, old favors. She was using all her influence to add dignity to the haste of Barbara's marriage.

Barbara floated through the days. Life was rich beyond imagining. She had only to count her new gowns, their colors like an artist's palette: cherry, sky, primrose, flame, dove, smoke, daffodil, topaz, violet. There were new petticoats to contrast with every gown; stomachers (panels that formed the

top of the gown) so stiff and crusted with embroidery and
jewels that they could almost stand by themselves, or else
trimmed with a ladder of soft, gauzy bows. There were small
caps of handmade lace; ribbon garters; chemises as light and
thin as air, gold and silver hairpins; gloves, white, fitting to
the elbow, perfumed; stockings of green and pink, scarlet and
white. There were dome-shaped hoops of rich damask and
silk; velvet cloaks. Shoes of salmon pink damask with shiny,
black wooden heels or of white silk edged with gold lace or
fawn-colored brocade with diamond bows. There were wedding presents to open, and teas and receptions and dinners to
attend: Tony held one in her honor, as did the great-aunts and
Fanny and Harold.

She had gone with her grandmother to meet Roger's staff.
Roger's servants had stretched out in a long line, waiting for
her. She had dressed in a new afternoon gown and worn the
lovely velvet tippet and muff Roger had given her. All of the
servants had watched her with shining, curious eyes as Francis Montrose introduced her. She had known exactly what to
say to them all, from Caesar White, who had winked at her—
she had ignored it in her best, dignified manner—to the tiniest kitchen maid, who had stared at her, eyes wide in a
grubby face, as if she were a fairy princess. Her grandmother
had been sitting in a chair watching, and every now and again
she would glance at her, and she would see the love and pride
on her grandmother's face and know she was doing well. She
had not even blushed when she had met the housekeeper's disapproving glance.

"Mrs. Bridgewater," she had said clearly, so that all could
hear and did not have to strain themselves, "how nice to see
you again." Later, if it were necessary, she would dismiss her.
Her grandmother had taught her how to deal with servants—
firmly but fairly. They were part of the family. They must be
taken care of. A loyal one was worth his weight in gold; a
disloyal or lazy one should be dismissed at once. Never keep
a bad servant, the Duchess said. They are like a bit of yeast
gone sour. They will ruin the whole loaf. Firmness tempered
with a drop of mercy was her grandmother's motto.

The days were flying by. Barbara considered it an omen
that her wedding day was St. Agnes's Day, when young
maidens across the country would be fasting so that that night

when they slept they would dream of their future husbands. When she slept that night, it would be by the side of her husband. Fanny had attempted to explain her sexual duties as a wife. Having grown up at Tamworth, which had its own farms, she had seen animals mate and knew what happened. She had also attended many a village wedding, where jokes and toasts to the wedding night were crude and graphic. She knew what was going to happen, and she was only a little afraid. She had been told it only hurt the first time because it was then that her hymen would be broken. To listen to Fanny, who would not look at her face, speaking of a wife's duty to submit—but never saying to what—in a high, breathless voice made Barbara want to giggle. Her grandmother had already cross-examined her and been much more forthright.

"You know what he is going to do, do you not?"

"Yes, Grandmama."

"It is the same as the animals you have seen mate, except one hopes Roger will have more finesse."

"Grandmama, please!"

"Are you afraid?"

"No, Grandmama . . . well, perhaps, a little."

"Some women find relations with their husbands offensive, Bab. The Lord above only knows that Roger Montgeoffry should have enough experience with women to know what is pleasing—what is that look on your face, chit? Are you jealous? You ought to get down on your knees and thank your lucky stars he knows how to kiss a woman the way she likes—what is wrong? Has he kissed you yet, Has he?"

"No, Grandmama."

"And you are sorry for it, are you not! Baggage! I wonder if I should warn Roger what is in store for—"

"Grandmama, please!"

"You just tell him what you like and do not like, girl. He is experienced enough to take it from there."

"Grandmama!"

Not all of her modesty was real. She looked forward to her wedding night, when, finally, Roger would be concentrated on her. For that, she would endure whatever pain came with bedding a man. Though they were to be married, she never saw him, except for a few moments at some reception. The most time she had spent with him was the afternoon she had been presented to the king. She knew he was busy, she knew he was important; but he had never so much as kissed her! Of course, how could he, when they were never alone? Still, she imagined that a man such as Roger would have known ways to get her alone if he wished to. He was not in love with her. She knew that. But he would be. She was going to use every wile she possessed, and any she could learn. Unfortunately, she had to wait until she was married before she could begin. Now, as a virgin, as a modest girl of a noble family, she was surrounded with rules, restrictions, family, always guarding her, as if she were a precious jewel that could be stolen at any moment. Marriage would bring some freedom.

"Merciful God in His heaven above!" Maude cried. Jane, who was helping the maid bake pies and had flour up to her elbows, came running into the hallway. Her Aunt Maude stood clutching an invitation to her heart.

"It has come!" she said to Jane, waving an envelope of cream-colored parchment sealed with red wax. "It has come."

"What, Aunt Maude, what?"

"An invitation to her wedding!" Maude ripped under the seal with one of her razor-sharp nails, even though Jane could see that the envelope was addressed to her. Maude had been dumbfounded when the news filtered down to her that Lord Devane was once again going to marry Barbara Alderley, and in indecent haste. She had told the tea party story to anyone who would listen; in fact she had become a minor sensation among her friends and in her neighborhood.

"I could tell straightaway," she said to her mesmerized listeners, building her story step by step, detail by detail, so that they could see themselves the white, sick look on Barbara's face, the flashing blue of Lord Devane's angry eyes. "I could tell that something was not right. I could feel it in my bones. The atmosphere in that great house was heavy. I had a feeling of doom—of doom—I tell you! And I was correct."

Maude had the gift, people were saying. They had begun to come to her about advice for arranging marriages, she was said to have the gift of foretelling whether or not they would be happy. So when the news of the wedding was once more current, Maude declared she had felt that, too, in her bones, a lightness, a kind of happiness, but she had not known for whom or what. Then she had heard about Lord Devane and Barbara. She was happy for them; she blessed them. She retold the story. People listened a third, a fourth time. And she dreamed at night of being invited to the wedding.

"Saturday, the twenty-first of January at eleven-thirty. It is the reception, Jane." Her aunt sounded aggrieved. "You might have thought we would be invited to the wedding. However . . . let me see, I will need a new gown and hat and shoes and gloves. Edgemont has his good suit. You will need clothes also. We cannot go in rags. A list. I will make a list of what I need. Now where is some paper? Peggy! Peggy? Where is that girl when I need her! I tell you, Jane, you cannot get good help these days! No matter what you pay. Peggy!"

Handing her the invitation, her aunt went into the kitchen, still talking to herself. Peggy was probably in the cellar, hiding. Peggy was a poor housekeeper, and she knew hardly anything about cooking. She was just a big, ignorant, country girl who had come to London to earn a living. There would be much fussing and swearing from her aunt, who would threaten to replace her, and Peggy would cry, and somehow they would find a pen and paper. Jane knew where both were, but she said nothing. She set down the invitation carefully and wiped the flour from her arms and hands with her apron. Then she read the invitation:

The Duke of Tamworth and his family request the presence of Mistress Jane Alderley and Master Augustus Cromwell at the reception honoring the marriage of Mistress Barbara Alderley to the Earl Devane. Saturday, the 21st of January at 11:30 of the morning. Number 17, Saint James's Square. The favor of an answer is requested.

Aunt Maude was not invited, but Jane knew better than to try to argue with her aunt. Wild horses would not keep her aunt away. It was kind of Barbara to invite her and Gussy. She felt sick. Harry, Harry, my love. She swallowed. Where are you? What are you doing? Do you ever think of me?

She wiped at the tears that trickled down her cheeks. Sometimes now she could go for hours without once thinking of him. She found comfort in mindless routines: kneading bread dough, feeding the fire under the giant kettle for the hot water they needed on washing day, mending sheets and stockings. There were spaces of time when her thoughts were calm. But they were just that, spaces between the pain. Something, anything would set her off, and she would be thinking of him again, and then she would long for the quiet times when he was not in her mind. She wandered into the tiny parlor that her aunt considered the best room in the house, sat down in a chair and looked out the window. Across the street, a cart was delivering coal. Two men were dumping wheelbarrowloads into the chute that led to the cellar. Gussy came once a week and sat with her here in the parlor. He had found an obscure reference to one of the earlier popes and was elated. His thin face became flushed when he was excited. Of course, then he also smiled and she saw his rotting teeth. Next month, her aunt was planning a betrothal party. It was old-fashioned but her aunt was excited about it. She and Gussy would exchange betrothal rings, the rings that each would wear, but that could be interconnected to form one ring, a symbol of their future joining together as one. They would go to church, and one of Gussy's friends would pray for them, they would take the sacrament, then come back here for cake and punch and dancing. Her parents were coming up for it. And then a month or so after that she would marry. She looked at the cream-colored invitation, its dark ink, the embossed pattern of lilies and roses on the border. Oh, Barbara, she thought. You are so lucky. Why are you always so lucky?

Barbara was awake long before the sun rose on the morning of her wedding, even though she had been up late the night before. Cousin Henley had arrived with Tom and Kit and Baby, and there seemed to be children and trunks everywhere. Then Aunt Cranbourne and Aunt Shrewsborough had arrived, and Fanny and Harold and their three children, and there had been much laughing and talking and hugging. Somehow Cousin Henley and Mary's governess had gotten the younger children upstairs, her Aunt Abigail had retired early with a headache, and she had sat up late with her two brothers—Tom was as tall as she was, Kit nearly so, they were growing like weeds—protecting her, proud of her, while her younger sisters and Mary hung on her every word. As had

Tony. Dear Tony. He had been with her everywhere these last weeks, by her side at all times, looking out for her, introducing her, buying her silly little things, fans, books, ribbons. She had felt bathed in love last night, with her half-grown brothers and her adoring sisters and Mary and Tony, and her grandmother and ancient aunts arguing over some long-forgotten, but remembered differently by each, incident at the court of Charles II. In just a few hours she would belong to Roger. It was not possible that three months ago she had been running the halls at Tamworth with her hair hanging down and her thoughts on simple, everyday things, like some child. Roger had simply been someone she loved the way she loved her absent father. Neither was ever there; she could not remember the last time she had seen her father, and surely it had been sooner since she had last seen Roger, but she loved them nonetheless. She did not miss them or pine for them; they were not part of her life. But she loved them with the same clear surety with which she loved her grandmother.

A chambermaid tiptoed in to freshen the fire. Barbara sat up and stretched. Soon Martha—Martha, her wedding present from her aunt, who had paid her wages for a year to be Barbara's personal maid, bah!—would oversee her bath. And she would dress slowly for her wedding day, for Roger, for her beginning in life as a woman, as an adult. The chambermaid smiled timidly at her. She smiled back.

"A box has come for you, ma'am," the girl said.

"Send it up!" Barbara cried. She could not accustom herself to the sudden excess of wealth in her life; she knew, of course, that her grandmother had money, but they had lived simply at Tamworth, though, of course, she had had every kind of lesson imaginable, French, Italian, drawing, watercolor, dancing, but still, now she could have as many gowns as she wished, and so many presents came to the house and she loved opening each and every one of them. And now here was another. The chambermaid came back in with a box and placed it on the bed.

"Light some candles," cried Barbara. The girl hurried to do so, obviously as excited as Barbara was by the box.

"Look! Oh, look!" she cried.

Inside, nestled in lightly moistened gray moss, was a posy of pink and white roses, mixed with winter violets, pansies and rosemary. Around the posy lay a matching wreath for her hair. Green and silver ribbons were woven through the lovely, delicately tinted purple and white and pink blossoms. The chambermaid gasped and clasped her hands together as Barbara carefully lifted out the wreath. The green and silver ribbons unfurled themselves down her hands and arms. Gently she set it on her head. Today, and only today, she would appear before Roger and the world with her hair down her back and shoulders, a symbol of her purity, the purity a bride should bring to her husband. Tomorrow, and for the rest of her life, she would wear her hair up, in whatever the style. Only in private, in bed, would she ever again wear her hair loose. She smiled at the chambermaid whose hands were on her cheeks and who was looking at her in delighted awe. (She would never know that Roger had not seen her flowers, but had left the choice to Montrose and White, who had fussed and argued and agonized over the choice as if it were their wedding. She would never know that they had been as excited as she when the florist had shown them his finished work; that Montrose had actually held the posy against his waist and walked up and down the library while White watched critically, and that the two of them had decided unanimously that there must be longer ribbons and that silver must be added to them, to the florist's disgust.)

The Duchess stamped her cane impatiently against the floor. "Never mind me! You are as slow as molasses! No one will be looking at me. I want to see her dressed! Hurry, Annie! Hurry!"

Annie slowly, deliberately, pushed another diamond-headed hairpin into the black lace cap the Duchess was wearing. She paid no attention to the Duchess's tirade, but continued her own task, that of making sure her Duchess looked as grand as possible. And she did. She was wearing a gown of dark green velvet, almost black the green was so dark, with an underpetticoat of black-and-green-striped satin. Over a chair lay a matching green velvet cloak lined with white fur. This was the first time since the duke's death that the Duchess had worn anything other than solid black or gray. Diamond-headed hairpins glittered here and there like tiny stars on her expensive lace cap. She wore diamond earrings, a diamond brooch, diamond rings and diamond bracelets. As soon as Annie had brushed some rouge on her cheeks and set a patch against her temple, she waved her away and summoned a footman to help her to Barbara's room. Her legs were bad, as bad as they had ever been. After each outing—the signing of the contracts, the court appearance, this tea, that reception she had attended— she had had to spend hours afterward trying to endure her aching legs. Hot compresses, dandelion wine, laudanum. Then she could rise, with Annie shaking her head angrily, to do her duty to Barbara. Well, today was her last day. After tonight, she would crawl into her bed and stay there for days, gathering strength for the long journey home. She almost felt that once she got into bed, she might not be able to rise again. Already, her legs were beginning that tiny ache radiating from her ankles and knees and hips that would soon spread and devour her. But she had to see Barbara dressed. She had to see the child on her wedding day. She had to reassure herself once more that she had done the right thing.

"Grandmama!"

Barbara ran to her and hugged her. The Duchess sniffed and pointed to a chair with her cane. The footman helped her to it. Mary, Charlotte and Anne, who were sitting on Barbara's bed, immediately climbed down and made respectful curtsies to her.

"Look at the flowers, Grandmama," said Anne, bobbing up and down like a cork, talking all the while. "They are so beautiful. I am to have flowers in my hair, also. Barbara said so."

"Our gowns are green, Grandmama. Green is my best color. Barbara said so. She says it is Roger's favorite color. Barbara loves Roger. I do, too," Charlotte said.

Only Mary was silent, having been raised in a household where it was unwise to address an adult unless the adult indicated interest. But even Mary's eyes were shining. Barbara is good for her, thought the Duchess, her mind for a moment leaving the figure whose red-gold hair was streaming down her back. For all the children. They need her.

Martha entered with a gown of heavy white brocade draped over her arm. The gown had a pattern of flowers embroidered with silver and green thread across the skirt, and there were flounces along its hem. A silver corded belt with long tassles at its ends tied about the waist. Barbara clapped her hands at the sight of her gown and danced around the room. She had on white stockings tied with green garters, a white corset whose stomacher was tied with green ribbons and a green-and-white-striped petticoat. Anne stepped into the white brocade shoes that Barbara would wear. She clumped over to Barbara.

"I am the bride. Look at me!" she said.

Martha frowned. Anne stepped out of the shoes. She looked as if she were going to cry.

"Martha," Barbara said, "send for my grandmother's tire-woman. I want her to do my hair."

Once Martha shut the door behind her, Anne, with a daring glance at her grandmother, stepped back into the shoes. Mary and Charlotte giggled. The Duchess chose to ignore Anne's behavior.

"Come here," she told Barbara.

Barbara came and knelt before her grandmother. The Duchess put her hand under her chin. Barbara's face was lovely, shining with happiness, almost full again. The Duchess kissed her on each cheek.

"Be happy, child."

Barbara hugged her tightly. "I am. I am so happy I could burst. Thank you, Grandmama—"

Annie came in. She barked for Anne to get out of her sister's shoes, and immediately ordered Barbara to sit down, so she could begin the task of brushing and curling and braiding Barbara's glorious hair. Everyone became involved. Charlotte ran to put the curling tongs in the fire; Mary held Barbara's hands while Annie brushed and pulled her hair, Anne held the ribbons and pins which would hold it all together. Annie deftly braided the sides, then she curled the back and joined the two side braids there, weaving them together with green and silver ribbons. One braid now, they lay atop the long, curling, thick red-gold hair that trailed down to the middle of her back. The Duchess unscrewed the diamond earrings she wore and motioned Charlotte to take them to Barbara.

"Oh, no, Grandmama. I could not!"

But in spite of her protests, Annie screwed them into her ears. They sparkled like giant teardrops in each ear.

"How can you bear all the noise?" Annie asked irritably.

Anne and Charlotte were quarreling over who should take Barbara her shoes. Barbara only smiled. But Annie sent the younger girls from the room. It was time they were dressed. They left after kissing Barbara.

"Promise we will live with you," said Anne at the door.

"Promise," said Barbara.

"You are lucky," Mary said to Anne.

"The gown," the Duchess said. "Put the gown on. Let me see her in it."

The Duchess's hands, folded over the top of her cane as she watched Annie fluff out the skirts of Barbara's wedding gown and petticoat, worked convulsively. The girl looked an angel.

"You are certain?" she asked gruffly, knowing there was nothing they could do if Barbara did have any last-minute doubts, and seeing with her own eyes that of the two of them, Barbara was by far the more calm. But that was because Barbara had never been married before. The Duchess had, and knew there were moments ahead in which Barbara would be greatly hurt, whether Roger grew to love her or not.

"Remember what you read to me when I left, Grandmama?"

The Duchess nodded her head. "Keep thy heart with all diligence," she had read to Barbara from the Bible, "for out of it are the issues of life."

"Well, that is what I am doing, Grandmama. Keeping my heart."

The Duchess nodded again and pursed out her lips. She would not cry, not now, when she had the ceremony and reception to get through. Sweet Jesus, the child looked like Richard.

"I wish your grandfather could have seen you today," she said gruffly. "He would have been so proud."

The servants of Saylor House, chamber and kitchen maids, ladies' maids, the footmen and butler and porters, the stableboys and coachman, the gardeners and cook, the laundry maids, the housekeeper, the grooms, slowly began to fill the hall, along with the family already waiting. It was tradition that they see the bride, that they strew herbs and flowers before her. They had already sprinkled rosemary and bay and dried lavender and rose petals on the front steps and inside the carriage she would ride in to the church. Now they waited expectantly to see her, and as she left, they would cheer for her and throw their flowers and herbs after her.

Again there was a commotion on the landing. The eyes of everyone in the hall, except Diana, who had found a mirror, turned to the stairs expectantly. The Duchess appeared, Annie at her side. Slowly, she began the descent down the stairs. Behind her came Anne, Charlotte and Mary. They wore small wreaths of roses in their hair, which was brushed long and full onto their shoulders, like Barbara's. All three were obviously proud of their new gowns and shoes and could not resist smiling at the people assembled below them. Annie caught Bates's eyes, and he nodded his head, as if to say, The old woman looks grand, as grand as she has ever looked.

A kind of sigh arose. Everyone was staring up at Barbara, waiting there at the top of the stairs, so that everyone could see and admire her. (The servants would talk about how she looked for weeks. For some of the serving girls, it would be the single most beautiful memory in their lives.) Barbara smiled all her love and joy at the family waiting down in the hall for her. Then slowly, grandly, with more dignity than she had ever shown (the Duchess was continually amazed at these glimpses of a more mature Barbara, glimpses of the woman forming inside), she walked down the stairs. Even Abigail's face softened as she watched her, until she happened to glance toward Tony and see the expression on his face. As Barbara reached the last step, her brothers and sisters surrounded her.

"Bab!" said Tom, bowing over her hand, and in an unusual gesture, kissing it. "You look beautiful."

"You do," echoed Kit, behind him. "First rate!"

"Oh, Bab," cried Anne. "You are the most beautiful thing I have ever seen."

"I love you, Bab," said Charlotte.

"I must have a kiss," Barbara said, opening her arms, seeming not to mind that her lovely white gown might be crumpled. "A kiss from each and every one of you while I am still a maiden. The next time you address me, Thomas Alderley, you must call me 'Lady Devane.'"

"Never! I will not do it."

"A kiss, please."

The servants let out a cheer as her brothers and sisters surrounded her and she kissed them. Even Mary, greatly daring, ran forward and kissed her cheek. Tony was last.

"A kiss for me, Bab?"

"Of course. With all my heart."

She kissed him heartily on the lips, and he blinked (to Abigail's irritation, he looked stunned) and then offered her his arm. With herbs and flowers falling on them like rain, the family assembled themselves into groups for each carriage. As the carriages drove through the gates, the people who had gathered outside to watch let out a ragged cheer.

"What is it?" asked Barbara.

The Duchess patted her hand. "It is for you, chit. For your wedding day."

CHAPTER EIGHT

" $\mathscr{I}$ have forgotten something. I know I have."

Montrose, Roger's favors pinned to the sleeve of his new coat, paced up and down near the font of St. James's Church. It was the most fashionable church in London, and on Sundays its pews were crowded with those who were truly religious and those who always showed up where it was fashionable to be, and today its altar and pews were wreathed with white roses and ivy and rosemary, an extravagant frivolity, since the wedding would be attended by few people, although already a crowd was outside in the churchyard, waiting to catch a glimpse of the bride, and of the king, who was rumored to attend. Roger, splendid in a dark blue coat and French wig, was talking with the curate. Robert Walpole, who was to be his best man, was beside him.

"How can he be so calm!" exclaimed Montrose, patting at the perspiration that dotted his upper lip, while White, beside him, smiled at his friend's complaints. "Are you hot, Caesar? I am hot. This church is too warm."

"Everything is fine, Francis. It is not too hot. You are nervous. And naturally. But do try to remember that it is Lord Devane, and not you, who must make the responses to the bride."

Tommy Carlyle appeared, blinking for a moment in the dimness under the church gallery. He wore a white satin coat and a blond wig. His notorious diamond blinked in his left ear. Roger, seeing him, left the curate. The two men shook hands, and Carlyle looked Roger up and down.

"I must say, dear one, you look quite well. I thought bridegrooms suffered from nerves."

"Not this bridegroom. Tommy, I think they have arrived. If I am not mistaken, there is Tamworth and his grandmother. Let me go and greet them."

Carlyle sighed and looked around him. Some distance from him sat Walpole's wife, Catherine. Her pretty, sulky face was turned toward the front of the church, where Roger was now busy greeting Barbara's relatives. Carlyle pushed the handkerchief back into his cuff, flicked at a speck of dust on his black velvet breeches, sat down and sidled over toward Catherine Walpole.

"I love weddings," he said to her. "Do you?"

Roger kissed the Duchess heartily on both cheeks and shook Tony's hand.

"You be good to that chit of mine—" the Duchess began, but her sister-in-law, Louisa Shrewsborough, thrust her thin body between Roger and the Duchess. With her was her sister, Lizzie. Aunt Shrewsborough poked at Roger's ribs with a gloved finger.

"She is my niece, Roger! Full of vim and vigor. I hope you can please her where it counts!"

Both the great-aunts cackled. They sounded—and looked—like well-dressed witches from a Shakespearean play. Roger chucked each of them under the chin. They loved it. The cackles rose again. He moved skillfully, gracefully, to Fanny and Harold, standing behind the aunts, and swept Fanny into his arms.

"I always make it a point to kiss my relatives, particularly when they are as pretty as you," he said as he kissed her on the cheek.

Abigail stood stiffly behind her daughter and son-in-law. A flush on her cheeks, she held out her hand to Roger, but he leaned forward and kissed her cheek, also.

"The best man of us won, Abigail," he whispered, and before she could answer, he moved on to Diana, who looked him in the eyes, seemingly not one bit ashamed of herself.

"I would strangle you with my bare hands," Roger said softly, kissing her lips, smiling into her eyes, "but it is my wedding day."

There was a loud cheer from the outside of the church, and Roger was past Diana at the doorway, greeting the king, Melusine von Schulenburg, and two attendants. Everyone in the church rose. The curate nearly tripped over his black robes running to the front of the church to greet the king. Roger kissed Melusine on the cheek and offered her his arm, and with the king following, escorted the royal party to the first pew. He looked completely natural and unselfconscious. King George nodded graciously to those standing around him before he sat down.

"Showy!" sniffed Abigail to Fanny, as they sat back down.

"Superb!" Carlyle whispered to Catherine Walpole and the Duke and Duchess of Montagu, who had taken their seats.

White knocked on the door of the small room in which Barbara and her sisters and Tony were waiting. Barbara stood at once.

"They are ready," White said softly. "And may I say, Mistress Alderley, that you look lovely."

As she walked down the aisle on Tony's arm, her sisters before her, Mary holding the long train of her gown, Barbara felt as if her moment in life had finally arrived. She was the center of everyone's attention, even the king, who was smiling at her. She stopped at his pew and curtsied. She knew exactly what to do and how to act because Roger, in one of the few times he had talked with her, had told her how she should behave. But of her own volition, as she rose, she plucked a flower from her posy and offered it, with a smile, to the king's mistress. The king nodded his head approvingly.

Her sisters and Mary were now clustered at the first pew. At Barbara's nod, they filed in beside the Duchess. Barbara leaned over and kissed her grandmother. The Duchess sniffed loudly.

"Dearly beloved," began the curate. (His voice carried. Christopher Wren had built this small church with its side galleries and rounded baroque arches to allow worshipers to see and hear clearly.) "We are gathered here in the sight of God, and in the face of this congregation, to join together this man and this woman in holy matrimony; which is an honorable estate, instituted of God—"

The Duchess stared blindly at the altar, seeing not Barbara and Roger, but other couples—herself and Richard, her sons and their brides, Diana and Kit. . . .

"Wilt thou have this man to thy wedded husband, to love together after God's ordinance, in the holy estate of matrimony? Wilt thou obey him, and serve him, love, honor, and keep him in sickness and in health; and forsaking all others, keep thee only unto him, so long as ye both shall live?" the curate was asking Barbara.

"I will," she said clearly, her voice low and throaty, like Diana's. It did not tremble or shake.

"Who giveth this woman to be married to this man?"

Tony looks ill, Abigail thought to herself, her eyes on her son's face. He had not taken his eyes from Barbara since the ceremony had begun. His response was inaudible, but he was placing Barbara's hands in the curate's, who would eventually place her hand in Roger's, symbolic gestures showing her obedience and dependence upon others for the marriage. The curate, as God's minister and priest on earth, would deliver her to Roger's care, through the power of God, as God had provided a wife for the first man who had walked the earth.

Tony sat down blindly by his mother, who reached over and patted his hand. Both his hands were gripping his knees so tightly that his knuckles were white. He was concentrated on Barbara. These last weeks he had shown a maturity that was new, and while annoying in some ways, encouraging in others. Abigail felt furious that his energies should be wasted on Barbara, who was not the wife for him. She was too lively, too headstrong, too . . . yes . . . say it, intelligent. Yet it hurt to love someone who did not return your love. Abigail could sympathize with her son's feelings. She had loved William; not deeply, of course. Passion had no place in marriage, which was based on respect and regard. But she had had some strong feelings for him at the beginning—how could she not?—he was handsome, virile, amusing. She had soon realized, however, that he would never care for her deeply, and she had been glad to know, thankful that she had realized in time, before she could have felt more and embarrassed both of them. She had been content with their relationship. The hurt had only been a little one, she had too much pride, too much self-worth to brood over it; she had duties and responsibilities. Still, seeing the look in Tony's eyes reminded her of those first few months when she had thought that, possibly, William might care for her. It was a painful time, a humiliating time. Her ups and downs. Her ridiculous, girlish hopes. Thank goodness only she knew of it, and she did not like to think of it, even now. Well, she was going to find Tony a nice little wife. An obedient girl. A good girl. She would make up for Barbara. Barbara. And Bentwoodes.

Of course, nothing could truly make up for Bentwoodes. It was a loss that would not be easily gotten over. All that land. Any fool could see that its development would harvest thousands of pounds. She had been lazy and lackadaisical not to have checked on it before. She had known it belonged to the Duchess—a freakish thing for her family to have done, pass land along to the daughters through a trust that did not allow it to become their husbands' unless by special consent of the daughter. And the Duchess had never consented it to her husband. Not that he needed it. He had inherited enough when the Duchess's father had died. Richard Saylor was no fool; they could say what they liked about his saintly character. He had married well. Married a girl who was richer and came from a better family. An intelligent move by any standards. More than intelligent. Pushy. Just as Roger Montgeoffry was with his handsome face and his charming manners. Well, charm covered a multitude of sins, and one of his sins—Catherine Walpole—was sitting across the aisle next to that odious Carlyle, watching with a downright sulky expression on her face, ripe for a scene. Barbara would have her work cut out for her. Montgeoffry was hardly used to a life of domesticity. But, then, what man was? It was the women who sat by the fire and spun, birthed and raised the children. Men were free to do as they pleased. A woman was only free once she was a widow, and then only if she was a rich widow.

"I, Roger, take thee, Barbara, to my wedded wife, to have and to hold from this day forward, for better for worse, for richer for poorer, in sickness and in health, to love and to cherish till death us do part, according to God's holy ordinance; and thereto I plight thee my troth."

The Duchess listened to Roger's vow, thinking of the expression on his face as Barbara walked down the aisle to him. He was not in love with her, but then Barbara knew that. Dear Lord in His heaven above, pray she did nothing foolish if he should never love her. She was so headstrong. Love was not the usual reason people of their station married. Yet she had found love unexpectedly in her own marriage and been so much the richer for it. To love and to cherish—how cherishing Richard had been of her. Life was so uncertain. Who could have known that she would grow to love Richard as she had? That Richard, of all people, should have seen past her bad-tempered, proud shell to the frightened, passionate person she was inside. That he should have held out his hand and said, Come with me, my love, and I will show you how to live.

"I, Barbara, take thee, Roger, to my wedded husband, to have and to hold, from this day forward, for better for worse, for richer for poorer, in sickness and in health, to love, cherish and to obey, till death us do part, according to God's holy ordinance; and thereto I give thee my troth."

Barbara and Roger were following the curate now to the Lord's table for prayers and blessing. After a short sermon and communion, it would be over. The Duchess prayed with all her heart that Barbara should have her heart's desire, or, if it was not the Lord's will, that she should have the strength to find other happiness in her life. She was so young, only a baby. Most girls married by fifteen, but most girls were not her granddaughter, and from her distance of years, Barbara seemed a child. Surely Roger's experience, his charm and kindness, would make the marriage easy.

There was a rustling sound around her as people stood up. Roger was leading Barbara toward the king. They were married. Her granddaughter was hers no longer. She now belonged to Roger.

A crowd had formed around the married couple and the king. People were kissing one another, and bowing to the king. The king kissed Barbara's hand.

"Countess Devane," he said. "Let me be the first to salute you."

Everyone applauded. Robert Walpole smacked Barbara on the lips, then turned to Fanny, then to Diana, who was being kissed by Harold, while the Duke of Montagu waited impatiently.

"I despise men," the Duchess of Montagu said, watching her husband kiss Diana.

"So do I," said Catherine Walpole, who was watching not her husband, but Roger.

"They have arrived!" someone cried, and the guests joining the waiting servants in Roger's hall cheered. Cradock opened the door, and Tony stepped across Roger's threshold, Barbara in his arms, her brothers on each side. The bride was not allowed to step over the threshold of her bridegroom's house, but had to be carried over it by her relatives. The servants stared at Barbara in her full, white gown with its green ribbons. She smiled at them. Roger appeared behind her, the Duchess on his arm. He went to stand by Barbara, and said, "I present your new mistress, the Countess Devane."

The servants clapped, and a shower of flowers and herbs fell on Barbara and Roger. Behind him, family and friends from the church were coming inside to join the guests invited to the reception.

"She looks lovely," Maude said loudly to Jane. Maude, startling in a purple dress with yellow embroideries and tassels and a turban hat, was on her second glass of claret. "Go up to her and say something."

"We will make her acquaintance in just a few moments," Gussy said. Jane smiled up at him gratefully. Her uncle was silent, as always.

"You have to push yourself forward in this world, Jane," her aunt was saying, Gussy having made no impression on her. They had arrived early, to Jane's chagrin, and she had followed her aunt about the town house as she inspected every room and nodded haughtily to servants and other guests. They did not know anyone here. They were out of place in this beautiful house with its elaborate furniture and beautiful guests and wedding candles and flowers. They ought to pay their respects and go. If her aunt had any sense, that is what she would do. But no, she just wanted to walk around looking at the other women's gowns and brag that Jane knew the new countess. If Gussy had not been here to lend a note of dignity, Jane would have died. She would have. Gussy might be dull, but at least he was a comfort. He alone had noticed how dispirited she had been since she had received the wedding invitation. She loved Barbara. She really did. She had always admired her spirit and courage. But she could not help feeling that it was not fair that Barbara should have her heart's desire so easily. Jane had always tried to be so good. Loving Harry had been the only really disobedient thing she had ever done, and she could not help that. Now she felt so bitter. So angry. And it was not nice to feel those things. Gussy had talked with her. Naturally she could not tell him what was wrong, but his sensitivity was comforting. He had prayed with her, and told her of his hopes for his own church, of how he would depend on his wife to help him with his duties to his flock. She had been excited at the thought that she could be a help to anyone. Some of the pain over Harry had eased. But today, being here, brought it back.

Gussy wanted to come, however, wanted to ask Lord Devane's permission to look through his library, which was becoming famous, said Gussy, and surely would hold an obscure book there that would help his researches. Her aunt had snorted. "Help his researches! You just ask Lord Devane if he owns any livings, that is what you do, Augustus Cromwell! Maybe then you can receive your own church, instead of substituting for every clergyman in town!" Gussy, like most clergyman, needed his own church, with a living that would be his for life, but they were not easily found. One had to have a noble relative, or know the bishops. Poor Gussy. He would be so much better than the Reverend Mr. Latchrod at Tamworth, who forgot his sermons and mumbled the host. Gussy was kind and caring. If she were not such a coward she would ask Barbara herself, but Barbara was a countess now, and would have no time for her. She belonged to Barbara's past, not to her future. She felt someone tugging on her gown and looked down at a familiar face. It was Anne.

"Come this way, Janie. Bab is asking for you."

"You see! You see!" shrieked her aunt. "I knew she would ask for you. Go on, Jane. Go on! Edgemont, is my hat straight? Where is that footman with wine? I need just one more glass."

They followed Anne, Maude grabbing a glass of wine from the tray of a passing footman. She drained it and handed the empty glass to her silent husband. Barbara was standing at one end of a crowded room, and the wall behind her was mirrored. It made the room seem full of people and movement.

"Speak up!" hissed her aunt. "Introduce us, and tell her what you need! Put yourself forward, Jane!"

Her aunt pushed her through the crowd of people surrounding Barbara. Barbara hugged her and said to the handsome, older man at her side, "Roger, this is my oldest friend, Jane Ashford. May I present my husband, Lord Devane."

He had the bluest eyes Jane had ever seen, eyes with many wrinkles around them in a thin, tanned face that was lean and beautiful. He smiled into Jane's eyes, and she felt suddenly welcome, suddenly warmed inside. Shyly, she introduced him to Gussy and to her aunt and uncle. He bowed over her aunt's hand, and she watched her aunt's mouth sag momentarily, then open in a series of continual sentences. Roger managed to get by them to her uncle. With a few graceful questions, he learned that her uncle was in the naval department and, motioning his hand, a neat young man in a brown suit appeared and at a few words from Roger, led her uncle out of the room, with Maude following.

"I have some friends here from the navy, I thought he might enjoy talking to them," Roger said to Jane, as if he had arranged it all just for her benefit. And quite without knowing how, she found herself on Roger's arm, Gussy following, walking through his elegant, richly furnished house, bowing right and left to all the people who wished to talk to him, but he was talking to her, and she was telling him of her family at Ladybeth Farm. And somehow, behind them, Gussy was talking of his studies and his book to Roger. He led her through the house until they found the Duchess, who was sitting in a chair, with her grandchildren gathered around her. The Duchess held out her arms, and Jane forgot her shyness and ran into them. And then naturally she had to introduce Gussy, and she had to hear all the messages from her family and friends, and Gussy had to explain his studies. She felt comfortable now, where she had felt awkward before. Roger left them. Every now and again, some way that Tom or Kit or the girls would move or smile reminded her of Harry. But then, everything reminded her of Harry. It hurt, but she could

bear it. She heard music starting in the other room, but she
let Gussy and the children rush off to see Roger and Barbara
dance their first dance. She stayed where she was, with the
Duchess. Later, she would ask her about Harry. She knew she
should have more pride. But she could not help it. She had
to ask. And she knew the Duchess would tell her. She had
learned long ago that behind the Duchess's bark was a kind
and understanding heart. Yes, she would stay here. The
Duchess was home, a painful reminder of home, but home
nonetheless.

By late afternoon, the satins and velvets of the guests had
begun to show food and wine stains; cravats were loosened;
faces were flushed; quarrels were starting here and there; talk
and laughter were too loud; the food tables with their ivy and
wilting white roses were beginning to look ravaged; no one
was ready to go; it was a successful party.

Catherine Walpole was dancing with Roger. She was whispering furiously. His expression, one of pleasant interest, never
changed.

"When will I see you again?" she hissed.

"Very soon, Catherine. You can hardly expect me to neglect
my bride on my wedding day, now can you? Think, Catherine. Remember when you were a bride. What if Robert had
flirted with another woman?"

She pouted. "That was ages ago. All I know is that you have
been avoiding me. And I will not be trifled with. What if I
told your little bride about you and me, Roger? What if I did
that?" She stared at him challengingly, her face hard.

"If you did," he said, "it would certainly spoil my honeymoon."

He surprised a laugh from her. "All right," she said. "I will
be good. But do not think you can drop me like an old rag,
because you cannot!"

"An old rag. You remind me of many things, Catherine, a
kitten, a flirt, a spoiled child, but never, never a rag."

Diana was dancing with Harold. He leaned forward and
whispered something to her. When she laughed, everyone in
the room stared at them, so provocative was her laugh. The
Duke of Montagu glared at Harold, as did Fanny. The Duchess of Montagu had another glass of wine. Maude was dancing with Robert Walpole.

"My husband, Edgeward—no, Edgemont, yes, Edgemont, is one of the most diligent workers in the department. But he was saying to me just the other day, Maude, what I really want is the treasury. The treasury—"

Francis Montrose gave a yelp and leapt away from Tommy Carlyle. White, who was sitting nearby and had had five glasses of port, was laughing helplessly.

"If you ever touch me again, you repellent reptile," Montrose said to Carlyle, his voice shaking with outrage, "I will break every bone in your body." His round face was rigid.

White cried with laughter.

"You are too sensitive—" began Carlyle.

"Sensitive!" shrieked Montrose, his voice unnaturally high, not caring that several people were staring at him. "You just keep your hands off me!"

Carlyle turned to White and shrugged his shoulders. White wiped his eyes. Carlyle continued staring at him. White sobered up.

"No, Tommy!" he stammered quickly. "Not me, either!"

At seven, Barbara and Roger cut their wedding cake, and footmen passed out tiny pieces to guests. The unmarried women in the room were supposed to put the cake under their pillows and dream of their lovers. Gussy, who had been upstairs with White and looked at Roger's books and who had also had several glasses of wine, brought Jane a piece.

"I am having a fine time, Janie," he said. He leaned over and kissed her on the cheek. It was the first time he had ever touched her. She said nothing, just stared at the piece of cake in her hand.

"B-b-beautiful," slurred Tony, who was looking at Barbara as she cut cake. "Beautiful."

Carlyle, standing next to him, hiccuped. "Roger certainly is."

At eight, Robert Walpole opened the door to the library. Harold lay on the floor, half on and half off Diana, the front of whose gown was pulled down to expose her full, white breasts.

"Who is it?" gasped Diana, trying to sit up.

Instead of backing away and closing the door, Walpole walked in, leaned over, and pinched the dark tip of one of Diana's bare breasts. She shrieked and pulled her hands across her chest. Kneeling, Harold tried desperately to rebutton his breeches.

"My turn next," Walpole said. He pulled down Diana's skirts. She lay still, watching him, not sure of what he would do. But he simply went back out the door, closing it behind him. Almost immediately he ran into Fanny.

"Have you seen my husband?" Her mouth was trembling.

"No," he said, blocking her way. "Tommy Carlyle is in the library there, dead drunk, snoring. Not a pretty sight, I warn you." Taking her by the arm, he turned her around and walked away with her.

"Let us look this way. If I know your husband, he is at a punch bowl and three-quarters drunk. And if we cannot find him, well, you can go home with me."

Abigail was concentrating on wiping a stain on her bodice. She could not imagine how she had come to spill her wine like that. Beside her, the great-aunts were quarreling over which of them had been the prettiest when they were young. Mary, Anne and Charlotte ran shrieking through the room chased by Kit. Barbara and Roger were standing in the hallway, shaking hands with departing guests, many of whom could barely stagger out the door. Abigail could just see them from where she sat. Roger's officious young secretary came up to her.

"Excuse me, Lady Saylor," he said. "But have you your bride's favors?"

Abigail stood up slowly. "Are you telling me it is time to leave?" She spoke slowly, carefully.

"Time to leave!" shrieked Aunt Shrewsborough. Her rouge was streaked into the wrinkles on her face. "What about seeing the bride to bed!"

"We are not going to do that tonight," Montrose said quietly.

"A disgrace!" cried Aunt Cranbourne. "In my day we knew how to end a wedding! And that was seeing the bride to bed and more drinking! Do not stand there staring at me, young man. I could take on two more like you. Come along, Louisa. It seems the wedding is over."

Sitting in a chair, the Duchess watched Roger's young secretary and clerk and butler skillfully herding people out. In the hall, she saw Barbara, surrounded by children, her broth-

ers and sisters and Mary. She was hugging them, unpinning
ribbons as favors to give them, kissing them goodbye, promising that tomorrow she would come to Saylor House to see
them. The rooms, which had seemed so overheated, so
crowded, full of people and noise and light, grew silent. The
Duchess saw Jane's uncle staggering out with his wife in his
arms. She had passed out, behind one of the punch bowls,
some hours ago. Jane and her young clergyman followed
behind. Who would Jane dream of tonight, thought the
Duchess, when she put her bride's cake under the pillow?
Harry? Or the thin, earnest, young man with her? A candle
guttered on the table near her, once a beautiful tableau of
food and flowers, and now a littered mess of plates and half-
eaten food. The silence pressed around her. How different
from her own reception, when laughing girls had seen her to
bed, had undressed her and combed out her hair and stayed
with her until Richard, in his nightshirt, had joined her, his
young friends crowding around. And her family had been
there, and everyone had made crude suggestions and wondered who would be more tired in the morning, Richard or
she. And they had drunk the bridal caudle, hot wine and cinnamon and egg yolk and sugar, and everyone had clapped and
had some, too. And then finally, amid good wishes and
laughter, she and Richard had been left alone.

"Excuse me, madam," said White, smiling at her. "May I
escort you upstairs?"

The Duchess gave him her arm. She walked past chairs
pulled this way and that, past spilled wine and food, past
candles slowly being extinguished by a footman, past wilted
flowers, past garlands being pulled down by a chambermaid.
Already they were cleaning up the wedding. But, then, Roger
was leaving in just a few days. There would be no round of
bride's visits for Barbara. She would be in France, far away.
The Duchess's heart squeezed. Her legs ached. She had drunk
too much wine. But she had this final duty to her grandchild.
Some relative must put her to bed, and Diana had disappeared hours ago.

Martha was brushing out Barbara's hair when the Duchess
entered Roger's bedchamber. The wedding gown and petticoats and stockings lay on the carpet, in a pool of white. The
room was silent. There was no one in here but Barbara and

that maid. Yes, a far cry from her own wedding night. Doubtless Roger thought himself too old for all the wedding-night fuss, the joking, the caudle. Well, he should not be too old for his other task, the deflowering of her granddaughter. She hobbled around the room, inspecting the paintings hanging on the walls. She stopped at the one of Richard. She had no idea Roger possessed it. She stared at it, admiring Richard's handsomeness, trying to pinpoint exactly where they had been in their lives when it had been painted. It was an early portrait of Richard in his twenties. Where had Roger found it? The Duchess only knew she had never seen it before.

Suddenly, the foreboding was in her, filling her, frightening her, making her breath stop. She groped for a chair and sat down heavily, taking in deep rasping gasps of air. Her vision was blurred. She could just see Barbara standing naked as her maid slipped a white nightgown over her head. She concentrated on breathing evenly. Gradually, as the maid began to gather up the clothes from the floor, her breathing slowed. Barbara came to stand by her. Her dear girl. Using Barbara's strong, young arm, the Duchess hoisted herself up. She was exhausted. Together they walked toward the bed. Its draperies were pulled back. The bed linens looked fresh and white. On a table near the bed, beside a candle, was a vase of flowers, the same flowers that Barbara had worn today. There was a wine decanter and two glasses waiting. The sight of it made the Duchess feel better. Roger knew what he was doing. He would see that her girl was not hurt any more than necessary. He had had many women. Many women. She was a silly, fearful old woman. She started to cry. Barbara, who had already climbed into bed, exclaimed, "Grandmama, what is it!"

It was a moment before the Duchess could speak. She was a noisy crier, sniffling and rasping. "I feel so old," she finally croaked.

"You are tired, Grandmama," Barbara said, hugging her, trying to wipe her tears. "You should be home in bed."

She jumped out of bed and pulled the bell pull before the Duchess could speak. Martha opened the door.

"My grandmother is exhausted," Barbara said firmly. "See that she is escorted home. And make sure someone goes with her. Kiss me good night, Grandmama. You must leave now. You are so tired. I will be fine. Truly."

The Duchess leaned on Martha's arm. Barbara was correct; she was tired; she did need her bed. And her granddaughter did not need her now. She was ready to start her own life, she did not want her old grandmother hanging about. Which was as it should be. She kissed Barbara and walked away feebly, leaning against Martha as if the maid were all that was keeping her up. It was time for her to be home, time to drink her special wine, time to have her legs wrapped. She could do no more. The future was up to Barbara and Roger.

When Roger entered his bedchamber, he found his young wife on her knees by the side of his bed praying. Her back and buttocks and legs showed plainly through the thin material of her gown. Except for a certain inherent female roundness and slight breasts, she was almost as lean as a boy. The sight of her on her knees made him laugh (even while her slightness touched something protective inside him). Was she praying for deliverance? It was too late. She was his. He had never been responsible for another human being before. Seeing her, the extent of his future responsibilities leapt to his mind. The full implication of his marriage was just beginning to crystallize.

Barbara jerked around at his laugh, jumped up and scrambled into bed. She pulled the covers up to her neck and stared at him with wide, serious eyes. Her hair curled about her face and neck with luxuriant richness. She had beautiful hair. It would feel good to run his hands through it. He felt so tired. All evening he had worked to prevent Catherine from making a scene and Barbara from feeling neglected. What a hypocrite Catherine was. He knew she was sleeping with Carr Hervey. But she still had to feel that it was she that was tired of him, rather than the other way around. Roger knew women, especially unfaithful women, too well. Would this child, staring at him with such big eyes, be unfaithful, too? In all likelihood, she would. But if she gave him sons for his dreams, she could do as she pleased and he would not grudge her pleasure. Lord, she had a sweetly shaped face. Like a valentine. He poured himself a glass of wine. She must have some, also, before he entered her. It would ease the hurt he must do to her. Dear God, it had been years since he had lain with a virgin. He sat down on the edge of the bed. She had put down the covers, and she was watching him. He could see her slight breasts through the thin material of her gown. The sight touched him. She was so young.

"What were you praying for, Barbara? An annulment?"

She laughed, deep, rich, throaty laughter, astonishing from such a young girl. The zest of it reminded him of her grandfather. Even when Richard had been old, he seemed young when he laughed. Roger drank more of his wine.

"I ought to be," she told him. "I have been warned by Fanny and Grandmama what to expect. Fanny says to submit. Grandmama says it is the same as the animals mating— only she hopes you will have more finesse."

Her ability to jest at such a moment caught him by surprise. He had not yet taken the time to know her. Who was she? More than the thin child of his memory. She had a sense of humor. That was good. A witty woman was so much more interesting to live with. Wit outdid even beauty in the long run; a thing few men realized until it was too late. God knew he had made the same mistake himself many times.

Barbara was watching his face. "What are you thinking? Are you angry?"

"Angry? Why?"

"At having to marry me so quickly."

He smiled at her. You are Bentwoodes' fairy godmother, he thought. Without you, I would not have it. It was his, finally. Tomorrow he was going to spend all day with surveyors and engineers. Even while he was in France and Hanover and Italy, Bentwoodes was going to take shape. Angry? he thought. I am elated. He touched her cheek with his hand. Such a soft cheek. She leaned toward him, a sensual, feminine, instinctive movement. He felt desire rising in him. That, too, was a surprise. Not that he should have an erection. He knew exactly what to think of to make himself hard. But that it should have happened without the thought. Perhaps she was going to be good for him. Perhaps her wit and resemblance to her grandfather would bury old ghosts that haunted him.

"I love you," she said softly, holding his hand against her cheek. "I have loved you since I was a little girl."

"You are still a little girl," he said.

"No."

"You have so much to learn, Barbara."

She leaned forward until her lips were nearly on his.

"Teach me," she whispered. "Please, Roger,"

He put down his glass, and held her face in both his hands. She was staring at him with love and trust. Gently, slowly, he leaned forward and touched her lips with his. What a sweet girl she was. Her youth, her open avowal of love, disarmed him, touched that part of himself he thought closed off to all feeling. He leaned her back against the pillows and pushed the heavy curling hair from her brow and face. He smiled again before covering her face and neck with soft, gentle kisses, as light as the touch of a feather. But then his kisses grew more demanding. She shivered. He was at her mouth again, his tongue gently exploring. She gasped with surprise. She had never been kissed so . . . she had not known . . . He raised his head. His eyes were so blue that they dazzled.

"What is wrong?" he whispered. "Have I frightened you?"

She twined her arms around his neck. "No . . . kiss me like that again . . . please, Roger."

He smiled at her, a lazy, slow, sensual smile that made the tips of her breasts grow pointed . . . from the smile and from what was in his eyes. He desired her . . . he desired her. . . . No one had ever desired her . . . and now Roger desired her. Leisurely, he put his mouth on her, one hand caressing her slim, bare hip under her gown. She had never been so exhilarated, with its tiny, electrifying undercurrent of fear, in her life. His tongue was exploring her mouth again, and his hand was moving up to her breast, and she could not think clearly anymore.

"I am going to touch you . . . here, Barbara . . . and here . . ." he said into her ear, his voice, his hands sending shivers down her spine. "I am going to touch you many places . . . and if any of them should displease you, you only have to tell me."

"And if they please me?" she said breathlessly.

He bit her neck. "Tell me that, too."

"Roger . . ." Her eyes were like night stars. Finally, he had to close his eyes at the expression in them. . . .

* * *

The Duchess lay awake. She had drunk too much wine. Was, in fact, drunk. To drown out fears. Worries. Old ghosts. Which had surrounded her today, in fact, all these days again in London. . . . Let him kiss me with the kisses of his mouth: for thy love is better than wine. On their wedding night Richard had memorized the Song of Solomon . . . Behold, thou art fair, my love; thou hast doves' eyes . . . to show his regard and desire, he had said. Our bed is green . . . our rafters of fir . . . behold thou art fair, my love. . . .

CHAPTER NINE

Barbara's brother, Harry, lay beside the plump body of Caroline Layton. It was late morning, and his head ached from drinking. He sat up, the sheet falling away to expose his abdomen and thighs.

"Darling," murmured Caroline, her hand lazily caressing his back, circling around to caress his thighs.

He lay down, perfectly willing to see what she would do. She played with him delicately, skillfully, kissing his thighs, his manhood, trailing her pointed, pink tongue along a path of her own devising. He became aroused. Caroline expertly slid her body over and atop his; he was inside her before he quite realized it.

She began to move slowly, sensuously, atop him, intent on her own pleasure, and he was content to lie still, allow her to do as she pleased. Her hands caressed his thighs, his buttocks, his chest as she moved and swayed to a rhythm that brought pleasure to them both. The tips of her overfull breasts jabbed his chest as she began to move more urgently, falling against him in little pants.

"Good . . . oh, Harry. Good . . . young . . . so young. I . . . oh . . . love young men."

She pushed against him, her face contained, intent on her feelings, and he joined her in her urgent, restless dance to completion, his mind empty, feeling only the full, glistening breasts, the slide up and down him, the hot moist heat surrounding him.

She cried out and dug her fingernails into him. He held her hips and jabbed his way to his own pleasure even as she fell limp against him. After a moment, she moved off him and lay down beside him.

"Darling," she said.

He did not answer, but rose, careless of his nakedness, and went to the window. His body was small and muscular with wide shoulders tapering to narrow hips. His face was his mother's, only masculine. It was a face that intrigued women. He was only beginning to explore the power of his looks. Caroline was the fulfillment of his most erotic, frustrated schoolboy dream. But he wanted far more than Caroline; he wanted a taste of all the women in the world. And he was learning that he had only to smile lazily and say whatever it was they wished to hear. Married women were best, insatiable if their husbands were dull enough. It did not matter that he had no money. It only mattered that he was wellborn and young, and, of course, too handsome for his own good. They were more than willing to pay for his clothes, his tobacco, his gambling. He would never bother with virgins again. He remembered Jane's shrill "no's" when his hand touched her breasts. He remembered his own suffering and guilt and wanting. It was not that he had not loved Jane. He had. And he still did. But she was like a pale daydream against the reality of Caroline Layton and others. When he had first arrived in Italy, angry, heartsore, he had gone straight to a portrait artist and commissioned a miniature of Jane. He had described her minutely. Then he had met Caroline. In a month, when the miniature was finished, it had taken him a moment to recognize it as Jane. The pale, frail blondness painted there could have been anyone. He had already forgotten exactly what she did look like, and the miniature, which he had meant to wear every waking moment, had been put under his shirts. And sometimes, when he was down to his last one, he would come upon it and gaze at it and try to remember how he had once desired her. But the young man under the apple trees at Tamworth was too far away from the young man, standing naked, looking out the windows of Caroline's villa.

CHAPTER TEN
PARIS, 1716

The Duc d'Orléans, regent of France for the boy king, Louis XV, snorted once or twice and, in doing so, woke himself. Outside, in the dark night, sleet tip-tapped against the windows. Inside, bodies lay sprawled in chairs and under tables. Another supper was ended. Orléans's suppers were private. No one was admitted except by invitation, and no servants were allowed because of what they might see. The guests did their own cooking, which was served on a specially designed set of china depicting men and women, women and women, men and men, in various stimulating, explicit sexual poses. As if the china were not enough to arouse appetites other than those of hunger, each guest consumed about three bottles of champagne apiece while watching a naked ballet performed by several of the young girls in the chorus at the opera, or a lantern show in which the figures outlined in the light of the lantern copulated like dogs, or perhaps, with dogs.

Orléans stood up shakily and began to rouse those guests who had not passed out. It was three in the morning. Those that could walk began to put on their clothes, pull down their skirts, button their breeches and leave. Orléans kept a special staff of footmen who would enter in a few moments, when he rang for them, and remove the unconscious to their carriages. He stepped over the naked bodies of two opera dancers intertwined around the half-nude body of Henri, the young Chevalier de St. Michel. Orléans paused a moment to study their

278

positions. The guttering candlelight softened the flesh tones, the explicitness. He shook St. Michel by the shoulder, and the man moaned and then tried to sit up. Orléans moved to his daughter, the Duchesse de Berry, who lay sprawled in a chair, snoring, her skirts pulled up, naked from the waist down. A man was still licking between her heavy thighs, moaning and pulling at the material of his crotch. Orléans pushed him away, and the man rolled against a sleeping comtesse, fumbled with her tousled skirts, settled himself atop her and began to pump against her with the mindlessness of an animal. The comtesse never moved. Orléans pulled down his daughter's skirts and closed her mouth. He glanced around the room. Most of the men were dressed and had left. As for the women, only his daughter mattered. He rang for the footmen and then wandered out into the corridor to his own apartments, every now and again pausing to look out the great windows into the dark night. Sleet made faint tapping sounds against the windowpanes.

Inside the supper room, the footmen, their faces impassive, began to carry guests away. Now and again, they would pause to look at a naked girl who was pretty, and a certain furtive look would pass between them, but nothing was said. When all of the guests were settled into their carriages, except for two of the opera dancers, naked, still asleep, the footmen, six in all, reassembled in the room. They took turns at the sleeping girls, those who were not engaged in sex pushing in chairs and stacking dirty plates and dousing the candles in the heavy, crystal chandeliers or in the wall sconces until it should be their turn. They were silent and swift and efficient, in both their lovemaking and their tidying. Very soon, they would be finished; the opera dancers would be sent home, never knowing of their final lovers except for an extra soreness the next morning.

When the last candle was extinguished, and no trace left of what had gone on in the room, the footmen shut and locked the door and went to bed. The room was now silent and dark. It needed the light of the candles to show off its beauty, for by candlelight it was exquisite. The walls, painted a cream color, were separated into different panels whose outlines were gilded with a thin layer of pure gold. Within the panels were small, perfectly carved figures of nymphs fleeing from fauns and satyrs against a backdrop of dark forest and winding rivers. An artist had painstakingly painted each tiny figure as if it were real. The flesh of the nymphs was as glowing, as pink, as those of the opera dancers who had earlier been there. The paneling itself was interspersed with large mirrors and paintings by the great Italian and French and Dutch masters, the subject of each, naturally, being love. The room was a reflection of the best and finest in French craftsmanship.

In another mansion in Paris, a mansion as beautifully furnished as the Palais Royal, in which Orléans lived, a French princesse tossed and turned on her bed. She was twenty, with olive skin and chestnut-colored hair, a petulant mouth and blue eyes that bulged slightly. And her small, childlike body had just miscarried a fetus because she had gone to her favorite abortionist. Her personal maid had changed the bloody sheets and taken the clotted blood that had been the beginnings of a child away to burn in the furnace. It was not the first infinitesimal fetus the furnace had burned. If it had lived to be born, the maid would have packed it naked and squalling in a basket and taken it across the Seine River to be sold to the beggars that specialized in child buying, in child slavery. If the princesse felt anything, she did not show it. Abortion was the price she paid for living as she pleased. She had no intention of changing her way of life, though she did try to change the price. She had experimented with every method of birth control available: drinking man's urine and willow tea; raising her thigh, coughing and sneezing after sex; seaweed plugs and various douches, from rock salt to lye water to pomegranate juice. Coitus interruptus, which her sisters swore by, was too uncertain. Sometimes, in the heat of the moment, she forgot to insist. Now her maid suggested a new method. It seemed that a household servant from Turkey said the women there tied a piece of thread to a small sponge, soaked the sponge in lemon juice, inserted it inside the vagina before the act, and afterward pulled the thread to retrieve the sponge. The princesse pulled her legs up to ease some of the sharp cramps which still seized her. Outside her windows, the sleet beat itself against the panes, and finally, tired from the loss of blood and from the pain, she slept.

It was January in Paris and a bad winter; fires burned day and night in the houses of those that could afford firewood;

the bodies of those who could not were stacked up in the street, frozen, like so much human firewood. The great king, Louis XIV, who had fought all of Europe for over thirty years, who spent his reign building the massive palace of Versailles, who said "I am the state," whose symbol was Apollo, god of the sun, had died in September of 1715. He left a nation bankrupt from wars; and he left a great-grandson of five to rule in his place, governed by a regency made up of his nephew, Orléans, and his bastard sons by one of his mistresses. His palace of Versailles was shuttered, left to the caretakers and mice. The grandeur, dignity, order and authority it stood for died with its creator. The other attributes it had fostered—greed, envy, malice, passion and ambition—moved on to Paris, where the regent lived, and the court followed. He set the tone for the times, one of wasted talents, dissipated pleasures, cynical boredom and open display of vice and perversion.

The next evening, Barbara pushed her way through a crowd of revelers at a masked opera ball held at the theater in the Palais Royal. Thirty violins were playing as laughing, costumed people danced on the new marvel, the large space created in the opera house by special machinery that raised the floor of the auditorium to the level of the stage. Anyone who dressed properly could attend; it had been hoped that holding public balls at the Palais Royal would stop some of the scandals erupting at other, more private ones in and around Paris.

Barbara was searching for Roger. This morning, she had slept so late that she had missed him, even though she had given Martha orders to wake her. I thought you needed your sleep, Martha had said to her when she raged at her. She spent the rest of the morning as she had spent every morning since they had arrived in Paris five days ago, in her rooms. When Roger had returned for dinner (he held an open table, which meant that anyone who wished to might dine with them, and the places around the dining table were always filled), she had to act as hostess and concentrate on her French and try to make intelligent conversation. Among the guests were John Law, the Scotsman who had some theory of money and credit and was the current darling of French society, and the Duc de Saint-Simon, a tall, dignified man who seemed mainly concerned about precedence among the princes of the blood, a subject Barbara found completely confusing. And then she had to dress for a reception and the opera ball following. The only time she had been alone with Roger was in the carriage. As soon as they had gotten to the ball, Roger had chucked her under the chin and told her to behave herself. She had watched his red-cloaked back disappear into the crowd. Behave herself indeed! She was beginning to feel angry at his casual treatment of her. A woman standing near her said, "Care to follow me, dear? I can show you things a man would never think of."

Barbara pulled her cloak closer about herself and reached up to make sure the intricate headdress she wore, drooping pearls and feathers attached to a velvet face mask, was straight. She wove her way through the crowd, back toward the dancing. Men continually grabbed her hands, but she pulled them away. How could Roger abandon her like this? A woman ran shrieking past her, followed by two men, costumed as birds of prey. Barbara found a chair and sat down amid a circle of old women, their mouths going like magpies as they shredded the reputations of everyone they thought they recognized.

Just now they were discussing how badly dressed one of the regent's daughters was. Roger had already taken her to the nearby palace of the Tuileries, where the boy king lived with his bodyguards, his tutors and governess and household. She had liked the king's shy manner, his dark eyes, his dignity. It was a far contrast to his uncle, the regent, who had been drunk the first time she was introduced to him. He sat, fat and red-faced, under a canopy in a reception room at the Palais Royal. One of the attendants announced them. He jumped up and embraced Roger, kissing him on each cheek. But when he bowed over her hand, she could smell the brandy and see the red, broken veins on his nose, and he would have fallen over, dragging her with him, if a footman had not caught him. She did not know what to do. Roger's face was impassive. She could not tell what he was thinking.

The regent burped and pinched her cheek. He held her arm, for support most likely, and led her to a stately woman with fat cheeks whom he introduced as his wife. The Duchesse d'Orléans was surrounded by young daughters in varying stages of ugliness. Of them, the only one who made an impression on her was the widowed Duchesse de Berry, who was quarreling with her mother.

Roger had been amused by her reaction to it all. He tried to explain to her. "Orléans is a libertine, a dissolute cynic, and the most intelligent man in France. He knows more of science and music than any man I know. His problem is one many royal princes share. He was never given any power, Barbara, never given anything useful to do. So he became a drunk and a lazy wastrel to pass the time, and now it is his habit. He cannot help himself. As for his wife and family, I will make no excuses for them, except to say that they have always done as they pleased. They consider themselves above the rules of ordinary conduct. It is something you must accept if you are to understand the French."

She tossed her head.

"Do not be a prig," Roger said to her. "As you grow older, and more experienced, you will learn that most things in life are neither black nor white, but a shade of gray. Never make judgments upon people, Barbara, because they may come home to roost."

Barbara leaned her head against the wall. The old women's chatter was giving her a headache, either that or her head-dress was. She wanted to go home. And there was Roger, standing near a far wall in his red cloak with his back to her. She went up to him and when she was behind him, she slipped her arms about his waist and whispered, "Will you take me home? I am so tired."

He turned in her arms, his mask different from the one Roger had worn.

"But of course, mademoiselle. Yet if I take you home it will not be to sleep."

"Forgive me, monsieur," she stammered, backing away. "I thought you were my husband."

The man followed her. "Your husband? How disappointing."

Whatever I answer, thought Barbara, I will appear foolish. So she said nothing, but stared at him, her chin lifted, until he bowed and moved to one side so that she could pass by.

I am a married woman, she was thinking to herself. I do not have to be escorted home like a baby. I can order my carriage and go. Roger will have to find another way home. She did not realize that the man in the red cloak was following her and heard her give her name to the Swiss Guards so that they might call her carriage.

"Henri!"

Someone tugged at the man's sleeve, a small child-sized woman with olive skin and a petulant mouth, made more petulant by the vermilion rouge coloring it and by the black mask she wore. Her hair was chestnut-colored and her eyes were blue.

"I am bored, Henri. Dance with me."

"Bored, Louise-Anne," he said. "How can this be? Have you broken with Armand?"

"Oh, no." She pouted. "But I am incapacitated just now, and Armand finds consolation in the arms of some little opera dancer. Nothing is fun when you cannot fuck."

He laughed. "Louise-Anne! You shock me."

"Pooh! Nothing shocks you. Dance with me before I die of boredom."

Barbara was silent as Martha untied the laces of her gown and unpinned the headdress and her hair. It was not simply that she hated Martha, though she did . . . it was Roger. Outside, sleet began to beat against the windows, as she burrowed under the eiderdown in sheets that had been warmed—and shivered anyway. Once again, Roger had either decided to stay in his own apartments or he was still out. She had no idea which. This was not the way she had thought to begin her marriage.

On the journey, he had been very kind, but then, he was always kind. She had been seasick as they crossed the channel, and he left her to Martha's care. Then she got a headache from the jolting sway of the carriage; the roads to Paris were rutted, muddy ribbons of dirt that rattled her head until her teeth shook. Then her flux began (it never came with the regularity of other women's). She kept up a pretense of good spirits, because the men (White, Montrose and Roger's valet, Justin, traveling with them) seemed not to mind the cold or the carriage or the discomfort of the flea-ridden inns. They stayed downstairs near the fire drinking hot wine, while she shivered upstairs under moldy, damp sheets and suffered from cramps.

Paris itself was a contrast of stone mansions—like the one she and Roger were leasing—broad squares and handsome gardens against dark, narrow, medieval buildings and wretched streets. It was a perpetual tumult of noise, even dirtier than London, and the beggars were more aggressive and noticeable. Signposts hung out into the streets; there were no lanterns on buildings as there were in London, so that at night the streets were dark as Hell was supposed to be. Beggars were everywhere; they dashed out in front of your carriage to beg for alms; they waited in front of house gates like human flies (blind beggars seemed to be a Parisian specialty). Church bells rang for morning, noon and evening prayers, and, as in London, street vendors selling lavender, brooms, doormats, fish and street ballads walked up and down the mud-filled streets, competing with the curses of the wagoners and the rattle of coach wheels.

She was homesick; Tamworth, her grandmother, Tony, her family, were too far away. It would take another miserable journey across roads and sea to reach them again. (When may I ask Roger about my brothers and sisters coming to live with me? she had questioned her grandmother the day after her wedding. Sweet Jesus, Bab, her grandmother had said, startled, give the man time!) Time. . . . He needed time, and so did she. When was her time? She did not seem to fit anywhere in Roger's life. It was as if she were an afterthought, a piece of baggage added to the journey at the last minute.

In London, there had been two or three days of frantic activity—Roger's servants packing and covering furniture with dust covers, and she trying to spend as many hours as possible with her grandmother and family. Everything for the journey was already planned; she simply followed along. On the journey, she had the feeling that Roger had forgotten he had married her. She would catch him staring at her with a look of stunned surprise on his face, as if to say, What is this girl doing here? It hurt her feelings. Not that he was anything but kind. And courteous. As was his staff. But she had not imagined this beginning to her marriage—Roger's neglect, the discomfort of the journey, her flux, Paris itself, this house, with its huge, cold splendor.

In fact, it was hardly a house; it was more like a palace
with rooms that led into more rooms that led into still more
rooms, and no wall without paintings, without marble or
mirrors, without intricate paneling and swags of carved this
and that—cupids, violins, flowers, animals—outlined in gilt—
impossible to describe, except that one had a feeling of such
immense richness, of such minute attention to detail. There
was something feminine in all the ornamentation, in its excess.
On every surface were fancy glass and gold clocks, vases of
hothouse flowers, bric-a-brac, china dogs, cats, shepherds.
Even Saylor House, for all its grandeur, was not the same. It
was simpler, less cluttered. If Roger felt at home among the
excess, she felt overpowered.

She pummeled a pillow with a fist. He had left her on her
own again tonight. Since arriving, she had drifted like a ghost
through this house, waiting for someone to tell her what to
do. All week, she had tiptoed to Roger's apartments late at
night and knocked on the door. If Justin, Roger's valet, had
not been so kind, she would have died of shame. Justin was
small and neat and precise, and he acted as if it were the most
natural thing in the world for her to appear as she did. He
talked to her about Roger, about his habits, as she waited.
(Roger was fussy about what he wore, but once he was dressed
to his satisfaction, he never gave it another thought. He liked
to stay up late, but he almost never overslept. He liked to
breakfast with Montrose and White and plan his day. . . .)
And what did my ladyship like? Justin would ask her. She did
not know. This was the first time she had ever been on her
own.

She hit the pillow again, and settled in it and into the covers like a small, determined animal making its nest. This was
her life now . . . with Roger, and she was going to have to
make it into what it should be because it seemed no one else
was. Perhaps it had been naive of her to expect to be one with
him immediately. But she was not a child, and they were
mistaken if they thought she was going to stay in the background quietly like one. She knew her duty. She knew her
position. Her grandmother had taught her what was expected
of a lady. And she was not afraid. (Well . . . only a little.)
After all, she had gone to Roger's town house on her own,

risking dishonor and her reputation, to tell him what was in her heart; she had told her grandmother her dearest desires when all seemed lost. Assuming her rightful position in Roger's household was just another step in achieving those desires. And no one could take it for her . . . though she had hoped Roger would help.

How was he going to be dazzled with her maturity and style (and fall madly in love with her) if she displayed none? Think on what you want, her grandmother would have said. Well, she wanted to be fashionable and worldly and have lots of babies and surround herself with her brothers and sisters and raise them and marry them off in style and be godmother to their children, all the while overseeing Roger's household and her own children with a splendid assurance that would amaze everyone. But the one who must be amazed was Roger. He was the axis around which she spun. She wanted him to love and need her (as she loved him, for sometimes when she looked at him and knew she was finally married to him, her love swelled her throat and hurt her heart). She wanted to surround him with that love, with the children of her body—and his—with the comfort and ease a loving wife could bring.

She had waited for him to make some gesture to show where she stood in his life, what he wished her to do. But there was none. And so now it was up to her. . . . She closed her eyes tightly and said a series of quick little prayers, just as she used to do when she was a child and the morrow brought things she feared to face. She felt better. She opened her eyes. She smiled. She knew her position and her duties. She had been well taught. (And on her own, she had begun to learn that success was sometimes simply a matter of having the courage to proceed in the direction of one's dreams. . . .)

The three of them rose like guilty schoolboys when she came into the breakfast room the next morning. She had been floating around on her own so much that they had probably forgotten who she was, she thought irritably. Well, she would remind them.

"Barbara," Roger said, smiling at her. "How nice of you to join us. I thought you would still be sleeping." He kissed her hand. Handsome liar, Barbara thought.

The footman held out a chair at the opposite end of the table. Roger was at the other end, with Montrose and White at his right.

"No," she said. "I wish to sit here."

She indicated the empty seat on Roger's left and intercepted a look between White and Montrose that made her grit her teeth. As she settled herself, she said, "Sleeping? No, I came home early last night. I could not find you, and I was so tired."

There was a silence. She smiled into her coffee as the men sat back down. After a moment, Montrose, whose place was directly opposite hers, cleared his throat and said, "Ah, I have arranged for you to visit the Château de St. Honoré, sir. The count requests that you share luncheon with him. And the Trianon will be opened for you anytime you wish. The regent says to simply select a day. And Madame has sent a note asking you and Lady Devane to St. Cloud."

Barbara took a deep breath. "Trianon is one of the king's residences, is it not? I would love to see it."

Roger smiled. "It would bore you. The talk will be of nothing but architecture."

"But you are searching for ideas for Bentwoodes, are you not, Roger? How could I be bored with that? It will be my home, too. I know more about architecture than you think." Under the table she crossed her fingers and said a prayer. You will go to Hell for lying, Annie always told her. She knew nothing about architecture. But she would learn.

A footman entered carrying a bouquet of camellias, their full, lush blooms a soft pink, edged in white. He handed them to Barbara with a bow, and more surprised than anyone at the table, she took them.

"Law has asked to see you at five," Montrose began, but Roger's attention was fixed on the bouquet and on Barbara's face as she buried it in the flowers.

"They have no smell," she said through Montrose's sentence. She was smiling at Roger, that smile of hers which so charmed people. Roger did not smile back. Montrose gave up. No one was paying any attention to him.

Barbara pulled a small white card from inside the bouquet and read it. Her brows drew together. The smile faded.

"Well, really," she said, "I thought these were from you. Who is Henri de St. Michel? Have I met him? There must be some mistake. I will tell the footman to return these—"

Roger held out his hand, and obediently she placed the card in it.

"'To the memory of last night—Henri de St. Michel,'" he read aloud. "The memory of—whom did you meet last night, Barbara?"

White began to polish his butter knife with a napkin and Montrose shuffled his papers; both would rather have died than leave the room at this moment.

Barbara tapped a finger against her mouth.

"I can think of no one. You were with me at the reception, and at the ball, I simply wandered around—really, Roger, the men are so rude—" She was suddenly silent. The image of the man in the red cloak had popped into her mind. But why would he send her flowers? He did not even know her name. She told Roger of it.

He handed her back the card. "It must be St. Michel. And apparently he is taken with you. You should be flattered. He is one of the young Turks of the city. You should also be careful. He is quite ruthless in his methods. I see I shall have to watch out for you more carefully at public balls, or I shall be fighting a duel over you." He laughed suddenly. Everyone stared at him. "I never expected to fight a duel over my own wife," he explained, but no one else found it amusing except Barbara, who clapped her hands together.

"A duel! How exciting! But, of course, I would not want you to have to do that. I will send the flowers back at once, Roger. He is impertinent."

"That would be gauche, Barbara, and never let it be said that I have a gauche wife. St. Michel has simply expressed an interest in you as an attractive young woman. I have done it myself a hundred times. Accept it as a compliment. I want you to be fashionable and sought after. I think you would enjoy it very much. But no duels, please."

She plucked three blossoms from the bouquet and sent two of them skittering across the table to White and Montrose.

Leaning toward Roger, she carefully fastened his in his buttonhole, inches from his face. Shyly, not quite daring to look in his eyes, she kissed his cheek. Her lips were soft.

"In memory of my first conquest," she said.

Roger stood up and pinched her cheek. "Your second. I was your first. I am meeting St. Honoré at noon, but I will be home for dinner. You look very pretty this morning, Barbara. Is that a new gown? No? I like it. Francis, follow me out."

Smiling to herself, she attacked her cold breakfast. White continued to drink his coffee, now and again glancing across the table toward her. He liked looking at her, liked the lean lines of her, the way she spoke so directly, so unexpectedly in that low, throaty voice. In a few moments, Montrose burst back into the room.

"Mr. Montrose, you must advise me," said Barbara looking up from her plate. "Ought I to hire a secretary? Or will you help me with some small commissions? I do not want to impinge on your duties with Lord Devane." At that moment, she looked very much her age.

In spite of himself, Montrose thawed. He sat down. "I am at your service, ma'am."

"Good. I have not explored this house fully or met the servants. What do you suggest?"

Montrose looked startled. "Suggest?" he said tentatively, as if she had implied committing murder. White covered his mouth so that they would not see his smile.

"Yes." She said directly, "I am mistress of the household, you see. And I do not feel it has been established clearly."

"Ah . . . I will arrange for an appointment with the housekeeper, madam, so that you may tour the house. And, ah . . . I will assemble the servants at your convenience and introduce them. And I will arrange appointments with the majordomo, the cook, etcetera, so that you may make your preferences clear to them. . . ." He trailed off, eyeing her to see if there would be more. There was.

"Very good. What is Lord Devane's schedule?"

"His . . . schedule?"

"Yes. What time does he breakfast each morning? Is he going to hold a levee? On which mornings? Is the open table scheduled every day? You know, Mr. Montrose."

"Ah, he is holding his levees on Thursdays only. He breakfasts at ten every weekday morning, and we go over his appointments at that time. The, ah, open table is scheduled on Mondays, Tuesdays and Fridays, madam."

"Excellent, Mr. Montrose. Thank you. In the future, will you and Mr. White make it a point to come down to breakfast half an hour later than you do now? And any guests we should have are to breakfast in their rooms."

"Half an hour . . . but why?" He quickly added, "If I may ask."

"I wish to breakfast privately with my husband each morning before the day's business begins."

"Would you prefer that Mr. White and I breakfast in our rooms, also?"

She wiped her mouth with a napkin. "Oh, no. It is Lord Devane's habit to meet with you in the morning, and I will not change it. Except slightly, to include me. I am sure he will not mind." She smiled, her grandfather's smile, and stood up.

"And would you please begin interviewing for a new lady's maid for me? A French one. I wish to send Martha back to England as soon as possible."

"B-back to England?" Montrose said in a dazed voice.

"Yes. She is unsuitable. Good day, Mr. Montrose. Mr. White?"

White looked at her. He had enjoyed watching her deal with Montrose. Now it must be his turn. She smiled at him, and unlike Montrose, he could not help smiling back.

"Could you please select some books on architecture, books Lord Devane would be familiar with, and send them to my rooms? I lied before. I know nothing of architecture."

The door closed behind her. White pulled up his lapel to smell the camellia she had given him. She was right; there was no fragrance. He said, "She may favor her grandfather, but do you know whom I am reminded of?"

Montrose swelled up like a pigeon. "Who?"

"Her grandmother. The Duchess of Tamworth."

She was pleased with herself. Enormously pleased. She had been cool and dignified, as befitting the lady of the household. She had spoken up to White and Montrose. Firmly, but not coldly (in her mind's eye, she could picture her grandmother's nod of approval). And now, she was going to go out. On her own. After all, she was a married woman. She could do so. She had an invitation to an afternoon at the Marquise de Gondrin's. She would be safe there; Marie-Victorie de Gondrin was only a few years older than she, and very kind. Her salon was as good a place as any to try her wings as a fashionable young matron. She took a deep breath. Forward, as her grandfather would have said (in the rose garden, holding his pruning shears before him like a sword, while she and Harry followed, the only soldiers left to him). Forever forward.

Marie-Victorie's red-and-gold salon was crowded. Some of the guests sat in a circle of armchairs listening to a speaker. Others played cards at the three tables set up for that purpose. Still others were strolling around the room arm in arm, talking, stopping to listen to the trio of musicians playing at one end of the room or to eat and drink from the buffet table nearby. The hostess, Marie-Victorie, Marquise de Gondrin, was nineteen, with dark hair and eyes and a figure that was fashionably plump. She was from one of the finest French families, and she had married into a family as distinguished. It was a marriage arranged by her parents, and she tried to be all that was dutiful to her husband, who had died some years ago. Most of her girlhood had been spent in a convent, where she had learned to embroider, say her prayers, dance, draw and read Italian and do accounts. She had also learned a love of God from the holy sisters, and though she lived fashionably, she tried to practice God's commandments, even though her friends, such as the Duchesse de Berry and Mademoiselle de Charolais, most definitely did not. She saw Barbara standing in the doorway alone, and excused herself from the guests she was talking with to go to her.

A young man, whose hawklike nose gave his ordinary looks some interest, had been leaning against a wall behind one of the card tables. As he saw Marie-Victorie hurry to the doorway and greet her newest guest, a thin girl, wearing little rouge, but with beautiful red-gold hair, he straightened up and moved closer to them.

"How lovely you look," Marie-Victorie said to Barbara, kissing her cheeks. "Fresh and unspoiled. Come, do you wish to play cards or listen to Monsieur Descartes declaim?"

"I will listen."

Marie-Victorie interrupted the thin man in a preposterous wig who was holding the armchair circle enthralled with his theory that Racine's dramas reflected both fantasy and life, to introduce Barbara. She was given cold nods and assessing looks. She wished she had worn more jewelry. She sat down in a chair next to an old woman, who had been introduced as the Princesse de Lorraine. The other guests were once more listening to the lecture with absorbed looks on their faces. The princesse smelled as if she had not bathed in a long time. She was looking Barbara up and down, paying no attention to the talk on Racine. Her rouge was crusted into the wrinkles of her face, and what few teeth she had were rotted.

"So you are Montgeoffry's new rosebud. You look a rosebud, all pink and gold and fresh. But you sound like a courtesan. That voice. It ought to tickle Montgeoffry's fancy." The princesse cackled like a witch. Barbara was reminded of her Aunt Shrewsborough. Why did old women always think they could say whatever they pleased?

"I heard he married a child," said the princesse, "and I see it is true. You look hardly old enough to rouge. You are not wearing enough, girl, and you ought to. It is the fashion, you know." The princesse belched loudly. A servant standing behind her leaned over. The princesse made an impatient movement with her hand.

"No! No! Damned pest! I pay him to follow me about and make sure I do not fall out of my chair. And what does he do, but continually annoy me. There are no more decent servants to be found these days. In my day, we flogged them. Today, it is nothing but leniency."

"I sympathize with you," Barbara began cautiously. "I am looking for a lady's maid myself because—"

"Just what you need!" interrupted the princesse. "A bright, pert lady's maid who knows what she is doing. She will bring you into style, put more color in those pretty cheeks. I will keep you in mind—"

"That would be wonderful. I—"

The princesse belched again. It was loud enough to halt the lecture in midsentence. Once more the servant leaned over her.

"Go away!" she cried. "Fool! Impertinent fool!"

Monsieur Descartes picked up his thread of thought smoothly. As did the princesse.

"Speaking of impertinence, have you heard the latest, rose-bud? Orléans's daughter, that slut de Berry, is said to be sleeping with a lieutenant of the dragoons, someone named Riom, they say. I thought she was involved with young Richelieu, but my daughter was telling me just the other day that de Berry has to ask this Riom's permission to go any-where. That he slapped her in front of a room full of people. And she puts up with it. Bad blood! Bad blood! That's what happens when cousin marries cousin . . . the mind goes. All the Orléanses are half-crazy. In my day, one might go to bed with a lieutenant, but he did not tell one what to do."

Barbara sat transfixed. She had no idea what she should say.

"Excuse me for interrupting," said a voice over her shoul-der, "but Madame de Gondrin wishes Lady Devane to meet an admirer of hers." Barbara did not recognize the speaker, but she was glad of any excuse to leave both Racine and the princesse.

"Go on, then," cackled the princesse, waving bony arms. "You are only young once, heh, rosebud?"

The young man led Barbara to one of the long windows that overlooked the gardens, rather than to Marie-Victorie.

"You are fortunate," he said. "The princesse considers it beneath herself to use a chamber pot and often relieves herself directly on the floor. That servant behind her cleans up, but it is hell on priceless rugs and whoever may be standing near."

She stared at him. He acted as if they were old friends when they had not even been introduced, and she was trying to decide whether she should be insulted by it or not, when he, as if by magic, held up a camellia before her. She had no idea how he managed it, and that did not matter. What mattered was the grace of the gesture and the fact that the camellia was a pink one edged in white. He grinned at her.

"You." Marie-Victorie's afternoon began to be interesting, after all.

"Henri Camille Louis de St. Michel, at your most humble service."

"But how did you know me?"

"I asked Marie-Victorie to tell me the moment you arrived. I watched you with the princesse, and, at the moment I gath-ered her smell was overwhelming you, I came to the rescue."

So this was her first admirer. She considered him. He was about twenty, ordinary in every way except for his hawklike nose, which gave him a predatory look. He seemed certain of himself.

"Did you receive my flowers? Camellias are my trademark."

"They were lovely. My husband thought so, too."

"The half-opened ones remind me of you. You have that half-wakened, fresh look about you. Very English, very appealing. Like a woman just learning of love."

"It must be the lack of rouge. The princesse says I do not wear enough."

He stared at her, not certain whether she was serious or not. She was not playing according to the usual rules, which required that she should either draw back, offended, or let him know that his pursuit would be welcome. Confused, he decided to laugh.

Barbara's eyes sparkled. Already she had an admirer. She tossed her head. It was exhilarating not to have a chaperone hanging over her. Before her marriage, she could not even speak to a man without her aunt frowning or her grandmother drawing her away. It was not that they did not trust her; it was that the reputation of a young, unmarried woman was so easily damaged. . . . If she laughed too loudly or smiled too much, if she seemed to like talking to young men . . . there were a hundred things she must do and not do. A young lady must always be modest, quiet, demure, obedient. Now, as a married woman, she had none of those restrictions—unless Roger wished to impose some—and he did not care to . . . yet. The freedom was wonderful, as was the knowledge this man found her attractive. If he found her so, then surely Roger must, also.

St. Michel backtracked a little. "Are you enjoying Paris?"

"I am now."

This he understood. He stepped closer to her. "When may I call on you?"

Her eyes were wide and blue and innocent. "Lord Devane and I would be happy to receive you at any time."

She curtsied and went to Marie-Victorie. She had enjoyed herself. St. Michel was fast, as Roger had said.

Armand, the Duc de Richelieu, sauntered over to St. Michel, who was still watching Barbara. Marie-Victorie was escorting her around the room, introducing her to more people. If St. Michel was ordinary, Richelieu was ugly, with a thin, narrow face and strange yellow-brown eyes, eyes that made people shiver when they saw them in certain lights. His voice, however, was soft and caressing. If a woman closed her eyes and listened only to his voice, she would swear he was the most handsome man in the world. Some women said his voice bewitched them.

St. Michel and Richelieu were all that was currently fashionable in young French noblemen, and of the two, Richelieu, with his more ancient pedigree and his sense of arrogant confidence, was the leader, while St. Michel was a determined copy. Both were married, but true to the mode of the times, neither lived with his wife. St. Michel, who was a second son, had married a rich young woman whose background was not as good as his, and he kept her in a family château miles from Paris, seeing her only once or twice a year. Richelieu, who had been forced to marry his stepsister when he was fifteen, had never slept with his wife and refused to have anything to do with her. His father had imprisoned him in the Bastille for over a year to force him to acknowledge and make love to the girl, but Richelieu refused. He was content that she should do as she please and did not mind that she had lovers. A current story said that he had recently and most unexpectedly visited his wife and found her making love to another man. His only comment had been to say that she was fortunate no one else had seen or she would have been embarrassed.

"To whom were you talking, Henri?"

"The young English countess, Devane."

Richelieu watched Barbara as she stood by Marie-Victorie. She was laughing. Her laughter was unrestrained. Her face was clear and fresh and free of care. His strange eyes glinted.

"Still innocent. A rarity in Paris."

"Spirited, also, I think," said St. Michel. They might have been discussing a horse. "And you have not heard the voice. Once you hear it, it lingers in your mind."

Richelieu tapped a finger against his mouth, his eyes still on Barbara.

"I saw her first, Armand," said St. Michel.

Richelieu laughed at him, a laugh that was soft, dangerous, challenging. St. Michel put his hand to his sword. Once more, Richelieu's eyes glinted.

"Temper, temper, Henri. Marie-Victorie would be furious—and rightly so—if we spoiled her drawing room with a quarrel. And over what? A woman. Let us toss a coin. The winner has the first crack at the little English. The loser stands aside . . . for a while. Agreed?"

After a moment, St. Michel nodded his head. Richelieu reached into a waistcoat pocket for a coin. St. Michel put a hand on his arm.

"We will use one of my coins, my friend."

"I can remember when I was first married," Marie-Victorie was saying to Barbara as they strolled through the drawing room. "I was overwhelmed, even though I went at once to live with my husband's family. My mother-in-law was rigid in her standards. She frightened me completely—that man staring at us is the Duc de Richelieu. I will introduce you in a few moments. Beware of him. He has a terrible reputation, but women love him anyway. Each desires to be the one that has the power to hold him. None do. Armand always moves on. But what was I saying? Oh, yes, how I used to long to be on my own, as you are, to run my own household. You are fortunate to be alone with your dear Lord Devane. You must visit me whenever you have a question. We will pretend I am your mother-in-law, your Parisian one. I had such a crush on your husband when I was younger. He used to be in Paris often on diplomatic missions for the court in Hanover. He never once looked at me. You are the envy of half the women in Paris."

"Whom did he look at?"

Marie-Victorie laughed and patted Barbara's hand. "To tell you the truth, I cannot remember. His name was always linked with someone's. A man as handsome and charming as your husband is much in demand. But I cannot remember that anyone was his favorite. He was great friends with the Prince de Soissons; that I do recall. Ah, here is someone I want you to meet. Louise-Anne, may I present Lady Devane. She is newly married, to the divine Roger Montgeoffry. Do you remember how we used to moon over him as girls? Barbara, this is Louise-Anne, Mademoiselle de Charolais."

The young woman Marie-Victorie was introducing her to looked to be no older than Barbara though her small, sulky face was heavily rouged and powdered. Her eyes flicked over Barbara in just a few seconds, and Barbara felt herself weighed, assessed and found wanting. Louise-Anne was one of the daughters of the head of the great house of Bourbon-Condé. Her bloodlines on both sides stretched far back into French history and royalty, for her grandmother had been one of the mistresses of Louis XIV, a position more honored by the French court than that of his legitimate queen. Louise-Anne had learned arrogance, the knowledge of who she was and from whom she sprang, before she could walk, for she was a granddaughter of France, of the great Louis, master of the world, builder of Versailles, creator of all that was cultured and civilized in the existing world.

"Marie-Victorie, where is Armand?" Louise-Anne said, giving Barbara a short nod. "I saw him a moment ago and now he has disappeared. He knows I wish to quarrel with him— ah, there he is. Excuse me."

Marie-Victorie linked her arm back through Barbara's, and they began to walk again.

"We grew up together," she said of Louise-Anne, "which is why I put up with her rudeness. She can be charming when she wishes to be, but now she is only charming for Richelieu. She is making a fool of herself over him. Everyone is talking about it. I wish she would marry and settle down."

"As we have," said Barbara.

Marie-Victorie patted her hand. "As we have."

It was late. Barbara lay alone in her bed, waiting to hear her door open, but it remained closed. Finally, she threw off her blankets and ran in her white nightgown to Roger's apartments, pushed open his bedchamber door gently and looked around. Justin, his valet, was gone. Good. Dressed in a loose robe, Roger was sitting in an armchair, staring into the fire. Littered at his feet were many papers, drawings and sketches of houses. She tiptoed into the room. She had to take a deep breath, her heart was beating so. What she was doing was . . . bold. If you want something, go after it, her grandmama always said. She had done so all day. This was her last citadel.

Roger did not hear her enter. He was thinking of what it felt like to be in Paris again. Of the memories being here revived. Paris was the center of the world; its arts, its fashion, its architecture, its language were copied by every civilized nation. He had first seen it in the late 1690s, when peace treaties were being negotiated between France and the rest of the world, and Paris was once more open to foreigners. He had been twenty-four, Richard's military aide for some four years, and before that, a soldier since he was sixteen. The war had been going on all that time, and he had seen enough blood, enough maimed or dying men and horses, enough burned fields, enough crying women, to last him a lifetime. He took a leave of absence from his regiment, Richard arranged some kind of official reason so that he should draw a salary, and he came to Paris. He loved it. Though the great Louis was in his pious years, there were still magnificent entertainments, ballets, suppers, balls at the luxurious châteaux surrounding Versailles, and he had dropped among the French women like a cannonball exploding. They all wanted him, a princesse here, a comtesse there, a duchesse, an opera dancer, an actress. For three years he drank, laughed, loved, spent other people's money. When war began again in 1701, he was among the last to leave. He went back to England, back to his post as aide, back to Richard. . . .

(Was it then that he realized his feelings for Richard were more than admiration? Or had he always known, ignoring them, burying them in service, in camaraderie on long campaign nights before a battle when the wind whistled through the tents, and Richard sat up grieving that the next morning he would be sending his soldiers into death. He ran Richard's errands; he rode through armies of crazed men to take commands to Richard's subordinates; he risked his life behind enemy lines as both soldier and spy, and he journeyed between God knows where and Tamworth or London so that Alice should have her letters. He had never known a man to love a woman the way Richard loved Alice. . . . Everyone in camp held his breath when her letters came, because their beloved, smiling general, the best, the finest soldier in England, had been known to make battle-hardened sergeants weep when a letter from his wife was not a happy one.)

But he was thirty now, and being Richard's aide was not enough any longer. And there was the war, its blood, guts spilling out of men whose faces mirrored the shock of that last final surprise. And there was the politics of ambitious men, stupid men, greedy men to contend with. And he was tired of it all and of himself. So he resigned his commission, and left for Hanover, with Richard's letters of recommendation and introduction in his pockets. He involved himself in Hanoverian policy, gambling that Elector George would be Queen Anne's successor. Until 1710. The year of Richard's death. Devastating him. The agony of the grief he felt, the feelings never expressed. He had thanked a God he stopped believing in that he had taken the time to visit Richard those last years. That he had never abandoned his old mentor, the finest man he had ever known. Who had never abandoned him. He was back in Paris when the ceasefires of war were ordered. Older now, forty stood as the next major signpost in his life. Wealthy. The heir to the English throne was his friend. Therefore, men scrambled to offer him ways to make money . . . as long as they benefited in return. He revived an old acquaintance, looking for . . . what? Had he known then what lay under that old friendship?

Even now, there was no answer, but being once more in Paris revived memories interlaced with pain. And passion. Dark and throbbing. Like blood seeping rhythmically from a wound. Ebb and flow. Life and death. I am over it, he thought. How demanding, forbidden and treacherous it had been . . . and exhilarating, as only such a combination could be. Striking him more deeply than anything in his life but his feelings for Richard. He could face that truth. And others. The ending of the affair was inevitable. He had known it even as it began, and yet he did not stop its beginning. And he had not been able to stop its ending. And that was when he finally knew his own mortality. Having taken the lid from his Pandora's box and gazed inside. At all he was. And was not. And chose to be. And chose not to be. . . .

Bentwoodes was his new love. Sealing over old hurts, old disappointments. Protecting him from himself. He was here for Bentwoodes (and to test his invulnerability—he admitted

it). Paris was the center of the world. He could not forever
ignore it. He would not. All his life, he had faced that which
he was afraid of. And triumphed. He would find his furnishings for Bentwoodes here; all those elements that made a fine
house beautiful, the moldings, the carvings, the rugs, the
tapestries, the furniture. Bentwoodes in its glory would
become Devane House. It would shelter his sons. He would
do as Richard had done. . . . He smiled to himself. A wistful, charming smile, sadness curving its edges beautifully.
Even in death, Richard influenced him. How oddly lives,
places, things intertwined in the space of mortality a man was
given. Who would have guessed that Bentwoodes—he could
remember fox hunting in its fields with Richard—would come
to mean so much? So much that he risked Paris again. I am
over it, he thought.

"Roger . . ."

He started. "Barbara! What is it? Are you unwell?"

She did not come any closer, but moved one bare foot back
and forth against the rug. She did not know it, but she looked
very young and very charming, with her hair all about her
shoulders and in her high-necked, thin gown.

"I . . . I feel so lonely, R-Roger. I wondered if you might
. . . c-come and sleep with me for a while." She bit her lip.
"You don't have to do anything," she said hurriedly. "I just
want some company. I am not used to being so alone all the
time, you see."

She rushed through the words trying to explain. "At Tamworth, there was Grandmama and my brothers and sisters,
and even at Aunt Abigail's, there was Mary. Here, there is no
one. . . . Oh, Roger, I miss my family so, and it is worst late
at night, and I thought, if you were not busy, you might come
and visit a while. Just until I go to sleep. You do not have to
do it forever. I am sure I will become used to everything
eventually."

"My poor baby," he said. "I forget how young you are." He
held out his arms, and she ran into them. He rubbed his chin
against her thick hair. She sighed and nestled against him,
poking at a drawing with her foot.

"What is this?"

"Bentwoodes . . . Devane House. My—our home."

She reached down and picked up a paper.

"That is a temple front," said Roger. "A man named Palladio designed it some hundred years ago in Italy. I find its classicism beautiful."

Palladio, she mouthed silently. Classicism.

"You know, Barbara," he said, watching her mouth as it shaped the words, "you are not at all what I expected."

But before she could ask what he expected he said, "To bed. I shall come and visit awhile." He stood up, and she stayed in his arms. As he carried her to her rooms, he said in her hair, "Even though I don't have to do anything I think I might after all."

The next morning she was at the breakfast table before Roger. She blushed when she heard the door open, her mind full of memories of the night before. She signaled the footman, and as Roger sat down, a cup of steaming coffee was placed before him. He was far more relaxed than she. But then he had far more experience with next mornings.

"You are up early," he said.

The footman began to serve them breakfast. Roger cut into a piece of bacon. After a moment he stopped.

"But where are Francis and Caesar? It is ten o'clock, is it not?"

Speaking very rapidly, Barbara said, "I asked them to join us in half an hour. I thought it would be a good idea to have this time alone, before you begin all your duties and appointments, and before I begin mine. It might be the only time we see each other all day, and we can start off the day together, no matter what happens later on. You do not mind . . . I hope . . ."

He smiled to himself and took another bite of bacon. "My dear child, you are free to order your household about as you wish."

She took another deep breath and plunged on. "I-I wanted to ask you about my invitations."

He looked at the stack of papers by her plate.

"I am not certain which I should refuse and which I should accept. I thought we might go over them together, if you do not mind. Until I know more people. Then I will not need your help."

"You could ask Francis's help."

"I should feel so stupid asking him. Please, Roger. Just until I learn my way."

He frowned. She held her breath. She looked young and appealing, and he remembered she had been young and appealing last night. He put down his fork and held out his hand, and she gave him the stack of engraved cards and tried not to rustle too impatiently as he leisurely looked through each one.

"You have calling cards from the Duchesse du Maine, the Duchesse de Berry, the Duchesse d'Orléans, Madame la Princesse and Madame la Duchesse. They are among the most powerful women in France. Return the calls of each one. We take no sides."

"Even the Duchesse de Berry?"

"She is the oldest daughter of the regent, and an afternoon call will do no harm. Under no circumstances, however, are you to go to one of her supper parties, if you should be invited. I doubt you will be. Use your own judgment, Barbara. Go wherever you wish, avoiding only suppers by de Berry, the regent or the Prince de Soubice."

"And what happens at these suppers I am to avoid?"

He smiled at her. "Nothing you need know about."

"Do you go?"

She was looking down at her plate. The smile on his face faded as he stared at her. Nothing about her was quite predictable. No maidenly tears on their wedding night, when he had expected them. Then her silence, her fading into the background on the journey, so much so that he had almost forgotten he was married. And now, again, her unfurling like a flower in the sun. Receiving bouquets from young men, appearing in his bedchamber at night in a thin nightgown, catching him at a vulnerable moment, charming him, and this morning, asking him dangerous questions. It shocked him to realize—afresh—that there was now a person in his life whose feelings he would have to consider. He had no wish to hurt her, but he also had no wish to curtail any of his activities. He would be discreet, but not even for Barbara, sweet as she was, did he intend to change his life.

"If I wish, I do," he said, very gently, waiting for her sulks, her tears; they seemed inevitable.

She still stared at her plate. He waited. When she looked at him, he was surprised to see that her eyes were not brimming with tears. They were clear.

"Will you come with me to Madame de Gondrin's this afternoon?" she said.

"Perhaps," he said, surprising himself.

She leapt up from her place and kissed his cheek and was back in her chair again before he had time to move, smiling at him as if he were the most wonderful man in the world, and smiling, she was the image of her grandfather. Why had he lied? He would not be going with her to Madame de Gondrin's. God, he would hurt her in little ways, a hundred little ways, and gradually she would come to love him with less intensity. Until she did not love him at all. Which would be best. For them both. But he found he did not like thinking of a time when she would not love him, and he sighed at his aging vanity.

"I have invitations to the opera and the theater and luncheons which are addressed to me only, Roger. Do I go alone?"

"If you wish. I will have many engagements which do not include you, and I would feel better knowing you are occupied with your own friends. It is not fashionable for a husband and wife to do things together." He watched her face as she considered this, thinking suddenly, sharply, of St. Michel's bouquet. "But do not become too fashionable, Barbara. There are limits." For her. Not for him.

She smiled again, happy at his proprietary words, words he knew were unfair, and he was touched. Be careful, Roger, he thought to himself. In his mind, he saw three toothless old hags grinning at him. The Fates.

"You mentioned not taking sides earlier. Tell me why."

For her to be asking him of French politics when most girls her age (and women far older) were interested in nothing but their gowns or gossip or love affairs was another surprise. What lay behind it? The wish to impress him? Or Alice's training? He thought of the quagmire that was French politics, of his own monetary stake in it, of women like the Duchesse du Maine, who schemed and lied and plotted so that her husband might have the power of his cousin, the regent. A power that had been left to du Maine in his father's will, for his father was the great king, Louis XIV. But du Maine was illegitimate, and though he had been given money, titles and position, he could never have that ultimate power, that of a pure bloodline, such as Orléans, nephew to a king. And, more important, legitimate. He thought of John Law, a gambler, a visionary, a rogue, who was in France to put its monetary system back together. He had schemes of a national bank, of public companies that would make millions for their investors and uplift the stagnant economy. Law was going to pull France out of its near-bankruptcy, caused by years of war under the great Louis. He thought of the financiers, the farmers-general (a monopoly of men who collected taxes and raised the money for royal loans), the bankers who wanted Law to fail, who had gotten fat and rich off the old systems of money lending. Roger was gambling that Law would not fail. He was going to invest heavily in the new bank, and in the public companies. To build what he envisioned required a great supply of capital. But Law's power rested on Orléans, and if Orléans fell, Law fell. And Orléans was in a shaky position, threatened with war by Spain, whose ruler was one of the great Louis's own grandsons—legitimate—and therefore was a cousin, but what was family when money and power were involved? And the Duchesse du Maine kept the flames fanned. And it was all over who should control the young heir's household and education. An heir who might die tomorrow of smallpox or the putrid sore throat or poison. And then France would be plunged in civil war again, as she had been all those years before Louis had been strong enough and crafty enough to bring the French nobility under his heel. He did not want a wife whose lifeblood ran on public policy, whose machinations undid kings (the ink on hundreds of letters—women always wrote letters—letters that lied, that pushed, that prodded, that slandered, that libeled). Barbara might grow as fashionable, as witty, as sophisticated, even as wanton as the cleverest of the French princesses, but he did not want her as devious, involved in what was the realm of men, and a dangerous realm at that.

"It is too complicated to explain," he said abruptly, "and I do not wish you to worry your head about it. Play, visit, gossip, buy whatever you desire, but do not become enamored of politics. It ruins women and I would not like it in you—ah, here are Francis and Caesar. Good morning, gentlemen.

Francis, I have a commission for you. I want you to go through the sketches of Le Vau and Le Notre that are compiled at Versailles. If you leave today, you can be finished by the end of the week. The regent has granted permission for us to see them. I want the earlier sketches—"

"I cannot do that, sir," Montrose said. There was a silence. "Lady Devane has asked me to interview candidates for a lady's maid, and the task will take several days." He did not look at Barbara.

How sneaky of him, thought Barbara, furious. Montrose put her status in the household to the test. Either she was its mistress, to be obeyed as Roger was, or she was forever relegated to a position of inferiority, respected by no one.

Roger put his hand over his mouth so that no one should see his smile. Household maneuvers for power. More lethal than French politics.

"You must certainly finish Lady Devane's business, then. Next time, I assume you will not need to ask." It was gently, charmingly done, but a reproof nonetheless. He looked over to find Barbara's eyes on him, adoring.

He stood up, chucking her under the chin before he left. Everyone was silent.

"Mr. Montrose," Barbara said. "That was unworthy of you. You may do Lord Devane's commissions before you do mine. You had only to ask." She left the room.

"Her grandmother's child," White said to Montrose, teasing, reminding.

Montrose sniffed.

That afternoon, at dinner, Barbara listened more closely to the conversation swirling around her. There was talk of the bastards' rank. What bastards? Saint-Simon slammed a fist on the table as he complained that the illegitimate should not be recognized before the princes of the blood, those related legitimately to the royal family. And someone mentioned a rumor that the regent would betray the young king for a chance to rule Spain. And there was talk of finance. Always finance. France was on the verge of bankruptcy, and John Law believed he had a solution. She knew that much because he continually told everyone so. He was at their table this afternoon, interrupting Saint-Simon to say so once more. He had a concept for a national bank. She listened to Roger promise to meet with Law and the regent later this afternoon. He had said he might accompany her to Marie-Victorie's. Finance outweighed her own charms.

Someone said the Duchesse du Maine was spreading more rumors about the regent's practicing witchcraft and incest. Someone else wondered why he did not arrest her. Someone else said he did not dare because the rumors were true.

"Richelieu went into her private apartments disguised as a dressmaker and stayed the night," the sister of the British ambassador was saying. A babble of talk followed her words. Richelieu topped witchcraft and incest. He made his mistresses wait together in his waiting room while he serviced them one by one in the bedroom; he was sleeping with the regent's daughter, de Berry—no, with the regent's mistress, Madame d'Averne—no, with them both. Strange, thought Barbara, that the ugly young man she had been introduced to only yesterday could be so notorious and yet so irresistible. When Marie-Victorie had brought him over to meet her, she had thought him arrogant, and his eyes made her shiver. Roger was signaling her. It was time for her to lead the ladies away. He was not going with her this afternoon. She would have to go to Marie-Victorie's by herself. She wished he had not forgotten. The patient in spirit is better than the proud in spirit, she could hear her grandmother say, but her grandmother was not young and in love.

That night, Roger did not return home from his appointment with the regent and John Law. After Marie-Victorie's, she had rushed to his apartments to find only Justin. She ate supper by herself, solitary at the long table. She dressed for the opera in silence. Martha was just fastening a necklace, when the note came. He was unavoidably detained. He begged her forgiveness. She was to go on without him. He did not know what time he would be home. She had Martha undress her, again silent as the gown and underpetticoat and jewels and pins and laces and stockings and corset had to be unfastened, untied, put away. She was not going without him. Not to a public ball. She had no set of friends yet to go with.

And where was Roger? Perhaps, after all, in spite of his words this morning, he was at one of the regent's suppers. She knew a little about them, never mind her professed ignorance to Roger. They were said to be sinful, wicked orgies with naked women and wine and every kind of vice. She might not know much about vice, but she knew about naked women, and she did not want Roger seeing one. Jealousy and all its attendant emotions seized her. She knew about jealousy, too, for she had been jealous of Harry's place in her grandmother's heart, and she had been jealous when Jane had begun to like Harry better than herself. But those feelings were nothing to the ones she experienced now. If Roger were to love another woman, she would die. She would kill the woman. And him. What if, at this very moment, he were smiling at another woman—touching her—

There was a discreet knock at her door. She was learning her household. It must be Montrose. Only he would knock with such politeness. She pulled a long shawl over her nightgown.

"Come in."

Montrose stood at the doorway. "Lord Devane requested that I present these to you—to keep you company, he said. They were to be a surprise, but Mr. White thought, since you did not go out this evening as planned—"

Barbara bounded up from her chair. "What? What?"

She was not yet used to the lavish way Roger gave her presents. It could be anything—a ball gown, jewels. Montrose pulled something from behind his body—a small, black boy, with huge brown eyes, eyes that stared at Barbara as if she were an ogre. Montrose half pushed the boy, who looked to be four or five, toward Barbara, and the child swallowed and bowed.

"Your servant, madame," he said in a soft, fluid accent.

Barbara stood transfixed. "But what is it?" she asked.

"A page, ma'am. His name is Hyacinthe, and he is yours to do with as you please."

Barbara bent down to the small boy. Why, he was the same age as Anne. His soft mouth trembled, but he did not cry. Very gently, Barbara held out her hand. After a moment, he put his into it. He was just a baby. Round his neck was a silver collar engraved with the Devane crest. It was the height of current fashion to own a small, black slave, that silver collar proclaiming his status.

"I am very pleased to have a page," Barbara said to him. "Particularly such a big boy as you. Are you seven?" Growing up with brothers had taught her much about the male ego. He shook his head.

"You look seven," Barbara said.

"I am five," he blurted out.

"Five!" Barbara rolled her eyes. He half smiled. Montrose coughed.

"Yes, what is it?"

"There is more, ma'am."

"More?"

What else could there be? What could possibly exceed a small, black page? Montrose went into the hall and came back with a basket. Barbara could hear small growls and yelps. Puppies! Roger had bought her puppies! Inside the basket were two fashionable pugs, with little pushed-in faces and bulging brown eyes. They howled when they saw Barbara, who leaned over and took them in each hand. They wiggled and squirmed and tried to lick her hands. They were tiny, hardly bigger than her hands.

"Pugs! Aren't they sweet! Look, Hyacinthe, look at my puppies!"

The puppies worked a change on the little black boy. He smiled at the wriggling, whining dogs.

"You must be in charge of them," Barbara said. Again, Montrose coughed. Barbara looked at him. What else could there possibly be?

"Where would you like them put, ma'am?"

Put? His stare took in the wriggling pugs and Hyacinthe.

"Here," Barbara said at once. She was not banishing her page or her puppies to that cavernous kitchen so far away. They would stay here in her room with her. She need not be alone any longer.

"Have a bed made in front of the fire for Hyacinthe. And leave the basket. Tell a footman to bring up some milk for . . . for Hyacinthe and the puppies . . . and me." There, let Montrose look down his nose at that. She knew how new puppies cried for their mother the first night from home. And she could not bear the thought of this little boy by himself in the servants' attic quarters. She knew how to protect what was hers. Someday Roger would learn that, the depth and fierceness of her maternal streak.

Later that night, after the puppies had been fed and played with, and Hyacinthe was snug in a little trundle bed before the fire in her bedchamber, she thought about Roger's gifts. Nothing was so impressive as having a small, black page to carry one's train or fan and bring wine to one's guests . . . and the pugs were dear. They had fallen into the bowl of milk in their puppy greed, and she and Hyacinthe had to clean them. Somewhere today or yesterday or the day before, Roger had taken the time to buy these for her. That meant he did care. And if he cared, she could be patient until he loved her. Grandmama was right.

She heard a sound. Someone was crying . . . very softly . . . but she recognized it. Anne or Charlotte, and even Tom and Kit before they decided they were too old, had done the same many times, cried softly in their beds over some hurt. She got out of her big canopied bed and went over by the fire. The little boy was crying in his pillow. She knelt down.

"What is it?" she said softly. "May I help?"

He started and took a deep breath and sat up. "Forgive me, madame. Do not beat me, madame."

"Beat you? But why would I do so?"

"They said I must be very good and not cry or I would displease you and you would be angry and beat me, as I would deserve, they said. They said I was lucky to be s-sold, and that I must be a m-man. It is only that I-I miss my friends, m-madame." His voice cracked and tears poured down his face. Barbara rubbed his rough, curly hair wondering who "they" were. She knew little about the beggar fraternity of Paris, who made money by buying children from women who did not want them or could not afford them, and then resold them to the nobility and rich bourgeois as pages and maids and companions. Black children like Hyacinthe were sold as slaves. But that was a fortunate fate. A child that was not bright or handsome enough was maimed and put on the streets to beg, the fraternity reasoning that deformity in a child would strike pity in the hearts of passersby. Profit had to come from somewhere.

"Shall I send you back?" she asked.

"Oh, no!" he cried. His fear made his tears stop. "Then I would surely be beaten! I was born to be a slave. Please, madame, do not send me back. I promise I will not cry anymore. Please, madame! They would be so angry. I am yours now."

"Then of course you shall stay. And I will not mind your crying tonight. I think you will stop when you are used to me and to this place. Now, you lie back down. You have many hazardous duties, beginning early tomorrow when you must bring me hot chocolate to drink. The cook will grumble at you. But you will say proudly, 'It is for Lady Devane.' And now, you must let me put these puppies into bed with you; I think they will wake up in the night and miss their friends also. And how will I sleep with puppies crying? You know they will not worry whether it disturbs me or not. And another thing. Early tomorrow you must take them outside in the garden, so that they do not spoil my rugs. And you must feed them. Now go to sleep, Hyacinthe . . . go to sleep."

She could see that her words soothed the boy. He had relaxed a little. She pulled the covers up about his small arms, each of which enclosed a sleeping pug. She thought of her brothers and sisters, of her grandmother, of Tamworth, its winter fields now covered with snow. Her eyes closed; she felt lulled by the warmth of the page and the pugs.

When Roger tiptoed into her apartment hours later, he found her asleep next to Hyacinthe's trundle bed, her head pillowed in one arm. One hand was still in Hyacinthe's. Roger stood still for some time looking at her. It made quite a picture, the sleeping child, the puppies, the sleeping girl, her hair tumbling down her back, a half-smile on her face, the fire behind her glowing red under its embers. He smiled down at her. She looked hardly older than the page boy. So young and innocent.

Her innocence made the women he had been with that night seem jaded and ugly. Their perfume seemed to saturate his clothes, and the smell made him sick. The high, floating feeling of the champagne he had drunk was leaving him. He felt old, tired . . . unfaithful.

This last was a new feeling, one he had never expected to have. What would she do if she should wake now and find

him swaying over her, drunk and smelling of other women?
Would she cry? Would she rage? He had no idea. He knew
only that she would care, and it was suddenly very important
that she should not know. She was such a strange, unexpected
child. She had said hardly three words on the journey here.
He had forgotten at times that she was with him. Then suddenly, in the last week, she had more than made her presence
known. The whole household was turned upside down by her.
Interruption of his breakfast customs. Camellias from St.
Michel. Interviews for a maid. If she should leave him tomorrow, he would miss her. He had not expected this. To like his
wife. To be fond of her.

She must be cold now that the fire was dying and she had
no cover. He bent down and scooped her into his arms. It was
no easy task; he was drunk, and she was almost as tall as he
was. He swayed a moment to catch his balance. She half woke
and said sleepily, "Roger, I'm so glad you are home." She was
asleep again even before she finished her words. He carried
her over to her bed, put her in it and pulled the covers up.

"So am I, Bab," he said to her softly. "So am I."

CHAPTER ELEVEN

*T*he final two candidates for the position of lady's maid to the young Countess Devane sat waiting in the ground-floor servants' vestibule until the countess should be ready to interview them separately. Both women were young, no more than twenty. Both were dressed stylishly, in good taste and with flair, as became a competent lady's maid. Both were already lady's maids in noble households, though neither was the chief one. They had experience with dressmaking, hair-styling, needlepoint, washing fine linen, starching tiffanies (a thin silk), lawns, points (needlepoint lace) and mending. In addition, both could read and write, speak English as well as French, play the harpsichord and dance. One of them, Thérèse Fuseau, was even experienced in going to market for kitchen staples. She had worked in the kitchens of the Condé household before being promoted to the bedchambers. Montrose had done his job well; each was highly qualified for her job, which was an arduous one. They might be called upon to read to a sick mistress or play the harpsichord or sing to amuse her. They must dress her for going out and see that her wardrobe and jewels were kept in good order, which meant supervising a staff of chambermaids, necessary women, starchers and washerwomen. They might have to nurse her through sickness or failed love affairs.

For a bright, ambitious woman, however, this was the opportunity of a lifetime. Lord Devane was wealthy, and his young wife had brought no favorite maids with her from her

313

home. A good lady's maid could make herself so indispensable that she became part of the family. It was a chance for permanence and security, along with responsibility.

There was little difference between the two women. Each was pretty in a petite way, with dark curling hair and dark eyes. Thérèse Fuseau had a most definite nose, but it gave character to her already pretty face. She sat quietly, twisting her hands in her lap in a way that was foreign to her normal behavior. But those who worked with Thérèse in the Condé household had noticed that she was not her laughing, sunny self these last few weeks. Usually, she sang as she worked the long hours of an assistant lady's maid (up before dawn to light fires, running errands between floors all day, staying awake until the early morning hours to undress one of the young Condé princesses). She was one of those rare people who take life as it comes and find the best in it.

But this last month, she had not been herself. And now, she was seeking to leave the Condé staff. Suzanne, her friend and roommate, who was employed as a starcher and idolized Thérèse for her climb from kitchen maid to assistant lady's maid, could not understand it. Thérèse cried at odd moments, was preoccupied, snappish.

What Suzanne could not know was that Thérèse was in trouble. She had given herself to one of the young princes de Condé, throwing away years of self-restraint. (She could have married the head footman; he had begged her. But she had no wish to end like her mother, dead in childbirth, tired and years old before her time, from children, pregnancy and the hard work of their farm outside Paris. It was better for a female servant to keep herself chaste; her life was easier; there was opportunity to advance, to save money. Thérèse had a secret dream of saving enough money to open a dressmaker's shop.) But it was a dream she had abandoned because she was, after all, only human, young and warmly passionate, and the prince was handsome and polished and said sweet things and she thought he loved her. And in a moment of weakness, she let him do as he wanted, as she wanted. For a while he could not possess her enough. He gave her money, which she would not accept, and gifts of flowers, which she would. The money made her feel like a whore, which she was not. She had given herself freely, out of love. Or so she thought. It did not take long for his interest to wane.

The moment she realized it was a moment of stunning clarity. That she could have been so stupid, she who had been raised in a noble household, she who had seen many a maid ruined. And combined with that was heartbreak, because she had cared for him. Yet she could have survived that. It was his disrespect for her as a person that hurt most. He told his brother, and his brother began to haunt her. Just one time, he begged. Money, he promised. Once he had found her alone in a hallway, sorting linens, and he had wrestled her to the ground, his hand up her skirts, before she had screamed, and he had run away. She realized that she had been nothing to her young prince but a hole into which he put his sex. And now, because of his brother, she felt terror, the sense of being helpless, which was black and suffocating, like a nightmare. At first, she could do nothing but tremble and cry. These tears were added to the ones she had already shed. But then her innate common sense asserted itself. She would leave. She would find another position before they drove her mad or before the old Princesse de Condé found out and dismissed her without references. The life of a single woman without a job or family on the streets of Paris was not to be thought about. If she thought of it, even once, she would lose her courage and do nothing but lie on her bed and cry, and be dismissed anyway for not performing her duties.

When she overheard the old Princesse de Lorraine gossiping with the old Princesse de Condé about the little English Countess Devane, and the princesse mentioned casually, just a few words, really, that the young countess was searching for a lady's maid ("God only knew she needed one"), she had another moment of stunning clarity. Her God had not deserted her, though she had doubted Him in the days of trouble. The Holy Mother had truly heard her choking prayers every night and interceded.

She waited now in the vestibule of the mansion Lord Devane was leasing, nervous, but also confident, as once she had always been, that God would provide. Monsieur Montrose, the neat, officious young man who had already screened her, came in and summoned the young woman sitting next to her. She stood up, smoothed out her dress, patted her curls in a confident manner and followed him out. Thérèse refused to let the other woman's confidence undermine hers. She was the better choice. She was bright, honest, diligent and shrewd. From the moment her mother had brought her to the Condé household, she had known what she wanted. Even before that. Her mother had been a lady's maid, and in the dark evenings when they gathered around the fire, her father already snoring because he was so tired from work in his fields, her mother would describe to them her life as it had once been. In place of the dark, cramped, one-room farmhouse was the great house, immense, shining, like a fairy palace, with more rooms than there were children sitting before the fire listening with intent expressions. In place of the watery stew and the black bread was food only to be dreamed of: apples, oranges, strawberries, hearty soups and ragouts, chocolates and bonbons. Thérèse and her brothers and sister had never tasted an orange, much less a bonbon. In place of the heavy, serviceable clothes, passed down from their mother and cut to fit them, was the dressing of my lady for a ball, her diamonds, her jewels, her feathers and fans, glittering and magic.

Her mother had lost that glory when she had fallen in love with and married an underfootman. They had taken their meager savings and put a down payment on a farm. The farm prospered, though the mortgage was never paid off, but her mother got smaller and sicker each year from the children that kept arriving. Thérèse was willing to escape the drudgery of the farm, the milking, the haying, the mucking out of barns and pigpens to live in a large city household. When she was seven, her mother and father drove her into Paris in their wagon, and she was left on the kitchen doorstep of the Condé house, in which her mother and father had once worked. The housekeeper was still a friend, and had obtained for Thérèse the position of kitchen maid. She worked hard. She was out of bed long before dawn, lugging firewood and building the fires in the great kitchen fireplaces. With sand and potash she scrubbed pots and pans that were larger than she was. She chopped vegetables until her arms ached. She mopped floors that seemed as long as her father's fields. She sang as she worked. She was merry and laughing. By the time she was ten, she was shopping with the cook at the markets, sometimes bargaining even more shrewdly than he, using her dark eyes and her small frame and her quick answers to amuse the vendors into giving her a better price. But always before her she saw the glory and glitter of the bedchambers. She wanted to be a lady's maid. The cook begged her to stay in his kitchens, swore he would teach her all he knew. But the housekeeper also had a fondness for her, and when a position as chambermaid opened in one of the young princesses' bedchambers, she moved Thérèse there.

Thérèse used every moment of her spare time to improve herself, learning to read and write, to speak English, to play music. She was ready when another position opened, that of lady's maid's assistant. The work was hard; the young princesses were spoiled and demanding, but she was happy. She had plenty of food, a small room shared with a friend, cast-off clothes that were worn only for a brief while before the princesses tired of them, one free day a month, wages, which she saved, and a footman or two or three who died for her pert smiles. But then she had made her mistake. . . . She closed her eyes and swallowed. She would not think of that now. She began to say her Hail Mary in a whisper. Hail Mary, full of grace, the Lord is with you; blessed art thou among women and blessed is the fruit of thy womb, Jesus . . .

It gave her courage when her turn came. She followed Monsieur Montrose through hallways and past ornate drawing rooms and up stairs until he opened the door to Lady Devane's antechamber. She had an impression of ornate furnishings and cold formality.

"Lady Devane," Montrose said to a thin girl in a rich autumn-green gown that made her hair the color of gold, two pug puppies with matching green ribbons around their necks at her skirts, "this is Thérèse Fuseau."

He bowed and left them alone. The girl stared at Thérèse with wide, blue eyes in a heart-shaped face. She was far younger than Thérèse had imagined she would be. Her face was pretty, but she did not make it up either fashionably or to accentuate its best features. The pugs bounded over and barked in such small, shrill yaps that Thérèse laughed.

"May I?"

At Lady Devane's nod, she bent down and patted them. They immediately began to whine and tremble under her hand, pushing at each other so the other should not get more patting, rolling over so that she might scratch their fat, puppy bellies. (Barbara had named them after her brother Harry and her sister Charlotte. Harry was always in trouble and Charlotte whined.)

"Bad dogs," Thérèse cooed to them. "Bad, bad dogs." They loved it, straining themselves into contortions to stay on their bellies yet lick her hands at the same time.

"Hyacinthe!" Lady Devane called.

A small, black page appeared in one of the doorways. He was a handsome child with full, smooth cheeks and dark eyes with long lashes.

"Take the puppies away," Lady Devane told him. He glanced at Thérèse and scooped up the puppies, who tried to lick his face. When he was gone, Lady Devane began to ask Thérèse about her background, how long she had been with the Condés, what references she could provide, and finally why she wished to leave.

"It is time, madame" was all she said. Then she stood waiting. Lady Devane was looking at her with those intent blue eyes, assessing her. Please, Holy Mother, prayed Thérèse, please make her like me. I beg you. I will say ten Hail Marys and light five candles to you if you will make her like me.

I like her, Barbara was thinking. I like the way she dresses and the way she answered my questions and the way she patted my dogs. Trust your instincts, she heard her grandmother's voice say in her mind, trust your instincts.

"When could you start?"

Thérèse clapped her hands together. "Within a week."

"Good. I will inform Montrose and have him arrange a footman to carry your things."

"You will not regret your decision, madame. I promise that. I will serve you faithfully and proudly."

Barbara smiled. It was her grandfather's smile. In that moment, Thérèse felt that somehow her life was intertwined with this girl's. She smiled back. Outside the antechamber, in the corridor, she leaned against the wall and burst into tears. Wiping them quickly, furtively, she walked down the hall. Outside the house, she had to stop and vomit in the kitchen gardens, but the only one who saw her was a beggar child staring through the fence.

Within a week, Thérèse was surveying her new domain— Lady Devane's apartments and the room on the ground floor which would be used for laundering and starching. The puppies yapped and bit at her heels as she walked through the formal room that separated Lord and Lady Devane's apartments, to the antechamber which was the first room of Barbara's suite. It was as she remembered, a cold, formal room clearly used for little but receiving guests. Crossing it quickly, the puppies still at her heels, she entered the bedchamber, which would also be used as a sitting room. This would be the center of her life.

The walls were the color of a robin's eggshell. A canopied bed occupied an old-fashioned, dark alcove. Near the fireplace was an overturned basket and an embroidery frame. The basket was frayed from small, pointed teeth. Thérèse shook her finger at the puppies. "Bad dogs," she told them. They stared at her, heads cocked to one side, tongues hanging out. She picked up the scraps of linen and dangling embroidery threads and put them back in the basket and shook her finger at the puppies once more. A pair of shoes lay in the middle of the floor, green satin shoes with stiff embroidered bows. A dressing table was littered with bottles and jars and feathers and ribbons and spilled powders. She would straighten it later. She crossed to two identical doors set into the wall. One would contain Lady Devane's most private room, where she could be alone. The other would be hers. Thérèse opened the door on her left. Lady Devane's room. Rich blue damask on the walls and on the two matching armchairs pulled before the fireplace. A window at one end, beneath which was a marquetry table littered with papers, quill pens and ink pot and Bible box. Thérèse closed the door. She was much more interested in the room adjoining. Hers. She opened it. A small fireplace, a luxury she had not expected. A narrow cot. Trunks and an armoire for Lady Devane's clothing. Pegs for hers. A table under a window. A window! Another luxury. A close stool. And a piece of mirror in which she might see herself to comb her hair. A small door, which she opened. The back stairs, leading down to the kitchens and basements.

That night, in her room, she said her rosary and thanked God again for His kindness. She felt calm. Not all her problems were solved, but she had food, warmth, a roof over her head. She was not afraid. She was in God's hands. In spite of the cold, she opened her window and leaned out into the dark night. It was good to have a window. It was good to be alive.

"Tell me what you know about her, Francis."

White and Montrose were in the sitting room they shared, a room that connected their bedchambers. Montrose was trying to read Alexander Pope's translation of the *Iliad*, but White kept interrupting. He was burning with curiosity about Lady Devane's new maid. The footman who had escorted her from the Condé mansion could talk of nothing else in the servants' hall. His description of her charms left White panting for more. The addition of a young, pretty, unknown female servant had the male household staff buzzing.

"There is nothing to tell. She is twenty; she has excellent experience; she speaks English."

"Why did you not tell me of her when she was hired?" White demanded.

Montrose sighed and closed his book. "I did. If you will remember, I told you that Lady Devane had made her choice, and I was finally free to deal with more important matters."

"Yes, but you did not tell me her choice was both charming and pretty. After Martha, it comes as a shock."

"Of course I did not. Who would say such a thing!"

"Jacques, who has better eyes than you in his head. He was almost drooling as he described her."

"One ought not to mix with maidservants," sniffed Montrose. "It is not conducive to good morale."

"Read your book, Francis. Read your book."

Thérèse sifted through Barbara's gowns and arranged them according to color and use. She sorted through stained clothes. She began an inventory of Barbara's growing collection of jewels. She added an expert starcher to the washerwoman who came on Tuesdays and Thursdays. She knew the best lacemakers and dressmakers in Paris.

"Thérèse," Barbara told her (she already loved the way Thérèse called her "madame"), "I want to look older, more sophisticated."

Thérèse understood at once and looked at her young mistress with more interest. So madame had a lover she wished to please. She was more French than she realized. Together, she and Barbara analyzed Barbara's assets: good complexion, glorious hair, prettily shaped face; and her liabilities: pale brows and lashes, small bosom. Thérèse knew a solution for everything.

Barbara was twisted, turned, powdered, corseted, rouged, patched. Within a week, she stood before the mirror staring at herself. She looked wonderful; even she could see it. Her gown was a pale shade of blue, cut long and deep at the waist as Thérèse had suggested. Heavy lace fell from her shoulders and breasts, and Thérèse had tied a matching piece of lace about her neck and fastened the diamond-and-sapphire brooch Roger had given her for Valentine's Day to it. The trimming on the gown was primrose and white. She wore rouge on her lips and cheeks, and her brows and lashes had been darkened with lead combs. The only other solution to her paleness was a set of false eyebrows made of mouse hair, but she could not stand them and would not wear them. To her great satisfaction, she wore three patches.

"Not too many," Thérèse had warned "or you will look like a comedienne on the stage."

I shall be very aloof and grand tonight, Barbara thought as she turned around so that Thérèse could give her a final inspection. She touched the brooch Roger had given her, and turned slowly, enjoying the way her skirts belled around her legs. The puppies barked from their basket. I look at least twenty years old, she thought to herself. Thérèse circled her slowly, her brow furrowed, to make certain everything was perfect.

Barbara was going to a birthday ball for the young king; yesterday she had gone to a Valentine's Day fete at Marie-Victorie's. Today her room was filled with flowers, camellias, from St. Michel, who had drawn her name as his Valentine at the fete. He said he came only to see her. She had flirted with him, once more trying her wings, unfurling them. There

was such a gap she must close between Roger and herself . . .
his worldliness, his sophistication, his elegance. She was hur-
rying as fast as she could; it was the height of fashion to have
admirers. Surely Roger must notice and approve. Surely he
must admire—a little—himself.

The Valentine's fete was a more adult party than those at
Tamworth, when the unmarried young people had gathered
and drawn lots as to who would be their Valentine. She had
always thought it silly. One year Harry had drawn her name
and been furious. You were supposed to give small presents to
whoever was your Valentine, for several days afterward, but
at Tamworth they had simply held one dance. No one took it
seriously, or believed, as some did, that the Valentine chosen
was destined to be your future marriage partner. Annie said
the birds chose mates on that day, and therefore it was special, while the villagers believed the first person seen was your
destined mate. One year, Barbara and Jane, following Annie's
advice, had taken five bay leaves and pinned them to their
pillows that night, four to each corner and one in the middle.
It was supposed to assure dreams of one's sweetheart, but
Barbara dreamed of no one, and Jane never said.

At Marie-Victorie's, there had been much laughing and
smiling and significant looks between the men and women. It
made her uncomfortable. She could feel a heightened sexual
tension in the air. But perhaps it had also to do with carnival,
already in progress. Carnival was the celebration before Lent,
the penitential season preceding Easter. And the Parisians celebrated with abandon. Someone had told her that carnival
was a time for sinning, to make up for time lost when the
repenting, fasting season of Lent began, and she saw what he
meant.

Already Richelieu had fought a duel with the Comte de
Gacé and been wounded. It seemed that the young Comtesse
de Gacé had gone to a party at the Prince de Soubice's, gotten drunk (as had most of the other guests), had been passed
around naked from man to man, then passed on to the servants. Richelieu had been laughing about it to friends, Barbara among them, at an opera ball, and the comte had overheard him and challenged him to a duel, which they fought
the next morning, not over whether the story was true or not,
but over Richelieu's ungentlemanly conduct in repeating it.

Barbara was fascinated and shocked by it all. The comtesse was only a few years older than she. In fact, the comtesse had been at the ball, dancing and laughing and looking young and ethereal in a white gown and diamonds. Now rumors were flying that Richelieu and Gacé were going to be imprisoned in the Bastille for dueling. Richelieu shrugged, but the Comtesse de Gacé cried; she did not want Richelieu imprisoned, even if he had talked about her. She really did not care where they put her husband. Everyone thought it was one of the best carnivals ever, and Barbara was intrigued by the sybaritic sophistication around her. There was an underside to it that she could only guess at, and its mysteriousness both attracted her and repelled her. Louise-Anne de Charolais, Richelieu, St. Michel and so many others understood it, belonged to it, and she felt like a child, standing on the outside, looking in. Here, she thought, lies another world, a world Roger knows and is at ease with, but its dark underside made her wary.

"Madame," Thérèse said, "you will be late."

Barbara opened her fan. Hyacinthe, dressed in suit of matching blue satin, and holding her cloak, was waiting. She stooped down and gave the puppies a last pat.

"Wish me good fortune," she said to them. They obligingly licked her hands.

Once the door closed behind them, the smile on Thérèse's face faded. She put a hand to her mouth, walked to the canopied bed, and pulled the china chamber pot from under it. She retched into it. The puppies, curious, came to the side of the bed, yapping at her. Finally, moving like an old woman, she rinsed out the chamber pot and then lay back down. The nausea was bad tonight, worse than it had ever been. She must act soon. People were not stupid. Today she had fainted in the washing room, and when she came to, the washer-woman and the majordomo, one Pierre LeBlanc, were staring at her with eyes that held the dawning of suspicion. The puppies barked until she leaned over and pulled them up beside her, but the effort made her sick again. She lay for a long time without moving, except for her hand fingering her beads as she whispered the rosary over and over again for strength.

There was a knock on the door. With a hand to her head, she sat up. White opened the door and came in, several books in his good hand. Thérèse stared at his deformed arm, at the tiny hand dangling from his elbow. She made a sound. White jumped. Then he saw her. The puppies never moved from the warm nest they had made in the bed covers.

"I beg your pardon," he said. "I thought no one was here. Have I frightened you? I am Caesar White, Lord Devane's clerk of the library. I was bringing Lady Devane some books about Paris I thought she might find interesting."

Thérèse nodded her head. She felt that if she said one word she would be sick again all over the bed, and him, even though there was nothing to spit up. He came closer.

"You are Thérèse Fuseau, are you not?" He smiled. He had a nice smile. "I have been wanting to meet you. My room is over in the other wing. I have a small sitting room with a good-sized fireplace. Perhaps sometime you will join me there for tea."

Thérèse shook her head. He stared at her, puzzled. "On your day off, then, you might care to go for a walk or supper. . . ." His voice trailed off at her lack of response. He blushed and set the books on a table.

"I am glad to have met you," he said more formally now. She was aware that she had hurt his feelings, but she felt too sick to care. He shut the door behind him without looking back. Thérèse lay back down. He seemed nice, but just now, she had no use for any man, nice or otherwise.

Barbara waited at the top of the stairs, as excited as if she were going to a fete in her honor. She was waiting for Hyacinthe to announce her name, at which time she would slowly, elegantly, maturely, walk down the stairs and dazzle Roger with her new sophistication. She heard her name. Slowly, she said to herself, walk down very slowly. Smile just so. Yes. Roger was at the bottom of the staircase, with Hyacinthe.

"You kept me waiting—" he began, but stopped. She stood still midway down the stairs, so that he should have a good look at her. Let him like me, she prayed. Please.

"Barbara," he said, letting her name out on a long breath. His eyes were a sky blue, lighter, more beautiful than her gown. "You look beautiful."

She flew down the remaining stairs. "Oh, Roger, do you like it? Are you pleased? Tell me the truth. Look, I have on three patches. They are called the gallant, the rogue, and the—"

Roger kissed her on the lips. "I know, Barbara, and the kissing." To her delight, he kissed her hands also. His eyes glowed at her. She wanted him to kiss her again.

In the Tuileries ballroom, she stood for a moment under the chandeliers, languidly waving her fan. She knew she looked beautiful. But what was more important by far, according to Thérèse, was that she felt beautiful. The Prince de Dombes, the Comte de Coigny, and the Duc de Melun were immediately around her, asking for dances. She sighed, and fanned herself. She would check her dance card, of course. At her side, Roger smiled to himself at her coolness.

"Save the first dance after supper for me," he said, chucking her under the chin, walking away without bothering to see if she wrote down his name. She frowned after him, but then the men around her moved closer, all talking, all wanting her attention. The Chevalier de Bavière joined them, as did the Duc de Richelieu. Obligingly, she wrote down their requests on her dance card. She fanned herself. Bavière offered to bring her punch. She sighed. Richelieu, watching her, grinned. St. Michel shouldered his way through the crowd around her. Marie-Victorie was on his arm, with her brother.

"You look superb," she cried. Her brother immediately asked for a dance.

"Bab," said St. Michel. "Tonight you are beyond compare—a goddess among mortals. Grant me the favor of the first dance, or I shall perish."

She smiled. The music was starting. Richelieu gave her his arm. "Henri, my card seems to be filled for now," she said, enjoying her triumph and his frown. "Perhaps after the supper interval . . ."

Enormously pleased with herself, she smiled at Richelieu, who escorted her into one of the circles of couples forming to dance.

"You do look better," Richelieu said as they began the opening movements to the dance. "At long last you match the promise in your voice. The woman in you is emerging. I await her arrival with bated breath."

Louise-Anne, standing behind in an adjoining circle, with St. Michel as her sulking partner, heard him.

"Does Henri know he is wasting his time?" asked Richelieu. He winked at St. Michel, who could not hear now that the music was beginning.

"No," said Barbara. "And I wish you would not tell him. I am having too good a time." Sometimes Richelieu made her angry. She never knew what to expect from him. His compliments were always double-edged. She did not like him at all. She could not understand where he got his reputation as a great lover. She wished she had not given him a dance.

"How was your duel?" she asked, hoping to embarrass him.

He grinned. "It only hurts me when I laugh. I think I will go to the Bastille."

She was silent. He watched her.

"Would you be sad?" he asked. She shivered. His voice was as caressing as a hand against her naked spine. She tossed her head.

"Sell me that black horse you ride. You will not need her if you go to the Bastille."

Richelieu forgot his attitude of the bored young duke. "You cannot possibly ride her!"

"Of course I can."

"You cannot!"

"Let me try."

"You will be hurt—"

"I will not!"

"All right," he said slowly, his strange yellow-brown eyes glinting. "For a bet then."

"A bet? I do not know if—"

"Ah, I see that under the woman is still the child. Never mind. I never do business with children."

"You have a bet, sir! What are we wagering?"

He threw back his head and laughed. Louise-Anne, trying to watch them, tripped over St. Michel's foot.

"I will give you the horse if you can ride her," said Richelieu.

"No. I will buy her."

"How tiresome you are. Forget the bet."

"No! I accept your terms. And if I lose?"

"You buy me a new hat."

She laughed at him. She had been afraid he would ask for something fast, forbidden, such as a kiss. She was so relieved that she decided she did like him, after all. St. Michel and Louise-Anne, who had run into another couple in their efforts to keep Richelieu and Barbara under view, agreed to leave their circle of dancers. They watched from the sides.

"What is he saying!" cried St. Michel. "Armand is pursuing her. I can see it. Bastard! He promised me!"

"What did he promise?" Louise-Anne demanded. "What?"

"Listen to me, Barbara," Richelieu was saying. "I will allow you to try riding Sheba only under certain circumstances. One, that your husband knows and approves, and two, that your groom is with you the entire time."

"Roger will not care—"

"He will care if you break your neck, and I do not want to fight a duel with him."

"Whyever not? Are two in one month too much for you?"

"What an impudent mouth you have. Someone ought to take care of that. No, because he always kills his man."

"No! Tell me more."

"I cannot imagine why I wanted to dance with you. Women who love their husbands are a bore."

"How fortunate then that this dance is ending. Is our wager still on?"

"Yes. Go away, little girl."

She stuck her tongue out at him. Several people saw her, but it only made Richelieu laugh. She turned to her next partner, who would treat her with more respect and with whom she knew she would enjoy dancing far more than she had with Richelieu. But she could not resist checking to see if he was still watching her. He was not. She tossed her head and smiled at her partner.

Louise-Anne grabbed Richelieu's arm as soon as he got near enough. "What promise did you make to Henri? Tell me."

Richelieu shrugged. "I have no idea. Did I promise something?"

"He seems to think so. I saw you romancing the skinny little English. God, what fools you all are over a new face. She would squeal if you touched her. I told Henri so, but he did not believe me. He seems to think she is burning with passion under all that innocence. Do you believe me, Armand?"

"Indeed I do, pet." He smiled down at her. "Did you really say that to Henri?"

She nodded, uncertain of his mood. He was sometimes so cruel. To her surprise, he kissed her hand.

"Thank you, Louise-Anne. You are a treasure."

Barbara was having a wonderful time. The other men did not talk to her the way Richelieu did. They smiled and said flattering things, and she enjoyed herself by smiling back and flirting and encouraging them to say even more flattering things. It was a delightful game, except that Roger was not around to see it. He stayed in the card room. When the supper interval came, and Roger had not appeared, and St. Michel, who seemed always to be at her side when Roger was not, suggested a stroll, she agreed. Let Roger come and find her. Let him find her enjoying supper with St. Michel. It would do him good. She was always standing around waiting for him. Tonight, she looked beautiful. He had said so himself. She had made herself beautiful for him. No one else. And he strolled off and left her on her own as if her transformation were nothing. She hoped he was losing at cards. She hoped he had to search an hour to find her. She was so busy hoping that she paid no attention to where St. Michel was leading her. Before she knew it, she was standing with him in a curtained alcove. There was room only for a settee, a kind of lengthened armchair that could seat two people.

"Sit down, Bab," St. Michel was saying. "I will bring you supper."

But then he was sitting down beside her. The settee was smaller than she thought. St. Michel sat very close. The dimness of the room made her nervous. St. Michel, at his ease, leaned back, one arm across the back of the settee. Barbara moved forward so that she was sitting on the edge. St. Michel laughed softly.

"What a baby you are. What can I do to you here, my dear Bab? The settee is far too small for any particular intimacy. I merely wish to rest a moment before I go for our supper."

"I am hungry," Barbara said in a small voice. Sweet Jesus, where was Roger? What if he should walk in and find her sitting so close to Henri? First he missed her social triumph and now he left her on her own with a man who was obviously up to no good. Five minutes. She would let Henri rest five

minutes—she jumped. His hand, the one that had rested across
the back of the settee, had just touched her bare shoulder, so
briefly that she might have thought she had imagined it if the
same hand were not now on her neck, caressing it. She tried
to twist away.

"How lovely you look tonight."

Now both his hands were on her shoulders, holding her, and
he was whispering against her neck and back. "Lovely and
exciting. Do you know how exciting you are?"

She could feel his breath on her neck. She pulled away and
stood up. He did, too, and his arms were around her, turning
her, and they were strong, and he was kissing her.

"Let me go!" She pushed at him.

"Barbara!"

St. Michel's arms dropped from around her. He stepped
back and put a hand to his sword. Roger stood at the alcove
opening, one of the curtains pushed aside by his hand.

"Are you well, my dear?" Roger stepped into the alcove and
touched her arm.

"Yes! No! He tried to k—" Roger suddenly squeezed her arm
so hard that it silenced her.

St. Michel and Roger stared at each other. She could hear
their breathing, short, staccato breaths, as if each had been
running hard. God only knew what she sounded like. She
looked from the face of one man to the other. What she saw
made her tremble. If Roger had not been holding her arm in
a death grip, she would have fallen to the floor. All the glamour of the evening faded beside reality. Roger was going to
challenge Henri to a duel. In which one or both of them
would be hurt. Or killed. It happened. All the time. Over
things far sillier than an attempted kiss. Oh, dear God, she
had never realized.

After a moment, which seemed an hour to her nerves, St.
Michel bowed and left. As soon as the curtain swung shut
behind him, Roger jerked her arm so hard that she stumbled,
and said, "You little fool! What happened?"

"He tried to kiss me!"

"Did he?" He was still holding her arm.

She wrenched it away. He must not talk to her this way.
It was not her fault. She was going to cry if he did not stop
staring at her. He was so angry.

"You are not in Tamworth," he said, his voice making her writhe with shame, "repulsing the attentions of the village yokels. You are in France, and if you do not wish a chevalier to kiss you, you should never enter darkened alcoves with him! Did he kiss you? Look at me! If he did, by God, I will—"

"No! No! Nothing happened! He tried to—I did not know—"

"Be quiet. Go at once and ask Hyacinthe for our cloaks and our carriage. We are leaving."

"B-but we have not seen the king—"

"Do as I say."

"What are you going to do?"

"Nothing that concerns you."

St. Michel went to the supper room, wiping the perspiration from his brow and upper lip. Trembling, he refolded his handkerchief and took a deep breath. Louise-Anne and Richelieu sat by themselves at a small table, and he joined them without a word, reaching at once for Louise-Anne's wine. He drained the glass. Richelieu motioned for a footman to bring more wine. St. Michel drained that glass, too. Then he straightened, his eyes widening. Louise-Anne and Richelieu both turned, in spite of themselves, to see what he was staring at.

Roger strode toward their table, and Richelieu rose, smiling, but St. Michel sat rooted to his seat.

"I came to tell you that my wife has a headache, and I am taking her home. I did not want any of you gentlemen who had solicited later dances to be disappointed." Roger's words were clipped and rude, unlike himself.

"Naturally," said Richelieu, slowly, glancing from Roger to St. Michel, when St. Michel did not answer.

"I wanted to dance with you," said Louise-Anne, pouting her full lips at Roger, but he did not notice.

"I am assuming you lost your way tonight, Henri, in more ways than one." Roger focused on St. Michel, his face grim, his voice edged with challenge. "Barbara is inexperienced socially. But I am not, and I guard what is mine."

His hand moved to his sword. There was a long moment of silence. St. Michel did not move. Neither did Richelieu or Louise-Anne. Abruptly, Roger bowed and left the room.

"What did you do?" breathed Louise-Anne, her eyes wide.

"I kissed her. He almost caught me." St. Michel wiped his brow again. "I will not fight a duel over one kiss. Not for anyone."

"You kissed her?" asked Richelieu, his eyes sparkling suddenly. "How was it?"

"I hardly know. There was not time—"

"What did she do? Did she lie for you?"

"Not precisely. She started to tell him, but he stopped her."

"A duel would have hurt her reputation. You should have pushed it. I would have," said Richelieu.

"Would you!" snapped St. Michel. "Well, I do not fancy dying over one kiss. A fuck, maybe, but never a kiss!"

"Roger and my uncle," said Louise-Anne, "used to share women between them, and now he is ready to kill for a stolen kiss from his wretched wife. It is too ridiculous for words."

"He was very insulting," said St. Michel, feeling braver now that Roger was gone, and some of the immediate fear was fading. "I ought to kill him for that."

"I can think of a sweeter revenge than death. Do you give up, Henri?" asked Richelieu.

"No! She will come around. She liked my kiss. I could tell—"

"And a moment ago you could not remember. Amazing!"

St. Michel put his hand to his sword. Richelieu stood up at once, knocking over his chair. Both had acted before Louise-Anne had time to blink. They stared at each other, the planes of their faces hard, contemptuous.

"Stop!" she screamed. "If you two fight a duel over that mewling little English child, I will never, never forgive you. Sit down, Armand! Take your hand from that sword! Have you lost your senses! She has not even kissed you yet! Armand, you are not healed from your last duel!"

"She has kissed me," St. Michel said petulantly. Slowly he moved his hand from his sword.

"You kissed her," Louise-Anne said. "There is a difference."

Richelieu sat back down. Louise-Anne shook her head. She was angry, near tears. Either of them could be dead by morning at the rate they were going. Men were idiots. She had always wanted to go to bed with Roger Montgeoffry. He had never given her a second glance. She wished he would kill St. Michel. And Richelieu. And himself.

"I despise you all," she said in a trembling voice. "You are insane."

"The hunt. The hunt is all," St. Michel said softly.

"And the fuck," said Richelieu.

"I will drink to that," St. Michel agreed, draining his glass. To have come close to two duels in one evening was enough.

In the carriage, Barbara and Roger were silent. Hyacinthe, sitting by Barbara, wriggled his hand into her cloak and found her hand and squeezed it. She swallowed. She was struggling not to cry.

Roger sat opposite her, his mouth a hard line. For him, the evening had turned bad from the moment he entered the card room. He had lost at cards, steadily, which was unlike his usual luck. And then the regent had taken him aside and whispered that one of his spies had brought news that the Pretender had given up his fight for the English throne and left Scotland in the dead of night, abandoning those Scots clans that had supported him, to the wrath of King George. Only a few of his followers would be with him, one of them Viscount Alderley. Even now they might be on the seas. Or on the roads. Their destination was said to be Paris. It was not a pleasant situation, from any point of view. The regent was bound by a treaty not to give the Pretender a safe haven in France. And Roger had no wish to deal publicly with the drunken, irresponsible man who was his father-in-law, a ridiculous relationship since he was almost ten years older than Kit. He had no wish to jeopardize his friendship with George, whose own spies would be reporting every move the Pretender and his entourage made. He was so irritated by the news that he went to search for Barbara, to tell her that he was leaving early but that she should stay and enjoy the rest of the ball. And he had walked into a scene that stunned him.

I guard what is mine, he had said to the childlike Princesse de Charolais. He had sounded like an actor in a bad play. This whole evening had been a bad play, and not entirely a comedy. It had shocked him to see Barbara in another man's arms. A rage had possessed him that he had not felt in years. He had just enough sense to keep from killing the young fool with her. It was really too ironic, to be spouting the lines of the distraught husband, when the other part, the lover, had always been his. It was really very amusing—except that he did not feel like laughing. He felt like strangling Barbara, who was stupidly impulsive, like her father. First she found her way to his house by herself and cried all over his best coat and upset his entire household, then she convinced that grandmother of hers—Alice made a better general than Richard—to persuade him to marry her immediately; then she appeared tonight, a vision of beauty, surprising him (even while he was amused by her transparency), touching him— she will grow into a lovely woman, he had thought, a graceful complement to Devane House—and then she was kissing strangers in dark alcoves! He was furious with her, even more furious because he knew she did not deserve his anger. But when he had seen St. Michel holding her, something in him had snapped. He had wanted to run his sword through St. Michel's no doubt fleshy belly and see the red blood stain his white shirt. Jesus Christ, what was wrong with him? If he had seen a woman he had wanted at tonight's ball, he would have gone up to her without another thought, except to behave discreetly so that Barbara should not know. Yet here he was, acting the outraged husband because his naive little fool of a wife allowed a young man to kiss her.

He did not suspect her of being unfaithful, but that would come. He was far more experienced than she, and he knew how easy it was. One tiny step led to another, until it was done, and then there was no going back. At the thought of Barbara's being unfaithful he felt as if something sharp had pierced his side. She was so young.

"He is married, you know." What made him say that? The words were out of his mouth before he could stop them. He sounded like a sulking twenty-year-old.

"Who is?"

"St. Michel." There was a silence. Let it go, Roger thought to himself. You have said enough.

Barbara squeezed Hyacinthe's hand and shut her eyes.

"He leaves his wife and children in a château in Normandy, and comes to Paris to live as he pleases. His wife runs the château and farms and sends him money for his town house and his horses and his mistresses." Why am I doing this?

The carriage lurched to a stop, and Barbara leapt out and ran, her cloak flying out behind her, until she reached her apartments. Hyacinthe ran behind her like a shadow. She stood for a moment in the doorway of her antechamber and leaned her head against the door frame. From the bedroom, the puppies came barking and tumbling over themselves in their haste to reach her. Thérèse appeared at the opening to the bedroom. She was wiping her mouth with a handkerchief, and her face was pale. There was a sheen of sweat above her upper lip. But Barbara did not notice.

"Madame is home early. Did you enjoy yourself?"

Barbara could not speak. She ignored the yapping puppies and ran past Thérèse into her bedroom. She pulled at the strings of her cloak, she pulled at the feathers in her hair. She sat down on the stool before her dressing table and stared at herself. I will not cry, she thought. I will not.

"What happened?" Thérèse whispered to Hyacinthe.

He shrugged his shoulders. "Madame tells me to fetch the cloaks and carriage. In the carriage she is very quiet. I hold her hand."

"And monsieur?"

"He talks."

"About what?"

"I did not understand. I was thinking of madame. She looked as if she was going to cry. Will she cry, Thérèse? If she cries, I will hug her until she stops."

Thérèse leaned down and gave the boy a quick hug of her own. "Madame needs to be alone. You take Harry and Charlotte in my room, and wait there for me."

"But madame might need me."

"Not tonight, my little one. Do as I say. Go on."

In the bedroom, Barbara's back was to her, but Thérèse could see her face in the mirror. Poor little one, thought Thérèse, perhaps a lover's quarrel. And her husband knows and is angry.

Quietly, Thérèse reached around and untied the strings on Barbara's cloak. When the cloak fell, and Barbara's shoulders were exposed, she squeezed them sympathetically. It was a gentle, quick gesture. Barbara bit her lip. Thérèse unfastened Barbara's gown and helped her out of her petticoats. She unfastened her jewels and unpinned her hair. Everything was done neatly and silently, and as if it were perfectly normal for Barbara not to say one word. Before Barbara even realized it, she was in her nightgown and Thérèse was brushing her hair.

It was comforting to have her hair brushed. Her grandmother used to do that. At the thought of her grandmother, Barbara nearly burst out crying. She missed her; she missed them all. And Roger and St. Michel had nearly fought a duel over her, and it was not romantic and exciting, as in the French romances she had read. And now Roger was angry with her. He thought it her fault.

There was a knock at the door. Thérèse looked at Barbara. Barbara nodded her head. Thérèse opened the door, and before her was one of the most handsome men she had ever seen in her life. He was older, his face was tanned and thin, he had blue eyes with tiny little laugh lines on each side, and his short hair was gray-blond. He was in a robe. Lord Devane. Thérèse's mouth fell open.

"I am Lord Devane," he said unnecessarily. "Would you ask my wife if she feels up to seeing me?"

She turned. Barbara's face told her everything. She is in love with him, thought Thérèse. And I do not blame her.

She stood to one side, and Roger went into the bedroom. Thérèse closed the door on them, and sat down in a chair in the antechamber.

She had forgotten husbands and wives could love each other. No one did in the Condé household. It was enough to make her forget her sickness.

"I was too harsh tonight," Roger said, walking toward Barbara. "I do not know what came over me. You are certainly to be allowed your own friendships. I will not interfere. I trust you, Barbara. I do."

She burst into tears. He smiled to himself as he took her in his arms.

When she woke the next morning, he was not at her side. She sat up, and the bed covers slipped from her. She was naked. She smiled. Roger had not been his usual, controlled self last night; he had made furious love to her. If he should love her . . . She put her arms around her knees and hugged herself. If he should love her, life would be perfect.

She had been in despair last night. Today she felt like singing. She got up. There was a soreness between her legs. She smiled again. Wrapping a robe around herself, she rang for Thérèse and sat down at her dressing table and began to brush her hair.

"Help me dress, Thérèse," Barbara said. "I have to breakfast with Lord Devane."

Thérèse took the brush from her hand. "Madame seems very happy this morning. Such a change from last night."

Barbara laughed. She could feel a blush starting to burn her neck and cheeks. "I am."

"So would I be. He is the handsomest man I have ever seen."

"Do you really think so, Thérèse?"

"Most certainly. You could have knocked me over last night when I opened the door and saw him. He is gorgeous."

"I agree."

They laughed together, like two wicked old ladies. Thérèse pulled Barbara's heavy hair from her face and began to twist it up.

"This morning we make you innocent, but with a bloom, like a rose opening. The carmine rouge, just a touch. One patch, no more, by your mouth. It will remind him of last night's kisses. I assume he kissed you. We add the rose morning gown with the green belt. The little rose slippers. He will be enchanted."

They were enjoying themselves immensely, but as Thérèse tied the belt around Barbara's waist, she felt the nausea rising, and she clutched her stomach. She could not help it.

"Thérèse, what is it? Are you unwell?" Barbara helped her to a chair.

"A stomach sickness."

"I will send for a doctor—"

"No. I will be fine in just a few moments. Please, madame, do not trouble yourself. Let me rest just a moment, then I will finish helping you dress. Lord Devane will be waiting."

Roger was already eating when Barbara ran into the breakfast room. At the sight of him, her throat tightened. He stood to greet her, and a slight flush appeared on his cheeks, but she did not notice. Roger cleared his throat. She waited.

"About last night," he finally said, quickly, in low tones, "if I hurt you—"

"Oh, no. It was—you did not hurt me."

"You look lovely this morning."

She smiled, all her heart, her happiness, in her smile. She had never loved him so much in her life.

"We have letters," he told her. "They arrived late yesterday. You have two. One from your grandmother and the other from someone whose scrawl I could not read." He handed her two letters.

"Harry!" she exclaimed. "It's a letter from my brother Harry. If you knew what a miracle this is, Roger! I do not think Harry has written two letters in his life—"

She ripped open the seal and read:

Dearest Bab,

What a shock Grandmama's letter gave me. You, a married woman, and to Roger, of all people. Does he know what he has taken on by marrying you, and being related to us all? I send him my condolences and confess that the thought of you as a married woman was enough to make me laugh for days. I also got drunk to celebrate. And celebrate I do, for I need a rich brother-in-law. I have met a friend, the son of Lord Wharton, who is touring Europe, and he wants to come to Paris. When he does, I shall join him. We are in the midst of celebrating carnival, however, and will not leave before it ends. But expect me, for I have a yearning to see you as a proper married woman. I need money, Bab, and ask you to lend me some. By the way, Grandmama wrote me that part of the marriage settlements included paying father's debts. What do you hear of Father? I owe Roger a letter of thanks and welcome to the family, which I shall write soon. Meanwhile, try to behave yourself, and send money.

I remain your loving brother,
Harry

The words "send money" had been underscored.

Roger was watching her face as she read it. It was soft and smiling. He realized her face always became tender when she thought of her brothers and sisters. She would be a good mother to their children. A nursery. He must build Devane House a fine nursery. Not dark, tiny rooms under the attic, but a spacious, sun-filled chamber where his children would grow strong and tall like greening plants. The thought surprised him. His eagerness to have a child. Not just a child that would be related to Richard. But Barbara's child.

She looked up. "He—he congratulates us, Roger, and thanks you for your generosity in the settlements and says he will visit us."

"Does he? And there is no mention of money, of a loan? When I was his age, I always needed money."

She handed him the letter. He read it while she opened her grandmother's letter and read to him from it.

"Let me see. . . . Her letter is dated two weeks ago. Our wedding made her tired, the journey back to Tamworth was miserable—their carriage lost a wheel. She was in bed a week with her legs, but now she is nursing the boys, who are ill. Some kind of fever—" She looked up.

"They will be fine. Children always have fevers."

She scanned the rest of the letter quickly. "That is the only mention of it. She says Aunt Abigail is trying to marry Tony to Sir Josiah Child's daughter, but Tony is having none of it. Good for him. Jane had her betrothal ceremony—I must write a letter. One of Squire's daughters is engaged! That *is* news—"

In spite of himself, Roger was interested. "Who is Squire?"

"Squire Dinwitty. He owns Trinity Farm, next to one of ours. He has three daughters, none of whom are married. Grandmama does not say which one is engaged. Let me see, what else . . . She says she looks forward to my letters and sends her love to us both, and she tells you to beat me if I should cause any trouble."

They smiled at each other.

White and Montrose, who had entered and seated themselves in the midst of Barbara's explanation of the letter, exchanged a look.

"Well, I have a letter from Carlyle," Roger said. "In his usual inimitable style, he writes that he has decided to cut his fingernails. He does not understand how the Chinese mandarin lords ate anything with such long nails, and he can find no one who is willing to feed him. He claims we are missed at court—"

"You are missed. They do not know me."

"You would be missed if they did, Bab.

"What else . . . The rebellion in Scotland looks to be a failure, and captured Scots lords are being brought to London for trial. The mob wants their heads cut off, but rumor, according to Carlyle, has it King George will be merciful. And your mother may be seeing Robert Walpole. No one is sure yet, he says, and London is rife with gossip." Carlyle's exact words were:

Now that bitch in heat, or in other words, your mother-in-law, has poor Robert in her clutches. She is playing with him the way a cat does a mouse. And such a mouse! No one knows what their—dare I call it a relationship—is. Bets are four to one in Robert's favor at White's. I put my money on Diana. Montagu is fit to be tied, and it looks as if Robert will find sponsors for her divorce. Trust Diana to land on her feet. She is wearing the most awful new emerald necklace, interlaced with diamonds, and will tell no one who it is from. I, for one, know Robert could not afford it. Everyone is dying of curiosity, including me.

"Walpole is the fat one?" Barbara asked, without much interest. She did not care whom her mother was seeing. "The one who spilled punch on Aunt Abigail at our wedding party?"

"The very one."

"An apt memory," murmured Montrose.

"Francis," said Roger, "what do you have for me?"

Silently Montrose passed Roger a stack of invitations. Roger sifted through them quickly, handing several of them to Barbara and saying as he did so, "Francis seems to have mixed some of your invitations in with mine. I see a note from Richelieu. Open it and see what he wants."

His voice was casual, but he was watching Barbara's face. Without hesitating, she ripped past the seal and read the note.

"He invites me riding this afternoon, Roger. I forgot to tell you that I tried to buy his black horse last night. You remember the one—we both thought she was beautiful—and he wants to see if I can manage her. As if I could not! But I thought I already had something planned—"

"You do," White said. "We were going to the Palais Royal to look at the regent's collection of paintings. We can easily do it another time." He smiled at her.

"Pooh," said Barbara. "I would much rather be with you than the Duc de Richelieu. He makes me angry every time I speak to him. I will see his horse another day."

"What time is this expedition planned?" asked Roger.

"After dinner," answered White.

"I want to buy some toys, also," Barbara said to White. "For my brothers, who are ill."

"The baby, too?"

Barbara nodded her head.

"Not the baby!" Montrose said, involuntarily.

"I know a place," White said. "A little shop on the Ile Sainte-Marie."

"I shall accompany you," Roger said.

Barbara clapped her hands, jumped out of her chair and kissed him on the cheek.

"Sir, you have an appointment—"

"Cancel the appointment. I have an urge to accompany my wife to the Palais Royal and see what drivel Caesar is telling her. You had better have your facts correct, Caesar, I warn you. And I am certain I know far better than Caesar here what toys will please sick boys."

White grinned.

Montrose looked down at his plate.

"Come with us," Barbara said impulsively. His comment about Baby had not gone past her. She spoke to White often about her family; he must have spoken to Montrose. There were no secrets in this household.

Montrose nodded. There was more talk of appointments; Roger mentioned that he wished to celebrate Shrove Tuesday by inviting some of their friends for pancakes; Barbara thought it a wonderful idea; they discussed whom they should invite, and asked Montrose to begin a list. White watched them with a smile on his face, and after they left the table, he said to Montrose, "I feel love in the air. 'Oh thou delicious, damned, dear, destructive Woman,'" he quoted, to

Montrose's annoyance, who hated it when White spoke lines he could not recognize.

"Congreve," White said, before Montrose could ask. Pleased, he began to buff his nails with the linen breakfast napkin.

"'Womankind more joy discovers/Making fools, than keeping lovers,'" Montrose quoted back. He smiled at White's expression of surprise and finished his breakfast in a good humor.

CHAPTER TWELVE

Two days later Roger walked into Barbara's small blue damasked room as she was finishing a letter to her grandmother. His appearing was so unusual—he was always busy in the afternoons—that she stared at him, her quill pen suspended above the paper. She knew from his face that something was wrong.

"Your father is in Paris," he said abruptly. "He wishes to see me."

"My father . . ." She said the words on a long, wondering breath. She had not seen her father in years. There were times when she even forgot he existed. "But where is he? When can I see him?"

"Barbara," he said gently, "he is in hiding—"

She stared up at him.

"France is an ally of England's now. An England ruled by a king your father has betrayed. There are spies everywhere. This morning I was told the regent has refused to meet with the Pretender, who is in Paris. It is a delicate situation."

"When does he want to see me? He may be ill or need money. He always needs money, as Mother does." She stood up. "Are we leaving now?"

"Barbara." Roger took a deep breath. "You are not going."

She looked at him.

"It is dangerous," he said. "The regent has heard a rumor there is a plot to assassinate the Pretender. That may include his followers. We must be careful. I do not care to become entangled in your father's politics."

She looked down at the papers on her desk, at the letter to her grandmother she was writing. "I want to see him." She looked at Roger and raised her chin. "I will see him. He is my father."

They locked eyes.

"It cannot be treason for a daughter to help her father. Tell me where he is, and I shall go to him. You do not have to become involved!"

"Damn it, Barbara! Do you think this is a game? Some masquerade in which you dress in a cloak and elude your pursuers! I could lose my head for helping your father. Ask the Scots noblemen whose heads are now hanging off Tower gate. They are dead, while the man they died for is here in Paris, very much alive."

"He is my father. He may need me."

"Need you! He does not even mention you in his note."

She took his hand. Her face was set, older than he had realized it could ever look.

"He is my father, Roger, and I must see him and help him, even if it is only to give him money from my allowance. I have not spent it all. Simply tell me where he is, and I will go to him. You do not have to be involved. It is not your responsibility. It is mine."

"Are you always so loyal?" The question was sarcastic.

"To those I love." The answer was not.

She shamed him.

He took a deep breath and closed his eyes. She could see the struggle going on inside him. At last he opened his eyes and took both her hands in his. "Listen to me. We must be very careful. I will have to go to him. No, Barbara! Listen! He is in a part of Paris that you could not go to, even with me."

"I want to see him."

"If there is any way, I will bring him here. It may be only an hour you have with him. Do you understand? You are to take what I can arrange and not ask for more. It is too dangerous, and I will not risk my head—or yours—for his sake."

"He will need money."

"I will give him money. Justin will know what is happening. Do what he says. Nothing more. Nothing less. You ask a lot of me, Barbara."

He pulled her to him and stroked her hair. He was thinking that he could not believe he was going to risk this to please her. The words in Harry's letter were coming back to haunt him. What had he taken on by being related to the Alderleys? His life had been settled, secure. He had little family to bother him. His brothers were dead; his nephews were happy to farm their land, their incomes augmented by the money he sent to ensure they left him alone. There was an old, long-buried Roger who would have done it without a second thought. But that Roger had nothing to lose: no money, no title, no wife, no responsibilities, no reputation. I must be insane, he thought.

Now the cause for his insanity sat trying to play chess, to act normally, but she could not concentrate on the game; everything was arranged. Roger would soon be bringing her father to his apartments by the back stairs, letting him in through Justin's room. Justin would come for her, saying simply that his master wished to see her. She did not know how long she would have with her father, but she had planned with Justin to have a supper ready for him. Already, Justin had sneaked a bottle of wine from the cellars and bread from the kitchens. In his own room, he had two small chickens roasting on a small spit. He had napkins and plate and silver ready and would make her up a table in moments. He promised. She could have hugged him. As she wished to hug her father. There were no paintings of her father at Tamworth; she had to depend on her memory, which was hazy. But he was her father; he was family, and she was going to see him, and that was all that was important. She was frightened. Your father is a damned fool, her grandmother had raged last summer when Sir John Ashford had brought the news of his flight. In her anger, Grandmama had smashed a soft-paste porcelain vase that Grandfather had brought from Lille. Barbara hardly knew her father; he had come to Tamworth even less often than their mother did. But when he came, he was always kind. Always. She loved him. Maybe this time, he could stay. If he were sick, she would nurse him. She might intercede with the king for him.

One of the logs burning on the fire snapped in two. The puppies, lying near Thérèse, who was mending lace, yawned and changed positions. Hyacinthe moved his knight. He and Barbara were learning chess at the same time. He giggled at her expression.

"I was thinking of something else," she told him. "Which is the only reason I overlooked that move."

Thérèse smiled to herself. Sometimes the young madame sounded the same age as Hyacinthe. The door opened. Lord Devane stood in the doorway, his hat in his hands, his cloak still on. He looked tired and so old that for the first time Thérèse fully realized the age gap between him and Barbara. Barbara stood up, knocking over the chessboard. What was Roger doing here? That was not in the plans she and Justin had so carefully arranged.

"I would like to speak with Lady Devane alone," Roger said. Thérèse picked up her mending, and she and Hyacinthe went into her room.

Barbara had an abrupt, sinking feeling in her stomach. He was not coming.

"Harry! Charlotte!" Barbara called, for the puppies were following Hyacinthe. She sank to the floor and cuddled them, running her hands over their small, warm bodies. It was suddenly important to feel warmth. They licked her hands and pawed at her.

"They will ruin your gown," Roger said. Something in his voice made her heart squeeze. She looked up at him.

"Tell me," she said in a level tone. She already knew what he was going to say.

He looked away from her. Jesus Christ, how could he tell her what he had seen tonight? The streets so dark, so narrow that he almost turned away. The coachman sweating in spite of the cold, keeping one hand on his pistol. The walk down the dark, cobbled lane. Rats scurrying across, rooting in the sewage floating down the middle. The stink of dirt, of rot, of filth, of poverty. His flesh crawling along his neck, his steps seeming to echo in the dark silence. The tavern, a hole in the wall, filled with ragged men who watched shifty-eyed as he entered and looked around, his hand on his sword, expecting at any moment to be struck from behind and robbed and killed. He had not even recognized Kit, aged, unshaven, days drunk, his once handsome face swollen and flushed, until he rose and called his name. Kit sat with two whores, their hair greasy, dirt making rings in the creases on their necks and arms. Roger's flesh crawled. Wine for everyone, Kit cried. Good of you to come, Kit said. It was bad luck, bad planning in Scotland. The time had been ripe, England could have been ours. He blamed Bolingbroke and Mar. A toast to the Pretender. The wine burned Roger's throat. Silently he gave Kit the letter Barbara had written to him. Kit put it in a pocket without glancing at it, asking for news of Harry. Roger told him what he knew. Barbara wishes to see you, he said. Yes, Kit replied. And I her. Soon. I will see her soon. Not tonight. Now and then, Barbara peeked out from behind Kit's swollen face, in the lift of an eyebrow, in the swiftness of a smile. It was grotesque.

Will you be in Paris long? Roger had asked. Kit laughed. They were going to Lorraine. Lorraine welcomed them. From there they would plan another invasion. This time it would succeed. You will be glad you married my daughter, Kit said into his glass. I will see you are not beheaded. I will find a place for you in the new court. Come with me, now, Roger said. Barbara wants to see you. She is waiting. Kit shook his head. Another time. Soon. Very soon. Tell me about Diana, he said. Is it true she is petitioning for a divorce? Roger nodded. You should meet my wife, Kit said to one of the drunken, disheveled women beside him. She is a bigger whore than you could ever be. Kit's eyes rolled into the back of his head. Roger felt the bag of money in a secret pocket of his cloak burning like fire against his leg. He could not risk giving it to Kit here. Someone would kill them both for it. He stood up. Where are you going? Kit had asked him, staring at him with unfocused eyes. Stay. We will share the women. It will be amusing. Like old times. All Roger could think of was how he would get the money to Kit. He could leave it with Mar or Bolingbroke, but he had a feeling they were not much better than the men here. A Pretender's court was a desperate court. There was never enough money. He could see the words being scribbled in the messages to King George from his spies, how Lord Devane gave the Pretender money for his cause. Well, he would have to risk it. And he would tell Lord Stair and King George the truth, that it was money for his father-in-law, who needed it. They understood the bonds of family. They would have to. Stay, Kit mumbled. Stay awhile. We need a man like you, Roger. Stay, stay, stay. Roger stood up, the money still in place.

Out in the dark street, Roger leaned against a sagging building and vomited the sour wine he had drunk. But he could not vomit up the taste of failure, futility and waste that Kit had given him. The memories. He and Kit in London, after the same woman. He and Kit in a marshy field in the Netherlands, both praying a cannonball would not scream across the sky and lob off one of their heads. Kit . . . younger, born with advantages Roger's family could never give him. He had had only his face and an ancient, respected name. Everything that had once been great in his family had been lost in the civil wars. Roger was what was called a poor relation. He had distant cousins who were barons and earls, but his father was a country knight, always trying to bring his estate to what it had been in his father's time, before the wars and Cromwell's plunder. Kit had everything. The face, the name, the family, the beautiful wife with an even more powerful family behind her.

There had been a time—long ago—when Roger had fancied himself in love with Diana. But then almost every man who met her at one time or another fancied himself in love. To have seen Diana at sixteen was to have seen glory. But Kit had married her. Thank God. And he had wasted Diana and all she brought to him in their marriage. Lured on and on by the same things that attracted Roger—wine, women, gambling. Why had Kit sunk deeper and deeper into a mire, while he, who had started with so much less, had prospered?

Ahead he could see a lantern shining. It was like a beacon, a symbol of hope after despair, light after dark. He began to walk toward the lantern. He heard footsteps, stealthy, careful footsteps. He put his hand on his sword and turned quickly. The footsteps ceased. He walked the rest of the way with his back to the walls of the buildings, his head moving from side to side as he listened. The footsteps followed him. They knew he had money. A human life meant nothing to them. When he got to his coachman, who stood holding the lantern, a cocked pistol in one hand, he felt as if he had run a hundred miles. He was sweating. Seeing Kit was like seeing a dark of himself. How easy it was for a man to lose himself in the bottle, in the futility of his life and sink into degradation. Welcome it. He could have ended like Kit; it was luck and the Hanovers that had changed his life. And Richard. Dear God, seeing Kit was like seeing what might have been. It was enough to make him want to go home and drink, drink until the stink of that place, those people, Kit, was obliterated. But first he had to face Kit's daughter, had to tell her her father was not interested in seeing her. Had to tell her now.

"Tell me," Barbara repeated.

"He . . . was in no condition to come here, Bab. I am sorry. I did what I could. I gave him your letter." Perhaps she would not ask. But then women always did. They had to know the little details, no matter how painful.

She was crouched on the floor, patting the puppies, her face tucked down so that he could not see its expression.

"Did he read the letter?"

"No."

"Did he ask about me?"

"Bab, he was drunk and—"

"I understand." She stood up.

Roger felt he should take her in his arms, but he was tired. He did not want to deal with a hysterical child.

"Do not look so, Roger," she said. "I will not weep all over your coat this time. In all the years I was growing up, I barely saw him. He used to come into our lives and fill us with promises, and then leave. He always left. You were more a father than he ever was. Your kindness never hurt, as his did. You never made promises you did not keep. I was a fool. I see that now. Do not worry over me. I will be fine. Did you give him the money?" Her face was turned from him now, so that he could not see it. He began an explanation, but she stopped him.

"Be sure he receives it," she said. "He will need it. Now go to bed. You are exhausted. I can see it." She gave him a quick, fierce hug and then stepped back. "Thank you. I should not have asked you to do what you did, but thank you, Roger."

Of all the reactions he had imagined, dreaded, this was not one. She sounded calm, self-possessed. He shuddered. He thought her a child, someone to cosset and protect, but at this ⟨...⟩ he felt the child, glad of the escape she had offered him. He did not want to cope with what might be behind the facade. He had his own tears to deal with, tears he would not shed, tears for what life dealt people, tears for how close the edge was.

As soon as he was gone, she walked slowly over to her bed. She held on to one of the bedposts.

"I hate him," she said.

The puppies' necks pulled back into their bodies at the sound of her voice.

She picked up one of the soft, goosedown pillows and hugged it to herself. He had not come.

"I hate him," she cried, her voice passionate, breaking a little. Then she slammed the pillow against the bed, imagining her father's face . . . what she could remember of it. She hit the pillow against the bedpost again, and again, and again, saying through clenched teeth, "I hate him!"

The pillow exploded in a rain of feathers. She beat the limp pillow sack against the post rhythmically until it was empty. She threw it to the floor and stamped on it. The puppies ran under the bed.

"I hate him!"

Thérèse ran into the room. Feathers were slowly settling all about the bedroom, about Barbara, and onto her, like snow.

Barbara glared at Thérèse, jaw jutting, teeth clenched, eyes narrowed, fists clenched, feathers sticking to her hair and her gown.

"I hate him," she said. Then her face crumpled. "I will not cry," she said breathlessly. "He is not worth tears. He was never worth tears. I—will—not—cry."

She pushed her fists into her eyes, then sank to the floor.

Thérèse knelt beside her, in a welter of skirts and feathers, and put her arms around her.

"The children?" she asked. "Your brothers—"

"No. No," Barbara said. She shut her eyes tight. She would not cry. Not for her father, who had never been a father. Just as her mother had never been a mother. She had been father and mother to her family, she and her grandmother. What a fool she was. She, with her worries for him, for her supper, for her planned talk of family. Have you heard about Tom and Kit and Baby? she had been going to ask. They are ill. I sent them toys. As if he cared. As if he had ever cared. It is all right, she said to herself. I will be father and mother. I will be. As I have always been. And I will bring you all here soon, and we will be happy together. We will need no one. We will have ourselves. She rocked back and forth, tears streaming silently down her face.

Thérèse rocked back and forth with her. Whom did madame love so? Only those we love deeply could cause such anguish. Madame, whom Thérèse thought so secure, so happy, with her handsome, older husband, her jewels, her life of ease, of receptions, of ball gowns, of admiring young men. There was sadness, there was pain, even for her. And why had Lord Devane not stayed to comfort his young wife, who adored him so? Was he frightened of tears, of emotion? A tear was water from the heart, from the soul. It was the way the heart expressed its pain. The young madame had lost something she loved; someone she loved had hurt her. There was nothing in that to be afraid of. God gave life—with its happiness and its pain—to all. Thérèse rocked Barbara in her arms as she would have rocked Hyacinthe. She knew what it was to feel pain, to feel disappointment in the ones you loved. Ah, she did.

Cry, madame, cry, she thought. It will make the healing easier. The Holy Mother knew she had done enough crying herself. And in a few days' time, she would lose her little baby, growing like a bud inside her. This baby she could not, must not have. And no one could know. No one could hold her in comforting arms and rock her back and forth. Holding Barbara, she began to cry for herself, for the little lost one, for this life that gave us all, every man and every woman, some sorrow to bear.

Thérèse paid the driver, who stared down at her from his seat atop the rented carriage. He had a rugged, weather-beaten face crowned with a moth-eaten fur hat to protect him against the cold.

"Are you certain, mademoiselle, that you wish me to leave you here? It is a bad neighborhood. I can wait."

The streets were dark and narrow, and the houses sagged against one another. It was too cold for anyone to be outside, but here and there a bundle of rags that encased a body huddled against a building.

Thérèse shook her head, and the driver shrugged and clicked his tongue for his horses to start up. She stood shivering a moment in the street. In an hour it would be dark. Already heavy clouds lay inert and low in the sky and threatened snow. She picked her way through the mud and garbage on the street cobbles and tried not to mind the way the eyes inside the ragged bundles followed her. Ahead she saw the sign of the tavern of the Red Boar, but her courage failed her, and she crossed the street and stood in the cold looking at it. This morning she had awakened before daylight, dressed quickly and slipped out to the church around the corner. She had knelt, staring at the statue of Christ, at his bleeding wounds and heart, and prayed to the Holy Mother and the saints for courage and for forgiveness.

Above her a window opened, and a chamber pot of urine and feces splashed down into the street in front of her. She leapt back, but not before some of it touched her skirts. The bile rose in her throat, and she put a gloved hand against her mouth. These last days she had begun fasting early for Lent, and the nausea had been easier. Now it was back in full force. She crossed the street with stumbling steps and pushed open the door to the tavern. The only light came from a feeble fire and it highlighted empty chairs and rickety tables. The only person in sight was the tavern owner who sat in a chair near the fire whittling. He looked up.

"I have come to see Mother Marie," she said, her hand against her throat.

He snorted and jerked his head to a flight of stairs on her right.

"Third floor. And try not to scream. It is bad for business."

She would have laughed, if she had not been sick. As it was she had to hold on to the sides of the wall to keep from falling. Sweat broke out on her forehead and upper lip as she concentrated on each step, trying to keep down the bile at the back of her throat. On the third floor, she leaned her head against the doorjamb as she knocked on the door.

It opened at once. Warmth hit her in the face, made even more marked by the cold and dark of the stairwell.

"Come in, dearie."

She did as she was ordered. The small room was crammed with furniture, a canopied bed with bed curtains, two armchairs, four tables and an armoire. There was a rug on the floor and a canary in a birdcage on top of one of the tables. The other three tabletops were covered with books and papers and dirty cups and little china dogs. Thérèse put her hands to the fire—there was a pot of soup boiling—and turned to face Mother Marie, fat and dressed in layers of dirty shawls. She might have been any age; it was impossible to tell. She wore a turban, once white, now stained here and there a red-brown, and her face under it was melon-shaped.

"You have the money?" she asked Thérèse.

Thérèse pulled a small bag of coins out of a pocket in her cloak. The coins represented a quarter of what she had saved toward her dream. The woman held out her hand, and Thérèse emptied the bag into it. She counted the money—dirt was crusted under her fingernails—nodded as if satisfied, and then said, "Cat got your tongue, dearie?"

"I-I feel sick."

The woman went at once to the armoire and poured a glass of brandy. She gave it to Thérèse, who shook her head.

"Drink it, dearie," the woman said. "It helps the sickness. I do not know why it catches some women so hard. Some go the whole nine months without a flutter; others cannot hold their heads up for weeks. Drink it, dearie. It will help the other, too. Now then, are you ready?"

In spite of the roaring fire, in spite of the brandy, Thérèse felt ice-cold inside and out. She nodded her head, staring with eyes in which the pupils were dilating.

"Drink another glass of brandy, dearie, for Mother Marie's sake. That's a good girl. Now sit down on that chair."

The chair was covered with red-brown stains.

"Lift your skirts," Mother Marie said, her melon face expressionless. "Put your feet up on that stool. No, keep your knees up. Open them. Come along, dearie, this is no place for modesty. Mother Marie has seen this sight a thousand times. Shift yourself forward a little. Good, dearie, very good. I won't be a second."

She rummaged in a bag near the chair. "There it is, now."

She turned and smiled, her lips like a half-moon, and held up a long, pointed knitting needle.

Thérèse's mouth went dry. She closed her eyes and gripped the arms of the chair with all her might. Holy Mary, Mother of God, she whispered, help me.

Barbara reread the letter she had been writing to her grandmother when Roger had interrupted her with the news of her father, three days ago.

"Dear Grandmama," she read by the light of her candle, "I am so happy." She smiled to herself, smiled at the girl who had written those words. Well, they were true. Her father was not going to destroy what she was building with Roger. When she had been small, her father had held her in his arms and told her he would come for her and she would live with him forever. And she had believed him. But he had never done what he promised. Each time there were excuses, and after a while she stopped believing him. She loved him, but she hated him, too. Hated him for his false promises and the pain they brought. She had been like a silly, wide-eyed child the other day, at once forgetting the past, expecting, hoping, wanting to see him. But no more. She did not care if she ever saw him again. She did not need him. She had Roger, who would be all her father could not be. She would write nothing of it to her grandmother. She would not change one line of her letter for him, who did not deserve her love. She had Roger and her grandmother and her brothers and sisters. She needed no one else.

She lifted her head, thinking she heard a noise, like a groan. She listened, but there was nothing more. She bent back over the letter.

"It is carnival here," she read, "and Roger and I stay busy every night going to balls and receptions." Except that tonight she wished to stay home, and Roger had gone without her. He seemed to need to get away. The meeting with her father had upset him. She could understand that. She had not even seen her father, and she had been upset. She did not write to her grandmother of how people behaved during carnival. That it was unsafe for a woman to go by herself into a darkened alcove or room at the opera house. That drunkenness and lechery were everywhere. She was shocked, but not as shocked as she would have been a month ago. She was learning to

shrug her shoulders and look the other way, as Roger did. Or
to laugh. And she also would not write that she had gotten
drunk for the first time in her life. Roger had found it amusing.

"All the talk here is of the Duc d'Orléans. He is sporting a
black eye, and he says he hit himself with a tennis racket, but
others say Madame La Rochefoucauld stabbed him in the eye
with her knitting needle for taking liberties. And the Duc de
Richelieu is going to be imprisoned in the Bastille for dueling.
I am riding his horse, a lovely black mare, spirited and lively.
You would like her very much." She had not written her
grandmother that she had won the horse as a wager; that
Richelieu had been angry, but would not take her money for
the horse. That Roger's only comments were that the price
was right and that she looked dashing atop the horse. She
could see he was amused by it all, but she had a feeling her
grandmother would disapprove. But then her grandmother
was not young and in love and in Paris, where everyone was
frivolous. She was going to visit Richelieu in the Bastille. She
had promised him another chance to win back his horse, and
they had decided to do it by playing cards. He was as cavalier
about his coming imprisonment as if he were going on a journey. No one took his imprisonment seriously, least of all himself.

I stay very busy. I am taking Italian and drawing lessons,
and I am going to have my portrait painted. I have a new
maid. She is very fashionable and has made me stylish. You
would not know me with my patches and rouge. I also have
a little page and two puppies which I have named after
Harry and Charlotte. I think Anne and Charlotte (the
Tamworth one) would love them. I have sent toys and
gowns and shirts and books for everyone. Tell the boys I
am sorry they are ill, and that each night when I say my
prayers I include a special blessing for them. Kiss Baby for
me. I have had a letter from Harry, who is still in Italy,
but says he will visit. I cannot wait to see him. Roger says
we shall visit Italy and Hanover this summer. I shall be an
experienced traveler by the time I return to England. We
are giving a pancake supper for Shrove Tuesday and two
receptions the following week. You would be proud of how

I am running the household. You and my brothers and sisters are often in my thoughts, dearest Grandmama. I send you all my love.

Your granddaughter,
Barbara, Countess Devane

She had signed the last two words with a flourish. There was such satisfaction in writing them. She was folding the letter to seal it when she heard the noise again. She stood up. It was a groan. Someone was in pain.

Hyacinthe ran into her room. His eyes were huge. She had left him in her bedchamber, asleep on the floor near the puppies. Thérèse, who had been strangely silent all evening, had said she would put him to bed. But he was still in his little satin page's suit. Thérèse must have forgotten. That was not like her.

"Thérèse," Hyacinthe said, his words falling over each other. "I hear her crying. I go to the door and knock, and she tells me to go away. She says it in a very mean voice, madame, so I do as she says. Only I hear her crying again. I think she is hurt, madame."

Barbara went to Thérèse's door and put her ear to it, but she could not hear anything. She knocked softly.

"Thérèse," she called. "It is madame. Is everything well?"

She opened the door and put her head in. Thérèse lay on her narrow bed, bundled up to her neck in bed covers. Barbara stepped into the shadows of the room, lit only by a candle on the table.

"Hyacinthe said he heard you crying. I heard something, too. Are you ill? Shall I send for a physician?"

Thérèse was sweating. "Oh, no, madame. It is my flux. Today is the first day, and the cramps are worse than usual. I did not want Hyacinthe to hear me. He is too little to understand. I will be fine. Truly, madame." She smiled weakly at Barbara, who closed the door and went to reassure Hyacinthe.

Thérèse, whose hands had been gripping the sheets under the covers, relaxed. Thank you, Holy Mother, she thought. The pain had been bad, much worse than any menstrual cramps. And there had been much blood, which she had managed to clean up, even though she had to crawl on her hands and knees. Even now, the bloody sheet was wadded under the bed. Her gown was just as bloody. She would burn it. But the sheet under the bed . . . that she would bury. The blood on it was not much different, perhaps a little more clotted, but she would bury it and pray over it. And she would go and light a candle to its tiny soul. It was not damned, as hers was, until the day she died. But now, she must rest. Rest and drink wine and broth over the next days, as Mother Marie—Thérèse shuddered at the thought of her—had said. The old woman had hurt her; the pain had been dreadful. But then what had she expected? She closed her eyes and said her rosary again. She would need its strength in the next few days.

In her blue damasked private room, Barbara was pressing her seal to the hot sealing wax. Hyacinthe was already sleeping in the little trundle bed. She stretched her arms. She was tired. Should she wait up for Roger, or go on to bed? He would not be in for hours yet, and he would more than likely be drunk. Richelieu and St. Michel and Marie-Victorie were coming to dinner, the first time that some of her own friends would sit at her table with Roger. She could study the architecture books White had brought. Columns and pilasters and porticos, the elements combining to make something elegant and beautiful. She had begun to copy some of the sketches. White said her sketches were good, but White would say that. She had not yet shown them to Roger, fearing his reaction. She patted the letter. No, she had not written everything to her grandmother.

For instance, there was no child growing in her yet. Her flux had begun yesterday, as if her rage at her father had churned up her body and caused the blood to flow. But life was still good. Very, very good.

CHAPTER THIRTEEN

*J*ane Ashford stood still as two of her sisters tied lacy ribbons to hold sprigs of rosemary in her hair. It was her wedding morning.

Last night she had dreamed a strange dream. She sat in a meadow with other girls weaving wildflower garlands, garlands of primroses, daisies, hawthorn and bluebells. Far off, she could see a maypole, its ribbons and wreaths of flowers waving in the breeze. The sun warmed her. The meadow grass was high and sprinkled with daisies and buttercups. The bees and butterflies zigzagged in the sky, dizzy drunk with the pleasure of the May flowers. Everywhere the hawthorn, or May, as it was called, was blooming, the white, the pale pink, the red. Its fragrance filled the air. Her cheeks were wet with the dew from the pink May, for it was the custom for maidens to rise at dawn on May Day and wash their cheeks with the May dew. Around the maypole boys and girls were dancing. One of them was Harry. He smiled and waved to her, and she rose, taking her May garland to him. But when she went to the maypole, with the sound of fiddles playing and people laughing loud in her ears, she could not find him. Someone grabbed her, and she began to dance around the maypole, telling her partner that she was looking for Harry. The circle was huge; the blue and red and yellow ribbons from the maypole twisted as everyone danced. Sometimes she caught a glimpse of Harry; he always smiled at her, but she was never able to get to him; he disappeared in and out in the dancing circle; others took his place. When she woke, she still had the curious, disoriented feeling of looking for Harry. She lay in the darkness under the covers, wedged between two of her sisters, watching the dawn filter through the window slats. This morning she was to marry Gussy.

The wedding was to have been at Tamworth church, the reception afterward at her home, Ladybeth Farm, but there was smallpox in the village, and her parents decided it was safer to travel to London even if it was winter, and celebrate the wedding there. The smallpox was a frightening thing, like a snake hidden in summer grass; no one ever knew when or whom it would strike. Her father said he thought some of the Duchess of Tamworth's grandchildren might have it. So the Ashfords had loaded up their traveling coach and come to London, her mother and her Aunt Maude falling on each other like children, crying and laughing, while her father and Uncle Edgemont stared at each other glumly.

Her wedding was smaller as a consequence. Aunt Maude did not have the room to put everyone up, as they would have done at Ladybeth, setting cousins and uncles and aunts among the attics and halls like stored fruit. There would be only her immediate family, a friend or two of Aunt Maude's, and Gussy's friends and family. They were packed together at Aunt Maude's like fish in a barrel. She and Gussy were to spend their wedding night here, and the last two days had been spent clearing out the storeroom that would be their wedding bedroom, setting up the great bed that was a wedding present from Gussy's parents. The bed filled the entire room. They would have to crawl into it from the door.

In fact, she and Gussy were going to live with her Aunt Maude until he should find a living or suitable lodgings. Gussy was living at Oxford, where he was a fellow at one of the colleges. It was agreed he would continue to live there, while Jane stayed with her aunt. Her mother and her younger brothers and sisters were going to stay awhile, camped out in Aunt Maude's precious parlor, while her father, who had had smallpox when he was a child, would return to the farm and write them when it was safe to return.

"Your visit will be wonderful, Nell," her Aunt Maude had told her mother, waving her scarves to punctuate her enthusiasm. "We shall shop every day and buy gowns and gloves and bring you back into style. John keeps you buried on that farm, you poor thing, but I shall resurrect you. I shall!"

Her father had pursed his lips and frowned, but her mother had laughed. Jane was glad her mother was staying, though last night, her mother had stumbled over a confusing speech about her marital duties to Gussy and how she must submit. Jane had really not understood what she meant. She knew she must be dutiful to Gussy, and she was prepared to be. Harry's memory was something to be folded up like an old letter and put away in a box of precious memories. Gussy was real life. Which was not to say that she was completely over Harry. But she was not crying every day. And she did not think about him all the time. The excitement of preparing for the wedding had helped. She had to open wedding presents and buy gloves as gifts for the bridesmaids and bridesmen and try on her wedding gown and go with Aunt Maude to select the food that would be served at the reception afterward. Aunt Maude's kitchen was too small to deal with the amount of food needed, Aunt Maude had declared. She was buying it all. Jane's father had been shocked.

"City ways," he said to her mother. "Lazy, slothful . . . a city woman." But then he had never had to spend days in a kitchen baking and roasting and boiling.

Her sisters handed her her bridal bouquet of gilded rosemary, ginger and wheat stalks tied with silver ribbons. It was almost time to leave for the church. She could hear her Aunt Maude shrieking in the other room about a lost ribbon. Jane felt calm; she was calmer than both her mother and her aunt, hovering and clucking over her like mother birds over an egg that has fallen out of the nest. She remained calm, waiting as her sisters strewed herbs and flowers in the aisle of the church. Her father, at one side, fidgeted nervously and kept glancing at her. They walked down the aisle to Gussy, tall and thin, in his new suit, his elbows sticking out. She was calmer than Gussy, who mumbled his replies and almost dropped her ring. The posy in her ring read "Two made one by God alone." She was calm as she recited her vows, even though she could hear her mother and her aunt crying, especially her aunt.

"Those whom God hath joined together, let no man put asunder," intoned the vicar, and she shivered. It was done. She glanced up at Gussy as the vicar began the blessing and psalms. Gussy smiled at her; all she could think of was how bad his teeth looked. He should not smile.

It was raining as they left the church, and they all scurried like rats to her aunt's. Her brothers carried her over the threshold, and the guests threw wheat (symbolizing fecundity) at her and Gussy's mother gave her a kiss and called her "daughter," and gave her a pot of butter, symbol of plenty and abundance of good things. Aunt Maude had set up a long trestle board in her parlor, and it creaked with food: barley cakes called brides' cakes, that would be cut into tiny pieces and passed through her wedding ring, macaroons, candied fruits, savoy biscuits, jelly molds, shoulders of beef and lamb, pigeon pie, ale and wine to drink, plus a huge bowl of punch, which her father and Uncle Edgemont were worrying over, arguing as to whether to add more or less rum with more vehemence than they did politics. Her Aunt Maude had hired a fiddler, though where they would dance later was anyone's guess.

Jane sat in a chair and received the homage of the guests. Her brothers and Gussy brought her plate after plate of food, which she did little but pick at. Her small sisters played with the wheat that had been thrown at her, making it into bridal bouquets and pretending they were the bride. Her father, after six cups of punch, asked Aunt Maude to dance. It was quite a sight, guests edged against the wall, her Aunt Maude as tall as her father, all arms and legs, as they capered around the room. Soon everyone was dancing the country gigs with their leaps and intricate twists, which made everyone thirsty, and more ale or punch had to be drunk. The food on the trestle table began to disappear. Hearing the noise, neighbors peered into the front windows and were invited in. The young Duke of Tamworth made a surprise appearance. (He had been invited; it was a move on her aunt's part to secure Gussy a living, but no one had expected him.)

He entered the parlor, looking tall and fat and bashful. He bowed over Jane's hand and stammered something she could not understand, but her Aunt Maude grabbed him by the arm and pulled him around the room, introducing him as if he were the King of England. You could mark his progress by the bobs and curtsies. Her father brought him a cup of punch, and after two of them, the young duke danced with Jane, to everyone's delight, and then with her mother.

"Came for Barbara's sake," he told her as he led her around the floor in a promenade. "Wrote me to come if I could. Sent you her best wishes. A letter coming soon. About Gussy . . . I will see what I can do. Good man, Gussy. That is a fine punch. I will have another cup."

Now it was evening. The rooms in the town house were bursting with people. Gussy's mother, a tall, quiet woman, was dancing with Jane's father, who had put one of Aunt Maude's caps on his head. The lace lappets dangled over his wig. Her mother sat in a chair watching, her lace cap crooked, her face mutinous, as if she were ready to quarrel. Uncle Edgemont was talking as if there were no tomorrow to the young duke; they were comparing punch recipes. Time to pull off the bride's garters and dress her for bed, her Aunt Maude announced in ringing tones. A ragged cheer rose. Jane stood up on her chair, while her mother hurriedly loosened her ribbon garters so that they were now down on her knees. (Young gentlemen with a liberal amount of punch inside them were known to reach too far up the bride's leg in search of the garter knot. And they were also known to take too long, causing jealous and more than likely drunken bridegrooms to become angry.) A wedding was no place for a duel, though Jane could not, in her wildest dreams, imagine Gussy fighting a duel. He was too even-tempered, too sweet. Duels were fought by hot-tempered, high-blooded young men . . . like Harry. She turned her thoughts from Harry.

She was married to Gussy now. She had promised to love, honor and obey him, and she meant to. Harry was nothing to her; she would forget him as easily as he had forgotten her. She squealed as the young Duke of Tamworth untied one of her garters. Everyone clapped while he tied it around the sleeve of his velvet coat. Some friend of Gussy's untied the other one. Now it was time for her to be led away and undressed and put into bed. The men were leading Gussy away to another room, where he, too, would be undressed and led to bed in his nightgown.

She stood in the little hall between the kitchen and storeroom. Her aunt, her mother, her sisters, her aunt's friends and female neighbors were all chattering and laughing. Her mother and aunt kept crying in the midst of the laughter, shaking their heads and saying, "Where did the time go?" Her sisters were unfastening her gown, being careful to find every pin and throw it away. There would be no luck if one remained in her gown or petticoats, though Jane did not really believe that. She shivered as they pulled her nightgown over her head. She stepped through the doorway and crawled across the bed. Her mother and aunt stood at the door, looking at her and crying. Suddenly, there was a shout.

"The bridegroom comes!"

Gussy now stood awkwardly in the doorway. She giggled at the way he looked in his nightcap. He climbed across the bed. Now they sat side by side, covers drawn up to their chins as they stared at the guests and family members crowded one upon another in the hallway. Gussy's friend sat down on the bed's edge in the doorway and threw one of Gussy's wedding stockings over his head. It landed by Jane, but not on her. Everyone groaned. It meant he would not be married soon. Jane's sister did the same thing, but Jane's wedding stocking landed on Gussy's nightcap. Jane laughed with everyone else at the sight of the stocking hanging down his face. Word traveled quickly to those crowded about who could not see. Jane's sister would be married soon.

"The caudle! The caudle!" shrieked her aunt.

Those in the doorway parted, and Uncle Edgemont appeared with a huge cup, steam issuing up into his face. It was the bridal caudle, made of milk and wine and egg yolks and sugar and cinnamon. She and Gussy both had to drink it.

"You will need it for strength, Gussy!" shouted someone.

"Lift up his nightgown," called a woman, "and let us see if Jane has anything to fear!"

Everyone loved that. Laughter filled the hallway. Gussy concentrated on drinking the caudle.

"I helped undress him," said Gussy's friend. "Jane had better begin her prayers!"

Another laugh.

"He is built like a bull."

"Drink the caudle, Janie, drink the caudle. You will need the energy!"

"We will see who is more tired in the morning, Jane or Augustus."

They finished the caudle. The laughter and the joking continued for a while, but it was too crowded in the hallway, and Jane's father wanted to make up a last bowl of punch. He led Jane's mother away; she was sobbing. With contrary admonitions to do their duty and to behave themselves, the young couple were left alone. The storeroom was dark; the only light was from the kitchen fire, which could be seen as a faint glow which just reached the doorway.

"Jane," Gussy said hesitantly beside her.

"Yes?"

He reached for and found her hand and squeezed it. "I want to be a good husband."

"And I a good wife."

But she was not prepared for how it felt to be kissed by him. It was all right while he was kissing her face and neck, but when he kissed her mouth, when he opened it, and for the first time she felt his tongue inside her mouth, she had to hold on to herself not to push him away. Her body stiffened. It was not like Harry; Harry whose mouth had been like honey, and whose tongue made her want to melt inside. She began to feel panicked, she turned her mouth away, but now Gussy was lifting her nightgown. He was mumbling her name and pushing against her, between her naked thighs. She had a moment of paralyzing shock when he entered her; the pain as he broke her hymen was sharp and vivid. She could feel her entire body quivering with the aftershock. He thrust himself in and out of her, kissing her neck, murmuring her name, groaning, "Oh, oh, oh-h-h." She kept her mouth turned away. Her hands gripped the bed sheets as she tried not to cry. It was not the hurt, though it did hurt; it was just such an . . . intrusion. Just when she was beginning to think she would scream, he cried out and sagged against her. Now his body lay on top of her like a rock.

"Jane," he whispered, "are you all right?"

"Yes, Gussy." To her surprise, her voice sounded calm, normal in the darkness.

He lifted himself off her; she could feel sticky wetness between her legs; it was throbbing down there. He kissed her on the forehead.

"Good night, my wife. I-I love you."

She did not answer. He tossed and turned, and finally settled against her, one of his long legs thrown over her. He began to snore. Her body relaxed. The tears she had held back welled and trickled down her cheeks. Now she knew why her mother had stumbled and mumbled about marital duties. Now she knew why her mother and aunt had cried. Christ above, if women knew, they would never marry. She had been raised on a farm; she had seen animals couple. But she had never before given a thought as to how the female might be taking the act. Poor things. No wonder they made the noises they did. Her mother said one became used to it. How? It was an intrusion into her most private place. And Gussy . . . had seemed to enjoy it. Naturally. No one was sticking anything into him! Irritably she pushed his leg off and wiped her face. The crying had made her tired. She yawned. Tomorrow, and for a week afterward, she had a new gown for each day. What a shame she was not at Ladybeth. She would have loved to show off her gowns, her wedding ring, to Squire Dinwitty's daughters, to the Duchess. Gussy had said he would take her up to Oxford. He would rent a room at an inn for the night. He wanted his friends, his tutors, to meet her. She had never stayed the night at an inn. She shivered with cold and moved closer to Gussy. He was too thin; she needed to fatten him up. He wanted her to hear him preach a sermon. She would be so proud, to sit in that front pew and listen. Too bad married life had to include the other but perhaps, as her mother said, she would grow used to it. "Harry," she whispered once in the darkness, but, of course, no one answered. How long ago it seemed since he had kissed her under the apple trees. Long ago and far away.

Barbara sat down at the breakfast table, skirts rustling, and unfolded her napkin. Inside the napkin was a rosebud, just unfurling a dark red petal or two. She looked up at Roger, and he smiled, the lines crinkling around his eyes. Last night, she thought. Her breath caught.

"In memory of last night," he said, watching a vein begin to pulse in her white throat. He thought about how it felt to kiss that throat, about how it felt to be inside her, about how she wrapped silky legs and arms around him and whispered

his name over and over. . . . He leaned across the table, and
ran his thumb over that vein. She shivered and took his hand
and held the open palm to her mouth and kissed it.

"I love you," she whispered.

He stood up abruptly, pulled back her chair, and led her
from the room, a hand on her elbow.

Thérèse was assisting the chambermaid in making the bed.
One look at her mistress's flushed, downcast face, at Lord
Devane, and she motioned to the chambermaid to leave the
bed unmade. Without a word, she pushed the maid and
Hyacinthe and the puppies out the door as if they were wayward geese. As the door closed, Barbara lifted her face, and
Roger's mouth was on hers, and she felt as if she were drowning in the sensations created by his mouth and tongue and
hands. Each time he made love to her she enjoyed it more,
felt more wanton, and free.

They lay on the bed and undressed each other, taking time
between the untying of a shirt or the unlacing of a gown for
passionate, long kisses. He held her face between his hands.
"Your face is a heart," he said, kissing her eyes, her nose, her
mouth. They were kneeling in front of each other as she
watched him untie the front of her corset. It fell open, her
small breasts were round and pointed through the thin fabric
of her chemise. Roger pushed her back gently, and she
watched him pull up her chemise and untie her garters and
slowly roll down her stockings. Then he leaned over and
began to kiss her legs and thighs, her stomach, between her
legs. She hid her face in her arms, ashamed a little. Gently
he pulled her arms away from her face. His eyes were like
sapphires; his face was taut with desire; he had never been
more beautiful.

"Do not be ashamed of what two people do between them
in private and for their own pleasure. Shall I stop?"

"No," she said. "Do not stop."

He smiled at her; she had never wanted him so much in her
life. All her sensations seemed to be in the tips of her breasts,
between her legs, soft, aching, swollen sensations. His tongue
was like a flame, searing her wherever it touched. When he
entered her, she was as soft and wet as spring moss. He
groaned and closed his eyes and kissed her deeply in her
throat. She kissed him back with all the passion and love and

expertise she was slowly gathering. She could not have enough of him, and he seemed to feel the same way about her. They strained together, touching, kissing, whispering; they were twined like vines, his mouth on hers, and he was groaning; as she moved her tongue against his the tingling inside her built and peaked. "Ah," she cried, scratching his back as he smiled down at her, "ah." She held him fiercely against her beating heart. He made her feel beautiful and desirable and wanton. And when she was with him, she was all of those.

Afterward, they lay still together, as if they could not bear to part. He covered her face with soft kisses and stroked her neck, while she arched her neck, as a swan does. She felt lazy and content. He lay with her until she seemed to doze, and then he got up and found his clothes and began to dress, noticing as he did so a volume of Palladio on the table by her bed, the newly translated *Four Books of Architecture*, with odds and ends of loose papers hanging out. Intrigued, he stopped to riffle through the papers. They were drawings, crude sketches of porticoes and temple fronts and what looked like an open-air villa. It had a temple front portico with classical columns and stairs leading to it. There was an open central hallway from front to back and windows evenly spaced on all sides. There was a small dome on its roof. He smiled to himself.

With one of the papers in his hand, he looked down at her. Her glorious hair was tumbled on the pillows, and she made no effort to hide her nakedness, which touched him, for he knew she was a modest girl, and the extent of her passion for him, her trust and love, was evident by the fact that she no longer covered herself before him.

"I thought you were asleep."

"Stay. Sleep with me."

"Is it not enough that you have made me late for breakfast and for all my morning appointments? Have you no shame, Barbara?"

"No. Not with you. None with you. Stay."

She looked very appealing, lying there. But he shook his head.

"Tell me of this," he said, showing her the paper.

She sat up and took the paper from him and blushed when she saw what it was. Without looking at him, she said, "It is a sketch I made."

He had to bend forward to hear her. "A sketch of what, Barbara?"

"A-a summer house. For Bentwoodes. Never mind, Roger. It is just a stupid drawing." She crumpled the paper in her hand.

"La Rocca Pisana is an open-air villa—a summer house—high above the Veneo plains. One of Palladio's students designed it. Your drawing reminds me of it."

"Yes, I tried to copy it. I thought a summer house would be a good thing. For the children. We could go there on the hot days and eat and read and do lessons."

"The children?"

Barbara took a deep breath. "I hope we have children, and I also hope my brothers and sisters will come and live with us. I miss them so, Roger. Perhaps they could come soon?" She saw the look on his face and hurried on. "Others do it. Marie-Victorie has two of her nieces living with her."

"Marie-Victorie is not newly married."

She looked down at her hands, one of which held the crumpled drawing. It was too early to have asked.

He took the drawing from her, and kissed her hand. "Later," he said. "Perhaps later."

She looked up at him, yearning. "Stay."

He pulled away and chucked her under the chin. "If I were ten years younger . . . Sleep for a while, darling. I will tell Thérèse to send breakfast up to you later."

At the door, he turned. "La Malcontenta," he said.

"What?"

"One of Palladio's finest villas. When we are in Italy I will show it to you."

She lay back against the pillow. Darling. He had called her darling. He had made love to her late last night, and then this morning. If he were ten years younger . . . She fantasized about a younger Roger, a Roger who would not leave her bed, but who would stay in it all day and make love to her over and over and over. She smiled to herself. She would have liked to have known that Roger, but it was enough that this one seemed to be caring for her more and more. She was going to win. She was. His feeling for her was like the trees in the gardens outside. When she had first seen them, they were nothing but bare, brown branches for winter; now that spring was coming, those branches were tipped with tiny buds of green. Soon, the tips would multiply and unfurl, and the branches would be covered with rich, vibrant green leaves, the rich green of spring and summer—of youth and love. Roger was going to love her. They were going to have many children. In a beautiful home. With a summer house. Where she would oversee Anne and Charlotte's lessons. La Malcontenta. He was going to show it to her. . . .

Roger stared at himself as he stood in front of his mirror. Justin tied his cravat and brushed his coat, acting as if it were the most natural thing in the world for his master, who was a fastidious man and who never left his rooms unless he was dressed perfectly, to reappear before ten-thirty in the morning, with his shirt half tied and his coat and wig and stockings off, to be dressed again.

I am a fool, Roger thought. There can be no bigger fool than an old man with a young wife. She is going to kill me. He was tired. He had drunk heavily last night, but still found that he desired Barbara, and so he had gone to her apartments and wakened her from sleep and made love to her. And then this morning, he desired her yet again. Her youth, her response to his lovemaking, her growing passion, were as intoxicating to him as champagne. He took her, expecting lust to lessen with familiarity, and found that he only wanted her more. There had been no other woman but her in a month or more. But he was not as young as he used to be; he was going to have to pace himself. At this moment, he felt like death; he would have to nap this afternoon or go to bed early this evening. Like an aged man, with a young wife. The oldest of jests. . . .

Why did she continue to interest him? He watched with both amusement and dawning respect her fledgling attempts to become fashionable. She had him acting as if he were a young stallion; and now he had just seen her crude drawings and been suddenly aware that under that child's face was a budding woman, with taste and a mind. He would build her just such a villa, but it would not be open-air. It would house his art.

And she had a will. Yes, Alice's will. She wanted her family to live with her. And he did not. But he felt certain that she would not forget.

She needs a child, he thought. A child to occupy her, and to give me rest. Unexpectedly, tenderness welled within him, and tears came to his eyes. He motioned Justin away and stared hard at himself, seeing every line, every wrinkle, every flaw. Seeing his age. And his possible folly. What did he feel for her? He desired her greatly, but she was young and adoring and new to him. Beyond that . . . she amused him, she infuriated him, she touched him. And he wanted children from her. Something stirred in him. Hope. . . . He smiled at himself, baring his teeth like a savage. The most handsome of savages. It was too ironic, too amusing even for the Fates. To fall in love with his own wife. (Justin, secretly watching, gave a sentimental sigh.) Give it time. Take what comes and be satisfied with it. . . . Jesus Christ, he would be the happiest man in the world if Barbara should have a child.

Thérèse tiptoed into the bedroom to see about her mistress. She was still asleep. Thérèse drew the curtains around the bed so that no light should disturb her. With all the lovemaking between Lord and Lady Devane, she should become pregnant soon. A child. She picked up Barbara's stockings and chemise and petticoat and gown from the floor and folded them. She went to the windows and looked out into the gardens. Hyacinthe was playing with the puppies. The Holy Mother bless him. She did not know what she would have done without him this last week.

He had run errands for her ceaselessly. The bleeding had not stopped; it was like her flux, except it made her more tired. Hyacinthe ran up and down the stairs for her, so that she could rest. She had buried the bloody sheet in a corner of the garden under a lilac tree, and said prayers over it. She lit a candle each morning in church, praying to the Holy Mother and her gentle son for forgiveness, praying that this cloud over her spirit would lift. She had thought to be happy again once the fear was gone, but she found that she was grieving for the child, as if it had been fully formed and had died at birth.

She found herself grieving for what might have been, even though she knew that if she had had the child she would have been dismissed, that she or the baby could have died, that they would have been reduced to starvation. She might have gone home to her father, but she could see his face, that of her married brothers and sisters, pious and fat like turnips. It was better this way, even though the Holy Mother Church said it was a mortal sin. But she had grown up in a great household; she knew the stories of the noble ladies, married and unmarried. They took abortion powders; they visited the evil old women in the back alleys; and if the babies did not die as planned, they were given away at birth. And they were shriven by priests who could not be unaware of their sins. If she could have donated a bag of gold or built a new church, she would have been forgiven.

She shrugged and shook her head. Perhaps her prayers would bring forgiveness, for the Holy Mother had been a simple woman, a woman of the people, a woman like herself. But she had not thought she would feel so sad, so old, so drained. She had not thought to find her mind going continually to that lilac tree, to that buried sheet. She found herself imagining what the child might have looked like. Surely time would heal her, as it did all things. She found comfort in her rosary and in the greening buds on the trees and in the tiny green stalks in the garden. But, Holy Mother, where was the joy she had once felt in simply being alive? That joy was all that a woman such as herself possessed. It made her special, set her above her fellow servants. Was it buried with that sheet which held all she would ever know of a child? She shook her head at her thoughts and went to oversee the laundering.

Louise-Anne de Charolais and Henri de St. Michel waited in the governor's room in the prison of the Bastille. They had come to visit Richelieu, who had finally been imprisoned for his duel with de Gacé a week ago, March fourth. His imprisonment had become a sensation; all of fashionable Paris flocked to visit him, to bring him flowers and sweets. In his arrogance Richlieu had had the cell furnished with his own bed and a table and chairs from his home. Rugs lay over the cold stone floors and tapestries hung on the stone walls. His valet stayed with him to attend him and dress him. In the evenings he strolled along the wall and in the garden with the governor. Paris loved it. Richelieu was an original. More women than ever vowed they were in love with him.

Bored with waiting, Louise-Anne went to the window, glanced out, and saw Barbara and Marie-Victorie de Gondrin being helped into a carriage.

"No wonder we must wait," she said to St. Michel. "He has been entertaining other guests!"

A jailer escorted them to the cell. Richelieu was dressed as he would have been on any day, in a plum-colored satin coat with black cording and brown breeches. His wig was new. His ugly face was thinner. That was the only sign that prison might not be all he said it was. He stood by a birdcage, pushing his finger through the bars and whistling to a small, yellow-gold linnet. His valet at once went to pour wine as Louise-Anne and St. Michel entered.

"Welcome," Richelieu said. "I have been dying of boredom."

Louise-Anne turned her face away from his kiss. "Do not mouth 'boredom' to me. I caught a glimpse of your last two visitors!"

"Ah, yes, the worthy Marie-Victorie and the Countess Devane. As I said, I have been dying of boredom. What could be more boring than a visit from two women determined to protect their virtue? Henri, I begin to think that Lady Devane will outwit us both."

"I thought you were trying to sneak in ahead of me," St. Michel said.

"Would I do that?"

"Yes."

Both men laughed. Louise-Anne pulled off her long, soft gloves and unpinned her hat. She tossed it on the bed and walked around the room to inspect it, stopping in front of the birdcage to make clucking sounds to the linnet, which burst into song.

"How charming! Who brought you this?"

"Lady Devane," Richelieu said casually. "She thought it would cheer me. She had some odd notion that prison is not enjoyable."

"Oh? And what other odd notions does she have?"

"Unfortunately, none of interest, my sweet. I was intent only on playing cards with her. Today I won. She was furious. Tomorrow she will win."

Richelieu's horse and Barbara's riding were a topic of much gossip, as was their running card game, in which they traded ownership of the horse back and forth, as one or the other won. Yet the lady in question made no secret of her devotion to her husband and favored none of her admirers, not even the persistent St. Michel. Paris was beginning to consider her both dashing and original. (Virtue was always original. Done with style it became dashing.)

"She really is boring," said Richelieu, "except that she plays cards so well. Tell me, Henri, the truth. How does your pursuit go?"

St. Michel was silent. It went badly, as all Paris knew. "I am thinking of dropping her—"

Richelieu began to laugh, cruel, mocking laughter. St. Michel stiffened.

"What a fool you are," Richelieu said. "I could have her in my bed within six months."

"Implying I cannot!"

"You will never be the man I am—"

St. Michel's hand went to his sword. Richelieu had no sword since he was in the Bastille for dueling. He grinned.

"I know a true man," Louise-Anne said softly, "who would laugh at both of you and kill either of you in a second if you dared speak to him as you do to everyone else. He would not wound, like you and Gacé, Armand. Throwing down your swords at the first show of blood. But kill you. Dead."

"Your Uncle Philippe," said Richelieu, diverted from his game with St. Michel. "Is he back in town?"

"The one who killed D'Arcy last year?" St. Michel interrupted excitedly, forgetting his anger.

"Yes. And before that he killed Montreal." Louise-Anne shivered. "The only time he was ever human was when he and Roger were friends. I always thought he killed Montreal because of Roger."

"Roger? Roger Montgeoffry?" said Richelieu.

"Yes, Roger and Uncle Philippe were fast friends, and then Uncle Philippe killed Montreal, and Roger left Paris, and my

uncle . . ." She stopped, unable to explain. "You would have
to know my uncle."

"I am glad I do not," said St. Michel.

"Well, you will have another chance. He said in a letter to
Mother that he is coming to Paris, for new clothes and the
theater and to see our wonder of wonders, John Law. But I
think he is coming to see Roger. Maybe they will duel. That
would be something to see. They are both real men. One of
them would die." She shivered again and put her arms around
herself. The tip of her little red tongue touched her upper lip.
Through the fabric of her gown, her breast tips had become
hard. Richelieu stared at her.

It was the last afternoon of a week in which the Duc and
Duchesse du Maine had thrown open the doors of their estate
to celebrate the coming of spring. All week long guests had
driven up the long front avenue to be feted with poetry readings and theatricals in which the guests had learned the parts
and played them on the private stage built at Sceaux. There
were concerts in the ballroom, dinners (observing the Lenten
fast, with fish fresh from the Seine each morning), hunting
and riding expeditions, strolls in the budding gardens, gambling and dancing every night.

Now, Barbara and Roger strolled along the edge of the
landscape pool at one end of the terraces at Sceaux. They had
been invited to spend the night, after the evening's dancing,
for Roger was buying two Arabian stallions from the Duc du
Maine, who had been given them as an illegitimate son of the
late king.

He was talking to Barbara of Bentwoodes and she listened,
adoring, aware at some deep level she could not give words
to that he was beginning to make a place for her in his life.
He was sharing his dreams. He liked the lavish hospitality, the
talk of art and literature, the fine wines and foods mixed with
scandal and politics, at Sceaux. It was a French, rather than
an English, tradition. Even at Saylor House there was not this
complexity, this magnificence. They were talking of this as
they walked, arm in arm, down the graveled paths, paths
punctuated by straight rows of young chestnut trees, which
led to the fountains, spurting water that glinted like crystal in
the fresh, cold, early spring air.

"It will take ten years to complete the house as I envision it," he was saying. "The first part I want to build is the temple of the arts—imagine it, Bab, a graceful, classical building filled with the finest paintings, statuary, ancient busts and drawings, a building that will uplift the spirit by its very essence. We will entertain in it, and the grounds surrounding it will be magnificent. I will link it with an arcade to the house, a house that will be the most beautiful in England. It will become the most famous in the country. Men of learning and sophistication, of talent, will always be welcome. Our hospitality will be as lavish as this—" He spread his arms to include the gardens and main house of Sceaux.

In ten years, Barbara thought, I will be almost twenty-six . . . and we will have children. Charlotte and Anne shall be married, and Harry and Tom. Roger will be fifty-two. That made her shiver—her grandfather had died at fifty-eight, and was considered to have lived to a ripe old age. Her grandmother, now in her sixties, was thought to be a miracle of health. Impossible that in ten years Roger might be dead and she a widow. To look at him now, with the sun shining strongly on his face, was to see a man who looked to be in his thirties, no more. He was handsomer than he had ever been in his life. Everyone commented on it, and he accepted the comments with the natural grace of a man who has never heard anything else. Barbara hoped it was her love that was making him younger. Only the myriad lines about his eyes suggested his true age. She shivered again and squeezed his arm.

"Make love to me."

He stopped in the middle of the path and stared at her. His eyes were bluer than the spring sky. "Now? In the afternoon?"

"Yes. Now."

The candles in the huge crystal chandeliers of the ballroom at Sceaux sputtered and dripped hot wax onto the shoulders of the guests. At almost midnight, the ball showed no sign of ending. The servants would have to replace the candles in the chandeliers before the first guest climbed into his carriage and drove back into Paris in the early hours of the morning.

Barbara yawned behind her fan. She and Roger were both tired. As soon as he returned with her glass of champagne, she was going to suggest they excuse themselves and go to bed. No one would miss them. Everybody was too busy gossiping about everyone else. John Law was here and people surrounded him as if he were a magnet. She caught bits and pieces of talk about his national bank, a miracle that would make everybody rich, that would make the national debt disappear, that would provide cheap money, increase trade, fix prices on goods and lending. She could feel the excitement pulsing in the room, pulsing from Law. But after two or so months in Paris, she had decided that the Parisians were always excited over something; if they could not find something, they made it up. She began to work her way through the crowd to find Roger and tell him she was going to bed.

Someone tapped her on the shoulder with a fan. She turned. It was Louise-Anne de Charolais, which surprised her. She knew the princesse did not like her; she was jealous over Barbara's visits to Richelieu, and her sudden popularity. (Richelieu had told Barbara just the other day that she must not, under any circumstances, stop visiting him in the Bastille. "My love life with Louise-Anne has improved immensely," he said, "and I owe it all to you. Swear you will continue to visit me.")

"I have been looking for you," Louise-Anne said, running her eyes up and down Barbara's lilac silk ball gown, trimmed in green and silver bows. The lilac was as pale as the buds on the lilac trees in the gardens, and Barbara wore a thick rope of pearls twined around her neck, and another twined through her hair, which was unpowdered, unlike that of the other women in the room. Heavy pearl earrings hung down on each side of her slim neck. With her rouged lips and cheeks— "Lightly, madame, lightly," warned Thérèse. "Your youth does better than any rouge"—and her darkened brows and lashes, she looked lovely, fashionable, and best of all, unique. Louise-Anne, with her hair powdered chalk-white, two vivid streaks of rouge across her cheeks, and her red slash of a mouth, looked haggard and shopworn beside her.

"Someone wishes to meet you," Louise-Anne said. "Lady Devane, may I present my uncle, the Prince de Soissons. Uncle Philippe, may I present Lady Barbara Devane."

He bowed over her hand. He was tall and heavy without being fat, with a proud, handsome, full-fleshed face marred by a dueling scar that drew his mouth up to one side. His eyes were brown, under heavy eyebrows—the eyebrows and the scar gave his face an ironic expression. He seemed to be in his forties. He was staring at her with a curious expression—part interest, part admiration, part something else she could not read, but perhaps it was just those eyebrows. When he smiled, she saw that he had white, even teeth, and that, combined with the smile, took her breath away. He was a very attractive man.

"I admired your grandfather. I cannot tell you how I have looked forward to this meeting," he said.

There was something odd in the way he spoke, as if he were making fun of her. She did not understand.

"You knew my grandfather?"

"We fought on opposite sides, but it was an honor to be his enemy; he was as famous in our army as he was in yours. The king used to throw vases at the campaign maps each time your grandfather besieged a city, for everyone knew it was as good as captured. Once I was his prisoner, and I was treated as handsomely as any guest. I felt honor-bound to stand by my pledge not to escape, even though your grandfather beat me regularly at chess. I assure you I came here tonight only to meet you. Louise-Anne will tell you that I have stayed on my estate the last year, and now I am like a country bumpkin in the city."

He did not seem like a country bumpkin. He spoke with assurance, seeming unusually polished and urbane. There was a slight touch of irony in everything he said, as well as in the way he looked at her. Surely it was more than the set of his eyebrows and the way that scar drew up his mouth.

"How long are you to be in Paris?"

"Who knows? I am tempted to go back to the country, the city is too much for me. I had forgotten the noise, the confusion, the people. I would have stayed home tonight, but I could not pass up the opportunity to meet the granddaughter of the famous Duke of Tamworth. A young woman—most lovely, may I add—who shares the distinction of also being Roger Montgeoffry's wife."

"You know my husband, then—but, of course, you must if you knew my grandfather."

He laughed, a laugh that was as rich, as full, as melted chocolate.

"Yes, Lady Devane. . . . May I presume and call you Barbara? Thank you. . . . I know him well. He and I were once very great friends. There he is now—against the terrace windows—still looking ten years younger than I. Marriage must agree with him. I always found his eternal youth most annoying. I still do. Take my arm, Barbara, and we will walk over and surprise him. Run along, Louise-Anne, my child. You have been a most helpful niece. You must walk slowly, my dear, for I limp—an old battle wound—of sorts."

Again she was conscious of irony in his tone. With one hand on his arm, she began to make her way through the people standing along one side of the ballroom. Roger had her glass of champagne, but was sipping from it as he talked with their host, the Duc du Maine.

"Roger," she called when she was close enough, "look whom I have found."

He turned, smiling, still talking to the duc, but when he saw her with the Prince de Soissons his face went white. The champagne glass dropped from his hand, splintering into fragments on the floor. Barbara hurried to him.

"Roger! What is it? Are you unwell?"

The expression on his face frightened her.

"Roger, my dear friend, is something wrong?" asked the Duc du Maine. A servant was kneeling in front of them, wiping up the fragments of glass, the spilled champagne.

"Nothing," Roger said, in an odd voice. "I felt a sudden pain. It is gone now."

Barbara noticed he leaned against the terrace door, as if he needed the support. The color of his face made her afraid.

"At our age," the Duc du Maine was saying, "we must be careful. That young wife of yours is exhausting you—ah, Soissons, my wife told me you were in town. An unexpected pleasure and surprise. You already know Lord Devane."

The Prince de Soissons smiled; the smile filled his face, lighting his eyes. "Roger . . ."

Roger was silent. Barbara glanced from one man to the other, and could feel the tension. She put a hand on Roger's arm, and her gesture seemed to wake him.

"Philippe," he said. "I did not think to see you. . . ."

"But here I am. Ready to revive old interests . . . old friendships."

"Roger," Barbara said quickly. Something in his face made her say it. "I am so tired," she babbled. "I was just coming to find you when the prince introduced himself. Could you escort me to my bedchamber? Gentlemen, you will forgive me, I know."

Roger straightened up and pushed himself away from the wall. Barbara could see the effort he was making. They left the Duc du Maine and Prince de Soissons and made their way through the ballroom; it was she who was supporting him.

"Shall I call a footman?" she asked him. No color had yet returned to his face. He looked terrible.

He shook his head, and they slowly climbed the stairs. Sweat had broken out on his face; he was ill; he had said something about a pain. As she opened the door to their bedchamber, he sagged against her, and she called for Justin and Thérèse, who both came running. The three of them helped Roger to the bed and laid him down. Justin began quickly to loosen his cravat, while Thérèse ran for a glass of brandy. Barbara stood at the edge of the bed, wringing her hands.

"What is wrong?" she asked him. "Tell me! Ought I to call a doctor?"

"No, no," Roger said breathlessly, trying to sit up. "I had a sudden pain . . . in my chest. I am better now. Leave me alone for a while, Bab. . . . Justin knows what to do. . . . Leave me alone."

He was not better. He could not catch his breath. She bit her lip, but did as he asked, going into the adjoining bedchamber with Thérèse behind her. He looked so white, so pale. They had done too much this last week. She could hardly be still long enough for Thérèse to unhook her gown. Once she was out of it, she ran to the door and peeked in. Roger was sitting up, leaning against Justin and drinking a glass of brandy. But when he sank back down onto the bed afterward, he groaned.

"Sweet Jesus," Barbara said. "He is truly ill—"

"Madame," said Thérèse, hanging up the gown and coming to her and making her sit down on the bed, "I will go downstairs and have a cordial mixed. I know a soothing recipe. And if he is still ill tomorrow, you will send for the physician and have him bled. That will make him better, if a good night's rest does not do so. He has been doing too much. That is all, madame. He is not as young as you, and he needs more rest."

"As everyone but me realizes. Go and make his cordial, Thérèse. I will just check on him once more."

She crept into the other bedchamber. Justin was sitting by the bed, and Roger appeared to be sleeping. She took one of his hands and rubbed it; it felt cold, clammy. Roger opened his eyes.

"Are you better?" she whispered.

"Yes," he said. "I need to be alone, Bab. Please."

She nodded and put his hand back down on the bed, patting it. "Thérèse is bringing a cordial," she said.

She went back into the bedchamber and sat down. He wanted to be alone. This was understandable, and there was no reason to feel hurt by it, and it was ridiculous to be reminded of her father. Roger was not like her father. She could sleep in here, and tomorrow he would be better. They would return to Paris, and she would nurse him, if need be, until he was better. And she would remember, from now on, that he was not as young as he looked. She closed her eyes. If something should happen to Roger . . . but nothing was going to happen. Everything was going to be fine.

Roger drank a few sips of the cordial Thérèse had prepared, then sank back down on the bed and closed his eyes. His chest still hurt. He had felt as if it were exploding when he looked up and had seen Philippe. Dear God. Philippe. Memories rolled over him, like waves pounding a beach. He was held by them, bound hand and foot, their captive. The darkness and forbidden desires, the arrogance and love. The blood pouring from Montreal's mouth and nose. The futility and anger. The despair. And the passion. . . .

CHAPTER FOURTEEN

*A*nnie sat in the Duchess's withdrawing chamber, guarding the Duchess against well-meaning, but intrusive, visitors. They had been coming—one by one—all morning: Squire Dinwitty, Sir John Ashford, Vicar Latchrod, tenants, some of the principal villagers. Braving the sickness, as soon as word spread. Annie gave them ale, listened to their condolences and sent them away. Only Vicar Latchrod stayed, in a drawing room, murmuring prayers. There was nothing anyone could do, and they must look to their own households, for the scourge lay coiled like a serpent in the brush, striking randomly and without warning. Many households had someone sick, someone in them dying. They could only pray, beseeching the Lord God Almighty, that soon now it would disappear.

Annie could hear the Duchess sobbing. She brushed tears from her own eyes and got up to shut the door more securely. In the bedchamber, which was dark and dusty—vases of dead flowers lay on tables littered with teacups and papers—there was no sound except for that of weeping. It was the clear, high weeping, such as a young girl does, except that it was not a young girl. It was the Duchess, and she was weeping for her grandchildren, the last of whom had died this morning of smallpox.

The sound filled the dark bedchamber with its desolation, its despair. On the other side of the door, Annie put her face in her hands. Sometimes life seemed nothing but a hard and weary burden. And there was so much to do. Even now, Henley was laying the little bodies in the lead-lined caskets. No one else would do it; they were afraid of catching the smallpox. It was said it would leap right out of a casket and kill you. And all the bedding and nursing clothes had to be burned. The house had to be disinfected with a mixture of pitch and frankincense. They would dispense with much of the ceremony; the bodies would not lie in state but would be buried as soon as possible, to keep the chance of spreading infection as low as possible. There would be no funeral invitations; the Duchess would write the necessary letters to the family.

A bell began to toll, the bell of Tamworth church, informing the village and countryside of the deaths. Annie wiped her eyes and blew her nose. Black hangings must be put up in the rooms, the mirrors covered. And the letters must be written. The one to Lady Diana and, especially, the one to Mistress Barbara. . . . Writing that one would be a test of faith.

Diana lay like a goddess, lolling on her new settee. She wore no hoops, so that her guests, Walpole and Montagu, could see the shape of her legs through the material of her gown. She stretched herself before them like a feast neither of them could have. It had been her custom lately to invite Walpole to a late supper, but only when the Duke of Montagu was also present. She then flirted with whichever man caught her fancy that evening. If it was a ploy to spur Montagu's cooling interest, it worked, for he found himself whipped into new frenzies (and new promises) by the sight of Walpole watching Diana with desire in his eyes. Walpole took it all like a good-natured bear; growling, cursing, but as yet safe.

She had fed them well. She was managing to live very nicely on her mother's allowance, supplemented by Montagu, and now the three of them drank brandy and discussed politics. Or rather the men discussed politics and Diana listened, waiting for the right spot in which to insert fresh pleas for her divorce petition. All the news was centered on the fizzling invasion in Scotland, of the Pretender's flight, his leaving his loyal Scots nobles to face the English and Hanoverian troops. Diana yawned behind her hand; Kit had been in Scotland, but luckily for her, he was gone with the Pretender. There was talk that he was in Paris. Good. Let Roger deal with him. To her, Kit was as good as dead. He had taken her too close to the edge, and now she felt nothing for him, except the need to be divorced from him and completely on her own. Walpole said Roger was reported to be buying half of France for Devane House and the other half for Barbara.

Clemmie scuttled into the room and handed Diana a note. She rose and walked closer to the candelabra to read it. Walpole and Montagu paused to watch her walk, and it was a sight worth stopping for. But they were unprepared for her shrill cry. She sank to the floor and suddenly the room was in chaos, as both men ran to her, and Clemmie screeched. Walpole reached her first, and carried her back to the settee. Montagu rubbed her hands, while Clemmie held a burning feather under her nose. She began to revive, her eyelids fluttering, her face white under its rouge. Walpole poured some brandy down her throat, and she sputtered and her eyes flew open and she coughed and cursed Walpole between each cough.

"That is more like it," said Walpole. "You frightened us—" He broke off because Diana put her hands to her mouth and began to cry, heedless of her makeup, or of how she looked. The sight was enough to make Clemmie's almost toothless mouth fall open.

Montagu picked up the crumpled note. "It is her children," he said to Walpole. "They are dead . . . the smallpox. My God!"

Clemmie began to wail again; Walpole patted Diana's hand, but Diana was oblivious of him. She was crying and rocking back and forth and her rouge was streaking her cheeks, and she did not seem to care.

That, and the smallpox, were more than Montagu could bear. He kissed her hand.

"My dear, I feel it is better if you are alone in this time of travail. I offer my sympathies. Indeed I do. I will call tomorrow or the next day to see how you are getting along." He was halfway out the door, finding his hat and cane and cloak by himself. "My sympathies—"

"Coward! Bloody coward!" Diana screamed, her face ugly, her throat muscles bulging. "Be sure and wash your hands afterward—the note might carry the pox—a pox on you—you half-man. They are dead! Dead!" Montagu scuttled out the door. Diana in a rage was impossible. Diana in a rage and crying was more than he could bear.

Diana pulled at Clemmie, and Clemmie sat down like a large lump on the settee, and the two women put their arms around each other and wept. Walpole lit his pipe and smoked, watching them. After a while, Diana made an attempt to wipe her face. She spat at him, "Why have you not left! Are you not afraid of the smallpox! Of grief! Or do you think I am going to forget myself and allow you in my bed!"

He did not answer.

"Leave me!" she cried. "I want to be alone. I have lost my children, and I never thought to, and now they are dead, and I want to go to Tamworth to see them buried, and it may already be too late!"

"There will be smallpox in Tamworth—" he began.

"I do not care! They are dead! Do you not see! I never thought they would die before I did! Go away!"

She buried her face in Clemmie's ampleness and sobbed. Clemmie sobbed with her. Walpole sat, silently, waiting. Finally, the sobs lessened again. Clemmie sighed and blew her nose on her apron. Diana looked at Walpole, her face ravaged, a travesty of its normal beauty. Wearily she said, "You are persistent. I give you that. Clemmie, fetch another brandy bottle. I am going to get drunk, and you, sir, may join me. I am going to get so drunk I will not be able to remember what a bad mother I have been. So drunk that it will take me days to recover. So drunk I will not remember how I feel at this moment."

Clemmie poured the three of them large glasses of brandy. Diana drained hers in a single gesture and held out her glass for more.

"I have a daughter," said Walpole, when they were both on their fourth glass. "A lovely girl, your Barbara's age, who is ill. The doctors try every cure, hurting her more with each one, and nothing makes her well. In my heart, I believe she is dying, and I pray to God that her suffering will be brief, but He does not seem inclined to hear my prayers." He spoke reflectively, sadly.

"I never cared," said Diana, slowly, choosing her words carefully now that the brandy was numbing her tongue. "I never visited them or thought about them. They were just there, like the sun and trees. Each time Kit bedded me, I had another. When he gambled, and there was no money, I cursed them, but my mother raised them. I cursed them and wished them dead so I would not have to worry about their marriages and settlements and allowances. And now they are. And it hurts. Robert, it hurts me so much that I almost wish I were dead myself. Do you believe in God, Robert? Is He punishing me? For my sins. There are so many of them. And I have enjoyed them all."

They shook their heads over her sins and drank more. The fire sputtered, but Clemmie was too intent on cuddling her brandy glass to add fresh coal. The candles began to gutter, as time passed, and they drank steadily. Diana, almost as drunk, now, as she had wished, shivered. She looked at Walpole, who had matched her glass for glass and then some.

"I have a most terrible urge," she told him. "I want to go upstairs and make love like a dog in heat. Am I mad, Robert? I am no prude, but I shock myself."

"They say it is a common reaction to death. A need to celebrate life in the midst of death."

"You speak beautifully. No wonder you hold the Commons in the palm of your hand. God, I feel so sad. I want to wallow like a dog. I want to know I am alive, and not dead like my children. Am I bad, Robert?"

He nodded his head, and she burst out laughing. She stood up and put down her glass, taking some time to put it down correctly. It kept wanting to fall over. She ran her hands over her body, cupping her breasts deliberately.

"I am going upstairs," she told him.

"Diana, this is not going to be the way you think. Are you prepared for that?"

She laughed at him. "No man is a match for me."

"I am, but I think you are too drunk to appreciate me. But you will, I guarantee that."

She walked toward the door, undulating her hips, glancing over her shoulder, her seductiveness spoiled only by her hiccup. "Now is your chance, Robert. Now or never."

Walpole set down his glass and followed her.

Clemmie sat in the shadows, nursing her brandy. "We are bad," she said aloud. "Lord have mercy on us."

* * *

Like three black crows, the Duchess and Annie and Cousin Henley sat in the winter parlor, their black shawls over their black gowns. Lover and friend hast thou put far from me, and mine acquaintance into darkness, thought the Duchess. My grandchildren are in the darkness. I am alone.

The thought pierced her through and through, like cold in her bones on a winter morning. She had no one left to care for, save Henley, who would only grow more dried and bitter and pinched with the years, now that she, too, had lost her charges. . . . The life of an impoverished female relative . . . servitude in a house that was not yours, among relatives who took you for granted. . . . She would assure Henley of her place at Tamworth, assure her that her service to the children had been seen, for the woman had put away her bitterness at the first sign of sickness and nursed them all unceasingly. What did Henley feel, sitting now with her tearstained, swollen face? She had thrown herself on the caskets at the funeral. Had she truly loved the children, of whom she so often complained? Who ever knew what was in the heart and mind of another? Suffer the little children to come unto me, Vicar Latchrod had read in his quavering, reedy voice, for such is the kingdom of God. He shall feed His flock like a shepherd. He shall gather the lambs with His arms, and carry them into His bosom. Smallpox. Lord, have mercy upon us.

Tom had been first, complaining of vague aches and pains so that she had not sent him back to school. And then the baby, whose fever rose so high that he went into convulsions, and she and Annie and Henley took turns bathing that small, thrashing body with cooling fever water. And with their tears. There were no spots on the baby, no telltale rash. He was dead after two nights of fever and convulsions. They could not weep enough tears to save him. They did not yet know. . . .

But on Tom's body had come that fatal red rash. And then she felt terror, cold tendrils curling themselves around her heart to squeeze it. Smallpox was merciless. There was no warning. No rhyme or reason as to whom it would strike, or how hard. Those who survived might have no scars or only a few or become blind or so pockmarked they forever wore a mask to hide the ravages. It had come to her house before.

. . . (Visions of Dicken. And his child. The rash swelling into raised pimples that became blisters of yellow pus. Swelling father and child into monsters of themselves. "I am on fire," Dicken had cried. Over and over. She and Annie and all their fever waters, their ague drops, their cordials and spirits of wine, had been unable to save them. Richard's face as they buried his firstborn and grandchild. . . . No more, she had thought, staring at that face. Saying at last what she had always known. His sons were his mainspring. He himself would not survive their deaths. Not like her, who would survive anything . . . even Giles. Her dear son Giles. An epidemic at Cambridge. They sent his body home. She made Perryman pry open the coffin. There would be no burying of him without a last look. The smell as the lid began to lift. Perryman dragging her away. The smallpox had turned Giles to black bile.)

So the smallpox had taken two of her sons from her, and now it appeared again, its death's head leering at her in the night as she tried to pray for strength and understanding. The end came swiftly for the little girls, who died soon after the first rash appeared. Their urine was bloody, and she had known at seeing it that there was no saving them. Smallpox was inside them. Tom and Kit fought valiantly, as brave in their fight for their lives as their grandfather, God bless him, had been on the battlefield. The pustules raised their skin until they screamed with it. Their skin sloughed off in large pieces. The agony—theirs, hers. The agony of watching someone you love suffer so. The odor in the sickroom so strong that everyone wore rags soaked in camphor around their faces to endure it.

Barbara's trunk of presents arriving. She held toys before fever-bright eyes, and the children smiled and whispered their sister's name. Be better, she urged them, croaking past tears swollen knotlike in her throat. Be better. . . . Sweet Lord Jesus, how would she ever have the strength to write Barbara? Little Anne, sitting up in bed, at the last, calling "Bab! Bab!" over and over. Kit, his face disfigured, ravaged with running sores and lost pieces of flesh, each breath a struggle as the smallpox attacked his insides, holding fast to a leaden soldier his sister had sent. Dying with it in his hand. The Duchess shivered even though the fires burned brightly, trembled with age and grief. . . . Let the day perish wherein I was born, and the night in which it was said, There is a man child conceived. . . . Let that day be darkness; let not God regard it from above, neither let the light shine upon it. . . . Let darkness and the shadow of death stain it. . . . Darkness. And the shadow of death. Smallpox. . . .

Dulcinea leapt from her lap, sulking because she had been locked away. It was bad fortune for cats to be around funerals, but Dulcinea did not believe such things and took it personally. Dulcinea was pregnant, and pregnancy made her impatient with human fancies. She began to groom herself in the middle of the floor, for all to see, but then lifted her head suddenly, and the Duchess looked up to see a woman swathed in black veiling push aside one of the curtains that served for doors. Dulcinea hissed. Diana, thought the Duchess blankly. Surely that could not be Diana under all those veils. And then Diana was sweeping across the room, her black cloak half on and half off, and throwing herself on the Duchess, who almost fell out of her chair in surprise. Diana was weeping in her arms. Now why, thought the Duchess. Cousin Henley stood up, her face expressing outrage. And now another person, Tony, her grandson, was coming into the room. He leaned past Diana and kissed the Duchess on both cheeks.

"Came at once," he said. "Soon as I heard. I am so sorry, Grandmama." He pressed her hand, and the Duchess felt tears starting. Tony. Tony had come to her.

"My children, my children," wailed Diana.

Everyone stared at her, as she threw back her veils dramatically and exposed a face swollen with tears. It was that sight more than anything that bereft the Duchess of speech. Diana crying. Diana feeling. It was beyond belief.

"I came as soon as I received your letter," Diana said, wiping her tears with a black handkerchief. "I cannot believe it has happened. Truly I cannot. I have cried the whole journey. Ask Tony."

Everyone in the room looked at Tony. He nodded his head, smiling at his grandmother shyly, and reached down and took her hand in his. The Duchess found that she liked the way his big hand felt on hers. Warm, comforting. From Tony, of all people. She stared up at him gratefully.

"Grandmama looks tired," he said.

"She is tired," said Annie, frowning at Diana. Annie and Cousin Henley were both rigid with disapproval. The Duchess was surprised their glances had not slain Diana on the spot.

"When are the children to be buried?" asked Diana.

"They were buried a day ago, Lady Diana," said Annie, a look of grim satisfaction on her face. "You know what small-pox is like. It could not wait."

"You buried them without my being here!" Diana looked at her mother. Her voice was even more low and throbbing than usual. "How could you!"

"And how would we know you were going to grace us with your presence!" snapped Annie, bristling.

"We had no idea you would come here," intervened the Duchess. She was too weary for quarreling. And she found that Diana's entrance had taken her breath away. Diana burst into fresh tears.

The Duchess stared at her, nonplussed. This new crying, caring Diana was more than she could cope with. She felt as if she were caught in the web of a nightmare, or a bad comedy. Nothing seemed real.

"Harlot!" cried Cousin Henley in quivering tones, her nose red with emotion. She stalked up to the weeping Diana. "Whore of Babylon! How dare you show your face here!"

To everyone's amazement, she slapped Diana across the face.

Diana slapped Henley back. Now all was true pandemonium, as Henley fell sobbing to the floor and Diana cursed her like a stableboy, and Annie screamed for everyone to be quiet. The Duchess thought she would faint. She knew she should rise and deal with it, as she had always done, but she did not have it in her. She was too tired, too old.

"Aunt Diana, leave the room. Annie, take Cousin Henley away. Put her to bed. She is distraught. Grandmama, come with me. I am taking you to your chamber."

Everyone stared at Tony. He is speaking in complete sentences, thought the Duchess. I did not know he could. He swept her up as if she were nothing. Annie led a sobbing Henley away. Diana picked up her cloak and glared, but there was no one left to glare at. The Duchess was being carried like a queen from the room. She lay in Tony's arms like a frail child, thinking, Tony . . . Tony. There is nothing of William in him but his height and fairness. Tony.

He put her down on her bed and covered her with a blanket and brought her a glass of wine. He had not even taken off his cloak. He sat down on the edge of her bed, and she was glad, because the room seemed too dark and empty. She was so glad her heart almost felt joyous. The Lord moved in mysterious ways. He had sent her Tony. Tears started behind her eyes. She was so old and weak. She spoke gruffly to cover her weakness.

"Your mother was angry at your coming, was she not? Do not lie, boy. I can read your face. It was a dangerous thing for you to do. There is still smallpox in the village, and you are his heir." She nodded toward Richard's picture over the fireplace. Tony looked at it, too. Richard stared at them, handsome, proud, eternally young.

"Why did you come, Tony?"

"Bab," he said.

She did not understand. Dulcinea leapt up on the bed and went at once to Tony, purring around him until he stroked her head. She mewed her approval to the Duchess and settled herself in his lap, purring so loudly that it was difficult to talk over her. Dulcinea never did such things. She disapproved of all strangers.

"Bab talked of you," Tony said, not meeting her eyes. "At Saylor House. Of you and . . . the others. Loves you all so much. Knew when Mother got your letter that you would need me. Here I am. For Bab's sake. She loves you, Grandmama. As I do," he added softly.

The Duchess stared at him.

"Aunt Diana wants to go to Paris to be with Bab," said Tony. "A bad thing, that."

The Duchess patted his hand. "Never you mind. I will handle Diana. I always could, and—now that you are here—I always will." Then she burst into tears. She was a stupid old fool, crying like this. What would her grandson think of her?

He pulled her into his arms (even though Dulcinea refused to move from his lap) as easily as if she were a child, which was what she felt like, and patted her back and said, "Do not cry, Grandmama. I am here, and I will take care of you.

Promise. Bab told me to watch out for you. Made me promise. And that is what I am going to do. I-I love you, Grandmama. I do. There, there. Do not cry. Hush, Grandmama,
hush. . . ."

CHAPTER FIFTEEN

$\mathcal{M}$ontrose cleared his throat. Roger frowned.

"Ah, you have an appointment this afternoon with the Duc de Guise, sir, and I found these letters, unopened . . . as you see . . . and thought perhaps you had overlooked . . . them. . . ." Montrose's voice trailed off because of the expression on Roger's face as he saw the letters.

"I never overlook things, as you well know," Roger snapped, as Barbara picked up a letter and examined it. It was on cream-colored paper, and the seal was red. A vein throbbed in Roger's forehead. It reminded Barbara of that evening he had caught her in the alcove with Henri. Poor Montrose. She knew exactly how he felt.

"Roger," she said, partly to divert his anger away from Montrose, who was staring down at his plate, his round cheeks a crimson color, and partly because she was curious, "these are from the Prince de Soissons. I thought you were old friends—"

Roger stood up abruptly and threw his napkin on top of his uneaten breakfast.

"We were. Once," he said in a cold voice. "Now we are old enemies. I do not want that man's name mentioned in my household again. Is that clear to everyone?" He stared at the three of them in turn, and they all dropped their eyes, as children do when they have been bad. He picked up the letters and held out his hand for the one Barbara had. She gave it to him. He walked to the fireplace and threw the letters into the fire, which was burning because the morning was cold. They curled and the edges turned brown, and then the fire devoured them. The three watched him furtively, turning their eyes away quickly each time he looked up from the fire. Once the letters were burned, he strode from the room without another word. The door slammed shut behind him. No one spoke.

Barbara kept her head bent. She could look at neither Montrose nor White. Why did he treat her so? What is wrong with him? she thought, excusing herself, unable to finish her breakfast.

As soon as the door closed behind her, White said to Montrose, "Are you all right?"

Montrose's cheeks were still red, but he nodded. "He has never spoken to me in that way before."

"What about the time Lady Devane came to St. James's Square, before they were married? Do you remember?" White was pushing at the fire with the poker.

"What are you doing?" asked Montrose, watching him.

"As I remember, he had some choice words for us both, afterward," said White, poking at the ashes. "And then there was the time you mixed those notes he had written to his mistresses, causing him to break with the wrong one—"

"You are not trying to retrieve those letters, are you? Stop at once! Caesar, what if he should return and find you? Come back to the table."

"Not a scrap left," said White, replacing the poker and dusting off his good hand on his breeches leg. Montrose wiped his face with the napkin, for all the world as if he had been the one searching for telltale scraps of paper.

"And then there was the time you allowed Lady Murray into his bedchamber, when the Duchess of Beaufort was already there. As I recall, I was astonished at the scope and grandeur of his cursing."

Montrose refolded the napkin. "It is not the same. He has been this way since returning from Sceaux," Montrose said. "Thérèse said he had some kind of attack there."

"Thérèse . . . ?"

Montrose blushed. "Sometimes I have to verify Lady Devane's accounts with her. She is very levelheaded," he added defensively.

"Yes, that is what I think whenever I see her. What a level-headed woman, I think."

Montrose sniffed. "She said he became quite ill the night before they returned. I think that must be it; he is feeling unwell."

"Well, I, for one, will be glad when he feels better."

What is wrong with Roger? Barbara thought. She had been thinking about it since their return from Sceaux, for he was so unlike himself, short-tempered and moody. It was at the back of her mind as she went through the routine of her days: breakfast with a now irritable Roger, choosing a gown for the morning, practicing her music and Italian, a walk in the gardens with Hyacinthe and the puppies, reading the latest play-bills and scandal sheets, perhaps something of a novel, or her books on architecture and history, changing her clothes for dinner, sitting through it knowing the charm Roger showed was only for his guests—once they left he would once more be moody and silent—on to afternoon visits, shopping or an expedition with White to the historical sites of Paris, or to sitting for her portrait, or to the Bastille to visit Richelieu, home to change to evening clothes, on to the theater, the opera, a ball, a reception, home again late, to sleep alone. Roger had not visited her bed since Sceaux, and she did not seek him out. There were no more intimate talks after lovemaking, of Bent-woodes and Devane House and mirrors and porticoes and marble statues for the gardens. She saved it all inside herself. She could wait. For him to be better. If he was ill, or over-tired, she could wait. But why did he not tell her what both-ered him?

It was so much on her mind that she lost at cards two days in a row to Richelieu, who laughed at her. ("You are about to lose Henri." Whatever do you mean? "I mean you cannot keep a man like that content with nothing. Tell me, has he ever kissed you on the mouth?" No. Not that it is any of your business. "Amazing. Well, when he drops you, my dear Bab, as he will do, do not come running to me for comfort. You will miss being the rage, for you will find your admirers following Henri's lead. Then you will kick yourself for not giving him more." Bah! "You will. Mark my words. And when you miss it all, come to me, my sweet, and I will make you the belle once more." And what would I have to give you in return? "Far more than you have given Henri." Dream on, Armand. Dream on. "I assure you that I dream of nothing else—damn it, you have won the hand. You took my mind off the cards. Another game, Barbara. I insist.")

She was beautiful . . . thanks to Thérèse. She was sought after . . . thanks to Richelieu and St. Michel. She was studying Italian and French history and architecture. She was doing everything in her power to be fashionable and sophisticated and worldly, to be what Roger wanted. But something had been wrong since Sceaux. He was hiding something from her, and all her growing sophistication and beauty (and sadly, her love) did not seem to make any difference, for he would not talk to her of it. The distance between them was now more and not less, and she had worked so hard for it to be less. . . .

She finished dressing for a ball at the Hotel Scully. Tonight, she thought. Tonight I will make him tell me what is bothering him. She wore a new gown of dark blue silk; it made her eyes sparkle. She wore diamonds sprinkled in her hair like dust, diamonds and dark blue feathers that trailed down the back of her neck. Both she and Thérèse were satisfied that she looked beautiful. And Roger loved beautiful women. (By now she had learned enough of his past reputation to know that women, beautiful and otherwise, also loved him.) She left Hyacinthe at home so that she could talk while they were in the carriage. Perhaps, if she looked lovely enough, if she were charming enough, she would lift his spirits, and he would tell her his troubles. Share them, as if she were truly his love, his dearest.

But in the carriage he was silent, brooding. He looked tired, older, and she felt frightened by the gap—of age, of knowledge, of life—between them. Her newly acquired finesse flew out the window.

"Are you ill?" she said abruptly. "Tell me."

"Do you realize how many times you have asked me that question in the last four days—"

"Share your troubles with me, Roger. Let me help. Is it me? Is it Paris? Are you ill? Where do you hurt if you are? Tell

me. How can I help you if I do not know what is wrong?
There must be some reason for your rudeness and your—"

"Rudeness? When was I rude?"

"You were rude this morning over those letters, and you
embarrassed me before White and Montrose by snapping at
me. You have been unlike yourself since Sceaux—"

"Why do you say that?" He grabbed her arm. She was
shocked by the sharpness in his voice.

She wrenched her arm away. "I say it because it is true."
Her voice trembled. I will not cry, she thought.

They were both silent. The only sound was of the carriage
wheels lurching over the uneven cobbles.

"At Sceaux," he said slowly (she found herself straining for
the slowness of his words), "do you remember when I felt ill?"

"Yes."

"Well, I am still not entirely well. My head aches all the
time, and I am tired."

He lies, she thought. Why does he lie to me? When I love
him so, and would do anything for him.

As if he divined her thoughts, he pulled her across the space
between them, into his arms, crushing her gown, and she did
not care. She felt so afraid, and she did not know why. I wish
I were older, she thought, babbling to God in the way she
used to babble to her grandmother when she was in trouble,
Lord Jesus, make me older now. . . .

"Barbara," he said into the diamonds in her hair, "there is
nothing you can do."

"Let us go home. So that you can rest—"

He covered her face with kisses, as light as air, and she
closed her eyes.

"Dance tonight," he said. "Enjoy yourself. You can help me
by being happy. Trust me in that, Barbara."

She pulled out of his arms slightly. "If it is not me—"

He kissed her hands. "No. Not you."

"—then I do. But I love you, Roger. And I want to share
all of your life. The bad as well as the good. For richer for
poorer, I vowed. In sickness and in health. I meant those
words."

He was silent. How young she was, to believe in someone
so. How trusting, of him, of life. That between the two of
them, he and life would give her what she wanted. Dear God,

had he ever been that way? He had never been more conscious of the age difference between them. She was truly still a child, though growing into a woman before his eyes. And he was a man who had seen and done too many things.

He left her in the ballroom, surrounded by admirers, and went into the card room to gamble. But he could not concentrate and lost money. He strolled through the drawing rooms, talking to friends, but found himself eventually back in the ballroom, looking for Barbara without being aware that that was what he was doing. She was dancing with St. Michel. He sat down in the middle of several rows of chairs to watch her, feeling better just at the sight of her. She was like a talisman, of all he had once been, and felt he was losing. There was comfort in her innocence, her belief in him. He watched her with that wistful smile on his face that made others watch him, and so he did not notice the Prince de Soissons, who had quietly seated himself two chairs away; he was watching Roger as intently as Roger was watching Barbara. Finally, the prince leaned across a chair, his proud, full, scarred face arrogant.

"She is the image of her grandfather," he said softly, so that no one else might hear. "I recognized her the moment I saw her at Sceaux. How fortunate for you, my dear Roger, that when you could not have the real thing, you could acquire such a close substitute. Does she make you happy?"

"Philippe . . ." Roger began to breathe heavily, as if he had been running.

"Smile to your lovely young wife, Roger. She is looking at you."

Roger bared his teeth in the direction of the dancers. "Go away, Philippe. I have nothing to say to you."

"Nothing to say to . . . an old friend?"

"We are not friends. I thought of killing you. It kept me sane. No one else in my life ever dared call me a coward. Or say I am dishonest. I should have killed you the first time you said those words to me . . . just as you killed Montreal. For nothing. I never loved him—" He stopped. In a different tone, he said, "Go away. I have another life now."

"With that child? Tell me what you talk of with her, Roger? What can you share? Old battles, old war stories, memories of a world that existed before she was born and can mean nothing to her? You are running away from yourself, just as you always did—"

Roger stood up, his hand on his sword hilt; the flesh around his nostrils was white and pinched, the look in his eyes was suddenly remote, dangerous. Philippe had only to say the wrong thing, and he would find himself facing Roger across an empty field at dawn, their swords whipping and hissing through the still morning air like snakes, until one or the other was dead.

"I apologize, Roger. For what I said . . . for what I did before. I apologize."

Roger stared at him. "Why did you come to Paris?"

Philippe smiled a slow smile that filled his face and made it handsome.

"To begin again, my friend."

Roger turned and strode away. He saw Barbara standing in a crowd of young people, waiting to go into supper, and he strode over to her, thinking, My God . . . my God. . . .

"I saw you talking with the prince," she said, her eyes scanning his face, seeing too much; he felt naked before her. "I thought you said—"

"Be quiet!"

Louise-Anne, standing behind her, tittered. Several of the young men surrounding her looked away.

Barbara's face went white; then she began to blush. Red stained her shoulders, her neck, her cheeks.

"I am going home," Roger said. "Stay as late as you like." And he strode away. She stood where she was, rooted to the spot. People moved around her the way water moves around a stone. She put her hands to her cheeks. Across the room, the Prince de Soissons, watching, smiled to himself. Someone took her by the arm and led her into the supper room.

"They sound married now," she heard Louise-Anne say to the Princesse de Condé. The princesse laughed.

Barbara joined a table with Henri, Marie-Victorie and the Duc de Melun. She laughed and talked and did not remember one word of what she said. She danced every dance after supper, and drank more than a little champagne. Be quiet, Roger said in her mind. Be quiet, be quiet. She tossed her head and smiled. Her face hurt from smiling. Her head hurt from the champagne. Her heart hurt from Roger's words.

"I will escort you home," St. Michel said, early in the hours of the morning. His eyes were gauging her mood, the amount of champagne she had drunk. She shrugged.

The carriage was dark. It rattled and lurched across the cobbles. She could hear St. Michel's breathing. The champagne had left her feeling tired and heavy, as if stones were attached to the ends of her limbs and were pulling her down, down, down.

"I adore you," St. Michel said in the darkness. With a lurching movement he sat beside her. In another moment his arms were around her as he tried to kiss her.

"No!" she said, twisting and pushing him. He only held her more tightly. His mouth was on her neck, then on the top part of her breasts where they swelled before they met the edge of her gown.

"No!" she cried, anger beginning to fill her—and fear, the faintest prickles of fear.

He raised his head to kiss her mouth, but she reared back and brought her head forward with all the force of which she was capable. Her head hit him squarely on the nose. He yelped and fell back against the carriage seat.

She was across on the other side, her body tense, ready if he should try anything again. Her heart was beating like a soldier's drum. . . . There was only silence.

"Henri?" she said tentatively to the shadows that were his body, his cloak, his face.

"My God," he said in the darkness, "I think you have broken my nose." His voice was muffled, and he sounded like a child, like a little boy, like one of her brothers.

"Henri, you should not have grabbed me like that—"

"My God, you have broken my nose! I am bleeding like a pig! If you were a man, I would kill you—"

"If I were a man this would not have happened. Hold your head back. Here, use my cloak to wipe the blood. Shall I stop the carriage?"

"Yes. You think I want to stay another moment in here with you, you, you . . ." He was silent, apparently unable to find a word. She knocked on the roof, and the carriage lurched to a stop.

"You are not a lady." His tone was shocked, as if he had made a terrible accusation.

She was silent. If she had let him do as he wanted, if she had cried or pleaded, would she then have been a lady? The footman was holding a flambeau, and she could see that Henri had his head thrown back, and part of her cloak bunched to his face. Carefully, he stepped outside. She leaned out the window as the carriage rolled away. He was still standing with his head back. Sweet Jesus, had she broken his nose? She felt a terrible urge to laugh.

She lay instead like a limp rag doll against the jolting carriage seat. Well, her foremost admirer was lost, in a style that only her brothers would appreciate. Now she would not be fashionable anymore. Why had Roger been rude to her in public? If he did not care for her . . . She bit her lip. But then another thought diverted her. Had she truly broken St. Michel's nose? What would Roger say to that?

Roger sat sprawled in a chair in his bedchamber, watching Justin put away his clothes. He wore his shirt, breeches and stockings, but had ripped off his coat, waistcoat and wig the moment he stepped into the room, as if they were choking him. Justin had taken one look at his face and, without a word, brought him the brandy bottle. Dear Justin, thought Roger, tipping the bottle back and feeling the brandy burn all the way down; Justin knew him better than anyone. Justin had been with him when he was nobody. Since before Philippe. He drank from the bottle the way he used to years ago when he was a brash young soldier, and he had made it through another battle, when the man next to him had died screaming with a pick-ax through his shoulder, slicing it off in one neat stroke, as a butcher does beef. Years ago . . . when the smell of blood and smoke and fear seemed to be everywhere; his hands shook with their memory as he drank, to forget. Drank and drank.

Justin folded his coat and put it away. He brought Roger his slippers. He pulled down the covers on the bed. Deftly, he scooped ashes into the warming pan, and warmed the bed with it. He drew the draperies. He did the hundred-and-one soothing tasks that made Roger's life comfortable. And all the time he never said a word, never asked one question. Did nothing more than glance at Roger from time to time. He knows, thought Roger. He has known since Sceaux. When

Justin was finished, he sat in a chair near the fire, silent, ready if Roger should need him. When Roger finished the bottle, he called for another. Justin brought it, and went back to his place by the fire.

"Justin," Roger said. His words were slurred. The room's edges were blurred. Good. "Justin. What am I to do?"

Justin was silent.

"He is here, you know," Roger said.

The sound of dogs yapping penetrated to the bedchamber. Justin straightened. He almost smiled.

"Lady Devane is home," he said to Roger. "Go see Lady Devane. She is a good girl, sir. A good wife."

He went to Roger and took away the bottle and retied the ties on Roger's shirt and helped Roger to stand.

"Go on, sir," he said. "She will make you feel better. She loves you, sir. Go on. That's it, sir."

The puppies ran yapping to the doorway of the bedchamber. They jumped up and down, their shrill voices filling the room. Barbara was in her underpetticoat, and Thérèse was pulling off her hoop.

Roger stood swaying in the doorway. He was drunker than Barbara had ever seen him. She motioned to Thérèse, who called the dogs and left.

"Barbara . . . ?" Roger said her name tentatively. He walked into the room, but stumbled into a chair. She ran to him and put his arm over her shoulder, half lugging him to the bed, where he fell back like a dead man.

"Dear Barbara."

She pulled off everything but her chemise, and snuffed the candle and crawled into the bed beside him. He took her in his arms. She put her hand to his face; it was wet. She forgot everything else, and wrapped her arms around him, cradling his head on her breasts.

"I feel so sad."

"I love you," she said. "I love you more than anything else in—"

His mouth stopped her words. She wrapped her arms and legs around him, and he made love to her as if he were going to die tomorrow. She had no time to meet his passion. Everything was touching, feeling, probing, wet. There was only his need, and her giving. I give you everything, she thought, covering his face with kisses, feeling the moisture from his tears. He was crying even as he made love to her. She whispered his name, her love, wrapping herself around him. He sank against her.

She touched his face, gently, tentatively. "Tell me why you cry."

"I am too old for you, Barbara. I have done too many things. . . ." His words were slurred. She did not understand them all.

"Hush," she soothed him, as she would have done Anne or Kit or Charlotte. "Hush. I am here." She thought of St. Michel. The urge to confess, to have her sins forgiven, filled her.

"Roger. Roger, I have done a bad thing—" She poured out her story, not certain whether to laugh or cry. Roger would know what to do. Roger knew everything. Even if he were angry, at least she would have confessed.

He did not answer. He was asleep. She pulled the bed covers up about his shoulders and felt his forehead with her lips and smoothed back his hair. He had not heard a word she had said.

White sat at a small table near the windows in his sitting room. He was supposed to be working, but he was looking at the gardens. Thérèse Fuseau was there, with the page, Hyacinthe, and the puppies. She was planting pansies in a corner of the garden under a budding lilac tree while Hyacinthe threw sticks, and the puppies ran after them, yapping and falling over themselves. They were roly-poly with fat. The gardens were ready for spring. Fresh gravel had been carted in and raked in the paths. Everywhere, bulbs were lifting their green heads, and already tulips were beginning to unfurl their glorious blossoms. The lilac trees showed purple buds. Everything was wakening after its winter sleep.

Thérèse finished planting the last pansy. Careful, she patted the dirt around the thin neck of its blossom, and sat back on her heels, satisfied with the tiny, private garden she had created. Even though the day was chilly, the sun was warm on her back. She listened to Hyacinthe's shrill, high, joyous boy's laughter. It made her smile. She wiped her hands off and went to sit on a garden bench to watch him. He ran back and

forth with the lithe energy only a young boy possesses, and
the puppies killed themselves to follow him. He threw the
sticks and then ran ahead of them as they gamboled after. She
had been to see a physician for the bleeding, which had lessened, but not completely stopped. When he had examined
her, his probing hands had made her writhe with pain. "An
infectious irritation to the female organs," he had told her
afterward. He gave her a powder to drink, told her to eat
plenty of eggs and beef broth to build up her blood and then
said, "When the infection heals, you will be unable to conceive children." Hyacinthe's happy laughter rose and fell in
the garden.

She heard steps crunching on the gravel and looked up to
see Pierre LeBlanc, the majordomo of the house, coming
toward her. He was fat, middle-aged and ugly, with freckles
on his face and hands. What can he want? she thought,
standing and shading her eyes as she watched him. Was he
going to chastise her for sitting in the garden? Or complain of
the slowness of the new laundress? As she was Lady Devane's
personal maid, his jurisdiction over her was tenuous . . . and
then she knew. She knew as surely as she knew her own name.
There could be no other reason. She kept her face calm and
smiling.

"A lovely day," he said to her, gesturing for her to sit back
down. "You have no duties, I see."

"Lady Devane has no complaints of me," she said coolly. "I
am stealing a moment of free time. Surely there is no crime
in that."

"No," he agreed genially, sitting down beside her even
though she had not invited him. "But there is a crime in stealing other things."

"What things?"

"The housekeeper tells me a set of sheets is missing from
your room." He pulled a penknife from his pocket and began
to clean under his nails. Thérèse did not answer. He was too
calm. He knew everything.

"Look at me! Look at me!" Hyacinthe called. She waved to
him.

"What were you doing out so early in the garden some
weeks ago, Mademoiselle Fuseau? But I may call you Thérèse,
yes? I look from my window, and I see Lady Devane's new

maid digging like a madwoman in the dirt—under that very lilac tree there. What lovely pansies you have planted. What can she be doing? I think. I am a curious man, Mademoiselle Thérèse. And a careful one. I run a clean house, a strict one. Is she burying jewels? I ask myself. Has she stolen from the young mistress? Does she plan to dig them up and meet a lover in the middle of the night? Yes, these are the things I ask myself. So, after you leave, I go to the garden, and I dig. And what do I find? I find bloody sheets, Thérèse. Bloody sheets. Sheets which I now have in a trunk in my room. And I remember how the pretty new maid faints in the laundry room. And how the chambermaid complains of vomit in the slop jar. And how the cook says you eat nothing on your tray. I run a strict house, as you see. Sooner or later, I know everything. About everyone. And so now I know what the pretty, stuck-up Mademoiselle Fuseau has done. I know. And I think to myself, Pierre, she should be dismissed. Lady Devane should know. But I like you, Thérèse. And then I think, why not give the young lady another chance? But I am a selfish man, and I also think that I should be rewarded for my kindness. What do you think, Thérèse?"

Thérèse did not answer. Each time he had said her name, he had said it with a knowing contempt. She watched Hyacinthe playing with the puppies. The morning was chill, but crystal clear, as if the spring sun was shining on the world with a radiance that made everything shimmer.

"Tonight," LeBlanc said, standing up, closing his penknife and pocketing it. "I will come up the back stairs. Leave your door unlocked."

He walked away. She did not stare after him, but closed her eyes and lifted her face to the sun. She could feel its warmth penetrating like the touch of warm, gentle fingers on her face. Hyacinthe was whistling to the dogs, trying to teach them to come to him. His whistle was clear and shrill in the quiet of the garden. Once more she heard someone's shoes crunching in the gravel. Involuntarily, she shuddered, but then there was a skittering sound, as if the person walking had stumbled. She opened her eyes. Caesar White stood a few feet away, his good arm against a small lime sapling. He grinned at her.

"I stumbled," he said. He nodded toward his crippled, shortened arm with its tiny hand. "Sometimes this makes me lose my balance."

Thérèse said nothing, neither encouraging nor discouraging.

"I saw you from my window," he said, coming closer. "You were planting flowers. They were pretty. Your face has a strange expression on it, Mademoiselle Fuseau. Did LeBlanc say something to annoy you . . . or am I the annoyance?"

He was remembering the evening she had been rude, as she was remembering it. That evening seemed a long time ago to Thérèse. So much had happened since then. Why had she been rude? Of course, because she was feeling sick. She patted the bench.

"Sit down, Monsieur White. And stop frowning. I was rude to you the last time we talked, but I was not feeling well. Now I am fine. LeBlanc was complaining because I was enjoying the sun." She shrugged, as if to say, he can complain all he wants, but here I am. "He put me in bad spirits. You, however, Monsieur White, have raised them." She smiled at him. Her maid's cap was very white against the dark of her hair, her lips were soft and rose-colored.

"Caesar," White said distractedly. "Call me Caesar."

"And you must call me Thérèse."

There were several moments of strained silence. Thérèse smiled to herself.

"I am glad spring is coming," she said.

"Yes. Yes, I am, too. The—the gardens will be beautiful."

"Yes, they will."

Both of them watched Hyacinthe for a while.

"Thérèse," White said in a rush of words, "sometime may I take you walking or for a carriage ride? On your day off?"

He is a nice boy, thought Thérèse. He has a nice smile. Niceness would be good after LeBlanc. And LeBlanc did not own her. It would do him good to know that. Because she must establish a certain superiority with him as soon as possible, or her life would be hell. She had had enough of hell.

"I would like that."

"Would you? That is wonderful, Thérèse."

When LeBlanc knocked on Thérèse's door that night, she was sitting up in bed, the covers folded neatly at her waist. Her hair was brushed and hung down in two plaits onto her shoulders. She wore a high-necked nightgown. She looked young and fresh and virginal. She felt a hundred years old. But calm. The worst that could have happened to her had already occurred. Once one had faced the worst, life was simpler. She nodded to Hyacinthe, who scampered out the other door, the door leading to Lady Devane's bedchamber. LeBlanc knocked again. She could hear the impatience in that sound.

"Come in." Her rosary beads were twisted together in her folded hands.

LeBlanc barreled into the room. He pulled off his wig and threw it to the floor. He shrugged off his coat and hopped on one foot trying to twist off a shoe. As he finally began to pull off the other shoe, he looked at Thérèse, who had not moved since he came into the room. Something in her face made him stand still.

"There are certain things we must get clear between us, Monsieur LeBlanc." Thérèse looked him in the eye. "First, you will never spend the night. Lady Devane's page sleeps in my room, and I will not have him shivering in a bedchamber corner all night when you have your own bed to sleep in. Second, you will always tell me when you wish to visit, and I will inform you whether it is convenient or not. Tonight is not convenient, as I would have informed you, had you given me time this morning. I am still in my flux. You may, of course, insist, but it will be messy for both of us, as well as painful to me. Third, the physician says I must have red wine and beef broth and eggs to heal properly. You will arrange that. The sooner I am healed, the sooner you may take your pleasure. Fourth, you will bathe and shave before you come to my bed. I will not sleep with a man who smells like a pig. And fifth, you will ascertain that no babies result from this liaison. You are never to come inside of me. Never. If you should give me a baby, I will go to Lady Devane and tell her everything. I will be dismissed, monsieur, but so will you. I know Lady Devane, and I am certain she will insist on it. I am finished. Do we understand one another?"

Various emotions had played across LeBlanc's face as she spoke: anger, incredulity, stubbornness.

"I could force you here and now," he growled. But Thérèse noticed that he made no threatening move and she was alert for that.

"Naturally," she said calmly. "But I am a strong girl. I would scream and fight; Hyacinthe would hear me. Everyone would know. I would be dismissed—but so, Monsieur LeBlanc, would you. I guarantee it. Lady Devane is very fond of me."

He stared at her, his mouth open, sagging. She decided it would be wise to be generous in victory.

"I know your power in the household. And I respect it. I have no intention of denying you. I am not stupid. I ask only that you consider my feelings, and my health. If I am well, the experience will be more pleasant for us both."

"I could give you to the footmen."

But his threat was hollow, and they both knew it. Hesitantly, with one eye on her as if she would spring from the bed and attack him, he picked up his wig and coat and shoe. He looked ludicrous.

"Mind you do not take too long with this flux," he said in an effort to restore his dignity. "I am an impatient man."

"Be sure to bathe," she answered. "Red wine, beef broth and eggs. Remember."

The door closed behind him. She leaned back, sagging, her mouth dry. He had taken it far better than she had expected. He was a bully, unused to others standing up to him. And not very clever. Her attack had taken him by surprise. Now he would view her differently. The balance of power between them had shifted slightly. She shuddered at the thought of his big, naked body on hers. She would think of something else, or recite her rosary. And she would go walking with White and enjoy his bashful regard. His regard would make her feel clean again. It would pass. Things always did. The important thing was that she survive. She thought of the girl she had been just months ago, singing and laughing and thinking the world her oyster. But that girl had never known a man's body or felt love or jealousy or hurt or fear. She got out of bed and called for Hyacinthe. She was teaching him his catechism. Listening to the lisping words of God, watching the earnestness of his sweet, dark face gave her comfort. The little boy meant a great deal to her; he might be the only child she would ever have. There was freedom in that fact; and there was sadness.

* * *

"What did you do to Henri?" Richelieu asked her immediately. Before she could even untie her cloak.

His question made her flinch. Did anyone in Paris do anything other than gossip? (St. Michel had said rogues had attacked him. He had ignored her as if he had never known her. His nose was broken.)

"Nothing!" she said irritably. Roger was as distant as if they had never made love, as if he had never cried in her arms and told her of his fears. "Now, do we play cards, or do you kiss your horse goodbye forever?"

"I would much prefer to kiss you—"

She turned around midstep and stalked toward the door. She was not taking anything from anyone. Richelieu could go hang himself. Thérèse was already unfolding her cloak. Richelieu caught up with her and grabbed her arm. She jerked it away and turned on him. He smiled.

"Stay," he said, putting himself between her and the door. "Please. I apologize."

He dealt the cards. She was silent, her face that of a bad-tempered child.

"You ought to control that temper," he said casually, ignoring the look she gave him. "I can see now why Henri emerged from his encounter so scarred. He will never forgive you, you know. Your days of popularity are ended."

She ground her teeth.

"If I ever try to rape you, I will succeed, temper or not."

She laid her cards on the table. "My trick," she snapped.

"Only in cards, my pet."

Her flux began. So, there was no baby growing. She had thought, after Roger's violent lovemaking, that surely, this time, there would be a child. But there was only blood. And now he stayed away from her, from their home; she fell asleep waiting to hear the sound of his boots in the hall. She felt like breaking something. Hyacinthe and the puppies were instinctively staying out of her way. Bah, her grandmama would have said, you need a good caning. Grandmama would have put her to work outside, beating the floor rugs with a stick, or inside, polishing silver until her shoulders ached. She did not have enough to do; and she was alone too much. Other women had cousins, nieces, children around them. She should send for Anne and Charlotte and Baby. Just write the letter and post it. Only Roger was so distant, he might grow more distant over it. Or then again, he might not even care. What was wrong? Why was he avoiding her?

Thérèse walked into the bedchamber, carrying letters. Barbara's spirits lifted. She snatched them from Thérèse, who said, unnecessarily, "They are from England, madame."

"This one is from Grandmama," Barbara said, ripping past the seal. "I hope the boys are—"

Her voice broke off as she scanned the page. Then she looked at Thérèse, and tried to speak, but no words came out of her mouth. She sank, like a stone, to the floor, not fainting, but just on her knees, her skirts belling around her.

"What, madame? Is there bad news?" cried Thérèse, staring at Barbara's white face.

"R-Roger," Barbara gasped. "Find Roger."

Thérèse ran from the room.

It cannot be true, Barbara thought. I will not allow it to be true. She rocked back and forth where she sat, her arms around herself, her body seeking ancient, comforting rhythms. The words in the letter were exploding like fireworks in her mind, and with each explosion she trembled. By the time Thérèse came back, with the housekeeper, Montrose and LeBlanc in her wake, Barbara lay on the floor, keening, a sound that sent shivers down the spines of the men. They tried to lift her from the floor, but she began to fight them, crying and screaming.

The house was in an uproar by the time Roger arrived late that afternoon. On impulse, he had gone riding, ignoring his engagements, his responsibilities, as he had done since Sceaux. He had meant to be gone for an hour or so, until the fresh air, the feel of the horse straining between his legs, had cleared his mind. But he had ridden on and on, almost to Versailles. And everywhere, in the city, in the dark forest, newly verdant on each side of him, Philippe had seemed to be riding, too, perched like a hunting hawk on Roger's shoulder, in his thoughts. Philippe had apologized. Proud, cold, arrogant Philippe, a prince of France. Roger laughed out loud, startling his horse. What power he had felt in that moment. And how Phillippe knew him . . . to tempt him so. Was it possible? Could he begin again? For this time, he would be the one in control, the one who ended it when it no longer pleased him. This time it would be on his terms. He felt his heart beat with the exhilaration of possibility, unfolding before him the way a woman unfolds her legs.

He had always wanted it all, wanted to taste and do everything. He had lost himself in so many women, so many beds. But Richard—Richard—had been the only person he had ever really loved. The terrifying fact of that had made him cry out in the darkness, like a child. And he had always found a woman to comfort him, to make him forget. Until Philippe. The only other man he had ever desired . . . ever loved. Philippe had cauterized the bleeding wound that had been Richard. Their desire had been flame, consuming them both. They had been like the Greeks of ancient times, equal in all respects—the ultimate lovers.

And now Philippe was offering that again. The risk made it all the more exciting. What a fool he was, just as he used to be about fighting. Trembling, praying; then the drums sounded, the trumpets called, and he lost himself in the blood lust, all fear forgotten in the physical act of staying alive, of killing before one is killed. Life stripped to the simple equation of survival. Nothing was more exhilarating than that. The brave soldier, Philippe used to say, mocking him, but admiring him, too—his courage, his joy, his skill in war. Philippe, who had left his heart like a desolate battlefield, dead men and horses littered everywhere, smoke swirling into the sky from the burning gunpowder and cannons. There could never again be between them what had once been. But even a shadow of what had been was a compelling enough reason to begin again.

Barbara. His thoughts stopped, skittering into the darkness like rats' feet against a bare floor. He did not want to think of Barbara, of what he might owe her, of how she would feel if she knew what he was considering. She would never have to know. And he, himself, did not know what he was going to do. But suddenly he felt young again, as powerful, as virile, as full of possibility as he had at twenty. But it was even better, because he was no longer twenty. The greens in the leaves were full of tints, browns, yellows; he hadn't noticed before. The air was crisp, fresh, burning his lungs; the sun surprising in the way it dappled through the trees.

When he finally rode into his own courtyard, the first shadows of evening were gathering. He was planning his evening. He had an impulse to go to Madame Ramponeau's on the Rue Rouge, to try the girls. Philippe had made his blood boil with a violence that even Barbara could not quench. He wanted to lose himself in sensation—wanted to lose himself in this new virility he felt. He wanted the softness of women, their salty taste, their yielding breasts. A young woman, like Barbara. Several young women.

He did not know what he was going to do about Philippe, but he knew he wished to savor this moment, this moment of youth with experience behind it; this feeling of renewal, of power, of possibility, of temptation; he wanted to savor it as long as it lasted.

He ran up the stairs to the bedchamber floors, not noticing how quiet the house was. LeBlanc and two footmen were hanging bolts of black material across one of the salon entrances as he ran by, but the significance of this did not register; he ignored LeBlanc's call. It was only when he walked into the connecting chamber between his and Barbara's apartments, and saw Montrose and White huddled together with Justin and Thérèse, that he realized something was wrong. His heart froze. LeBlanc and the footmen, the black cloth.

"Barbara!" he said. "Where is she? What is wrong? Is she ill? Answer me!"

"She is resting now," Montrose said, his face white and still, his eyes large in his face. "The physician gave her a sleeping draft."

"It is her family, sir," White said. He had seen the shock passing over Roger's face, as had Justin, who was already pouring Roger a brandy. "A letter came from the Duchess of Tamworth this morning. Lady Devane's family, her brothers and her sisters, have died. From the smallpox."

Montrose handed Roger the crumpled letter. They had had to tear it from Barbara's hand. She had been shrieking. Montrose had thought he would faint.

Roger read quickly; the handwriting was shaky, the ink blotted.

My darling granddaughter, my most dear child,

It is with a heavy heart that I write you. I know no other way than to tell you simply—they are dead, my dear. All of them—your brothers and sisters. Of the smallpox. Tony will write you the details, which you will want to know, but which I have not the strength to include. I cannot even write their names my hand trembles so. My tears fall on this page as I write, as I know yours are now doing. I would give my own soul to be with you at this time, Barbara, and I can only tell you to trust in the Lord God Almighty, His power, His wisdom, His mercy. "I will lift up mine eyes unto the hills, from whence cometh my help. My help cometh from the Lord, which made heaven and earth. He will not suffer thy foot to be moved: he that keepeth thee will not slumber. Behold, he that keepeth Israel shall neither slumber nor sleep. The Lord is thy keeper: The Lord is thy shade upon thy right hand. The sun shall not smite thee by day, nor the moon by night. The Lord shall preserve thee from all evil: he shall preserve thy soul. The Lord shall preserve thy going out and thy coming in from this time forth, and even for evermore." Remember these words, my dear. Think of them in the coming days of sorrow. I know our dear ones are in heaven with Our Lord. They are lambs He has gathered to His bosom. Only that thought sustains me in these, my hours of grief. I pray that you are well, that you find the strength to overcome this news. I am very tired. I can write no more. Tony is with me. I pray for you, dearest Barbara.

Your loving Grandmother

"There is another letter," said Montrose.
Roger ripped past the seal to read,

Dear Bab,
    I will take care of Grandmama. You are not to worry. You take care of yourself. You are in my thoughts, Bab, and my prayers. Grandmama has asked me to write you how they died. She said that later you would want to know, that you would have to know. The baby was first, Bab. He never regained consciousness—

Roger folded the letter, trying to think what this news must mean to his wife. She had loved her brothers and sisters; she had wanted them to live with her. He had avoided this plan, not wanting his life cluttered with children, when his bride was child enough. But this . . .

He raised his head. Everyone was staring at him, their faces strained.

"How did she take the news?" he asked.

For a moment, all of them were silent, which told him more than any words could. Finally, Justin said, "She was most distraught. That was when we sent for the physician. He—he bled her and gave her something to sleep. She is quiet now."

Montrose said tersely, in shock himself, "We had to hold her down."

"She was very upset," White said, his voice trembling slightly. "Very, very upset."

Thérèse said nothing at all.

Roger walked into the bedchamber. Someone had pulled the draperies, and it was dark, but he could see that the mirror on her dressing table was cracked. Bottles and jars and broken glass lay everywhere, and a chair was overturned. He took a deep breath and went to the bed. She looked as if she were sleeping. Her face and eyelids were swollen. My poor dear, he thought. My poor, poor baby. He reached down to touch her face; her eyes opened and she clutched his hand. He sat down on the bed.

"Bab," he said softly. "Bab. I'm sorry."

"Do not leave me," she said.

He sat by her, stroking her hair, until she slept.

A week later, Roger stared at the gardens from his room. Around him, scattered on the floor, lay a wig and a coat of gray watered silk, a black armband still attached to the sleeve. This morning a memorial service for Barbara's family had been held. He had been surprised at the number of people who had come. He had wandered among them listening to them chatter about the national bank, that miracle that was going to make everything wonderful, and about the possibility that the Duc de Richelieu would stand trial for his duel, about the news from abroad that the Prince of Wales was said to be furious that his father was not going to make him regent for the summer when the king journeyed to Hanover, and of how wan and thin Lady Devane looked, and of how exasperating it must be to Lord Devane that he had to cancel so many planned entertainments due to his young wife's mourning. He shook his head; they were here to observe him, to observe Barbara, to observe each other. He knew them well.

Among the many flowers that had come was a huge bouquet of purple iris, interspersed with sprigs of rosemary. Iris, or fleur-de-lis, as the French called it; they were on the coat of arms of the Bourbons, Philippe's family. The flowers came from Philippe. Iris, fleur-de-lis, whose meaning was flame; I burn. Philippe had been at the back of the church. Flame. I burn. Barbara had fainted during the service. She wanted him with her day and night. He escaped each night, once she finally slept, into the arms of other women, any woman he could find, a compliant duchesse, an opera dancer, a whore. He was drawn to them; he reeked of them, coming home at all hours, Justin putting him to bed like a child; most nights he was incoherent from drink.

Philippe standing there. Flame. I burn—and nothing quenches the flame. Philippe was forcing a decision; he had given an ultimatum. Clever, clever Philippe. Among the fleurs-de-lis lay a small note card anyone might have seen: I leave soon, it read. See me one time. Only that. Nothing more.

You have a young wife, Roger said to himself, staring out into the gardens, and seeing none of their fresh greenness, their blossoms, their design and beauty. She loves you. She needs you. You will have children together. It is not enough. (Who may know the heart of another? How can any man judge another? Only the Lord God Almighty. And He does not exist.) She will be devastated. . . . She does not have to know. . . . Sooner or later, they always know. . . . Sooner or later, they do not always care. . . . Temptation opened her silky white arms and beckoned. . . . My poor, poor Barbara. . . .

Roger stood on the steps of the doorway to Philippe's Paris home; it had once been the stables of the palatial Hotel de Nevers behind it. Philippe had leased it and had every interior wall torn out to rebuild a small, furnished house that

exactly suited his city needs. Roger remembered it as being
filled with the finest furniture, old paintings, chairs and tables
that were built by the great Louis's own craftsmen, with different woods, oak and walnut, pearwood and limewood,
repeated in the paneling of the walls and the room molding.
The Duc de Nevers included the use of his gardens in the
lease. There had been moonlight strolls, recitals, picnics. The
most beautiful women in Paris found their way there, as did
poets, playwrights, the cream of the nobility. In Louis's dying
years, the best and wittiest of the court were not at Versailles,
but at Philippe's.

Roger knocked on the door. One of Philippe's servants
opened it. In the dark hallway were crowded trunks and
boxes. Philippe was leaving. It was no bluff, as Roger had half
expected. The servant pointed the way to the upstairs green-
and-gold salon, but Roger knew the way. It had always been
his favorite room. He found himself running up the stairs and
checked himself. He rapped on the salon door with his cane.

"Come in."

Across the room, at the windows, Philippe rose awkwardly
from a chair. His face was as somber, as troubled as Roger's
was smooth. Roger felt strangely calm as they stared at each
other. This man had once been his love, the love of his life.
The whoring of the past week had cleared his mind. He would
say goodbye. It was better not to begin what he might not
finish. The danger was too great. For his sake, and for Barbara's. She stayed in his mind, her face pale, like that of a
ghost.

It took Philippe a few moments to speak, a fact that moved
Roger. Philippe was never without words, never ruffled.

"I did not think you would come."

Roger was silent.

"Your wife . . . is she better?"

"I came to say goodbye," Roger said easily. Philippe's having mentioned Barbara made it easy. "I wish you well."

"And you, Roger."

Roger crossed the room to shake Philippe's hand, so that
Philippe, with his limp, should not have to move, and when
their hands clasped, something electric leapt between them.
What a fool I am, Roger thought, as Philippe moved closer.

What an incredible fool. And then, this is all there is. This is
reality. The other is a dream.

They lay quietly in the bedchamber, listening to someone,
Philippe's valet, begin to lay out places for supper in the
adjoining room. They could hear the chink of glasses and sil-
verware. Their first lovemaking had been violent, passionate,
angry, as their bodies and tongues and hands expressed mutual
hurt and desire and need. Now, the anger was gone, but not
the passion, or the need. Philippe ran his fingers over Roger's
face, tracing his profile, his cheekbones.

"You are as handsome as ever. Do you never age?"

Roger stared at Philippe's dueling scar. He had been present
when Philippe had received that; Roger had been his second
in a ridiculous duel over a wanton countess. Women had
always wound themselves in and out of their lives. He had
cradled Philippe's bloody head in his lap and known how
much he loved him. Loved him more than he had ever loved
anyone except Richard, and Richard was dead, and had never
loved him back. (Would he have been a different man today
if Richard had returned his love? Yet Richard's granddaughter
loved him, the way he had loved Richard. The Fates, how
they must be laughing at the coil of his life). Yes, Richard was
dead and Philippe was alive, never the man Richard Saylor
had been and yet Philippe had stared up at him with eyes that
understood, this man that was all Richard was not. Proud.
Arrogant. Jealous. It had been an unforgettable moment, that
moment of knowing. The physician had bandaged Philippe,
and Roger had helped him to his house, and there had been
the countess, weeping and wailing for Philippe. And Philippe
had made love to her, bandage, pain, and all, there in front
of Roger. Roger had joined in, and then, suddenly, over her
body, they were making love to each other. It was the beginning. Odd that so many times before they had shared women
and never touched each other. But it had all been a prelude
to that final conclusion, to each other.

Roger stretched. He felt soothed and relaxed, replete. "As
for aging, I have just lost twenty years, thanks to you."

Philippe laughed, and his laughter was rich, full, like melting chocolate, his teeth even and white. In his own way, he
was a handsome man.

"Do you remember the countess?" he asked, and Roger joined the laughter, thinking, How well he still reads my mind, my moods.

"She always thought it was her own beauty that aroused us. I wanted you from the first moment I ever saw you, Roger. That moment you walked in behind the Duke of Tamworth. I wanted you for years. War divided us, and time and events, and still we found each other. We are destined together."

Roger closed his eyes under the spell of Philippe's voice, his hands, which were caressing him and making him hard again. Desire held him, dark desire.

"Do you remember," Philippe whispered against his ear, "how much we enjoyed sharing a woman? Having her first, one after the other, watching each other." Roger groaned. "And then making love ourselves, love that was more exquisite than anything else on earth. Your wife, Roger, your Barbara . . . might she ever . . . join us . . . ?"

Philippe's tongue was in his ear, but Roger felt as if he had been dropped into an icy river. He moved away and sat up.

Philippe, leaning on an elbow now, stared at him. That scar gave an ironic twist to his mouth, but then why not? What could be more ironic than for his lover to mention his wife and for him to feel defiled. As if Philippe had touched a part of himself that must remain inviolate. Barbara was his innocence, his talisman. Emotions twisted themselves inside him. He was a fool to have come here. To have begun again. But it was not too late to leave. To end it.

"I apologize," Philippe said, watching him carefully, not making a move to touch him. "I should never have said such a thing. Some men do not care, but you do. Do you love her?"

Roger was silent. Philippe's easy apology caught him off guard, as did their nakedness. The old Philippe would never have apologized. He was touched . . . and aware that he wanted to make love with Philippe again. He despised himself.

"Come here," said Philippe, opening his arms.

They lay together without desire, while Philippe stroked Roger's face.

"It will be all right," he said.

"I do not want her hurt."

"No, of course not. I promise. We are together. Nothing else matters."

CHAPTER SIXTEEN

*A*t first, it was like swimming up through muddy water. She managed to put her head above the surface: events, people, conversation were clear; she understood. But then she was sucked back down, down into the murky waters of grief, and everything was filtered through pain. She remembered the service held by a visiting bishop; she had no memory of her fainting or of Roger's panic. She remembered Thérèse telling her of people who called to offer condolences, the regent and his wife; Lord Stair; the Duc and Duchesse de Saint-Simon; John Law; Marie-Victorie; the Comte de Toulouse; the young Comte de Coigny, the Chevalier de Bavière, the Prince de Dombes. She lay in bed and turned her head away. She wished to see no one. She wanted no one but Roger. Her Roger. And even her memory of Roger was unclear. Sometimes she called his name, sitting upright in panic, and he was there. And sometimes he was not.

She cried herself to sleep. They have died, she sobbed to herself, and I never even got to say goodbye. There was so much she had envisioned: arranging their marriages, being godmother to their children, seeing to their futures with Roger's wealth and power behind her. Always, always she had cared for them, since she was old enough to carry one of them straddled on her hip. They were part of her growing up, of her girlhood, of who she was. It seemed that for all her life until Roger she had held on to hands smaller than hers. . . . She was going to give them what they deserved out of life;

she had made so many plans. And now she felt as if she had lost a part of herself, as if a piece of her heart had been hacked off, and she must live with the bleeding remainder. The ache. If only I had insisted they come to France, she thought, over and over, they might be alive today. She could not sleep; then she took laudanum and slept too much; she could not eat; she could do nothing but lie in her bed. Thérèse and Hyacinthe were there; two loyal sentinels guarding her. And Roger. He was there. He rocked and held her. He talked to her. He was her anchor; he was her soul. When he was gone, to an appointment, to a reception (after all, they were not his flesh and blood, she did not expect him to stop living), she was at the bottom of a muddy sea, and the sunlight seemed far, far above her.

"What a dreary place this is . . . all this black crepe," said White, at the breakfast table, which was still littered with the remains of breakfast, highlighted by a streak of sunlight which came through the windows to gleam dully on the huge silver epergne in the center of the table. Swags of black cloth draped the doorways and windows of the room. The mirror above a serving chest had its surface covered with black cloth.

"It is no wonder Lord Devane is gone out so much. He seems in strangely good spirits, does he not, Francis? He liked my fourth canto. He wants me to compose a poem for Lady Devane's birthday—she will be sixteen in May. I forget what a child she still is. 'Superbly executed,' he told me after he had read it. What are you working on?"

"An inventory Lord Devane wanted of the items stored in the Pont Neuf warehouse. For his journey." Montrose sniffed.

White understood that sniff. Neither of them approved of this journey. It was a new emotion in both their lives . . . to feel the slightest disapproval of what Roger might do. He was going to visit the estate of the reclusive Comte de Bourbon, an elderly, eccentric and extremely wealthy relative of the Prince de Soissons. The comte's estate was one of the most beautiful in France, designed by Le Vau, and visitors were rarely allowed. Neither thought—though they had not said as much as one word to one another—that he should be leaving his wife at this time, even if it was only for four days. The extent of her grief had touched them both. White understood it better, because of his own large and loving family. But Montrose had a younger brother, and Barbara's family tragedy touched some place deep down inside of himself which he kept private. He, too, had plans for his brother; he, too, wanted to use his influence and position to help his brother advance. And once, there had been an even younger brother, who had died, a sunny, open, good-natured child, whom Montrose had adored. He remembered his pain at the boy's death, his mother's tears.

Barbara had woven herself into the fabric of their lives. Her presence at the breakfast table, teasing them, ordering them about, casting adoring looks at her husband, which they mocked, but secretly respected. Her late afternoon teas, held impulsively, randomly, in the blue-and-gold salon off the terrace. The trays overflowing with food, with mouth-watering biscuits and cakes and tarts that were recipes from Tamworth. Her curiosity, her interest in what they were doing, while they stuffed their faces with her food as if they were once more hungry schoolboys. Thérèse and Hyacinthe would be there, and White would recite verses from his poems, and Hyacinthe would make the puppies do tricks, and Thérèse would make them laugh with some story of her life with the Condés. Lady Devane sat behind the teapot and applauded them all, and told them stories of herself, of her family. Lord Devane had even joined them sometimes. There was something comfortable and easy about her teas. (Is there one today? they would ask each other, never knowing until they saw the parade of footmen, laden with trays and urns and teapots on their way to the blue-and-gold salon.) Before she had married their master, the household had been formal, distant, masculine; she brought a hominess, spontaneity. If Lord Devane was their father, she, for all her youth, was becoming their mother. She had become an integral part of their lives; no one quite knew how it had happened. They found that they missed her, for in the shock of her first grief, she was staying in her apartments. Each, in his own way, had grown used to her presence.

They would not openly criticize Roger, who was as happy and laughing and busy these days as either of them had ever seen him. They might find his good spirits strange, compared with his young wife's grief, but it was a welcome change from his mood of the previous weeks. Therefore, Montrose went back to his inventory, doing nothing more than allowing himself that one, expressive sniff, and White's mind jumped to the birthday poem he would compose . . . and to Thérèse, who was much in his thoughts these days. He lived for the times when she strolled in the gardens with him, or allowed him to buy her supper at some crowded, noisy tavern. He found himself telling her things he had told no one else—of his ambitions, his admiration for Lord Devane, his family background. She was a good listener. He dreamed of the day when she would allow him to kiss her . . . and more.

(It is just for four days, Philippe had urged. He rarely allows anyone to see his estate, and it will be an inspiration for your Bentwoodes. Roger had wavered, feeling guilty about leaving Barbara. She will never know you are gone, said Philippe. I know what grief is. In those first weeks, you are conscious only of yourself. How do you know what grief is like? asked Roger. I lost you, said Philippe. It nearly killed me. And once, long ago, there was a girl I loved. I could not marry her; she was an innkeeper's daughter. Her name was Angelique, and she looked like an angel. I loved her with that boyish intensity with which all men love their first, true loves. I set her up in a house in town and visited her whenever I could, and when she became pregnant with my child, I used to lie with my head against her belly and feel the child kick, and I could have wept with happiness. What plans I had. I would educate him with the best tutors—naturally I dreamed it was a boy—and he would become my personal secretary, and I would oversee every step of what would be a long and glorious career for him, while Angelique grew old, but beloved, beside me. Ah, the dreams of youth. She died in childbirth. It was a boy. The child died. And my dreams died. I know what grief is, my Roger. You never told me this, said Roger. Philippe had smiled, a sad, wistful smile such as Roger had never seen. He thought, We are closer than we ever were. I am learning more about him than I ever knew, and he about me. It is better than it was. My life is richer, fuller, more wonderful than it has ever been. He shivered suddenly, one of those superstitious chills, when the Fates brush their cold hands against one's cheek and say, Beware, beware such happiness. But Philippe was urging him to hurry, and the sun was shining, and their horses were stamping their hooves against the ground, impatient for their morning exercise, and the feeling vanished before it even completely registered in his mind.)

The little kindnesses helped. They came from unexpected sources and in unexpected ways. White composed a eulogy in honor of her brothers and sisters and sent it tied with a blue ribbon. There was Tony's letter, his assurance that he would see after Grandmama, unexpected and, therefore, even more dear, for now Grandmama was alone, and she, for all her grief, still had Roger. There was her grandmama's letter. After a while she found that rereading those words, "I will lift up mine eyes unto the hills, from whence cometh my help"— beautiful, inspiring words, words that contained tiny, healing droplets of comfort as they echoed in the mind—rereading that letter, feeling her grandmother's sorrow and strength reach across the miles that separated them, helped. Montrose, stuffy Montrose, sent a message saying he was answering the cards and letters of condolence for her, and that he had saved them, cataloging them as to importance (as only he would) and would send them in to her whenever she felt strong enough to read them. She began to notice that every day Thérèse brought in a fresh bouquet of spring flowers—all the fragile, lovely bulbs, nested with ferns, the fat tulips, regal hyacinths, fragrant narcissuses, proud daffodils and lilies. They were from the Duc de Richelieu, said Thérèse, who sent a note every day along with the flowers asking after her health. That Richelieu could be so thoughtful surprised her. And there were little homemade bouquets, new lilies, fresh roses, sprigs of lilac, from the housekeeper, a gardener, a favorite footman, the cook, Montrose and White.

And there was Thérèse. Barbara was beginning to understand the complicated relationship that had always existed between her grandmother and Annie. When another woman, a woman whose heart and organs were the same as yours, who shared the same cycle of blood and moods, comforted you and dressed you and saw you at your worst as well as at your best, a special bond slowly formed, even though that woman was your inferior, a servant. Thérèse brushed her hair each morning and night. (Bringing memories of Tamworth, of her grandmother. She could picture her grandmother's room, the welter of tables, their tops spilling over with books and vases of flowers and potpourri. Dulcinea, purring, complaining, jumping from person to person. Grandmama and Annie arguing, as they always argued, as one or the other of them brushed her hair. Anne and Charlotte curled on the bed, watching.) Thérèse insisted she change into a fresh gown each day, insisted she sit by the window, rather than lie in bed, and watch the gardens. This, too, brought comfort. Tamworth rose and fell to the cycle of the seasons, of crops. Her grandmother was always bottling, drying, pruning, and flowers and plants were part and parcel of her life. Cowslips, daisies, marsh marigolds, bluebells in spring. Summer was roses, masses of them climbing over the garden walls, and snapdragons and pinks; autumn was chrysanthemums, berries, oak and beech leaves; winter was red nettles, blue forest periwinkle, shy wood violets, snowdrops. There was comfort now in watching the buds unfurl and open, the trees leaf out, in watching the gardeners and weeder women at their year-round tasks. It gave her a sense of time as a continuing thing, a thing beyond her own self, a thing that had its own rhythm, in which she was only a tiny cog.

And there was Hyacinthe. He tried, valiantly and often without success, to be still. Having grown up with brothers, she, even in her grief, her new need for stillness, could appreciate his efforts. He would sit by her for hours, if that was what she wished. He practiced in secret with the puppies, now into their first real growth, but still tiny, yapping things, and was proud when he could make her laugh with some new trick he taught them. He ran up and down the stairs for books that might interest her, bonbons that might tempt her fragile appetite.

She was touched by all these kindnesses, small, but dear, showing she was loved. To find that the pretty compliments she had listened to when she was well and dancing and happy had now disappeared, along with their creators, when she was sad and thin and dispirited was a bitter thing, though Richelieu had warned her. You will be fortunate, Barbara Alderley, her grandmother had once said, if you have three true friends throughout your life. There will be many acquaintances and easy, laughing people who will call themselves friends, but a true friend is there when you are in need. At Tamworth, secure, like a fledgling bird in its prickly nest, she had not known what those words meant. But now that grief began to open new depths within her, now that, for the first time, she thought to ask, What is life about? she began to understand a little more of what her grandmother meant. Nothing was as you expected it, she thought to herself. Not yourself. Not life. Not other people.

Rags between her legs held the fresh, red blood of her flux. No child. She wanted a child now more than she wanted anything. It was a pledge to life, to her brothers and sisters, as well as to her love for Roger. She felt only a child could truly heal her.

She was looking at the gardens, which stretched before her eyes in a style made fashionable by Versailles. First there was a handsome stone terrace connected to the house. At the edge of the terrace, which swept downward into broad steps to a graveled edge, were great bronze vases which contained whatever flower was in season. From the steps and gravel edge were parterres, those flower beds whose shapes are outlined by rigidly pruned evergreen box shrubs. Inside the centers were masses of bulbs, blooming ferociously and riotously under the spring sun. Between the parterres was a wide, single path leading to a landscape pond at the other, far end of the gardens. On each side of the path, behind the terrace's vanguard of parterres, was a grove of trees and shrubs, inside of which were fountains with benches so that the visitor might rest and enjoy the view. These fountains were hidden by the massing of the trees and shrubs; they were a surprise, a visual treat.

In the distance, she saw two men walking down the central path, from the landscape pond toward the house. She recognized one of them as Roger; he was talking animatedly, waving his arms and stopping here and there to point out this or that view of the gardens. The other man was larger, he limped. Once, halfway between the pond and terrace, the limping man put his arm around Roger's shoulder, and together they stared toward the house. Barbara leaned forward, waving to them from her window, but they did not notice her. Gradually, she realized that the limping man was the Prince de Soissons, whom she had met at Sceaux—Roger's enemy. Now they were friends again, it seemed. She did not quite know this friendship had been revived; the details had been lost in the furor of her first intense grieving. Roger had gone on a short journey with the prince to view someone's estate. She had hardly paid attention when Roger had told her, hearing only that he was leaving her. But now, as she saw them strolling together, arm in arm, like old, close friends, she felt a sudden, sharp pang of envy. Roger looked so happy. His whole body gestured his well-being. She leaned back in her chair, feeling the blood ooze out of her. She must have a child, and soon. She must have something of her own to love, someone she did not have to share with everyone else in the world. Someone who would not leave her alone. Then she was ashamed of herself, to feel envious that Roger had a close friend, to feel sorry for herself. That was a weakness her grandmother despised. Bah, her grandmama would have said, frowning at her. I have no use for weak, whining women. Get up and do something!

She stood up and clapped her hands at the puppies. She would go downstairs. She would order tea served in the salon that fronted the terrace, surprising Roger. It would do her good. Clear away these useless feelings. Frowning at her image in the mirror, she pinched her cheeks. With the weight she had lost, she looked a scarecrow in her black gown. The bloom was gone from her cheeks. Well, the prince would just have to see what an ugly, thin wife his friend was saddled with. She tossed her head.

The majordomo was surprised to see her and even more surprised at the vigor of her orders. There were no scones or Tamworth tea cakes baked, he stammered to explain. She frowned; already the household was becoming lax. He hastened to assure her he would provide adequate substitutes. It would be nothing to set up tea in the blue-and-gold salon, madame.

Once there, she watched Roger and the prince from the window. They were at the bottom of the terrace steps, still talking animatedly. With the puppies following her, she wandered around the room as the footmen arranged a table and chairs in a sunny spot for tea. On a long, low table were spread plans and sketches . . . Bentwoodes. His dream. Her dream. Their future. The home for the children she ached to bear. Footmen entered with the silver teapot, the urn of boiling water, trays of food, biscuits and crumbling cakes. Roger would be surprised and pleased. She opened the terrace doors a fraction.

"My dear Roger," she could hear the prince saying, "that is an absurd idea. You of all people should know better. The essence of good design is more ornamental, more baroque, not this nonsense of ancient Rome and Palladio. I am surprised at you—"

His tone was patronizing, superior. She felt angry. Bentwoodes—Palladio—was hers. And Roger's. No one else's. A sudden, mischievous impulse, such as the ones that used to embroil her in such trouble with Harry and Jane, came upon her. She hissed to the puppies, who were chewing the edge of the priceless, handwoven carpet. Holding each of them up, she whispered, "After him. Get the bad man. Go on!"

They whined and yelped in her hands. She opened the terrace doors wider.

"Get him."

The puppies shot out, and there was an immediate confusion of noise, shrill growls and yelps, along with Roger's "Damn it! Heel! Heel, I say! I do not know what is the matter with—Hyacinthe! Hyacinthe! Come and get these damned dogs!"

Barbara grinned to herself and ran to sit in the central armchair before the tea table. Spreading her skirts, she tried to look innocent. She began to pour boiling water into the teapot (from the terrace came continued growling and Roger's cursing). She pictured herself the essence of domesticity; she could see the etching in the shop windows—it would be enormously popular, "Faithful Young Wife Awaits Her Lord (After Having Set The Dogs On His Best Friend)."

Roger strode into the room, a puppy held by the scruff of the neck in each hand, as if they were lumps of offensive, smelly cheese. He stopped short at the sight of Barbara, sitting before a full tea table. Behind him was the Prince de Soissons, his proud, heavy, scarred face angry. Barbara bit her lip not to smile. (She was terrible! Her grandmother always told her so. What on earth had possessed her? Ah, it felt good to be so bad.)

"I have had tea prepared for you," she said, trying to look innocent. "Good afternoon, Monsieur de Soissons."

"These dogs are incorrigible. They went after Philippe like hellhounds. Look, Bab, one of them—Harry, I think—has torn Philippe's stocking. They ought to be beaten!" Roger jerked his hands up and down, and the puppies, hanging like sausages, whined. Barbara ran to take them from him.

"I am so sorry," she said. "I cannot imagine what happened. Here, I will put them outside. Bad, bad dogs," she scolded.

In the hall, she handed them to a footman, patting each small head and saying, "Good dog." She covered her mouth with her hands, choking with laughter.

Once her face was smooth, she reentered the room. Both men rose as she seated herself. She found she could not help glancing at the prince's torn stocking. Bubbles of laughter rose inside her again. The prince was watching. He knows, she thought, and for some reason she shivered. Her jest was no longer quite so funny. She was conscious of that feeling she had had the first time she met him, of something strange behind his eyes under those heavy brows. Or was it simply his dueling scar that made his gaze so ironic, so oddly curious? Grief had left her fragile and more sensitive to the moods and feelings of others. She had a sense, sudden and sure, that he disliked her (well, she could hardly blame him; on second thought her trick was childish and petty) and that Roger was nervous. Of what?

"I am sorry about the dogs," she said, not looking at either of them, but hiding behind the details of pouring tea.

"Bad manners can always be forgiven," said the prince, leaning back in his chair, secure now, relaxed. "They are due to a lack of discipline, and I will not blame an animal for its training. May I have an extra biscuit? I love an English tea."

He knows, she thought, and he is angry with me. It is my manners he is commenting on. She tossed her head.

"I thought I smelled scones—" said Montrose, walking in through the open terrace doors, though he tried to back out again when he saw the prince. Roger waved him in and introduced him.

"Your name is a familiar one to me, sir," said Montrose, bowing to the prince, "as Lord Devane has had an appointment with you nearly every day." He laughed. (Such talk was Montrose's idea of wit.)

"Sit down," Roger said irritably.

"No raspberry scones?" Montrose eyed the tea trays. "Lady Devane, it is good to see you downstairs."

"No scones. The kitchen was not expecting me yet."

"Nor was I," said Roger, smiling at her, as she handed him his tea. "But I, too, am glad to see you out of your apartments at last. Are you certain it is not too soon?"

"Yes," said the prince. "You are not now in the blooming looks I saw at Sceaux. Which is completely understandable. May I offer my condolences in person on your tragic loss, Lady Devane, but then we agreed before that I should call you Barbara. May I still do so?"

"Yes," she said breathlessly, feeling the same way she had felt the day she pulled Charity Dinwitty's pigtails and her two older sisters had turned on her. It was six years ago, but she remembered the sinking feeling in her stomach as she faced them. They had beaten her bloody. As the prince intended to do. . . .

"I think Lady Devane looks very well," said Montrose. She offered him another biscuit.

"I thought I smelled raspberry scones," said White, popping his head into the room from the hallway. "Oh, excuse me. I did not realize you had company."

"There are none," Montrose called to him.

"Come inside anyway," Roger said, "and let me introduce the Prince de Soissons."

White bowed. He smiled at Barbara. "It is so good to see you, Lady Devane. We have not had a decent tea since—well, since."

The prince said, "May I have that piece of cake? I enjoy my food, as you can see. It has always been a source of aggravation to me that Roger remains as slim as a boy. Looking at him, you would never guess he was some twenty-odd years older than you, my dear. Old enough to be your father. When were you married, child?"

"In January, Monsieur de Soissons."

"You have torn your stocking," said Montrose.

"Yes," said the prince. "So I have." He remained focused on Barbara. "You must call me Philippe. I insist. There can be no formality between us. As the wife of a man I consider a friend it would break my heart. . . . January. You are still a new bride, then. What a sadness that tragedy has marred your marriage so soon. Roger tells me that your brothers and sisters died of the smallpox. A terrible thing; a terrible way to die"

"Absolutely," agreed Montrose. "My uncle lay like a stone for three days, then suffered for ten more days before he finally died. Every festering sore on his body bled."

"I will have a piece of cake," broke in White, loudly.

"Terrible, terrible," agreed Philippe. "My youngest brother swelled up like a sausage and bled from the mouth and nose. He never got a single spot. We knew then it was fatal. What were their names, Barbara?"

She swallowed past the rising lump in her throat. "Tom . . . Kit and Charlotte . . . and Anne and . . . the baby, William," she ended on a whisper. Sweet Jesus, she was going to cry. She was going to disgrace herself before this cold, thoughtless man and cry. She stood up, knocking over a teacup.

"Lady Devane!" cried White.

The eyes of all the men focused on her.

"Barbara," said Philippe, setting down his cup, a concerned expression on his face. "I have distressed you! I am a clumsy fool! You must forgive my bad manners!"

She nodded blindly in his direction. Liar, she thought. She must get out of the room before she began crying. He must not see her tears. He must not. Outside, she slumped against the wall, tears coursing down her cheeks.

"Darling," Roger said, directly behind her, taking her in his arms.

"Are you ill? What can I do?"

"Help—help me to my rooms. Then go back to your guest. I am so sorry, Roger," she sobbed through her hands.

He picked her up and she buried her face in his shoulder, thinking, I cried on his good coat before. At St. James's Square, when I could not have him. Oh, it hurts. It hurts. I wish they were not dead. I wish they had not died in such a way. I wish I had brought them to France even if Roger disliked it. Why did that man want me to cry? Why?

"You are too thin," Roger was saying, his mouth a straight, grim line. "You are not eating enough."

She smiled into his shoulder through her tears, at his tone. It reminded her of her grandmother. Even though she was thin and tearful and weak, surely he loved her, just a little.

Inside the blue-and-gold salon, White turned on Montrose, who was standing up, staring at the doorway Barbara had run through, with a bewildered expression on his face. His round face had flushed red.

"Idiot! You should have known such a topic would distress her!"

"It is entirely my fault," said Philippe. He, too, was standing. He, too, was staring at the doorway through which Barbara—and Roger—had run, though there was no bewildered expression on his face.

"I did not mean to make her cry," said Montrose, looking as if he might cry himself at any moment. "I-I was excited over having tea again, and she seemed so well."

"She is well, you bloody idiot, but it has not been a full month yet!"

"Lord Devane's devotion is admirable," said Philippe.

The two other men stared at him, then at each other.

White bowed coldly and strode from the room.

Montrose pressed his trembling lips with a linen napkin. "I did not mean to make her cry," he said again in a whisper. Then he, too, excused himself and left.

Philippe was alone. He spoke aloud and softly. "I, however, did. And it may have been one of the more stupid things I have ever done."

He sat back down to finish his tea, eating the extra biscuits Montrose had left on his plate and another serving of cake, but all of it in a mechanical way, without the relish with which he had eaten before. When Roger returned half an hour later, he said to him, an expression of genuine concern in his voice, "How is she?"

Roger did not answer.

"Roger, I am a fool. I was upset at seeing her unexpectedly, and those dogs made me angry. I said what I did deliberately, and now I regret it. You must believe me."

Roger walked past him, straight to a tray set with brandies and wines, and poured himself a glass.

"She will be fine," he said tiredly. Barbara had cried for a long time, and she kept saying she was sorry about the dogs. He had had to pretend he did not know what she meant. Damn Philippe. Damn that cruel streak of his. Christ, he was worried about her. She was too thin. Her grief seemed excessive, her emotions too volatile. She needed him . . . to be more than he could be. He had felt it the night of the ball after Philippe had tempted him. But not with the depth he felt now. Guilt . . . love . . . desire . . . was passion worth the pain he might cause . . . he had done so many things in his life . . . not all of them good . . . but none made him feel this sadness with himself.

Philippe watched his face, the expressions playing so openly over it.

"It must be fatiguing," he said, "to have a wife that young. Rather like a child one must raise."

Roger glanced at him, frowning, but Philippe's face was empty of malice.

"It is . . . at times," he said abruptly, draining the glass of wine.

Philippe stroked the dueling scar that had ruined his profile, but had brought him Roger.

"Will you believe me when I say I am sorry?" His tone was sincere, grave.

"You had better be."

"I have been thinking while you were gone. You mentioned a brother once—older—"

"Harry."

"Yes, Harry—such a common name. He is in Italy, is he not?"

"As far as I know. Italy is where I have money sent."

"Why not write him and have him come here? She might do better with the added company of someone in her family. And it would relieve some of the burden you must feel."

Roger set down his glass, obviously surprised at Philippe's thoughtfulness. "It might be just what she needs; she is so very family-minded . . . and still such a child . . . as you say. This has all been a terrible shock for her."

He poured himself more wine. Philippe, watching his face, waited.

"Well?"

"Well, what?"

"My dear Roger, I know your every mood. What else is on your mind? Come, tell me. What did she say upstairs? Does she dislike me so much?"

"On the contrary, Philippe. She said you do not like her."

It was out, the thing that had been between them since he had reentered the room, dividing them, dividing his loyalties. He had hated the feelings her words produced—the knowledge, deep inside himself, that she was correct, the knowledge of Philippe's cruelties, his jealousies that she was no match for, and yet which he inadvertently exposed her to; the sudden, wearying guilt, the sense of being trapped, trapped by her innocence and faith in him, trapped by his own vanity and needs. . . . He needed Philippe. God help him . . . he loved him, knowing what he was, what he was capable of, he still loved him. But the main feeling, the one whose taste he now drank brandy to cover, was one of unworthiness. He was not worthy of what she felt for him. And that perhaps hurt most of all.

"Not like her?" said Philippe, who had come close to guessing Roger's every emotion. "Who says I do not like her? My manners this afternoon were boorish, appalling. Sometimes I am an old fool. Tomorrow I will send her three dozen red tulips—"

"Good. She likes flowers."

"—begging her forgiveness. It is her grief, Roger. It distorts perceptions. She mistook my nervousness—and my irritation—I admit it—for anger. For dislike. I found her a delightful child. Subdued, now, not in her best looks; but that is understandable! Her voice is extraordinary. It sent shivers down my spine. I did not notice it at Sceaux, being too intent on other things. And when she smiled at you this afternoon, she was lovely. Truly lovely. You are a fortunate man, Roger."

Philippe's generosity surprised Roger. "Yes," he said. "The first time I saw her smile was like seeing Richard again, in his youth. She has her faults, but, all in all, she has been a pleasant surprise. She knows her duty. Her grandmother—a veritable tigress—has raised her well. You should have seen her take over my household. It was like watching Richard maneuver crack troops into position. One attack, and we all surrendered. And she loves me. In a year or two from now, when there are children, and life has matured her more, she will be a superb countess. I envision her running my estates, my children . . . myself, as I dodder around Bentwoodes with a cane, gardening, the pastime of an old man—" He stopped, aware he had said more than he meant to.

Philippe hoisted himself out of the armchair and limped over to where Roger was standing.

"Pour me a brandy," he said. "I find that making a fifteen-year-old cry has upset me more than I realized."

They both laughed. And when Roger had poured it, Philippe clinked their glasses together and said, "To gardening, my friend. To gardening."

When her flux stopped, Barbara went to Roger's apartments. He was dressing to go out; Justin was just helping him shrug into a coat edged with gold lace. He looked handsome, elegant and formal. His hands were covered with jeweled rings. Justin, seeing Barbara standing in the doorway in her nightgown and shawl like a lost child, hurried to her, fussing over her like a hen over its chick. She must sit here out of the draft; she must have a glass of wine. And Roger held her hand to his lips and kissed it. Smiling at her, his eyes crinkled in the corners. She felt her breath catch. He was so handsome. She wanted a child—their child—so much. He read her as if she were a book. He called for Justin to bring him pen and paper and dashed off a note (she caught Philippe's name) and sent Justin scurrying to have it delivered. (She was glad it was Philippe he was breaking an appointment with.) Roger pulled off his wig, and she helped him out of his coat. He pulled her onto his lap and petted her, and his petting led to more sensual caresses until finally they were in bed. She wept as they made love, which distressed him, and later, lying on his chest as he stroked her hair, she tried to explain. The sense of being fragile, like delicate glass, these days. The way other emotions, such as love, were underlaid by grief. Do you want to go home? he asked her, to Tamworth. I will send you there. She closed her eyes. To be with her grandmother again. To feel her grandmother's strength, her safety. But she was a woman now. With her own life. And her duty to Roger as his wife. She had to learn to stand on her own. She reached up suddenly to kiss him for his thoughtfulness, and he was not able to hide the expression on his face. For the briefest of seconds, she saw that he wanted her gone. The shock of it squeezed her heart. She lay back on his chest, hiding her face from him. If he had told her he hated her, he could not have hurt her more. And Roger was thinking, God forgive me, but I want her gone. Not forever. Just for a few months. Just a few months of complete freedom. And she knows it. I let her see it. Jesus Christ, what is happening to me? I had better be careful. Very, very careful. He hugged her closer. I will buy her something tomorrow, he thought. Philippe can help me choose it. Something that will make her forget.

He thinks I am a child, she thought, staring into the narrow, black velvet box in which was nestled a diamond-and-ruby bracelet. A child to be bribed with pretty trinkets. Why does he want me gone? What have I done?

"Madame!" exclaimed Thérèse. "You must wear this. I insist! It is absolutely beautiful. Here, hold out your arm so I may fasten it on. There! Look how lovely it is, how it shines against the black of your gown. You are fortunate to have such a thoughtful husband. I can tell you the only time the Princesse de Condé received something like this from her husband was when she caught him being unfaithful!"

Thérèse laughed; the sound was like silver bells; and Barbara, after a moment, laughed with her.

"Now, go," said Thérèse, giving her a little push. "Madame de Gondrin is waiting downstairs, and it will do you good to get out. Go, madame, go."

In the carriage, Marie-Victorie de Gondrin, as always, placid and self-possessed, seeming years older, kissed Barbara on both cheeks as if she were a convalescing child. When I am twenty, will I be this way? Barbara thought. Calm, assured, understanding everything.

"I am so glad you are coming out with me," Marie-Victorie said. She held Barbara's face in one hand, examining it as if it were a piece of fruit she wished to purchase from a vendor. "What is wrong, Barbara? You have a strange look on your face."

"I-I have a headache. Perhaps I ought to go back in. I do not feel like seeing anyone."

Marie-Victorie patted her cheek. "My dear child, grief is not something one puts away in a few days like a winter cloak for storage. It has its own time. You will feel better for making the effort. I promise you. Come now, I have sworn to Armand that I will bring you by to see him. He says he has not played a decent hand of cards with anyone since you stopped coming by—"

Barbara smiled.

"There. Is that not better? You need to get out more, go on with your life again. Your dear Roger will be glad to see it. Men never like it when their wives are unwell—but what is this on your arm? Let me see it! Did Roger give that to you? Naturally! You are so fortunate, Bab. Gondrin never gave me anything so beautiful. Now, let me think, what has been going on lately."

She chatted on about the possibility of a parliamentary inquiry on Richelieu and de Gacé for dueling and the speculation as to whether or not the regent would take the sacrament at Easter since it meant his swearing to give up his mistresses. Barbara thought about what Thérèse had said, and the suspicion that had sprouted in her so suddenly, like a poisonous plant, was fully grown in seconds.

In the Bastille, Richelieu strutted up to her, ugly, his thin, narrow face thinner, his head cocked to one side. His strange eyes glinted at her.

"You look terrible," he said.

She laughed. He was thin and stringy and ugly, and she did not know why she had come to see him. He kissed her hand.

"I have missed you abominably, Barbara Devane. Sit down and let us play cards! At once!"

She beat him four games out of five. It almost took her mind off Roger. Marie-Victorie was correct; she must get out more. In her mourning, she could no longer attend balls and receptions, but quiet dinners, an afternoon visit here and there, would do her good. She had lessons she could begin again: Italian, watercolor, pianoforte and singing. She could sit for her portrait once more. White and Montrose and she might resume their excursions. She would finish the volume on Palladio. And begin another. Devane House. It was the reason Roger remained so long in Paris, to order or buy all that was beautiful for it. She would make Devane House the focus of her attention. Until there should be a child. And for diversion, she had Richelieu, awful Richelieu and the card games. And she had Roger. . . . She stared at the bracelet on her arm until Richelieu reminded her that it was her turn to deal.

No, madame, Justin told her, he is not here.

She tried to wait up, but fell asleep. He did not come to breakfast the next morning. She went up to his apartments. Justin was folding linen shirts and putting them into a cupboard. Where is he? she asked. Justin concentrated on his folding. He had gone riding. With whom, Justin? He did not say, madame. Whom did he go riding with? she asked Montrose. Why, I believe it was the Prince de Soissons, Montrose answered, surprised. She caught up with Roger later in the day. Why did you not come to breakfast? she asked him. He kissed the top of her head. No reason. Do you like the bracelet? It is beautiful. Why did you not come to breakfast? I did not know you would be there, he said, staring at her. I was late and breakfasted with the prince in his home.

Roger stayed in that evening and was at breakfast as usual the next morning, but it did not help the suspicions she now felt, eating at her, like a canker.

"Do you really think I look so awful?" she asked Richelieu, a few days later, unable to concentrate on her hand. Thérèse and Hyacinthe were with her, as chaperones. She felt drawn to Richelieu the way metal filings are to a magnet. He was a man of the world, he was honest, brutally so. Women fought over his favors, except for her, and yet he had not abandoned her when others had.

"Yes."

She frowned at her cards.

Hyacinthe, fascinated by the linnet, kept pushing his finger through the cage. The linnet squawked and flapped his wings.

"Leave that bird alone!" Richelieu snapped.

"Do not raise your voice to my servant!" Barbara snapped back. Richelieu narrowed his eyes at her, but did not say anything else. Hyacinthe went to stand by Thérèse, who was talking with Richelieu's valet.

"Aces are high," Richelieu prompted when she still had not played a card. She stuck her tongue out at him.

"Lovely, Barbara. No wonder your husband strays."

She struggled to keep her face from showing anything. Richelieu was like a viper, always knowing where to strike to kill. She felt as if the breath had been knocked out of her.

"Who says my husband strays?" She was proud of how cool her tone was. If he was looking for gossip, he would not get it from her.

"All husbands stray," he told her, watching her. "You have been ill, neglectful, full of yourself. We men are creatures of the flesh. I assume—"

"Never assume." She slapped her first card on the table. Richelieu stared at it. It was a good one. He had given up trying to guess her strategy. He suspected she played without one. He waited patiently. Patience was his strong point. They played steadily, without speaking. Finally she said, as if it were unimportant and she were merely speaking to pass time, "Why are you unfaithful to your wife?"

He smiled to himself. At last. "I am unfaithful because I was forced to marry her. Because there is no love between us. Because I wish to be. I do as I please, and so does she, with my blessing. I do not want her. Let someone else enjoy her."

Barbara shivered.

"And what would you do if you found your Roger was being unfaithful to you?"

She could not answer. Richelieu mocked her.

"You would cry. All women do. My wife did. And do nothing. Which is why men go on being unfaithful." His scorn stung.

"And what would you do!"

"I would be unfaithful back, Bab. Sauce for the goose."

"And what would that achieve?"

"Nothing. Except that sometimes revenge is sweet. Very sweet."

His eyes glinted at her. This conversation was becoming too uncomfortable. She tossed her head.

"Do you believe in anything?"

"Of course not. I lost my innocence at ten, when I was at court, and I learned that men and women—especially women—are capable of anything."

His hand was lying near hers. She had an impulse to carry it to her cheek. Part of that impulse was pity for the child of ten, and part of it was something that startled her. She glanced at Richelieu and then away, but not before he saw what had been in her eyes.

"Do not pity me," he said staring at her. "You are the one to be pitied. When you lose your innocence, it will hurt far more than losing mine did."

He made her angry. Good. She fastened on it the way one of Annie's yard hens leapt upon a fat June bug. Anger covered the fact that just a moment before she had suddenly wondered what it would be like to kiss him.

"I am not innocent. I am a married woman. I have nothing to lose."

"Barbara, you have everything to lose."

She stood up, throwing her unplayed cards on the table. "This is a stupid conversation. I have a headache, and I am going home."

"Good. I have never seen you play so badly. See if you can find someone to practice with." He stood up as she gathered her fan and gloves.

"I wish I had never come to see you."

Richelieu chucked her under the chin. She slapped his hand.

"I will see you tomorrow or the next day," he called after her. "Give your husband my regards."

He went over to the linnet and tapped against the wires of the bird's cage.

"Pretty bird," he said, smiling, "pretty, pretty bird. Sing for me. Sing."

They were talking of Barbara. Richelieu always maneuvered the conversation around to her. He was obsessed with her; no one could tell him too little or too much. He studied her the way a general might study a terrain map; no morsel of gossip about her was too small, too insignificant. Louise-Anne was used to his ways, he had always had other mistresses; yet this infatuation of his was too much. She despised Barbara because of it.

Louise-Anne sat on the edge of Richelieu's chair, sulking, but they ignored her. The three of them, St. Michel, Richelieu and she, were more than a little drunk. They had whiled away the afternoon playing cards and drinking wine, and now it was twilight, and the pretense of playing cards was finished. Richelieu baited St. Michel about his broken nose, about Barbara.

Why did you drop her? Richelieu asked. I found her boring, St. Michel answered, but it did not satisfy Richelieu. They talked of her inexplicable, continued faithfulness to Roger, and here Louise-Anne was unusually silent. Roger had been to one of the Duchesse de Berry's notorious suppers. Her heart had begun to beat wildly when he walked in late, with her uncle, the prince. No one came to a de Berry supper in innocence. Anything might happen. And did. By the time he arrived, nearly everyone was drunk and beginning to pair off for the evening. She immediately left her partner and went to him. He and her uncle were the oldest people in the room, but Roger was the most handsome, the most desirable. She wanted him. Wine made her bolder than usual, wine and his presence in that place. She was glad Roger was cheating on his nauseating little wife; there was no other reason for him to be here. She could have crowed with triumph. She was glad her uncle was back, that he had converted Roger to their old ways. Roger and her uncle always chased women. And now, once more, they chased them again, if the rumors were true.

She stood before Roger, smiling wantonly. And he smiled back. She loved his smile; she always had. When she was younger, still a girl, and he and her uncle were always together, she had dreamed of him smiling at her just so. She stepped closer, swaying with wine, offering herself, her meaning plain. And he had shaken his head. Just a tiny shake. No more. No less. But her lust was ashes in her mouth. As was her pride. And her uncle stood behind him, his proud, full face contemptuous of her.

She shuddered at the memory. It was so seldom that anyone made her feel shameful, but they had. The rest of the evening she had watched them. They settled on a silly little countess and took her off with them to one of the bedrooms the Duchesse de Berry kept available for her guests. Louise-

Anne had writhed with jealousy, and anger, and humiliation. Why not choose her? Why was she not good enough? She had had half a mind to write an anonymous note to Roger's wife—his doting wife who was busy parading her grief for her family—and tell her of her husband's activities at night with his friend, the Prince de Soissons; but she had not done it—yet.

"I want to get drunk!" she said loudly.

"You are drunk," said Richelieu.

She leaned over and kissed him, slowly, lingeringly, running her pointed little tongue along the edge of his jaw and into his ear, as St. Michel watched. She looked into Richelieu's eyes. At least he understood her. Dear Armand, he understood her very well.

Richelieu motioned for the valet to pour more wine, and Louise-Anne moved to sit in his lap. She put her hand inside his shirt and rubbed his bare chest. St. Michel watched; his breathing quickened.

"I want to get totally and vilely drunk and do something awful," she whispered. She rubbed herself against Richelieu like a cat.

"Henri just told me something interesting," Richelieu said. His voice was caressing, sensual. Louise-Anne shivered at the sound of it. Armand had something planned.

"We were arguing over his true feelings for the Lady Devane. Do not frown, Louise-Anne, I promise this will be worth your while. And he admitted—I had to pull it out of him—that he does dream of the lady occasionally."

Louise-Anne put her hands over her ears, but Richelieu pulled them down.

"Listen," he commanded. He stared at her, his yellow-brown eyes mesmerizing her, knowing her. "He dreams of raping her. A recurring dream of rape. Yes . . . I thought you would find that interesting, Louise-Anne. I was surprised when you did not react before, but your mind was elsewhere."

"Rape," she whispered. She said the word slowly, savoring it.

"Louise-Anne is fascinated with rape," Richelieu told St. Michel, and laughed at his friend's expression.

"Tell us," he said softly. "You will not regret it, Henri. That I promise." There was silence in the room. Louise-Anne was staring at St. Michel now, her eyes wide. Richelieu reached up and caressed her neck. She shivered again.

St. Michel was silent, as if he did not know what to do or say.

"The dream," Richelieu prodded, patiently, as if St. Michel were a slow child. "Describe the dream to us. Go on."

St. Michel swallowed. He took another drink of wine. "I-I see her coming to me . . . and she is crying . . . crying like a child . . . and her hair is loose . . . loose and flowing—I always wanted to see her hair that way. I always wanted to touch it, run my hands through it. I always loved her hair."

Louise-Anne had put her hand inside Richelieu's shirt again, against his heart, and she could feel it beating violently, although his face showed no emotion. I hate her, she thought. Why does he want her so? And Roger wanted her, too. He might tomcat through Paris with her uncle, but she knew he cared for his wife. Why? If she had not been so drunk, she would have gotten off Richelieu's lap. But she was too far gone. St. Michel's words had started something. Something she could not run from. She closed her eyes to it. Her breath was warm against Richelieu's ear. "The story is better told in bed," she said. She put her mouth on Richelieu's, drowning out thoughts of Barbara, that it was Barbara he wanted, and they kissed, their tongues twining. St. Michel watched them.

Richelieu, Louise-Anne in his arms, walked over to the bed. St. Michel stood up hesitantly, watching Richelieu. Richelieu nodded his head, and St. Michel stumbled in his haste to join them. Louise-Anne lay now in the bed's center, her eyes closed, as if she had swooned. Richelieu leaned against the carved headboard of the bed, his face slack and empty.

"We want to hear more of your dream, Henri."

St. Michel swallowed and sat down on the edge of the bed. Louise-Anne sat up and turned her back to St. Michel, who licked his lips.

"Unlace me," she said to him, her eyes on Richelieu's. "My gown feels too tight."

Richelieu leaned his head back and watched them with narrowed eyes. St. Michel's hands trembled as he unlaced Louise-Anne's intricate corset. She sighed as it loosened and let her gown slip down her shoulders. Her slight breasts were white just above her chemise. She reached up and began to unfasten the pins in her hair. It fell on her shoulders, tangled, luxuriant. She leaned back against St. Michel, her eyes closed, and his hands came around to touch her breasts. He fondled them, breathing shallowly. She slipped away from him, and shrugged out of her gown and hoop. Now she wore only her chemise and stockings and garters. Both men's eyes were fastened to her slender leg, to the soft white of her thigh and calf as she slowly unrolled her stockings.

"Tell us the dream," Richelieu said hoarsely.

St. Michel licked his lips, his eyes on Louise-Anne, who was kneeling near him.

"I-I see her coming to me and crying . . ."

"Yes?" said Richelieu. Louise-Anne had begun to caress her breasts through the chemise. Her eyes were closed.

"Is she clothed or naked?" asked Richelieu.

"Clothed for now," said St. Michel. "And I take her in my arms, and I hold her tenderly, softly, so that she trusts me, but all the while I want to hurt her, to pound her into nothingness. I lead her to my bed, and we lie down upon it—" He stopped and gasped. Louise-Anne had unbuttoned the front of his breeches, and her mouth was on him, sucking.

"God!" he said.

"Go on," urged Richelieu.

"She—she is still crying . . . oh, that is good . . . and—and I slowly undress her . . . God, Louise-Anne, do not stop, harder, harder . . ."

"Describe it, said Richelieu, his eyes closed, his body limp and relaxed.

"I-I unfasten the front of her gown as she lies on the bed. Louise-Anne, why did you stop—"

But Louise-Anne had moved to Richelieu, who lay with his eyes closed. She unfastened his breeches and began on him. Richelieu never moved. St. Michel groaned and pulled off his shirt and breeches and moved so that he was beside Louise-Anne. He put his hand under her chemise, on her small, white buttocks

"Her eyes are closed," St. Michel said. "I pull down her gown and turn her over and unlace the corset. Her arms are trapped by the sleeves of her gown, and so I turn her back over and begin to kiss her breasts—"

"Describe them," whispered Richelieu.

"They are young and firm and they have pink tips. I kiss them, and free her arms from the gown, and she wraps her arms around me. I make her stand and I pull down the gown. I pull away everything but her chemise and stockings. Her legs are long, long and slim. I pull up her chemise. . . . I see her most private parts, her hips swell gently . . . how soft and white her thighs are . . . the hair on her . . . I tear the chemise from her. Her eyes widen with shock, for I have been so gentle, but before she can react I throw her to the bed and enter her savagely—" Louise-Anne groaned, but Richelieu pushed her head away from him. He lay with his eyes closed. Louise-Anne lay back beside him, her eyes on St. Michel. She pulled up her chemise and opened her legs.

"No kisses now," St. Michel said, crawling over Louise-Anne, and beginning to do what he had just described. "I make her cry with the pain, writhe under me, desperate to be free, but it does not—God!—matter. Only I matter, my need, my anger. . . . I hurt her again and again and—God!—again." Supported by his arms, he thrust himself in and out of Louise-Anne viciously. She was making soft, little cries, cries slowly escalating into screams. She reached over for Richelieu's hand and brought it to her breasts. She screamed louder.

The valet, who had been sitting outside, ran into the cell, but stopped the moment his eyes caught the writhing bodies on the bed, for none of them had bothered to close the bed draperies. He turned at once and closed the door behind him, crossing himself as he sat down once more in his chair. The Princesse de Charolais screamed for a long time, but he stayed where he was. He knew better than to intrude.

No one was in Roger's apartments. Barbara opened the cupboard and felt under the pile of shirts. Nothing. She pulled the drawers and rummaged through the clothing there. Under a pile of stockings, she found a handkerchief. Opening it, she saw an embroidered initial in the corner, an "S" surrounded by tiny fleurs-de-lis. She smelled it; there was no fragrance. She ran to the small study next to Justin's room, in which Roger kept all his letters, and was just beginning to riffle through a box of letters when Justin said from the door, "Lady Devane, is there something I can help you find?"

Blushing scarlet from her shoulders to the top of her head, she stammered no and hurried from Roger's apartments, the handkerchief wadded into a small ball in her hand. Roger did not come home at all that night.

The next morning, as soon as she was fully awake, she ran to his bedchamber and pulled back the bed draperies, half expecting him to be gone, but to her relief he was there, sleeping. She tugged on his shoulder. He tossed and muttered and after a moment opened his eyes blearily.

"Jesus Christ, my head. What time is it?"

"Seven."

He groaned and turned over. She stood by the bed. After a moment, he opened one eye and looked at her.

"If—if you are going riding this morning, I would like to go. My black riding habit is ready, and I could . . . I could join you. . . ." Her voice trailed off.

"Not this morning," he said. "The only thing I want to do is sleep."

"Well, I will see you at breakfast—"

"Do not talk to me of food." He closed his eyes.

She rubbed one foot against the carpet. "Yes. Well, I will just let you sleep."

Once she was certain he was sleeping again, she rummaged through the pockets of his coat and breeches. Nothing. She smelled his shirt. Sweat, brandy, perhaps jasmine and orange water. Nothing more.

Curled up in an armchair in the window of her bedchamber, she thought about it as she embroidered. Her needle plunked in and out of the thin material. Was he being unfaithful? It seemed as if she had wakened from the first shock of her grief to find something changed between them . . . in such a subtle way that she did not trust her own intuition . . . and yet she had seen the look on his face. He wanted her gone. Why? She had thought he was growing fond of her, was loving her a little. And she had been so happy with that. And now she did not know what to think. He had never been more cheerful, more tender and solicitous of her. Why did she suspect him? Was it her imagination?

"S." The handkerchief was in the pocket of her gown. She took it out and stared at it twenty times a day. Who was she?

The material she was embroidering tore as she thrust the needle through it savagely, and she threw the frame onto the floor in a fit of temper and stared out the window. Harry, who had been hiding under her skirts, leapt on the frame, got it between his teeth, and shook it back and forth, killing it. Charlotte crawled out at his growls and ran after him, barking. She managed to grab an end. The game was on. Barbara sat brooding, her face mutinous, the hard line of her jaw showing. Was he unfaithful? Was he? Outside, in the garden, Roger and Philippe walked into her view. They stood at the edge of the terrace talking. Philippe, Roger's dear friend. She realized how much time they spent together. She ground her teeth. Philippe sent her flowers; he never failed to inquire after her health; he did not intrude on her presence too often, and yet she disliked him. What is happening to me? she thought. Has my grief unhinged me? Am I seeing devils where none exist? She was pitiful. She was disgusting. To be jealous of a man who was Roger's friend. Roger would despise her if he knew, but not any more than she despised herself. Roger and Philippe were no longer in view. She leaned back in her chair. "S." There was a reasonable explanation, and she was making herself sick. I must have a child, she thought. I need something to love. Why did he want her gone? What had she done?

"Why are you sitting up here alone?"

She started. It was Roger. He walked into the room, and Harry and Charlotte dropped the embroidery frame (the piece of linen it had held was shredded satisfactorily to pieces) and trotted to him, whining for his attention. He leaned down and absently scratched their heads.

"You should not sit up here and brood," he told her. "It is not good for you. It will not bring them back."

She stared at him, anger rising in her. She had never shown him her temper before. She had always managed to control it before him but now, the grief, the worry, the fear had loosened her hold upon it. And she did not care. It would feel good to scream at him. Very, very good. It rose in her like sap up a tree filling her throat, her head, her mind.

"I am not brooding." She said each word through clenched teeth, the line of her stubborn jaw plain through the soft youthfulness of her face. He stared at her, startled. At this moment, she was the image of her grandmother, or of Diana.

She reached into the pocket of her gown, while he watched her, eyes narrowed, obviously trying to understand her mood. Well, let him understand this. She threw the wadded handkerchief at him. It fell to the floor a few inches from him with a soft plop.

In that single instant, Roger's heart seemed to stop, then to explode with a roar, a dull pain, that filled his ears. To give himself time to think, he picked up the handkerchief and unfolded it. The "S," the fleurs-de-lis, stared up at him like his own sentence of death.

"Justin told me you went through my clothes," he said calmly. The calmness came from shock.

That calmness maddened her. It was as if someone had lighted an explosive in her mind.

"Who is she!" She screamed the words at him. The two dogs froze. Their tails tucked under, and their heads ducked down. They looked at each other.

"W-what?" Roger stared at her as if he did not understand.

She wanted to tear his heart out. She wanted to chop it into pieces and eat it raw. She wanted to scratch his handsome face until it bled, like her heart.

"Who is she!"

She was on her feet, screaming the words so loudly that the blood rushed to her head, and she was dizzy. She was also murderous. The dogs skittered over each other in their efforts to be the first under the bed.

Roger half laughed. I will kill him, she thought. She took a step toward him, but his next words stopped her in her tracks.

"That handkerchief is Philippe's."

It was as if she were an inflated leather ball, filled with fire, and someone had just stuck a knife in her and all the fire fell out, leaving her empty. She could only stare at him.

"I thought—" But she could not finish.

He laughed out loud then, throwing back his head, looking like a handsome god. The sick, white color of a moment ago was gone.

"You thought I had a lover," he finished for her. "Who? A dancer from the opera or a fat little serving maid? Thérèse perhaps?"

He crossed the distance between them and pulled her into his arms. She felt like a rag doll, all her stuffing gone. That instant from fury to relief had been too sudden.

"There is no woman in my life who means anything to me but you," he said into her hair.

She burst into tears and pushed him away. "I thought you were unfaithful! I thought you had someone else! I wanted to kill her! And you!"

"Barbara," he said, laughing at her tenderly. She held her hand up.

"No. Listen to me! I am not meek or obedient or good. I am not patient or dutiful. Grandmama tried to make me so— truly she did—but it was no use. She said I would just have to muddle through life as I was: feckless, impatient. You are right to want me gone out of your life. I would not blame you if you sent me away. I am not always a good person, Roger." She wiped her face with fierce swipes, but the tears continued to pour down.

He pulled her to him. "Barbara," he said tenderly, holding her close, stroking her hair. "My dear, dear child. I adore you."

She began to cry harder than ever. He tried to choke back his laughter. He felt so tender toward her that he laughed to cover deeper emotion—at her love, her innocence, and at his reprieve. The relief was so intense he covered her face with kisses, her jealousy dear and sweet to him. His dearest child crying for the moon. I am her moon, he thought. He closed his eyes in bittersweet pain.

"I love you," she said. "I have always loved you. I know I am young and foolish, but I would be anything you say, do anything you wanted me to. You are everything to me, Roger."

He stepped back from her, tenderness gone now. In its place was guilt. Heavy. Interminable.

"Do not say that," he told her, his face hard and cold. "Never say that to me again. I am not worth it. Dear God, Barbara, no one is."

She tried to hit him. His words made her crazy. She had offered him everything . . . and he had refused it. He managed to catch her arm.

"I hate you!" she screamed, struggling, trying to claw his eyes. "I hate you!"

She was like a madwoman. He managed to pin her arms back. She tried to kick him, to bite him. He grabbed her and held her. He was panting. He managed to wrestle her toward the bed, she shouting and kicking the whole way. He picked her up and threw her on the bed, falling with her. The force of it knocked her breath away. The two of them lay there breathing heavily.

She lay still, deflated, too exhausted by her emotions to move. He sat up, letting go of her gingerly, as if he expected her to strike him at any minute. He stared at her as if she were an escapee from Bedlam, a madwoman who ought to be in chains.

She giggled. The expression on his face when she had tried to hit him . . . She laughed out loud.

"Are you insane?" he said.

She bellowed with laughter. "Yes! Yes! Yes!"

Laughter was better than tears.

"Y-your f-f-face," she tried to tell him.

He threw back his head and laughed, too, laughing until he hurt. Finally, they lay side by side, every now and again laughing; but the storm was past. Roger wiped his eyes. It had been a close call, and not even Philippe amused him this much. But none of it could last. Choices were being forced upon him. Not yet, he thought. Let me savor it, just a little longer.

Barbara lay relaxed, the tension, the tears drained from her. It was a wonderful release, her bad temper. A wonderful release.

"Why did you try to hit me?" he asked her. "Was it because it was Philippe's handkerchief? I know you do not like him."

"He does not like me."

Roger was silent.

They would never agree on this point, thought Barbara, and he can have his friend. I tried to hit you, my dear, stupid husband because you told me not to love you. And I do. I always will.

"I am supposed to go to the opera this evening," Roger said, staring up at the bed canopy.

"Tell me again." Barbara's voice was low, throaty, seductive.

He half sat up, leaning on his elbow to stare at her. She stared back at him, her lips parted.

"Tell me again."

He touched her face. "There is no other woman but you."

She opened her arms. "I want a child. Give me a child, my darling, darling Roger. And then you may go to the opera . . . if you have the strength."

She kept busy. She readied her household for Passion Week and Easter. There must be plenty of bacon to eat on Good Friday and Easter Sunday, as well as the traditional Good Friday hot-cross buns. Eggs must be boiled and dyed different colors with herbal juices and then painted with gold leaf. Hyacinthe was excited about the eggs, and she gave him the job of seeing that they were decorated and displayed in a serving dish in one of the salons. She ordered mutton, ale, fish and loaves to give to a certain number of beggars (she and LeBlanc decided on one hundred) whose feet she and her household would wash on Maundy Thursday, the Thursday before Good Friday. Thérèse told her that the Parisians dressed in their best clothes on Maundy Thursday and went from church to church saying prayers in each and giving beggars alms.

She and Roger and Philippe and Marie-Victorie and the Comte de Toulouse rode in an open carriage to the chapel in the Bois de Bologne to hear Passion Week psalms sung. Marie-Victorie had said they were lovely, uplifting, and that everybody in Paris came. And she was right. Everyone was there: carriages jostling one another as coachmen tried to squeeze in; people in and out of them, strolling among the trees in their new Easter gowns and coats; the women with tiny, dainty parasols and pastel gowns. Barbara felt like a crow in her gown of black. But it was good to be out. She said a silent prayer for her brothers and sisters. She cried a little when the psalms were sung, but no one seemed to mind. Roger put his arm around her; Philippe patted her hand. She and Philippe managed a truce of sorts. For Roger's sake. They looked into each other's eyes and knew what the other thought, but said nothing. She could live with Philippe, as long as she had Roger. And perhaps his child. She prayed with all her might that a child was growing within her at last.

She saw Thérèse and White strolling together, hand in hand like two lovers, with Montrose trailing some distance behind. She pointed them out to Roger.

"Why will you not let me come to your rooms?" White asked Thérèse, his plain face strained, whispering so that the crowds around them would not hear him. They saw the Devanes with friends in an open carriage and smiled and bowed. Thérèse snuggled against his good arm, smiling at him, her dark eyes glinting.

"Caesar," she teased. "For everything there is a time, and it is not our time."

"I-I think I am in love with you."

She looked away. Sunlight glinted in her dark curls. White was silent, afraid he had gone too far, afraid of frightening her away.

Barbara ordered Easter flowers sent to Lord Stair's mansion. A vicar was attached to his permanent staff, and Easter services for the English in Paris would be held in the chapel near the mansion. And she ordered a Pascal taper, a huge, white candle made of finest wax, to light for the vigil of Christ's death and coming to life again. It would burn on the gospel side of the altar from the Saturday before Easter until some forty days later on Ascension Day.

She sat on a bench in the garden Easter Sunday afternoon. The lilac trees, the tulip trees were in full flower. The chestnuts and limes showed tender, green leaves. Pinks, daffodils, roses, sweet Williams and pansies bloomed. Christ our Passover is sacrificed for us, thought Barbara, repeating the Easter service in her mind, therefore let us keep the feast, not with old leaven, neither with the leaven of malice and wickedness, but with the unleavened bread of sincerity and truth. At Tamworth there would have been many Easter festivities, forfeits, rolling down Tamworth Hill, games of handball, foot races in which the winners were given tansy cakes, made with the tansy herb, which cleaned the humors left in the stomach and guts from eating fish for Lent. How was Grandmama this Easter? Was Tony with her still? Did she

miss her grandchildren? Did she miss Barbara? Barbara wiped
tears from her face. Would there ever be a time when thinking of them did not bring pain? Glory be to the Father, and
to the Son and to the Holy Ghost. As it was in the beginning,
is now, and ever shall be, world without end. Amen.

Thérèse stood in her thin nightgown and gazed out her open
window at the rooftops of Paris. The night breeze was pleasantly cool. She smelled the Easter lilac, now fading, its first
riotous bloom going. LeBlanc would not visit her tonight. She
was free. He was tired from Lady Devane's Easter activities,
and had one of his stomach humors and was suffering in his
own room. She had seen that he wanted her to come to him,
to hold his hand, to fuss over him, but she ignored his sulks.
A man was a man was a man. Nothing more. Nothing less.
She laughed at herself, sounding the experienced woman when
LaBlanc was only the second man she had ever had. But he
was the same as her young prince, minus the youth and slim
stomach and her adoration. Full of himself. Of his problems.
He was afraid of displeasing Lady Devane, who was too
demanding. He was afraid he would lose his position to the
younger, abler butler of the wine cellar, whom Lady Devane
liked. He was afraid he was going to die of stomach pains.

At night, after he was through, she lay like a dead woman
under him, but he never seemed to notice. He settled himself
and talked of his troubles, like anyone. He was becoming fond
of her. She could see it. He worried about her bleeding and
wanted her to go to another physician. He scolded her for
going up and down so many stairs. It could not be good for
her female parts, he said. He talked, and she listened, telling
him nothing of herself. It was hers to keep, hers to give as she
wished, and she wished to give nothing to LeBlanc.

And yet, his bedding her had given her a kind of security.
The footmen were not so free with their compliments. The
chambermaids might eye her with disdain, but there was an
amount of envy mixed in. No one bothered her. She was
treated with a certain amount of respect.

She thought of Caesar and his nervous, half-declaration of
love. Why could she not love him? He was a nice man, a good
man. He read his poems to her, trembling like a boy at her
praise. And yet when she had allowed him to kiss her, she felt

nothing. Just as she felt nothing with LeBlanc. And she could not give herself. Not to nothing. Not again. Would there ever be anyone who stirred her heart as the young prince had? Whom she could love the way madame loved her husband? I would like to feel again, she thought. I would like to love someone, something.

She rubbed her arms against the chill of the breeze. Hyacinthe was snoring. She needed to turn him over on his back. Dear little boy. She loved him. Already, he was acquiring a smattering of English, and he knew the first answers in the catechism. Someday, she thought, leaning out and looking at the dark rooftops, darker shadows in the night, I shall save up enough money and open my own shop. I shall live by myself with Hyacinthe and a cat or two. Madame shall be my most honored patron. My dresses will become famous. I will have several girls working under me. And no one shall have me whom I do not want to have me. I shall be free, free as a bird. She thought comtemptuously of LeBlanc, his boasting, his temper. Already she was stronger than he. He needed her soft body, her fingers around his manhood so that he could spend himself and die like a beached fish, needed her soft arms around him as he whispered his fears. And she had no such need of him. But she was not free of him either. He was like a hair shirt she wore, reminding her of her sin. Her punishment. Her hell. But at least hell grunted and groaned and took only five or ten minutes. The Blessed Mother was kind. Most nights of the week.

It was May. Paris in May. The chestnut trees were full and green, the limes and oaks. The baskets of the flower sellers overflowed with daisies, lilies, peonies, periwinkles, lavender, mint, lads love. The Seine sparkled in the warm sun, as boats bobbed on its shining surface, its banks crowded with fishermen, beggars and naked, laughing children. The breezes were as soft, as warm, as a woman's hand. The first bridge over the Seine, the Pont Neuf, was crowded with its mélange of vagabonds, street musicians, dentists and quack doctors, who stood on wooden boxes or rackety wagons and called out their skills to the passing crowd of duchesses, merchants, pickpockets, princes. Everyone who could be outside was. It was May.

The talk was all of John Law's newly created national bank—a miracle of instant credit which was going to extinguish France's crushing national debt. Everyone was rushing to invest in it, wishing they had been as wise as the Englishman, Lord Devane, who was said to hold many shares. Law's bank was a wonder of financial genius, everyone exclaimed. He had a twenty-five-year monopoly; authorized capital was fixed by edict and could not be increased without government sanction. The bank issued its own notes, and these notes had to be converted into cash on sight at the bank. Its stock was offered for public subscription, and the sums in payment for bank stock had to be in bank notes. It was under legal obligation to buy all the Louis XIV paper (notes the late king had issued to cover his wars, now worth little of their original value) at eighty percent discount, payment to be made—once more—in the bank's own notes.

"Debt has disappeared by magic!" everyone cried, not realizing that paper was eliminating debts contracted in gold. Everyone was ecstatic, except other financiers. Prices were already falling; trade was increasing; money was cheap.

Geraniums were blooming in the huge bronze vases on the terrace. Barbara sat at one of the tiny wrought-iron tables, painted deep green, in a matching wrought-iron chair. She and Roger were having company. Part of it was to celebrate Law's bank, part of it was to celebrate May. John Law, Marie-Victorie, the Comte de Toulouse, Philippe de Soissons, Montrose, White, Thérèse and Hyacinthe strolled about, eating her grandmother's famed lemon tarts and drinking tea or fruit cordials or rose brandies. She had stayed busy. She had resumed her Italian lessons and asked White to begin teaching her Greek, which pleased him very much (or was it being close to Thérèse which pleased him?). Her portrait was nearly finished, and she had ordered a duplicate painting to be sent to her grandmother. There were no paintings of her at Tamworth, as there had been no paintings of her brothers and sisters. She wanted her grandmama to have her there, in spirit, if not in flesh. She wrote regularly to her grandmother and to Tony and to little Mary. It was now two months since the news of the deaths. She still wore black. She still avoided evening balls and receptions. But she visited, and played cards with Richelieu, and she and Roger held quiet dinners. She was

working on a floor plan for Devane House, based in part on
La Malcontenta. White helped her. He found the original
plans and corrected her sketches. She felt full of purpose,
almost content when she worked on it. It was a combination
of Palladio and Tamworth and Saylor House. It was good.
Even White said so. The pain was better. Her brothers and
sisters were often in her thoughts, but not always with tears.
There was no child. That was a new grief in her life. Roger
was attentive and adoring, but something was happening. She
had changed. She wanted more from him. He was always
buying her presents, extravagant things, diamonds, a new
coach, Richelieu's horse. (Richelieu had had to sell; he was so
in debt. It had taken the zest out of their gambling for a
while, until Richelieu suggested they gamble for Roger's
nightcap. She had loved that.) But she wanted more than
trinkets and Roger's occasional regard. She felt so alone. She
read her Bible often, trying to be patient, to be long-suffer-
ing. Charity (which her grandmother said meant love) suffereth long, and is kind. Charity envieth not; charity vaunteth
not itself, is not puffed up. Doth not behave itself unseemly,
seeketh not her own, is not easily provoked, thinketh no evil.

From her chair, she watched Hyacinthe throw sticks for the
dogs. (Bad Harry. He still growled at Philippe every time he
saw him, and Barbara could never find it in her heart to discipline him.) Thérèse and White stood on the terrace steps
watching also.

"Something has to change," White was saying. "I cannot
stand this much longer. I want you, Thérèse. I love you."

Thérèse did not answer. She never answered. White turned
away and walked up the steps. Even in his own misery, he
noticed that Lady Devane seemed forlorn today, for all the
company about her house. She had changed since the deaths
of her brothers and sisters. She was quieter, more mature. And
Lord Devane had not changed with her, White thought with
sudden insight, looking toward Roger and the Prince de Soissons, who were strolling across the gravel path toward the
terrace steps. As usual, they were talking animatedly, and
Roger must have said something amusing because the prince
threw back his head and laughed. And he put his hand on
Roger's shoulder. Just for a moment. For some reason, the

gesture bothered White. He stared at them and then at Lady Devane. She was watching them also.

Philippe's gesture imprinted itself on her mind, repeating itself over and over in a sudden, stopped moment of time. She felt faint and did not know why. She stood up to call to Roger.

LeBlanc appeared at the terrace doors, the ones that led from the blue-and-gold salon.

"You have a visitor, madame."

She turned. Two young men were framed in the doorway, both dressed in the height of fashion with all its excess: the laces, the red heels, the large buckles on the shoes, the heavy, curling wigs, the patches, the walking canes. One of the young men was unusually handsome, with dark skin and oddly colored violet eyes and a straight nose over a firm, full mouth. He was smiling, and his smile was like Barbara's. The other young man beside him was eclipsed, ugly by comparison, young, thin, with staring dark eyes and thick lips.

"Harry!"

She screamed the words. One of the dogs bounded to her obediently, but she was already running.

Everyone's attention was caught. They watched her fly across the terrace, two dogs yapping at her heels, to throw herself in the arms of the handsome young man, who caught her, laughing, and swung her around and around. She covered his face with kisses. Then she held it in her two hands, and he smiled at her. Like her, when he smiled, he was beautiful.

"Harry," she said. She turned to her guests, who were more or less assembled up and down the terrace steps, their eyes riveted.

"This is my brother," she said to them all. "Henry John Christopher Alderley—Harry!"

On cue, one of the dogs leapt suddenly in the air, almost to her waist, flipped and landed on its feet before her. Everyone applauded.

CHAPTER SEVENTEEN

Arm in arm, Barbara and Harry strolled through the gardens. She had introduced him to everyone, along with his friend, Philip, Lord Wharton, or Wart, as Harry called him. Wart now sat in one of the wrought-iron chairs describing Rome to White and Montrose, who hung on his every word.

Reactions to Harry had been varied. Thérèse stood still, staring at him in a way that made White nervous and then half angry. But Harry was concentrating on a glass of rose brandy and keeping his big-buckled, red-heeled shoes clean, and he did not really notice Thérèse—or at least, White did not see him notice. Roger had been glad to see him, while Philippe said coolly, "Yes, I know of your father." Harry had flushed red and looked irritated. Later Philippe had taken Roger aside and warned him about young Lord Wharton, who openly flirted with Jacobite politics. Both the English and French governments were keeping an eye on him. "Not the best friend for your brother-in-law to have," Philippe said. And Roger had watched Harry stroll off with Barbara with an eye that was now not quite so fond.

"Harry, Harry, Harry," Barbara said, squeezing his arm, "I cannot tell you how I feel." She smiled at him. (Taking stock. He was heavier than he had been when he left Tamworth, but it made him more manly looking, less the boy. He was dressed in the height of fashion, expensively, and she wondered where he got the money—forgetting Roger's generosity.

455

He seemed calmer, less angry inside. Perhaps he was over Jane. He had already had two glasses of rose brandy, but she could not see the old symptoms of quarrelsomeness and melancholy yet. Italy had done something for him. In November, she had said goodbye to a boy, and now she walked with a man.)

The two dogs gamboled and frisked at their feet as they walked down the path to the large landscape pool.

"How are you going to keep us apart?" Harry asked her, indicating one of the dogs. Barbara laughed. "I could change his name to Ralph."

"But would he answer?"

"No. I guess we shall have to call him Harry-dog."

"Flattering. He is Harry-dog. Who am I? Harry-man?"

She leaned down in the path, her skirts in the dirt, and grabbed Harry's front paws.

"Listen to me," she told the dog, shaking a finger at him. "You are Harry-dog. Understand? Harry-dog!" He whined and tried to lick her face. Charlotte nudged Barbara. Barbara scratched both their heads while Harry watched her, taking stock, as she had done just a few moments before.

Finally, she stood up and linked her arm in his and they continued their walk. At the pool, she sat on its edge, tearing apart a leaf and tossing bits of it into the water.

"You are thin, Bab," Harry said.

She tossed her head. "I know."

He sat down beside her and took her face in one hand. "It was terrible news, was it not? Out of the blue like that. I got drunk. And I stayed drunk for two days."

A solitary tear plopped onto the bodice of her gown. Gently Harry traced its path on her cheek with one finger. He quoted softly:

> "Let me pour forth
> My tears before thy face, whil'st I stay here,
> For thy face coins them, and thy stamp they bear,
> And by this Mintage they are something worth,
> For thus they be
> Pregnant of thee . . ."

"Why Harry," she said, surprised. "I did not know you liked poetry."

"It was useful in Italy. Lady Rising liked poetry. Poetry . . . and other things."

She recognized this note in his voice—that old ironic melancholy of his, let loose by drinking. She touched his face briefly, her touch as light as a butterfly's wings. She knew him; he had done things in Italy he was ashamed of. He was still torn between his boyish ideals and the reality of growing up. Poor Harry.

The afternoon sun glinted softly in the depths of the pool.

"Tell me about you," he said. "About your marriage. Are you happy?"

"Oh, yes. Roger is good and kind and generous. I am so happy." She did not look at him.

He cocked his head to one side. "Barbara . . ."

She tossed her head again. He waited, knowing her. She gestured impatiently as the words spilled from her. "There are no children yet . . . and he is so busy . . . and sometimes I feel so alone . . . and oh, Harry, I love him so!" She threw herself into his arms. They almost fell backward into the pool. Harry stroked her hair. She was crying. The old Barbara never cried this easily. What had softened her? The deaths? Or time? Or love?

He comforted her. "What is it, Bab? Tell me. Why are you crying?"

She sighed and wiped her eyes. It was good to have Harry here. Shades of late nights at Tamworth, when she had crept into his room, or he into hers to talk. When there was always someone to make things better, to bandage her wounds, to send her smiling on her way. When she had not had to worry about her life, but lived day to day, happily, like her grandmother's latest cat.

"I do not know how to explain. I-I just feel alone. Roger is so involved with—with all his projects. He is always gone."

"Does he neglect you?"

"N-no. But sometimes I feel as if I must make an appointment to see him, to be with him. I am in mourning, of course, so I do not go out as I used to. It is probably my imagination. The—the deaths and all. But I want so much, Harry. So much. And Roger does not . . ." She trailed off, not knowing what she wished to say.

"He is a man, Bab. Men and women have different lives, different needs."

"I understand that. But sometimes two people—together—build something. Between themselves."

"You are too impatient. What you want comes with time—"

"And how do you know! When did you become so knowledgeable in things between men and women!"

He grinned at her. "In Italy, I learned a lot about things between men and women!"

"Bah! I am not talking about that! I want a husband who shares my life with me, who shares his life, who talks to me, who—"

"Only lovers do that together."

"Grandmama and Grandfather had it! And you and Jane! And—"

"Jane was a passing thing. A first love. Nothing more. What a romantic fool you are. And what our grandparents had happens to few people, Bab. At least, few people who are married to each other."

She said what was in her deepest heart. "I thought, for a while, Harry, that he had a mistress. But then I decided it was my grief and my jealousy. Now I am not so sure. I think there are other women in his life. Meaningless, perhaps, but there. And I hate it! I hate it!"

"A wife and a mistress are different things. Roger is years older than you, set in his ways. You cannot expect him to give up everything for love of you."

"Why not, Harry! Oh, why not?"

He laughed at her. "What a baby you are."

She did not reply. He put his arm around her. They sat together in the twilight. The sun still sparkled through the trees, but the sparkle was softened by evening. Birds were singing, and the night insects had begun that first raspy practice before their symphony began.

"You have not asked me about Italy," he prodded, trying to steer her mind in another direction. Dutifully, she asked. He described it, the colors of the sky and mountains, the rivers. The cities of Rome and Venice and Milan, their statues, their churches, their society. Carnival. She listened to him, thinking, Who is he? He has experienced things I have not, and now I do not know who he is. But perhaps it was only the twilight, which could bring a wistful mood, and her own melancholy. Part of her grief, Roger had assured her, when she tried to talk to him of these strange, sad feelings she experienced.

Harry told her about Wart, about what a good friend he had become, how he lent him money and had been his second in a duel.

"You have already fought a duel!"

"Yes." Harry's face was proud.

Wharton was seventeen, extremely rich, and had married against his parents' wishes. So they sent him abroad. He and Harry had met in Rome and liked each other immediately, Harry being attracted to Wart's money and background and good manners, and Wart being attracted to Harry's success with women and hot temper. Wart was shy and admired what he considered Harry's boldness. They had become boon companions. And when Roger had written for Harry to come, Wart had come along. He would stay in lodgings his parents' agent had already arranged for him.

"Roger asked you to come? For my sake?" She felt better. Roger cared for her more than she allowed. If only she could learn to be satisfied with what she had.

Servants were lighting lanterns that were strung in the trees.

"Who is this Soissons?" Harry asked her as they strolled back toward the house.

She could not see his face in the dark, but she could hear the dislike in his voice. Already. Sometimes she and Harry were very much alike.

"Why do you ask?"

"I did not like him."

"Do not let Roger hear you say so! Phillipe is his dearest friend."

"Well, then, let me say I do not approve of your husband's friends."

"Harry, do not be difficult. You are going to be staying with us, and it would be awkward if you quarreled with the prince."

"Well, you have Roger tell the prince that he had better watch what he says to me. I take nothing from anyone anymore, Bab."

She felt, rather than saw, the movement of his hand to his sword hilt.

She was silent. Italy had changed him. The softness of boyhood was gone and in its place was a man. And not all parts of the man were admirable.

The next morning, he strolled, whistling softly, into Barbara's apartments. The antechamber was empty, and the door to the bedchamber was open. Hands in his pockets, he walked in, and the whistle died in his throat. Appreciatively, he stared at the shape of a woman's posterior, as she, on her hands and knees at the bottom of the foot of the bed, slapped a slipper against the floor and exclaimed,

"Harry! Come out at once! Now! You stupid dog!"

"I protest at being called a stupid dog."

Thérèse turned around in surprise and then, when she saw who it was, sat back on her hands. They stared at each other . . . the way they had stared at each other yesterday the first time their eyes had met, and held.

Holy Mary, Mother of God, thought Thérèse, her heart pounding in her ears from the effect his eyes had on her, he is the most beautiful man I have ever seen. Not beautiful in the thin, angelic way of Lord Devane, but beautiful in a different, lustier way. His lips were firm and full, his cheeks smooth and flush with youth, his eyes the shade of the blossoms of a wood violet, his lashes long, his nose straight and full. He grinned at her, a grin that acknowledged her femaleness, and its effect shocked her. For the first time in a long time she felt alive, well and full of her old youth and vigor.

He strolled forward, very much at his ease, very much aware of her embarrassment, and held out his hands. She allowed him to pull her up. For a second their faces were close enough to kiss.

"Tell me who you are again," he said. "I saw you yesterday, and last night all I could think of was your face."

She became prim and proper. She stepped back, shook out her white apron, settled her little lace cap, the efficient lady's maid. "Thérèse Fuseau," she said shortly. "Lady's maid to your sister."

"And I am Harry Alderley."

"I know." His silence made her nervous. "I was calling the dog. He got into madame's box of bonbons, and now he will not come out from under the bed."

"'Madame'? You call my sister 'madame'? I love it. Little Bab Alderley, her hair knotted, her dress torn, is now 'madame.' And the dog's name is Harry?"

"Madame named them for you and for your sister, Charlotte."

He stepped closer to her. "But how will I know which of us you are calling for?" His tone was teasing, provocative.

"You will be Monsieur Alderley, and he will be Harry. It is simple, no?" She knew how to put fresh young men in their place.

He stepped closer still. She did not back away. She came to his chin.

"And what if—for some absurd reason—you should begin to call me Harry? Then where would we be, Thérèse?"

"We can only trust that will not happen, monsieur." Adroitly, she stepped around him, leaving the room with great dignity, which she spoiled by glancing back at him. He was watching. He grinned. She hurried away.

Richelieu leaned down, his arms on each side of the armchair, trapping Louise-Anne.

"Are you certain?" His eyes gleamed at her, frightening her. "Are you absolutely certain?"

"I saw them," she stammered. "At de Berry's. I stumbled into the wrong room. They were making love. They are lovers, Armand."

Richelieu turned away from her and stared at the linnet in its cage. It preened itself, ruffling out its feathers, and began to sing. Its song filled the cell, clear, sharp, high, almost hurting the ears.

"What are you going to do?" Her voice was as shrill, as sharp, as the bird's song.

"I am going to compose a poem."

"Will it hurt Barbara?"

"Yes. Yes, it will."

"Good. Let me stay. Let me—"

"Go away, Louise-Anne. I cannot work with you distracting me." He looked up and saw her face. In an instant, he had her arm and was twisting it. She cried out.

"You will leave this to me. Do you understand?" His face was inches from hers. His eyes glittered. She was afraid. She nodded her head.

"Go home," he said, his voice now caressing. Still holding her arm, he kissed her lips. She shivered.

"Let me stay."

"No."

She walked to the cell door, lingering a moment, but he was hunting for a pen and paper, and she might never have existed. She slipped through the cell door like a shadow.

"A rhyme," Richelieu said to himself. "Just an ugly little rhyme." He hummed, thinking of its effect. Lampoons, scurrilous poems and obscene rhymes were printed about everyone in society. They were printed on presses secretly at night and by morning hundreds could be found pasted to public statues, walls, buildings, in bedchambers, drawing rooms and council cabinets. The great Louis XIV had tried unsuccessfully to have them stopped. His court was a favorite topic. Suspected writers were imprisoned, presses were destroyed; but the rhymes continued. Their source was inexhaustible—gutter poets, gutter noblemen. There was a new writer of particular talent; his verses stung. His name was Arouet, and he was the son of a notary. He had been imprisoned, but nothing stopped him. The Bourbons suspected him of composing the latest rhyme about Louise-Anne, but Richelieu felt the verses were too mild to have been written by Arouet, who was said to be thinking of changing his name to Voltaire. The Arouet rhyme about Louise-Anne went:

> If frisky and young Charolais,
> For Richelieu love doth display,
> Why, 'tis bred in the bone;
> But what trouble for one,
> When her mother had more
> At her age than a score!

Everyone had loved it, for her mother, a princesse of France, was notorious for her love affairs, as Louise-Anne was becoming.

Richelieu sharpened the point of a quill pen, quoting softly, to himself, " 'A virtuous woman is a crown to her husband: but she that maketh ashamed is a rottenness in his bones.' I covet thy crown, Roger." He bent over a piece of paper and began to write.

Harry talked her into accompanying him to Marie-Victorie's afternoon reception. It was the first time she had gone out, other than to visit quietly with friends, or to shop, or to stroll in the Tuileries with Marie-Victorie and Thérèse and White. She was excited. Harry was good for her. And Thérèse had seen a charming gray hat with black ribbons and roses that were a shade of pink that was almost gray. She wore it.

She and Harry made a striking picture as they walked together in Marie-Victorie's salon. Across the room, Louise-Anne, standing with St. Michel, watched Harry. She watched when he threw back a glass of brandy as if it were nothing and immediately called for another. She watched the way his eyes swept the room, lingering on the prettier women. She was ready when his eyes found her. She pouted and bit one full, red bottom lip. His eyes widened with interest. He dragged Barbara over.

Reluctantly, Barbara introduced her brother to Louise-Anne and to St. Michel, wondering why Louise-Anne smiled at her in such an odd way. Why did St. Michel seem to be gloating? Harry noticed nothing. His eyes were full of Louise-Anne. He had meant what he said about Jane, Barbara thought. He was over her. Was love so easily dismissed? She thought of Jane's face that time in the apple orchard. Was she over Harry? And what did it all matter? She left them and went outside to stand on the terrace, alone. For the first time in her life, she felt bitter. She could feel the doubts, the hurts, hardening her heart. If only she could have a child. In her search for solace, she kept returning to one chapter in Corinthians—St. Paul's definition of love, which bore all things, believed all things, hoped all things, endured all things. She wanted to believe if she were good enough, if she were patient enough, Roger would love her. As she wanted to be loved. It seemed that once he had almost loved her. She had thought he did. She had no idea what had happened. Patience did not come easily to her, and she could feel all the stirrings of her nature fermenting. A child. She had to have a child.

* * *

She and Hyacinthe and the dogs were playing in the gardens. It was a game of hide-and-seek, and the dogs were worthless, for they followed the hider to his hiding place and then yapped shrilly until the seeker found it. But the sun was shining, and Hyacinthe was laughing hysterically as he chased after the dogs, and it made her feel happy inside, like a carefree child again. She hid herself behind one of the tall vases on the terrace and tried to shoo her stupid dogs away. Harry stiffened and growled. She turned to look at what he was growling at. Philippe stood at one of the salon windows staring at her, the dislike on his face so plain it startled her. For a moment, both of them stared at each other. Mischievously, Barbara stuck out her tongue at him. Philippe stepped back, out of sight. She covered her face with her hands and giggled. Poor Roger, Barbara mimicked what she thought Philippe must be thinking. Married to such a child. Why will she not behave, Roger? Why will she not grow up? Bah, bah, bah, thought Barbara. I am grown up.

Hyacinthe came bounding up the steps.

"I found you! I found you!" he screamed.

The dogs barked and leapt up in the air. She grabbed Hyacinthe and turned him up on his heels, while the dogs licked his face. He laughed, the sound so full of joy that it made her laugh. But her happy mood was disturbed; Philippe had destroyed it. He dislikes me as much as I dislike him. Why do we pretend? she thought.

She and Roger quarreled later that night.

"I do not like him!" she said, slamming her brush down on her dressing table. The top of her dressing table was cluttered with crystal bottles filled with scent, loose jewels, feathers, patch boxes, rouge and powder jars, ribbons, bits of lace. It was a lavish display that usually gave her pleasure. But not tonight. Nothing gave her pleasure tonight. Roger sat in an armchair. He had been watching her brush her hair. She saw his face in the mirror and ran to him and put her arms around him.

"I am sorry, Roger. I do not know what is the matter with me. I did not mean it."

He pulled her into his lap and his eyes searched her face. "What is it, Bab? Tell me."

"I do not know. I feel so empty. So useless. You are always gone. I want children."

He stroked her hair. "They will come. They will come. You are not over the deaths yet. That is all."

She stifled the sudden, maddening urge she had to slap his hand away and scream. It is marriage, she thought. It is me. It is you. Nothing is turning out the way I expected, and I have not the character to make the best of it. Grandmama would be so ashamed of me. She would be so ashamed.

"We will be going to Hanover in another month," he said, watching her face, guessing more accurately than she knew the moods passing through her. He was becoming too careless. Too many suppers at de Berry's or the regent's. Last week he had been so drunk he had made love with Philippe without their usual mask of a woman with them. It had been a stupid thing to do. He woke the next morning and wondered for a moment if Philippe had deliberately allowed it. Philippe. He wanted too much. As did Barbara. The choices. They were closing in.

"I think it will do us all good to get away from Paris." He pulled her head to his shoulder. "I have not been a good husband, Bab."

The old Barbara would have said yes, you are, you are. But this stranger that now inhabited her skin was silent.

"Be patient with me," he said to her. "I need time. We both need time for everything to be better between us."

She lay in his arms. Just once, she thought, I wish you would say you loved me. Charity . . . love . . . beareth all things; believeth all things; hopeth all things; endureth all things. . . . I would endure anything for those words. I love you, Barbara. Such simple words. Sometimes I think you never will. And it hurts me, Roger. I am afraid. When I was a child, I spake as a child, I understood as a child, I thought as a child: but when I became a man, I put away childish things. I am not a child, Roger. I am a woman. For now we see through a glass, darkly; but then face to face: now I know in part; but then shall I know even as also I am known. . . . Love me, Roger. Please love me.

* * *

In the first early morning light, Thérèse hurried across the gardens and into a side door. She reached down and wiped the dew from her shoes, pulled the mantilla from her head and stuffed it into her apron pocket. Whirling into the kitchen, she gave the orders for madame's luncheon. The cook stared at her, his eyes hostile behind the fat that almost closed them. He knew better than anyone what to cook to tempt Lady Devane's fragile appetite. But this one was under LeBlanc's protection, and no one could say a word to her.

In the hallway of the floor on which the bedchambers were, Thérèse stopped to look at herself in a mirror. Her cheeks were flushed from her running; her hair was curling more than usual from the morning damp, the damp in the church, which had crept in and chilled her to the bone. Her eyes were swollen. She always cried a little when she said the prayers for the baby's soul. Abruptly, she turned. She suddenly felt the presence of someone else, someone watching her.

Lady Devane's brother stood some distance away, his feet bare, his wig off—ah, his hair was dark, thick, like hers. He wore a huge, incredibly colored robe, blue swirling into red swirling into green. She blinked at the sight of it. He stared at her. She grew still. She knew that look. Ah, she knew that look. Holy Mary, Mother of Jesus, how many men had looked at her so? Would he command her now to follow him to his room? Would he trick her into coming there? Or would he force her, now, in the silence, the emptiness of the hall? He was just like the rest. No better. Only handsome, and young with a youth that had charmed her heart. She was a fool. Suddenly she was so disappointed that she drooped, like a flower, and he ran forward to grab her. His mouth, so close to her, was full and red. Once she had allowed herself to think about kissing it. Now it would violate her. Take . . . before she was ready to give.

"Where do you go every morning?" His question was completely unexpected. "I can see you from my windows. I do not sleep well, and every morning I have seen you scurry across the terrace like a thief and disappear behind a garden door. You are gone for a while, and then you reappear. And most mornings, you have been crying, like this morning."

What right had he to pry in her affairs? If he knew the truth he would truly rape her in the hallway like the whore he would consider her to be. His question was a ruse, a preliminary to one thing, and one thing only. But she surprised herself by answering, "I go to chapel. I pray every morning for a loved one." She waited, tense as a cat, for his next move.

"A loved one . . . fortunate loved one, who makes you cry. You are so lovely, Thérèse. Much too lovely to cry. I will not make you cry. When we are together, I will not make you cry. I promise that."

He walked back to his room, and she stared after him, angrier than if he had tried to steal a kiss.

Roger sat in the richness of Philippe's green salon. Everything here pleased the eye: the arrangement of the paintings, the masses of flowers in low vases atop small tables; the upholstery of the chairs, richly green; the matching draperies; the extravagance of gold fringe; the glass clocks; the porcelain figurines; the way in which the sun poured in, like gold spilling from a pot, through the open doors and windows; the fragrance of the gardens' flowers drifting in through the windows, along with a bee or two.

The two of them were near the opened windows, where they could feel the breeze and the sun and smell the gardens. They had spent many afternoons thus, watching spring tint the white winter landscape with soft color, talking of everything—their pasts, their future, Bentwoodes. Today Roger was silent while Philippe talked. Of the margin of success Law's new bank might enjoy; of the tangle France's finances were in; of the profit Roger might make; of the cost to build Devane House; of the plans Lord Burlington's protégé, William Kent, had drawn up; of the scandalous conduct of the Duchesse de Berry. She had strolled through the gardens of her palace of Luxembourg, gardens open to the public. She had dressed herself as a lower-class bourgeois to hear what people said of her, and what she heard so infuriated her that she attacked three men and their wives and had to be dragged off screaming and cursing by her own guards. He talked of anything and everything, anything to fill the silence between them with words, words which allowed other words not to be said.

"She needs a child," Roger said. As easily as that she came into their conversation.

Philippe's knuckles tightened on the curling arm of his chair. There was no need to identify the "she."

"Of course she does." He tried to make his smile genuine. "She should have several children, all of them, we can only hope, as handsome as you or her famous grandfather."

Richard, thought Roger. What would he think of me now? Of this coil I twist myself on? Of the unhappiness I have caused. Would he understand and forgive? Could he? Could any man? Who can understand but two men such as Philippe and myself? Who are we? Who am I?

"She is unhappy, Philippe. More than I have ever seen her. I think it is mostly the deaths, but some of it is my fault also. And I find it hard to forgive myself. She is a child, and for her, the world revolves around me."

As for us all, Philippe thought bitterly, but he said, "What do you want me to do?"

Roger smiled at him, his wistful, charming smile. "How well you know me. Nothing. Everything. We talked of meeting this summer in Hanover and then traveling together to Italy. Could you understand and forgive if I wanted to be with Barbara, alone? Just for a few months. I feel that I must give her that time; that I must devote myself to her. And perhaps, out of it will come a child, and she will not need me so completely then."

Philippe's knuckles were white against the arm of the chair. As white as his face. How ironic, he thought, that he should be the stronger of us. That I should need him more than he needs me. And all because of a skinny, red-haired girl who is young enough to be his daughter. He loves her. I think he loves her. And what I shall do when he learns it himself, I do not know. Ah, pride is bitter. It tastes like copper in my mouth. I want to kill him I love him so. And yet if I lose him I shall die, wither in the sun of my life. And so I will be silent. I will swallow my pride. I will do whatever he asks and pray that it is enough. Pray that she does not become stronger with the years, taking away all his love for me with her youth and beauty and devotion and leaving me nothing. Ah, Barbara Devane, I wish you had strangled at birth. I hurt more than the time I caught the splinters of a cannonball in my leg. More than the time I lay bleeding with my face slashed open. I hurt. I hurt.

"Take her to Hanover. To Italy. I will stay away. Do what you must, and I will be here for you, my dear friend. I cannot fight you, Roger, or fight what I feel for you."

Roger closed his eyes at all he heard in Philippe's voice.

"She suspects something," he said. Philippe saw the sorrow in his face.

"Then we will be more discreet," Philippe said calmly, although inside, his heart was like a stone, even colder. I will show you no mercy, Barbara Devane, he thought. No mercy at all.

White walked through the early morning loveliness of the gardens attached to the house. It was as if, during the night, someone had come and frosted the trees, the shrubs, the flowers, with diamonds, for that was what the morning dew resembled, thousands and thousands of diamond droplets. But White's thoughts were not on the dew or the morning beauty of the gardens. His thoughts were on a piece of paper he had found yesterday afternoon nailed to the stable doors. On the ugly, clumsy verse printed upon it:

> Devane, Soissons, Devane—'tis all in vain,
> Old and young, young and old,
> Friends forever, tied with ropes that hold.
> Devane, Devane—when all is done and said,
> Soissons comes between—in life, in love, in bed.

Into his mind, like a falling star, had flashed that moment two weeks ago when he had stood on the terrace with Lady Devane and seen the prince touch Lord Devane on the shoulder and felt the earth shake. To his poet's eyes, the gesture had been larger than life, full of something he did not understand. He had put it away as his overwrought imagination; a poet's watchfulness, always observing other people, their reactions, their emotions. But it had stayed with him, lying coiled like a sleeping serpent at the back of his mind, and even as he finished reading the last clumsily composed line it reared up and struck.

He had crumpled the paper, only to see another pasted farther down and another and another. They were in the garden, on the front steps, in the stable yard. Anywhere and everywhere Lord Devane—or Lady Devane—might find them. He hunted them down, each and every one, and burned them, his own sweat dripping into the flames. If she should see . . . if she should see, would she even understand? He felt as if he had been punched in the stomach. He admired and respected Roger, who was everything he was not. Handsome. Charming. Noble. Generous. This was something he could not even think about; to do so made him want to cry, to vomit. His hero with an Achilles' heel so monstrous that he could not bear it. His hero, a hero no more. All his verses, the epic poem he had been working on for so long, were nothing if it were true. They were a paean to something false, a man who was not a man. A man who loved another man. He could not think of it without shuddering.

Thérèse was leaning out an upstairs window, shaking out a rug. She waved to him, and after a moment, he waved back. Thérèse. He had seen her strolling in the gardens in the late evening twice with Harry Alderley. Laughing and talking together, looking at each other like two people who— He would not finish the thought. It hurt him. She had never let him do more than kiss her once or twice. And now she flirted, as he had wanted her to flirt with him, flirted with a spoiled young nobleman. It was not fair. Nothing was fair. What was happening? He felt as if his whole world were crumbling.

Hours later, across town, Harry Alderley watched Louise-Anne de Charolais being undressed by her maid. He sipped his glass of wine, grinning at her. Seductively, she smiled at him, now in her hoop and petticoat, her breasts pushed up, white, at the top of her corset. He reached across the dressing table to pour himself more wine, and in doing so the name on a crumpled piece of paper caught his eye. Devane, Soissons, Devane. . . . He put down the wineglass and smoothed the paper, his face changing as he read. Louise-Anne, in her chemise and stockings, a silky robe over her shoulders, motioned for her maid to leave.

"What is this?" he asked her, a vein throbbing in his forehead. He shook the paper.

She had been walking toward him, ready for his embrace. She shrugged. "The latest street verses." She looked into his eyes and then away, quickly.

"The latest street verses," he said slowly. "About my sister and the Prince de Soissons!" He kicked the fragile chair he had been sitting in and it skittered across the room. "It is a lie!" he shouted. "Who would write such filth!"

"It is not about your sister," Louise-Anne said, watching him. "It is about Roger—and his lover."

He stared at her. "Roger and his—"

In two strides he was beside her, one hand roughly on her arm. There was nothing of the lover on his face now. He shook her.

"Explain yourself!"

She tried to pull her arm away. "My uncle is Roger's lover. It is so simple, Harry. Are you as naive as your sister? Do you not know that men may be lovers? Could you have spent all that time in Italy and never have seen them? It is called the Italian vice." She had put her hand on the front of his shirt as she spoke, her own words beginning to excite her, as did his violence. Now she stared at him, her mouth slightly slack, moist, ready. He dropped her arm as if it were a snake and backed away from her.

"I do not believe you—"

She laughed at him. He smashed his fist down on her dressing table. Fragile jars and boxes went flying. She stopped laughing.

"Did you write this filth? Did you?"

She shook her head.

"Who did?"

"I do not know," she whispered. The expression on his face frightened her. He picked up the wine bottle and sent it crashing into the wall. She flinched at the sound. Wine dripped to the floor like blood.

"Go away," she told him, but he was already out the door.

On the street behind her mansion, it took him several minutes to calm down enough to orient himself. He began to walk in the direction of his sister's house, not yet noticing the pieces of paper—old and new—pasted to the buildings he passed. Finally, he looked at them.

"Devane, Soissons, Devane . . ." he read. He ripped the paper from the wall and tore it to shreds. He walked farther down, carefully reading the notices now. Some of them he tore from the wall, crumpling them into balls and throwing them into the mud of the street. By the time he had walked six blocks, sweat was gleaming on his brow. They were everywhere. It would be mere chance if Barbara missed seeing them.

"Barbara," he whispered, the veins standing out in his forehead. "Barbara."

"Now let me see," Montrose said, "if I put Madame de Gondrin here, I will have to put the Comte de Toulouse there." Like a child, Montrose sat in the middle of the floor of the adjoining parlor he and White shared, playing with pieces of paper that were his seating arrangements for Lady Devane's birthday dinner party two days away. There could be no ball, no reception, because of her mourning, but Lord Devane had insisted on an opulent, small dinner with a recital afterward. The household had been planning it since the beginning of the month. Montrose was working feverishly; he had managed to secure the talents of Adrienne Le Couvreur, the most famous actress in Paris, who would enact passages from Racine's tragic heroines afterward. There would be violins and bass viols on the terrace, where the guests would dine at a series of small tables. The regent and his wife would be coming, Lord Stair, John Law and his wife, the Prince de Soissons, the Duc and Duchesse de Saint-Simon, Lord Alderley, Lord Wharton, the Duc and Duchesse de Noailles, the Prince and Princesse de Condé and the Prince and Princesse de Bourbon, Madame de Gondrin, the Comte de Toulouse. Small, but select. A proper reflection of his master's influence.

"The regent here, at the table with Lord and Lady Devane and her brother. But who else shall I put with them? The Princesse de Condé or the Duchesse de Saint-Simon? The duchesse, perhaps. She might inspire the regent to behave himself—Caesar, are you listening to me? Where shall I put the duchesse?"

"In a dustbin for all I care." White sat nearby, brooding. It might not be true. It might be some piece of political filth. Something twisted to disfigure a sincere friendship.

"What is wrong with you? You have been like a bear since yesterday. Have you quarreled with Thérèse again? Or has something gone wrong with your poem—"

"There is more to life than poems, Francis."

"How very original. I must write that down somewhere. There is more to life than poems. I sit here struggling with an impossible seating plan, and all you can say is 'There is more to life than poems, Fran—"

Pierre LeBlanc, the majordomo, burst into the room like an explosion. "Quickly," he panted. "Come quickly! They fight! They fight! It is everything terrible!"

"Who? Who?" Montrose, still sitting on the floor, looked and sounded like an owl.

"Lord Alderley! The prince! Lord Devane! He is tearing up the blue-and-gold salon! He is like a man gone mad! Help me!"

The three of them ran from the room, Montrose's pieces of paper scattering like dust.

Harry had not come back intending to fight. He stood in the doorway of the salon, swaying from shock, and watched Philippe put his hand on Roger's shoulder and say, "My dear, they are everywhere. What shall we do?" And something exploded in his mind then, red, orange, ugly. It was true. He burst across the room and threw himself on Roger's back, screaming, "You filthy, prick-licking son of a bitch! You are not fit to touch the hem of my sister's skirts!"

He threw Roger facedown on a table in front of him. Blood spurted, red and dark.

Philippe grabbed Harry, pulling him off, and like a frenzied bull Harry staggered back, sending them both barreling into a china cabinet, plates and vases crashing around them, porcelain victims. Harry and Philippe grappled like two wrestlers, their faces strained, panting.

"Bastard!" Harry screamed. "French fucking bastard!"

Shaking, Roger wiped blood from his mouth. LeBlanc and a footman ran in.

"Stop them!" Roger panted. LeBlanc and the footman seemed unable to move. Harry and Philippe were on the floor, rolling over and over, into tables and chairs. LeBlanc ran out. Picking up a vase, Roger ran forward and smashed it against Harry's head. Harry groaned and lay still atop Philippe. Kicking, Philippe pulled himself away.

"I . . . will . . . kill . . . him," he said in a shaking, breathless voice. "With . . . my . . . own . . . hands . . . I will kill him." Blood was gushing from Philippe's nose, staining his linen shirt, his velvet coat.

"No!"

Roger's voice rang out. He had to get Philippe past that red rage. Men had died for far less than what Harry had just done.

"Think of the scandal! Think of me, if nothing else!" Roger's face was hard, commanding, the way it was when he had led troops. Philippe looked at him, and Roger saw the danger in his face.

"I will not let you do it," Roger said. And he put his hand on his own sword.

Philippe swung back his leg and kicked Harry in the ribs as he lay there. The sound thudded dully. The footman flinched. Harry groaned.

"English dog," Philippe said through clenched teeth. "I will eat your liver for supper—"

Montrose, LeBlanc and White burst into the room. They stood staring, at the white-faced footman, at the overturned tables and chairs, at Roger and Philippe, both wigless, both bleeding, at broken plates and vases and scattered paper, at Harry, lying like a dead man.

"Is he . . . is he—" stammered Montrose.

"No! But I wish he were. Drunken fool! Carry him to his room!"

Roger's voice was like iron, the only normal thing in the room. It snapped people back into themselves. LeBlanc and the footman picked Harry up and carried him away; he was strung between the two of them like a dead deer.

"Your face," Montrose said to Roger. Roger wiped his mouth, which was bleeding. Montrose ran to hand him a handkerchief, his own, starched, white, pristine, unused.

"What happened, sir?" he asked, his eyes wide as he looked around the destroyed room.

Roger and Philippe exchanged one glance, a glance that White, standing quietly by the door, was on the alert for. My God, he thought. It is true. They are lovers. He wanted to weep, like a child who has been told all his fantasies are false.

"He was drunk, and he attacked us without provocation," Philippe said, rage still on his face, in his voice. He dabbed at his bleeding nose.

"Perhaps he read this." White moved from the door to hand Roger a piece of paper. There was silence in the room.

"What? What?" cried Montrose, looking from one to the other, feeling the tension.

Roger flushed, tried to speak, but White had caught him off guard. White turned on his heel and left the room, and Roger gazed after him.

"There has been some ugly gossip, Francis," Roger said, tiredly handing Montrose the paper. "Gossip that is not true, but which Lord Alderley apparently believed. I trust you will see that the servants do not speak of this. It will be all that is needed to fan the fires. And will you see that this house is thoroughly searched? I will not have my wife exposed to this filth."

Dazed, Montrose bowed and left the room. Roger slumped into a chair.

"Dear Christ," he said. "What am I going to do?"

"I am going to kill him," Philippe said. "If he ever dares so much as to look at me the wrong way, I am going to kill him. And nothing you can say will stop me."

Montrose searched for White. Finally he found him in his bedchamber. He was stuffing shirts into a battered valise. A fire burned in his small fireplace, and Montrose could see whole manuscript pages there, untouched except for curling edges.

"Your verses!" he cried, running to the fire and trying to pull them out. "My God, Caesar, what are you doing? It is your poem!" He managed to pull about half the pages out. He stamped on their smoldering brown edges. White continued to stuff shirts into his valise. Then he put in his brushes, his shaving razor, his soap cup.

"Where are you going?" Montrose cried.

"I am leaving."

"But why? Is it something I have done? Is it Thérèse? I thought you knew about LeBlanc. Has Lord Devane insulted you? What! What could it possibly be?"

White stood still, a shirt in his good hand, poised above the valise. "Thérèse and LeBlanc? What about Thérèse and LeBlanc?"

"Good God, I thought—that is—nothing. Idle gossip. You know how people are." Montrose never lied well.

"This seems to be my week for idle gossip. Tell me, Francis."

Montrose looked miserable. "Thérèse is sleeping with LeBlanc. She has been for some time. I did not know whether you knew, whether to tell you, so I said nothing. Do not leave here because of her. She is not worth it. Lord Devane values you. I value you, Caesar. You are my only friend."

"Thérèse is sleeping with LeBlanc," White repeated slowly. He sat down on the bed, as if his legs would no longer hold him. He put his hand to his face to cover his eyes. He made some sound. It might have been a laugh. It was hard to tell. Montrose stared at him, his round, earnest face anxious.

"I ought not to have told you. It was shock—the fight, and everything. I hardly know whether I am coming or going."

"Yes . . . the upheaval downstairs. The quarrel. That paper." White's voice was odd.

"Surely you do not believe those verses? Lady Devane would never have anything of that nature to do with the prince. She loves Lord Devane."

"Lady Devane and the prince . . . is that how you read it?"

"How else?"

What could he say? "How else indeed."

Roger was at Harry's bedside, waiting for him to wake. As Harry shook his head, groaned and tried to sit up, Roger said in that voice that would not be disobeyed, "You are a drunken, dissolute, stupid man. You burst into my home like a common criminal and you insult me and my friend, a prince of France. I ought to have you horse-whipped, Harry!"

Each word was like a blow from a hammer, implacable. Roger sounded like his mother, like his grandmother. Pain radiated throughout his body, from his face, from his ribs, making it difficult to think clearly. Roger's voice, his icy control, his contempt, made Harry unsure of himself. What had seemed so certain seemed now like shifting sand.

"This is Paris," Roger continued, each word spat out through clenched teeth, "and all kind of foul rumors abound. To believe every one of them is the mark of a fool, which I begin to believe you are. You owe me, and you owe the Prince de Soissons, an apology. Only the fact that you are my wife's brother keeps me from throwing you out on the street as you deserve. It was all I could do to keep the prince from challenging you to a duel. Do you know how many men he has killed? You would be one more easy mark on the blade of his sword. You were wrong!

Whatever you thought—and I do not want to know because then I will kill you myself—you were wrong! I am a rich and powerful man, and I have enemies. Who will say and do anything. You add credence to their filthy lies with your actions. You young fool! I expect a note of apology from you to the prince by tomorrow morning. If you do not write it, I will throw you out of my house, sister or not." He stared down at Harry contemptuously. "If your grandfather knew of your conduct today, he would be ashamed."

Harry lay where he was, listening to Roger's retreating footsteps. He felt the way he had felt at Tamworth, when his mother had raked him over the fiery red coals of her anger, and he had been too surprised to think clearly. There was still a spark of defiance, but it was defused by the terrible pain in his ribs, and by Roger's words. Was he wrong? Did Louise-Anne lie, for some reason of her own? He did not know.

"You are sleeping with LeBlanc!" White cried. "And all the while you had me groveling at your skirts for one kiss!"

Backed against the corner, Thérèse was silent, watching his anger, every sense alert to save herself. White grabbed her wrist and pulled her from her corner, making her stumble.

"Why did you do it? Why?" He twisted her wrist, making her cry out with pain. His face was transfigured with the emotion, the anger on it. "I ought to beat you. I ought to make you grovel in the dust like the teasing slut you are!"

"Do it!" Thérèse spat at him. "Do it! Be like LeBlanc and make me do what I have no wish to! You are all alike! All of you! Taking, taking, caring nothing for the feelings I have! I did not want you! Do you hear me, Caesar! I did not want you! And I do not want LeBlanc! But I have no choice! Can you understand that! I have no choice! I am a woman! I have no choice!" She screamed the last words at him.

He dropped her wrist, stunned by her words, by the vicious, cruel anger behind them. "Thérèse. I did not mean to—please do not cry. Please."

She turned away from him, wiping her face with her apron.

"Go away," she whispered.

He touched one of her dark curls gently before he left the room. She sat down in a chair. "Oh, Caesar," she said after him. "I am sorry. So sorry."

* * *

Harry struggled out of bed. His face felt as if it had been used as a bowling pin. There was dried blood crusted on his shirt. It hurt him to move, to breathe. He limped down the hallway to his sister's apartments. In the bedchamber he saw Thérèse sitting in a chair by the window. He limped to her, and when she saw him, she rose with a cry, and in a second had him in the chair, was pouring water from a pitcher, and bathing his face with her apron. He groaned, but sat still under her handling, like a child.

"What happened?" she whispered.

"Oh, Thérèse," he said. He put his arms around her, though it nearly killed him to move them, his head in the skirt of her gown, and held her. She stroked his short, thick, dark hair.

"There," she soothed. "It is all right. I am here. I am here."

The words were the same she used to soothe Hyacinthe when he had a bad dream. Nothing else was said. She bandaged Harry's raw knuckles. She cleaned the dried blood from his face, touching the swelling with gentle fingers. Carefully she eased him out of his coat and shirt and wrapped torn strips of bedsheet around his middle. He gasped and turned white. He was trembling when she finished. Very gently, she touched his lips, his beautiful firm, red lips with her fingertips. He did not try to make anything of it, he simply accepted her gesture. She helped him stand up, and he limped away.

She straightened the room, putting away the bloodstained rags, the creams, the bloody water. There was no need to follow him. She knew where he was, as he knew where she was. It would be so easy. She sighed. Her heart was not healed from the baby. And he was hot-tempered and in debt and would be faithless. Time, she thought, smoothing back the hair at her temples. I have all the time in the world. She felt her heart swell. It was good to be young and alive. She began to sing, her voice as light, as lilting, as a bird's.

CHAPTER EIGHTEEN

The moment she walked in, Barbara felt it: some odd tension that came from the way the footmen stood back in the shadows like small boys caught and punished for something; the way their eyes cut at her and then away. Something has happened. It was her first conscious thought. And with it . . . Roger . . . he is ill. She heard people in the blue-and-gold salon nearby. LeBlanc and the housekeeper and a footman were in the process of trying to mend the damage. A broken chair lay stacked neatly in a corner; most of the pieces of porcelain were off the floor; most of the chairs and tables had been righted, but Roger's papers were still strewn about as if a wind had come in and thrown them everywhere. LeBlanc began to stammer even before she demanded an explanation.

"I am not at liberty to say."

"You are not at liberty to say!" She drew herself up to her full height. "This is my household, Pierre LeBlanc, and you will give me an immediate explanation."

LeBlanc exchanged a glance with the housekeeper. A glance Barbara caught.

"Well?" she snapped.

"There was an . . . ah . . . altercation of sorts, madame."

"An altercation? Do you mean to tell me there was a fight . . . here?"

"Yes, madame."

"Between whom?"

479

"Ah . . . Lord Harry, and Lord Devane and the Prince de Soissons, madame."

Whipping her full skirts over one arm, she ran up the stairs. The doors to Roger's apartments were locked. She hammered on them with her fists. Justin let her in. Lord Devane, he explained, not looking at her, was resting with a poultice on his mouth. She swept past him.

"What is this I hear of a fight between you and Harry?" she began, but was stopped by the sight of his face, sick and white.

"Roger!" she cried, throwing herself on the bed beside him, ignoring Justin. "Tell me what happened. This is all so unbelievable!"

There is a hell, thought Roger, and it is here on earth. Now, in this room; seeing her face; its innocence. That is hell. I do not want to pay for it. Not with her. He touched her cheek.

"Do not worry your head about it," he said, trying to smile. "It will all blow over in a few days."

"A room downstairs is destroyed. Your face is bruised. I hear that you and my brother and Philippe have engaged in some kind of quarrel. And you tell me not to worry! Roger, I want to know! I have a right to know!"

He made a decision, gambling with fate, with his luck, as he always had done.

"Read this." He gave her a small piece of paper, which he had found pinned to his pillow. Justin had no idea how it got there, and Roger had realized the futility of Barbara's not seeing the verses sooner or later. Why now? he had thought, smashing his fist against a wall in a rage of helplessness and fear. It was just as true five years ago. Why now, when there is someone who can be so hurt by it? Dear God, what shall I do?

She scanned it quickly. Devane, Soissons, Devane—'tis all in vain . . . she finished, "in life, in love, in bed." Her face changed. Dear Christ, it is coming, thought Roger.

"I . . . do not understand," she said slowly, as slowly she began to. "Who would write this?"

Roger shrugged, his face showing nothing. "I have many enemies, Barbara. Any influential man does."

"Yes, but to write this . . . this filth! To use my name as if I were a common whore! To—to imply that Philippe might be my lover!" Her voice had gotten louder with each word, propelling her off the bed. She was screaming by the time she finished.

And then, at the expression on Roger's face, "Sweet Jesus, you do not believe it! Surely you do not think—Roger, you are the only man in my life! I swear it!" She threw herself back on the bed, on him. "Tell me you believe me!"

Some kind of struggle was going on inside of him; she could see it.

"I believe you," he said, but it was said too slowly to satisfy her.

She took his hand in both of hers and held it to her heart. "I swear by all that is holy, by Our Lord Jesus Christ above, that you are the only man that I have ever loved, and that I have never been unfaithful to you." Steadfastly she refused to think of the time she had thought about kissing Richelieu. Surely the Lord would not want her to count that.

"You are a good wife, Barbara."

She nodded her head in agreement, making him laugh. Reprieved, unexpectedly so, he leaned forward to kiss her mouth, tempting and soft.

"Who would have written this?" she demanded under his lips. "It is outrageous. Someone ought to be hanged! We will cancel the dinner! We will go to the regent, demand satisfaction! We will—"

"See that vase there," said Roger, pointing to an ancient Chinese vase on his mantel. "Smash it and get your tantrum over with now, because I am sick to death of Tamworth temper. There is nothing we can do, except ignore it and act as normally as possible. Does anyone in your family understand the concept of rational behavior?"

She felt as if she had been dashed with cold water. Harry. She had forgotten Harry. What had he done?

"What did Harry do?"

"He attacked Philippe, and me. You saw the downstairs. Imagine the rest. I can only assume he was drinking. It was all I could do to keep Philippe from challenging him to a duel—"

"Sweet Jesus."

"Precisely."

"He was defending my honor—"

"Do not talk to me about honor, Barbara. He lost his temper and acted without thinking. As a result, he has given the gossips more than enough fodder to make these despicable verses seem to be based on some fact. We will hold your dinner party; Harry will be on his best behavior, and you will behave as charmingly as possible to the Prince de Soissons. That will give people something to think about, if they can get past the marks on all our faces."

She put her hand to his swollen mouth. "Oh, Roger, I am so sorry. Does it hurt?"

"Of course it hurts, but not nearly as much as being embarrassed in my own home. You will, I hope, emphasize to your impetuous brother the need for continued good manners in the coming weeks."

Now she was beginning to feel angry. "He did it for my sake. What was he to think? At least Harry fights for what he believes—"

"Implying I do not? No, Barbara, I will not follow your reasoning. Harry acted without thinking. If he had thought, he would have realized that you would never be unfaithful to me."

Her face was mutinous.

"You are not the only one touched by this, Barbara. It is my name being dragged alongside yours. My honor—as well as yours—being questioned." His handsome face was grave. She was instantly ashamed of herself.

"Roger, I did not think. You are good not to be furious with us both. I will speak to Harry. I promise. Thank you for not sending him away."

"Make no mistake, Barbara. I am still angry with him, but at my age, I know what time will do. This will pass; if we behave as always, some fresh sensation will take its place for lack of anything else. Within a month, we will be gone, and all of this will be behind us. Try to think of that, rather than this filth. Promise me you will try."

It had been written down, distributed across the city. The written word was so powerful; it lingered in people's minds as truth. This rumor might follow her like mud clinging to her skirts for years, no matter its lies. He asked much of her. She said, "I will."

She went to see Harry. He was sulky, rebellious, drinking. She was shocked at the sight of him, so much worse than Roger. His face was cut and bruised; one eye was closing and turning black and blue; his knuckles were bandaged, and he could not move without pain. He refused to discuss any of it with her except to tell her through clenched teeth that Roger and Philippe would receive an apology from him.

"And what about me?" she said softly. "Do I not deserve one?"

"What for?"

"For thinking that I would be unfaithful—"

"I never thought that, Bab."

"Then why would you attack Philippe?"

He was silent. A muscle worked in his cheek.

She left him. Poor Harry, thoughtless as always. Only this time, he had shamed her by his conduct.

In her bedchamber, she thought about it as she took off her hat and gloves. It was a shameful, dreadful thing that verse implied, sullying her honor. She understood Harry's anger. She could not get the verse out of her mind. Devane, Soissons, Devane—

A knock sounded. Caesar White peeped in. She welcomed him, even though all she wished was to be alone for a while to sort everything out.

"Lady Devane," he said, talking and bowing and coming into the room all at the same time, "I came to say goodbye."

"Goodbye? But where are you going?"

"I am leaving."

"Leaving," she cried, staring at him. "But what do you mean? Not leaving the household—but why? What have we done? Surely you are not going to leave before my birthday? What has happened? Tell me, Caesar, and I will make it right."

He took her hand and kissed it. "I have enjoyed our association, Lady Devane, and I will always remember you. I hope you remember me as kindly—"

"How can I not? Caesar, have you talked to Lord Devane? He is going to be so upset. Do not leave like this—"

But he shook his head, becoming even more adamant at the mention of Roger's name. She could not believe it; she felt as if she were losing a dear friend. He had been her first ally in the household. This could not be happening.

"Please, Caesar. Stay for my sake. At least until my birthday—"

She could see that he was moved by her emotion, but Thérèse came into the room, and he stiffened, and said he could not change his plans, but that he wished her all happiness.

"He is leaving us!" Barbara cried to Thérèse.

Thérèse looked at White and then away.

"I must go," White said to no one in particular.

"Is it because of the verse?"

"The verse?"

"Yes. Are you leaving because of that? Surely you know it is all lies. I would never be unfaithful to Lord Devane."

He took both her hands in his good one. "I admire you from the bottom of my heart," he said, looking into her eyes, "and I would never believe evil of you."

"Then why are you leaving?"

He did not answer. And she knew then that nothing she could say would change his mind. Something had happened; but she was not to know what it was.

"Wait." She rummaged through a cupboard until she found her bag of coins.

"Take this," she said, handing it to him.

"No! I could not—"

"Lord Devane would be furious if you went away from us empty-handed. Go on, take it. I can always get more tomorrow. You know how generous my husband is. You have my good wishes, Caesar. I hate that you are going."

He could not look at her. Swallowing, he bowed and left. She watched him walk out of the room, as did Thérèse. Then she ran to find Montrose, who was in his parlor halfheartedly arranging pieces of paper.

"What happened?" she cried.

But he could tell her nothing; he was as bewildered and hurt as she was by White's sudden flight.

"He quoted poetry," he said, looking at her blankly.

"Poetry!" she exclaimed. "What did he say?"

"He said, 'From morn to noon he fell, from noon to dewy eve, a summer's day; and with the setting sun dropped from the zenith like a falling star.' "

"But what does that mean?"

"It is about Lucifer and his fall from heaven. That is all I know."

Lucifer! She wanted to stamp her feet and shout at the sky. What was happening? In their own household? It was coming apart and she did not know why.

Now it was the afternoon of her birthday. Outside, footmen and maidservants bustled—stringing new paper lanterns across the gardens, raking the gravel, pulling old blooms off the flowers, setting the tables with linen cloths that brushed the bricks of the terrace, arranging flowers and ivy and candles in the center of each table. The fountains in the gardens would spew wine tonight. In the kitchen, the cook and his helpers roasted meats and the fish, duck and capon dishes that would be served tonight. In the pantry, on silver trays, lay mountains of fresh fruit, jellied tarts, cakes, iced and sugary. Her finished portrait, festooned with flowers, hung in the hall, the first thing guests would see as they came in the door. Yesterday she had overseen the sending of its duplicate to her grandmother. Her grandmother was very much on her mind; she longed to talk with her. Something was wrong—it was the verse—she could feel its effect as surely as she felt the sun on her face. They were all touched by it.

She thought about it as Thérèse dressed her for the dinner, a glittering affair, even if it was small, since the most important people in Paris would be there. And she did not care. She dreaded the thought of having to smile and nod and pretend nothing was wrong, pretend that she did not know what she knew, pretend she did not realize that they were all watching, assessing her—and Roger's—every move. Everyone in her household was nervous and edgy, from LeBlanc and Montrose to herself and Roger. It was as if everyone was waiting for the other shoe to drop. Roger was like a cat, high-strung, snapping at everyone. He and Harry avoided each other, which hurt her heart to see. Harry sat sprawled in one of her armchairs, patches over his bruises, as if to emphasize them, dressed to an inch of his life: an expensive wig and coat, lace that was finer than hers, high heels on his shoes, the young dandy. He might not have had a care in the world, except for the marks on his face—and the scowl.

She was on the edge of a ferocious mood herself, for all that under Thérèse's skilled hands she looked like an angel. Her flux had begun this morning, bloodred. She had wanted to cry with disappointment. But it was her birthday, and she had to pretend that everything was well; that her name had not been dragged in the mud with her husband's friend; that her husband was not humiliated; that her brother had not made an ass of himself; that one of their most devoted servants—and friends—had not inexplicably left them. She pressed her hands together not to scream at Thérèse as she brushed her hair up, arranging fresh, white roses in it. Tonight, she wore black and white: a black low-cut gown, the underskirt shot through with threads of silver, its petals frosted with pearls and diamonds. Patches were sprinkled on her forehead and cheeks, to emphasize her red rouge. Huge diamond drops were in her ears, her birthday present from Roger, as were the bracelets she wore on each arm. Hyacinthe matched her, black and white, like a tiny harlequin. He would carry her fan and whichever of the birthday bouquets she had been receiving all day she chose to carry tonight.

Most of her presents were littered across her dressing table, along with her ribbons and jewels and scent bottles and laces. There was White's poem. It had been tied with a blue ribbon, and in its lines, she was compared to Aurora, the goddess of the dawn, for her red-gold hair and shining spirit.

There were the various birthday bouquets from friends (Richelieu's had come with a pearl bracelet—most improper, but very like him). Harry had given her a fan scented with lavender and verbena, the fragrance reminding her of her grandmother. When she had opened it, the scene painted across it resembled the view from Tamworth's library windows—the rose gardens and yews, the deer park beyond. ("I described it," Harry explained, "and the man painted it." He said it nonchalantly, as if it were nothing, but she kissed him for his thoughtfulness.)

She had received many letters from her relatives to wish her birthday happiness, from her aunts and Tony and Fanny and

Mary. But the two most unexpected letters were from her parents. Her father wished her felicitations of the day and gave her an address to send him money, which he would repay, he wrote. She folded away his letter without a word, hiding it under some jewels in one of her boxes. (Later she would take it out, reread it, and send him the money.) It was her mother's letter that most surprised her—ink-stained, badly spelled, for Diana had never bothered much with her lessons, being more intent on flirting with her tutors. Her mother wished her a happy birthday, and said that she was in her thoughts. She signed it, "Your loving mother, Diana Alderley." Harry was reading it now.

"I received one, too," he said, folding it and handing it back. "Has she seen God, do you think?"

Barbara shrugged. Her mother had never remembered a birthday before, not when she was at Tamworth, not in all the time she could remember.

"There," said Thérèse, touching a last rose. "You are perfect!"

"Not quite," said Harry, reaching into his coat. "She needs more jewelry." Hanging from his finger was a long gold chain ending in a single diamond drop, held by two small pearls. She recognized it immediately.

"Grandmama!"

Harry handed her a letter, grinning at her. "They both came yesterday."

"I knew she would not forget!" said Barbara, tearing past her grandmother's seal to read the beloved, much-needed words.

I send you birthday greetings and all my love, and I would give anything to see you, but I do not travel well these days and so must content myself with your letters, and with my trust in the Lord's watching over you. Sixteen. . . . You are a woman now, with a woman's sorrows and joys. I kiss both your cheeks and your eyes and I wish that I could sit watching you dress for your birthday fete. Remember me among the princes tonight, as I remember you each night in my prayers. I send you my blessings. When you first left for London, I read to you from the Lord's Word. Do you remember? I read you: "Keep thy

heart with all diligence, for out of it are the issues of life."
Advice which is as good today as it was then. If Harry is
with you, kiss him for me. Tell him he does not write, and
I expect him to. Watch over him, he has not your character. Everyone at Tamworth is well. Dulcinea has had more
kittens. Tony is with me still, braving the threat of smallpox and the Lord protecting him for it, and the more I
know him, the more I love him. I can see that with my
guidance, he could make something of himself. Your mother
prospers in London. Her divorce petition has been
approved. Jane is with child. Tell Harry if you think he
should know . . . or care. Keep thy heart, my dearest
granddaughter, for your heart is my heart also. I enclose a
little something from my own youth, mine when I was sixteen—so very long ago. Written this day, the twenty-sev-
enth of April, in the year of Our Lord, 1716, at Tamworth
Hall.

Carefully Barbara folded the letter.
"What does she say?" asked Harry.
"That you never write and that Jane is with child."
Harry's face was so still that Barbara was almost sorry for
her flippant words. Thérèse, who was fastening the necklace
around Barbara's neck, thought, Who is Jane?
"One more present! One more present!" chanted Hyacinthe,
bringing it in. The dogs yapped at his heels.
"Shut up!" Harry told them. They barked at him. The box
was long and thin, like a fan box, and it was tied with a black
velvet ribbon. But when Barbara opened it, she saw not a fan,
but a piece of paper folded over and over to resemble a fan.
Even before she read the words, she knew what they said:
"Devane, Soissons, Devane . . ."
Harry grabbed it from her and crumpled it. His eyes were
flashing with anger.
"Damn it! I would like to kill the writer! Bab, are you all
right?"
She had her eyes closed and one hand around her grandmother's necklace. Keep thy heart. She could do that. She
squared her shoulders, snapped open Harry's fan, and selected
Wart's bouquet of vivid red roses.
"Your arm, Harry."

His eye scanned her face and he must have approved of what he saw, because he smiled at her. Together, they went downstairs.

Talking in low tones at the foot of the stairs, Roger and Philippe moved apart as they appeared. Something about that movement set off a momentary ripple in Barbara's mind—that verse touched them all. Even Roger and Philippe could no longer be completely natural, but then Harry and Philippe were staring at each other like two stiff-legged dogs on the verge of a fight, and she forgot it in trying to get everyone past that moment. Philippe bowed over her hand, and there was something so amused, so malicious, at the back of his eyes that it was all she could do not to snatch her hand back. He is enjoying this, she thought. Why?

The dinner was as awful as she had imagined. The sly glances at her and Roger and Philippe; the awkward silences; Roger's charm lost against Philippe's coldness and Harry's smoldering anger. The tension between those two was frightening; Barbara expected every moment for them to whip out their swords and begin dueling. I shall get through this, she kept thinking, through the long, six-course meal, through the recital of music and scenes from Racine's plays, through the fireworks display in her honor. And then, at last, the guests were leaving. Only a few of the men stayed to gamble in the library. She escaped upstairs, her face aching from false smiles, her heart aching from the shame at the way people had watched her tonight; her loins aching from her flux.

Toward dawn, she had a bad dream. She dreamed she was in a crowded room, people everywhere, laughing, talking, dancing, and she was looking for Roger. She looked in a mirror, and the mirror became a window, and on the other side was Roger, and he was talking to Philippe. For some reason she began to cry. She slammed her fist against the mirror, and he looked at her, but he did not see her. She felt as if she were nothing. Sweating and whimpering, she lunged out of her sleep into the dawn. The bed beneath her hips, her rags for the flux, were soaked with blood. She got out of bed, knocking over the books on her bedside table. Her feet skittered among the papers that fell from them as she went to open the drapes. Her sketches. For Devane House. She pulled back the drapes. It was just dawn; not all of the shadows of

the night were yet gone. She changed into a fresh nightgown.
Roger. She wanted Roger. He would be asleep, but she would
lie next to him and his body warmth would comfort her. How
silly she was to be frightened of a dream.

He was not there; no one had slept in his bed. The candle
Justin had left was burned to a stub. She crept downstairs.
The house was silent, still dark. In the library, the card tables
were littered with empty wineglasses and finished candles. She
went into the blue-and-gold salon. The breeze from the open
terrace doors fanned her cheeks. She thought at first the servants had forgotten to close the doors, but then she heard
Roger's voice, outside. And Philippe's. A sudden, old impulse
to eavesdrop seized her. She crept closer to the open terrace
doors. The chill of the dawn touched her feet.

"'Rosy-fingered dawn appeared, the early-born,'" she heard
Roger say. He sat on the top terrace step, with Philippe. Their
coats and wigs were off, and two wine bottles, empty, lay on
their sides. Philippe was drinking from the third, and he
poured more into Roger's upraised glass.

"Bravo, my friend! Let me think . . . Homer."

"Very good, Philippe. I salute you."

"No, let us salute the dawn." They drank to the dawn.

"I will miss you," said Philippe.

Roger put his hand on Philippe's shoulder, and Philippe
leaned his cheek against it for a moment.

Barbara's eyes focused on that gesture.

"Who said parting is such sweet sorrow?"

"Shakespeare."

"You should have let me arrange a marriage with a docile,
convent-bred French girl. She would have understood. And if
she did not, you could have sent her back to the convent."

"But I have grown so fond of my country-bred English girl."

"To my profound sorrow."

"And mine. Life is never simple."

"Never mind," said Philippe, putting his arm around Roger's shoulders. "She will never learn our dark secret. You are
safe. You can make her believe whatever you want. She is
putty in your hands as we all are. What is there about your
fatal charm, Roger, that makes it so fatal?"

There was the beginning of a roaring in her ears. She made
a small sound. Philippe turned his head toward her, and they

locked eyes. He saw her; she saw him see her; and for that second she read his heart clearly. He hated her, and he loved Roger. My dear God, she thought, as Philiipe turned back to the gardens as if she were not there. As if she were a ghost. Or nothing. Roger was oblivious of her. He put his hand on Philippe's face.

"I shall miss you," he said.

Philippe smiled at him, and then, before her disbelieving eyes, Roger pulled Philippe's head down, and their mouths met, and they kissed. She could not move. The kiss did not break. The morning sun, now in its first strength, surrounded them like a halo. She stepped back, back into the cool shadows of the room. Her thoughts were incoherent. . . . They kissed like a man and a woman. . . . She had seen it in Philippe's eyes. . . . They were . . . Her thoughts stumbled to the few, small gestures which had fastened themselves in her mind, ready, waiting for this moment. The day Harry had arrived. Last night. Devane, Soissons, Devane. It did not mean that she and Philippe were lovers; it meant that Roger and he—

"No," she said, stumbling back over a chair. It was as if she were a piece of glass, and she was splintering into fragments. Everything was pressing in on her, becoming dark, yet through a tiny tunnel of light she could still see them on the terrace, still embracing. They were before her eyes even as she sank to the floor. Someone was screaming . . . over and over . . . the sound filled her mind with pain. . . . Roger . . . oh, Roger. . . . She fainted.

CHAPTER NINETEEN

The Duchess and Tony walked through the meadows bordering Tamworth Hall. It was early morning, the morning after Barbara's birthday, and the dew clung to their feet and wet the hem of the Duchess's skirt. It glistened on the green meadow grass, a grass green as only May could make it, a grass through which white meadow daisies and golden buttercups bloomed. The buttercups grew higher than the grass, and the Duchess was like a child, slashing at their heads with her cane, ruthlessly. But she could afford to be extravagant; the month of May was extravagant. The smallpox was gone, borne away on April winds. It had spared her Tony. The bees were out, already drunk on flower wine, zigzagging greedily from field to hedge to field again. Cowbells sounded in the morning stillness, as the milkmaids herded cows to their morning pastures. A few birds called to one another. The hawthorn was showing its fat buds, its promise of sweet fragrance; the butterflies and bees and the Duchess checked on it anxiously.

"A week more," she said to Tony, "and the hawthorn will be open. Smell it already." She would fill Tamworth Hall with hawthorn branches, as would every villager and farmer their own homes. There would be branches of hawthorn in cottage windows, in country parlors, filling houses with its wonderful sweetness, the beauty of its red or white or pink blossoms.

"This is my favorite time of year," said the Duchess, leaning on Tony's arm, surveying her rich fields, the woods between here and Tamworth Hall, woods whose trees had leaves the color of spring, a tender, moist green, under which bloomed violets and wood sorrel and sweet woodruff. She must be out soon, with Annie and a maidservant or two, to gather the woodruff. Its perfume would scent her drawers and trunks and cupboards for months afterward. She had it growing in her kitchen gardens, among the rhubarb and tender radishes and young onions and potatoes, among the cabbages and rows of spinach, but to her mind, no woodruff smelled as sweet as that which grew under the trees in her woods. Ah, she loved Tamworth. It was a part of her soul; even now it was healing her with its birds and flowers and bees and meadows. She missed the children, yes. Not to see them running in the meadows, climbing the trees, fishing in the stream. But they were gone. With their grandfather now in the family vault, and the only meadow flowers they would ever see again would be the ones she brought them. Vanity of vanities, all is vanity—yet not all. She was not alone. The Lord was good.

"Look at that sky, boy. It is as blue as the color of Barbara's eyes, or your grandfather's eyes. Someday this will all be yours, and now, I can say those words gladly. You are a good boy, Tony. A good boy to look after your grandmother so."

Tony, hulking above his thin, frail grandmother, blushed like a child. A shame, thought the Duchess, that he is so plain. None of William's handsome looks at all, except for his height. All Abigail, watered down to nothing. Ah, well, we work with what we have. And we thank the Lord for His blessings. She squeezed Tony's arm and gestured for them to continue their walk. Abigail would be here tomorrow, anxious no doubt to see why her son tarried so long. The Duchess smiled grimly to herself. Abigail would have to loosen her hold a bit, for the Duchess claimed Tony now. He was hers. Given to her by the Lord God Almighty. Though she was prepared to share . . . to a certain point. . . . Ah, she looked forward to quarreling with Abigail. She slashed the heads off a patch of buttercups with vicious satisfaction.

Dulcinea appeared from nowhere, her silvery-white fur sleek with dew, her tail slashing with jungle majesty. She was stalking birds, hoping with her cold cat's heart that perhaps a hatched babe or two had fallen from their nest. Above her, a pair of rooks circled and cawed and swooped down at her. Dulcinea was no fool; there was a nest close by; a baby on the ground perhaps. She ignored the Duchess and Tony, intent on her hunt, and went leaping into the woods with the grace of the primeval beast she was.

"Want one of Dulcinea's kittens, Grandmama. Do not forget."

"Say 'I,' boy! Can you not say the plain English word 'I'! You are going to have to learn. I will not have the Duke of Tamworth sputtering around this country like a damned fool! Let me hear you say, 'Grandmama, *I* want one of Dulcinea's kittens.' Say it. Or I will give you nothing. Go on! Say it! You can do it, Tony."

Hesitantly, Tony said, "I . . . want one of Duclinea's kittens."

The Duchess nodded vigorously. Poor Tony. Why should he hoard words as others hoarded gold? What was he afraid of? What kind of upbringing had he had that he could not declare himself? She remembered him as a child, fat, unblinking, staring about him silently, someone on Abigail's staff always correcting him, teaching him, pushing him, if Abigail herself was not worrying over him. Harry and Barbara teasing him unmercifully. She herself ignoring him. Poor lout, no wonder he was the way he was. Well, he was under her wing now, and she would bring him out of himself. Abigail had done her duty as she saw it, but she had raised a shy, uncertain man, and the Duchess meant to do better. God had granted her this last chick in her hour of need, and she would do her best by him, never mind that he was not all his father had been. He was hers. They walked on through the woods, coming out of its cool shadows to the gardens near the house. She was tired now. She could feel her age dragging her down. She needed her morning rest.

"Never mind me, Tony," she said, softening the edge of what she had said before. "I am a crotchety old woman this morning. I did not sleep well last night. Barbara was on my mind. I felt a worry. Annie says the tea leaves bode evil. I do not like it!" She stamped the ground with her cane. "I hope she is happy. She should be happy. I pray she is. Sometimes one feels so helpless . . . a feeling I never like, Tony. I do not believe in helplessness."

He was silent. She knew what that silence meant. He still loved Barbara. Ah, what a tangle life was. Never giving us what we wanted, or worse yet, giving it. Well, there was no use coddling him. The truth had to be faced. That was how people healed, by facing the truth, as difficult as that was to do sometimes. But Tony was frailer than Barbara; not used to her gruffness, as Barbara was. She had much to make up for in her handling of this boy—this dear boy. She squeezed his arm.

"You cannot have her. She is married, and even if she were not, she is too strong-willed for you. You would both be unhappy. Oh, I know you do not think so, but I am right, Tony. I see with the eyes of an old woman, and I am right. Come on, boy, pull me along. Tamworth is just a few more steps, and I must rest a bit. Ah, feel that breeze. Look, one of your grandfather's roses—they are called the Duke of Tamworth, named after him—is opening. Look at that color. Ah, there is nothing prettier than a Tamworth morning, is there?"

He smiled at her. It caught her heart. There was a glimmer—just the tiniest glimmer—of Richard in that smile.

"Bah!" she said, smiling back at him. "Never mind trying to charm me. It will do you no good. I am a tough old bird. All we Tamworths are. You will see. You are one of us. God bless you, boy, you are one of us. Pick me a rose, Tony. I want to go inside smelling your grandfather's roses. . . ."

PART II

*E*NDINGS

ENGLAND

1720–1721

CHAPTER TWENTY

"**B**ab," a voice called her softly, pulling her up from sleep's dark nothing, "wake up."

She ignored the hand on her bare shoulder, clinging to the dark in her mind, but it shook her again, insistent. As insistent as the throbbing bright sunlight coming in through the open windows. Closing her eyes more tightly, she snuggled into the rumpled sheet, still cool from the early morning damp. Then someone kissed her shoulder.

"Darling," a soft, shy, young voice said, "I must go. At least wake to tell me goodbye. Please, Bab . . ."

Thoughts went skittering into one another inside her head. Dark. Shrill. Like a summer night's bats disturbed in their cave. Sweet Jesus, she thought, her face pressed into the pillow, this is a nightmare. Wake me when it is finished.

"I am meeting Wart at Garraway's. South Sea is making another stock offer to annuity holders, and I must convert mine before it is too late," the voice said, "otherwise I would not leave you like this. But I told John to serve you tea. Wake up . . . love." The last word was hesitantly, shyly, said.

It was enough to make her turn over and open one eye to see Jemmy Landsdowne (seventeen and no nightmare) sitting on the edge of the bed, watching her with eyes that adored her. Oh, dear, sweet, merciful God, she thought, turning her face away as he leaned forward to kiss her lips. Quickly, she shut her eyes. He contented himself with touching a strand of her long, tousled, red-gold hair instead.

She listened to the sounds he made as he left the room, the rustle of fabric as he pulled on his coat, the sound of his heels tapping across the floor, the merry off-key tune he was whistling as the door closed. Nausea gripped her by the throat. It was last night's drinking, but it was this also. The door reopened, and she did not move. She played being asleep, while the nausea choked her, and thoughts circled in her head, a head which pounded, which felt as if it were being tightened in a vise. She heard the sounds of china rattling against a tray, the dull clink of silver. What have I done? she thought. This is not happening. The door closed.

She sat up and slowly shook out her hair. It billowed out around her like a lion's mane. Wrapping a sheet around her naked body, she got up from the bed and poured herself a cup of tea. Her hands were shaking so badly that she spilled some, but the hot liquid burned her tongue and throat and some of the bile in her stomach. She went to the open window and leaned out. The hot, still air of London's August fell on her like a blanket. She could smell the stench from the Thames River, matching what lay on top of her stomach. A cart rolled slowly by, the barrels on its back pierced with holes that sprinkled water on the street to keep the dust down. Across, on the front steps of a house, his basket of tools and fresh rushes at his feet, a chair mender stood mending the broken rushes of a chair while the housewife watched him from her front window. The shrill cries of street vendors on the main street just around the corner could be heard: "New river water!" "Ripe strawberries!" "Knives, combs or ink horns!" "Crab, crab, any crab!" Somewhere, a man and woman were quarreling. Barbara wedged herself in the open window, like a gypsy or lazy maidservant, and sat there, watching the chair mender and sipping tea.

Have I bedded Jemmy Landsdowne? she thought very slowly, for thinking hurt her head. Asking that question made the nausea rise in her throat. Never run away from the truth. . . . That was her grandmother's voice in her mind. Bits and pieces of the countless homilies, lectures and sermons she had listened to as a girl always drifted in and out of her mind at random to remind her that she was not living up to her grandmother's standard of a gentlewoman. She needed no sermon. . . . Her everyday life these days was reminder enough.

Never run away from the truth because you carry it on your shoulder, and someday it will put its ugly face into yours and say, "Boo." A lecture pulled out and recited by her grandmother whenever she and Harry had lied about their latest mischief. They both used to jump back—even though they knew what was coming—at Grandmama leaning forward, her fingers curling on each side of her face like a witch's, to cry, "Boo!" in a loud voice. But facing the truth of stealing from Tamworth kitchen or Sir John's orchard was a far cry from facing the truth of waking up in the bed of a boy she had no feeling for. (A fondness . . . there was that. . . . The resemblance to Kit . . . but fondness could not justify . . . Boo. . . . Thank you, Grandmama, I can say boo for myself.)

How can this have happened? she thought, leaning back against the window frame. Suddenly she wished with all her heart that she could be fifteen again, with the vigor and sureness she had felt then. The sense of knowing exactly what she wanted; the sense of knowing exactly what was right and what was wrong. Now she was twenty, and she knew nothing. Except that she was sitting in a window, under Jemmy's sheet naked as a Covent Garden whore, and in similar circumstances. And I know this, she thought, and the thought rang sharp and clear like a bell in the morning in her mind. I know I do not like what has just happened. What has been happening to me all this spring and summer. I know I am afraid. Do you hear me, Grandmama? Does anyone hear me? I am afraid. But her grandmother did not answer. How could she? One did not answer what was never asked. Ugly little truths jumped down from her shoulder and went leaping like demons before her eyes. Boo, she told them. Boo.

Wearily, she concentrated on remembering what she could of the night before. She had left Richmond Lodge in the early afternoon with Charles. At the thought of Charles, she stiffened. A new and dangerous element was introduced into her predicament. Did he know? Well, he must *not* know . . . for all their sakes. Go on, she told herself, trying to get past Charles. Face the rest. Everyone was crammed into carriages: Charles, Harry, Pamela, Wart, Judith, drinking from silver flasks and laughing—except herself. She had not wanted to go.

She was in one of her moods, as they were known . . . those
dark times in her life, coming lately again with increasing fre-
quency (she had thought them left in France), times when she
felt she had lost her place in the world, when living from day
to day was not enough. But how did she explain such feelings
to people who never felt so? There was no explaining.

And she and Charles had begun to quarrel, and naturally
they had stopped at taverns along the way to London (she
could just picture the others piling out of the carriage like
pumpkins spilling from a cart, so glad were they to be away
from the quarreling). There was the memory of smoky rooms,
ale foaming, Pamela's whiny, high-pitched voice, Judith's
inane laughter, Harry losing a quick game of cards, her headache. Her boredom. Her distaste. Everyone was laughing and
talking and having a good time. Only she sat apart. And so
she began to drink, to be like them, to feel a part of their
fun, glass after glass, until at last everything was soft, a golden
blur, and she could laugh and joke as they were doing. Where
Jemmy came in she had no idea. Only that somewhere, in
some tavern, he was there, with his own group of friends. All
younger than she by three or four years, and one of the young
men began to flatter her—as did any young man who considered himself fashionable these days, for she was "Fair Aurora,
the dawn's sweet, young queen. . . ."

If she tried, she could still hear the echo of Wart and Harry
baying like hyenas when they had read the stanzas to each
other, stanzas from Caesar White's last book of poetry, which
had made her famous even before she put the toe of one of
her satin shoes on English soil . . . the poetry . . . and
Richelieu. She closed her eyes at the thought of Richelieu; the
corner of her mouth trembled slightly. You still love him, he
had said, his face so different from that first time when he
had whispered, I have waited such a long time . . . touch
me, Barbara . . . touch me. But she had been too numb, too
crazed inside to appreciate his skill. Revenge had been on her
mind . . . only revenge. . . . She shook her head to chase
away thoughts that would only bring tears, and took a sip of
her cold tea. There was no use in crying. She had not cried
since those terrible weeks after she had seen the truth of Roger
and Philippe, weeks in which she had thought she would go
mad, weeks in which she had screamed and wept and been

for all the world the same as one of those wretched women chained in Bedlam Hospital.

She put one hand to her face at the thought of that time—and its aftermath, seared in her mind, as seared as the moment she had seen Roger kiss Philippe—for the aftermath was Roger walking away from her as if she were nothing. Walking out of her life. That was the moment she stopped crying. The hurt was too deep for tears. It went to her core, her essence, her being. All that had existed was loss—choking her with darkness, the way water does a drowning man. She had thought she would die. (What a child she had been to think a broken heart would kill her, but it had felt so; yes, at the time, it had felt so.) She had not died. Nor had she cried again. Not even when she and Harry journeyed to Italy to bury their father. We bring nothing into this world, the curate had chanted (the wooden coffin was slowly being lowered down, down, down into dust and nothingness, and no one was there to mourn save the curate . . . and her . . . and Harry . . . and she knew what nothingness was because that was all that was in her heart), and it is certain we can carry nothing out. (I will bring him home, Harry told her, his face a shadow against the dark sky. I swear I will bring him home. He did not. She arranged it herself, Roger paying for it, as he paid for all things. A sack of gold arrived for her each month, wherever she might be, and there was always a banker she could call upon for extra funds. The first time the gold had arrived, she had the clear memory of flinging it against a wall in such a fit of rage that the sack burst and gold coins went skittering everywhere. She could still picture Harry and Wart on their hands and knees hunting for coins. Two years later, she was staring at a newly arrived sack and wondering if Roger had touched it, if the mark of his hands might still be upon it, and she could not keep herself from touching it also, as if her act would lessen some of the distance separating them. Touching it gently, delicately, as if some of his warmth might have crossed the miles from England to France to make her well again.) The Lord gave, the curate had chanted, and the Lord hath taken away; blessed be the name of the Lord.

She watched a scrawny street cat leap suddenly into the shadow of a house and emerge triumphantly with a struggling rat in its mouth. The chair mender, his task finished, was packing his tools into his basket. "Old satin, old taffeta, old velvet!" came clearly to her ears from somewhere near. It had been a long time since she had thought of her father's death. There were no tears then, and there were no tears now. But they were in her heart. She could feel them. Like many small stones. Thoughts tumbled over each other in her mind: her father, the grave, the wind that day roaring and howling around her, sucking at her, pulling at her, Richelieu rising from his chair that first time and saying in his caressing voice, ah, the birthday girl at last, Charles and Jemmy snarling over her in that tavern last night like dogs over a choice bone. Charles was drunk, drunker than anyone except Harry, and more lethal. . . . Harry's edge was gone . . . spilled from his body in Paris, side by side with his blood. But Charles still possessed a dangerous edge that had at first intrigued her, and now left her weary. If all things left her weary, and she was only twenty, what would her life be at thirty. . . .

"Mistress! Mistress!"

She looked down. The chair mender was smiling up at her, gap-toothed, waving something in his hand.

"How much, mistress?"

The sunlight caught what was in his hand. A coin. Probably the coin he had just earned. Laughter suddenly filled her, like bubbles rising in a glass. She smiled down at him.

"Not today. Another time, perhaps."

He sighed, winked, then pocketed his coin. She watched him walk away, his basket strapped to his back. Harry would have appreciated this moment. Or Richelieu. But not Charles. The laughter inside her evaporated.

Charles had thrown a glass of punch in someone's face last night for less. She could remember shouts and Pamela's screams, chairs turned over and Charles and one of Jemmy's friends rolling on the floor, amid the sand and stale tobacco and spilled ale. And laughing, she remembered laughing like a madwoman, and Jemmy (dear Jemmy, who flattered her with his boyish admiration, who reminded her of her brother, Kit, whom she was fond of . . . no more . . . nothing more) took her outside and began to kiss her. She remembered saying no. Yes, she could remember that. And then she was in a carriage, and everything was reeling into darkness around her, and Jemmy was trying to kiss her again, and she was confused because she was thinking of Roger, trying to remember how his mouth had felt on hers. . . . My dear Barbara, Richelieu had told her, his mouth twisting ironically, I cannot fight a ghost. Nor do I intend to. . . .

She shivered so violently that the teacup perched on the window ledge fell to the floor. She stared at the little pool of tea, the tea leaves, the bits of broken cup on Jemmy's floor. Annie believed in the tea leaves. What did these say about the future . . . and did she wish to know? As she stood up, everything in her stomach, which had seemed soothed by the tea, rose up in her throat. Stumbling, she ran to the chamber pot and retched. Her mouth tasted vile; she was racked by the spasms of her body; her head felt as if it would explode. If only they could see me now, she thought, wiping her mouth. Aunt Abigail, the Frog, all those people who believe I am so fashionable . . . and so wicked. She would have laughed, except that she felt too wretched. Sick and wretched.

Once she could stand again, she began to pull on her clothes. The mirror above an old Dutch chest reflected her motions, the jerky movements of her hands. Taking a last look around the room to be certain she had left nothing—as if leaving nothing might erase the fact that she had been there— what a fool I am, she thought—she caught sight of her image in the mirror. A woman with magnificent hair pinned carelessly into place stared back at her. A woman in that first, true flush of young beauty, with a heart-shaped face and large blue eyes with a strained expression in them. A woman unfashionably slim when all the world celebrated full, fleshy white arms and breasts and thighs, and she could offer only a certain beguiling slenderness that turned to gauntness at the first zigzag of her emotions. But there was always her smile and her voice. I do not know why I desire you, Charles had whispered that first time into her ear, as she lay under him. But I do, he said, biting her white neck. I do. You taste as sweet as honey. . . .

She sighed. Desire would not be on Charles's mind at this moment. Or honey. Only rage. And she did not blame him. She had not been fair with him from the beginning. She had not been herself since that first moment of seeing Roger again . . . and Philippe. Charles could not know who she was. He only saw the image she presented to the world at large, but behind the image was a shadow, and the shadow was herself and all summer she had floated between the image and the shadow, knowing that if she was not careful she would do something she would regret. That she was on the edge. And there had been enough to regret in Paris. Enough. She had fallen off the edge there, and the climbing back had been so long, so arduous. Revenge had not been sweet. Richelieu had lied.

"Boo!" she said to the woman in the mirror, the one with the shadows over her shoulder, old ghosts, old memories, old guilts. She opened Jemmy's door and ran down the stairs, like a child determined to get as far away as possible from the scene of her mischief. Her mind raced ahead of her feet—the image of her Aunt Abigail rising up as she had done years ago when Roger had still been a dream. Pride goeth before destruction, and a haughty spirit before a fall. She could see her aunt saying those words . . . and her grandmother, too. Oh, yes. Grandmama would have plenty to say about this escapade, though, of course, she had no intention of allowing her to find out. . . . For shame, Barbara. . . . Have you no pride, Barbara? He is only a boy, Barbara. . . . But she was too wise—or too foolish—to stay at Tamworth and listen to her grandmother's sermons. Oh, no, a brief visit when she had first arrived in England had been enough. She was the fashionable young woman of the world. Hiding behind a mask of joking and high spirits and the flippancy she had become known for (thank you, Richelieu), allowing Harry to pull her along any way he wished, as a diversion, with their entourage—a lady's maid, a page, two yapping dogs—headed for London before the dust of traveling was even off their clothes. I will come soon and visit, Grandmama, she had rattled, not looking her grandmother in the eyes, not wanting to see what must be in them, because if she could not yet live with all that had happened since Roger's leaving, sweet Jesus, what must her grandmother think? Those sharp old eyes would pierce through any mask she might wear, and she could not bear that. Not yet. Boo. . . .

Outside, waving her flimsy summer scarf like a banner, she flagged down a hackney carriage.

"Devane House," she said to the driver, sinking onto the musty, worn leather seats, still thinking of when she had left her grandmother. She had told her she would come back soon and waved at her from atop her horse, Harry's horse dancing impatiently beside her, but not any more impatient than she was inside. Inside she was fifteen again, and London was her destination. Her ultimate destination. It was all that was on her mind. It had called her from across the sea. Called to her in all the letters from Mary and Tony and her grandmama. For Roger was in London, and she had a longing to see him, to see what time had done, that pride could not suppress. And dreams . . . dreams that would not lie still, as they should in their grave in her mind, dreams which rose at night and haunted her in her sleep like old, white ghosts. She put her hand to her head. Philippe smiled at her across the crowded, domed salon of Roger's newly built pavilion of the arts. Oh, yes. Philippe had sent those dreams flying away like the wisps of nothing they were. Not even Roger's amazed smile of welcome, the something she had seen blaze into life behind his eyes, something she was now old enough to recognize, could compensate for Philippe's being there. She had felt betrayed. Again. Not by Roger, who had never once made her any promises. But by herself. By the foolish girl inside herself. The girl she ran away from. The girl she pretended not to be. Never run away from the truth because you carry it on your shoulder and someday it will put its ugly face into yours and say, Boo. Well, the truth had put its ugly face into hers that day. But she had still run away. She could blame it on Harry. He was with her, and he and Philippe must not meet face to face. Not again. Not after Paris. But it really had nothing to do with Harry. It had to do with the way her heart felt when she saw Roger again for the first time in four years. And then saw Philippe, too. And she could not bear it, all that which was still within her heart.

She tore the leather of the carriage seat, gripping it with her nails. I will bear it, I will bear it, I will bear it.

In her mind she saw Charles as he had looked that day, staring down at her with arrogant, raking blue eyes, the same shade of blue as Roger's. I went to Paris to meet only you, he had said, but you were gone. Well, here I am, she had answered, turning away, not knowing what she was saying, who was speaking to her. Feeling only the terrible, numbing shock of seeing Roger again, and then Philippe. How pitiful you are, she said to herself, her hands gripping the carriage seat. She had flirted with Charles because he was the first thing handy. She stared out the carriage window. Poor Charles; he possessed someone who did not exist. He did not understand her. But how could he? She did not trouble to explain herself. Richelieu had understood her, but then Richelieu had known her before, before she became the creation of lies and gossip and certain of her own foolish acts . . . laughing, stylish, flippant . . . with that hard Parisian polish that everyone found so fashionable, when the real Barbara was . . . who? Who was she? A fifteen-year-old child with her arms still held out, still believing in love and honor and truth . . . when she knew better? Oh, Jemmy, I am so sorry. Oh, Charles, it was the drink. I drank because of emptiness inside me, emptiness you cannot begin to understand. Her mind lurched to a stop. Where in the name of all that was holy was she? This was not the way to St. James's Square.

Irritably, like a Fleet Street fishwife, she leaned out the window.

"You!" she called to the driver, her voice sharp. "Where are you going?"

"Devane House," he answered, missing her by inches with the spit of chewed tobacco that accompanied his words.

"No! No! That is wrong," she shouted at him.

He turned his head to look at her. "You said Devane House," he told her stubbornly, but he began to tug on the long reins of the carriage horses.

She pulled herself back into the carriage. Damn his impudence! She did not live at Devane House, and never had. Roger lived there. She stayed in his old town house at St. James's Square. (To the delight of London gossips, who buzzed about their separate living arrangements and waited expectantly each time she and Roger ran into each other to see what might happen. They underestimated Roger, his courtesy, his style. He treated her every time with teasing, provocative politeness, even if she was with Charles. He complimented her hair, her gown, inquired after her health, her family. It took her breath away, that polished surface of his manners. And in his eyes, there was always a look that hurt her heart.) Yes, the gossips had underestimated Roger, as she had also. If she had wanted rage and anger from him—and of course she had—some surge of feeling to show her worth—she had forgotten his facade of urbane sophistication, which could gloss over anything and still smile . . . and so beautifully. When he smiled at her, that look in his eyes, holding her hand to kiss it, she felt the touch of his lips all the way to her heart. Time had not erased that. No, there was never outward rage from Roger. It was not his style. (Only when he had noticed the bruises on her neck, bruises Richelieu's kisses had made, had she seen rage. In his eyes, in the sudden frozen posture of his body. And she had been glad. Now he would know. Now he would feel what she did. An eye for an eye. She was ready for his rage, for ugly words of accusation. But he never said one of them. He simply turned on his heel and left her. She could bear the lack of emotion. It was the leaving that killed her. But they were too far apart for anything to bring them together. The duel between Harry and Philippe was too fresh in both their hearts, not to mention on everyone's tongue. What would Paris have done without them to gossip about that summer?) She closed her eyes, squeezing the lids tightly shut at the thought of the girl she had once been, the girl who had lain sobbing on her bed for hours because she had been unfaithful, and now . . . now she could not finish her thought. An eye for an eye and a tooth for a tooth. Richelieu, you lied. Revenge was not sweet. But, darling, he answered, grinning at her (even in their final parting, he was able to find a certain, grim amusement), it was for me.

The driver's exasperated sigh made her open her eyes. He had pulled the carriage over and was outside it, staring at her with those world-weary eyes that all London hackney carriage drivers seemed to have. His expression said, My lady, I have seen everything, and it no longer bothers me and I just want to know where you wish me to drive you so I may collect my money and go home and smoke a pipe of tobacco in peace. She looked at him. He waited. An impulse seized her.

No one will be there, she was thinking. Roger is in Richmond. Everyone was in Richmond with the court. Even she was supposed to be there. Who would know if she should stop in for a visit? After all, it was also her home. She had a perfect right to see it. It was the talk of London, and she had never set foot in it, not since that first time. Today seemed to be her day for reminiscing, so why should she not go all the way home, home to what had once been her dream, as well as Roger's? He would never have to know. She could bribe the housekeeper. She could walk in, ask for something to eat—her stomach was clawing at her insides like a lion—explore its finished rooms to her heart's content in private, then go home, her curiosity about Devane House sated, home, to think of some way to see that her latest idiocy did not harm anyone else. Yes, just a small visit. No one would ever know. And if they did, she could blame it on a mood. A whim.

She smiled at the driver, her grandfather's smile.

"Devane House, after all," she said.

The driver eyed her a moment, before climbing wearily back up to his seat and clucking at the horses.

Inside the carriage, Barbara sighed. He thought she was insane, or spoiled. Yes, that was it, a pampered, lazy noblewoman who did not have enough to do, so in her boredom she provoked hardworking hackney drivers who were simply trying to earn a living. He was a good judge of character. She began to repin her hair, straighten her gown, pinch her cheeks for color. She would not go to Devane House unkempt.

The carriage was now on Tyburn. Traffic along Tyburn was never heavy, except during those times each year when the sessions for trying criminals were held, and the condemned, sometimes as many as twenty men and women, were taken to be hanged at Tyburn Tree, a scaffold farther away toward Hyde Park. Then Tyburn and New Bond Street and the roads to Oxford and Edgware were crowded with humanity, on foot, on horseback, in carriages, come to see the hangings. It was like a festival or a fair, and the number of people depended upon the notoriety of who was to be hanged, but a good show was expected by all. The condemned rode to their destiny in a rough cart, the fatal ropes around their necks. Some dressed for the occasion, and these were the ones the crowd loved, for their style and bravado, the men in fine coats of velvet or taffeta, the women in white, with great silk scarves and with baskets of oranges and flowers to be thrown to the crowds thronging around the cart. Friends and family ran on foot alongside, often carrying the coffin their loved one would rest in, but, more important, they were there to perform the function of pulling on the feet of the hanged ones, to bring death more quickly. The condemned might make a speech, and the crowds always hushed expectantly for last words; the speech might even be printed and distributed afterward as a keepsake. Some thought Roger a fool to build anywhere near Tyburn, but others said it would provide the perfect seasonal entertainment to bored houseguests.

The carriage turned off Tyburn onto Montgeoffry Road, which ran parallel for a half-mile to the road to Hampstead. On Barbara's left was Devane Square, still unfinished, its surrounding streets named for her grandmother and grandfather; Richard Street on the public side, which faced Tyburn Road, and Alice on the other, opposite from Montgeoffry. Only one section of the town houses was finished (Philippe lived in the largest and most expensive; Wart had found that out for her). Their white fronts of gleaming Portland stone and brick shone in the hot sunlight—none of the stonework yet dirty from London's perpetual coal smoke. All of the houses were similar, with entrances on their upper first story, under classical temple-front porticoes, up handsome steps. Another section of houses was framed out, and she could see workmen hammering and sawing and carrying boards, sweating in the sun. A construction captain, sitting on one of the benches in the gardens that formed the center of the square, doffed his hat at her as her carriage drove by. Already the gardens of the square with their fountain and green lawns and trees and flowers that Roger had assembled from over the world were gaining a reputation as a botanical curiosity. Londoners came to stroll here in the cool of the evening, came to watch the progress of the houses, admire the outside facade of Wren's small church at one end of the square, came to cross Barbara Lane, behind the church, and peer through the gates at the magnificent grounds and house beyond, rising before their eyes.

The carriage began to circle around the grounds of Wren's lovely church—workmen were busy here, too—until it turned in to the short road that was Barbara Lane, her lane, before the gates of Devane House, into which Roger had been pouring his money and energy these last few years. Her house, also. She gave her name to the gatekeeper, who allowed himself one glance of startled curiosity before he ran to open the massive wrought-iron gates. The carriage rolled onto a circular drive, on each side of which were planted rows and rows of young lime trees. Barbara had the carriage stop, and she stepped out. She walked through the young trees to the fountain opposite the gates. Gardeners were everywhere, digging, hauling, planting.

The fountain had added to her reputation. Out of its waters rose a naked sea nymph atop a giant scallop shell. It was very Louis XIV, and very Barbara, for the nymph, with her streaming hair and slim body, was said to have more than a close resemblance to her. The fountain was not on. She stood on its stone rim and stared at the face of the sea nymph. Charles was correct. It looked like her. Why would Roger have done that? She turned to stare past the landscape pool and gardeners through an alley of larger trees, straight ahead to Devane House, completed only to its first story, but magnificent in its frame of trees and garden and blue August sky. She remembered her primitive sketches of so long ago, of La Malcontenta. She had not seen La Malcontenta with Roger, after all, but with Harry. She had gazed at its beauty, its perfection, with a heart that threatened to burst. The large, serene temple-front entrance, grand stairs reaching up to it on each side, the house around it simply a magnificent frame. There were willow trees and a lake. La Malcontenta. Roger.

Off to one side, hidden by the trees, was the small pavilion of arts, resembling a Roman summer villa, connected to the main house by a loggia—an arcaded roofed gallery. This she had seen, though she had no memory of it. She remembered only Roger . . . and Philippe. The pavilion, too, was the talk of London, for no one else had ever built a separate building to house his art, though Lord Burlington was now said to be doing so. Roger was in the forefront of a new fashion. All people could speak of was its classical shape, the ornate decoration of its rooms, the rare paintings and statues and medals and busts it housed, the great octagonal dome of its center salon. All through the spring, Roger had hosted parties there, and people had strolled through his temple and its adjoining gardens and admired his taste and wealth and hospitality. Barbara had also been invited; a personal messenger had come to St. James's Square before each reception. But she had never gone, not again. Neither she nor Harry. Charles had. And Wart. And both had described the beauty of the house and the temple and the grounds. But now, standing here in the hot sunshine, she could at last see it and feel it, and she was proud, proud that Roger had achieved what he had, proud that she was married to him, no matter the state of their marriage.

She went back to the carriage and had the driver take her around the drive to the front of the house. It rose before her, half finished, massive, solid, splendid. Workmen, off to one side of the entrance, worked high up on wooden scaffolding, encasing brick by brick the second story of the house. Wagons of brick stood waiting beneath them. She got out and ran up the elaborate double staircase of the portico, the roofed porch resembling the facade of a temple. This staircase and portico matched that of the smaller temple and those of the town houses. It was an example of Roger's style, connecting all the different buildings of his overall design unobtrusively but solidly. She had to knock on the double door a long time before someone answered, and then the housekeeper could only stare at her with her mouth open. The housekeeper was round, round everywhere, round mouth, round face, round body. She reminded Barbara of the apple dolls she and Jane used to make after apple harvest.

"I am Lady Devane," she said coldly. "I need someone to pay the driver. I want something to eat and a cup of tea and a carriage to take me to St. James's Square." And then at the expression on the woman's face. "I am Lady Devane," this time slowly, "Lord Devane's wife."

"Oh . . . yes. Yes! If you will follow me, my lady," said the woman, recovering herself and beginning to smile. Her smile was round, too. "This way, my lady."

She led Barbara through the huge, cool hall into another huge, cool room to a long gallery that ran along one side of the house. Barbara could feel the woman's surreptitious glances, and she cursed herself for following her impulse and wished she were more like her mother, whom nothing bothered. And then, with the realization of the enormity of her last thought, her legs felt weak, and she had to sit down in the window seat of one of the long windows that lined the outer wall of the gallery. She felt sick. The housekeeper followed.

"Please," she said to her, struggling with nausea again. "Pay the driver waiting outside. And see if you have anything I can eat. Anything at all. I-I was in the neighborhood and—and I wished to stop and rest for a moment."

The woman smiled at her. "You just never mind me, my lady. It is the surprise of it that has got me acting like a chicken with its head cut off. You just sit right there and rest yourself. I will take care of everything. That I will. Now, what can I feed you? I have nothing fancy, what with Lord Devane gone and me not expecting you. Oh, Lord Devane will be angry with me when he finds out—"

"We will keep it a secret," Barbara said hastily, trying to stop the woman's flow of words, wanting her only to go away and leave her alone. "Between you and me. So he will not know, and therefore not be angry—"

"He told us time and again we were to be ready for you, whenever you might call. But what with time passing and all, well, we let ourselves slide into sloth. Sloth. I could just shake myself. Me with nothing prepared. But I have bread," she said, brightening. "Freshly baked bread. And some roasted chicken—"

"Chicken would be wonderful," Barbara said quickly. "And do not blame yourself. I gave you no warning. I promise I will say nothing to Lord Devane." She smiled at the irony of those words.

The woman dropped a curtsy. "And I have not even introduced myself. Well, you see, I am surprised. Head over heels. Elmo, my lady. Mrs. Lettice Elmo at your service. Now, will you sit here, or do you want to rest in your apartment? I could make down the bed and—"

"My—my apartment?"

"Oh, yes. And a grand one it is. Lord Devane had it decorated last year when the house was far enough along to live in. It is the only set of rooms that is finished. Not even his own are."

"I will sit here, Mrs. Elmo. Perhaps—perhaps later I will see it. Now, if you do not mind, I am so very hungry—"

And to her relief, Lettice Elmo rustled off, in a bustle now to do her duty.

Barbara leaned her head against the window frame and stared out into the gardens, but she did not really see them. She was thinking of what the housekeeper had said, and of the fact that she had so casually thought of wanting to be like her mother. It is time to stop when you can think such a thing without shuddering, Barbara Devane, she told herself. And Jemmy was in her mind again. And Charles. She pressed her hand to her mouth. He must not know what had happened. She would write a note to Jemmy and beg him to be discreet. If I survive this without being killed by Charles, she thought— and only part of her thought was in jest—I am going to have to make some changes in my life. I cannot go on this way. Jemmy. Sweet Jesus. He is a boy. A boy. Nothing to me. Charles will be so angry. She shook her head rebelliously. He always wanted her to bend to his will. She would not. He said he loved her. You did not select me, he told her, his mouth pulled up to one side ironically, I selected you. You had no choice, Barbara. No choice at all. She had been wrong (another mistake in her summer's seemingly endless series of mistakes) to think she could handle him, but her anger, that bright blinding anger that often led her to do things she had no real wish to, had her by the throat. She remembered the white, even gleam of Philippe's teeth as he smiled at her under the great candlelit chandelier in the domed salon. She shuddered. Today, her life was a shambles. How glad Philippe must be.

The chicken and freshly baked bread made her feel better, stronger. She tore white chunks from the bread's warm heart as if she were a starving beggar. She picked every last morsel of meat from the chicken bones, sitting cross-legged in the window seat, like a gypsy. At last she dipped greasy hands in the delicate porcelain bowl of lemon water (two tiny rosebuds floated in it) Mrs. Elmo had brought in with the food. She could see Roger's taste in everything, from the china dishes she ate from and the lace-trimmed linen napkin she wiped her hands on to the ornate wall and ceiling carvings, and the symmetry of the graceful, tall windows in the room in which she was sitting. Roger had always had an eye for what was beautiful. She remembered those months in Paris, when every aspect of her life had seemed full and rich and beautiful. When she had been so in love.

I must go, she thought, standing, but then Mrs. Elmo was back, and she let herself be persuaded to view the rest of the house. She walked through the rooms behind Mrs. Elmo, seeing everywhere grace and beauty, light and spaciousness,

the finest of craftsmanship in whatever was built. She felt
Roger's touch everywhere, felt surrounded by it, as if he had
taken her in his arms. None of the rooms she saw were finished. Some lacked paintings on their ceilings or chimneypieces or draperies for their windows or furniture or carpets.
But it did not matter. What was done was splendid. Perfect.
She could feel and see the time and care that had gone into
the house as she walked through its silent rooms. In one large
salon, her portrait hung, the one that had been painted in
Paris, suspended by a long, dark velvet ribbon. She stared up
at it, its presence shocking her. She and Mrs. Elmo stared up
into the face of that girl (painted before her brothers and sisters died), at the laughter, zest, innocence which radiated
from it.

"I should have recognized you at once," Mrs. Elmo said.
"Not a day goes by but I do not look at that portrait."

"Time changes us," Barbara said softly.

"You are more beautiful," Mrs. Elmo said.

Barbara was silent.

Mrs. Elmo led her to a door. "This is your apartment," she
said, beaming. "I saved the best for last."

Hesitantly, Barbara stepped over the threshold of the first
room of the apartment. It was an antechamber, a sitting
room. Beyond would be a bedchamber. This room was lovely:
a thick Turkish carpet atop the parquetry floor, festoons of
carved flowers across the walls and surrounding the mirror
above the fireplace, small, delicate pieces of furniture, tables,
armchairs, stools, a tiny writing desk. The window draperies,
the furniture upholstery, were a fresh, light color, the shade
of sea foam. The paintings mounted on the walls were all her
favorites, ones—long ago—that she had told Roger she liked.
She walked into the bedchamber. Above the fireplace hung a
portrait of her grandfather. The draperies surrounding the bed
frame were embroidered with hundreds of roses. Fresh flowers sat in a vase by a table near the window. A climbing rose
bloomed outside the windows. She could smell its fragrance,
heady and sweet from where she stood.

"I put flowers in here every day," Mrs. Elmo said. "Those
are Lord Devane's orders."

Barbara felt something in her throat catch. Mrs. Elmo
opened another door. Here was a smaller chamber, and step-

ping into it, Barbara felt an affinity, a perfectness that shook her soul. It was small, intimate, made for reading or writing or checking household receipts or embroidering. The walls were damasked, and they sloped upward to a low ceiling painted with children and lolling cherubs. It was unfurnished, except for a long, low bench and a cradle, in a corner, swathed in gauze. Barbara's heels tapped on the uncovered parquetry of the floor as she went to it. She touched its edge carefully with one finger. The cradle rocked gently. Dear God, she thought, closing her eyes, feeling tears, hot and burning, years old, behind her eyes. Dear, dear God.

"I did not know where to put that," Mrs. Elmo said quickly behind her. "It ought to go in the nursery, but those rooms are not finished. So I said to myself, Lettice Elmo, you just put that pretty thing in here. Not expecting you. Shall I take it away?"

"No."

"You are sure—"

"Yes."

Both of them stared at the cradle. Mrs. Elmo sighed. "There is nothing like children to let you know what life is all about. I had seventeen myself, and ten of them lived to make me proud. I see my daughters every Sunday. Every Sunday. They are good girls. Well, now, Lady Devane, if you will come this way. This door leads up back to the main salon—"

In the carriage, once it was on its way and she no longer had to smile and listen to Mrs. Elmo, she lay back against the seat, drained. Thoughts, images, memories circled in her head like blackbirds against a clear sky. Charles. Jemmy. Roger. The cradle. She felt sick again, but this was the sickness beyond that brought on by too much drink. This was a sickness of heart. Of spirit. For what might have been.

At St. James's Square, Dawdle, her majordomo, opened the door for her, almost as if he were expecting her.

"Your mother has been here," he called after her, as she ran up the stairs. "Twice. And Lord Charles Russel."

That stopped her midstep. She turned on the stairway. "When?"

"This morning. Very early, Lady Devane. He woke me up pounding on the door."

She ran on up the stairs to her bedchamber (not Roger's . . . never Roger's, but another room she had chosen for herself). She ordered the hip bath and pulled a dust sheet off a chair so she could sit while she waited for Dawdle and the one chambermaid on duty to carry up buckets of water to fill it. Dawdle was full of questions: how long would she be staying? should he hire another temporary chambermaid and a cook? what did she desire for dinner?, but she just shook her head at him, holding on to herself inside, the wound, the hurt, reopened and pulsing larger and larger. I should have stayed away, she thought. What a fool I am. Later, she told him. I will decide everything later. He ripped dust covers from the furniture and opened windows and apologized for not being more prepared, but she waved him away. She wanted only to be alone.

She ripped off her clothing and sank down as far as she could into the water. It felt good, cool. Not a breath of air from the open windows stirred the draperies. She washed her body, scooped water up to her breasts and neck and face, concentrated on slowing her breathing. Everything was pushing up inside. Push it back, down, down. This was it . . . wash it away. . . . So Charles had been here, had he? Striding past Dawdle to check her bedchamber himself. She knew that from what Dawdle did not say; servants had a way of communicating unpleasantness about their betters. And her mother. What on earth could she have wanted? Well, none of it mattered. None of it. Because she was going to lie here in the cool water for a few more moments, until she was calm and collected inside, until those bad thoughts just on the other side of her mind went away. And then she was going to rise and dress and write Jemmy a note (going by his lodging on her way out of town or giving it to Harry to handle) to tell him that he must deny everything, for her sake. That it was all a drunken mistake. That she was fond of him, but no more than that. That she humbly begged his pardon; it did not matter if he hated her, indeed, that might be best. And then she was going to Richmond (before Charles could find her) to pick up Thérèse and Hyacinthe and the dogs. And then she was going to her grandmother's. And if Charles wanted to follow her, he could damn well come face to face with her grandmother. Because she was leaving London and Charles and this mess of a spring and summer to see if she could make sense of it in Tamworth with her grandmother. . . .

She put her hands to her face. The cradle. The pain. The pain of seeing that empty cradle. . . . Shake with it, fight it, think of something else. . . . Oh, she should have stayed with her grandmother to sort out emotions that had come with her from Paris, along with her trunks, instead of rushing head-long to London like that fifteen-year-old girl she had once been who believed her dreams would come true if she only dreamed them long enough. And they had not. She gasped. The pain was agony. Her heart was being squeezed with it. She could not breathe . . . retreat. Yes, retreat. From Charles, from the Frog, from the cradle, from the agony, from everything. A masterly retreat is part of fighting the bat-tle, her grandfather used to say, waving his pruning shears above the bowed, blossom-heavy heads of his beloved roses. He had no more armies, no more sons, only his roses. He expounded military theory to them and to any of his grand-children who would stop long enough to listen to him. Her dear, sweet grandfather. . . . Yes, retreat would defuse Charles. By the time he discovered where she was, his anger would have diminished. Irritation would have taken its place.

She managed to smile through the red mists of pain at the thought of Charles damning her to hell, but searching for her anyway. As she knew he would. As she would wish him to do. Oh, Charles, she thought, you will not be angry with me anymore. You will want to kiss me and make up, but, my dear Charles, my dear love, I think it is too late for that. Too late for us. She could not run away any longer. The pain took her and shook her. She gasped like a fish in her bath. She was a rat caught by a cat, and the cat was shaking her, shaking her to death in its mouth. The ghosts of her brothers and sis-ters danced around her; the ghosts of the children she had not borne, the dreams that had not come true. She was on a brink, an edge. Now. And she must step back. She must gather the courage to step back. Before it was too late. As it had become in Paris. Before she so changed that the girl who lived inside her, who stared at her some mornings from behind her eyes as she looked into her mirror, would never again be free. Boo. The pain, ah, the pain. Face the truths, whatever they were. Face them. However ugly, they were better than lies. Lies slowly strangled the soul with their gossamer tendrils. She knew. She had felt her soul this afternoon.

She gripped the sides of the bath to control the trembling of her body. To hold inside tears that pushed up like hard, jagged chunks of ice. Hold on. Hold on. Run. Hide. Hide away. To Tamworth. To Grandmama. Grandmama will make it better. . . . She was able to smile, beads of sweat on her upper lip with the effort she was making, at that thought. She was no longer a child, her grandmother could no longer kiss the hurt and have her convinced it would go away. But Tamworth, the peace, the haven it seemed this moment. No one quarreling over her. Jemmy. Charles. The Frog. No one yammering at her of what she must do. No Philippe with his cruel, white smile reminding her of what was gone. . . . Tamworth . . . the wych arbor, the great octagonal bay windows where one could sit hidden all morning, the twisted chimney stacks, the ancient ivy, her grandmother's bedchamber, her grandfather's rose garden, the path to Jane's, the apple orchard, the green cool of the woods in summer . . . yes, Tamworth. There she would rest. There she could be free. . . . Her breathing was slowing. Carefully, not quite trusting herself, she loosened her hands on the sides of the tub. The trembling was over. She wiped the perspiration from her lip, from her brow. She felt as weak as if she had been sick with a fever. Weak and trembling like an invalid, which was what she was. And what would heal her? Would truth? Would anything? The pain was less now. She could bear it. She sank back into the water, her head held by the bath's high edge, her eyes closed, her body exhausted. She was glad she was alone, so glad for the quiet here, the silence. There was time to pull herself back together, nothing but silent moments of time. . . . The bedchamber door slammed open.

Diana stood framed in the doorway. Her famous violet eyes, like Harry's eyes, narrowed at the sight of her daughter naked in the hip bath, staring at her.

"Well," she said, and her low, throaty voice made the hair rise on the back of Barbara's neck, "you make a pretty sight, but I am the wrong one to waste it on. Charles Russel was at my door this morning before dawn, and I have never seen an angrier man in my life. You had better get out of that bath and find him at once. Or there is going to be more trouble than either of us can handle."

CHAPTER TWENTY-ONE

"Mother," Barbara said flatly, "how did you get in here? I thought you were in Norfolk with Walpole."

Diana was already inspecting the gown Barbara had pulled off; she considered her daughter's wardrobe and jewel case extensions of her own, and much more interesting.

"Norfolk is boring," she said. "Robert is boring. All he can think of is building his house and buying more property. I swear I would break with him if he had not just been reappointed to the ministry. Is this new?" She held the gown up. "Where is the waist in front?" The gown was shapeless, falling from neck to hem almost like a tent.

Barbara took a deep breath, trying to hold her temper. How like her mother to barge in, say something outrageous, then talk about fashion. She was not to be trusted. She was selfish and greedy. She had never once asked what happened in Paris. Never once questioned the rumors that had swirled about Roger, about Philippe, about Harry, about Barbara. Not so much as one question. Which Barbara could not forgive. But she was not going to deal with her mother today or for many days to come. She was going to Tamworth. Hang Charles. And hang her mother.

"It is the latest style from France, called a sack gown. I am told it was devised by a French duchess to disguise pregnancy, and that Madame will not receive any woman who dares to wear one in her presence. She says they are indecent and look

521

as if the wearer had got straight out of bed. Go away, Mother, I am bathing—"

"How comfortable it looks. I ought to have one made myself—"

"So you should. Do so immediately. Take my gown—as you will doubtless do anyway—so that you have a pattern. I should warn you I left my jewel case in Richmond, but there may be a few jewels in the drawers of the dressing table. Take those also. Take anything of mine you want. Then go away."

Diana looked at her daughter. Barbara had learned much in Paris, among her accomplishments the rude, arrogant manners of the French princesses, and she had been known to use them effectively (especially to the Prince of Wales, who was a glutton for punishment). Even so, she was no match for her mother.

"Certainly," Diana said coldly. "The fact that Charles Russel nearly tore my door off at its hinges this morning would be of no interest to you. The fact that he frightened me, and I am, you may be assured, not easily frightened by raging men, would be of no interest to you. The fact that I think he intends to kill whomever you spent the night with would, of course, also be of no interest to you. Good day, Barbara."

"Kill? Kill!" Barbara floundered in the shallow hip bath. "I do not believe you!"

"As you wish. Now I will go home as you have all but thrown me out—"

"Mother! You stay where you are and tell me what makes you say such a wicked, wicked thing!" She felt the fear prickling through her, blossoming hydra-headed in her breast. Charles had dueled before; he was capable of killing someone if he was angry enough. I am a jealous man, he had said, his hands playing in her hair. Leave, if you must, if you do not care for me. But do not be unfaithful. Not while you are with me. I can forgive all things but that. She gripped the sides of the tub. "What did you tell him?"

"What could I tell him! I had no idea where you were. Where were you, by the way?"

Barbara did not answer.

Diana sat down abruptly, her face changing. It was as if she had momentarily lost strength in her legs. "It is true," she whispered, staring at Barbara. "You were with another man.

I cannot believe you would be such a fool! Charles will kill him! And the scandal will ruin all our plans—"

"Your plans, Mother, never mine! If you choose this moment to say one word to me about the Frog, I will scream—"

"Do not call him the Frog!" Diana said sharply, rallying. "He is your prince and deserves respect—"

"He looks like a frog, he acts like a frog, he is a frog, and that is what I will go to bed with before I bed him. There is nothing, nothing, you can say or do that will change my mind—"

"How dare you speak to me so!" Diana's tone was arrogant, scornful, annihilating. "I am your mother, and I have only the welfare of the family left me at heart. You selfish creature! Harry can go to hell in a basket for all you care! You think only of yourself. And I am sick to death of it—"

"Get out!"

Diana stared at her daughter.

"Get out of my room! Get out of my house! Get out of my life! You cannot tell me what to do! And you, above all people, cannot judge me! Get out! Get out! Get out!"

By the last words, Barbara was screaming, out of control, standing up in the bath, water dripping from her, the veins jutting out in her forehead and throat. It was too much; it was all too much, and for her mother to begin nagging about Harry when there was a possibility of a duel between Jemmy and Charles was the last thing she could bear at this moment. A duel. Not again. And not over her. The thought of it was impossible to stand. Charles would set in motion something that would forever affect her, just as the other duel had. The scandal, the lies, the gossip swirling around her, the distortion, the filth clinging to her, making her into something she was not. The aftermath of a duel never ended. People were forever changed, and she could not go through it again. She would not. She did not deserve it. Just as Jemmy did not deserve to die. He was a boy. A child, still. What had happened between them was not planned! Was there anyone who would help her? Was there anyone who realized the seriousness of the situation? A man might die—unjustly—because of her. Duels were not glamorous affairs of honor, not when there was anger and revenge behind them. They were blood and possible death and the smell of fear. They were women left alone, crying. As I am alone, she thought. And she began to tremble with the emotion of her fears and the anger at her mother and all that had been uncovered at Devane House today. Her weaknesses were naked and exposed, like shells upon a beach, as she stood there, shaking.

Something like compassion moved across Diana's face, though in a saner moment Barbara would have sworn it was not possible for her mother to feel such a thing. At any rate, she picked up the drying cloth and threw it over Barbara's shoulders and helped her from the tub and into a chair. Barbara sat, pulling the cloth about herself like a second skin, while her mother gave her a glass of brandy. She stared at it as if she did not know what to do with it, brandy spilling over her fingers with the violence of her trembling.

"Drink it," Diana said. Her voice had an odd, harsh sound to it. "Drink it all. You will be better in a—"

There was a rapping at the door. Diana's words died in her mouth. She and Barbara stared at each other.

"Charles," Barbara whispered.

She could not face him. She was not afraid of him, but his anger would require such strength to withstand, and she was, at this moment, without anything left inside herself to make her strong.

Diana's face became hard and arrogant. She had enough inside herself to face a regiment of angry men. She strode across the room and whipped open the door. Dawdle, standing there, took a step backward at the expression on her face.

"A-a note, m-madam," he faltered, "for Lady Devane—"

Diana snatched it from his hands.

"Idiot! You frightened your mistress! Give it to me. Then get out of my sight." Each word was like the lash of a whip. Dawdle stood struck dumb before her.

"Fool servants," she said, turning away, though Dawdle could still hear her. "They never know how to do anything properly!" She ripped open the note.

"It is from Harry. He says to come to his lodgings as soon as you can—"

Harry. He would help. He would want the duel no more than she; he would remember Paris and its effect. . . . Tony's image rose suddenly in her mind, fair and large. If only Tony were in London. His cool head, his unexpected practicality, would stop everything. He could handle Charles. Stay, Bab, he had said to her the other afternoon, taking her by the arm and staring at her with his wide, pale blue eyes, eyes that were almost gray. He had known what she did not; but she would not listen. . . .

"Harry!" snapped her mother, seeing her expression. "Harry will be about as much help as your cousin Mary. You just listen to me. I know all about duels. You have two options, and two options only: find the man and spirit him out of town, or find Charles and change his mind. Because if the two of them meet first, you are finished. Their sense of honor will be all that is important. I know! If a challenge has been issued, you will not be able to change their minds, though you plead or cry or tell them your husband will beat you. God, Barbara, I could beat you myself! I told you from the beginning that Charles Russel was not a man to be unfaithful to—"

"I did not plan to be unfaithful—"

"Just tell him that!"

"I will!"

"A fat lot of good it will do you."

Barbara picked up the sack gown tiredly. She and her mother always quarreled on the level of children. "Mother, go home. I do not need—"

Diana took the gown from her. "You need me more than you know. Have you no mind at all? You must wear a gown that will accentuate your bosom, your waist, not this new style. A look at a little breast will do more to influence a man's mood than a dozen words. You must look seductive, contrite, tearful."

She was already in the adjoining room searching through gowns. Barbara could hear bits and pieces of her sentences: ". . . never listen to me . . . stir up their desire . . . a man is like a . . ."

Sitting down to pull on stockings, it was all she could do to make her hands move. There were visions in her head. Paris. Dark early morning hours when she and Thérèse were waiting for word of the duel, both of them crying in turns. The horror of those hours, the certainty that Harry would be killed, the desperate sense of futility, the knowledge that there was nothing that could be done. And then true horror. Harry being carried in, blood covering his face. She could not move. It was Thérèse who had the strength to go forward, to look at his bleeding head, to say in a shaking voice, "He is alive, Holy Mary, Mother of God, he is alive. His ear . . . it is gone. But he is alive. . . ." Not this way, Charles, she said in her mind. We deserve better than this. . . .

". . . but then you never can predict exactly what they will do," Diana was saying in front of her. She held up a gown, cut low across the front, with a tight, narrow waist. "This one is out of style, but who will notice. No stays, just you underneath. Lean forward often enough to give him a good look at what is inside this gown, Barbara. It will readjust his goals."

Barbara stood up while her mother tugged the gown over her head, onto the contours of her body.

"Sit down," Diana said. "I will put your rouge and powder on. You are still shaking. You must get hold of yourself. Cry. Not now, then. Can you cry? There is nothing to soften a man like tears." Diana was unscrewing jars that held rouge. "Tears make some men think of bed. Let us hope Charles and the other one—are you going to tell me his name? No? Oh, well, I will know soon enough—be still! Is this rouge new? What shade is this? I like it."

"You may have it." In her mind, she was very far from her mother.

Diana began to feather on the powder, the rouge that would make Barbara sophisticated and beautiful. She darkened her brows and lashes, twisted and pinned her thick hair, perfumed her arms and neck and the tops of her breasts. On her face she fixed the tiny black silk shapes of hearts and stars and half-moons. She was as fast, as expert as Thérèse. Barbara sat looking at herself in the mirror, at the rouged, fashionable woman who stared back bleakly at her. She did not recognize herself.

Diana admired her work. "All I can say is if either man can resist you, they do not make men the way they used to."

She held up a pearl bracelet that Thérèse must have overlooked in her packing. "Where did you get this? I like it."

"Richelieu gave it to me," Barbara said, jerking it on. Years ago. When I was young. For my sixteenth birthday. When I learned my husband's lover was another man. That was another time, and I was another person.

"Richelieu, heh? I always heard he was good in bed—"

Barbara stood up. "Goodbye, Mother."

She touched Diana's cheek with her own. In her head were visions tinged with red: blood, deep and red, thick, spilling everywhere, on Harry's face, on his hands, across his velvet coat and linen shirt, pulsing, pulsing from the side of his head while she and Thérèse worked like silent, crazed women to stanch the flow. Blood all over them. On their hands. On their gowns. On their faces. In their hair. Its smell. Its slipperiness. It must not happen again. She could not bear it.

"If you find Charles," Diana called after her, "get him into bed. It is your only prayer—" But her daughter was gone.

Diana sat down abruptly on the dressing stool, and then, from the force of long habit, stared at herself in the mirror. The woman who looked back was no longer a flawless beauty; time was there in deeper facial lines, in the myriad wrinkles around the eyes, in sags along the jawline, in the extra flesh that padded her body. But the woman who looked back was also still extraordinary-looking; the bones underneath the flesh were good; time would never erase them. She frowned at herself and patted the extra softness under her chin. She lifted her chin and looked at it from each side. Suddenly she smiled.

"Not bad for a woman of thirty-four," she said out loud. (She was a month away from forty.) She stood up. At the door, she paused. Back to the dressing table she went. She picked up the jar of rouge whose shade she had liked. And on her way out, she picked up the sack gown and folded it across her arm.

Harry's servant opened the door. Barbara whirled in, past the parlor and into the bedchamber where Harry, wigless, in his stockings and breeches, was searching through the drawers of a cupboard.

"Charles was here not half an hour ago," he said, his back to her. "He woke me up banging on the door—damn it, have I no clean shirts! Marchpane! Where are my shirts? He wanted to know where Jemmy's lodgings were. I would not tell him."

The breath left her body. She sat down limply on the bed. Harry was still rummaging through the ruins of a drawer.

Four years had done little to change him, except to turn him from a boy into a man.

"We nearly fought ourselves," he was saying. "I tried to make him rest a moment. He has been up all night looking for you. And he is past drunk. I was just coming for you— ah, here is one." He held up the shirt, and in doing so, saw Barbara's face. Down came the shirt, he went to her, taking her cold hand in his.

"Are you well, Bab? Answer me. Marchpane! Marchpane! Get some water for my sister—"

"No! No." She swallowed. "I cannot stand another duel."

They looked at each other, both thinking the same thing. He patted her hand, then walked to the window. The sounds of midday London came to their ears, the street vendors selling lavender and brooms and doormats and gingerbread, the rumble of carts and wagons, the curses of drivers. Absently he rubbed his mangled earlobe, his fingers lightly playing with the healed tissue of the ear opening, the scar of the groove the pistol ball had indented in his skull. Philippe had either aimed to miss and failed, or aimed to kill him and failed. But he had succeeded beyond his wildest dreams, because something essential had poured out of Harry with his blood, some wild, boyish, carefree recklessness that was so much a part of his charm. He was still boyish and still reckless. And still charming. But it was an act. To cover the empty place inside. He knew it, and Barbara knew it. And they never mentioned it. Never.

"I have been thinking, Bab. We must reach Jemmy or Charles before they reach one another. If that is done, I do not think we can stop it—"

"So Mother says. But I could convince Jemmy. I know I could—"

"No honorable man is going to walk away from a duel, my dear. You must face that. If Charles has time to sober up and rest, he will cool down. He is not the kind of man to prey on another man's inexperience. I know that."

He was thinking of Philippe, she thought. Dangerous memories. Philippe had taken more than his ear. He had taken his faith in himself. Harry had gone marching into battle like a young prince, even though his knowledge was swords, not pistols. But the choice of weapons was Philippe's. And he chose pistols.

"Where can we find Charles?" he asked her.

"Garraway's. He will stop at some point in Garraway's. He always does."

"Then you will leave a note for him there."

"Saying what, for God's sake!"

"That you must meet with him—begging him to meet. He will not be able to resist; he is in love with you, you know."

"A fine way to show it." Her face was haggard. "And Jemmy?"

"Write another note, saying essentially the same thing."

"And then what?"

"Pray they show up. You will deal with Charles, and I will deal with Jemmy."

"How? What will you do?"

"Spirit him out of London if I have to. Young fool! I will not let him face Charles." His face was grim.

He is remembering, she thought. God help us all. She reached out her hands and he took them in his, squeezing them. He had always blamed himself for Roger's leaving her afterward, but she knew now that life was not that simple. It had been both their faults . . . and neither's.

She went to write the notes while Harry finished dressing, searching for a blank piece of paper on a table littered with papers. Riffling through them she began to notice they were bills. She opened more and more of them. Bill after bill, gambling debts of honor, pawn receipts, reminders that stock payments were due, bills for hats and snuffboxes and gold-topped canes. Oh, Harry, she thought. You said everything was under control. You said you made money this summer; you said you were going to pay off everything. She closed her eyes. Well, whatever money had been made had not been spent on clearing debts. Harry was living on the brink of financial disaster, the specter of imprisonment for debt a certainty, if it were not for her generosity and their mother's and Tony's. But to lend him money was to see it thrown away. He was always sure some stock purchase would catapult him over the brink; the next horse he backed would win; the next throw of the dice would change his life. She picked up a bill, months old, for two pairs of soft leather gloves, green-colored. Green gloves.

A needless expense. Whom had he given them to? Pamela? Judith? A whore?

"I have an idea," he called to her from the bedchamber. "With your permission, I will get Wart to help. He will know where to find Jemmy."

Wart. Yes, Wart would know. Just as he knew where the next card game was, or the next horse race or cockfight. Wart spent even more money than Harry, but as a duke he had much better resources to fall back on. Sometimes she wanted to blame Harry's friends for his recklessness, but all the young men she knew were in debt, always gambling, spending their money on clothes and snuff and gold toothpicks and actresses. Richelieu had. And Charles did. And Wart, who was running through his inheritance as if there were no tomorrow. He was no longer the shy boy of Paris, brilliant and endearing. His baby son had died from smallpox in March, and Wart, who had settled down to live with his wife and son on his estate, had plunged headlong into dissipation. With Harry as a too-willing companion. But she understood that. It was grief. Which did strange things to one, twisting the heart the way it did. Would she have acted differently in Paris if she had not still been grief-stricken over the deaths of her brothers and sisters? Still fragile and off balance? Who was she to judge Wart or Harry? Or anyone. The five graves at Tamworth had changed her, as had the grave of what had been her love for Roger. Vanity of vanity, saith the Preacher, all is vanity. She no longer turned to the Lord above for comfort, but in the first days of her most searing grief over Roger, she had searched for answers and found only a grim irony in the bitter words of the Preacher: What profit hath a man of all his labor which he taketh under the sun? One generation passeth away, and another generation cometh: but the earth abideth forever . . . forever . . . unlike love or youth . . . forever. . . .

"Sprinkle some water on those notes," Harry said over her shoulder.

"It will look better if it seems you have cried over them. Waterlog Jemmy's. He is still young and impressionable—smile at me, Bab. Perhaps nothing happened between you two. You were both so drunk . . ."

"I am in no mood for your vulgar jests," she said irritably. "If you had seen the way he looked at me this morning—"

"He always looks at you that way. God knows why."

He made her laugh. Dear Harry. He had been with her when Roger left; he had been with her when she left Richelieu; he had been with her in Italy to bury their father; he had been with her the afternoon she had first seen Roger again. Harry had no illusions about her. It was so comforting. . . .

"Harry . . . these bills . . ."

"Never mind those." He sprinkled water liberally over both notes and her gown. "I will pay them soon. Just as soon as I sell some stock. Just wait, Bab. We are both going to be laughing about this thing in just a few days. I promise."

Now she sat waiting in a tavern not far from Garraway's coffeehouse on Cornhill Street in the financial heart of London. The tavern was on the corner of a short blind alley with other small taverns and coin and specie dealers and, since this summer, offices of stockjobbers, those who bought and sold stock on their own account. Noblewomen were not a usual sight in this part of London, which belonged to merchants and bankers, but as people flocked here from Westminster and the suburbs, from all over the country and abroad to buy South Sea and other stocks, the sight of noblewomen, in their carriages or accompanied by their maids, was now nothing new. They were as eager to invest as their husbands, pawning jewels or heirlooms, spending their jointures, to finance moneymaking. She had spent many an hour in this very tavern waiting thusly for Harry or Charles. They were used to her here.

She stared out the bow window to Garraway's across the street. It was crowded, not only with its patrons, but with buyers and sellers of stock. She could barely see inside for the press of people and carriages and horses outside. A mood of frantic activity was everywhere in this part of London. It made her more nervous than she already was. A fourth subscription of South Sea stock had been offered, and people were clamoring to buy or sell. And no wonder. Last spring, the South Sea Company's plan to take over the national debt had been approved, and the stock rose with each subscription all summer. In April the price of the stock had been £300 a share. By June it was £1,050. The success stories were known to all: one actress retired from the stage, having made £8,000 on South Sea; a fortunate man had the honor of announcing his marriage to a woman whose attractiveness was increased by having made £100,000 in the South Sea Company; an Exchange Alley porter bought himself a carriage fit for a duke and a velvet coat with his gains, £2,000 on South Sea . . . South Sea marriages, South Sea carriages, South Sea jewels, South Sea estates. Its name was magic. The directors even allowed investors to borrow money against stock.

Lloyd's, Jonathan's, Garraway's, Virginia's and other coffeehouses were crowded all day and into the night with men at clerks' tables, eager to invest not only in South Sea, but also in the other companies that had sprung up to take advantage of the public's craze to invest. It was madness, and it was wonderful. London was euphoric, its financial heart beating loudly, heard all over the country. The streets of Cornhill and Threadneedle and Leadenhall were packed all day long with carriages and horses and people. Invest. Invest. What stock have you bought? Have you heard the latest? Staring out at Garraway's, Barbara was sharply reminded of Paris the summer before when carriages and people on horseback or on foot crowded outside John Law's mansion waiting for the door to open so that they could trade Law's bank notes for stock in his newly formed Mississippi Company. The news from France now was not quite so optimistic. John Law had been dismissed from his spectacular post of controller general of France, but some said it was French politics, and others claimed the French simply could not abide a foreigner in such a high position. Everyone here knew Law was a financial genius. After all, he had solved France's bankruptcy and introduced that miraculous new idea of credit. Now everyone in England wanted to experience its wonder firsthand; it made money cheap and available. And the prime example of its splendor was the South Sea Company. South Sea lent money on its stock, and therefore there was more money to buy more stock, and its rise was magic and enriching and self-perpetuating. The government was behind the scheme; the king was governor of the company; an earl was a director.

"Well, I do not like it," Barbara heard one of the two men at a table just behind her whisper loudly and sibilantly. "It is going to burst. It is already under nine hundred."

South Sea. They were talking of South Sea. She was so weary of it, but then what else did people speak of these days? Only last week Harry had been angry that his name was no longer on the lists of those who had first options to buy in the fourth subscription. The clerk said there were no lists this time, Harry told her, angry and impatient, an underlying desperation in his voice that she did not understand, but I do not believe it. It is Roger's doing . . . and then, seeing her face, he had caught himself. Harry and Roger were enemies now, enemies since that moment her screams had brought him bursting into the blue-and-gold salon to see her struggling and sobbing in her husband's arms. Yet still his name was on the earlier lists . . . a generous gesture . . . by someone. What had she and Roger said to each other as Harry lay bleeding on her lace-edged sheets in that house that had become a hell in Paris? She could not remember. She remembered only a contrary longing to be somewhere safe, and the safest place she knew was her husband's arms. . . . She put a hand to her head. I will not think of that now.

"Do not be so cautious," said his companion. "The price will rise again."

"The Bubble Act is a mistake," answered the first man, the pessimistic one.

"Nonsense," said the other. "John Law says credit well managed is worth ten times the amount of capital stock. The rise could go on indefinitely."

"But they have lent money they do not have. Millions of pounds. Any man of sense knows a house built on sand will eventually fall—"

She caught her breath. Charles was standing at the door, blinking in the dimness, searching for her.

"The Duke of Marlborough drew his money out in May. In May! What does he know that we do not?"

She lifted her chin and stared at him. Their glances locked. His face was white and tired, and once he saw her, it became grim. He began to stride toward her table, calling impatiently for a glass of wine. The closer he came, the more clearly she could see he had not slept; his eyes were bloodshot, rimmed with red, and unfriendly, the eyes of a stranger.

"All right. Granted it may have to fall eventually, but surely not before November."

Barbara turned around. "Will you hush!" she hissed.

The two men stared at her blankly, but she was already facing away.

He was nearly at her table, walking with the loose-limbed masculine grace some big men possess. She could feel her heart beating with loud, irregular thumps. There was such a resemblance to Roger; Charles might have been a less handsome, much larger brother, but for his nose and his mouth, wide and sensual and—he stood before her now. He is drunk, she thought. I cannot deal with him. She felt a sudden sense of doom and closed her eyes to will it away.

He sat down heavily. A waiter glided over to serve the wine, opened his mouth to speak, glanced at Charles's face, then quickly to hers, and at once glided away, no fool. Charles drained the glass of wine. Do not drink anymore, she thought, but she did not say a word. The hair on the back of her neck and along her arms had risen.

"Where were you last night?" His words were flat.

"I had too much to drink. . . ." She could almost hear her mother telling her to lean forward, to show him her bosom, but she could not bring herself to do so. It seemed dishonest and unworthy.

"Let us leave," she said to him, softly. "We can go to my home, or to yours, whichever you please, and I will make you something to eat, and then we will talk. As friends. But not here, Charles. And not now. Not in this way—"

He interrupted her. "I know where you were."

His shoulders seemed to block out light and air and space.

"If you know that," she tried to say calmly, "then you also know you have no reason to be angry—"

"I can forgive a whore, Bab, but not a liar."

She felt as if he had slapped her. A sense of both sorrow and futility filled her. "You know I am not a whore or a liar."

"But you are," he said, his mouth pale with the effort he was making to keep his temper. "They told me so in France, but still, I wanted to meet you. I dreamed of you. And when I did meet you, I knew I wanted you. I did not love you then, did not expect to love you, but I wanted you. I thought them wrong. Liars. Gossips. Now I love you . . . and I thought you loved me." His voice was soft. And dangerous. She hated the way he was looking at her, as if she had failed him, and he despised her for it. She had failed him. And herself.

"I do care for you, Charles—"

"Then why did you sleep with Jemmy?"

What can I answer? she thought. I do not know why I slept with Jemmy. I do not know why I slept with you. I do not even know why I slept with Richelieu. That is a lie—sometimes my life seems filled with lies, Charles—I slept with Richelieu to hurt Roger. Only it hurt me more. And I slept with you to hurt Roger. Only that hurt me more, also. The truth? You desire truth? All right, I will tell it, ugly as it is. Perhaps it is the only thing to help us.

"I was drunk, drunker than I have ever been. As you are now. It was a mistake. A terrible, terrible mistake. Do not add to it—"

But she had guessed wrong. He was closing his eyes, his face was twisting with pain. He was blinking his eyes rapidly, almost as if he was going to cry. But instead he said, "He is a dead man."

The words rang in her ears.

"No! He is only a boy! Listen to me, it would be shameful to duel with him—"

"It was shameful of you to lie with him. The boy acted the man." His face was gleaming with sweat. He seemed sick. "And he must pay for it. I stand for no one touching what is mine."

"Yours! I am not yours! You are not my husband—"

He stood up, knocking over his chair. The tavern around them was quiet, everyone staring at them, all motion suspended. Someone held a glass in midair. The waiter's hand was still, quiescent upon the table he had been wiping clean.

"Wait!" she cried.

Words babbled out of her as danger pressed down on her, over her anger, squeezing out her breath.

"I did not mean it. I did not. Listen to me. You are angry, and I am angry. We never quarrel well. You have had too much to drink. And no rest. We will go someplace that is quiet, together, someplace that is private, and I will explain it all to you. You owe me that, Charles—"

But he was already walking away from her.

"Charles!"

She sceamed his name. Everyone was staring at her, all mouths a small O.

"Charles!"

She did not care what they thought.

"Charles!"

The veins stood out in each side of her neck.

The door made a thudding sound as it closed behind him. Outside, he leaned over and vomited in the street.

She had been waiting in Harry's room for an hour. I have failed, she thought over and over. Afternoon was fading; soon it would be the beginning of the summer twilight. She paced up and down in front of Harry's window; already she had sent Harry's man with another note for Jemmy. He was ordered to slip it under the door if no one answered. Wild plans went through her head. If Harry found Jemmy, she would have him knock him unconscious and then kidnap him, taking him somewhere in the country until Charles was calmer. She would learn where they were dueling and leap in front of their pistols or swords at the last minute so that they could not kill each other. She would tell the constable and have them both arrested. The whole thing was a nightmare tinged with melodrama, too poorly acted to garner anything but orange peels and boos from an audience. It could not be happening; yet it was. One act on her part setting into motion a chain of events that was leading to tragedy. If Jemmy died, she would not be able to forgive herself. Or Charles. If Jemmy died, the scandal would be enormous. She would have to withdraw from court. The Frog would read her a righteous lecture. The maids of honor would snicker behind their fans. Roger could divorce her. Easily. How Philippe would love that. She could envision him, a black raven on Roger's shoulder, advising him. Ironic that she had lain in her bath—was it only this morning—and planned to go to Tamworth to sort out her life. Her life was now unraveling. She had it in her hands, but the threads, tens of them, slipped through her fingers. Do not let Jemmy die, she prayed as she paced back and forth. Please. Please. Please. She thought of all she might have said to Charles and had not. She should have listened to her mother; she should have gone on her knees there in the tavern, pleading. Weeping.

The door opened, and Harry stood there looking at her. She had to sit down, knowing what he was going to say even as he said it.

"I could not find him—"

Sweet merciful Jesus, pray for us now in the hour of our need. She held out her hands, and Harry crossed the floor swiftly to take them.

There was a knock on the door. She and Harry stared at each other, one thought on both their minds. She found herself choking, unable to breathe as Harry opened the door. Jemmy. . . .

Diana walked in.

"I could not wait another moment at my house," she said, going at once to her daughter and ignoring Harry. "I must have been to yours at least seven times. What is happening?"

"The duel is set for tomorrow morning," Harry said with a glance at his sister. He still had the door open, as if by wishful thinking his mother would walk back through it.

"Tomorrow morning!" Diana cried. "Did you see Charles? Did you?"

Barbara did not answer.

"I knew it!" Diana said. "I knew that temper of yours would ruin everything. Time and again I have told you how to handle men. And do you listen? No. You think you know everything. You have to cajole them, plead with them, make them think you are weak and frightened when they are angry. There are times to lose your temper, Barbara Alderley, and there are times to keep it, and a wise woman knows—"

"Shut up!" Barbara cried, putting her hands over her ears. "Shut up!"

There was a note in her voice that rose above their heads. Hearing it, Harry went to her and put his hand on her shoulder. I am hysterical, Barbara thought, as if from a distance.

"It is not true," she heard herself saying to Harry. "Tell me it is not true."

"Bab," he told her gently. "They are placing bets on the duel at White's, which means that Jemmy has accepted Charles's challenge—"

"Where will it be?"

"Who knows?"

"If you could find out—"

"You would do what?" Diana cut in sarcastically. "Show up in your carriage, scream, have hysterics while their seconds hold you, and they end up killing each other for certain because you are there! You cannot stop the duel, Barbara. And if you dare to be where it is held, your reputation will never recover. People will think you went there to gloat, to cheer Charles on, to—"

"Damn what people think!"

"No, Bab. She is correct. Listen to her."

Barbara was silent, looking from Harry to her mother and back again. "The Earl of Camden," she said. "I could go to him." The earl was Jemmy's father.

"And do what?" demanded Diana.

"I-I could explain what has happened, and how it is my fault, and beg him to order Jemmy away."

Diana pursed her lips. "It is unlikely he would . . . and yet . . ."

"And yet?"

"It might be worth a try. I know the old man, I will write a note so that he will receive you. Yes, it might work. Jemmy could be sent away immediately, confined for a while to his father's estates; Charles would cool off, you could disappear—"

"To Tamworth."

"Yes. To Tamworth. And I would explain to the prince that your friendship with Jemmy was distorted, tell him how you worked to save him, and when you came back to court, say, in December, he would be as hot for you as ever."

"Harry." Barbara's voice was barely controlled. "Tell her that I am not going to bed with the Frog. She will not listen to me."

"Mother, she is not going to bed with the Frog."

"And why not? You seem to have bedded everyone else."

Harry flushed. "Out," he told Diana. "Get out."

Diana sat down, deliberately fluffing out her skirts so that the elaborate edging on the hem should not be crushed.

"It is my fault," Harry said to Barbara, "for answering the door without asking who was on the other side. Shall I drag her out forcibly?"

"Get me some paper," Diana ordered, unimpressed with either of them. She waited. "Why are you two staring at me? I thought time was of the essence here."

"I am going to lie down a moment," Barbara said, her hand over her eyes. "You deal with her." She went out of the room.

Harry motioned his mother to the cluttered table, finding the pen and inkwell for her, while she irritably riffled through the crumpled papers littering the top of the table.

"You remind me of your father," she told him, frowning. "All these unpaid bills. I have been bankrupt, Harry, and I tell you it is a terrible state to be in. Once we get this nonsense with Barbara settled, I am going to find you a wealthy wife. And you are going to marry her if I have to order you dragged to the altar. These receipts for South Sea stock—it is rumored Sir John Blunt has been quietly selling his. Since he is the principal director behind the massive selling, I would take note. I myself have already written a note to Roger, telling him I wish him to buy back my stock. What is this, ten guineas for green gloves? That shopkeeper is a highway robber; I would not pay it."

"I have no intention of doing so. The letter, Mother. . ."

Diana concentrated on her task. Harry was silent, watching her. Once she asked him how to spell "favor," and once she asked him about the betting at White's.

"Three to one that Charles will kill him," he told her shortly.

She signed her name with a flourish; it was perhaps the only word which came easily from her pen, other than "money."

"Good odds," she said. "Do you think he will?"

"Yes."

"Fool. Men in love are fools, but then so are women. I told Barbara to watch herself with him. Here. I am finished."

He waved the ink-stained, blotted note to dry the ink.

"What do you think will happen if this fails?" he asked his mother.

"Jemmy will die. The scandal will be enormous, until some fresh scandal replaces it, as it will. Barbara will have to retire from court for a few months. The prince will sulk, miss her, allow her return too soon. Roger may petition for a divorce, but I doubt he will. In fact, Harry, our best ploy is to reconcile them—do not scowl. It would be better for Barbara. By spring, most people will barely remember why she left court, though there will be a certain unsavoriness added to her reputation. But she can return, resume her place, and if we are fortunate, she will be more amenable to the prince's overtures after her brief exile."

She eyed Harry knowledgeably. He flushed. She knew how easy it would be for him if Barbara became the Prince of Wales's mistress. There would be money, sinecures, other estates for the asking.

"Barbara!" he called angrily. His mother read him too well. "You never give up, do you?" he said to her.

She smiled at him. "No."

In the carriage, Barbara said to him, "By the way, today I overheard two men talking. One of them said he thought the South Sea Company underfinanced. I thought you might want to know."

He shook his head. "I have a hunch stock will rise again, Bab. I cannot always be unlucky, can I?"

She counted hedges and ditches and ponds on the wearying hour's journey to Islington, where the earl and his wife were in summer residence. She watched milkmaids herding their cows home, groups of them laughing and singing and swinging their buckets, barefoot in the summer dust. How free they look, she thought. The carriage had to stop for flocks of geese and sheep, ragamuffin boys herding them toward the village common where the animals would graze awhile before going to night pastures or barns. In the fields, harvesters were still shucking corn, working as late as possible in the summer's long twilight, to bring it in. Their voices were raised in song, and women and children followed to gather the gleanings, that corn not harvested because of size or color, and therefore traditionally left to whoever wanted it. In other fields, yellow faces of corn peeped through green stalks, waiting their turn to be harvested. She thought of Tamworth, remembering its harvest seasons, the concentrated, sunburned faces of the workers, the harvest suppers as the sun set, the corn piled high and yellow in carts, children playing in the stubble, the rich heaviness to the pears and apples and plums that would be waiting on the tree limbs for their harvest, the scurry and bustle all over Tamworth as her grandmother directed foremen, distributed corn and fruit, some to the kitchens, some for drying, some for her stillroom, some for the poor who would have need of it during the cold winter. I wish I were there now, she thought, closing her eyes, seeing it, seeing the meadows, the corn waving in the breeze, the apple trees heavy with fruit.

"We are here," Harry said, shaking her shoulder. "Wake up."

The interview with the earl was difficult. Harry held her hand while she tried to explain. The earl's face became grayer with each word she spoke. Finally he stood with his back to her, staring out his windows at the darkening gardens, while the clackety song of crickets came clearly through the windows to compete with the sound of Barbara's low, throaty voice.

"Please do something," she finished, and her voice was shaking. "You are the only one who can. It is a misunderstanding from start to finish. Lord—Lord Russel is sometimes hot-tempered and impetuous, but I know he will regret his actions once he has time to think of them. And I will not be the cause of hurt to your son if there is any way I can prevent it. Please, my lord . . ."

It was some time before the earl turned around to face her. Finally he said, "He fancies himself a man. He is a man. He will consider it an affair of honor—"

"In another year or two it will be an affair of honor. Not now. I beg you to do as I ask. No one will think badly of him . . . or of you for saving him. He is too young to—to face Lord Russel."

The earl took a great while to answer her. Finally he said, "I will write the note. I do not condone what has happened, but I will do what I can. He is still so young, as you say. Wait here for me, Lady Devane."

He went into an adjoining smaller room. When he returned, the sound of a woman's crying came through the door with him. He handed a folded and sealed note to Barbara.

"My wife," the earl said simply. "He is our youngest, you know."

The earl walked them to their carriage.

"Lady Devane," he said, putting his hand on Barbara's arm as she began to climb into the carriage. Harry stepped back to allow them some privacy. "It took a great deal of courage for you to come to me as you have. I thank you for that. And if you will forgive an old man's tactlessness, I think you a better woman than this situation reflects."

She waited now in her bedchamber in St. James's. Armed with the note, Harry had sworn to her that he would find Jemmy if he had to search all night. Her mother was with her. She did not wish it so, but there was no keeping her away, short of ordering Dawdle to throw her out, and her mother outweighed him. Diana lay on the bed, fully dressed, dozing on and off. Barbara sat in a chair, near her window, open to catch the night's breezes. For a while she had listened to the sound of carriages, of people walking in the square and hailing one another, but finally, even that had stopped. There was now only silence, and the night watchman's hourly cry. She tried not to worry with the passing time, tried to believe that it boded good not evil. A kind of litany went continually through her mind: Lord have mercy upon us, please make Harry find Jemmy, please make Jemmy read the note, please make Jemmy obey his father, Lord have mercy upon us. That out of her drunken act could have come this was beyond belief. She shivered, and finally she dozed, starting awake every once in a while, then dozing again. Diana snored, sleeping the sound sleep of those with clear consciences.

At dawn, Harry tiptoed into the room, the Duke of Wharton behind him. The faces of both young men were pale and drawn. In her chair, sleeping, Barbara was just beginning to be outlined by the light of a dawn that was growing stronger. A great, long snort of Diana's jolted her awake. She sat up and saw Harry at once, Wart behind him.

"Tell me!" she demanded of them both. "You found him? He read the note? Harry . . ."

At the expression on his face, her voice dried up. The pupils in her eyes began to dilate.

Harry pulled her up, holding on to both her arms.

"Listen to me. I gave him the note. He would not listen to reason. He said it was your honor as well as his. That he would defend your good name with his life. He would not listen, Bab. It is not your fault. Do you hear me? You have done everything you possibly could."

"He is not . . ."

"He is dead," Wart said tiredly, "though to be fair to Charles I do not think he meant to kill him. Jemmy moved at the last second."

Barbara said nothing. She sank to the floor.

Snoring loudly, Diana woke herself up with a start. She saw Harry and Wart staring down at Barbara, who sat on the floor in her nightgown and shawl, slumped over like a limp rag doll.

"He killed him, did he?" she said. "Well, that is that. There goes the prince."

CHAPTER TWENTY-TWO

*P*hilippe sat in the pleasant gardens of the house Roger was leasing for the summer from the Countess of Dysart. The gardens reached down to the shining, silver waters of the Thames. From his seat under a shady arbor, he could watch the river swans, their regal necks arching in the sun, as they floated in random, languorous formation to London. It was a leisurely day, bees drifted from roses to pinks to sweet Williams, insatiable, slowly swelling with the amount of nectar they contained, until they resembled nothing so much as tiny, striped barrels. Bright butterflies flitted in the air until they were lost to the eye over the river.

There were few large houses in the vicinity, and finding a place to stay was difficult, but Roger, with his usual charm and luck, had managed to lease this small house. Philippe was having to board in a tavern. The house was in Richmond, a sleepy village on the verge of waking because the Prince and Princess of Wales spent the summers here, staying in a lodge in Richmond Old Park. They talked of rebuilding the lodge, and there was further talk of building a row of modern town houses to house the princess's maids of honor, along one side of Richmond Green, the center of the village, a large, open common that had once fronted a palace of Henry VIII. The palace had long since fallen apart, but the green remained vital, the center of the community. Richmond's only boast to fame, other than the fact that it was favored by the prince, was its hill not far from the green and in a curve of the

Thames. The view from Richmond Hill was one of the finest Philippe had ever seen. From the top one drank in the serene beauty of the shining, curving ribbon of the Thames, surrounded by green fields and woods and pastures and, in the distance, under clouds floating like white sheep in a summer-blue sky, were the medieval spires of Harrow and Windsor. Wealthy merchants and noblemen, their eyes not on the view but rather on the prospect of the future King of England, were already beginning to buy parcels of land and build spacious summer houses. Roger planned to do so and had borrowed yet more money on his South Sea stock to buy up property in the area.

Philippe said nothing to these plans. There was no dealing with Roger's boundless enthusiasm these days. Everything he owned was invested in the building of Devane House and the square, yet he continued to borrow on his stock to invest in land and in the new companies created over the summer and to buy more paintings, more furnishings, more rare books and folios and manuscripts. Philippe had a typical nobleman's attitude toward money, in that it was simply there and not something one worried about, yet he was alarmed at the amount of money Roger was spending.

In the old days, he and Roger would have discussed the news Philippe had received in his letters from France: Law's carriage had been overturned and attacked by a mob; Law had barely escaped being killed; he had taken refuge in the Palais Royal; he was said to be talking like a man who had lost his mind. There were riots in Paris, new edicts every day from the regent. Could it be possible, Philippe would have asked Roger, that Law's revolutionary theory was a failure? Had he caused a further collapse in the economy? Could England fall the way France seemed to be doing? Sir John Blunt, the force behind the South Sea takeover of the national debt, based his theories on Law's success in France. Should we sell stock? Philippe would have asked. Should we liquidate? But Roger would not hear even the slightest doubt he had, and Philippe had done something that he had never expected. Since July he had been selling South Sea stock . . . and he had not told Roger . . . but then Roger would not care if he did tell him. Philippe stared out at the lovely view before him. In four years, he had aged; his face and body were much heavier, and his mouth was bitter, and the bitterness had nothing to do with the old scar that drew it up to one side.

Yesterday at Richmond Lodge he had heard the news of the duel as he strolled with the lovely young Mistresses Bellenden and Lepell, two of Princess Caroline's maids of honor and the brightest, prettiest young adornments of the court . . . until the Countess Devane had made her entrance last spring. Clusters of people on the terraces were whispering, their faces secretive and grave and underlit with glee, as people's faces always are when they are delivering particularly malicious gossip. Jemmy Landsdowne . . . dead . . . Hyde Park . . . Charles Russel . . . the Earl and Countess of Camden retiring to their estate to mourn . . . possible arrest, never, he is the son of a duke . . . and over and over again . . . Barbara Devane . . . Barbara Devane . . . Barbara Devane. She was in everyone's mind, on everyone's tongue: the laughing, flippant, poised young woman whose gowns were always more fashionable than anyone else's, who led the prince around by the nose, who inspired foolish poetry and verses from young men, who was the lover of one of the most eligible men at court, who was rumored to be the next mistress of the Prince of Wales, who did not live with her husband, who wore the slightly rakish air of one who had seen and done her share of living, but who had such lovely, clear blue eyes. Eyes that the young men wrote insipid verse to, never reaching the heights Caesar White had achieved in his last epic poem, "The Dying of Young Aurora."

Barbara added a certain dash to what Philippe had considered a fairly dull court, though courts could be interesting places, particularly courts of the heir to the throne. The fight for power had to be so much more subtle; after all, one must not offend the still living king with too much solicitude about his heir, the corporeal reminder that even kings are mortal. All summer, Philippe had watched that viper who was Roger's mother-in-law weave her web about the Prince of Wales. And he had smiled ironically to think that he and Diana might share a common goal, for he, too, wanted Barbara to become the prince's mistress. Perhaps even more than Diana did. Roger's pride would never allow him to reconcile with the public mistress of a royal prince, particularly such a dull and stupid

prince. Therefore, the news of the duel made him ill. He had
to stop and rest a moment, the lovely Mistresses Bellenden and
Lepell fluttering around him like soft butterflies in their pastel
gowns. For he had faith in Diana, in the sheer, dogged determination with which she pursued her goals. And now, a
moment's anger between two jealous men, and it was gone.
And Philippe, with the expression on Roger's face when he had
seen Barbara this spring engraved in his mind, felt poisoned
with the final, harsh dregs of his cup of bitterness. For Roger
wanted her again. . . .

A lone bee, clearly dazzled by the fragrance and color of
nearby snapdragons and pinks and sweet Williams, busied
himself in flower after flower, so fat with nectar that he could
barely fly from one blossom to the next. "Gather ye rosebuds
while ye may,/Old Time is still a-flying,/And this same flower
that smiles today/Tomorrow will be dying." Roger had gathered his rosebuds in Hanover, going from flower to flower,
crazed with grief, no joy in his random couplings. Old Time
was still a-flying. English poets sometimes put things aptly,
though never with the splendor of the French, thought Philippe, gazing at the bee. He had suffered Hanover, knowing
the fit must work itself out, that what he had set in motion
must be played to its conclusion. But he had never expected
that conclusion to be the loss of the physical closeness between
them. Yet when Roger was finally finished that summer in
Hanover, he was finished with everything. He was empty, and
Philippe had seen for the first time that Roger was no longer
immune to time, that this grief, whose depth he had so mis-
calculated, had changed him. The bee droned close to Philippe's head, too fat with nectar and therefore unable to fly,
drifting lower and lower toward the ground, settling near the
toe of Philippe's shoe, his wings fluttering in helplessness.

"You were too greedy," Philippe said to him in flawless
English, learned all those years ago when he had loved the
handsome young aide to the Duke of Tamworth. Now ashes
in his mouth. For nothing. He was a stranger alone in a foreign land. The bee droned in agreement. Philippe reached
down and carefully set him on a nearby carpet of fallen blossoms. Die in peace, he thought, surrounded by what you love.
Death will be welcome to you. When you can no longer taste
the divine nectar of life, when love no longer exists, then life

is death. You have had your glorious moment in the sun. Die in peace. So I will, droned the bee.

Roger came out of the house and stood in the sunshine. He, too, knew of the duel, but it had not been Philippe who had told him. Philippe knew better than to mention Barbara's name, for with the mention of her name all that they both held so closely inside might burst out, and then Roger would be forced to sever the tie he allowed to remain between them out of kindness. Though, as Philippe had learned, sometimes kindness can be very cruel. Shading his eyes against the sun, Roger saw him and smiled and began to walk toward him. Philippe watched him. The building of Devane House had helped Roger. Philippe had watched it erase the ravages of grief that had shown so clearly after Hanover. But this summer, as Devane House was in its final stages, and London talked of nothing else, and indeed, nothing else was more beautiful, Roger had miraculously shed all signs of aging. He was leaner, fitter, more tanned and smiling, possessing new energy and drive. There was light and laughter once more in his handsome face. The years disappeared. Once more, people were dazzled by his charm, his smile, that perennial youth so lightly frosted with time. He had taken a mistress, something he had not done since the excesses of Hanover. At every fete, every ball, every concert or opera, all women's eyes followed him and men were drawn to him again once more. Philippe had thought, as he had watched Roger grow quieter and grayer, that perhaps, at last, his sun was setting, and that if he were patient, Roger would turn to him for warmth in his waning years. But suddenly Roger was shining brighter, more dazzling than ever. And the cause—it was far more than Devane House—was probably at this moment on her way back from London, a fresh scandal to her name, and her husband smiling because of it. What cause did he have to smile? Philippe could see the expression on Roger's face. He was happy. Why? Almighty God, why? And once more he tasted the dregs of his pride, bitter, corrosive, copperlike in his mouth. He was a prince of France, his lineage was linked to kings, stretching back hundreds of years, he was learned, sophisticated, a product of the best of his civilization. His pride was immense, and it lay humbled in the dust, a monstrous ruin whose shadow he faced daily. Once there had been no secrets between them. Had they ever been young, laughing over women, sharing them? Had they ever been lovers? There were times now when he thought his memory played him false, when he knew its truth only through the pain which was a daily reminder of what had once been. We pay for our sins in this lifetime, he thought, watching Roger—no longer his lover, yet still his love—stride toward him with the slim vigor of a twenty-year-old, while he sat full and heavy on his bench like a stone. With each breath I take, he thought, I pay for my sins of pride and love. Ah, Roger . . .

"I must be getting old," Roger said. The neck of his shirt was open, and his sleeves were rolled up, and he wore no wig, and he looked like a young man whom nature had grayed too soon. "I have a pain here," and he touched his chest.

"You ought to rest more," Philippe said irritably. All summer, Roger had been acting as if he were twenty again. He had taken and discarded a new mistress in a four-month span. No wonder he had a pain.

"I have decided to put off my return to London for several days."

Philippe stared at him. "The note said the meeting was urgent—"

"The South Sea directors are old ladies, merchants and bankers trembling in the wind at the idea they might lose a penny."

"But the stock is falling."

"And it will rise again. I told them when they insisted on this Bubble Act that in prosecuting other companies they might make their own stock fall. It is a tremor, no more. It will rise again."

"Roger, take time to read my letters from France. I have an ominous feeling—"

He stopped. The look of impatience that crossed Roger's face at his words made him ill with pain. Once he had been the leader, the strong one, and Roger the follower. Now all was changed. He would not be the harbinger of doom, the complaining, dreary one. He would not play that role. He did have some shred of pride left. He managed to smile and shrug. "As you wish."

"Good!" Roger said at once. And Philippe saw that he never meant to discuss it seriously at all. "Let us take a boat to

Spring Gardens this evening. Monty will be there with his new mistress, and Tommy says the birds are singing as if they know summer is at an end. We can bowl, drink some good English ale, and watch Monty make an ass of himself with this new woman. What do you say?"

Philippe smiled easily in agreement but he thought, Scraps from your table, Roger, thrown to the faithful dog.

Francis Montrose came bustling out of the house.

"Francis is upset by my decision," Roger murmured. "You might condole with him in private on my unpredictability. It will do him good to vent his spleen."

"Lady Alderley is here, sir," Montrose called as he neared them.

"What?"

"Your mother-in-law," Philippe said dryly, as if Diana needed an explanation. "She must want money again."

"Well, well. Order tea in the gardens for our guest. And, Francis, send out some brandy and claret with that tea. Lady Alderley prefers stronger refreshment toward afternoon. And I had thought this afternoon would be spent dully, Philippe, just you and I."

Under the shadow of the arbor, a muscle worked in Philippe's cheek.

Montrose did not move. He cleared his throat. "One does not like to . . . you, ah, are in your shirtsleeves, sir."

"Am I? Shocking. Lady Alderley would be scandalized, not to mention Justin, who would go into a decline. Have your way. Send out my coat." He smiled, and Montrose grinned back. The charm was in full effect.

Philippe watched him with narrowed eyes as he inspected a flower bed, plucked a fat, luscious pink, and when his coat was on, tucked it into his buttonhole. Why was he so happy?

Diana strolled out of the house toward them, a huge hat shading her face and softening the fact that she wore too much makeup for the harsh sunlight. She also wore a gown cut in the style that Barbara had introduced; Barbara looked like a sylph in hers; Diana resembled several but she possessed that supreme confidence some beautiful women retain, in spite of extra lines and wrinkles and sags. In her own mind, she was always beautiful.

"Diana," Roger said, meeting her halfway and bowing over her hand, "your visit is unexpected and pleasant. Come and sit with us. You know Philippe, of course."

Philippe and Diana nodded coolly, each having long ago recognized the other as a worthy opponent. Diana had never once mentioned Philippe's duel with her son. But Philippe felt her knowledge in many cunning, cold ways.

"I had thought to speak privately with you," she said to Roger.

Philippe raised one eyebrow. "If you will excuse me, Lady Alderley, I have an urge to stroll along the river."

"Prince," Diana said, purring, giving him her hand and smiling at him, "how understanding, how kind you are. And do take your time."

She sat down in Philippe's vacated place. Nearby, footmen were setting up a table for tea under the shade of some oaks. A breeze lifted the edges of the white linen tablecloth as they attempted to lay it across the table. Swans, their long, slender, curving necks rising out of the cool, green weeds, clustered at the edge of the river. Diana saw Philippe clap his hands to them.

"That is a lovely necklace."

Roger's words startled her. Instinctively, she put her hand to it. "Barbara let me borrow it," she said defensively, before she thought. Then she collected herself to gaze sadly up at him. She spread her arms wide, a gesture Roger recognized a popular actress using in the last tragedy presented at the Haymarket Theatre.

"Roger, you see before you a crushed woman."

He saw before him a plump, still beautiful one, as ruthless and amoral as a tigress. He said nothing, but watched her gravely, his eyes narrowed slightly.

She sighed dramatically. "My mother's heart is broken. You have heard the news. I know it. I am consumed with forebodings. Are you going to divorce her?"

The question had the grace of a cannon shot. She was alert for his reaction. He caught his breath.

"Understand my concern," she said quickly. "I must know . . ."

"Why? What possible business is it of yours?"

Then he saw some emotion she was unable to control under the false ones she used so well.

"Diana . . ." He was staring at her, his face amazed, and then he smiled slowly, and for that moment, with his high cheekbones and blue eyes, he was completely beautiful, like an artist's dream of an archangel.

"You love her. . . . Yes, she has that effect on people."

Diana was suddenly restless, agitated, unsure of herself, as if he had caught her in a compromising position.

"She is headstrong, stubborn and will not listen to a word I say!" she said in aggrieved tones.

"I know."

She stared at him. Her mouth fell open. He was looking toward the river, and the expression on his handsome profile was somehow vulnerable, yearning, passionate.

"No," he said softly, as if he were speaking to himself, "I am not going to divorce her . . . ever." He turned to her. "Amusing, is it not? But then life is, if one only has the perception to see it."

"I will be damned . . ." she said slowly.

"You probably will be. And I with you. But until then, have the grace to close your lovely mouth and say nothing more on this subject. I will not discuss it. Come, take some tea. I have brandy or claret for you, and you may tell me the latest gossip from Norfolk. How is Robert?"

They made idle talk under the shade of the trees, almost as if her visit had been a social one, as if no nerves—from them both—had been touched. There were tea and cream and brandy and claret and hot scones and a mound of small iced cakes on a silver tray. Roger threw crumbs to a trio of greedy squirrels while Diana told him the gossip she knew and drank several glasses of claret and made the mound of iced cakes grow steadily smaller. Finally there was a silence between them. Roger tossed a final crumb.

"When is she returning?" he asked, unable to stop himself.

And quite naturally, Barbara was once more the topic of their conversation.

"Tonight."

"And her plans?"

"I do not know. To retire to Tamworth, I think. She would discuss nothing with me, though I did my best to help her. I told her she has only to lie low for a few months but she does not listen. She is taking it harder than I realized she would. She is . . ." She had to stop, unable to find a word to describe her daughter.

"Too sensitive?" suggested Roger. "Ashamed? Mortified?"

"Whatever. I do not understand her. She did not kill the boy. You know, Roger, I am so relieved you are not going to do anything hasty. It is time she settled down and had some children. Surely you two could get along together for enough time to make a child or two. I have a feeling she might be happier with children. She always liked them . . . God only knows why. You lose your figure, your breasts leak, it hurts to have them, they are ugly and red-faced for years. Still, when they grow, sometimes they change. Barbara had so much spirit. She is hard underneath, like a rock. My arm would ache when I whipped her before I could make her cry even when she was a little girl. I wish Harry had her spirit. But he is all flash. No spirit. He is in debt, you know."

"What young man is not?"

"It is more than I had realized. Much more. I worry, Roger." She looked at him. He did not rise to the bait. He never did, but she never tired of trying. Usually she managed to hide whatever irritation she might feel about Roger's ability to ignore the fact that Harry existed. Today, however, the journey or the duel or Roger's perception of her true feelings or perhaps just the claret must have made her irritable because she said, abruptly, "I sent you a note over a month ago asking you to buy back my shares. Did you receive it?"

"I am short of cash just now, Diana."

"Send a note to your banker, and he will pay me. I need the money."

"You distrust the market? Why, Diana?"

She shrugged. "What goes up must come down. And I have no one but myself to depend on."

"You have Robert Walpole."

She was silent.

Never had she mentioned the duel, the estrangement between him and Harry. If once she had, he could have refused her.

"I will write the note. But you owe me a large favor, Diana, because it will stretch me to the breaking point to pay for your shares. So I warn you, I will collect on the favor."

She squeezed his hand. "Trust me. Whatever you need will be yours. I cannot afford a loss just now. Somehow I am overdrawn, and I have already borrowed from Barbara, and Mother will not advance a farthing on my allowance. I may just have to make up my mind to marry again."

"I am amazed. And Robert?"

"What difference would marriage make?"

"Yes. I see your point."

"Oh, here comes the prince. I must go. I have never understood why you allow him about—ah, Philippe, I was just saying what a shame it was you took such a long walk. I had wanted to visit with you a little, but now I have talked Roger's ear off and managed to forget another appointment in the bargain. So I will leave you two gentlemen. No, Roger, do not get up. About that note . . ."

"Montrose will send it to your lodging."

"Excellent."

They touched cheeks. Philippe bowed over her hand. He and Roger watched her walk back toward the house. The claret had put the voluptuous sway back into her walk. It was a sight to see, and both of them watched appreciatively.

Philippe sat down. "What did she want?"

"What does she always want?"

"I thought so. Where is she rushing off to?"

"I would imagine she is going to see the Prince of Wales. Diana always plays all sides against one another, as I learned only too well before I married. But the Frog will be difficult to handle. He will croak with fear and offend the lovely maiden."

Philippe stared at him. The happy mood was gone, but Diana's visit would explain that. What was not explained was the sudden restlessness, the yearning that appeared on his face and at the edges of his voice.

Roger looked up at the sky, quoting softly:

> "Come live with me, and be my love,
> And we will some new pleasures prove
> Of golden sands, and crystal brooks,
> With silken lines, and silver hooks . . ."

He stood up abruptly and rubbed his chest. "John Donne, a major poet lost to the church, whom I admired in my youth.

I am going to walk by the river awhile. No, by myself, please. Order more tea. Later, we will go to Spring Gardens and listen to the birds—not that they can match these." He rubbed his chest again.

"What is wrong?"

"I have a pain. It must be love."

The words were flippant, hard, no stranger than the manner in which he said them, walking away even as he spoke, as if he could not bear to be where he was another moment. Philippe watched him stroll into the coming twilight, that time when everything was so beautifully, so softly lighted, and over his own face came the terrible gray shadows of sorrow.

A small boy, four years old, played in the ditch that ran along the edge of the main lane from Richmond to the tiny, neighboring village of Petersham. Jane Cromwell, overseeing laundering—it was washday—wiped her face and noticed that her son was not in the yard with his brother and two sisters. Amelia and Thomas were tied to a large oak tree and the baby, Winifred, sat in the glorified chicken coop Gussy had made to hold her outdoors. But Jeremy was four, and he did not have to be tied to a tree or sit in a coop. He was old enough to be trusted. Still her heart gave a funny leap when she did not see him. He was her firstborn, and as a fetus, his little presence growing inside her had taken her mind from her past and toward her future with Gussy. Jeremy was special.

"Keep stirring," Jane told Betty, her maid, who was stirring clothes in a large iron pot of boiling water with a great oak stick. Betty came from Ladybeth Hall. She had a harelip, but not a bad one; her palate was not split, only her upper lip, but it was difficult to understand her. She was a good, obedient girl for all her deformity, but the other servants at Ladybeth claimed she was unlucky and would not work with her. Finally, the Ashfords sent her to Jane, reasoning that Gussy could cast out any bad luck with his prayers. Jane walked by Cat, her other maid, who sat on the porch churning butter. She could hear Cat mumbling, "Come butter, come. Come butter, come. Peter stands at the gate waiting for a buttered cake. Come butter, come." It was an old country charm to make the butter take. Jane sighed. Cat might have sweet, red lips, none of them split grotesquely up toward her nose, but she was lazy and willful. Charming butter when she had only been at it an hour! Cat was Gussy's Mary Magdalene, only all of Cat's devils had yet to be cast out. She could depend on Betty to watch the children, to see they put nothing they should not in their mouths or wandered away, but not Cat, who watched only men.

She went to the white picket fence surrounding her yard and garden and saw Jeremy playing in the ditch along the lane. She smiled at the sight of his wayward hair, the seriousness of his expression. He was far away from her in his thoughts. She called his name, and finally he looked up.

"You be careful," she told him. "And next time, tell me before you leave the yard."

"Yes, Mama."

Petersham was not large; there were only fifteen or so houses and the chapel, St. Peter's, next door, but when the court was at Richmond many carriages made their way through on their way to Kingston, some six miles away, which was the corporate town of the county of Surrey. She always worried that Jeremy would be run over by a passing carriage. He did not hear as well as he should. Since birth, he had suffered from earaches, and she had spent so many nights walking with him in her arms while he screamed with pain that now she dreaded the least sign of a cold.

"Jeremy, I am going to need you in a moment. Do not stray."

"No, Mama."

She smiled again at the high, clear sound of his child's voice. It reflected his heart. He was a good boy. Today, for instance, he was helping her hang out the wash to dry. Before the day ended, there would not be a bush or tree or fence post that did not have drying wash on it. She hated washday, the laborious, tiring work of stirring the clothes over and over, the carrying of kettle after kettle of water from the pump to the kitchen fireplace to the iron pot, the stoking of the fire—though Jeremy fetched wood without complaint—the rinsing of the clothes in cold water, the wringing of them to take out excess water, the way there was never enough bush or fence post for the next load and she would have to hang clothes over the yews at St. Peter's next door. She was tired, and her back hurt, and she needed rest, but that was not merely washday. She was with child again.

Thomas was crying. Amelia had taken away his cloth ball (a gift from Barbara, who spoiled the children with her constant presents). Jane went to pick him up, untying him, cradling his fat body in her arms, wiping his dirty mouth with her apron. He had been eating dirt and grass. He was teething, and everything went to his mouth. At night he woke up crying, but Gussy, knowing her condition, usually put him back to sleep. Even so she did not rest well. And not even her mother's favorite recipe for teething, black cherry water into which spirits of hartshorn had been mixed, was making Thomas any easier to live with.

"I know, sweetie," she told him. "I know."

She did know. She wished someone would pick her up and cradle her. Another child on the way . . . another birth, but she would not think of that now. There were months ahead yet in which to worry, to cry, to dread the moment until it came as she was swept up in its throbbing pain and the memories of it paled beside the reality. I will greatly multiply thy sorrow and thy conception, in sorrow thou shalt bring forth children. . . . The pain grew and grew; your body was no longer your own; it heaved and pushed without you, pressure always mounting until you thought you would be split in two; your body's heaving becoming the focus of all the world until you whirled downward into nothing but pain and blood and screams. . . . Afterward, she would lie there, feeling nearly dead and think, Never again, please, dear merciful Lord, never again. But childbirth was a woman's lot, her legacy from Eve's sin, and it was God's own commandment to be fruitful and multiply. And Gussy was so good. He prayed throughout her childbirths. He sobbed in her arms when it was over and said, "If I could take the pain from you, Janie, if I could just take the pain," and she thought, If you just could. . . .

"Cat!" she called sharply. "I see you!"

Cat, who had been looking at a passing farmer, his wagon loaded with corn, gave Jane a look of dislike and pumped her arm up and down a fraction faster than she had before. Jane closed her eyes and counted to ten. Gussy had brought Cat to them. Her parents had thrown her out of their cottage and

Jane now knew why! Gussy was certain their Christian influence would give Cat the necessary example to mend her ways, for Cat liked to walk out with young men and lie in the bushes with them, and Jane did not know why Cat never conceived when she herself seemed to become pregnant every time Gussy hung his breeches on the bedside peg. Perhaps, as Betty said, Cat was practicing witchcraft or saying a spell.

She sighed. A mood was coming over her. She would have to ask Gussy to pray with her tonight. It was a despair she had begun to feel since Thomas was born. . . . Hers was not to question God's will and she loved her children with all her heart and yet her life stretched ahead of her, and childbirth seemed its yearly mark, and she was so afraid. She had talked to her mother, who had squeezed her and cried a little and said that she must accept life as it was. She could do that, but she was so afraid of the pain.

They would read the Lord's Prayer tonight. The words soothed her, as did David's Psalms. Gussy would pamper her, knowing her fear, which would increase as the months and the child within her did. They would walk together; it was beautiful here, so near the Thames, and Richmond only a short distance away, a walk along the edge of Richmond Park, a royal park created long ago by Henry VIII. Before she became too large, he would take her on excursions: to Kew to look at Princess Caroline's developing botanical garden, to Chelsea to see the Worshipful Society of Apothecaries' Physic Garden and to Fulham, where Gussy worked for three days every two weeks in the library of the palace of the Archbishop of Canterbury. They would go to Kingston, where Lent and winter assizes were held; these were sessions to administer civil and criminal justice, and Gussy had been appointed one of the chaplains to the prisoners who would go before the magistrates.

Gussy worked so hard. He was curate of St. Peter's here, and even though St. Peter's was a chapel of ease, which meant it had been built for the use of those parishioners who lived too far from parish churches, Gussy still had to conduct services and perform the duties of churching women after childbirth and visiting the sick, and what with his clerking at the archbishop's library in Fulham and his work on his book, he had little time for himself, let alone her and the children, but he made time. And he thanked the Lord each night for His bounty. There were starving curates all over the country, eking out a living, while he had three positions—due to the generosity of the young Duke of Tamworth—which paid for everything they needed and allowed them a little left over to save. And parishioners were always giving them baskets of eggs and fresh milk and fat pullets because they said Gussy was a good man, a man who was a shining example of God's word at work. And he was. Oh, he was.

He had bought her a gold-and-glass clock to put on their table in the parlor. And when she had first realized she was going to have Winifred, he had bought her a gown of black silk with a red-and-white petticoat and cherry-colored stays and daring stockings of black silk. How she loved that gown. She saved it for only the most special of occasions. She had been wearing it the day she first saw Harry again, and though she tried very hard not to succumb to the sin of vanity, she was so glad that she had had it on. So glad.

At that thought, she frowned at herself, and Cat, who happened to look up and see her, put some more energy into her butter churning. Jane sat down on the bench around the oak tree to hold Thomas, who had fallen asleep. She really ought to help Betty, but she was tired. She would rest just a moment. She untied Amelia, who began to bring her blades of grass to admire, which she did, over and over, even though her thoughts drifted from Amelia. She and Gussy had gone to Ham House, the great house of the Earl of Dysart which he opened to visitors, and she was happy because she was not pregnant. Usually, within two or three months of childbirth, she was increasing again, but she was going into a sixth month of freedom. It was heady stuff. They had walked to Ham House to stroll in its gardens, which were lovely—the front lawns sloped down to the Thames—and everyone went there; Jane had even seen the Prince and Princess of Wales. And there was Harry, so unexpected, standing with Barbara and a tall, bold-looking man who was staring down at Barbara as if he did not know whether to strangle her or kiss her. Barbara had cried out her name and come running over, and she was so very glad she had her black-and-cherry gown because Barbara looked so lovely and fashionable. And Harry had walked up to her. She knew he was surprised, and touched,

as she was. He kissed her on the cheek and shook Gussy's hand
and told him she was his old sweetheart. And then the young
Duke of Tamworth strolled up, and they walked through the
gardens together, but all she could think of was the way her
heart was beating and how Harry's eyes were more beautiful
than she remembered. . . .

"Move, Thomas," Amelia demanded petulantly, pushing at
her brother's sleeping form. "Now." Amelia was tired also,
and she wanted to be in her mother's lap. Harry said Amelia
showed disturbing signs of becoming like his Aunt Abigail.
Jane blushed. Harry came to visit her. Not often. Just every
once in a while. She would look out her window, and there
he would be, leaning on her fence, grinning, his horse tied to
a picket. Gussy knew. She told him every time. And it was
very innocent. A friendship. He sat with her in the garden,
talking, while the children played around them, of Italy and
France and mountains and cities and rivers and palaces that
she would never see. And she talked of her chickens, of the
barley meal and milk she fed them to make them fat, of how
she wanted to try growing marigolds and garlic among her
lettuces next season to keep away bugs, of Thomas's teething
and Jeremy's earaches. And he did not laugh at her. His
handsome face became softer, as he listened to her and smiled,
and she forgot that he was said to be a notorious womanizer
and in debt, and remembered only that he was the boy she
had once loved. They captured something of their childhood
closeness again, without the pain, and with the love strangely
changed. And then one of the children would cry, or Gussy
might appear to talk of politics with Harry, of how wise it
was of the Prince of Wales finally to reconcile with his father,
of the way the South Sea Company was becoming too powerful, of how Robert Walpole and Stanhope ought to stop
quarreling and work together for the good of the nation. And
she would listen, smiling, happy to see her Gussy and Harry
together, until her children claimed her, and she had to put
them to bed, or clean them or feed them or do one of the
hundred-and-one endless tasks one did with small children.
You are good for him, Jane, Gussy would say afterward. He
needs to settle down, and you are a good example of the kind
of wife every man needs. Dear Gussy. . . .

A good example. There was one thing she had not told Gussy. In a box under the loose floorboard in the parlor lay a pair of soft, dark green leather gloves smelling of cinnabar. From Harry. He had not given her anything else, nor would she accept anything else, but she could not resist those gloves, presented out of the blue, without a word, in the middle of summer. Sometimes, when she was certain there was no one around to see, she took them out, and she touched them and put them on and rubbed the soft leather against her face and smelled the cinnabar and thought of all the places she would never see, where things happened that she would never do. And she did not tell Gussy. And she did not know why because she did not love Harry, at least in any way Gussy need fear. These four children tied her to Gussy in a way Harry could never share, and Gussy's life was her life now, and she loved him, perhaps not in the wild, romantic way she loved Harry, but in a practical, comfortable way of knowing his back was warm at night and that he liked his afternoon tea lukewarm and that an evening of working on his book made him happy. Perhaps the gloves were simply a symbol of her vanity, a reminder that once there had been a wild, handsome boy who had held her close under the apple trees and whispered that he loved her. And she did not know if she could explain that to Gussy. . . .

"Mama! Mama! Mama!" cried Jeremy.

The screeching of his voice made her jump, waking Thomas, who began to cry. Betty dropped her oaken stick and ran to the fence. Cat stopped churning. He has fallen and broken his arm, Jane thought, stumbling over her long skirts and Amelia, who was determined to come with her. At least Winifred was sitting placidly in her coop, but Winifred was never anything but placid. It probably came from being fourth in line. She managed to reach the fence without dropping Thomas or stepping on Amelia. Betty pointed and smiled. Jeremy was climbing up into the coachman's seat of an elaborate black carriage with a green and gold crest on the side. Barbara! Amelia began to clap her small, fat hands together.

"Bab! Bab!" she said.

Barbara put her head out the window; she was wearing a straw hat with long green ribbons of silk and pink roses of silk, and Jane was instantly aware that her dress was old and that

Thomas had spit up on it. Barbara smiled at her, waving, and it was difficult for Jane to believe that this was the same woman who was said to have just caused a duel between Jemmy Landsdowne and Lord Charles Russel. Who was said to be in disgrace, whom it was rumored the Prince of Wales would dismiss from his court tomorrow (even though he was in love with her himself). Gussy had brought the news back with him yesterday from Fulham, shaking his head. He read his Bible aloud to Jane, "'Who can find a virtuous woman? For her price is far above rubies. . . .' " Jane had sighed, trying not to doze off, for she had been up the night before with Thomas's teeth. . . . The attributes of a virtuous woman, yes, Jane knew. She rose early and worked late; her household was not lazy (doubtless no one burned the bread and the children teethed without problem); she clothed it in scarlet she had woven herself; she spun wool, advised her husband wisely and succored the needy. No wonder she was virtuous, Jane's last conscious thought had been before she fell asleep, in the middle of Gussy's Bible reading, there was no time to be anything else.

The coachman, Jeremy on his shoulders, helped Barbara down from the carriage. She had a large basket on one arm, and at the sight of it, Jane became almost as excited as her children. Forgetting Gussy's admonitions to be cool to Barbara, she opened the gate and, with Thomas in her arms and Amelia dragging determinedly on her skirts, welcomed her friend.

Barbara kissed her cheek and at once set down the basket to pick up Amelia.

"Pretty girl," she said, kissing Amelia's fat cheek (there was nothing about Amelia that was not fat). "Carry in the basket, Jeremy. Betty, how are you? I have brought tarts. Will you make Mrs. Cromwell and me some of your tea? Jane, you are washing. I have come at an awful time, but I was so close, and I had an impulse to see you all that I could not deny. Come here, Jeremy, and give me a kiss or I will not give you one single tart, and there are lemon ones, your favorite."

With Jeremy and Amelia hanging on her and Jane following with Thomas and the basket Jeremy had dropped, Barbara went to sit on the bench built around the oak tree, near Winifred's coop.

"Winifred, you precious," Barbara said, lifting the child up in her arms. Winifred was startled out of placidity into a gurgle. Barbara kissed her neck and set her down in her lap. Amelia grudgingly moved over. Winifred got one hand on Barbara's necklace.

"Take care," Jane said. "She will break it."

"I have many necklaces and no babies. Let her do what she pleases. No, Amelia, do not cry. You may wear my bracelet. There. Look how pretty it looks on your arm. What a big girl you are, Amelia." Jane smiled to see her difficult Amelia so neatly cajoled into good nature again. It would be interesting to see how Barbara would wrest the bracelet from her when she left. And then Betty was coming out with a steaming pot of tea, and the basket had to be opened and there were—naturally—toys for the children, lead soldiers for Jeremy, who whooped and yelped and gave Barbara another kiss, and a china doll for Amelia, who was wide-eyed with pleasure, and a set of wooden beads strung together for Thomas and another for Winifred, and then for Jane there were three gowns Barbara no longer wanted, two of them almost new, velvet and silk that Jane could recut to fit herself and use for the children. She sighed with pleasure as she ran her hand over a gown of blue velvet. And then there were lemon tarts to eat and tea to drink, and before Jane knew it, she and Barbara were sitting on the ground, Barbara in her beautiful gown, her hat off (Amelia had it on), with children all about them, some eating, some asleep, some, thank goodness, just sitting quietly in whatever lap happened to be free. And Jane, gazing at her friend, could not believe that two men had just fought a duel over her, and one had died.

"Your garden looks pretty," Barbara said, leaning her head against the back of the bench. Winifred was asleep in her arms, the necklace clutched firmly in one hand, the wooden beads in the other.

"My hollyhock and snapdragons took well this year. Your grandmother sent me some of her seed. No, Amelia, leave Winifred's beads alone. You have your doll. I need to harvest the herbs."

"Grandmama always says the dew must be dry on them before they are picked."

"I know. She sent me two pages of instructions along with the seeds and told me to order *Five Hundreth Pointes of Good Husbandry*, which I did."

"What is Jeremy doing? Jane, he has a ladybug. Jeremy, bring it here. You must be very careful with ladybugs. If you harm them, bad luck will come. Jane, do you remember. . . . Fly, ladybird, north, south, east or west—"

"Fly where the man is found that I love best," Jane finished with her. They laughed. Jeremy ran off, the ladybug cradled carefully in his hand.

"How are his ears?" asked Barbara.

"Well all summer."

"I have heard the putrid sore throat is in London. Keep him warm, Jane, once autumn begins."

"I will."

They fell silent, watching Amelia toddle over to Jeremy to see if she could have any of his soldiers. It was late afternoon, and a bird was singing. Jane's garden was full of late summer blooms. There were fat pinks and red sweet Williams, and the regal blue hollyhocks and bold purple asters and pretty white daisies and nodding purple-blue delphiniums. Butterflies and bees droned over them. Thomas lay asleep in Jane's arms. Jeremy and Amelia quarreled amicably over which soldiers Amelia might play with. Cat was straining butter from the cool sides of the churn; Betty hung a load of wet wash on bushes in the chapel garden; ants carried away the lemon tart crumbs the children had left everywhere; a breeze lifted the leaves in the trees and made them rustle the way a woman's long gown will.

"I really should help Betty," Jane said drowsily. She felt like lying down on the ground to sleep. It was the new child taking her strength. They always did at the beginning.

"I should not have interrupted you, not on washing day. I love it here, with you and the children," Barbara said quietly. Something in her voice made Jane look at her. She was staring down at Winifred, and the expression on her face caught Jane's heart.

"You are welcome anytime," Jane said defiantly. If Gussy could have his Mary Magdalene, she could have hers.

Barbara smiled at her. "You should be so proud of Jeremy. He is a little gentleman. He reminds me of Kit. Kit had that same kind of sweetness."

"He is his father's pride and joy. And mine. Gussy is already teaching him Latin."

"Will Gussy be angry with you because I have come?" Jane blushed.

"He has heard, has he not?" Barbara said, stroking Winifred's hair with her hand. "As have you."

Jane felt as if her tongue were bigger than her mouth, she could think of nothing to say.

Barbara put Winifred down beside Jane gently. She kissed her friend's cheek and stood up, brushing crumbs from her gown. The ease between them was gone. Jane pried loose the necklace from Winifred's hand. Barbara clasped it around her neck and strode over to Amelia. Somehow, without making her cry, she repossessed her hat (the roses would never be the same) and her bracelet. She leaned down, and both Jeremy and Amelia hugged and kissed her. Jane felt tears start in her eyes. Thank You, merciful Lord for all Your bounty, she found herself thinking. She put down Thomas next to Winifred and hurried to Barbara.

"Come again," she said. "Whenever you wish."

Barbara kissed her cheek. For a moment, they clung together.

"How fortunate you are," Barbara whispered to her, "that you never do anything of which you must be ashamed later."

And then she was climbing into her carriage and the coachman was turning it around in the lane, and she was leaning out the window and waving to Jeremy, who was running behind it. Thomas had wakened and was sitting up, staring down solemnly at the sleeping Winifred. Amelia had wrenched the beads from Winifred's hand and was playing with them. Cat was patting the sides of a cool, white mound of butter. Betty stirred a load of wash and sang a little tune. Jane thought about the green gloves under the parlor board. It was such a little sin. . . .

How clean and simple Jane's life is, Barbara thought, leaning against the back of the carriage seat. She wished she could stay in her carriage, stay in it until she reached Tamworth and crawled into her old bed and pulled the covers up over her head. But she could not. She must oversee the packing of her household and tomorrow take her leave of the Frog and his princess, with the court looking on, ripe for any glance, any word that might show the Frog's displeasure. She dreaded his lecture. The court waiting for her disgrace. If Philippe was there, she did not know how she would bear it.

The carriage pulled up before the house she was leasing. She ran up the stairs.

"Madame!" Hyacinthe came running to her in the hall, all legs and arms and growing boy. Charlotte and Harry were yapping shrilly behind him. She knelt to pet them, the comfort of being here making the humiliation of her disgrace fade slightly. Harry and Charlotte whined and fussed and contorted themselves into ridiculous positions as she found their favorite places to be scratched. Hyacinthe stood waiting, staring at her with dark, bright eyes.

"I was worried, madame," he said, frowning. Hyacinthe had long ago assumed the responsibility of worrying about her. "As was Thérèse. Many notes have come for you. The prince's equerry called this morning. There is a note from Lord Russel and also, madame, a note from Lord Devane."

From Roger. Her heart stood still. It was a moment before she could make her legs strong enough to hold her when she stood. She went into the bedchamber, pulling off her hat, the dogs and Hyacinthe following her. Thérèse was folding gowns into neat stacks. She looked at Barbara, an expression of relief on her pretty pert face.

"I am so glad you are back, madame. Hyacinthe and I, we were worried. Sit down," she said, coming over to Barbara and taking the hat from her. "You look tired. Hyacinthe! Fetch madame a small glass of wine."

"Am I already disgraced?" Barbara asked, pointing to the stack of gowns. "Have I a note of dismissal?"

"I—I thought only that we might be leaving—"

"Is it common news, Thérèse? Tell me."

Thérèse nodded her head, her mouth grim. She pointed to the small pile of notes on a table by the window. Barbara went to sift through them. She crumpled Charles's without reading it. There were no apologies on his part that she would accept. She put her aunt's aside. She would not read a lecture from her Aunt Abigail. She opened the note from the Frog. She was to call on him tomorrow morning at eleven. It was signed with his Christian name, and underneath were scrawled the words, "You have broken my heart." She sighed. He had no heart, only vanity. He would be impossible tomorrow. How could she bear to listen to his words of reproach? She touched the note from Roger, thoughts tumbling in her head. Was it over between them at last? Were the ties between them finally to be severed? Funny how in Paris she had wanted nothing else . . . and now . . . it was a moment before she could steel herself to open it. Thérèse, eyeing her as she folded gowns with deft motions, sniffed. Slowly, Barbara unfolded the note.

My dearest Barbara,
   I will escort you to court tomorrow morning, as it is both my duty and my wish. I believe I remember you well enough to know you are thinking harshly of yourself. Do not. No one who truly loves you does. I will call on you at ten. Until then, I remain, whether you wish it or not, always yours,
   Roger

She stared at the note.
Watching her, Thérèse felt her heart give a little skip.
"He is coming to escort me tomorrow," Barbara said slowly to Thérèse. Just as slowly, a smile spread across her face, lighting it from within. Her grandfather's smile. She held the note a moment to her bosom, then carefully folded it, as if it were made of glass and might break.
"Monsieur Harry? Does he come with you?" Thérèse asked.
"I left him in London. He tried so hard to help me, Thérèse—"
Hyacinthe came into the room with the wine. Barbara smiled at him.
"She is better," he said to Thérèse. "Look."
Thérèse glared at him. Barbara laughed. Charlotte and Harry barked at the sound of her laughter and stood up on their back paws.
"Bad dogs!" said Thérèse. They barked louder.

Later, after Barbara had eaten, she sat in her oldest night-gown and shawl by an open window while Thérèse stood behind her brushing her hair. Charlotte was in her lap, and Harry was lying on top of her feet. Hyacinthe, on a nearby stool, was reading, slowly, from *Robinson Crusoe*, the literary rage of last year. They had started the book some weeks ago, and all three of them lived for its adventures. They had made a pact that no one would read ahead of the others.

"'I walked about on the Shore, lifting up my Hands, and my whole Being, as I may say, wrapt up in the Contemplation of my Deliverance, making a Thousand Gestures and Motions which I cannot describe, reflecting upon all my Comrades that were drowned, and that there should not be one Soul sav'd but my self . . .'" read Hyacinthe, pausing now and again over a word he did not know, until Thérèse prompted him.

Soothed by the familiar sound of his clear voice, Barbara felt herself relaxing. Outside, she could hear the night crickets, the sighing of branches against one another, a gate yawning and creaking in the wind. Her hair crackled as Thérèse ran the brush through it with familiar strokes, soothing strokes. Roger was coming for her tomorrow. He would be with her when she faced the court. No, she might not have the comfort of children, might never have them. But she had this moment, its quiet, these people, their love, her family, Hyacinthe and Thérèse and the two dogs. They were hers forever. And tomorrow, Roger was coming for her.

CHAPTER TWENTY-THREE

"**H**urry up, Thérèse! He will be here soon!"

Thérèse sighed and continued to lace up Barbara's stays at her own pace. He would not be here soon; they had almost another half-hour to go, but it would do no good to say so.

"Thérèse! You are too slow! Hurry!"

The dogs, picking up Barbara's nervousness, ran around Thérèse's feet and barked in agreement.

"Hush!" she told them.

The stays were tied. Now she draped a loose robe over Barbara and handed her a large paper cone, and Barbara put her face into it. Hyacinthe, looking up from his book, seeing what they were doing, moved to a far corner of the bedchamber. (Yes, he had been reading, and yes, it was *Robinson Crusoe*, but Thérèse could hardly discipline him when she was secretly reading ahead herself.) The dogs scurried under the bed as Thérèse felt the texture of Barbara's hair to be certain she had rubbed in enough pomatum to hold the hair powder. She opened the box of white powder, violet- and orrisroot-scented, and tapped a large powder puff in it.

Little clouds of white powder rose around Barbara's head as Thérèse lightly powdered it. Hyacinthe hid himself behind a window drapery. When she was finished, Thérèse walked around Barbara. Yes. It was perfect. Barbara raised her face from the paper cone, and Thérèse pressed the puff along her hairline to blend excess powder back into her hair. She stepped back and looked critically at her work. Yes. Yes, it was good. It made Madame Barbara older-looking, but without harshness, for her face was still young and soft enough to carry the stark white powder. Barbara unfastened the robe to finish dressing, and Harry and Charlotte came out from under the bed to growl and attack the powder-scented garment until Hyacinthe managed to drag it away from them and fold it away. Thérèse tied a black armband around the sleeve of Barbara's gray gown, and while Barbara slipped on jewelry, she rouged and patched her face and ran the little lead combs through her lashes and brows.

"I wish this day was over," Barbara said.

As do I, thought Thérèse. We should have stayed in Tamworth with your grandmother; you were not well enough to come to London and see him again. And now this has happened—but the note from Lord Devane is what is disturbing you most. I feel your mind searching, probing, wondering why, not daring to acknowledge hope. Ah, Lord Devane, you must somehow give my dear Barbara her life again. You do not deserve her love, but what has that to do with anything? Love is not given because one deserves it. She needs a child. If you come back, I shall pray every day to the Blessed Virgin to heal her barrenness and bring a child. . . . And then she made a strange face at her own tiny sorrow remembered.

Hyacinthe saw her face. "Thérèse, what is wrong? Did a pin stick you?"

"No," she said. "Life did."

"Go to the window and see if you can see Lord Devane's carriage," Barbara told Hyacinthe, but before he could, someone knocked at the door, and Barbara started at the sound. It was a footman with a note. Thérèse recognized the writing; it was from Lord Russel, but Barbara put it on her dressing table without opening it.

There was another knock. The footman again. "Lord Devane is below."

Barbara stood up abruptly, knocking over the dressing table stool. Harry and Charlotte, their tongues hanging out, waited expectantly by the door; they wished to go downstairs with her. She knelt down to pet them while Thérèse slipped three black feathers in her hair and clipped them with a pearl clasp.

"Will Monsieur Harry join you in Tamworth?" she asked.

"I am sure he will, Thérèse, if only to escape his creditors. Be ready when I return. I want to leave immediately." Barbara stood up. "Hyacinthe, go downstairs and tell Lord Devane I am coming. Then wait in the hallway for me until I call you." She clapped at the dogs to lead them into a small adjoining room and shut the door on them quickly. At once, they began to whine and scratch at the door.

"Go with God," Therese said softly. "I will pray for you."

"Do that. God does not seem much in my life these days. I think I need him." Barbara was out the door.

Thérèse leaned in the doorway to watch her go down the stairs. The dogs had begun to howl. In the middle of the staircase, Barbara stopped a moment and took several deep breaths, then ran rapidly on down and out of sight.

Hail Mary, full of grace, the Lord is with thee; blessed are thou amongst women, and blessed is the fruit of thy womb, Jesus. Holy Mary, Mother of God, pray for us sinners now and at the hour of our death. Amen. Thérèse took a deep breath. She felt better. Barbara was now in the hands of the Blessed Virgin, and after Thérèse had finished her packing, she would kneel and say her rosary several times just to ensure that the Holy Mother continued to intervene as long as need be. Blessed Mary, ever virgin, had once been a mortal woman. She would know. She would understand. The dogs were now yelping, Harry the loudest. Thérèse opened the door, and they bounded out, running all the way to the other door, but it was closed. They looked hopefully at Thérèse, but she ignored them, so they satisfied themselves with going to lie wherever she needed to step.

"Bad dogs!" she told them, shaking her finger at them. They watched her, their eyes as bright as little black buttons. She began to sort jewels carefully into the compartments of Barbara's jewel case, thinking of Barbara as she did so. . . . Some women needed children, and some, such as herself, did not. She would never forget the small bud that had formed within her or the way of its dying . . . or the necessity that it die. She stopped to cross herself. Always she lit candles; always she said the prayers for its soul, and for her own, which would pay in Purgatory; she had accepted that penalty at the beginning. But she never ceased to believe that the Blessed Virgin, the Holy Mother, a woman herself, would intervene with the

Lord when her time to pay came. And truly, Hyacinthe and Madame Barbara and Harry were enough for her. They were her family. She felt no need of a child, and the older she became the more she realized that, indeed, if her soul was damned, her life on this earth was blessed. Never again had she to worry about bearing a child she could not raise, whose birth would pull her down into disgrace and poverty. She had only to walk down any street in London to see the women, hundreds of them, like herself, but dirty, unkempt, old before their time, watching with eyes that were bitter and tired, watching children—the destiny that damned them—play in street gutters, as filthy, as abused as the women themselves. She always said a prayer when she looked into one of those women's eyes. How many of them had once been ladies' maids like herself? She knew the answer. Too many. One fall from grace was all it took. One rape. Or yielding to temptation. And their life changed forever. But not hers. The Lord in His mercy, the grace of the Blessed Virgin sheltered her. She was her own mistress.

How many times had Harry begged her to let him set her up in lodgings? She should abandon her position and become his, he told her. And when she lay in his arms, she was tempted. She did so love him. But when she was home again, dressing Barbara or directing the chambermaids or teaching Hyacinthe to read, she knew deep in her heart that if she did, he would cease to love her as he now did. That she would lose something essential. She did not blame him; it was human nature to desire what one could not have and to take for granted what one possessed. If she had been a woman of his station, she might have yielded. But then, if she had been a woman of his station, they might have married. But would she have married him? He neglected his estate and gambled and spent money he did not have, and as a wife, she would have resented such ways, for his future would then also have been hers. And his unfaithfulness. As a wife, there would have been that, too. As it was, and God was so infinite in His wisdom, they were both free. They loved each other freely. She knew he was unfaithful, and yes, there were times when it hurt her. But she also knew that she did not want to lose him, that his heart was hers; and she comforted herself with that, finding patience and acceptance through her prayers. Harry had not the strength to be faithful. Or the mind. Yet, always he returned to her. Always. And loving him had been her choice. After the duel, there could be no other choice. Not for her. He had not forced her. How she loved him for that. And for the deliberate, delicate gentleness and delight with which he had first made love to her. . . .

Now, when would she see him again? There were so few times to treasure these days. Once she had spent the whole day with him at May fair. She smiled at the memory . . . striped tents, sausages, ale, blood puddings, acrobats, freaks, mimes, Scaramouche, the harlequins, the summer sky, a pair of soft, green leather gloves he had bought her as a souvenir. How happy she had been for that whole day! (That was the day she had seen Caesar White again. She had been laughing at the antics of the puppets in a Punch and Judy show, and there he was, staring at her through a crowd of people. She had smiled and called his name but he turned away. It had made her sad to see that after all this time he had still not forgiven her. And she had looked at Harry, who had never said one word about LeBlanc, who had never questioned her about Caesar, who was simply Harry, and she had thanked the Lord for her blessings.) And now she must wait until he came to Tamworth. Well, what was, was. It did no good to brood. And she had much to do, and the time would pass, and before she knew it, there he would be, grinning at her in the doorway of her room while she opened her arms and held him close to her breasts and loved him carnally with her body—the love sweeter for the absence—as she loved him spiritually with her heart. She closed the jewel case, and before she realized it, she was humming a little tune as she began to pack the last of her mistress's belongings. In the midst of her humming, she stopped suddenly and said out loud, "Be well, Caesar." I will add his name to my prayers, she thought, and the thought soothed her again, and happily, she resumed both her humming and her tasks.

Roger stood at an open window, one foot up on the low sill, when Barbara opened the door. She walked in easily enough, but stopped in the middle of the room, unable to will herself to move one step farther. They stared at each other, and then, very slowly, he smiled. Why is he always so handsome? she thought, and she felt as if her heart were going to jump out of her body. In her mind, it was a bird fallen from its nest and fluttering frantically in circles on the ground. She noticed that he, too, wore a black armband, just as she and Hyacinthe did, and that courtesy touched her. He proclaimed to the world that Jemmy Landsdowne was a mutual friend, that the loss was shared. His gesture would muffle some of the scandal. It was the gesture of a generous—and confident—man.

He straightened up and walked toward her. Surely he sees my heart, she thought wildly. It must be visible leaping just beneath my skin. He stopped an arm's length from her. Too close, and yet so far away.

"You look beautiful," he said, and his eyes were like sapphires, polished to a fine glow, burning, burning her with all that was in them. He took a step closer. In spite of herself, she stepped back. She might never have been alone with him before. He was a stranger to her, and yet this was the same man she had loved with all her young heart. He had been the first to make her cry with passion in his arms from the skill of his lovemaking and from the love she felt for him. If he kisses me, she thought . . . and she could not finish the thought.

"Barbara," he said. "You are trembling. Are you ill? Shall I call for your maid?"

It was as if cold water were dashed in her face.

"No," she said calmly. "It is nerves. Thank you for coming this morning, but I have decided your accompanying me is unnecessary. I can handle myself—"

"I am certain you can," he said. His tone was cool, detached, self-assured. It threw her off guard. "Whatever may have happened between us, Barbara, you are still my wife. I would be a cad not to offer you the protection of my name and presence at such a time as this. Are you ready? Good girl. You look superb. My carriage is just outside."

He went out to tell Hyacinthe to call the carriage forward. She stared after him. How dare he be so cool and collected. How dare he. She raised her chin. When he came back inside for her, she swept by him without a word.

* * *

Irritably—very irritably—Abigail eyed Tommy Carlyle, the only other person sitting in the antechamber in Richmond Lodge that was used for the Prince and Princess of Wales's drawing room receptions—the chamber those who had an interview with their royal highnesses in the private apartments must first pass through. Carlyle fanned himself slowly with a huge fan that had dangling silk tassels, and he wore the usual large diamond in his left ear and an impossible wig. Even Louis XIV would not have worn such a wig, thought Abigail, unable to pull her eyes from it. Carlyle smiled at her, and to Abigail the smile seemed to say, I know why you are here, and I am here for the same reason. I would not miss it for the world. Unfortunately it was beneath her dignity to inform him that she was here only because her daughter, Mary, now sixteen, was a new maid of honor to the Princess of Wales, and she was merely waiting for Mary to finish her day's attendance. She had no wish to see her own niece humiliated (even if she did deserve it). Barbara was, after all, still family.

Of course she had been appalled when she heard of the duel, so much so that she sat down at her desk and composed an impulsive letter of indignation and outrage to the Duchess and posted it to Tamworth by special messenger. Let the Duchess see what her pet was doing now, she had thought. Let the Duchess read about the latest scandal and weep! Barbara was growing into a copy of her mother, she had written with angry, sweeping, underlined capitals, and four years ago she could have told them when they insisted on marrying her to Roger Montgeoffry that no good would come of the match. Had anyone listened then? No. The Duchess had come marching up from Tamworth and scattered them all about her like so many bowling pins. Time has proved her correct, she had written. Part of her livid anger—and she would be the first to admit it—had to do with the fact that her niece had somehow snatched the single most eligible man at court, a man Abigail had been cultivating for some years, waiting patiently, carefully, until Mary was old enough, before she set anything into motion. She had laid her plans so well. As she always did. Charles's mother and she were old friends, and they had agreed between themselves that the match would be perfect on all sides. Mary had only to reach sixteen, and then the pair of them would begin their work. And who had shown up a month after Mary turned sixteen? Every time she saw Charles Russel grin like a lovesick fool at her wicked, immoral, rude, headstrong and already married niece, she wanted to smash something, preferably on Barbara.

Barbara. The stories that had reached them from Paris. Shocking. She could not even think of the scope of some of them now without blushing, such as the one intimating that Roger and his distinguished friend, the Prince de Soissons, were lovers. Roger had his faults, and she would be the first to name them, but he was no effeminate horror like Tommy Carlyle, even now smiling at her across the room with his ugly, rouged face. And he was family. (She had forgiven him for Bentwoodes. Having bought up the surrounding property and having sold it to the Cavendishes for a pretty penny last year.) And as for the Prince de Soissons, well, she had never met a more charming and sophisticated and masculine man in her life. Philippe was poised, well mannered, of an impeccable background . . . even if he was French. It was certainly too bad she did not have a daughter to marry off to him. Mary was far too young; the Lord above knew Roger and Barbara had proved the mistake of that great a difference in age. (She also realized the closer she became to him that Philippe needed an older woman, a seasoned woman, a woman of calm reasonability. Those attributes all took time to develop. No girl would have them.) Not only was he an interesting and intelligent conversationalist, he was an expert dancing partner, and a perfect addition to any long dinner party . . . and a very attractive man. She could not say enough good things about him, and she was glad that at least one of Roger's friends had some refinement. The older Robert Walpole became, for instance, the more vulgar he was. As much as Abigail disliked Barbara, to be fair (and Abigail prided herself on her fairness), some of the blame for her conduct had to rest on Roger's shoulders. He was her husband. It was his duty to guide his wife, his duty to correct her conduct (instead of allowing her to romp around as free as a bird snatching up eligible young men).

At that moment Diana swept into the room. She and Abigail nodded coldly to each other, and Abigail noted critically that her sister-in-law wore a tight gown of royal purple with a ridiculous matching turban and, naturally, too much rouge. And, unfortunately, she looked far better than she ought to. Abigail sighed and stared at the rings wedged on her own pudgy fingers. Nature gives you the face you possess at twenty, she always quoted to her daughter, Fanny. Like the face you possess at thirty. But the face you have at fifty is the face you deserve. Diana was some ten years from fifty, and if she was going to receive the face she deserved, all Abigail had to say was that nature had better do some fast stepping. She herself was settling along decidedly matronly lines—yes, she accepted it. She was not one to run away from the truth. Besides, as Philippe reminded her, it was a woman's character that was important, not her face. He had such charming manners. She smiled and smoothed the collar of her gown—a gown cut low at the bosom. At least her bosom had not failed her.

Abigail watched as Diana knocked haughtily on the prince's private apartments door, gave her name, and was instantly admitted, as if she were a queen. Mary said that Diana had spent most of yesterday evening closeted with the prince in his private chamber, and Abigail knew what she was doing. Trying to repair the damage her daughter's latest scandal had caused, as if such a thing were possible. Like mother, like daughter. Diana had dragged the family name in the mud of scandal for years, and it looked as if Barbara was going the same way. Well, she had tried to warn them. She had told the Duchess Roger was too old, that his morals were unstable, his friends unsuitable. Had that stubborn old crone listened? No. Abigail could not blame herself. She had done her duty. As she always did.

She frowned. Tony and his friend, Lord Charles Russell, had walked onto the terrace outside and were deep in conversation. Carlyle, sitting opposite her like the repellent reptile he was, caught her frown and swung around to see what she was staring at. When he turned back around, he smiled at her with an expression of complete understanding. She felt an urge to slap him. Of course, she was upset to see Charles here. He was like a son to her; his mother was an old friend. He ought to be on one of his father's estates, letting time heal the damage to his reputation that the duel had caused—not that it was his fault. It was Barbara's. Where there was smoke, there was fire, she always said, and the things that had come filtering in to them from Paris. Well! No wonder Charles was infatuated. At least nothing would happen to him now, even though there was a law against dueling, because who would bring charges against the son of a duke? The prince had summoned him here to reprimand him. She only wished he had summoned Charles at a different time from Barbara. But the ruling family had no tact. It was their German blood.

She sneaked another glance at the terrace. Charles and Tony were still talking. Or rather—naturally—Charles was talking, and Tony was listening. Abigail's ample bosom swelled as she contemplated her future: one son a duke, one potential son-in-law heir to a dukedom, one daughter therefore a duchess. (And then there was Fanny. She should have looked for a higher title, but she had been younger in those days, less experienced. She would see that Fanny's children made good marriages. If only Fanny would stop having children . . . but that was neither here nor there. At least, for the time being. Now she must concentrate on Mary. Fanny was pregnant again and so could wait.)

As a brother-in-law, Charles would be an example to Tony. She looked him over approvingly. He was as big as, or bigger than, Tony, who was now one of the tallest men at court. And for her part, she did so like a tall man. So solid. So . . . well . . . big. Philippe was tall. And William had been tall. (Time was making her memory of William's physical attributes hazy, but she always thought of his height—if nothing else—fondly.) She hoped Charles was unburdening himself about Barbara, repenting his mistake. It was time Tony's own eyes were opened about his cousin, as Charles's must surely now be, for Tony had retained his foolish infatuation over his cousin, not that he ever said one word. (But when did he say more than a few words at best?) Abigail knew, however. She could not be fooled. She had a mother's instinct.

Tony looked up and saw her. A slow smile spread across his face, transfiguring it to something near handsomeness. In spite of herself, she smiled back. The Duchess had done wonders with him; Abigail had to give her credit for that, and she always was one to give credit where it was due. It might make her heart burn with jealousy, but she encouraged his relationship with his grandmother. The old witch was good for him. She could not deny it. He was still very quiet, but when he spoke, it was in complete sentences, and his sentences usually betrayed a good deal of common sense. Perhaps the sense had always been there, and she had been so busy trying to change him into something he was not that she had missed it. Well, she had her faults. Who did not? And behind her pushing had been a mother's love. Always. Tony was so much improved these last years. . . .

Of course, compared with Charles, one was not quite so impressed. Tony had lost much of his weight, but there was still a layer of fat to him compared with Charles, who was lean and fit. Tony could not be called handsome, no indeed, but without the extra fat he had carried for so long, his face was attractive. He had a snub nose and a nice mouth. And his shy, grave manners were quite winning. No, he was not dashing, like his friend Charles, but in his own way, he was at last developing satisfactorily. She no longer had to push and prod so. In fact, sometimes she had the distinct impression that maturity would only make Tony better and better.

She saw him shake his head at something Charles was saying. She saw Charles begin to argue. She sighed. It would do Charles no good; Tony had developed a mind of his own. She did not know sometimes whether to laugh or cry over it. She might talk to him about something until she was blue in the face, and he would listen politely, but then do as he wished. Now, for example, he had taken it into his head to stop wearing wigs. They were hot, he told her, and made him sweat. She frowned at his choice of words. She reminded him that they were the fashion. That no man wore his own hair. I do, said Tony, and he let his blond hair grow long and wore it pulled back and tied with a ribbon. Seeing Charles's curling wig, she sighed again. She did not care that Tony's long hair somehow made his face more chiseled and masculine. Wigs were the fashion. One follows fashion if one does not wish to be stared at, she told him. And he had said, smiling at her (she did have a soft spot for that smile), perhaps I will set a fashion. Tony. Of all people. Eccentric. He was going to be eccentric like the Duchess. Well, thank goodness he was a duke and would be allowed to get away with it. And now she had heard that he had a mistress. (Through Fanny from Harold.) Not some quiet little shopkeeper or milliner, as might be expected, but an actress. Devil's spawn, all of them. Whores.

Of course she wanted her only son to garner a little experience, but not with an actress. But it would do her no good to say one word. He was as stubborn as his grandmother.

On the terrace, the Prince de Soissons limped by Tony and Charles. A war wound, he had told her. She shivered. She did have a weakness for military men. After all, William had been a soldier. She waved her silk scarf and called Philippe's name. He stood still a moment, looking at her without smiling, but then a smile spread across his face. He had such even, white teeth, and Abigail found his dueling scar both attractive and a little frightening. She shuddered deliciously as he walked slowly toward her, leaning on his cane. As he passed Carlyle he nodded coolly, and Carlyle simpered. Abigail sniffed. Odious, odious man.

"How charming you look," Philippe said, bowing over her outstretched hand. "Are you waiting for your daughter? I am searching for Roger. Have you seen him this morning? I called at his home, but his butler said he was coming here."

"Leave a message with one of the equerries and join me instead for luncheon. I have some fresh boiled mutton, and it seems such a while since you and I have had a chance to visit." She could not stop herself. She batted her eyes at him.

He smiled at her as if he understood her completely. She felt her breath catch. "You tempt me. But I must say no this time."

She sighed. "Well, then at least sit down a moment and visit with me until Mary comes. I cannot stand being alone in this room with Carlyle. One would think he came to witness a freak show."

"And has he not?"

She frowned. He was not usually so blunt. Perhaps the duel had upset him also. After all, Roger was his friend. "Barbara is not a freak show, merely an undisciplined, spoiled woman, as you and I have so often agreed. Discretion. She lacks discretion. Surely this disgrace will teach her the necessity of acquiring some. I know I am mortified by it. That poor boy. I hope the prince dismisses her from court for a year." (In a year, Abigail could accomplish so much.)

"A year," said Philippe. "Yes. That would be adequate. Look, Abigail, interest grows. Carlyle was merely early."

The room was filling. Several members of the prince's household were strolling in in twos and threes: Philip Stanhope, John Hervey, Mistress Lepell, Colonel Campbell and Mistress Bellenden and Mrs. Howard. They seated themselves in random chairs or at the card tables placed throughout the room.

Yes, thought Abigail, Mrs. Howard, the prince's mistress, would be more than interested in Barbara's disgrace. And the young Mistresses Bellenden and Lepell had been the beauties of the court until Barbara's arrival. She could almost feel sorry for her niece, but then she saw Tony and Charles coming into the room, and the expression on Charles's face as he leaned against the wall made any stirrings of compassion she felt fade completely.

The door from the Prince of Wales's private apartments opened. Conversation, spasmodic anyway, suspended itself to begin again almost at once as Mary Saylor closed the door and went to her mother. Abigail sighed. Mary was not pretty, and there was just not much that could be done about it. On Tony pale brows and lashes did not matter (and Barbara, hussy that she was, combed hers dark) but on Mary, unmarried, and therefore not able to wear artificial aids to beauty, and possessing a square face anyway, they were fatal. She did have a good figure, and large, blue-gray eyes, like Tony's, but compared to Mistress Bellenden or Mistress Lepell (or Barbara), she fell short. Not that it mattered. She was the sister of a duke and that was by far the most important asset of all to possess. But Abigail had been pretty when she was Mary's age, and Fanny still was. (You cannot make a silk purse out of a pig's ear, she could just hear the Duchess say.)

"Oh, be quiet!" snapped Abigail.

Philippe leaned toward her. "I beg your pardon."

"Nothing. A random thought . . ."

The door to the private apartments opened again. Again, conversation halted. It was Diana, and she took one look at the gathered crowd, so casually resuming their conversations and said loudly, "Damn!"

Everyone heard, which did not seem to bother her in the least. It comes from running with Robert Walpole, thought Abigail, who stiffened as if someone had slapped her.

Carlyle laughed behind his fan. He watched Diana walk over to her sister-in-law, and he rose leisurely.

"Why are you still here?" Diana said, not bothering to lower her voice. "If you left, some of the others might follow. I never thought you would stoop to gloating, Abigail, but then Barbara has dampened quite a few of your plans, has she not?"

"I never gloat!" Abigail flashed before she could help herself. Her bosom swelled. She was not going to allow Diana to divert her into an unseemly quarrel. Not that she minded quarreling; there was a lot she had to say to Diana about her daughter—but not here, in Richmond Lodge.

"I was waiting for Mary," she managed to finish calmly, "and she has just now appeared. We are leaving. I have no wish to see my own niece humiliated, I do assure you."

"She is not going to be—"

"Ladies," said Carlyle, in a purring voice, looming like a giant bear just behind Diana. "May I join your little circle? I felt so lonely over there, and I must say, it does my heart good to see families clinging together in times of trouble."

Diana scowled and turned to answer, but then her mouth dropped open. Everyone saw it, saw her expression of complete amazement combined with chagrin, and turned as if they were one body to see what she was looking at. There was an audible gasp.

Barbara stood framed in the doorway, one hand resting on her husband's arm, the other hand on the shoulder of her page. All three of them wore mourning.

"Wonderful," murmured Carlyle. "Simply wonderful." He sighed and put a huge hand over his heart.

Charles, his eyes fastened to Barbara's profile as she passed him, stood like someone turned to stone. As did Philippe.

"Mama!" Mary said, too excited to be quiet. "Roger is with her!"

"We all have eyes in our heads," Abigail said acidly, irritated at feeling slightly overwhelmed herself by the impression their entrance was making. But then she happened to glance at Charles's face, and the anger and despair on it shook her to her soul. She felt the blood rush to her head from the shock of it. It was not some infatuation, then. He was head over heels in love. She shook out her gown and swept forward grandly. What Roger had started, she could finish. And would finish, for Mary's sake. She met them halfway in the room, kissing Barbara's cheek and smiling determinedly at Roger.

"I am delighted to see the pair of you," she said loudly. (Everyone was listening anyway. It was simpler to speak clearly so that nothing would be repeated incorrectly when it was repeated, as it would be.) "Barbara, my angel, you have all my sympathy and support."

"Abigail," said Roger, leading his wife past her smoothly, "your sympathy and support are taken for granted."

The sight of Philippe, standing there, staring at her with a white, grim face, his eyes like stones, made Barbara stop in her tracks. I will not speak to him, she thought. I will not. She began to tremble. Roger pushed her forward, and she found herself among her family.

"Barbara," Diana said, her violet eyes on Roger. She tried to pull her daughter off to one side unobtrusively. "It would be much better if you saw the prince alone. I have spoken with him and—"

"Diana," Roger said, "I could not help overhearing. I will not allow my wife to see the prince alone. Hyacinthe, you may go and inform the prince's secretary that Lord and Lady Devane both await his pleasure." He raised Diana's limp hand and kissed it. "I am sure you understand," he said. Diana was silent.

No one in the room was making any pretense of watching anything other than every move Roger and Barbara made. All eyes focused on Hyacinthe, as he ran to do as he was told, then swung back immediately to Roger, who seemed to be the principal actor in a drama no one quite understood, but all felt.

"Do you ever miss anything?" Roger said to Carlyle.

Carlyle forgot his affectation long enough to grin, but then Roger looked at Philippe, and the smile that had been on his face since he entered the room thinned at the edges.

"I did not expect you here today," he said.

"Nor I you."

Abigail caught her breath at the expression on Roger's face.

"You know me," Carlyle said quickly, stepping in between Roger and Philippe and waving his fan outrageously so that all attention centered on him. "I follow the drama, on stage and off. Your entrance was magnificent! There has been nothing like it for years. The armbands are an exquisite touch. My compliments. I would give my back teeth, yes, my back teeth, to be in that room for his expression when you walk in beside her. It will outdo anything seen in here. And I must say, my dear one, that it is very well done. Do you not agree, Philippe? It is certainly well done of Roger."

"Very well done."

Hyacinthe came scurrying out of the private apartments. Roger, glancing around the room, gave his arm to Barbara.

"If you will excuse us," he said to the room in general, "we have an appointment."

There was complete silence as they walked to the door, and a kind of collective sigh as the door closed behind them.

"Magnificent," said Carlyle, snapping shut his fan.

Diana frowned at the closed door.

"Philippe," said Abigail, who like everyone else had found herself watching the Devanes until the door literally closed in her face, "do reconsider and have luncheon with—why, Philippe! What is wrong? You look ill."

He bowed blindly in her direction. The dueling scar showed red-pink against the extreme whiteness of his face. "If you will excuse me this time, Abigail. I find I have a sudden headache. I will walk awhile in the gardens. . . ." And his heels made a clicking sound as he limped away from them all, straight through the terrace doors and down the steps out onto the lawns.

Other people were leaving also. Diana's glance swept the room and returned to Colonel Campbell, a close friend of the prince's. Her eyes narrowed. She swayed toward him, smiling beautifully, and they left the room together. Mrs. Howard, leaning on Philip Stanhope's arm, laughed at something he was saying as they walked away.

"There, at least," said Carlyle, "goes one person who is happy to see the Devanes reconciled." He waved his fan pensively.

Abigail took her daughter's arm, ignoring Carlyle. He might have been invisible.

"Come along, dear. I never meant for us to stay so long. I must say Barbara was fortunate Roger has such a strong sense of duty. I want to speak with your brother and Lord Russel before we leave—"

"Oh, no," Mary said, pulling back.

"I cannot abide unnecessary shyness. Pull yourself together, Mary," Abigail snapped. "Do move out of the way, Lord Carlyle! Charles will be delighted to see you."

"Not today," Mary said. But her mother was sweeping her along . . . just as she always did.

"A wise woman," Abigail was saying in a low voice, while she smiled in the direction of Tony and Charles, "ignores a man's infatuation with a woman he cannot possibly marry. And even Charles Russel cannot compete with Roger Montgeoffry if Roger has decided to reconcile. Not that she will make him a good wife, but that is neither here nor there. What is here and there is your future—Tony, my dear boy. Give your mother a kiss. Charles . . . so good to see you. I had a letter from your mother just the other day. Before all this nonsense, of course. You remember my daughter, Mary, do you not? I was just telling her that it seems an age since you have visited us. Your mother and I are such dear friends. . . ."

Carlyle smiled behind his fan at Abigail's maneuvers. Superb. Charles Russel could barely wrench his eyes from the door to the private chambers, but Abigail Saylor was forcing him to, forcing him to smile and act as if everything around him were normal. How fortunate that I decided to come today, thought Carlyle. So many pieces of a puzzle lying about, no rhyme or reason to them, and in ten minutes the overall design becomes plain, if one only has the sense to see it. Ah, life, how wearying it all is. And he snapped shut his fan and strolled out of the room. And finally, so did Abigail and Mary.

Only Charles and Tony were left. The two of them lounged against the wall, both big, one of them angry but self-possessed, the other shy and grave. Both of them stared at the door to the private apartments, and a muscle worked in and out of Charles's cheek.

In about a quarter of an hour, the door opened. Roger and Barbara, with Hyacinthe, came through, and the moment the door closed behind them, Barbara took her hand from Roger's arm. She wiped at her face quickly, angrily. Tony and Charles straightened up. Both looked at her. Her face, for a second, crumpled. She ran toward Tony, and he opened his arms.

"I will not cry," she whispered into his chest, crushing his satin lapels in her clenched fists. His hand came up to stroke her hair, but he caught himself. Roger's eyes went to Tony's face at that arrested gesture. Charles stood to one side, his face grim and uncertain at the same time.

"Lord Charles Russel."

Charles looked at the footman standing at the door to the private apartments. His hand went out to Barbara, but he, too, caught himself, and then he strode toward the door. He and Roger locked eyes. The resemblance between them was striking. Charles might have been his son. He stopped in front of the older, and yet still more handsome, man.

"I owe you an apology," he said abruptly. His face was flushed, but he met Roger's eyes squarely.

"You do," Roger said. "But there has been enough scandal, therefore I will accept on my wife's behalf." The stress he put on the words "my wife" was lost on no one in the room, except, perhaps, Barbara. "I need not remind you a gentleman does not intrude where he is no longer wanted. Need I, Charles?" Roger's voice was soft, and deadly.

Charles's nostrils flared. He looked as if he wanted to kill someone, but he bowed shortly and strode through the door to the private apartments.

Barbara said into Tony's coat, "I was so ashamed for him to reprimand me! If Roger had not been with me —"

"Well, it is over now. All over."

She stepped away from him at those words and looked up into his face. "So it is. Everything is. Tell me the truth, Tony. Are you ashamed of me?"

Very slowly, a smile spread across his face. It changed the contours and lit his eyes. For a moment, he was almost handsome. He shook his head.

"Do not make me cry—"

"Go to Tamworth, Bab. I think you would do better there."

"Yes. Yes, that is exactly what I am going to do." She hugged him. "You will write me? You will visit me?" She hugged him again. "I love you, Tony."

He stepped back, nodded once to Roger and left the room, his blond head bowed.

"There is no need to see me home—" Barbara began, but Roger interrupted.

"Let me decide what I will and will not do. I will escort you to the carriage, if you please. And then, since it is your desire, you may go home alone."

She was silent, meek almost, as he gestured for her to precede him.

Outside, at the carriage, he leaned one foot on the carriage step and watched her. Her face was very pale where the rouge did not cover it, and she was holding on to Hyacinthe's hand, as if she were a child and had just been punished. He could not help smiling, and she looked at him, and then quickly away because the passion in his eyes burned her so. And there was Philippe. Always Philippe between them. Even today, he was between them.

"I was proud of you," Roger said. "You displayed courtesy and far better breeding than the prince. Try to understand his irritation. A man who fancies himself in love at his age is often a fool."

Her other hand was lying in her lap. Gently, he picked it up and smoothed open the palm against his knee. He looked down at it. "I do love you so," he said. And he lifted her palm to his lips and kissed it. She could feel the pressure of his lips leap through her entire body. Once, so long ago, he had kissed her palm thusly at St. James's Square, when she had been young and foolish and crying. Now she was older and just as foolish, only there were no tears. She cupped his cheek with her palm. I loved you, too, she thought. Sweet Jesus, I loved you.

"We could deal better together than we have," he said harshly, and his eyes were the color of the summer sky above them. What was in them, what was in her, frightened her. She was not yet ready. She snatched her palm away. Her gesture did not seem to bother him in the least.

"Go on to Tamworth, Barbara. I must go to London. I will write to you. There is much I have to say, and some things are easier said in a letter. And I am going to say them, one way or another. You cannot run from me forever."

"Go, John," she said to the coachman, and Roger stepped away and shut the door. She leaned out the window but did not look at him. "Thank you for today." The carriage lurched away.

He stared after the carriage, growing smaller and smaller as it rattled down the oak-lined lane that led from Richmond Lodge. Finally, he walked away, and as he walked he began to whistle softly. As if he were satisfied. . . .

Philippe sat in the shade of some bordering trees that overlooked the fine tender green lawns of Richmond Lodge. Every feeling was numb, as they had all become the moment he had seen Roger beside Barbara this morning. Under the numbness, he was aware of a great pain, yet for now it was blessedly deadened. I understand, he thought slowly. It was as if all his thoughts, everything about him, even the blood flowing through his body, were moving with a stately slowness. Every detail—the green of the lawn, the sun dappling through the trees, the myriad tiny lines upon his hands as they lay quiescent in his lap—was significant. I understand it all now. He wants her, just as he wants all beautiful things. And he will have her. And I am to be the sacrifice. She has won. She does not even know it. But she has won.

At the end of the lane, Barbara's carriage lurched to a stop. She leaned out to see her aunt's carriage pulled to one side, Mary jumping down and lifting her long skirts, running toward hers. Not now, thought Barbara. She leaned back against the seat and closed her eyes.

"Bab. I have to speak with you. Open the door."

She motioned to Hyacinthe, and Mary climbed in. But instead of speaking, she fidgeted with a bow on her gown.

Barbara watched her through half-closed eyes. "Have you come to run away with me to Tamworth?" How normal her voice sounded. "Do so, and I will have Thérèse show you how to make up your face so that all the young men swoon at your feet. I will show you how to laugh and smile and flirt. They will be putty in your hands—" Her voice broke. She took a deep breath.

Mary stared at her.

"Never mind me. I have had a bad day. Several bad days, in fact." Those words were flippant, curt. Mary flinched. Go away, thought Barbara. Go away before I hurt you.

"I am a fool," Mary said, staring down at the shredded bow in her gown. She looked up at Barbara and said with the same abruptness Tony often displayed. "But I have to know. Do you love Charles Russel?"

Barbara closed her eyes. She wanted to claw her little cousin's face suddenly. She wanted to scream at her and kick and stamp her heels on the floor, like a child.

"Dear me, no," she said, and her voice was cutting. "He was amusing . . . for a while. You are a sweet dear to worry over me." Now go away, Mary, before I begin screaming and do not stop.

Mary leaned forward and hugged her. Her blue-gray eyes, clear and limpid like Tony's, gazed into Barbara's. "I had to know. I love you. Be well, Bab. Please."

I will not cry, Barbara thought, as the carriage jumped forward. I will not.

Carlyle, in the Richmond Lodge stable yard waiting for a groom to bring his horse, looked up and saw Roger, about to mount a horse, sag suddenly against its side. He broke into a run, all affectation gone, to reach Roger and take him by the arm.

"Roger! What is it? Are you ill? Where is your carriage?"

Roger raised his face. It was drained of color, and the sight of it frightened Carlyle.

"Barbara . . . has it," he said slowly, as if speaking each word hurt. "I am fine. I-I felt a small pain."

"Let me call another carriage for you. You sit there on the steps, and I will—"

"No . . . Tommy. I will be fine. I . . . I am feeling better already." With an effort, and to Carlyle's horror, he hoisted himself into the saddle. His face was pale, and there was a sheen of perspiration suddenly all across it.

"I . . . must be getting old," he said, looking down at Carlyle.

"Not you," Carlyle said quickly. "Never you. Roger, go home and rest. Promise me."

Roger smiled. The smile was a grimace. "I will." Carlyle shivered and stared after him until someone cursed at him angrily to move out of the middle of the stable yard.

* * *

The carriage lurched crazily over the dried mud ruts on the road to Tamworth. Barbara was silent in a corner, her feet tucked under her, both dogs asleep in her lap. Hyacinthe rode outside with the coachman, and Thérèse, sitting opposite, understood her mood and said nothing. They would have to stop in another hour or so at a tavern to spend the night; they had gotten away from Richmond too late to reach Tamworth until tomorrow afternoon. Barbara leaned her head against the corner of the seat and carriage side. How weary I am, she thought. Bits and pieces of the day kept flashing in her head, the expression on the Frog's face as he watched her advance with Roger; the way she felt when she walked into her parlor and saw Roger this morning; the brief glimpse she had caught of Charles's face; the way her heart hurt at the mere sight of Philippe, the ugly memories his presence ignited; Mary's question. . . . We deserved to end so much better than we did, she thought. . . . Oh, Charles. And then there was the numbing fact of Jemmy's death. His death haunted her, perching on her shoulder in her mind like a black crow. He was so young. . . .

"Hello! Stop! Stop the carriage!"

The words penetrated her thoughts. Thérèse was leaning out the window.

"Three men," she said tersely. "On horseback. One of them is trying to stop the carriage."

Barbara began to jerk off rings and bracelets, looking for a place to hide them. She slipped a ring down the front of her gown.

"Not there!" cried Thérèse. "Your shoe. Put them in your shoe—"

And then both of them looked at each other and said, "Hyacinthe!" at the same time. If John should fire off his pistol, if the highwaymen should have firearms—Barbara pushed the dogs from her lap. Thérèse was already half out of the window. Barbara moved across the seat to hold her waist and legs to steady her. She saw a horse and rider go by. The carriage began to slow down. It stopped. Thérèse fell back into the carriage. Her face was white and pinched about the nostrils. Hyacinthe leaned over, his head upside down in the window. He grinned at them.

"Lord Russel," he said. "It is Lord Russel."

Barbara wrenched open the door and stepped out into the dirt of the road. One rider had the reins of the carriage horses. Another two were just riding up. She recognized Charles immediately.

"How dare you stop my carriage in this way!" she yelled at him, fright making her shrill. "You are fortunate John did not blow your head off!"

Charles leaned down toward her, his face strained, a smear of dirt across one thin cheek.

"Listen to me. I have to speak with you. We cannot leave things as they are."

"There is nothing left for us to say—"

Her words ended in a gasp, for he put one arm around her waist, and with her dangling like a sack of meal, trotted away toward a small copse of oak trees. The horse's gait, the way Charles's arm clasped her waist, knocked the breath from her.

She almost fell down when he let her go. He dismounted and tried to take her in his arms. She stepped back.

"Forgive me," he said, and his wide, sensual, beautiful mouth was so grim it was a thin line, but not any grimmer than the expression in his eyes. "Say you forgive me."

"You killed him—"

"God, Barbara, do you think anything else has been on my mind since the moment I saw him fall? Do you think I have no feelings at all? I have to live with the knowledge of what I have done for the rest of my life. But I cannot live knowing you hate me."

"Oh, Charles, I do not hate you."

He took a step toward her, but she turned and leaned into a thick tree trunk, her cheek against the rough bark.

"How could you do it, not only to Jemmy, but to me?" she said, and her voice was trembling. "Can you not see? It is over."

"I will not believe that," he said quickly. "We both have much to regret. But we can change, Barbara. If we only try—"

He put his arms around her. She did not lean back into him, as once she would have done, but she did not pull away either. He rested his chin on the top of her head as he spoke softly, gently, persuasively.

"I love you. I love you in a way that frightens me. I could not stand the idea that another man had touched you. I was wrong. Drunk and crazed. Never have I humbled myself as I am doing now. Say you forgive me, Barbara. Say you love me. I need to hear the words. . . ."

She turned around and looked up at him. His eyes searched her face. It is too late, she was thinking. I do care for you. But there has always been Roger between us, though you did not know. . . . There is so much you do not know, Charles, and now there is Jemmy . . . and the hurt and shame there is so deep . . . atop too many other hurts. . . . It is too late for us. . . Oh, God, I am no different from Roger, allowing you to love me that way he allowed me. . . . Oh, God. . . .

"There is someone else," she said slowly, her face white, as if all the blood had drained from it. "There has always been someone else—"

He stepped back, the angles of his face changing, so that for a second, she might have been facing Roger. But he was not Roger. He never would be.

"What a fool I am," he said, moving now toward her, anger, more than anger in his face. "I am nothing to you. Nothing at all. Goddamn you—"

She stepped back at the expression on his face, but the tree trunk was behind her, and he was before her, shaking her shoulders savagely.

"I may have to live with killing him, but you have to live with his lovemaking and what that makes you! Go on! Run away to wherever it is you are going, and when enough time has passed, crawl back to the safety of that husband of yours, if that is what you plan, for it is certainly what he plans! But you will miss me, and by God in heaven, you will need me! Because I am young, like you. And he is old. And I love you. As much as—or more than—he does. And I am the better man. . . . God, I would like to strangle you!"

He let go of her contemptuously, and she almost fell. He looked down at her.

"All summer you have been playing a dangerous game, Barbara. Yes, you hate me at this moment for saying the truth. Well, I could not keep myself from loving you, in spite of it, which only makes me a fool. But what does this summer make you?"

His words were flames in her mind, crackling and burning, and too close to truth to be borne. She wanted to kill him for saying them. She had run away from Richelieu not to become so and yet here she was and there was the gleam of Philippe's white, even teeth as he smiled at what was achieved, slowly but surely, if one only waited long enough. She grabbed Charles's cloak and twisted it in her hand, pulling him to her, surprising him with her surge of angry strength.

"In my life, I have known only four men, and one of them just died for it, and perhaps that does make me a whore, but I don't think so! And I mean to be so much else! You will never know all I mean to be! And Roger, for all you despise him, would never have killed a boy, no matter what I had done! Which makes him the better of us both! You will never be the man he is, not if you live a thousand years! And I will never love you the way I once loved him!"

She dropped the cloak, panting, and Charles stared at her, and all that was in his face hurt her. But she could not stop. Not now. The anger and despair and his words were all too much.

"You go away," she told him. "You go far away and marry, as your mother keeps urging you! Some sweet, docile girl who has no fears and hurts and so can never disappoint you! As I have done! You are right in one thing, Charles! I hate you for saying the truth! And I always will!"

Her words carried clearly. The men who had come with Charles looked down at the ground, and Therese put her hand to her mouth and accidentally leaned against the carriage door so that it opened, and Harry and Charlotte went leaping out, yapping and barking, straight to their mistress. They sniffed Charles's legs, and even though he was familiar to them, they growled at him. He kicked at them.

"Goddamn you!" screamed Barbara. "You leave my dogs alone!"

He turned and walked away. She knelt down and gathered Harry and Charlotte into her lap. They whined and licked her face.

"Good dogs," she whispered. "Good dogs."

She wiped her face. She was crying. Damn him.

CHAPTER TWENTY-FOUR

The Duchess was inspecting her beehives or, rather, she was watching her doddering beekeeper (as old, as ancient as she was) inspect the hives, sheltered in specially built sections of a garden wall constructed in her great-grandfather's time. The spring had been cold, and she and the beekeeper had used tried and true methods to keep the bees thriving. They had fed them honey boiled in rosemary in little wooden troughs put near the hives; they had fed them toast soaked in ale; she had ordered more thyme and lavender planted nearby—although there was already an ancient wisteria vine that had attracted them years ago—and lamb's ears and soap-wort and Queen Anne's lace and mint and violets, surely more than enough to tempt any capricious bee's driven little heart. But the queen was new, and the Duchess and her beekeeper wanted to ensure that the colony expanded itself properly and continued to make sweet, mint-flavored honey, a Tamworth specialty.

The bees were her new interest, an interest necessary these last years. She had Tony to keep her going, and he had, especially when Barbara had not returned amid such terrible, wild rumors reaching them from France and Hanover. But Tony was a man, and to protect that manhood, the Duchess pushed him to depend on no one, her least of all. And so, she had her bees. It ought to have been Barbara. Any fool with one eye in her head could see she was not well when she appeared this spring, but Barbara was a woman now and bent on her own way. Something had happened to her in Paris, but had she come home, home to Tamworth where she belonged and where the Duchess could have nursed and cared for her? No. She had racketed about the city of Paris with some rascal called the Duc de Richelieu and earned herself quite a reputation in the bargain. And a year later, she had handled her father's death and burial and sending of the body home by herself, without so much as a word to the family, other than a terse letter informing them of the death. And still she stayed away. And so the Duchess busied herself with her bees, demanding, exacting little creatures, temperamental, apt to move their hive if it became too crowded or the herbs and flowers nearby did not suit them. They had to be treated carefully, fed their special diet in a cold spring. Bees would not thrive if they were quarreled over; they had to be informed when a death in the family occurred. They were nervous, busy creatures who would sting you in a second, if you disturbed them improperly, even though it meant their own death.

Lately, death had been much on her mind. All the deaths—Kit's, Richard's sister Elizabeth, Cousin Henley's, her own. For it was coming. She had lived far past her prime; she was a doddering, nearly toothless, old hag. She never knew when her legs would fail her, and she would have to be helped about by a footman, like a cripple. (Now, for example, at a discreet distance, was the latest in a series of footmen Annie assigned to watch over her. She hated it, but her body was failing her more and more, and there seemed to be nothing she could do. She was a prisoner inside it. Some mornings she woke and felt young again, but then, as she struggled out of bed, she knew the truth. She was very old.) It was time to let go and fade away. No one needed her anymore, and that was the plain, simple truth of it. She had outlived her usefulness. Just the other day, she had been discussing it with Richard, which was another sign of her old age. She talked out loud to him now and did not care a sixpence who heard her.

Richard, she had said, sitting beside his marble tomb, I am thinking of joining you. All the children are gone, and Barbara and Harry and Tony—and God knows, Diana—do not need me, and I am old and my legs always hurt and sometimes I cannot walk. And even your memory is growing dim, my love, and I thought that would never happen. Never. I want to be with you and the boys. I am tired of bees. And then she told him the latest scandal about their granddaughter, described in lurid detail in a recent letter from Abigail. (The footman, over in a corner out of her way—she hated to be reminded visibly of her infirmities—had averted his head at the sight of tears slowly trickling down the Duchess's old, wrinkled face.)

Leaning heavily on her cane, the Duchess walked slowly away from the garden wall toward Richard's rose garden. The beekeeper, who had been in the middle of explaining when he would take the honey, exchanged a glance with the footman. More and more, the Duchess's mind seemed to wander. She would be talking, or listening, and without warning, she would drift off. But woe to the person who dared correct her. She came back with startling, killing suddenness.

The rosebushes are glorious now, she thought, in their last season of blooming, their litter of falling petals only one reminder of the end of summer. Yes, already August was on the wane, and autumn was coming. She could feel it in her bones; she could see it around her. The sun set a little earlier in the evenings, and in the mornings sometimes a mist rose from the stream trickling in the woods. Many of the birds were gone—she missed their shrill, sweet songs—and the ferns in the woods were beginning to show new splotches of russet color among their fans of green. She took a deep breath of rose-scented air. Autumn, around the corner, was a good time. A busy time. Idle hands were the Devil's plaything, as was an idle mind. She would have no time for idleness; there would be all the harvesting to oversee. Where now there was a sea of green stalks bursting with yellow ears of corn and waving golden heads of fat wheat, there would soon be nothing but blackened stubble. Then came the picking of plums and pears and apples, and the frantic making of jellies and jams and preserves. Her stillroom would be worse than any beehive, as Annie and she and helpers mixed potpourris and made rose brandies and lemon drops and strawberries in wine and cordials for fever and pearl in the eye and coughs and agues. Candles and soap had to be made. Ale brewed. Hogs slaughtered. All before winter. Before the time of hibernation. Of rest. Of death. Well, she would savor each small thing this autumn, the ripe darkness of a gooseberry, the high squeals of dying hogs, the smell of hive wax and bayberry essence in candles, the distilled perfection of drying rosebuds. Each detail would be sweet. Bittersweet. As life so often was.

Ahead of her, a small, fluffy white kitten cleaned herself on the broad flagstone steps of the terrace. The new Dulcinea. The old one had gone into a decline after her last litter, of which this new kitten was the Duchess's choice to continue the cycle. She had outlasted even her ancient cat. She sighed and hobbled her way up the steps. Time to ascertain if there was enough in the pantries for the coming harvest supper, when the last of the corn was harvested and laborers and tenants and farmers and all of Tamworth celebrated with a huge supper on the lawns, a tradition that went back to the beginnings of Tamworth itself. Richard would want plenty of good ale for the workers, and Giles would not yet be off to school and could help her. . . . No. Richard was dead. A long time dead. And Giles. She knew that. She knew it as well as she knew her own name, yet sometimes the past was more real to her than the present. Dulcinea leapt up as she passed by and batted at her long skirt.

"Bah!" she said. "You will never match your mother."

"Your grace!"

It was Annie calling. Annie, and her butler Perryman, ancient enemies over household precedence, had formed an unholy and uneasy alliance these last years to watch over her. Annie was a fretful old hen, always clucking. And Perryman was a great fool, without the bells on his cap. The Duchess scowled at the sound of Annie's voice. She would be wanting her to rest, which was exactly what she had in mind, but she did not like to be reminded of it. The footman assigned to follow her, a big, bold young man with a round, merry face and an impudent smile, in spite of broken front teeth, suppressed a smile at the expression on her face.

"You!"

She had turned on him with startling suddenness for such an old woman and was glaring at him. He stiffened.

"You, there. Jim! Or is it John?"

"Tim, ma'am."

"Tim, is it? Well, you just go tell Annie where I am before she bellows the house down. Go on. Do as I say. I am not liable to fall down these steps, and if I do, I daresay I will be healed in a month or so. . . . What did you say your name was?"

"Tim, ma'am."

"What happened to John?"

"Ah, John was . . . needed in another part of the house, ma'am."

"Could not put up with me, could he? More fool, he. You, Jim, go on now—"

"Tim, ma'am."

"I know. Do not keep interrupting me, boy! Go and do as I say. I do not have all day to talk with footmen!"

She sat down on one of the stone benches, and Dulcinea jumped up in her lap and rolled on her back and began to bat at her hands. The Duchess scratched her belly. You are already fat, she thought. You will be fatter than your mother. Poor Dulcinea. It was the last litter that killed her, for she was too old to be bearing kittens, but she always got an itch at the cry of a tomcat. I hope you are going to be the proud, selfish, immoral hussy your mother was, the Duchess thought, looking down at the white bundle of fur which had wrapped herself around her hand. What a shame I will not live long enough to see you in your prime. Well, Tony will take you. Tony is a good, dear boy who comes to see me often and lies and says how Barbara is always asking after me when I know Barbara never gives me one thought anymore. What happened in Paris? And was it my fault, Dulcinea? Was it?

Annie, thinner, browner, bossier than ever, came outside to the terrace. Too bossy. But the Duchess had not the strength these days to deal with insubordination. Emotion tired her. Anger tired her. Sweet Jesus, getting out of bed in the morning tired her! What would happen to Annie when she died? Who would have an irritable, thin old brown stick that knew every charm in the east of England and could recite the recipes for half the Duchess's concoctions by heart? Well, doubtless Tony would see after her, too. I only hope that little actress is making him happy, thought the Duchess, giving a grim chuckle. (Her sister-in-law, Louisa, had written her that gossip, and she had gone off in a choking fit of laughter that nearly killed her.)

"It is from Barbara," Annie repeated impatiently.

She ought to be more patient, thought the Duchess. I am old. Then the sense of the words penetrated. She held out her claw of a hand and ripped past the seal. Dulcinea batted at the single sheet of parchment.

Dearest Grandmama,
   Doubtless you already know the news of my latest scandal, but what you do not know is that I am coming to you. The thought was there before the scandal. Look for me the day after this letter.
   Your loving granddaughter,
   Barbara, Countess Devane

Annie glanced at the Duchess's face, which was without expression.

"Help her to her bedchamber," she ordered Tim, the footman.

Tim put his hand on the Duchess's bony elbow.

"Bah!" she snapped, slapping at him. "Take your hands off me. I am no cripple!"

Startled, he stepped back.

She stood up. Without a word, she hobbled into the house, Dulcinea following.

"I knew the letter would cheer her up," Annie said.

Housemaids were bustling and had been since early morning, cleaning and polishing places already cleaned and polished, but Lady Barbara was expected today, said Annie, and her grace was in a demanding mood. Windows in the late duke's bedchamber were opened to air out the room. For the first time since his death, it was going to be used. For Lady Barbara. The duchess had been in the gardens all morning, ruthlessly ordering the cutting of roses and snapdragons and pinks and dahlias. Stableboys were sent to the woods to gather gillyflowers and harebells and ferns. Every room still used had its vase of flowers with trailing tendrils of dark green ivy down its sides.

A dinner had been in preparation since before dawn: a great roast beef and spinach tarts and patties of calf brains and a fricassee of rabbit and a salad of radishes and lettuce and boiled summer peas. And as a special treat, a gooseberry-apple pie, as big as a wagon wheel, with preserved flowers sprinkled across its crust. Even now Perryman and one footman sensible enough to handle the responsibility were mixing Tamworth punch, peeling the lemons, stirring the sugar and brandy and rum, arguing over the amount of nutmeg and gin. Not that she deserves a bit of this, the Duchess could be heard to mutter on and off throughout the morning, as she was everywhere, in the garden, the kitchen, the great hall, the duke's bedchamber, her keen eye on every item, while Dulcinea curled in the crook of her arm and she leaned on Tim.

She rested at noon, refused any luncheon and allowed Annie to dress her in her second-best gown and place a black lace cap on her head. Now she sat in a parlor off the great hall that overlooked the avenue of lime trees Barbara's carriage would drive down. Her hands clasped and reclasped the golden head of her cane, as Dulcinea dozed on and off in her lap and played with the lace on her sleeves (and got slapped for her mischief). Young house servants tiptoed past the open door, whispering and pointing at her solitary, motionless figure gazing out the windows until she told Tim irritably to close the door.

Sometime in midafternoon, a young stableboy came running down the avenue, leaping barefooted across the gravel in the courtyard to dive into a side door of the house, startling both Perryman and Annie, drinking tea in the servants' hall.

"It is her! It is her! I saw the carriage!"

Perryman rose majestically. "Very good. I will inform her grace—"

Annie glared at him. The rivalry between them was as ancient and fierce as that of any savage tribe. "I am her tire-woman, and I will do the informing. Her system must have no shocks to it."

"She has the constitution of a rock, and my news can hardly be a shock since Lady Barbara is expected. I have been in this household since the Duchess became a duchess. My father served hers! I believe I know my responsibilities."

Perryman swept majestically from the room. At times such as these, any pretense of dignity was forgotten between him and Annie. She hitched up her skirts and passed him in the great hall. He broke into a run, and the two of them reached the parlor door at the same time. They wrestled over the door handle, both jerking it open. Perryman managed to precede Annie, but was pulled up short. Annie ran into his back.

Tim and the stableboy stood before the Duchess.

"It is a grand black carriage with a crest on the door," the stableboy was saying. "With four black horses pulling it. Grand enough for a king."

"Yes, that would be Roger's. Here is a coin for you, boy. John, give the boy a coin."

"Tim, ma'am."

"My cane," said the Duchess. Tim handed her her cane. Annie and Perryman stood coldly some distance away. The Duchess stopped in front of Perryman.

"Things have come to a pretty pass," she said to the middle of his chest, "when I have to depend on a stableboy and a footman for news of my granddaughter's arrival."

Perryman stared frostily at Tim. "Those who do not recognize the order of a household must learn. I was just coming in to inform the Duchess—"

"It is my duty to inform the Duchess—" broke in Annie.

"I saw him running by outside," Tim said, grinning impudently at the two of them. "I thought he might have some news. The old girl was anxious."

"Do not call her the old girl," Annie began, but the sound of a carriage, horse's hooves against gravel, and the jingle of harness came clearly into the room. Annie and Perryman looked at each other; they might miss the arrival. They crowded back through the parlor door together. Several stableboys, a groom or two, the cook, footmen and maidservants came running out of doors, clustering behind the Duchess like chickens behind a mother hen.

Trembling, pawing the gravel, the horses stopped, and a groom and stableboys ran to grab the lead bridles. Perryman stepped forward to open the carriage door. Out tumbled the two pugs, their little eyes bright and bulging. They ran forward, yapping shrilly, and Dulcinea leapt from the Duchess's arms to Tim to a nearby bush, her tail straight up in fright. Hyacinthe descended and bowed before the Duchess. The stableboys, remembering again his black skin and his fine clothes from the spring's quick visit, glared at him. Thérèse stepped down daintily, showing pretty ankles, to the delight of watch-

ing grooms and footmen, who had discussed her frequently
since their own brief glimpse of her in the spring, when she
had accompanied Lady Barbara and Master Harry. She curtsied to the Duchess. And finally, one hand in Perryman's,
Barbara descended from the carriage.

She is too thin, thought the Duchess. When I last saw her
at least she had some flesh on her bones. This summer has hurt
her. I see it in her face.

"You! Boy!" she snapped to Hyacinthe, who bowed again
and told her his name.

"You find those dogs and shut them up. I cannot abide yapping, misbehaved, spoiled animals. The duke's dogs were
always well trained. You! Coachman!"

Barbara's coachman froze.

"You just mind where you drive those horses on the way to
the stables. I will not have my lavender beds ruined by careless driving! You footmen get these trunks off this coach! Have
you all turned to stone!"

Galvanized, people were scurrying right and left. Only she
and Barbara were unmoving, as people moved around them
as water does stones in a stream.

"You! Frenchy!"

Smiling, Thérèse repeated her name softly, and several
footmen and grooms were seen to roll it on their tongues
silently.

"You follow my Annie, and she will show you my granddaughter's chambers."

She looks so old, thought Barbara. I had forgotten, or per-
haps I never noticed. Oh, Grandmama. You can still bark.
And I'm sure you can still bite. How glad I am to be home.
She smiled at her grandmother.

Impudent chit, thought the Duchess. She is the image of her
grandfather at this moment. I ought to cane her. Ah, Richard, our girl is home. She opened her arms, and without a
word, Barbara walked into them.

Barbara did not eat much of the dinner prepared in her
honor, though she did smile at the sight of Cook and two
footmen bearing in a pie the size of a wagon wheel. But as
the servants in the household gathered around for a slice,
along with a cup of Tamworth punch Perryman was now

importantly ladling out, she slipped away in the laughing disorder, climbing the back, uneven stairs to the attics, opening the door to her old room. But there was nothing left to remind her of herself. The bed stood bare, without its draperies and mattress. The Dutch chest was empty now. Her bird's nest and treasures were long gone. She sat a moment at her window, gazing out onto Tamworth, trying to remember the girl who had once sat here by the hour, but all she could recall was the expression on Charles's face as he stared down at her, and she told him she hated him. In the nursery, she sat for a long time on the floor, the dust motes from the sun coming through the window to dance around her. On top of low tables were stacked small wooden chairs. A cradle sat empty and forlorn in a corner, not even its gauze draperies to swathe it. The pale ghosts of her brothers and sisters floated dimly in her memory. Here all was stillness, all was time wound down, stopped, no more.

Bab, said dead Charlotte in her mind, do not leave. Little Anne's hand clutched the cloak of a fifteen-year-old girl off to London. I am the bride, Anne said, clomping about in her big sister's shoes, look at me. Bab, Tom and Kit said to her in her bride's finery, you are beautiful. I love you, Bab, said Charlotte. I love you. Dear, shy, difficult Charlotte. Nothing now. Worms and moldering bones. Oh, Charles, I wish we had not quarreled. In her mind, he said the hurtful, ugly truths to her again, and in her mind, she covered his lovely, firm mouth with her hand to silence him. She looked toward the empty cradle. Baby smiled a ghostly toothless smile. A spider was making a web in one corner. Jemmy lay bleeding to death on the ground. It only hurts when I laugh, said Richelieu. Roger, she thought. It hurts. It all hurts me so.

That evening she walked with her grandmother to Tamworth church. All was soft and mellow now with dusk. In another hour it would be dark; the evening was cool and quiet, but with country sounds—the lowing of cattle in their fields, the frogs. Harry and Charlotte were around her feet, their coats covered with briars and weed seeds, as she stooped to gather gillyflowers and pimpernel that grew along the ditches of the lane. Inside Tamworth chapel, while her grandmother murmured to the eternally young marble figure of her grandfather lying across the top of his table tomb, Barbara read the memorial tablets on the walls, for her uncles, her brothers and sisters, Cousin Henley. She filled the basalt vases in the corners with the wildflowers.

The household was waiting when they returned, gathered in the great hall for evening prayers. Perryman brought the Bible box and opened it and took out the huge Tamworth Bible and laid it in the Duchess's lap. She sat tiny and wrinkled, dwarfed in the duke's massive oak chair. The hall, with its dark timbers of wood vaulting above, was almost like a church itself.

" 'Have mercy upon me, O God, according to thy loving kindness,' " she began to read in a quavering voice, and Barbara closed her eyes to listen, evening prayers a constant she had grown up upon, and now, the full sounds and cadences of King James's scholars soothed her heart because the words brought back memories of such evenings stretching back as far as she could remember. After the reading, the Duchess added her few short, personal requests, that the weather continue mild, and that one of the kitchen maids—who would go unnamed but who would know herself—not be so forward with the stableboys. Everyone bowed his head to pray silently.

"Lord, have mercy upon us," the Duchess finished.

"Christ, have mercy upon us," repeated her household. "Amen."

Tamworth's day was over.

Barbara lay in her bed. The dogs, at her feet, were already snoring loudly, exhausted with their first day in the country, with their exploring and attempts to follow a scent, with the fruitless effort to corner and kill the kitten, Dulcinea. She had returned to her bedchamber to find Hyacinthe trying to wash an eye turning black and blue. She listened to his excited version of a fight with two stableboys, and tonight he was sleeping over the stables with them. He had fought, successfully, to make his first friends. She and Thérèse had smiled at each other above his head.

From her bed, she could see the moon. If I were in Richmond or London or even Paris, she thought, my evening would only be beginning. I would still be dressing for the theater or a game of cards in the Frog's private chambers. There would be hours ahead of me, long hours, in which to gamble and flirt and be bored. Charles would be watching me, and I would see in his eyes that he wanted me. And I might walk with him in the gardens, letting him kiss me until my legs were weak and all I could think of was to be alone with him, naked in his arms. Or I might flirt with someone else. Just to see his anger. As Richelieu taught me. . . . How well he taught me. . . . People around me would be gossiping, drinking, becoming louder as the night wore on. And I would go to my bed in the early hours of the morning, and if I were sober, I would think, Another night has passed. And my life goes on. And nothing happens. Words from her grandmother's reading this evening drifted into her mind. Purge me with hyssop and I shall be clean. Wash me and I shall be whiter than snow. Oh, Charles, there were times when I almost loved you. I did not treat you fairly. Make me to hear joy and gladness; that the bones which thou hast broken may rejoice. Roger, you smile at me with your handsome face and expect me to fall at your feet. . . . If only I could . . . but I cannot. . . .

She climbed out of bed and creaked open the door to her grandmother's chambers. Her grandmother lay back against a snowy mountain of pillows, but she was not asleep. A solitary candle glimmered on the table beside the bed, and one hand moved in a rhythmic motion over a purring, white bundle of fur, the new Dulcinea . . . while her grandmother read from her Bible, her lips moving with the words. Barbara smiled. . . . Nothing changed, and everything did.

The Duchess looked up as she saw her granddaughter walking toward her. Nothing changes, she thought, and everything does. Here is my Bab with me once more, but not the Bab I knew. That Bab would have come bounding into my bed, spilling over with thoughts, with her hurts and needs, heart and face an open book to me. This is a woman who approaches me, and her hurts are not open for all the world to see, but still she comes to me, as always, the ritual remembered, beloved. Thank you, my heavenly Lord, for your multitude of tender mercies. . . . Richard, our girl is home.

Barbara got into the bed and moved Dulcinea and lay down, and without a word, the Duchess reached out and touched her hair, her hands stroking the red-gold curls. Barbara closed her eyes. There was a comfortable silence between them. The Duchess felt herself begin to doze. It was the warm familiarity, the old, beloved memory now real again, for the young Barbara had spent many a night thusly, and then it was over misbehavior also. . . . What a mischievous, headstrong child she had been. . . . What had she done this time. . . . Had she and that rogue Harry given the pigs her precious rose brandy to drink so that the poor creatures staggered like fat, pink drunken barrels in their pens, while the grooms leaned against the fence, watching, crying with laughter. . . . Had she and Harry gotten into John Ashford' s orangery to steal his newly formed fruit? Well, she would talk with John tomorrow. . . .

"You know of the duel?"

Her words jerked the Duchess awake, and she found herself looking into her granddaughter's blue eyes.

"Duel?" she said, parrying for time. "Has Harry been sent down from school again for dueling?"

Barbara leaned on one elbow to stare at her. "No, Grandmama. That was long ago. I meant the duel between Charles Russel and Jemmy Landsdowne."

"Oh . . . yes . . . that duel. Of course I know about it! I am not in my dotage yet! Your Aunt Abigail broke two pens in her haste to see I had all the news." She sat up straighter and pulled forward her lace-edged cap, which had slipped during her doze. "Who was this Jemmy?"

"An admirer . . . a friend . . . a boy. He reminded me of Kit. I flirted with him. And more. Which he died for."

Ah, yes, thought the Duchess. I know. I know all they say of you. Abigail sees to that. A good name is rather to be chosen than great riches, and loving favor rather than silver and gold. . . . As a jewel of gold in a swine's snout, so is a fair woman which is without discretion. . . . Oh, there were many verses she could now recite to her granddaughter . . . about women and their wiles and their wicked ways . . . but she found that not even one of them would go past her lips. She could not say them to this girl, this woman, she loved so. Yet how easily she had always said them to Diana and turned away from her daughter contemptuously. If she had never said them to Diana, never judged her, would things have been different? If she could have loved Diana the way she loved Barbara . . . The thoughts pained her. Old, she said to herself.

I am too old for regrets now. Too old to change. Softly, in a hesitant voice that was so unlike herself that Barbara stared, she said, "In this life many things happen in which we play a shameful part. Those of us who are strong forgive ourselves and go on. The weak wallow in their shame and allow it to devour them. There is no one of us without sin, child. There ought to be some comfort in that."

Surprised, Barbara smiled at her.

How lovely she is, thought the Duchess, for all her thinness. No wonder a man was killed for her. But she could not read her granddaughter's heart, as once she had done so easily. Barbara closed her eyes again, and the Duchess began to stroke her hair. Roger, she thought. Does she still love him, or does she love this Charles Russel? What happened in Paris? Am I ever to know . . . and can I bear it if I do?

Hide thy face from my sins, and blot out all mine iniquities, Barbara was thinking, the words from the evening reading still in her mind. Create in me a clean heart, O God; and renew a right spirit within me. Cast me not away from thy presence; and take not thy holy spirit from me. Restore unto me the joy of thy salvation . . . Oh, Grandmama, how glad I am to be here, to be with you. I know what you will do from the moment you rise in the morning until you go to bed at night. Your world is a ritual and you are unvarying in your strength and steadfastness, and you and Tamworth will make me well again. I know it. She closed her eyes and went to sleep.

She sat with her grandmother in the afternoon shade of some ancient oaks. The oaks were not far from the house, atop a small hillock from which could be seen both the house and the fields of wheat and corn, colored with the moving shapes of workers, busy at harvest. Letters had arrived; there were always letters; the Duchess maintained a network of correspondence; people throughout the county rode over to hear the news from her letters. Her system was to read them in the afternoons and reply to them in the mornings, and all through each day, as she oversaw her household, going from stillroom to kitchen to parlor to garden, she could be heard calling impatiently for Annie to write down some thought or comment she meant to include in a letter.

"From Tony," said the Duchess, picking up and ripping past the seal of a letter with pleasure. A smaller note inside fluttered into her lap. She tossed it to Barbara and spread open her own letter and began to read it with relish.

"London is hot. . . . Of course it is! It is the end of August. . . . he says South Sea closed their stock transfer books after a day, the crowds to transfer were so thick, and that the terms for this new subscription are far stricter. . . . He says he does not like it and to sell out any stock I might have, no matter the loss. . . . Bah! I sold out in May! Bunch of greedy goldsmiths and stockjobbers! That John Blunt is a scrivener and nothing more, and all the knighthoods in the world will not rub the ink from his fingers nor the figures from his heart! What else does my boy say. . . . Alexander Pope and Lady Mary Wortley Montagu continue to flirt with each other at their poetry readings. . . . Hem . . . I do not like Pope. His spirit is mean and small. Caesar White is the better poet. He was a fool to leave your household, you know. A writer needs a patron. What is he doing these days?"

Barbara looked up from her letter. "I have no idea. I have only seen him once—to thank him for the Aurora poem. I-I had other things on my mind."

"Exactly why a writer needs a patron," the Duchess repeated stubbornly, but Barbara was not listening. Her grandmother opened another letter.

"Abigail says all the gossip is of the writs the South Sea will bring against the . . . what is this word? Her handwriting looks like a hen's scratching. Is it English Copper Company? Yes. That must be it. And the Welsh Copper Company and the Yorks Buildings Company. She says the Prince of Wales has been advised, and he has resigned as governor of the Welsh Company. Roger sent a personal note to Tony to inform him, so that he might sell any stock invested. A handsome gesture. Abigail says the prince was furious, but the directors were determined. Stock for the Royal Assurance Company and the London Exchange Company are both dropping. Everyone is watching with bated breath, she says. . . ."

"Breath," murmured Barbara. "Yes." In her letter, Tony said not one word about stock or Alexander Pope but instead wrote how much he missed her. The Countess of Camden— Jemmy's mother—had been taken ill, he wrote. She looked up and out over the cornfields a moment before continuing to read. Charles had left Richmond to go to one of his father's estates. The Prince of Wales would not allow her name mentioned in his presence, but her mother was in and out of his private apartments continually. Tony had seen Roger, who looked well, and told him when he wrote her to tell her to expect a letter soon. A letter, thought Barbara, and she reread Tony's.

"Yes," said the Duchess. "Any fool can see it is not possible to carry that much paper credit with so little specie behind it. It is a bubble and will burst."

Harvest Home. . . . The Tamworth corn harvest was finished, and reapers prepared to celebrate before they moved to the next farm and its fields. The brightest of reapers' handkerchiefs and flowers and yellow ears of ripe corn decorated the cart containing the last of the harvest. The corn baby, a rough image fashioned from corn sheaves, sat atop the cart. It was wrapped in white linen, had a scythe tied to one outstretched arm and wore one of the Duchess's old straw hats, into which convolvulus—the flowering vine that loved to wrap itself around corn stalks—and ears of corn were twined. The cart rumbled down the road to Tamworth, and neighboring farmers left their fields to cheer its progress and join its parade. The reapers, flowers and ears of corn in their hats or behind their ears, played pipes and tabors, or small drums, while their women and children danced with them and all around the harvest cart.

Tamworth servants scurried to be ready before the cart and reapers and neighbors arrived. The Duchess and Dulcinea sat watching the activity in the duke's massive oak chair, brought outside for the festivities. She would give up her place to the corn baby when it arrived and would make the first toast to the hard work and successful harvest with a tankard of her best ale, ale that would flow freely all evening and late into the night. Servants staggered by her, toward the rough tables set up on the lawn and covered with her best linen tablecloths, carrying plates piled high with boiled potatoes and cabbage and turnips and carrots. Perryman and the footmen were bringing out roasted and boiled beef, mutton, veal, and pork. For days Cook had been making custards and apple pies, both now being carried to the tables hot and smoking from the ovens. There were ale and tea and cider. The village fiddler sawed on his fiddle, warming up for the night of leaping country dances ahead. The Duchess smiled at the bustle around her, proof of her good management, of Tamworth's bounty against a cold winter or late spring. There would be enough for Tamworth and for any neighbors or tenants not as fortunate.

Sir John Ashford from Ladybeth strolled over to her. The next harvest suppers would be his and Squire Dinwitty's. He had arrived early to read her latest letter from Abigail (and to sample her ale).

"The ale is bitter this year, Alice."

She glared up at him. Her ale was always excellent. He had some fool notion that Ladybeth's was sweeter.

"Abigail and Maude seem to agree on the situation. Maude wrote us that the city was on pins and needles about the price of stock, too. Royal Assurance is down. And South Sea," he said.

"I sold out in May," the Duchess replied. "I do not hold with so much loose paper scrip. Give me a solid bag of gold coins every time." Scrip entitled its owner to shares in a joint-stock undertaking and was exchanged for a formal certificate when payment for the stock was made. It was now functioning as money, but scrip from goldsmiths, banks, South Sea and other joint stock companies were all competing chaotically against one another.

Sir John frowned at her and moved on. They did not agree on economics, but then what did they agree on? she thought. It was the arguing that mattered. Doubtless after he had drunk more of her bitter ale, he would return to expound his own theories. Well, she had spent the morning resting, and she would be ready for him.

She noticed the footman Tim ride up from the village. Bringing her letters, but today she would forgo the pleasure of reading them, for she would have to listen to the head reaper's speech in her honor and admire the corn baby and welcome everyone with a speech of her own. She saw Vicar Latchrod, newly arrived, sneak a glass of ale and smiled grimly as he noticed her notice him. Drink up, Vicar, she thought. Perhaps the ale will shorten your long-winded prayers. Barbara and Thérèse went by carrying a huge tray of freshly baked bread. Barbara was laughing, and the Duchess smiled to see her. She is fatter, she thought. Though she has been with me less than two weeks, she is fattening up, growing sleek again under my and Tamworth's good care. Hyacinthe and a stableboy and the two dogs went shrieking past. Dulcinea did not even jump away to hide. She and the dogs had come to an understanding. Already she was nearly their size, and they could not match her for simple, cold cruelty. You leave me alone, she had told them, and I shall not slice your stupid pugs' noses into warm, bleeding ribbons each time I see you. Harry, nursing a torn nose, agreed, and Charlotte followed his lead. To salve their pride, they pretended Dulcinea did not exist. But she did, and now she sat up to watch them, her eyes slitted with interest.

Tim gave Barbara a letter. The Duchess saw her face as she glanced at it, and her heart gave an odd leap. Without a word to anyone, Barbara turned and walked away, away from the tables and merry, bustling servants—many of whom had been sampling the ale—toward the oaks on the small hillock. The pipes and tabor could be heard clearly now; the harvesters were in the avenue of limes. The Duchess glanced toward the oaks. Barbara, a small figure, was sitting on one of the benches built around a tree, her head bent as if she were reading. . . .

The letter was from Roger. . . . He had written . . . as he said he would. She could put it away. . . . She did not have to read it. . . . She could always say she had never received it. She ripped past the wax sealing it together.

My dearest Barbara,

I meant to write you long before now, but my salon is crowded from morning until night with South Sea and Bank of England and East India directors and members of the ministry and friends who want favors because the exchange is so erratic. You see how I begin. . . . I have forgotten how to write a love letter. I bore you with news about stocks, when all I want is to open my heart to you. And so I shall. Over the last four years, there have been many times I thought of you and wanted you with me, but I remembered your last words to me, and I felt any message on my part might only further estrange us.

She raised her head. The clear high sounds of the pipes and tabor caught her attention, and she looked down to the lawn, filled now with women and men and children and a cart dressed as if it took a bride to her wedding. There was a sudden clapping on everyone's part, and the lead reaper stood before her grandmother and spoke. She could not hear the exact words, but they changed little from year to year. Her throat closed. I will not cry, she thought. He does not deserve my tears. She looked back down at her letter.

I thought we would go our separate ways, or at least always live apart. And then, when I saw you this spring, so close and yet so far from me, I knew that I loved you and wanted you. I knew that I had always loved you, even in Paris. I looked at you, grown up, no longer the dear child of my memory, and you were lovely, and I felt that I had built everything thus far for this one moment, for you, and my life, which had been empty, filled again. I have watched you this summer, Barbara, and if I thought you were happy, I would leave you be. But you are not. I know it. And I feel there is still something left for me in your heart. I pray to a God I have not believed in in years that there is. I find myself dreaming the dreams of a young man—that I may hold the woman I love in my arms and make love to her and see her bear my children. I want you. And I need you. I believe, this time, we could be happy. Come to live with me again at Devane House. It is a big house, and we could live as far apart, or as close, as you so desired. Take your place of honor by my side. I will woo you as no woman has ever been wooed, and if it is my honor to win you back as my wife, I will cherish your dearest love for the rest of our life together.

I am not a fool. I know there is much to be explained between us, and I will answer whatever you ask of me, no matter how painful. But not in a letter. Face to face, so that you can see my heart in my eyes and know what I feel for you. Know this now. That each hour of the day, I have some thought of you, and at night, before I sleep, I envision you once more in my arms. Remember what was between us, and know that while it can never be as it was— for you, dear heart, are a woman now and not a child—it could be something just as fine.

I remain, always and forever, your husband,
    Roger Montgeoffry, Earl Devane

"Barbara," said her grandmother. "Are you ill?"

The sound of a fiddle, laughter, clapping, reached her dimly, as if she were far, far away.

How dare he, she thought. How dare he write me such a beautiful letter. She put her face into her hands, and the letter fluttered to the ground. A blue butterfly, the color of the woods' harebells, perched on its upended corner before the Duchess leaned down and snatched it up. Her eyes ran over the words, and she looked at her granddaughter whose face was still hidden. She sat down on the bench and folded the letter. Down on the lawn, Perryman was dancing with Annie. It was amazing what four quick tankards of Tamworth ale accomplished. She waited. What happened in Paris, she thought, that even now, after this, she cannot forgive him?

Barbara raised her face from her hands, a face that was white and sick, with blazing eyes. "Keep thy heart. . . . Do you remember how you said those words to me? And I did. I knew my heart. And I went after what I wanted. But it was not as I expected it to be, and now there has been so much anger, so much hurt, and I can no longer reach out—like that girl of fifteen—for what I want. I cannot forgive. He wants me. I have seen it in his eyes. I have felt it in his touch. But I cannot forgive—"

"And why not?"

The urge to confess was so strong. But she could not. She would not. Betray Roger. She had never been able to make that final betrayal—of the truth.

"You would never understand. Your life has been so different from mine. You had my grandfather, and children, and dreams that did not turn to dust in your hands. I have nothing but regrets."

"And whose fault is that! What happened in Paris, missy, that you cannot forgive him? What happened that he writes you as fine a letter as any I have ever seen, a letter that would melt most women's hearts, and yours is not melted? You with your own lovers! Your own scandals! What happened!"

Barbara's eyes dilated as she stared at her grandmother.

He was unfaithful, thought the Duchess. Only that could cause this. I knew he would be, but I imagined he had more finesse than to allow her ever to learn. And enough experience to handle her if she did. I never thought Roger would be clumsy. Well, she wanted him, and she got him. Let us get this thing in the open once and for all. I have lost patience with her.

"What a whining, unforgiving little fool you have become, Bab Devane! If you loved him, you should have fought for him. . . ." She faltered a moment at the expression on Barbara's face. But only for a moment.

"Bah!" Deliberately she struck her cane against the soft earth beneath their feet. "Do you think every one of us receives what he wishes out of life? That there are those of us so above the rest of God's creatures that we suffer no hurt, no injustice? Welcome to the world, such as it is, Barbara Devane. You are grown into a fool. And I could never suffer fools!"

"Damn you for the interfering, self-righteous old woman that you are!" Barbara cried. "Yes! My husband was unfaithful! But not with another woman! Ah, now I have your attention! Well, listen to me, Grandmama! He was unfaithful with another man! Yes, now that I tell it, you are stricken silent, aren't you? Suddenly you have no lectures, no Bible verses to recite me! No trick to pull from your sleeve to make my life come back together again! Do you, Grandmama? Do you!"

There was a roaring in the Duchess's ears. She heard Barbara from a long way off because a pain was gripping her insides with sharp claws, paralyzing her. Richard, she thought. I knew. From long ago. And I could not face it. Would not. Lord, have mercy upon us. Christ, have mercy. She stared at her granddaughter, who was beginning to say such things, things she ought not to hear, things that ought not to be said, words of betrayal and humiliation and hurt—such hurt—oh, she writhed inside at the hurt. I am too old, she thought feebly. I should have let it be. But she was helpless to stop what she had set in motion. . . .

Barbara dashed at the tears running down her face. She could no more stop her words than she could have stopped the sun's journey across the sky. She had been silent too long, wandered like a lost child through the maze of other people's desires too long. She was tired, and she was angry, and she was afraid. The letter was so beautiful. Promising so much. And she no longer trusted. Anyone. Not even herself. Someone must share her pain. She would die if someone did not share it. The pain of the last four years. Her mother would not hear. Harry could not. There had been no one to tell, for she had found, even in her most violent rage, that she could not betray Roger to anyone else. With the truth. Let them guess, let them gossip, she would not say it. For it was her youth and her love and her pride and her sense of herself as a woman that Philippe had killed that morning. And her dream of Roger, the handsome knight, the hero. The man that must be more than all other men. She did not think she would ever get over it. So she must pour out her grief, she must tell someone the truth, his truth and hers, if it killed her and her grandmother both. . . . She wiped her eyes savagely.

"I thought I would die. But I did not. I wanted to. I felt killed with what I had seen. I cannot even talk of it now, after all this time, without crying. Look at me! Harry guessed it. I never said a word, but he guessed. He nearly died himself trying to salvage my honor. Honor! I have no honor anymore. So much of what has been said about me is not true. But enough is. I have had lovers, yes, but only Richelieu and—and Charles. . . ." Her voice broke on his name. "I have no excuse for Jemmy. I was drunk. It was a mistake. This summer I have felt so wild inside. I do not understand it myself. Oh, Grandmama, I tried to forget Roger. Not to love him. But I still do. I weep like a child because he sent me a love letter! I still love him! God help me. I am so afraid. To love a man who is not a man, a man who . . ." And she could not finish, but put her face in her hands and sobbed like a child.

The Duchess heard her and was helpless. She felt as if someone had thrown her to the ground and knocked the breath from her. Feebly she thought, Thank God she has stopped talking. Each word is a knife in my heart. Let her cry. It is good to cry, to let the poisons out. Poison kills, it

kills the heart. . . . Abigail's wonderful Prince de Soissons
. . . strange are the ways of the Lord. Christ, have mercy on
us. If I were not so old and knew the emotion would kill me,
I would cry with her. Dear God in heaven above, I was
wrong five years ago. Wrong. Richard, I allowed our girl to
be hurt. My pride, my arrogance. They are ashes in my
mouth. Come and comfort me. I need you, my heart. Where
are you?

Hyacinthe and Perryman made their way up the hillock to
them. Perryman had the corn baby's hat on his head. Old
fool, thought the Duchess feebly.

"Madame." Hyacinthe waved his hand. "Come and join
us."

Barbara leapt up from the bench and ran down the other
side of the hillock. Somehow the Duchess managed to get to
her feet.

"Perryman, escort me back to the supper. You, Hyacinthe,
you just never mind your mistress. She has a pain." It took
all her strength to say the words. She saw the letter lying on
the bench. She picked it up and put it in the pocket of her
undergown. She motioned to Perryman, who held out his arm
to support her. If he had not, she would have fallen.

"Old fool," she said without feeling. "Take off that hat!"

The Duchess lay in her bed, floating, floating above the
pain in her heart and in her legs. She had fallen at the harvest supper, and Annie and Tim and Thérèse and Perryman
and Hyacinthe and she did not know how many other people
had converged upon her like sheep stampeding over a ledge.
Somehow she was in Tim's strong, young arms, and she
remembered to smile and even had the sense to have Tim
carry her to her bedchamber window so that she could wave
down to the chastened people clustered on her lawn and have
the satisfaction of hearing their cheers and the fiddle start up
again. Let them enjoy their supper. Thérèse and Annie had
rubbed her legs with liniment, but she could not stop moaning, because the pain was everywhere, and she thought she
would die from it. Wine, she gasped, the wine. And she trembled and spilled it over herself as she drank down the soothing
drafts of dandelion wine. It would dull the pain; it would dull
everything, and then she could bear it. From her window

came the sounds of the festivity, the fiddle, the pipes, the tabor, laughter, shrieks. She had sent Annie and Thérèse back down. They knew only that their Duchess had overtaxed herself and was now sleeping well. She was not sleeping, however; she was floating above herself. Perhaps I have drunk a bit too much wine, she thought.

"Richard," she said out loud, "you ought to have watched out for me. I have no head for wine."

She stopped because someone was in her room. Was it the wine, or was that Barbara floating to her bed? It looked like her granddaughter, though the face was so swollen it was difficult to tell exactly who it was. Well, I am here, she thought from her dreamy, floating distance, and now I can deal with whatever you might tell me, though I may die later in my sleep from it. (Barbara, it was only a letter, a snippet of gossip, and I could not believe what might be true. I knew, but I did not know. I could not face it. I let you face it. Forgive me. Richard, I hurt our girl.)

"I came to apologize for what I said to you this afternoon."

Her voice was so hoarse it was unrecognizable. She sat on the edge of the bed. "You are not self-righteous and interfering. I said some terrible things to you. I ask your pardon. I- I was upset." She laughed, a short, bittersweet laugh, as if she had just remembered something.

"What are you laughing at?"

"Nothing. Everything. A memory. Someone once told me he only hurt when he laughed. I know how he feels. I have been crying all afternoon. I feel terrible."

"Five years is a long time to carry such things in your heart," the Duchess said from her safe, royal, floating distance. She bit her lips to bring the feeling back to them. Richard had let her drink too much wine. Give me no more surprises, Barbara, that is all I ask, she thought. I am self-righteous and interfering and far, far too old to change.

"I hate to cry," Barbara said.

"You always did. I blame Harry. He teased you about it until you fought him, crying all the while, when you were a girl. There is no weakness in crying. If we do not sorrow over what hurts us, how do we ever go past it? I have shed many a tear myself, Barbara Devane, over what life has brought me. Compassion can come from great pain. If you allow it. But compassion takes courage. Bitterness is easier." How grand she sounded. How wise.

"I do not feel very compassionate at this moment, Grandmama."

"No. I should not imagine you do." She squeezed her granddaughter's hand and looked at her lovingly. It felt good to be grand and wise.

"There is more," said Barbara.

Kill me, thought the Duchess. Kill me now and be done with it.

"He talks of my coming to Devane House, of our children," Barbara was saying.

She looked into her granddaughter's eyes. Such sadness, thought the Duchess, forgetting that she did not wish to know. What? What? What could hurt her girl so? After Roger, what else could there be?

"I think I may be barren."

The Duchess opened her arms, and Barbara moved into them, and the Duchess held her and stroked her hair and smoothed the tears from her young cheeks, just as every once in a while she smoothed a tear from her own cheek. She held her and rocked her and soothed her just as if, once more, Barbara was the child, and she the strong, all-knowing woman she had once been, who had healed all childhood hurts. For a long, long time she rocked her. And then finally Barbara moved and wiped her own eyes and blew her nose and poured them both a large glass of wine, and her young face was swollen and only she and the Duchess and the Lord above knew all her sorrows. Life, thought the Duchess gulping down her dandelion wine with uncharacteristic greed. Life is what is going to kill me. I am too old.

"I want to sleep in here tonight."

Of course you are going to sleep in here tonight, thought the Duchess. I am certainly not going to sleep alone. If I die tonight, as is almost certain, I want someone to know it. She tried to speak. Something was wrong with her lips and tongue. She had to concentrate not to roll out of the bed like a bowling pin.

"I want more wine,' she said, petulantly.

Gently Barbara took the glass from her hand. "No more wine. Lie back and close your eyes. Go on. I am here. I am here, Grandmama."

Everything was whirling behind the Duchess's closed eyes. The world was topsy-turvy. Her granddaughter was now taking care of her. Once it had been the other way around. Life and its endless complications. Barren. She could not be barren. It would be too cruel. Diana spewed children from her body as easily as a cat did kittens and cared nothing for them. And her granddaughter, who loved them so, could not conceive. Life hurts, Richard. Roger loved you. I understand that now. I saw the hunger in his eyes, but I did not recognize it then. The seeds were there, for what happened to our Bab. But we did not understand. And yet, when he looked at me, there was sometimes the same hunger. I could feel his desire. He was a handsome man, Richard. All the women wanted him. And he wanted them. He is a man. A complicated man. It would be easier for us all if he were not. . . .

Her grandmother had saved the letter, giving it silently back to her; she read it and reread it until it tore along its creases. I am not a fool, he wrote. I know there is much to be explained between us. Philippe. Who smiled at her under the great dome of Roger's pavilion of the arts. If Roger thought she would pack her trunks and rush headlong to London to his waiting arms, he had another thought coming. (Besides, she had rushed headlong once, already, in the spring, and he had not even realized it. Rushed headlong into Philippe's smile. Like running into a wall.) She would wait. She would let her heart tell her what to do, and she would not make one move from Tamworth until she was certain. Roger could wait . . . as she had waited. She still had much to deal with. There were dark dreams of her father and of Jemmy. Of Charles and Richelieu, who opened their arms to her, but somehow she could never reach them. She had to understand it all. And herself. Roger, wait. As I have waited. Ah, Roger, the girl who loved you in Paris does not exist, and the heart of the one who does is so hard. . . . It needs to soften. I need time now to heal, forgive and forget. . . .

* * *

Outside her window, in the fields and woods of Tamworth, autumn was coming. In the hedges, the hawthorn berries showed red, as did the bramble berries, and those in the sun were turning ripely black. The petals from the roses fell and fell and fell like rain—or tears—until only the scarlet hips were left. The sunsets were ruby and gold. As she watched one from her window, verses came to mind; verses she had once known as well as she knew her name. . . . Charity suffereth long, and is kind . . . beareth all . . . believeth all . . . endureth all. . . . When I was a child, I spake as a child, I understood as a child. . . . When I became a man I put away childish things. . . . For now we see through a glass, darkly . . . but then face to face. . . . Keep thy heart with all diligence . . . for out of it are the issues of life. . . .

The sunset she watched was beautiful. Tamworth was beautiful, bathed in its glory. In another few weeks, it would be time to gather hazelnuts. The leaves would all be turned, the air crisp and cool. Come to live with me again at Devane House . . . compassion comes from pain. . . . Though I speak with the tongues of men and angels, and have not charity, I am become as sounding brass, or a tinkling cymbal. . . . She would write a letter to Jemmy's mother tomorrow. It would be a different letter, a painful letter, but she would do it anyway. . . . A hand wriggled itself into hers.

"Do you have another pain?" asked Hyacinthe. "Is it terrible?"

"I think my pains are better."

She kissed his cheek and breathed in the glory of the sunset. She drank in its beauty . . . its serenity, its quiet. . . .

A furious honking burst the quiet. Below, three of the Duchess's Michaelmas geese waddled as fast as their splayed feet would take them across the lawn, honking frantically the entire time. Shrill yaps now joined the honking. Harry and Charlotte and Dulcinea leapt from a clump of bushes and ran after the geese—it was a hunt, and a joint effort.

"Hyacinthe! They are after the geese Grandmama is fattening for Michaelmas! Run at once and chase them away, or Grandmama will murder us all!"

She smiled at the thought of what her grandmother would say when this came to her ears, if it were not already there. What a racket they were all making! It might be enough to bring her grandmother out of her bed; she had been feeble lately. She saw Hyacinthe run and leap across the lawn, and then he was out of sight. Now, mingled amid barks and honks came the sound of Hyacinthe's crude curses, such as the stableboys used. And then she heard her grandmother:

"I will kill those dogs! Perryman! Perryman!"

She laughed out loud. The court would be returning to London soon. There would be about the same amount of barking and honking and jockeying for position around the Frog, supreme until his father returned from Hanover, as there was right now in the courtyard. How glad she was, how thankful, to be here, rather than there. Here, one might find one's way in peace. There, one would find only chaos.

CHAPTER TWENTY-FIVE

*E*ngland's economic house of cards was falling, falling faster than a comet out of the skies. In February, when the South Sea Company had taken over part of the national debt, the example of John Law and France's amazing financial spurt of inflation and spending was foremost in all minds. For months, the British government and British companies had watched Englishmen take their gold across the channel to invest in Law's new Mississippi Company. Credit was capable of infinite expansion, backed by the state, preached the prophet, John Law. The idea of a huge financial monopoly in close association with the state and trading on its credit was working in France; and in England, the South Sea Company, ever growing, rivaling even the Bank of England, was bold enough to try to create the same success. Rising markets were the key, and South Sea assured such a market through issuing new stock without authority, lending on unsound securities and bribery in the correct circles. As it rose to fantastic heights, other British stocks rose with it. And no one realized the cycle had a devastating end, an end France was now experiencing—scarcity of money, high cost of all goods, credit destroyed, public confidence in money systems shattered.

When speculators began to sell South Sea stock to cover losses in other investments, the stock began to fall. And because its rise had been based on fool's tricks, nothing could stop the fall once it began. Other stocks, even those based on sound securities, fell with it; the comet had hit the ground and was exploding, and no one was safe from its impact. By the first week in September, banks in Paris and Amsterdam, scenting disaster, were ordering London agents to sell South Sea. The market, already unstable, became flooded with panicked people selling as the value kept dropping. By September 16, even the most optimistic of South Sea's directors sensed the abyss ahead and began trying to negotiate with their rival, the Bank of England—a rival that would only welcome their fall—to engraft the two stocks together to restore public confidence and stop selling.

By September 21, ministers in England were breaking their pen points in their haste to write the king in Hanover and tell him his island kingdom which he had left in a mood of speculation and spending, was now on the verge of bankruptcy, despair and possible rebellion. By September 24 , the Sword Blade Company, the financial arm of the South Sea Company, handling its cash transactions, closed its door against a rioting press of withdrawers, and suspended business. Panic gripped London, and the country at large. Fortunes were melting, and no one understood why. Assets froze overnight. South Sea stock had been 900 on August 17. By the end of September, it was 190. In the space of a month, people stood bewildered and bankrupt amid the ruins of financial chaos in what would be known forever after as the South Sea Bubble.

Bah, thought the Duchess, sitting on the terrace overlooking the faded rose garden, Dulcinea in her lap. Her hands, on top of her cane, opened and closed impatiently. She watched a fat green caterpillar inch through the white petals of chrysanthemums in a nearby pot and, lifting her cane, she whirled it and whipped off the head of a flower. Tim, standing just behind her, ducked. The flower landed near, but the caterpillar (and Tim) were unharmed. It lay motionless on the fallen green stem. The Duchess debated as to whether she should risk getting up to step on it. The fact that she had to debate made her more irritable than ever. Bah. Fat slug. Greedy worm. Eating her autumn flowers.

"Step on that." She pointed with her cane to the caterpillar, now inching away.

"Go on. Good. Step on him one more time. Excellent." She smiled grimly to herself, and Tim grinned, a grin that disappeared the moment he saw her glaring at him.

"Where is my granddaughter?"

"In the kitchen, ma'am, with Thérèse and Cook making jelly. Shall I bring you inside now? Do you want tea—"

" 'Do you want tea?' " mimicked the Duchess. "No. I want to be alone. Quit hovering over me. Go away!"

She settled back in her chair, less irritable now that she had killed the caterpillar and routed Tim. Impudent young fool, treating her like an invalid. They all did—Annie, Perryman, Barbara. Ever since Harvest Home. Well, she was no invalid. Sweet Jesus, she was merely old. Old. Barbara had given her enough shocks to kill her, but it was a sure sign of her strength that she was alive today, sitting in the sun. It would take more than Barbara's confessions to kill her. More than Abigail's panicked letters about South Sea stock. Bah. She had sold out in May. She did not hold with such goings-on. Law and his infinite credit. Richard had been the gambler in the family. Not her. Fat slug eating her flowers. Invalid. Bah. She raised her face to the sun and closed her eyes. Barbara was making jelly. . . . That was a good sign. . . . She hoped it was plum jelly. . . . She liked fresh plum jelly on a hot scone. . . . She must be sure to tell Richard tonight when she visited chapel that Barbara seemed to be doing so much better. . . . He would want to know. . . . Ah, the sun was warm . . . fat . . . greedy . . . slug . . . eating . . . her . . . flowers. . . .

A lone man on horseback trotted up the avenue of limes and into the courtyard of Tamworth Hall. He tied his horse's bridle to a bush and walked around to the side of the house. On the terrace, the Duchess dozed, not waking even at the sound of his clinking spurs. He stood a moment staring down at her; then he reached to tickle Dulcinea on her belly, and she mewed loudly and clutched his hand with sharp claws, and the Duchess started awake.

"Tony!" she cried. She smiled up at him. Then her smile faded. "What is it!" she said sharply. "Tell me."

He knelt down in front of her, his face so sorrowful that she pulled his head to her breast and held it, stroking his thick, blond hair, tied back with a ribbon. Like Richard's. When she and Richard had been young, it had been the style for men to wear their hair long, as Tony now did. His hair smelled of sweat and mint and sunshine and man. She raised his face.

"Tell me. Now."

In the kitchen, Barbara overturned a jar of flour and it went spilling everywhere, across the broad oak table they were working on, over her apron and gown and shoes, over her hands and the purple plums waiting to be sliced. Cook made a strangled sound. Barbara giggled and pushed back a stray lock of hair, and Thérèse, across the table, pointed to her with a big wooden spoon and said, "Now it is on your face," and the two of them burst out laughing. They had been laughing and giggling and irritating Cook all morning, like a pair of unruly schoolgirls. The reasons were varied: Outside it was autumn, and the air stung their cheeks as they walked the dogs or went to chapel; the fireplaces were being used once more, and the logs crackled satisfactorily as they sat before them in the evenings eating hazelnuts and listening to Hyacinthe read *Robinson Crusoe*; and each week there came a letter for Barbara—from Roger—an ardent, compelling letter that shook her heart's hardness and made it feel like a girl's again.

Annie ran into the kitchen. "It is your grandmother! Dear merciful God, hurry!"

The two of them ran with Annie, Cook lumbering behind, through the great hall and past the winter parlor and past the room that was used as a library to the terrace. Even before they were on the terrace, they could see the Duchess through the open doors. They could hear her. She was struggling, struggling in a tall man's arms, twisting and trying to pull from his arms, fighting him, weeping, saying over and over, "Oh, no, oh, no."

Barbara stopped where she was at the sight of Tony and her grandmother, but Thérèse and Annie and Cook went on, and then Tim was there, and they had the Duchess somehow—she was fighting them all—and they half carried her, half dragged her past Barbara. She was crying, crying like a child, and her face was so old, so wrinkled and anguished that Barbara felt the blood leave her head.

She stared at Tony. Roger, she thought. It is Roger. I have waited too long. She would have dropped then to the floor like a stone, but Tony caught her and led her outside to sit on the terrace steps. The day was glorious, clear, cold, the trees showing their autumn colors: cherry trees a rich scarlet; oaks every shade of green and brown; beeches, orange, and horse chestnuts, the color of gold, newly minted.

"Roger," she said, staring at Tony. He took her hands in his and held them tightly. "Roger," she said again, and her voice rose.

"Listen to me," he said urgently, abruptly. "Listen. Not Roger. Roger is well. But—I have some bad news. Very bad news. You have to be brave. Do you hear me, Barbara? For everyone's sake. It is Harry. He—Barbara, I do not know how to tell this. He is dead. Three days ago. Wart found him. In his lodgings. He—God, Barbara—he slit his throat with a razor—"

She stared uncomprehendingly at the tears in his eyes. He was crying. Big, blue-gray eyes. Not like the summer sky, as Roger's were, or Charles's. Nor violet like Harry's . . . Harry! She slumped forward, and Tony caught her in his arms, and he held her and he stroked her hair and he murmured to her and she thought he said he loved her but she really did not know, she did not know anything but pain. . . .

Thérèse knelt by her bed, saying the aves, the gloria, the Our Father over and over, but her rosary beads kept slipping from her hands, just as the words, their comfort, kept slipping from her mind to leave only hurt, black and choking, blotting all. She had helped carry the Duchess to her bedchamber. She saw Annie mouth the words "Master Harry" to Perryman and shake her head, and suddenly a nameless, faceless dread seized her, and she had to leave that room. She felt as if her stomach had caved inside itself. She stumbled into a hall. Two maidservants ran to each other and said something, and one of them began to cry, and the other threw her apron up over her head and wailed. No, thought Thérèse. She began to walk. She did not know where she was going. Hyacinthe found her, his face tear-streaked, her rosary clutched in one hand, his faithful companions, the pugs, with him.

"Thérèse, oh, Thérèse," he said, and he took a sobbing breath. "Sit down."

He made her sit and take her rosary in hand, and the dogs were there, somewhere, yapping, and he tried to put them in her lap, and she knew. She knew before he said it. What had to be said.

"Monsieur Harry," he said, his voice trembling, crying, crying like the child he was. "Monsieur Harry is dead. They say—oh, Thérèse, they say he cut his throat."

Hush now, she told him. Hush, and she opened her arms and took him in them to hold him close while his thin, boy's body shook with sobs. But she could not cry. Not yet. The hurt went too deep. It was now, now as she knelt, that the tears came. As she said the prayers that had always comforted her, but between the comfort now were terrible, blank spaces. Grief welled in them, inexhaustible, like a spring. Our Father, who art in heaven, Hallowed be thy Name. . . . Harry . . . Harry . . . Harry . . . you were my heart.

Tony had handled every detail. He had sent a special messenger to Norfolk to inform Diana; his mother and sisters and brother-in-law were escorting Harry's body down from London, and he had arranged for the coroner in London to rule "not of sound mind" so that Harry could be buried in consecrated ground by a priest. Suicides were buried on public highways with a stake driven through their hearts. No priest could perform funeral rites over them. It was the law. Not of sound mind. The words wore a groove in Barbara's mind as she sat in the winter parlor with Tony and a little man, all smoothness and oil, from Maidstone, who was displaying his funeral palls and the souvenirs for the mourners, gloves, enameled rings, hatbands, the details of the ceremony of burial, the details she and Tony were dealing with, for their grandmother was bedridden. She lay in her bed like a wrinkled, anguished, limp rag doll and cried for Harry. And all Barbara could wonder was, Why? Why had he done it? Tony said things to her about stocks falling, about something called the Sword Blade Company suspending payment, about panic in London, and she could only stare at him. She would have given Harry her last penny, sold her last jewel, visited him in debtors' prison, schemed to release him. He was her brother. In Paris, it was he who had kept her from going mad.

The little man showed a sample of his flannel; there was another law that bodies must be buried in woolen, but Barbara shook her head and blew her nose. Tamworth flannel ·ould cover Harry. Annie had already purchased some from the most skillful weaver in the village, and she and Thérèse were cutting a shroud. When Harry's body arrived, they would clothe him in it; the cloth touching his body would be soaked with tears of love and grief. From family. They would wash him and dress him in his new shroud and fold his hands, and he would go into the family vault with the touches of those who loved him as a final gesture. Hair rings, said the man. The deceased's hair arranged so nicely in a tiny circle under clear glass. Rings with posies inside, "Prepared Be to Follow Me." White gloves. Black gloves. Anything needed. Wax candles. Funeral invitations, skulls and thighbones engraved with great skill in the corners. Coffins. Whatever her ladyship might desire. For a favorite brother. Tamworth would provide, Barbara thought, as she rose impatiently and walked to the window. Even now, the village carpenter was making the coffin. The rosemary to strew in it would come from her grandmother's stillroom. The flowers. The love.

Tony led the man from the room and came back to stand behind Barbara. He put his arms around her, and she leaned her head back against him. It fitted perfectly under his chin. She looked out at the autumn landscape, so bright with its autumn leaves. But in a few weeks, a month or more, it would be winter. Cold. Frost. Snow. Death.

"Why would he do it, Tony? Tell me why?"

Harry was home. The black hearse from London had arrived, black and white feathers attached to the horses' bridles, her aunt and Mary and Fanny and her husband, Harold, and her grandfather's ancient sister, her Aunt Shrewsborough, in carriages that had followed behind. Already Harry was in a back room where the women who had served his grandfather and grandmother were washing him, shrouding him, murmuring prayers over his body. And then he would lie in a Tamworth coffin in the great hall for a day, candles burning at his head and feet, a plate of salt over his heart to symbolize immortality and eternity, salt preserving that which it seasoned from corruption and so symbolizing immortality of the soul. She embraced her aunts and Fanny and Mary and for a moment all was fresh tears and black veils and trailing crepe. Then she went to find Harry. They were washing him, and Annie quickly covered his face, but Barbara pulled back the cloth. She would see it. His face was so still, so white, the whitest thing she had ever seen, whiter even than snow. So this was death. This stillness, this whiteness. And under his chin was the killing thin red line, stitched crookedly with black thread, jagged toward the end when his hand must have faltered.

Some of the maidservants were crying. Thérèse was sobbing, but then she loved Harry, too, Barbara thought, the new grief at the sight of Harry making her faint and light-headed. The three of them—four with Hyacinthe—had been like a family in Paris and Italy. Harry had loved to tease Thérèse, until she would make him stop. Thérèse could always handle him. Something flickered in the back of her mind as she looked at Thérèse, but she had not the strength to decipher it now. Not with Harry lying naked and still in front of her. There was so much to do. And she had to be strong, even though she felt as if lead were attached to the bottom of her long skirts, as if she were dragging them through thick mud. Even though she felt as if someone had battered her soul with a hammer. So much yet to do. See to the food for the funeral feast. Be certain that all spare bedchambers were cleaned and aired. Doors and windows and beds draped in black cloth. Mirrors covered. Dulcinea, protesting, looked away. A count of the rings and gloves and hatbands that would be given the mourners.

Tomorrow, Harry would lie in state, and friends, villagers, relatives would come to pay their respects. Tomorrow evening, he would join all the others in the dark vault under Tamworth chapel. A memorial plate must be ordered. And a marble bust. She wanted a marble bust in the chapel. To commemorate her last brother. Gone now. Earth to earth, Tom and Kit, ashes to ashes, Anne and Charlotte, dust to dust, Baby and Harry, as it was in the beginning, is now and ever shall be: world without end. Amen.

She walked past the winter parlor.

"They are dropping like flies," she overheard her Aunt Shrewsborough say. "One cannot pick up a news sheet these days without reading of another suicide."

"There is a run on the Bank of England," answered her Aunt Abigail. "The prince and Marlborough made deposits, but people are frightened. Hoare's bank is unloading stock, and it is rumored there will be no interest payments made this month."

"My banker tells me I have lost a good fifteen thousand," said Aunt Shrewsborough.

"Fifteen thousand?" said a man's voice. Harold, thought Barbara. Fanny's Harold. She ought to go. She ought not to stand here and eavesdrop like a child. Harry had always told her it was a habit that would bring more harm than good. . . .

"I have lost over thirty thousand," said Harold, and Barbara could hear in his voice that particular timbre of someone who was frightened. "I understand now why Harry did what he did—"

"Hush, Harold," said Aunt Abigail firmly. Oh, yes, thought Barbara. You will know the decent emotion, the correct emotion. And you will not allow anything else.

"You must not think like that," her aunt was saying. "For Fanny's sake, and the children's."

"I blame myself," said Aunt Shrewsborough. "He came to me before he died—"

"He came to us all," said Aunt Abigail.

Not to me, thought Barbara.

"—wanting money, and I gave him some, but I was angry with him. The goldsmith my banker uses had slipped away in the night with all the gold he could carry. Go to your brother-in-law, I said to Harry. He is as rich as Midas. It is his company that has brought all this crashing down on our heads. Ask him for money, I said."

"You did not!" said Aunt Abigail.

"I did, and I shall regret my words until the day I die. I knew he and Roger did not speak. It was my temper. My temper and that damned goldsmith."

"I have heard Roger has made a fortune in all this," said Harold, and Barbara shivered at the unexpected animosity she heard in his voice.

"And I have heard," snapped her Aunt Shrewsborough, "that he is near bankruptcy. Which is probably more likely than these wild rumors that are circulating—"

Barbara opened the draperies, and the three of them stared at her with the stupefied, guilty expressions of those caught gossiping. Abigail recovered first.

"Come and sit here," she said, smiling kindly at Barbara and patting the cushion of a nearby stool. "We were just talking of your dear brother Harry. No one knew the extent of his debts, Barbara. No one."

He was alone in London, Barbara thought, staring at them with a face that was set and hard. Alone with you, who care nothing for anyone but yourselves. Alone and afraid. No wonder he thought there was no place to turn but death. No wonder he killed himself. Oh, Harry, why did you not come to me? Why? I would have helped you. And now I am alone. You did not think of me . . . and to her horror, she burst into tears before them.

She lay on her bed, so weary now that she could hardly move. Her mother had arrived. Weeping, crying, falling on Harry's body in its coffin like a mourner in a Greek tragedy, having to be pulled off, fighting those who pulled her off. Hysterical. So hysterical that Fanny had fainted from the sheer commotion her mother created. Fanny was used to quieter families. The screaming. The crying. Why did he not come to me? her mother wailed, beating at her breast, pulling her hair, as those around her scurried and scampered to calm her. South Sea, her mother screamed. It is the South Sea that killed him. Where is Roger? Where is Roger Devane! I will claw out his eyes. I will cut out his heart and eat it myself. Where is he, Barbara? Where? I do not know, Mother. Where are you, Roger? Come to Tamworth, please. I need you.

Now it was morning, the morning of the afternoon on which Harry would be buried. Today, someone would place the final, small square of flannel over his face, and she would have to watch as they lowered the coffin top and then he would be gone from her forever. Her heart was a stone in her breast, her throat ached with tears not yet cried. Thérèse was useless, sobbing, stumbling into furniture, and she sent her away and dressed herself, thinking, How shall I survive this day?

Downstairs, they were already assembling, villagers, friends, relatives, gathered in small groups about the coffin, murmuring, some of them crying. She began to distribute mourning gloves. Gussy clasped her hand. My dear, I am so sorry, he said. Jane would have come, but our children are ill and she could not leave them. She sends her deepest love. Wart and some of Harry's London friends surrounded her, and she smelled the wine on their breath as they said their condolences, pulling on the black gloves she gave them. Colonel Campbell, representing the Prince of Wales, bowed over her hand and told her how shocked his highness was to learn of the tragedy. He would have come in person, said Campbell, if conditions in London were not as they were, and she remembered with a start that there was also a crisis somewhere else, and it was called the South Sea Company, and Harry lay in a wooden box for it.

Bab, go and get something to eat, Tony said. Leave me alone, she replied. You are not my brother or my husband. Out of the corner of her eye, she watched him as he walked away from her. Wherever was the tongue-tied, abrupt, fat man she had once known? She resented his solicitousness, his calm. Anyone would imagine this was his home, she thought, watching with narrowed eyes as he greeted his guests. But then someday it would be. Everything would be his. She stared at Tony. He was becoming more and more good to look at—his height, his eyes, the sweetness of his smile. It was unreasonable to resent him, but she could not help it today, when she would bury her brother. Tony was alive, and Harry was dead. Tony's life was full of promise. He had unsuspected strengths that would carry him through life's south seas. While Harry . . . Harry lay final and still in a wooden box.

There was Charles, across the room, staring at her. She saw people glance from him to her and back again, saw Jane's mother, Lady Nell, mouth the words "duel" to one of Squire Dinwitty's daughters. She could feel something inside herself cracking, but she did not let go. She lifted her chin and walked over.

"I did not expect to see you today," she said. "Thank you for coming." She gave him the ritual pair of black gloves.

"He was my friend, also. My sincerest condolences, Barbara."

She would not cry. Not now. Before all these people. If she started, she would not be able to stop.

"Did you—did you see him before he—before, Charles? Did he say anything? Anything at all. I have to understand, you see. And I do not."

He shook his head. "London is a different place these days, Bab, a place you cannot imagine. It is like a city under siege. People hoard gold. They make demands for immediate repayment of loans, or they refuse to pay what they owe. Goldsmiths leave in the night for Brussels with whatever they can carry. People are frightened. There is talk of rebellion at tea parties. There have been riots in Exchange Alley. Every man has lost something, and he no longer trusts his neighbor. Do not blame Harry." He looked at her. "We all have an edge to which we can be pushed."

She flushed.

"I wrote you a hundred notes." His voice was lower now, more urgent. She shivered at the sound of it. "I tore them all to pieces. I have to speak with you. Where can we be private? I have to explain—"

"There is nothing to explain." She was afraid suddenly, afraid of the emotions floating up inside her.

"But there is. More than you can imagine. Where is Roger?"

His abrupt question caught her off guard.

"I-I do not know," she stammered. "I am sure he—he is on his way. The—the crisis in London delays him."

"You are not reconciled, are you?" he said, stepping closer. Suddenly, she could not catch her breath.

"There you are."

Both of them jumped at the sound of her aunt's voice. Abigail, all in black, round, plump, determined, smiled at them, though her smile thinned a little on the edges as she looked at Barbara.

"Come and sit with me, Charles. We have much to say to each other. Barbara will excuse you. She has her other guests to attend to."

Barbara allowed her aunt to lead him away, glad of the reprieve. She felt vulnerable, dazed, no longer in command of herself. Roger, she thought. Please come. I need you. She walked back toward the others.

"The banks are going down," she heard Squire Dinwitty say to a group of men as she walked forward. "Atwill and Hammond, Long and Bland, Nathaniel Bostock have all suspended October payments."

"There needs to be an inquiry," Sir John Ashford replied, slapping black gloves in the palm of his hand. "A public inquiry. The directors must be held responsible for their actions."

There was a murmur of agreement.

"Is Devane coming to the funeral?" someone asked.

Sir John shrugged, and then they saw her, and all of them nodded solemnly at her, quiet until she had passed. Lady Nell Ashford swept forward and embraced her. We loved Harry, too, she whispered. He was like another son. And yet you were glad he could not marry Jane, thought Barbara. Harry. The prodigal son only in death.

Where is Grandmama? she asked Annie. In bed, where she needs to stay. And my mother? Annie smiled dourly. A cordial to calm her nerves, she will not stir until this afternoon. Good, said Barbara. Very good. She felt faint and went to stand outside in the chill. Wart was there, with a friend of Harry's.

"Coal prices are down, and the sale of ships has been canceled at Lloyd's for lack of bids," Wart said to someone standing beside him.

"I had to cancel my order for a new coach," the other man said. "And the coach maker said his yard was full of canceled coaches. Do you think Devane will come?"

"I doubt he dares to," said Wart.

The words echoed in her mind.

In the afternoon, Perryman approached her. "Another visitor is arriving."

She went outside to the courtyard. Two riders were coming down the avenue. One of them rode a stallion, Spanish, black, magnificent with a deep chest and strong, muscled legs. The horse cantered and fidgeted and tossed his head, and his rider handled him with graceful ease. Barbara's breath caught. She walked forward to the edge of the avenue. The rider of the stallion looked up. From where she stood, she could see he had eyes the color of the summer sky and high cheekbones, like an archangel's. The handsomest man there ever was. Still.

A sob caught in her throat. Roger. She lifted her black skirts and ran, like a boy, down the avenue. He leapt off his horse and opened his arms, and she flung herself into them. His arms, his beloved arms, were tight around her. His gloved hands stroked her hair. He was saying her name over and over as she began to cry, while he covered her face with kisses. She was safe. Safe at last. Now nothing else could hurt her.

"You taste of salt," he murmured, and she cried harder and held on to the lapels of his coat and told him Harry was dead, her Harry was dead, and she had no one, no one in the world, and he hushed her and kissed her and dropped his stallion's bridle to the ground and held her in his arms.

Montrose, on the other horse, reached for the bridle and trotted past them. He nodded to the young Duke of Tamworth, in the courtyard, his eyes shaded with his hand as he stared down the avenue, a grave expression on his face. In the avenue, Barbara and Roger stood together, and finally, when they turned to walk toward the house, she saw Tony, standing tall and still in the courtyard, and something about the way he was standing, the way he watched, made her heart ache.

" 'Behold, I shew you a mystery; We shall not all sleep; but we shall all be changed, In a moment, in the twinkling of an eye, at the last trump: for the trumpet shall sound, and the dead shall be raised incorruptible, and we shall be changed. For this corruptible must put on incorruption, and this mortal must put on immortality. So when this corruptible shall have put on incorruption, and this mortal shall have put on immortality; then shall be brought to pass the saying that is written, Death is swallowed up in victory. Death, where is thy sting? O grave, where is thy victory?' "

Tamworth church was filled; household servants and the servants of neighboring houses had to stand in the side aisles, heads bowed, sprigs of wilting rosemary in their hands, as Vicar Latchrod read the funeral lesson. Harry's coffin was in the vault now, somewhere below them, final prayers having already been said over it, clods of earth thrown on it. All that was left of his burial was this—the psalms and lesson. Where

is Death's sting? thought the Duchess wearily. In my heart.
Man that is born of woman is of few days, and full of trouble. He cometh forth like a flower, and is cut down. . . .
Harry . . . why did you not come to me? Beside her, Diana
wept uncontrollably, and in her mind the Duchess saw the
ghostly whiteness of Harry's face as he lay in his shroud. In
June, that face had been laughing, flushed. He had come to
see her, brimming over with plans, with ambitions. He
wanted to borrow money to play the market. He had the deed
to a colonial plantation he had won in an endless card game
to give her as collateral against the loan. This time it will
work, Grandmama, he had crowed, kissing her cheek and
laughing. I shall win and pay off the worst of my debts and
settle down to become a gentleman farmer. I promise. I do
not trust the market, she had told him. In my day, hard work,
the right marriage, land, gold, a few investments in solid
companies—proven companies—were the ways to building a
fortune. South Sea is solid; he told her. You will see . . . you
will see. . . . She put her hand to her eyes . . . I am too old
to bury any more of my grandchildren, she thought.

"The Grace of Our Lord Jesus Christ, and the love of God,
and the fellowship of the Holy Ghost be with us all evermore.
Amen," intoned Vicar Latchrod.

In the silence following his words came the final funeral
peal of the bell in the church tower. The Duchess shuddered,
as the congregation rose.

Roger stepped outside to an afternoon grown colder and
darker. Low clouds hung in the horizon. He looked around.
Yes, there was Montrose with the horses saddled, ready to
leave. Now there was only his goodbye to Barbara, who would
not understand. Several men converged on him, their faces
wearing the grimness those in London wore. Jesus Christ, he
was tired of grimness, tired of fear, tired of talk of stock and
South Sea.

"I know landlords, myself included, who were paid for their
land with stock, at the top of the market," said Sir John.
"Stock that is now worthless. What do the directors plan to
do about that?"

"I have every confidence," said Roger, tiredly—he was so
weary of saying this same thing over and over, to himself, to
everyone—"that the plan to engraft stock with the Bank of

England will go forward. I know Robert Walpole and others are working on it."

"If South Sea is at two hundred," said Wart, "why should the bank buy at four? Walpole is holed up in Norfolk with all the gold he could carry out of London. Tell the truth, Roger."

"But the Bank of England must engraft the stock," said Sir John. "Or people will be ruined—"

At that moment, half carried, half dragged between Tony and Harold, Diana came out of the church. "Harry!" she was screaming, her face a mask of anguish. All eyes turned to her.

"If you will all excuse me," Roger said. "I see my wife."

Barbara was standing by the low, spreading branches of a cypress tree, and her hair was shining red-gold against the green of the limbs.

"What did they all want? I am cold. Are you cold? Do you think Harry is cold? In that vault?"

"No, Barbara," Roger said gently, taking one of her gloved hands in his. "Harry will never be cold again. Walk with me a moment."

"Lord Devane," said Charles, looming suddenly in front of them. Barbara moved closer to her husband.

"I am leaving," Charles said, and a muscle worked in his cheek. "I wanted to say goodbye to—to you both."

She stared at him a moment and then looked down. How young they are, thought Roger. Was I ever that young? He rubbed his chest. The burning sensation in it never seemed to leave him these days. It burned on and on, like coals in his stomach. Barbara began to tremble as Charles walked away from her, and Roger led her into the graveyard, among the leaning gravestones and evergreen yews, where they could be alone. He glanced up. Yes, there was Montrose with the horses, waiting.

Charles stood blindly at the church gate. He had no idea where he was.

"There you are," someone called, and he turned, and Abigail was converging upon him, her black handkerchief waving.

"Where are you going, Charles?"

"I thought I would return to London today, Lady Saylor. There—there is no need for me to stay any longer." Behind her, he could see Barbara and Roger talking to one another in the graveyard. He closed his eyes.

"But I wanted you to ride back with us tomorrow. We brought two carriages, and there is more than enough room."

"No, thank you. I must return today."

She looked up at him, and under the round softness of her face was firmness. "You will call on us in London." It was not a request, nor a question.

What have I gotten myself into? thought Charles. "Yes," he heard himself saying. "I will . . ."

"I do not understand."

Roger closed his eyes. Be gentle, he told himself. Stay calm. She does not understand. She has not been in London. She does not know. She is, in many ways, a child still. He took her hands, which he was holding, and held them to his lips.

"I have to go back to London. If there were any way I could stay, I would. But I cannot. Please try to understand."

She stared at him. He saw the mutinous expression creeping across her face.

"Goddamn it, Barbara," he burst out, unable to control himself, "I am in trouble! I stand to lose everything. Do you understand that? I thought to offer you a fine home and security, and I find myself standing on the brink of nothing!"

Her mouth trembled. "At least stay the night—"

"I cannot! I have to go back. You must accept it."

He walked away from her, taking the chance, just as he always had done, gambling on his luck to support him. She either loved him, or she did not. The choice was hers.

He was atop his horse before she came running, calling his name and running. Everyone in the churchyard stared at her. Even Diana was momentarily silenced. The pain in his chest eased somewhat. His magic girl, who made him feel young again. She did love him. He did have her. It was only a question of time, which he did not possess anymore. But again, his luck would support him, as it always had. With her by his side, life might assume different proportions, less frightening, less final. He looked down at her.

She stood holding on to his stirrup, her head bowed, like a child. Barbara, he thought. My dearest. He bent down and lifted her chin. Her eyes, Richard's eyes, glittered with tears.

"Kiss me," he said. "Kiss me," he said again. "And come to Devane House."

She put her mouth on his, and the tenderness of his mouth, the pain, the need, the longing of the kiss shook her.

"I love you," she whispered against his lips.

He smiled at her, his eyes crinkling in the corners. She put her hand on his face. He pulled himself back up in the saddle. He was as handsome as a god, as handsome as her memories, as handsome as her dreams, all that she had ever loved, she thought, staring up at him. Keep thy heart with all diligence; for out of it are the issues of life. You, Roger, are my heart. And you always have been.

"I will be waiting," he said, and he spurred his horse, and then he was galloping away with Montrose, leaving her in the churchyard among the tombs and leaning gravestones and dying flowers.

Under the church porch, Tony and Mary stood together watching.

"Did Charles see?" asked Tony.

"I do not know. He saw enough. He thinks them reconciled."

"They are."

Mary looked at her brother. "Tony . . ."

His face was closed. Some people thought it his stupid look, but Mary knew better. He was thinking, thinking things that no one would imagine.

"Do you want to back down?" he asked her. "There is still time."

"No," she said. And then, in a low voice, "She cannot marry him. And I can." She looked at her brother again. "And you?"

"Rabelais says he that has patience may compass anything."

"Did Rabelais know Roger?"

Tony smiled. "No."

"Come, Grandmama, just a bite more."

Barbara was feeding her grandmother hot soup, and the Duchess was being difficult, the emotional toll of the day expressing itself in her querulous complaints, she was not hungry, the soup was too hot, she was tired.

The funeral had taken the strength from them all. Annie sat listlessly in her chair by the bed and did not fuss at her mistress to hush and eat. Diana sat quietly by the fire. For a while this evening, she had wept and moaned, but no one had paid any attention to her, and now, she just sat, staring into the fire, picking at a thread in her gown. Dulcinea and the dogs snuggled in a heap at the Duchess's feet.

"Lady Nell wants your recipe for pepper posset," said Annie.

"Who is ill?"

"Just another bite," said Barbara. "Please."

"Two of the children."

"Which two?"

Annie did not know.

The Duchess looked at Barbara. "You will be going back." It was not a question.

"Who?" said Diana, lifting her head. Her face was swollen grotesquely. No one would recognize the beautiful Diana Alderley this evening. "Who is going back? Where?"

"You are an irritating old woman, Grandmama. I thought you too grief-stricken to notice anything."

"I am not blind. That was quite a scene you and Roger played in the churchyard today. It eclipsed even talk about South Sea."

"You?" said Diana, focusing swollen, narrowed violet eyes on her daughter. "And where are you going?"

"Will you order a memorial tablet in London?" said the Duchess. "Have them put on it, 'The night shineth as the day: the darkness and the light are both alike to thee . . .'" Her voice, clear and thin in the silence of the room, trailed off. A tear trickled down her cheek and lost itself in the wrinkles.

"Oh, Grandmama," said Barbara, kissing her hand and holding it against her cheek.

"You are not—" Diana turned to her mother. "Tell me she is not returning to London? Why? Why on earth—" Her face changed. "Roger!" she said. She looked at Barbara accusingly. "You are going back to him!"

"It is hardly a sudden thing," said the Duchess dryly.

Barbara was silent.

Diana stood up. "He killed your brother!"

"Mother, that is not true. I will not allow you to say it again."

"Well, he might as well have! Do not be a fool—"

"All summer long," Barbara said, her temper rising, "you told me to return to him. All summer long you told me to have my cake and eat it, too. Use them both, you said. Enjoy Devane House. Enjoy what Roger can give you. Do not be a fool, you said then, too."

"It was different this summer. Roger was a wealthy man. Things have changed. You have not been in London, Barbara. The directors go in fear of their lives. Did you notice the way people stared at him today? He is a marked man. A man on the verge of disgrace. If you had any sense, you would stay right here and—"

Barbara stood up abruptly, spilling soup on her gown. She kissed her grandmother's cheek. "Day after tomorrow," she said. "I will leave then. Shall I come and sit with you tonight, before you sleep?"

"Please."

Diana was silent until the door closed behind Barbara. Then she said bitterly, "Well, I am singularly blessed in my children. She is a headstrong, impulsive, wrongheaded fool."

"Not children." The Duchess spoke softly from her bed. "Child. You are singularly blessed in your child. All the others are dead."

Diana caught her breath, her mouth trembling suddenly.

"Harry killed himself," the Duchess continued. "With a razor. Across his throat. You were away. Away from town."

Diana began to cry, not prettily, as she was capable of doing, but in a noisy, ugly, gulping way. Annie, sitting beside the Duchess, smiled dourly.

"Why—why are you s-so cruel to me?" Diana wept. "I loved him. I-I love her. She is a-all I have I-left."

"I know."

There was silence but for Diana's sobbing and the crackling of the logs in the fireplace.

"How old I am," said the Duchess to herself softly. "How tired. . . ."

"I am here," said Annie, bending over her.

Diana stood by the edge of the bed. She looked like a large, sullen, repentant child. "I-I am here, too, Mother," she said. "If you want me."

The Duchess patted the bed, and Diana sat down on it. She looked at her mother, so tiny, so frail, against her mass of pillows. To Annie's surprise, she put her head against her mother's breast and began to weep again.

"I know," the Duchess said, stroking her hair. "I know."

The carriage waited in the courtyard, Thérèse inside, trunks strapped to the back and top, while Barbara and her grandmother took a final, short walk together. It was cold, morning cold, and the Duchess was very weak, but she insisted. They walked along the terrace and stood looking at the duke's desolate rose garden. Weeder women were on their hands and knees, pulling up weeds between the rosebushes, while the gardeners were shoveling a covering of crushed leaves and dirt on the stem bulb from which the spring's new rose canes would develop. Behind the rose gardens, smoke from burning piles of leaves spiraled into the autumn sky.

"I should gather the rose hips. Send Jane some rose-hip fever water if the posset does not work," the Duchess said.

"It will work. Your concoctions always work. I will write to you every week. I promise. Give Hyacinthe plenty to do. Tell him I shall write to him also."

(Barbara had decided that Hyacinthe should stay at Tamworth, for the time being. He had cried at the idea of being left, but she promised to send for him as soon as she could and told him he must look after her grandmother and that he could sleep in the stables with his new friends. And she left him the copy of *Robinson Cruoe* to keep. She whispered that she was also leaving Harry and Charlotte for him to look after, but that he was not to tell her grandmother until she was long gone. And then, after the telling, he was to run and hide, and by dark, the duchess would be too tired and too worried and too glad to see him to do anything at all. That was how I always handled her, Barbara told him, which made him smile through his tears.)

"Will you go straight to Devane House?"

"I do not know, Grandmama. More than likely."

"London is not a pleasant place these days, I am told. Promise me you will be careful. Your coachman has his pistol, has he not? Loaded?"

"Yes."

"I have two things to say—"

"Only two?"

"Never mind. I want to say them before I forget. The first is about forgiveness. It is never done well in little bits and dabs. Do it all at once and never look back, or do not do it at all. Those are your grandfather's words, and not mine. And the second is about change. Change is an easy thing to decide and a difficult thing to do. It is the day-to-day struggle of it that defeats people. Do not despair if old ways look good to you. Despair only if you fall into them too often."

Barbara put her arms around her grandmother. How small she was. How thin and frail. How much of her zest was buried with Harry. How much of them all was buried with Harry. "Take care of yourself," she said gently.

They walked back to the courtyard arm in arm. I hate to leave this place, thought Barbara. Annie and Tim and Perryman and her mother waited by the carriage, and Annie frowned as she saw the fatigue on the Duchess's face.

Barbara embraced her mother. Diana looked sharply older; there were hollows in her cheeks and dark circles under her eyes. She is grieving, thought Barbara, genuinely grieving. Harry would laugh if I told him.

"You are a fool," Diana said.

"Goodbye to you, too, Mother."

She climbed into the carriage, and it lurched forward. The Duchess staggered back as she watched it rattle down the avenue, and both Annie and Tim clasped an elbow, and she did not say anything, but leaned into their combined strengths. They saw Hyacinthe burst from behind one of the limes and run after the carriage, Harry and Charlotte following, yapping furiously. And behind the dogs came a fluffy white ball of fur, Dulcinea. The carriage stopped, and Barbara and Thérèse both climbed out to embrace Hyacinthe while the dogs leapt and howled around them, and Dulcinea skulked nearby.

"She forgot the dogs," said the Duchess.

Hyacinthe stepped back, wiping his face, and Barbara and Thérèse climbed back in—it looked as if Thérèse was crying now—and away the carriage lurched, again, and after it ran the dogs, but they ran halfheartedly because Hyacinthe stood in the middle of the avenue. He darted back behind the limes, and those on the terrace saw him running toward the woods, the dogs following him and Dulcinea following the dogs.

"She has left those dogs," the Duchess said. She sighed. "Tim, you watch for that boy in the next few days. I do not want him sick from grief. Inform those stableboys I will cane the first of them that dares to tease him."

"Time for bed," said Tim, taking her arm firmly.

"I choose my own bedtime!" snapped the Duchess.

Tim jumped back as abruptly as if a pet dog had just bitten his nose.

Diana laughed.

The Duchess scowled at her. "Give me your arm, Diana. I am tired," she said. "It is my bedtime."

Philippe stood a moment before the windows of his town house which overlooked the back garden. Everything was ready. His trunk was packed; the notes were written; his butler had precise instructions as to the rest of the books and furniture and clothing. His carriage waited outside. He had only to walk out of this room and down the stairs and out into the morning and proceed. Away from here. An hour or so on to Gravesend, one of the villages along the Thames closer to the sea than London, where ships loaded and unloaded passengers. There a ship was taking him back to France.

The only regret he felt, oddly enough, was that of leaving Abigail. The note he had written her would not ease her hurt, he knew; but in time, she would forget him and remember him only with fondness and a delicious sense of escaped danger. She would have been a good mistress, well bred, discreet, in control of her emotions, enthusiastic in bed once he taught her how to be, but he had not the strength for a mistress. Not yet. He must heal first from Roger, and that would be a long time's mending.

Roger.

Abigail had described the scene outside the church in vivid detail. He had been able to picture it in his mind: Roger, dashing, mysterious, faintly scandalous again because of South Sea, atop his restless stallion, his young, grieving wife running across the churchyard, her black gown belling around her long legs, calling his name, the words exchanged that no one heard, making them all the more intriguing and sweet, the kiss. Yes, he could see it all. The reconciliation was, in effect, achieved. It was only a matter of time before it became a physical reconciliation also. He knew Roger, knew his single-minded charm in pursuit of an elusive woman. He had watched him often enough in France in those early years, admiring the technique, the charm, the flattery, the knowledge of dazzling good looks used so ruthlessly, but so charmingly. Always the charm. That fatal charm.

How did the English King James version of the Bible express it? There be three things which are too wonderful for me, yea, four which I know not: The way of an eagle in the air; the way of a serpent upon a rock; the way of a ship in the midst of the sea; and the way of a man with a maid. The way of Roger, with any maiden, was amazing indeed. If only the maiden were not Barbara. As he had listened to Abigail, his choices showed startlingly clear before him. He could leave, now, with his pride and dignity intact, or he could stay, pretend it did not matter, and see it played out to the end.

He was almost tempted by the last, for the ending of it all was in question. Roger was too besotted to see it, too lost in this final grasp of lost youth. There was no doubt of his ability to bring Barbara back to his bed and to satisfy her once there. There was, however, some doubt as to how long she would stay. The innocent child of France was gone, and in her place was a woman both innocent and knowing. She had stubbornness and tenacity, yet there were devils within Roger's nature which might be subdued, but were never vanquished. They might prove more stubborn even than she. And, as a playwright might say, there were other twists to the plot. Lord Russel, for one. And, amusingly enough, young Lord Tamworth for another. A quiet young man, a grave young man, an extremely determined young man. Even Abigail, as clever as she was, underestimated him. Yes, there were interesting twists to the plot, if one had the heart to stay and see it played out. He had not. He had no more heart. Sometimes, at night, as he lay unable to sleep, he felt as if he had nothing inside. Nothing but dark emptiness. Sentimental, foolish, unmanly, perhaps. But real nonetheless.

Life's but a walking shadow, a poor player that struts and frets his hour upon the stage and then is heard no more; it is a tale told by an idiot, full of sound and fury, signifying nothing. English at its best and most lyric. Shakespeare expressed the realities of life very well, without the gleam and dazzle of the French language, perhaps, but very well, very well indeed, for an Englishman.

The note to Abigail was written. As was another to Carlyle—asking that he write if there were any news of Roger that Carlyle felt he might wish to know. And finally, there was the last gesture, worthy of a soldier and a prince. To another soldier, a soldier fighting the final battle, a battle which might defeat him, he was leaving two bags of gold. They would go anonymously to Roger's banker. A gift from the gods. A forestalling of the inevitable, though with Roger's luck, he might pull through this financial crisis. But not as he had been, never again could he acquire the splendor of wealth he had once possessed. Yet, who knew what tale the idiot next would tell? Roger might rise, like the phoenix of legend. Rise from the ashes and win, with his young wife by his side, the powerful Tamworth family his allies, the King of England his friend. But no children. Here, at last, was some small satisfaction. Barbara, clearly, was barren. There would be no Montgeoffrys to give them joy.

The satisfaction, however, carried within it a small, poisoned barb he floundered upon. For, in his heart of hearts, he would have loved to look upon a child of Roger's; the irony was that the mother did not matter; she was a vessel, a receptacle, nothing more; she did not matter . . . if she had been anyone other than Barbara. To see the imprint of Roger upon a small face. What satisfaction, what joy, what completeness there would have been in that sight. But such was life. His carriage awaited, as did his ship. His beloved France, his estate, wooded and cool in the summer. His gardens. His books. His treasures. Another world from here. Another life.

Jacombe, the banker, cleared his throat and glanced at Roger. "The amount," he said, "as best I can find, comes to £250,227."

There was a short silence as, appalled, Roger stared at him. The amount was so much more than he had figured, even in his wildest additions and subtractions, with Montrose late into the night.

An unexpected addition of £200 pounds in gold, Jacombe was saying. Delivered two days ago to your account. Other than that, as you know, no cash of any kind. Loans outstanding totaling some £70,000. Jacombe's voice was dry, the amount shocking even him, banker that he was. £70,000, thought Roger. Money to this friend or that, gambling debts, horse racing, personal loans, a scrawl across a sheet of paper promising payment, word of a gentleman. Gentlemen who now said they could not repay a penny. They were all bankrupt. How weak I feel, he thought, wiping the sudden sweat on his forehead.

Overdue payments to contractors, piling up since before August. The carpenters, the bricklayers, the painters, the laborers, the craftsmen, the makers of furniture and draperies, a bill for French damask, the color of sea foam, with embroideries, coming to some £15,000. Barbara's bedchamber, thought Roger. Barbara's bed. He had envisioned Barbara, naked, white, red-gold against that soft green.

Jacombe's voice droned on. Stocks, thousands in the Mississippi Company, now valueless, in South Sea and London Assurance and Royal Exchange and other companies he had speculated in over this summer, their value gone or dropping. Payments due on the land he had bought surrounding Richmond over the summer, which would increase in value in the long term, but had to be paid for in the short term. Bills for wax candles and Venetian marble. Had he actually spent £20,000 on Venetian marble?

Payments past due on the loans he had arranged to pay for the building of Devane House and Devane Square. And mortgages when his initial funding had run short. Most of the square stood empty, and it was still unfinished. Few had the cash to lease his town homes, and he had not the cash to pay the laborers to finish. A cycle, pulling downward. If you walked through the streets of London, you met people trying to sell coaches, gold watches, diamond earrings; servants roamed the streets, looking for work; Long Lane and Monmouth and Regent Fair, the streets of the used clothing markets, offered richly embroidered waistcoats and petticoats, the clothing of the wealthy, the titled, along with their rags and secondhand gowns. Everyone was selling. No one was buying.

Who had told him just the other day that credit was frozen solid? Whoever it was had not been able to send £25 from London to Dublin by a bill of exchange. The pamphlets, the street ballads, the lampoons knew who to blame—South Sea villains, South Sea thieves, the directors, his face, his name, featured among them as prominently as John Blunt's. Though his part in it was much smaller. Blunt had pushed through the schemes. He had only helped with bribes, the lists of subscribers. Devane House had been his avocation, his hobby, his world, not the rise and fall of stock, though he, like anyone, profited from the rises. But not enough. Not nearly enough. Now the directors of the Bank of England said they would not engraft stock. They had survived the run on their cash coffers, by the skin of their teeth, and they did not care what happened to anyone else now, as long as they survived.

London was a changed place these days, a ruthless place. Men who smiled upon you yesterday demanded payment on old loans today. Women who once lowered their eyes seductively now asked you straightforwardly to buy their diamonds and pearls. The banks in Amsterdam had recalled cash advanced to London, denying credit, selling stock held as collateral. The Prince of Wales refused to see him. When he appeared at court now, it was as if a space surrounded him, a space into which few people ventured. Members of Parliament were in town, angry, perplexed, bearing petitions from their townships asking for punishment to the creators of the present misfortune. Yet who was to blame? Parliament for wanting to rival France? Blunt for manipulating credit? The ministers for ignoring it? The other directors for allowing it? Himself, for concentrating on Devane House, on Barbara? He pulled at his cravat. He could feel the familiar breathlessness. It would be followed by pain, by the burning in his abdomen and chest. He needed to calm himself, to rest. There were solutions. There were always solutions. If a man did not panic.

What was Jacombe saying? Something about drawing up a list of assets, a list of disposables, though as a banker and businessman, he knew this was the worst of all possible times to sell anything. Roger dismissed him and stood a moment at his desk, a finely made French desk of intricate, inlaid woods and mother-of-pearl and marble. He took deep, gasping breaths of air. He could hear himself, and the sounds he made frightened him. He could not get enough air. He managed to open a window that overlooked his gardens, his pavilion of the arts. A fog was rolling in. The air he sucked into his lungs

was wet, moist on his cheeks, in his throat. He drank it thirst-
ily. November was supposed to be the season of fogs; it was
a week away yet. This was an early fog, blurring his vision
of his pavilion, distorting his sight. . . . He shook his head.
He felt as if a fog were rolling in over his mind. He saw Philippe. And Richard. Standing in the fog. Philippe was wise to
leave as he had. He had not even said goodbye, but one could
not blame him. He had not done well by Philippe. The burning grew stronger. He must not think of that. He must rest.
Calm himself. Not allow panic to overwhelm him. He was
tired. He had been working too hard, going from meeting to
meeting, argument to argument, the trip to Tamworth, the
disgrace, the worry over his account books. His mind raced in
spite of his effort to calm it.

Two hundred fifty thousand pounds. An incredible sum. He
could never pay it off. His belongings would have to be sold.
If he could hold creditors off—and he could. He was related
by marriage to the Tamworths, the King of England was his
friend, as were Robert Walpole, Lord Townshend. The list of
those that owed him, in some form or another, was endless.
He would begin calling in his markers. If he could hold his
creditors off, he could wait, wait until the market calmed, and
then sell discreetly. He rubbed his chest. The pain was
spreading. He might even have to sell Devane House. Options.
What were his options? The governorship of a colony. Surely,
the king would grant that. Barbados. Jamaica. He smiled, but
the smile turned to a grimace. He grunted with pain. God, it
hurt. He must lie down. Barbara would come with him. Her
youth was his talisman. He dreamed of her at night, her long,
white slenderness, the thick red-gold hair loose on her shoulders, her bare breasts, the red-gold between her legs. Soon he
would kiss that red-gold; he would possess her again, totally;
and they would start anew.

The pain doubled, trebled. It was blinding, staggering. He
fell to his knees in front of the window, clawing at it. A rock,
the mightiest rock in the world, was on him, on his chest,
crushing him, crushing him. Down, down, down. He fought
it. Richard. He struggled to push it off. Philippe. He struggled
to breathe. Barbara. He had no power, no strength. No, he
thought, as the fog rolled in over his mind. Not now. Not yet.
I am not ready. I am still young. Barbara. Young enough to—

and then the fog, gray, cold, crushing, slipped over into soft darkness, soft like a woman, soft. And his last conscious thought was how glad he was of the softness, because the other, the pain, life, was unbearable.

CHAPTER TWENTY-SIX

"No, Mama," Jeremy said.

Shaking with fever and chills, his voice rose high and strained in the room as he recognized the doctor, with his black bag of pain. Jeremy looked at Jane with begging, fever-bright eyes.

"No, Mama. Please!"

The baby within her kicked, in sympathy with Jeremy, with her own feelings. Whenever the doctor came, he brought more pain: in the black river leeches that made Jeremy scream with fright; in the stinging, burning plasters; in the bad-tasting medicines, in the hot liquids poured down throats and ears. She did not blame Jeremy; she could barely stand the sight of the doctor herself, but Jeremy was not better. The others, after weeks of nursing, lay wan, weak, but well, in their cribs and beds. But not Jeremy.

His cough had deepened. He complained of new, sharp pains in his chest. It hurts me to breathe, he said. His fever did not go away. And yesterday there was blood among the yellow mucus he had coughed up. The sight of that blood made Jane's heart stand still. As she stared at him, with his too-thin body and his too-bright eyes, and the tiny rattle in his breath, she thought, dear merciful Lord Jesus, we are beyond pepper possets and barley water and fever cordials. Dear merciful Lord Jesus, make him well.

"Mama! Mama!"

Jeremy tried to climb out of the bed, but Gussy caught him and held him, and his thin arms and legs flailed wildly against Gussy. The doctor had opened his bag and was taking out a jar filled with small, black river leeches, which were applied to the body to suck out the bad humors of the blood.

"No! No! No!" screamed Jeremy. "Mama, Papa, do not make me!"

Jane put her hand to her mouth. The little bit of supper she had eaten rose in her throat.

"Mama! No! Oh, no-o-o."

Jeremy was screaming and flailing and thrashing on the bed, his face transformed into something primitive and feral. Large drops of sweat gleamed on Gussy's forehead, rolling down his face, as he tried to hold a child whose voice was shrill with terror as he struggled to get away.

Thin wails joined Jeremy's; his screams had frightened the others. The baby inside Jane kicked again, harder. The bile rose in her throat. Jeremy's eyes rolled back white in his head, and he began to foam at the mouth. The doctor laid the leeches across Jeremy's chest, carefully, one after another. The boy screamed for his mother, over and over. She managed to open the door and step into the dark hallway. Now she heard how loudly the others were crying, their terror mirroring Jeremy's. Her throat closed, and she leaned against a wall, feeling something rise inside her.

"Jane!" she heard Gussy call, her name drowned out by the sound of Jeremy, a terrible, breathless sobbing that tore out her heart—"Mama, Mama, Mama." Nothing but her name over and over and over.

She ran. Down the stairs, standing a moment in the hall, breathing heavily, her eyes wild, darting, into the kitchen. Cat and Betty sat before the fire, roasting nuts, oblivious of the screams from the floor above as they whispered and laughed.

"See," Cat was saying, with her pretty smile pointing to the grate on which hazelnuts were roasting, "Jonathan's is burning brightest. Jonathan is my true love." Beside her, Betty nodded. Damn them, thought Jane. It was All Hallow's Eve, and they were practicing the country customs which would foretell their sweethearts. You put hazelnuts in the fire, naming each one after a boy, and the one that burned brightest was your true love. Long ago, she and Barbara had done the same thing.

"Damn you!" she said.

They turned to stare at her, their mouths dropping open.

"Damn you both for the lazy, worthless sluts you are!" She heard herself screaming, but she could not stop. "I will beat you both! I will turn you out in the night! I will— Go take care of those children. Go-o-o!"

The veins stood out in her throat as she screamed the last word, holding it in a long, high sound that was becoming hysterical. She heard herself but she could not stop. She put her hands over her ears and ran out of the kitchen, into the dark, the cold. All the while the baby within kicking its fluttering kicks, over and over. I am killing it, she thought, as she ran blindly in the dark. Killing it. And then: It must be easier to birth a baby gone five months than nine months. That would be a blessing. And then: God forgive me, I did not mean it. And then, Jeremy, Jeremy, please do not scream. Please do not die. I love you so. And then she stumbled, falling over a tree root, and plunged to the ground, catching herself at the last moment with her arms. But the weight of her body made her arms tremble with pain, and she sank down, down to the earth, the cold, dark earth, and she curled up into a ball, feeling the fluttering kicks of the child inside her, but thinking, I have killed it. I have killed it for sure. And she lay there, numb.

How tired I am, she thought after a while. For four weeks, she had run up and down stairs, holding one child or another, staying up with their fevers and frets, stirring broths and cordials and possets over the hot fire, the child within her growing, growing, while she became thinner and thinner, too tired at night to eat. There was never time to rest; everyone was ill, crying, tossing with fever. And then had come news about Harry. She could not comprehend it. Not Harry. She did not believe it still. She found herself looking up at odd moments during her day, expecting to see him ride up, a grin on his face. What a jest I have pulled, Janie, he would say, the old, mischievous light in his violet eyes. I made them think I killed myself.

She wanted to grieve over him, wanted to sit quietly and hold the soft, leather gloves he had given her in her hands and rub them against her cheeks and smell the cinnabar and think of the apple trees and how they had once sat under them, and pledged their undying love. But Harry had died. Perhaps she should have gone to the funeral, perhaps then she could have accepted it. But there was no time, no time for Harry. South Sea, Gussy had said to her before he left, trying to explain, knowing by her stunned silence that the hurt went deeper than she showed. He talked of rivalries between great companies, Bank of England, East India Company, South Sea, about stocks rising and falling, and everyone believing in their magic. Even he, he told her. He had lost their savings, he said, confessing in the shock of the news about Harry. All our savings, he had said, which I will save again. She stared at him. Above them, a child was crying. Always, a child was crying. Harry could not be dead. Not Harry. Yet Gussy said he was. . . .

And there was Jeremy. While the others healed, he kept the fever. He held his little chest and cried when he had to cough. She bathed him with lemon water, fed him all the remedies she knew for coughs and fever, the combinations of maiden-hair, coltsfoot, saffron, sugar, pennyroyal, rose leaves, nut-meg, ribwort, ale, but nothing worked. He tossed and turned and shook with chills, even though she lay in the bed with him, sweating under the number of covers over them both, holding him in her arms, humming little tunes, telling him little rhymes, telling him stories of her adventures with Bar-bara and Harry when they had all been children. Tell me again, he would beg, between bouts of shaking. Tell me again. And she would, until her voice was hoarse.

But he did not get any better. And then yesterday, in that moment of heart-stopping stillness, she saw the blood he coughed up, mixed with the mucus and phlegm. Blood. Frightful thoughts raced through her head: consumption, years of dying, the children separated, sent away so the others should not catch it, consumption. Not Jeremy. Not her dear Jeremy who had grown under her heart and helped her heal over Harry. Her firstborn. Her little son. Her helper. Her brave, dear boy, with his wayward hair and thin legs and sweet, high voice. She would not let it be so. It must not be so. She had not endured those hours of bone-wrenching labor, the clumsiness of that first midwife, the pain, the total depth and breadth and width of that pain, for Jeremy to die now. What was the use of enduring childbirth if the child you bore did not live? It was the sight of it, its helplessness, the way it nestled blindly in your arms, that made the pain bearable. The child was the reward. God could not take her reward from her. She would never survive it. Never.

She shivered with cold. She was a fool to be out here lying in the dark. Country folk believed the spirits of the dead were out on All Hallow's Eve. Harry, she thought, are you out here wandering, wandering. . . ? Take a candle, go to the looking glass, eat an apple before it and comb your hair—the face of your loved one will be seen, looking over your shoulder. Long ago, when she was a girl, she and Barbara did all the country charms, Barbara laughing at them but doing them, she more serious. Harry. She never saw his face in that mirror, but she had once loved him nonetheless. He slit his throat, Gussy had said. Harry. Wild. Boyish. A dream. He will never have any money, her mother told her, trying to comfort her long ago, as she cried and cried and cried. There is bad blood there. Bad blood. Fly, Ladybird, fly. North, south, east or west. Fly where the man is found that I love best. How the blood must have gushed from his throat when he cut it. Harry. The blood. In Jeremy's throat, too, coming up with the phlegm and mucus. Jeremy.

Someone was lifting her up from the ground. Someone was murmuring her name, wrapping a woolen cloak around her, kneeling beside her and chafing her cold, cold hands. Gussy. Her dear Gussy. Fly where the man is found that I love best.

"Jane," he began, and she heard his voice break in the darkness. She put her hand to his face. He was crying. Her rock, her steadfast husband, was crying, as one of her children did. She listened, her mother's ears straining for the sound of children, but the house was quiet. She must have frightened Cat and Betty into seeing about the children, even on All Hallow's, which was sacred to servants as a time of play and games. There was no sound of Jeremy screaming for her. To save him, to make him well, to take the hurt away. As she would if she could. What had the doctor said? What had he found that made Gussy, with his faith in the Lord and his serene calm, cry this way? She knew. Jeremy was going to die. She knew.

Gussy still knelt before her. She found his hand in the darkness and pulled him down so that his head was in her lap, against the baby, which fluttered weakly. In her lap, Gussy cried and cried. She put her hand on his hair. He did not have on his wig, and his own hair was thinning. She stroked that thinning hair, the high bulb of his forehead, thinking of all the knowledge, the sweetness under her fingertips. She smiled to herself. Cat and Betty were probably standing at an upstairs window, staring down at the two of them, murmuring that the witches had possessed them, and cast an All Hallow's spell over them.

"What did the doctor say?"

"He said that Jeremy has an inflammation of the lungs."

"And—"

"He will give him medicines to bring down the fever, but—" Gussy could not finish.

"But there is a possibility he will die," Jane finished for him, calmly. The knowledge that he was going to die settled into her firmly, securely, and . . . for now, calmly. This is real grief, she thought, her thoughts seeming to her to be like stars shining brightly on a clear, summer night, pinpoints of clearest light against dark sky. True grief. The death of a child. My child. . . .

Gussy pulled her up to stand beside him. For a moment, they stood together, and she felt his tears dropping onto her face. Dear Gussy. He would have need of the Lord in the next weeks, as would she. Only the love of God, the thought of a peaceful afterlife—suffer the little children to come unto Me—would reconcile her to Jeremy's dying. And the reconciliation would not come easily. Even now, she could feel denial of it rearing back inside of her. She would fight Death with every breath she took, every recipe, water, cordial, herb that existed. With her mother's love.

"I love you," said Gussy.

"I love you, too," she said.

Together, they walked back to the house.

Barbara's carriage lurched into the courtyard of Saylor House in London, the horses' mouths foaming against their bridles because the coachman had driven them so hard. It did not matter that his mistress had said they could drive into

London late; he refused to be on the road after dark on All Hallow's.

In the carriage, Barbara fell against Thérèse. Damn him, she thought, knowing it would do no good to scold him; country superstition was stronger than harsh words on All Hallow's. How weary I feel, Barbara thought, the excitement of coming to London lost now, evaporating with the miles, as the carriage lurched on and on and Thérèse sat so silent, so quiet, none of her usual chatter, her rosary beads clinking over and over; and thoughts of Harry rose, in spite of herself, in her mind. She did not want to think of him, but the thoughts pushed themselves up. She did not want to cry over him, but tears welled anyway. Roger, she kept thinking, I will tell Roger, and he will hold me and make the hurt well. Harry.

She walked up Saylor House's broad steps, Thérèse behind her, thinking of how a cup of tea would refresh her, take the tiredness, the dreariness from her. In the great parlor, as the murals of her grandfather's battles rose up on the walls all around her, she had a sudden vision of Harry, lying on that table, and the thin, red, stitched line under his neck. Hysteria rose in her throat along with a wild impulse to cry, to scream, to pull her hair, to shock her aunt and Tony, who were rising out of their comfortable armchairs before the fire, staring at her as if she were a ghost. She was not a ghost. Harry was. Roger. How she needed him. And how she feared that need. There were so many things yet between them. Things which must be settled for her peace of mind.

"You are here so quickly," her Aunt Abigail was saying, an odd note in her voice.

"It took no longer than usual. There has been no rain. The roads are not impossible yet. Are there scones? I am famished."

And she kissed both Tony and her aunt, and sat down abruptly, even though the two of them still stood, and began to butter a scone.

"Did you not receive my letter?" said Abigail.

"What letter?"

"Roger has had a serious attack. He is ill, Barbara. Tony and I have just come from Devane House. I wrote you. I sent the letter off yesterday by special messenger, but—"

"Roger? Ill?" She stared up at her aunt, not quite able to take in her words.

"Merciful heavens, worse than ill. The doctor fears for his life—"

"Mother!" Tony interrupted swiftly, but Barbara was up, knocking over a cup of tea in her haste, running from the room. "Thérèse!" Abigail and Tony heard her call as she ran out into the hall. "Thérèse!"

"I did not mean—" Abigail began, but Tony was striding past her.

"I am going with her."

"No—Tony!"

Abigail followed him into the hall. There was no sign of Barbara. Tony ran to the front door and wrenched it open. Barbara was climbing into her carriage, Thérèse behind her. He called her name, but she shut the door, and the carriage lurched away. Tony ran down the steps, Bates and Abigail behind him. He turned to Bates, frowning.

"Have a horse saddled immediately."

"Wait, Tony," said Abigail. "She does not need nor want you at this moment—" She stopped. The face he showed her was determined and stubborn and desperately in love. She was silent as she followed him back into the house. She left him in the hall and went back into the great parlor and closed the door behind herself. She looked at the war murals, the great cabinets filled with porcelain, the fine furniture. Everything was as it should be. Everything showed her—Tony's—wealth and power. She sat back down at the tea table and began to pour herself a cup of tea, but the hand that held the teapot trembled, and she poured tea over the table, and it spread quickly and began to drop onto the priceless rug under her feet. She grabbed at a napkin and another cup of tea spilled on the rug before she knelt on her hands and knees to blot the liquid. There. There. She was getting it all. Everything was fine—she hit her head on the table and sat back on her heels and burst into tears, her powder and rouge running, as she cried and could not stop.

It was so many things. London was dismal, gloomy, full of fear. No one could help catching the feeling. This South Sea thing. It kept on and on, touching all their lives, ballooning larger and larger. Wherever one went—to court, a private party, shopping—it was all that was discussed. She had lost half her private fortune. Half. And Harry had killed himself over it, and Roger had had an attack of apoplexy, and Harold was moving to his country estate in the north. I cannot afford London, he told her. I have to live in the country. And Fanny was pregnant. And the north was wild and cold. It had moors, wet marshlands that Abigail hated. And Charles Russel had been within an inch of signing a marriage contract when the news of Roger's attack had buzzed through London. Then yesterday he was distant, elusive, and she knew what was in his mind. Barbara. If Barbara was going to be a widow anytime soon, he would wait. For sixpence, she would have ended the negotiations yesterday, but what did Mary do, her quiet, her obedient Mary, but have hysterics. Hysterics. It had taken Abigail hours to calm her. I will kill myself, she had screamed. I love him, I love him. Abigail blew her nose again. Mary had reminded her at that moment vividly of Barbara five years ago, but when she told her so, pointing out what had happened to Barbara, Mary just cried harder. And when she went to Tony to back her up, he said that he was on Mary's side. Mary is a child, she had shouted—yes, she had shouted. Her children drove her to shout. We are better able to decide what is best for her than she is, she told Tony. And Tony, who loved his sister, who could be counted upon to do the right thing, was as obstinate as Mary. If Mary wanted Charles, Tony said, she could have him. And Abigail had seen, in the middle of a shout, why. Tony wanted Barbara. And if Mary were married to Charles, then Charles would be out of the way.

You fool, Abigail wanted to shout (but did not, luckily; some sense returned). Barbara will never love you. Never. And if Abigail had her way, she never would. She would die rather than accept Barbara as a daughter-in-law. And worst of all, she did not even have Philippe here to talk to. She cried and blew her nose again. She could have poured out all her troubles to him, and he would have listened with interest. Talking to him was such a comfort. And it had been years, years, since any man made her feel the way Philippe de Soissons did, sometimes. Yes, she was human. She had feelings, too. She had needs. But she had always been able to sublimate them in the welfare of her children, in the running of their lives—

to their best interests, of course. But Philippe had made her think . . . of other things. She was not such a fool that she could not tell when a man found her attractive. And what did he do? He left for France on some pretext about pressing personal business, without so much as a last goodbye. She had cried like a girl over his letter. Men. Tony was going to break his heart, and she could not do one thing to stop it. And Charles was a selfish fool. Harold had no regard for anyone's feelings but his own. He was taking her dear Fanny off to the marshlands, and life was dreary and dismal and difficult, and she had lost half her personal fortune in a stupid gamble and she ought to have known better. She had more sense than that. It was those speculators pushing stock higher and higher and the excitement. . . . She rose from the floor and shook out her gown, noticing, with dismay, tea stains on it. She took a deep breath. She sat down, and calmly, regally, picked up the teapot to pour herself another cup of tea. She stared at the teapot a moment. Then, following a rare impulse, she threw it at the fire. It missed the fire, but broke into pieces on the mantelpiece. She stared at the pieces, at the tea spreading everywhere, at the tea leaves and grounds which would surely stain the woodwork and floors. It had been a porcelain teapot, from China, unusual and expensive. Breaking it had not made her feel any better, and she had ruined a good teapot in the bargain.

Barbara was out of the carriage and running up the stairs before the carriage came to a full stop at Devane House. Running past Cradock and staring footmen in the hall, running through the library to Roger's bedchamber. She flung open the door. There was no one in the room. She stood staring at the empty bed, her eyes widening. He could not be—she turned and ran through the bedchamber apartments, through the room that connected his with hers, to hers, lovely with the intricate wood carvings and that sea-foam-colored damask. She took a deep breath and opened the door to her bedchamber. Justin, folding a nightgown, stared at her, his face slowly breaking into a smile as he recognized her. Aunt Shrewsborough, in a chair by the bed, rose.

Barbara walked to the bed. It was as if she were walking down a dark lane, and all sides were dark, and only the bed was the light at the end. She looked down at the man in the bed, at Roger, not so very different from when she had seen him last. His face was flushed, his eyes were closed. She put her cheek against his. It was too hot, but the heat was a sign of life. He was alive.

"You look as if you have seen a ghost," her Aunt Shrewsborough said. "He is not a ghost yet, but I will not lie to you, Barbara. He is fighting for his life."

She opened her mouth to say something, but her legs suddenly had no strength, and she was sinking, would have fallen to the floor in fact if Justin had not caught her, murmuring to her—dear Justin, he had always been so comforting; how she depended on his comfort those years ago in Paris—telling her Lord Devane was alive, giving her a glass of something to drink. She drank it down in a gulp, and it burned her throat like fire, burned all the way down, landing in a ball of fire in her stomach, but the fire was good. It sent warm tendrils of life into her legs, her arms, her head. She was better. Roger was alive. It was not too late. Nothing was too late.

Her Aunt Shrewsborough led her out of the room to the withdrawing chamber.

"Fever," she was saying. "It is the fever that is so bad. It does not break. We give him the fever water the doctor left, the medicine. Justin and I wash him down with lavender water every few hours, but the fever does not go away. He was burning with it when they found him."

"When was that?"

"Three days ago. In the library, near an open window. No one knows how long he lay in that damp air. Damp air will kill a body quicker than anything. I blame it for the fever, but the doctor says it is the apoplexy which has given him fever."

"Apoplexy . . ."

Aunt Shrewsborough sniffed. "Doctors. He thinks it apoplexy, but I do not. My first husband went like that," and she snapped her fingers, "from the apoplexy. Bad blood to the brain. Or so the doctors tried to tell me. He died in the arms of some whore. I think the excitement killed him. But my second husband had an attack that was more like Roger's, the fainting, the fever. A long bout of fever. And he finally woke to make my life a torment for five more years. It is too bad we are not at Tamworth, Barbara. Your grandmother and her Annie could cure anything. I do not trust doctors. Never have. Never will."

Barbara stood up abruptly. "I am going to sit with him now." She kissed her aunt's wrinkled cheek. "Thank you for being here with him."

"Nonsense. He is family. You can thank your Aunt Abigail and Fanny and Tony, too. We have all been here."

Tony walked into the withdrawing chamber just as the bedchamber door closed behind Barbara. He still had on his hat and cloak. He stared at his aunt.

"Barbara," he said abruptly. "Where is she?"

Aunt Shrewsborough looked at him; everything he felt was written plainly on his face. She shook her head and sighed and stood up and walked over to him. She did not quite come to his shoulder, even in her high heels.

"She is with her husband," she said. She took his arm and said more gently, "Come away, boy. This is no time for you. Take me home, and you and I will drink a glass or two of brandy together. Brandy is what we need now. A good, strong glass of brandy. She is with her husband, where she belongs."

Five years, thought Barbara, sitting in the chair her aunt had vacated by the sickbed. In five years I will be twenty-five . . . that is nothing. Nothing. I want so much more . . . and then a memory flickered in her mind, of Paris and Richelieu and his saying, You are too greedy, you want everything, all of his love, all of his devotion, you expect too much, Bab. She could remember her answer so clearly. I will have it all, or nothing. . . . Then nothing is what you will end with, Bab. Nothing. Like Harry. She pushed back the thoughts of Harry. Later. She would think them later, when Roger was better. I will take the five years, she said to herself. Or one. And be glad for it.

On the bed, Roger opened his eyes. She bent over him, but he did not see her. His eyes were dull, glazed, the eyelids rimmed red. His hands clawed feebly at the covers. "Behind," he whispered. "The French are massed behind . . ." His breath was harsh and rasping; it was clearly a great effort for him to speak.

"Hush," she said, putting her hand to his forehead. How hot it was. "I am here. I am here now."

He closed his eyes, but his breathing still had that harsh rapidity to it. The sound frightened her. Even more than the fever.

What battlefield did he walk in his mind? What battle did he relive? Where was he? Alone . . . all alone someplace she could not reach. Someplace that he must survive. And the enemy was not the French, it was Death. Death. Like the thin, red line stitched with black under Harry's chin. All the fears and doubts and questions she had carried inside herself from Tamworth. . . . Tell me about Philippe. . . . It was the first thing she had been going to demand of him. And now, Philippe was unimportant. If he were to walk into the bedchamber in the next second, he would be nothing. Nothing beside the fact of the way Roger lay in the bed breathing short gasps of air, his hands clawing the bed covers, hot and dry with fever. He might die. But not if she could help it. She had youth and strength and determination on her side. Forgive and never look back, her grandmother had said. And she had thought, How easy that is for you to say. And now she knew it was the truest of wisdoms. Her grandmother knew what she did not. As always. I forgive you, Roger, she thought, staring down at him. For us, there is no longer any past. There is only now. Live for me. For us. And I swear to you that I will never look back again.

She walked in the gardens of the house the next day, taking an hour away from the nursing, Thérèse and Mrs. Elmo and Justin there if Roger should need anything. He was no better. Still the fever burned in him. The doctor came by. His pulse is still too weak, he said. This fever will kill him if we do not bring it down. How long can he last with the fever? she asked, and the doctor shrugged. Who knew? A messenger was already on his way to Tamworth with her letter requesting her grandmother's strongest fever waters and cordials. Her tears had fallen on the paper like rain as she wrote. Aunt Shrewsborough was right; if only she could take Roger to Tamworth. There he would get well. He would. Annie and Grandmama could cure anyone.

She shivered as she walked, and it was not just the cold. The gardens were so empty. The legion of gardeners working in them had been a favorite topic in London, and she still remembered how many people had been in them the day she visited. Now there was no one, anywhere. It was as if time were suspended; here and there one saw a wheelbarrow overturned; burlapped plants that had been left unplanted and had died. Devane House rose behind her, massive and unfinished piles of brick and stone waiting, ladders, scaffolds . . . everything waiting. Last night Cradock complained to her of surly footmen who wanted back wages and of food vendors who refused to deliver food because their bills were unpaid. Mrs. Elmo cornered her to say the housemaids were stealing little things, a book, a porcelain statue, a medal here and there from the collections. They, too, had not been paid. And there were broken drains in the kitchen and a leak in the roof that needed fixing, Mrs. Elmo said. Bills, Montrose said to her this morning, nothing but bills. He showed her the sheaf of papers, overdue notices for candles, food, oats, clothing, carriages, all the things whose payment she had always taken for granted.

Not only was the staff at Devane House due back wages, said Montrose, but so was the staff at St. James's Square. The contractors and craftsmen who had worked on the town houses and Devane House itself were due money. There were bills for furniture, drapery fabrics, porcelains. Roger's banker, Jacombe, wished to speak with her as soon as possible, Montrose said. As did the solicitors in the law firm Roger employed. Mr. Civins of that firm had written a polite but urgent note requesting a meeting—lawsuits pending for nonpayment, guessed Montrose. There were mortgages and settlements and indemnities to see to, as well as stocks and annuities. He was compiling a list of assets that Lord Devane had requested before his illness, and she ought to look at it; she ought to begin deciding what could be sold. She might have to go to creditors and appeal to them personally. They would not be able to refuse a woman, Montrose said. In the cash box were two bags of gold, the only cash we possess, Montrose told her. Tell me what to do, he said. Tell me what to do, said Cradock. Tell me what to do, said Mrs. Elmo.

She noticed squares of paper plastered over the front gates and on the fence; she tore one down. It was a crude printing taken from a better woodcut; the finer version would be on sale in bookshops. Entitled "Britannia stript by a S. Sea Director," it featured Britannia as a Roman matron pulling away from a South Sea director, who looked like Roger. There were lines printed at the bottom.

> See how a crafty vile projector picks
> Britannia's purse by South Sea shams and tricks;
> Drains her of wealth till he has made her mourn,
> And humbly cheats her with a false return;
> Takes much, leaves little for her own support;
> Gives her fair words, but all he says comes short;
> Conveys her riches to a distant shore,
> And daily courts the silly dame for more.

Behind the caricature of Roger was a waiting ship. Barbara crumpled the paper up. How did they dare? He was ill, perhaps dying, and they wrote vicious lies, blaming him for everything. She stared past the gates, to Wren's unfinished church on the other side, its windows and doors boarded up. I hate this place, she thought. I want to take him away from here. Before it kills him.

The Duchess held out her hand, and Hyacinthe gave her the copy of *Robinson Crusoe*.

"Defoe, heh?" she said, examining it. "He is a scribbler, and nothing more. In and out of prison for debt. And a dissenter, a Presbyterian to boot. Does he write a good story?"

Hyacinthe nodded his head listlessly.

The Duchess sighed. Barbara had been gone two days, and the house was a tomb without her. Hyacinthe moped in corners; she herself stayed in bed and cried. She had not been to chapel or held prayers for her household since Harry's death. She felt too weak and too tired. It was as if a part of her were buried with him. She patted the edge of the bed. Gingerly, eyeing her, Hyacinthe sat down. She gave him back the book, and Harry and Charlotte leapt up on the bed to settle themselves next to Dulcinea. She stared at the dogs, and Harry, tail wagging, barked happily at her. She felt too tired even to protest his impudence.

"Read it," she said to Hyacinthe, closing her eyes and leaning back on her pillows. "Let me see what this Defoe has to say for himself."

" 'Preface,' " began Hyacinthe. " 'If ever the Story of any private Man's Adventures in the World were worth making Publick, and were acceptable when publish'd, the Editor of this Account thinks this will be so.

" 'The Wonders of this Man's Life exceed all that (he thinks) is to be found extant; the Life of one Man being scarce capable of a greater Variety.' "

"Bah!" said the Duchess, her eyes still closed.

" 'The Story is told with Modesty, with Seriousness, and with a religious Application—' "

"A Presbyterian application, no doubt," sniffed the Duchess.

" '—Applicant of Events to the Uses to which wise Men always apply them—' "

Diana burst into the bedchamber, waving a letter. "Roger is ill," she said dramatically, her violet eyes shining with excitement, "perhaps dying."

"What? What?" said the Duchess, trying to push herself up on the pillows, her lace cap falling forward into her eyes, Dulcinea and the dogs protesting at her movement. "Give me that letter."

It took her a moment to make sense of it, and it was only after she had reread it that she realized the letter was addressed to Barbara, and that Diana had opened it.

"You opened her letter," she said to Diana.

Diana stared at her. "You are becoming senile. What has that to do with anything? I thought it might be important—"

"You thought nothing of the kind—"

"Are you going to lie there and scold me for opening a letter when my daughter's husband is ill? May, in fact, already be dead? God, this is unexpected. I have a thousand things to do—"

"Dead! Dead? Who says anything about dead?"

"Abigail says—quite clearly, Mother—that he has had a serious attack, and that Barbara must come immediately."

"She does not say he may be dead. *Aqua mirabilis*. And imperial water. Yes, imperial water and a syrup of violets and woodsorrel and lemon for fever. I have a palsy water recipe. . . . She must bring him here. Annie! Where is that woman when you need her? Hyacinthe, you run and fetch Annie for me. And Tim. And Perryman."

She threw back the bed covers and sat on the edge of the bed and took a deep breath, preparation for standing. Her legs were not to be trusted.

"Have you lost your mind?" said Diana. "What are you doing?"

"Doing? Doing? I will go to London. Annie and I. Between the two of us we will cure whatever ails Roger Montgeoffry—"

"You are mad! You cannot even stand up. The journey would kill you. See! See," said Diana, for the Duchess had tried to stand and had fallen back on the bed like a tipped-over bowling pin. Dulcinea complained loudly, and the dogs jumped off the bed and barked at Diana.

"Go away!" she told them. "Mother, listen to me. Your health is poor. I will go to London. I will take your fever waters and cordials. I will take care of Barbara."

The Duchess looked at Diana with narrowed eyes. She had forgotten now exactly what they were speaking of, but she knew it was important and that it involved Barbara. Diana, regal in her black gown, confused her, staring at her with a face which showed nothing but concern. Ha, thought the Duchess, her face becoming mutinous.

"I know what you are thinking," said Diana, "but she is my daughter, the only child left to me, and I have nothing but her welfare at heart. I swear it. Now, I am not going to stand here arguing with you. I am going to pack and order my carriage." She swept forward and kissed her mother on the cheek. "I have Roger's welfare at heart, also. You will just have to trust me." Her gown hissed against the floor as she left the room.

Roger, thought the Duchess. I remember. Abigail wrote that he is ill. Very ill. She scratched Dulcinea under the chin.

"I do not trust her. Do you, Dulcinea?" Dulcinea mewed loudly and worked her long claws into the bed covers.

Hyacinthe and Annie and Perryman and Tim ran in, and Hyacinthe stood to one side of the bed while the Duchess—clear-minded now—issued her orders. Annie was to pack the necessary waters, and she was to accompany Lady Diana to London. Lord Devane was ill. Bring him back if you can, she told her. Perryman and Tim were to see that Annie and the waters and Diana got out of Tamworth as soon as possible.

Sooner. Breathless but triumphant, the Duchess settled back again in her pillows as the three left the room. Annie would put a crimp in Diana's style. She smiled grimly to herself and looked up to see a single tear rolling down one of Hyacinthe's cheeks. Her smile faded.

"Will Lord Devane die?" he asked.

She patted the bed, and Harry and Charlotte immediately jumped up.

"You and I are going to say some prayers. As soon as you finish reading me some more of that Robert Crenso—"

"R-Robinson Crusoe."

"Yes. We will read a little more of that. Just a little. And then we will say prayers for Lord and Lady Devane—"

"And Thérèse?"

"And Thérèse. Our prayers may help more than any syrup of violets. We have to trust in the Lord, Hyacinthe. We do what we can, but we have to trust in the Lord."

Carefully Justin and Thérèse turned Roger over, and Barbara dipped a rag in lavender water and washed his back. His skin seemed to be on fire. If anything, the fever seemed higher than this morning before her walk. Roger murmured and moaned, and his hands clawed at the bed sheets as Justin slipped a fresh nightgown on him. Barbara settled him back on the pillows and washed his face with the lavender water.

"Tommy Carlyle has sent you flowers," she told him. By the bed was an enormous bouquet of roses and holly and ivy. "He says he will call on you the moment you are well enough to receive visitors. He is saving gossip for you." Roger did not respond.

Barbara sighed and stood and happened to notice Thérèse's face. Her skin was sallow, and there was a stricken look in her eyes. It has been too much, thought Barbara. Harry and the funeral and the journey and now this.

"Go and rest," she said sharply. "Take the rest of the afternoon off. I will be fine." And she meant it. She felt as if she had the strength of ten, had purpose once more in her life. Roger was going to live. She would not let him die.

Dully, Thérèse walked toward the kitchen. She did not like this house; in the day and night she had been here she had discovered suspicion and distrust everywhere. The housemaids were sullen, the footmen surly. They had not been paid their wages in two months, and many of them had lost money in South Sea, and they half believed that Lord Devane had piles of money hidden somewhere. Their whispers were like the hisses of geese. She ignored them. She felt nothing; every feeling she possessed was with Harry. She went through the days with a space between her and everyone else in the world.

She opened the kitchen door quietly, intending to leave at once if the cook was there. Last night, he had asked her oh so careful questions about Lord Devane's health, and Lady Devane's spending. She wished he would leave, all the servants would leave, as they had threatened to do last night as they drank forbidden brandy, Lord Devane's brandy, in their tea. He has thousands, a footman said, forgetting Thérèse. He has our money hidden away. It is a trick. I hope he dies, another said. Thérèse shook her head. These people were trash, without loyalty or kindness in their hearts—her eyes widened. In the kitchen, Montrose was packing a basket of food, and something in his furtive movement made the hair rise on her arms. Was he stealing, too? It was like a canker spreading throughout the household, the stealing, the disloyal talk, the suspicion. She felt anger stirring tiredly inside herself.

"She would give you anything you asked!" she said loudly. "For what must you steal?"

Montrose started and dropped half a roasted chicken on the floor. Thérèse stared down at it disgustedly.

"It—it is not for me," he stammered defensively. Then he blushed. She walked into the kitchen, hands on her hips. "Well! Are you going to let it rot on the floor? This morning, she told me to begin cleaning her jewels. She thinks she may have to sell them. This evil mistress we have. This South Sea whore. Holy Mary, Mother of God, how can you steal from her? How can you steal from him!"

"I am not stealing! I just take a little. For someone who needs it! Lord Devane would not care! He would have me take more if he knew who—"

"Who! Who do you take 'a little' for?"

Montrose did not answer.

"A whore, perhaps," said Thérèse. "A food vendor, who sells it in turn and gives you half the money, a—"

"Caesar! It is for Caesar White."

And then he stopped, as if he had said far more than he meant. Thérèse's mouth fell open. Montrose frowned and picked up the chicken and put it in the basket. Thérèse saw a bottle of wine and some bread in it, also. He put the basket over his arm and walked away from her, his expression both injured and dignified.

"Wait!" she called, running after him. She caught him by the arm. "Tell me—"

"Tell you what? Why should you believe me? After all, I may be lying. Someone like me, who has served Lord Devane for some six years. Be sure and lock up the silver, Thérèse. I intend to go after it next."

"Tell me."

"There is nothing to tell. Caesar lost everything in the fall of stock. He is living in a garret in Covent Garden without money for coal or food. And he is so despondent that I think sometimes he will—" He stopped, glancing at Thérèse, and changed what he had been going to say. "He made a little this summer, and I told him to stop playing the market and put it away, but he was stock mad, and when the prices fell, his fortune fell with it. Not an unusual story these days."

Thérèse crossed herself. Then she grabbed a cloak from a peg. "I am going with you."

Thoughts whirled in her head as she walked beside him. Despondent, so despondent that . . . the thin red line under Harry's chin was vivid in her mind. The flash of a razor. The whiteness, the stillness of his beloved face. Her own face became grim. She would not allow another person she knew to take his life. There was no misfortune worth that. It caused so much pain, so much guilt to those left behind. And it was a sin before the sight of the Lord.

She ran up the dark stairs, stairs that smelled of cabbage and urine, ahead of Montrose, pausing only to glance back at his face to be certain she was before the correct door, then she strode in, an avenging household goddess. Caesar lay on a cot, staring out a tiny window at the leaden sky. His withered arm, its tiny hand, lay outside the covers. He turned listlessly at the door's opening.

"So," Thérèse said, walking toward him, "this is how you end up when you have nothing more to do with your friends.

Poor as a churchmouse and feeling sorry for yourself in the bargain. I hear you have lost everything. Well, so have I. But you do not see me lying in a bed like an invalid, crying in my pillow. No! And why? Because I have people who care for me. I have God, and the blessed Lord Jesus and his Holy Mother, and there is nothing more in life that is necessary, nothing—" She stopped, on a breath turning into a sob, horrified with herself. She had not meant to say these things. They had just come out.

"Thérèse! I-I was sorry to hear of Harry. . . . Oh, Thérèse, it is so good to see you," Caesar said slowly, and she burst into tears, crying, crying for herself, for the enormous hurt in her, the ache, crying for this life that was so hard to live sometimes, in spite of God, in spite of faith.

"You are loved," she sobbed. "And that is more important than anything in the world."

He got out of bed, and took her in his good arm. She sobbed against him. He stroked her hair, and murmured her name and said he was sorry, and she knew he meant Harry. Yes, they were all sorry. Harry.

Montrose remained transfixed at the door. Finally, he managed to get hold of himself and come inside the room. He opened the basket.

"A little food, a little wine," he said. "That is what we need."

Thérèse blew her nose.

Caesar smiled. His smile was ragged at the edges, without the inner mirth that had once made it so special. But it was a smile nonetheless. "Food, wine, and the two of you," he said. "A feast for the gods. In truth."

That night, tired, Barbara went into the bedchamber where her trunks were, searching for paper on which to write a letter to her grandmother. Thérèse sat in a chair, cloths for cleaning and jewels scattered in her lap, looking at something in the palm of her hand and crying. Crying as if her heart were broken.

"Thérèse!" Barbara said, running to her, but she jumped up, the cloths and jewels falling to the floor, as well as what was in her hand, and ran from the room. Barbara knelt down to pick up the jewels and saw Harry's mourning ring. She picked it up and stared at it. Harry . . . Thérèse. . . .

She found Thérèse in the housemaids' bedchamber. Two housemaids sat in bed, laughing and talking as if Thérèse, lying across another bed, did not exist. They stopped laughing at the sight of Barbara, stared sullenly at her a moment, then rose from the bed to make slow curtsies. Why are they not working? thought Barbara, her eyes narrowing. She looked at them coldly, other things she had seen and heard in this household coming to mind.

"Get out," she said.

They scurried from the room. Thérèse sat up and wiped her eyes. She began to stammer an apology. Barbara held out her hand and opened it.

"Here," she said.

Thérèse stared at Barbara's palm. In it was the ring.

"Do you—do you wish me to clean it?"

"I wish you to have it."

Thérèse stared at the ring. She opened her mouth, but Barbara interrupted her.

"No! Do not say anything. I could not bear it. I-I loved him so."

She put the ring down abruptly on the bed and left the room.

Gently, Thérèse picked it up. She held it tightly in her hand. She would wear it on a gold chain, on the chain that held her tiny crucifix. It would lie between her breasts with the crucifix, near her heart, a reminder of how she had loved him. She lay back on the bed. . . . She had promised Caesar that she would see him tomorrow, and she would. When a person was on the edge, as Caesar was, it was important to see others' love, others' caring. If Harry had had someone in London . . . She could not finish the thought. Tears seeped down her cheeks. She began to pray. Hail Mary, full of grace, the Lord is with thee. . . .

Downstairs, Barbara banged open the door to the library. Montrose, huddled among his inkpots and lists, stared at her.

"I want a list of all the servants in this household and the back wages owed to each. Tomorrow."

"Lady Devane. Lady Devane!"

Justin shook her out of sleep. She was out of the trundle bed instantly, moving toward the sickbed. He is dead, she thought. "The fever is broken," said Justin behind her.

She felt Roger's forehead. It was damp. His hair was matted with sweat. She touched his cheek with her own. It was cool. The fever was broken.

Justin smiled, she clapped her hands and covered her mouth to laugh. The fever was broken. Justin bowed, and she curtsied, and they did a country jig once around the room together, in the dark, stumbling into furniture, holding their laughter in like children doing something forbidden, and thus laughing even harder. The fever was broken.

That morning, the doctor felt Roger's pulse and frowned. He is still an ill man, he said, but Barbara did not care what he said. Roger's fever had broken. He was going to live. She would not allow him to die. She left the doctor clucking over Roger and threw on a shawl and went outside. He was going to live. When he woke, she would tell him how much she loved him, and she would nurse him carefully. If there was any way, any way possible, she was going to take him to Tamworth. She glanced up at the sky. There was not much time. One or two good rains, snow, and the roads would be impossible. The muddy ruts would rattle him to death. She would take him away from this house with its surly servants, take him away from London with its lying news sheets and gossips, to convalesce at Tamworth. Secure. Safe. Among those who loved him, and by spring, he would be well.

A horseman trotted up the circular road to the house and she ran forward, thinking it was Tony. Charles was off his horse in one lithe movement and holding her hands before she had a chance to speak.

He smiled down at her, and she saw herself reflected in his eyes. No rouge or powder, faded old gown, someone's woolen shawl. And she did not care.

"He is going to live, Charles," she said, taking her hands out of his. "The fever is broken." She looked up at the leaden sky and laughed out loud. "He is going to live!"

She felt suddenly like dancing, like running. Something that had been squeezing her heart had eased its hold, and she had not even realized it, until now, when it was gone. I feel like celebrating, she thought. Celebrating survival, for I begin to think simple survival a feat in itself. He is going to live.

Charles watched her face. Everything she felt was clear on it. Goddamn me for a fool, he thought, staring at her face. Only she makes me act such a fool.

"Come and have tea with me," she said, her grandfather's smile on her face.

He shook his head. "I am happy at your happiness, Barbara. I rode over only to see how Roger—and you—did. And so I see. I have some happy news of my own. I wanted to tell you in person. I think I am going to be married."

He said the words calmly, as if he were telling her of the purchase of a new horse, his arms crossed on his chest, his eyelids half closed. At his ease.

She was silent. Finally, she said, flippantly, the Barbara of this summer, to cover what she really felt, "My condolences to the bride."

He threw back his head and laughed. She wanted to slap him. He stepped toward her, his eyes no longer half closed. "Give me a kiss of congratulations, for old times' sake. We both have what we want, do we not?"

He was looking at her in a mocking, half-challenging way, and she wanted to slap him again, and she stepped forward and kissed him quickly, hard, on the lips, but he caught her by her shoulders and said, his voice as mocking as his eyes, "Not like that. Never like that, Barbara. You have forgotten old times, I see. I will remind you." And he put his mouth slowly, deliberately, on hers, and she felt the shock of its warmth all the way through her body, and she thought . . . Charles . . . we might have been, we came so close, but I could never give you the whole of my heart . . . and then his tongue grazed hers, and she leapt back out of his arms, fiercely, frowning, saying, "Roger! Roger needs me! I do congratulate you. I do! Goodbye, Charles."

And she ran all the way to the house, not looking behind her even once. And in the house, she peeped through thick draperies at him, and he was still there, staring at the house, but a fog was in, slowly rolling over and over, through the gates, down the lane, slowly obscuring him.

* * *

When Roger woke, she was there. He opened his eyes and saw her and struggled to lift his hand, but could not and she lifted it for him and kissed it. "I am here. I love you," she said. "You are with me. I will take care of you."

"Barbara." He croaked out her name. "H-hurts."

"Hush, now. Go back to sleep. Rest. You must rest. And then you will get well. If you rest."

A carriage drove into the circular road and wheeled before Devane House. Diana and Annie descended from it, and strode purposefully up the steps and into the house.

"Where is my daughter?" said Diana, pulling off black gloves and glancing down the hall.

"In the library," said Cradock, bowing.

"And Lord Devane?"

Cradock smiled. "His fever has broken."

"Oh," said Diana.

In the library, Barbara and Montrose were going through the list of servants.

"There was a riot in the lobby of Westminster yesterday," Montrose said.

Barbara shivered. "I want to take him away from here. I was thinking of closing the house, leaving only you and Cradock. If I sell my pearl tiara, it ought to more than cover the cost of wages to the other servants. As far as I am concerned, there is not a one among them worth—"

The library door opened dramatically, and Diana swept in, Annie following dourly behind.

"Annie!" Barbara said, jumping up. "Annie!"

"I have come to nurse that husband of yours. Your grandmother sent me."

"I want to go to Tamworth, Annie. I want to take him away from here. The doctor says a journey will kill him, but, oh, I want him out of here. Go and see him. Through those doors there. Did you bring Grandmother's medicines? Oh, Annie, I cannot tell you how glad I am to see you. Francis," Barbara said, turning to Montrose, "Annie can cure anyone."

Montrose coughed and glanced toward Diana, who stood to one side, watching Barbara with eyes that were both reproachful and mocking.

"Mother," Barbara said. "I am glad to see you, too."

"Yes," said Diana. "So I see."

She looked at Montrose, who coughed again and left the room. Diana sat down. She picked up the piece of paper that held the names of the servants. Her face was hard, cold.

"Have you been to court?"

"No, Mother."

"And do you plan on going?"

Barbara's jaw hardened. "No, Mother." She tensed for the argument she knew was coming.

"I see."

Diana stood up and pulled back on her gloves. At the door, she said, "Do me the courtesy of letting me know when you leave town."

Thérèse fed White another spoonful of soup, talking all the while. "—and his fever broke early this morning. How glad we were! Madame Barbara was dancing around that house like a little girl. And this afternoon, her mother and Annie— Annie is the Duchess's tirewoman and she knows everything about nursing—arrived. Madame Barbara says Annie will make Lord Devane well again." She smiled, and White smiled back.

She leaned forward to put down the bowl, and her necklace swung out of her gown.

"May I?" asked White, and he held the mourning ring between two fingers.

"Harry's," Thérèse said. She kissed the ring and crossed herself and put the necklace back inside her gown. "Now," she said, "I have a proposition to lay before you."

White arched an eyebrow.

"We are closing down Devane House if we can leave, and only Montrose and one other servant will be there. I told Lady Devane about you—no, Caesar. Do not look at me that way. I told her only that you were in London, and she suggested that you come to stay at the house with Montrose."

"I do not need anyone's charity—"

"Shut up. I hate false pride. She made the offer out of her regard for you. She has no idea—of this," said Thérèse, making a gesture with her hand that took in his shabby room. White frowned.

"And why not? I thought. It would give Montrose company, and you a place to become stronger. You might begin writing again. Well, you might. You can at least write to me. And in the spring, you could come to Maidstone, which is close to Tamworth, and convalesce."

Thérèse stood up. "You think about it. I will be back tomorrow."

She put the bowl and spoon back into a basket and straightened the covers about White's body and fluffed his pillows. He watched her with eyes that were not as listless as the day before. She shook out her gown and tied her cloak and pulled the hood up over her face and picked up the basket. She kissed his forehead and went to the door. She paused.

"I overheard someone say Alexander Pope lost half his fortune, and John Gay everything."

White frowned at her.

She smiled back. "We are never alone in our misfortune, Caesar. Sometimes it only seems so." And she closed the door before he could think of a reply.

Annie sat down at a table in the room Barbara had given her and dipped her pen in ink. She must write a letter to her Duchess, who would be waiting for it, who would not rest or sleep properly until she heard from her. They would be bringing Lord Devane to Tamworth, just as soon as Mistress Barbara closed the house and dismissed the servants. The Duchess must prepare for him. And other things. Annie shook her head as she wrote. Lord Devane was dying. Mistress Barbara would not see it, but he was. If she was careful, if she delicately added the mandrake to the foxglove, she could deaden the pain this journey would give him. And who knew? The foxglove might prolong his life . . . for a while. Mistress Barbara was correct in her impulse to want to take him to Tamworth. A man needed to die with people who loved him by his side. In a house filled with tradition and memory. Where others had died, so that Death was not unfamiliar, not frightening, to its walls, its household heart. She could give him the strength to survive the journey. Yes, that she could do. But no more. There was no medicine, no herb, no power—but the Lord above's—that could save him now.

CHAPTER TWENTY-SEVEN

*R*obert Walpole flung one large, naked leg from under the bed covers and put his hands behind his head to watch Diana brush her hair. She whipped the brush back and forth, totally concentrated on her image in the mirror, and he smiled slightly at the intensity of that concentration. She sat at a dressing table skirted with gauze and lace. Two long arms of gauze wound down on each side of the large mirror affixed to the table's top, and a litter of crystal jars and bottles competed with rouge pots and brushes and ribbons of different colors, cherry, green, primrose, for space. Why she had the ribbons he did not know. She only wore black now. For Harry. But black became her, as she well knew. Clemmie scuttled in and out of his vision, a ponderous lump in moth-eaten satin slippers that had once belonged to Diana, picking up clothes and clearing the table of the supper he and Diana had eaten. She glanced at Walpole sideways and then put her hand in one of the pockets of his waistcoat to steal a couple of coins. Walpole pretended that he did not see her. Grinning with her gap-toothed smile, she clutched the coins in one hand, and the dirty pewter in the other, and still somehow managed to open and close the door behind her, Diana's slippers slapping against her bare heels.

"Does she always steal?"

"Always," said Diana, not taking her eyes from the mirror. She had lost weight since Harry's death, and it made her face harder, colder.

"And you?" he asked.

"Whenever I can." Though he had been joking, Diana answered seriously, concentrated now on rubbing l'eau de Ninon into her cheeks, and particularly into the deep lines on each side of her mouth. She missed the irony, that the water was named after a famous French courtesan, said to have remained beautiful far past the time to age, but Walpole did not.

"Do you think Barbara has reached Tamworth yet?" he asked, his mind on age and beauty and death, and therefore Roger.

"Who knows?"

"You seem remarkably unconcerned."

Diana rubbed the water into her face with deft, hard strokes. "On the contrary, I am remarkably concerned, but when has she ever listened to me? She does exactly as she pleases. Now people are saying his illness is a false one. That he has fled the city and taken thousands of pounds with him and that Brussels, not Tamworth, is his final destination. I could have told her they would say that, but she would not have listened." She screwed the lid irritably back on l'eau de Ninon and rummaged through her many jars and bottles and pots for another. "Will the Commons press for an inquiry?"

Walpole rubbed his eyes tiredly. "I will do all I can to stop one."

"But can you stop an inquiry?"

"I do not know. All I know is that the best way to end this crisis is to concentrate on stabilizing the economy and not on punishing the directors—"

"That sounds like a sentence from a speech you are planning for the Commons."

"As a matter of fact, it is," Walpole said. "Lord, I wish I had seen Roger before he left. Carlyle said he was so ill. Roger Montgeoffry. Ill. In all the time I have known him he has never changed, except somehow to grow more handsome. I became fatter with the years, and older, and he more handsome. He has been a good friend to me, Diana. I will screen him when Parliament begins."

"You have so many to screen: the ministry, the king, the prince. Some of them will slip through the cracks."

"Not Roger. I promise."

"I hope to God you can keep your promise. I have spent this entire morning dealing with Harry's creditors. I do not want another bankrupt in the family. Who is Alexander Pendarves?"

The question surprised him. Suspicious, he leaned on his elbows to stare at her. She, however, appeared fascinated by something she had just discovered on her chin.

"He is a member from Newcastle," he said slowly, "a rich, miserable old miser who has not been to a Parliament in some twenty years, but is at this one to see vengeance done to the men who made him lose a half-guinea on the exchange. Now, why, Diana, do you ask?"

"Robert, whatever can this be on my chin? Just look!" And she swiveled around and thrust out her chin; there was nothing on it.

"It is enormous."

"Which chin, Diana?" And then as she glared at him, "Put a patch on it. It is probably a witch's wart."

He lay back on the pillows chuckling, suspicion forgotten, in his delight at his own wit.

Heavy rain pelted down as two carriages pulled into Tamworth's avenue of limes. Barbara wiped her eyes, kicked at her horse's sides with her heels and rode up to the carriage holding Annie and Roger. She knocked on its door with a riding crop. Annie rolled up the leather shade.

"We are here," Barbara said, rivulets of rain streaming down her face and neck in spite of the hood on her cloak. Annie nodded her head.

Inside the carriage, she leaned over the makeshift board bed created for Roger and felt his pulse. It was weak, a thread. He lay with his eyes closed and his mouth drawn in, pinched and blue at the edges. She felt his forehead, but there was no fever.

" 'This was a dreadful Sight to me, especially when going down to the Shore, I could see the marks of Horror,' " read Hyacinthe, curled up beside the Duchess and the dogs and Dulcinea in her big bed, " 'which the dismal Work they had been about had left behind it, viz. The Blood, the Bones, and part of the Flesh of humane Bodies eaten and devour'd by—' " He stopped, lifting his head to listen, put down the book and got up to run to the window. He turned, his dark eyes shining.

"They are here! They are here!"

The dogs leapt from the bed, as if they understood. The Duchess forgot about savages and blood and bones.

"Run down and see for sure. Hurry, boy! Run for me! And tell that rascal Tim to come and fetch me."

She leaned back against the pillows, feeling the tiredness begin from the little bit of excitement just experienced. She shook her head and closed her eyes. Tim walked in. She opened her eyes.

"It took you long enough," she snapped. "Hurry, now. Master Giles is home from school, and it seems an age since—" She broke off, aware from Tim's face that something was wrong with what she had just said.

"It is Lady Devane, ma'am," Tim said gently, "with her husband, who is ill. Master Giles is—" He did not finish.

"He is dead."

She and Tim were both silenced by her words. But Tim recovered first.

"Here, now. Lady Devane has come all this way just to be with you. Are you going to sit up here and brood, or are you coming downstairs with me?" And then, to her astonishment, he winked at her.

"Impudent—you have no manners! No manners at all! In my day, a footman would have been flayed alive for such conduct! My household is falling to pieces! To pieces, while I lie up here and rot!" She sighed. She felt better. Invigorated almost. She glared at him. "Take me downstairs."

The great hall bustled with activity. Perryman was loudly and importantly ordering footmen about. Hyacinthe and the dogs—yapping shrilly—ran from Barbara to Thérèse, clearly unable to make up their minds which of them to stay with. Barbara, her cloak and hair drenched, was ordering footmen to be careful as they carried Roger in, covered with blankets, lying on a board, Annie and a thin, neat man who the Duchess guessed was his valet holding a cloak over him to shield him from the pouring rain outside the door.

The Duchess pointed toward Roger, and Tim carried her over. Annie folded her lips tightly at the way the Duchess looked and glared at Perryman, who glared back (each had

secretly missed the other), but the Duchess had eyes only for
Roger. He looked worse than she had expected, and she had
expected the worst from Annie's letters. He groaned and
opened eyes of startling blue contrasted to the whiteness of his
face.

"Alice . . ." he whispered slowly, and he tried to smile, but
the effort cost too much, and he closed his eyes.

The Duchess met Annie's eyes. She met the eyes of the little
man who was Roger's valet. She met the eyes of Thérèse.
Then she looked at Barbara, dripping with rain, and Barbara
smiled brightly back at her, Roger's hand held in hers.

"I have brought him home for you to nurse. Roger"—she
leaned down to him—"you are at Tamworth. Where you are
going to get better."

And then she was all movement, outdoing even Perryman,
as she ordered the footmen to be careful as they carried Roger
up the stairs, called instructions to Thérèse and Annie and
Justin, hugged Hyacinthe, bent down to pet the dogs, who
kept leaping up on her skirts, shrugged out of her wet cloak,
running her hands through her wet hair. All the while, smiling.

"Take me upstairs," the Duchess said to Tim, and they fol-
lowed behind Roger. She felt weak. Weak and sick at heart.
I do not possess the strength to deal with this, she thought.
Harry's dying; it all has taken too much.

In the duke's bedchamber, Barbara rushed about seeing
Roger comfortably settled. The room smelled of clean linen
and lemon and lavender, and the fire crackled in the fireplace, but Roger shivered and moaned as he was laid on the
sheet. Justin tucked blankets carefully about him while Barbara rubbed his cold hands and called for Annie and told him
she would feed him tea and toast herself.

"You are home," she said to him. "You will be better soon.
I promise. Tamworth is the cure for anything."

Roger's mouth was a grim line, as was Annie's when she
came up behind Barbara to stare down at him.

"Give him more of the medicine," Barbara said. Then,
"Annie, was I wrong? To bring him here? He looks so—" and
she could not finish.

"He would be the same anywhere." Annie moved her to one side and motioned to Justin. "Help me to lift him up on the pillows—"

Barbara walked from the room, and as she closed the door on Justin and Annie trying to lift Roger, she sagged a moment against it. Terrible, dark fears rose in her mind. She swallowed and breathed deeply in and out for a few moments, until they went away. She smoothed back her hair and went into her grandmother's bedchamber. The Duchess lay back against her pile of pillows, eyes closed, one hand stroking Dulcinea, and Barbara sat down on the bed and held one of her grandmother's gnarled hands against her own soft cheek. Constancy. There was such comfort this moment in her grandmother's constancy. She could count on that . . . as she could count on nothing else. The Duchess opened her eyes.

"The journey tired him, Grandmama. We had rain these last two days. Pouring rain. We packed warm bricks all about him because Annie said it would be bad if he caught a chill. I know there must be a cordial or a draft somewhere"—she could hear herself babbling, but she could not stop—"somewhere in those receipt books of yours that will give him some relief, that will help him rest—"

"There is."

"I knew there would be. I had to take him from London. I had to. The news sheets. They were writing such things about him. They were—"

"Hush, now. Hush."

Childlike, Barbara laid her head against her grandmother's chest, feeling the brocade of her bed robe prickle against her cheek. The Duchess stroked her hair, the drying curls. Now, she thought. While I have a little strength. Now.

"He will be better in the spring, I think," Barbara said.

"And I do not. Listen to me, Barbara, and be brave. Roger—"

"Do not say it!"

Her ferocity surprised the Duchess. Barbara sat up in her arms, her eyes blazing.

"The last time someone said those words to me Harry was dead. I will not listen. Not again! Do you hear me? I will not listen!"

An edge of hysteria lay in that voice. The Duchess could feel herself reeling, somewhere far off in her mind. Hear this now, foolish people, and without understanding; which have eyes, and see not; which have ears, and hear not. . . . Barbara will not hear . . . she will not see. . . . Richard . . . and she closed her eyes and gray mists seemed to swirl in her head, bringing forgetfulness . . . blessed . . . she drank the waters of the River Lethe, which gave the gift of forgetfulness to those who drank from its cool depths. . . . Lethe . . . in Hades . . . Heaven and Hell. . . . Someone was shaking her shoulders gently . . . bringing her back. . . . She did not want to come back . . . pain was here . . . more dying . . . Richard . . .

"I did not mean it, Grandmama. Please open your eyes! Please talk to me! But not of Roger. Later, we can talk of him. Please, Grandmama—"

The Duchess opened her eyes. "I must write to your mother of Harry and Jane," the Duchess said. "The match will not do—"

Barbara caught her breath, and the Duchess knew something was wrong. And then, she knew what. And she could not bear the look on Barbara's face.

"I remember, Bab. I do. Harry—" Her face crumpled like a child's, and she began to cry. "Harry is dead. I know. I remember. I am old. That is all. Old." And you will not hear me, Barbara, and my heart hurts for you.

Dear God, thought Barbara, holding her grandmother in her arms and rocking her. I am going to break. Like glass. Into hundreds of sharp pieces. She took a deep breath. I will not break. I am strong. I can help myself. And those that need me.

"I loved him so," her grandmother was sobbing in her arms. "I should have given him more money when he asked me, but I did not. I did not understand."

"No, Grandmama," said Barbara, feeling tears for Harry swell up in her own throat, but refusing to shed them, knowing that if she began, she would never stop, not with Roger lying as he did, in the next room. "None of us did."

"I am glad you are here," said the Duchess, clinging to her. "So glad you are here."

* * *

The November rains brought sleet and frost, a prelude to the coming snows of December. Tamworth opened its wintry arms and sheltered those who needed it. Barbara now led the evening prayers. Barbara oversaw the last winter chores of candlemaking and hog killing. Barbara decided when the weather was mild enough for the Duchess to be carried to chapel. Barbara met with the vicar to talk of Advent sermons. Barbara sent to London for a special book for little Jeremy, still ill, a book with brightly painted pictures and characters which folded out. Barbara sat for hours in the stillroom, deciphering the spidery handwriting of some long-ago Tamworth housewife, reading of angel salve and oil of St. John's wort and waters to preserve the sight, cure the stomach, prevent consumption, plague, apoplexy, scurvy, reading of cordials and drafts and pastes, and trying any of those that Annie approved upon Roger. Barbara cajoled the cook into preparing plums stewed in wine and the white meat of capons and delicate stews and broths for Roger, and for her grandmother.

Barbara listened to the complaints of the household staff and decided what should be done. And as the days grew colder and the nights grew longer, and the ancient corners of Tamworth made people shiver with their drafts, Barbara ordered Hyacinthe to begin reading aloud—to any of the household who should wish to listen—the amazing and fantastic adventures of *Robinson Crusoe*. Grooms and stableboys and housemaids and footmen could talk of nothing else through their dreary winter chores. His adventures were the exciting rhythm to which the household moved as November faded into a leaden December. Roads became mud-filled mires. It was a chore to walk to a neighboring farm. The sun set early. Frost covered windows and doors. Cold household corners were avoided as all sought the warmth of the fire. The only news of the outside world came through letters, letters not easily delivered, sometimes a week or more late, and therefore, all the more treasured. . . .

The Duchess did not recognize the handwriting or the seal of the letter before her, and she slapped at Dulcinea, who was determined to play with it. Dulcinea leapt haughtily to Barbara's lap, staring with slitted, green-gold eyes at the Duchess.

Madam,
   I take a great liberty in writing to you, but I have heard much of your fairness and strength, and I knew your husband long ago. He was the finest general I ever had the honor to fight against. And, therefore, I hope you will consider me, in an odd way, an acquaintance, and grant my request. I have recently heard that Lord Devane is gravely ill, and is residing at Tamworth. It would be the greatest kindness if you would write me to let me know how he fares. I enclose my address in the hope that you will, and remain your obedient servant,

Philippe Henri Camille Louis de Bourbon, Prince de Soissons.

Well, thought the Duchess. Well, well, well.
She glanced guiltily at Barbara and folded the letter away before she should see it. Barbara frowned over the letter she was reading, and the Duchess recognized the handwriting; its neat precision could only be Francis Montrose's. Each week he wrote a long letter, and Barbara worried all day after receiving it and stayed up late into the night writing an answer. She and Montrose were trying to deal with Roger's debts.
"Mr. Jacombe is now recommending that we sell Devane House," Barbara said irritably. Mr. Jacombe had something new to recommend each week. "I will never do it. I will pull down every stone and brick myself before I allow anyone to have that house. We are going back there in the spring when Roger is well."
The Duchess did not reply. She knew better than to try to talk with Barbara about Roger's illness. She would not hear. Never had the Duchess seen such obstinate denial. She tried not to think on it too much, of all that lay behind it, tried not to think what would happen when Roger died. She prayed each night to the Lord for strength when that time should come. Because she would need it. Barbara would have none left.
She skimmed through Abigail's letter—without the heart now to enjoy its gossip—Parliament's opening, the king's

speech, Neville and Pitt moving that the directors of South Sea be ordered to open their books before the house, a reference or two to Roger's flight, as his going to Tamworth was now called, Walpole's surprise and dismay, his speech that he had a plan for restoring public credit that was more important than punishing those believed guilty, anger and catcalls from members, a suggestion later, from Lord Molesworth, that directors be tied in sacks and thrown in the Thames.

"The ministry is upset by the Commons' determination to pursue an inquiry," wrote Abigail. "And I agree. The names on the directors' lists for special preference would be embarrassing. I know my name is there, and I should not wish it bandied about by the Commons."

She closed by asking of Roger's health, and then, almost as an afterthought, she wrote that Charles and Mary had signed marriage contracts. "We are planning a quiet wedding by special license in a few days, out of deference to our mourning for Harry. I know you will understand why I ask you to break the news to Barbara. Both Mary and Charles send their love to her, as do I, and we all pray for Roger's recovery."

I would imagine you do, thought the Duchess, folding the letter. Now, how do I begin to tell Barbara this?

"Here is a letter for Roger from Tommy Carlyle," said Barbara, smiling. "I will read it to him when he wakes." She looked out the window, but it was misted with cold. She could see nothing. It was like looking out at nothing. As if there were no world past these windows. "Last spring when I first saw Roger again, I went to a great fete he held at his pavilion of the arts, and all London was there, Grandmama. They hung on his every word; they followed him with their eyes; they admired his wealth and taste. Lord Sunderland stood on one side, and Lord Stanhope on the other. In the gardens, the king strolled with his mistress and his secretaries and his Hanoverians. The prince and princess were there, and Walpole and Townshend and Montagu, and I was so proud. In spite of my anger, I was so proud—" She stopped. "Only Carlyle and Walpole have written him. I do not think I will ever forgive all the others."

"It is politics, Barbara. Those who fall from power are always shunned, by all but a few true friends. We were, the

Marlboroughs were, even Walpole went through his hours of darkness. A year ago he had nothing—"

"But my mother. Speaking of whom, I have a letter from her. Let me see what she writes."

"—and today, Walpole's name is on all lips, and he has a position again in the ministry—"

"Good God." Barbara looked up at her grandmother, a stricken look in her eyes. "Charles and Mary are going to marry. . . . Mary . . . I never thought of Mary!"

"Give me that letter."

She read Diana's brief, curt, tactless sprawl, no date, no greeting, just the words:

Congratulate yourself, Barbara. I know I do. Charles Russel will marry your cousin Mary in a few days. Abigail crows with pride, and so she should. It did not have to happen, as well you know.

Your mother, Diana Alderley

God curse her, thought the Duchess, stealing a march on me, dropping the news like a cannonball into Barbara's heart. God curse her.

She leaned forward. "Barbara . . ." But Barbara was standing up, dropping Dulcinea out of her lap like a stone. It was too much for Dulcinea, who mewed loudly and jumped to the windowsill.

"It hurts me," Barbara said. "I never thought of Mary." And she left the room.

A week before Christmas, when the sky was low and gray, threatening snow, Barbara rode to all the neighboring farms to deliver handwritten invitations to Tamworth's Christmas Eve play, in which she herself would figure, as she had done in the old days. The Duchess was glad to see her go out of the house, away from Roger and her nursing of him. She came back from her outings with bright red cheeks and a brighter red nose and high spirits. She is taking the news of Charles and Mary well, thought the Duchess proudly, as she watched her ride away to Ladybeth Farm to deliver the last of her invitations.

An hour later, Barbara walked into Tamworth kitchen, her fur-lined cloak hood pushed back from her head. Thérèse and Hyacinthe, preparing mincemeat pies for Christmas Day dinner, looked up at her.

"Did you give Lady Ashford the recipe for Jeremy's cough?" asked Thérèse. "And the New Year's gifts—"

"Jeremy—" Barbara began, but her throat closed. She went out the door, toward her grandmother's bedchamber. They had all been crying at Ladybeth, when she arrived, the maidservants, Jane's younger brother and sisters, Lady Nell and Sir John. There was a note from Jane. Jeremy was dead. He had died two days ago. Only last night, she and Thérèse had spent the evening wrapping New Year's gifts for Jane's children, hair ribbons with mottoes on them, wooden animals, a hoop and a stick for Jeremy when he was well. She held a note in her hand. A note from Jane to her. It said:

You will know by now that my Jeremy is dead. He died peacefully in our arms. It is the Lord's will, and he suffered so, that at last, I was thankful to let him go. He loved the painted book that you sent to him. I read it to him over and over. Thank you for that, Barbara. The others are well. I cannot write anymore. Not today.

"Shall we cancel the Christmas play?" asked the Duchess, holding her.

"No," Barbara whispered, huddled against her. "Let us have this one Christmas together, as it used to be."

Everyone sat in the great parlor, wreathed with evergreen and holly, a huge yule log burning in the fireplace, amid whispering, rustling, waiting. Hyacinthe sat near the Duchess, his eyes shining with anticipation, and the younger servants giggled and fidgeted restlessly among themselves. This year, once more, Lady Devane was playing a lazy, insubordinate maid to Perryman's Duchess. The older servants whispered to the younger ones that one had not seen anything until one had seen Lady Devane and Perryman play off each other. Vicar Latchrod agreed, his nose red; he had already been tippling at the Christmas punch.

The Duchess sat dressed in her finest, as she did every year for this Christmas Eve play held in her honor, parodying her, one of the highlights of Tamworth's year. She wore a black velvet gown, and diamonds glittered on her fingers and around her throat and even in her lace cap. Her legs were aching, and she was tired. Very tired. Death, too much death. One never knew from where it would come. Young Jeremy had died from an inflammation of the lung. Harry by his own hand. Richard of a broken heart. Dicken and Giles and her grandchildren from smallpox. But it could have been measles, consumption, gout, humors of the blood, fever, rickets, palsy, a cut or sore or cold that did not heal. . . . She glanced down at Roger, propped in that bed that had been carried down and set up for him. How careful the footmen had been not to hurt him as they moved him, yet still he could not suppress a groan or two. He lay back now against the pillows with his eyes closed. His mouth was pinched in, and his cheeks had a flush the Duchess did not like, and he had lost so much weight in these last weeks that he no longer resembled himself.

He opened his eyes and seeing her, tried to smile. The old wistfulness was still there. You were the handsomest man I ever saw, barring Richard, thought the Duchess. He thought the world of you. She blinked her eyes at the sudden tears welling in them. She would not cry tonight. This was Barbara's night. She had worked so hard for it. She and Thérèse and Hyacinthe had wreathed every room in the house and all the mantels and windows and Tamworth church and chapel. There were bay-scented candles burning. They would have their Christmas dinner tomorrow in this room with all the servants. A Christmas as it used to be. The Duchess thought of all those Christmases she and Richard had shared, when her sons rose tall and handsome around her, with their young wives and families. There was no Christmas as it used to be. Roger made a restless movement, and she leaned over him.

"Save your strength for the play. In her girlhood, Barbara could convulse a saint when she was in the mood—Roger, what is it?"

She leaned over farther so that she was near his face.

"Take care . . . of her," he whispered.

"Take care of her," snapped the Duchess. "You are a fine one to give me orders. On Christmas Eve. You are dying, and

I am old. What can I do? You just take care of yourself! That is what you do!"

He gave a weak laugh, a ghost of itself. "I should . . . have married you, Alice. . . ."

He was charming to the last. Even dying could not extinguish that. "Bah!" she said to cover her feelings. "I would not have had you! Not on a silver platter! Now hush. The play is beginning."

Barbara was wonderful. The serving maids and footmen screamed with laughter. She was outrageous, hilarious, running over to snatch the vicar's wig and wear it herself, dancing with St. George and his dragon, parodying the lord of misrule so that even those who acted with her could not help laughing. Hyacinthe cried with laughter, wiping tears from his face and holding his stomach. When Barbara whacked Perryman's Duchess across the rear with a broom, the Duchess went into such a fit of coughing laughter that the play stopped until she was well again. Even Annie was surprised into a grim chuckle or two. When the play was over, everyone stood up and whistled and cheered and clapped, and called her name. Barbara curtsied to the audience and picked her nose and tried to wipe it on Perryman. Hyacinthe bayed with laughter; Justin pulled off his wig and waved it; Thérèse laughed and clapped; the Duchess wiped her eyes with a handkerchief. Hyacinthe released the dogs, and they ran to Barbara, excited by the noise, and leapt and flipped in the air, and everyone clapped even harder. It was the best play ever, they all agreed.

"Punch and ale," said the Duchess, stamping her cane on the floor. "Punch and ale."

Barbara walked over to Roger, breathless, perspiring with her performance.

"He looks tired," she said to Justin, who nodded his head and went to fetch the footmen to carry him upstairs. Barbara bent down.

"Did you like me?" she asked. "Did I make you laugh?"

Roger stared at her, his mouth compressed. "I . . . hurt . . ."

She felt his forehead with her hand. Then with her lips. Was she wrong, or was he too warm?

"Annie!" she called, a rising note in her voice. "I should have left you upstairs," she said to him.

His eyes were bright, so blue against the terrible whiteness of his face. A bright, burning blue.

She put her ear to his mouth. He seemed to want to say something.

"I . . . love . . . you," he whispered. She held his hot, dry hand all the way up the stairs.

She sat tiredly in the window seat in Roger's bedchamber. Finally, the snow had stopped. It had snowed all this Christmas Day. They had not gone to church; no one had come to carol to them. Even the Christmas dinner was muted and quiet, because the Duchess did not feel well enough to come downstairs, and Barbara got up from the table every few moments to check on Roger. She could not help it.

I would like to walk to Tamworth chapel, she thought, and sit awhile. Say a prayer for Jeremy, for Harry. For Roger. The snow outside was as white as Harry's face in death. She closed her eyes. Charles and Mary would be married now. She remembered her own white wedding gown, trimmed with green. How excited and happy she had been. Her brothers and sisters had crowded around her, loud in their love and excitement. How tired I am, she thought. It was as if the Christmas play had taken the last of her strength. Jeremy's death and doing the play in spite of it and Roger's fever. She must write a note to Jane and Gussy. Dear little Jeremy. How white the snow was. Tomorrow she would go outside and build a snowman with Hyacinthe before Roger's window. He would like that. And she would pick more holly to put in his room. He was sleeping now. When he woke, she would tell him about the snowman and the holly. And how in just four weeks, it would be their anniversary. They would be married—

Justin made a sound. She lifted her head.

He stood staring down at the bed. She felt her heart begin to beat so rapidly that it hurt her head. She stood up. Justin looked at her.

"He—" He did not finish.

She tried to run to the bed, but it seemed to take her a long time, an eternity of time. Roger lay on the bed, not restless now, not tossing and turning as he had done all night and into the day, so that she could not eat her dinner, could not say Christmas prayers, could not think of anything but him. He lay still, and peaceful.

Timidly, she reached out and touched his face, his beloved face, which was too thin. He would look better when he had some of his weight back. The fever was gone. He was cool to the touch.

"Lady Devane," Justin said, his voice breaking as he took her by the arm. "He is—"

"Do not say it, Justin."

She could hear how calm she sounded. How cool. Like Roger's forehead. She sat down on the bed and took Roger's hand in hers. "Do not say it just yet, and then it will not be true."

She felt something splinter inside herself, but did not know what it was. She heard Justin leave the room, and she was glad, glad to be alone with Roger, for a moment, just the two of them, because until someone said the words, cried and screamed, it would not be true. He was alive until someone said he was dead and began to grieve.

"I loved you so," she said to Roger, who did not answer, who did not move, who did not even breathe, but lay there, so silent, so peaceful, handsome to her even in illness, even in death. She rocked back and forth now, his hand against her breast, the beginning of grief welling in her, grief that seemed dark, bottomless, opening like a dark chasm beneath her. "Since I was a little girl," she said to Roger, and in her mind was a sudden shining memory of how handsome he had looked atop his great black horse, smiling down at her, the child who loved him, smiling and leaning down and lifting her up, up into the sky it seemed, and putting her before him in the saddle, holding her close with one strong arm, his horse leaping forward under them; she could feel the power of that leap still if she closed her eyes, propelling them forward, faster and faster, past gardens and cottages and hedges, and her hair streamed out behind her and he laughed, and she felt—in her childhood—there would never be a moment as good as this one. Never. Galloping with Roger Montgeoffry holding her on his great black horse across the tender green fields and pastures of Tamworth. . . .

CHAPTER TWENTY-EIGHT

The snow fell and fell and fell. It was impossible to get in or out of Tamworth, even by sled, for the horses stumbled in the drifts. Roger lay in the great hall, huge candles burning at the head and feet of his hastily built coffin, a coffin of raw boards. He lay packed in snow, but even so, he was changing, his face somehow sinking in, pulling toward the earth, the faintest but most inevitable of shifts. We must close the lid, the Duchess said to Barbara gently, tomorrow if the snow should stop even for a short while, we must bury him. Vicar is ready. But I am not, thought Barbara. The notes informing family and friends of his death lay piled neatly on a table. How late into the night, as the candles burned down to guttering stubs, had she and Thérèse and Annie written, their pens scratching over the paper, writing words, terrible, final words . . . and now the snow made their being sent impossible, just as it made the ordering of elaborate coffins or funeral palls or invitations or mourning rings and gloves from Maidstone impossible. The church bell would toll, muffled by the snow which had transformed the landscape, and only she and her grandmother and the servants and those neighbors who might brave the snow would attend his funeral service. He would lie in Tamworth vault; there was no place else to entomb him.

It is not fair, Barbara thought, leaning her swollen face against the icy panes of a window. He will be buried with no pomp, no ceremony, and it is not fair. She wanted crowds, she wanted a long lying-in-state as mourners filed past his coffin, she wanted an elaborate funeral procession, the carriages draped in black, black bridles, black feathers on the horses, she wanted weeping and wailing and gnashing of teeth. Sitting cross-legged on the cushions of a window seat, staring out at the snow which made all impossible, she rocked to and fro. He would lie in Tamworth vault; yet surely he had planned to lie beneath the stone floor of the church Wren had begun to build for him at Devane Square. They had never discussed it, yet surely it was his plan. Not to lie in the vault of her ancestors, near the coffin of her brother. He and Harry had not spoken in the last years of their lives, yet now they were equals in death. Would their ghosts rise up from their coffins and bow coldly and make peace? Surely death had taken the edge from Harry's temper . . . as it took the edge from all things. . . .

The dogs leapt unexpectedly into her lap and licked at her face.

"Come," said someone.

Thérèse. Her dear Thérèse. And Hyacinthe, standing solemnly, taking her hand, leading her away, as if she were the child and he the grown-up. You must rest now, said Thérèse. The two of them led her to her bedchamber—actually, four of them, with the dogs winding in and out of her skirts, knowing something was wrong, wanting to lie in her lap, to lick her hands, to offer their devotion for Roger's going. Such a final going. So much more final than she could have ever dreamed. . . .

"Do not cry," said Thérèse. "Hush, now, madame. We will stay with you while you try to rest."

And so they would. Her family. No more brothers and sisters. No Roger. No child. . . . But two dogs and a page and a serving maid. . . .

Rosemary, that was for remembrance, and all the holly she could gather, as she stomped through the snow, her hands blue with cold, and ivy leaves, forever green. Nothing else to lay atop his coffin. Only bare branches rimmed with frost. No need for black gloves. No need for mourning rings. No way to buy them. No one to give them to. Look who bore his coffin in: Squire Dinwitty, Tim, Perryman, Justin, two grooms. Roger Devane, who dined with princes and laughed with

kings and served under generals. The church was as cold as
ice. All of them shivered in their cloaks. Vicar Latchrod's teeth
chattered as he hurriedly read the funeral service. . . . I am
the resurrection and the life, saith the Lord, he that believeth
in me, though he were dead, yet shall he live. . . . Roger had
not believed in God. . . . Murmurs of condolence surrounded
her, a blur of chapped faces and doffed caps. They were in a
hurry to go home, to sit before their fires, and she could not
blame them. . . . The sun shone as she walked out of the
church. Everyone's boots crunched in the snow, which glistened, wetly, like tears. Icicles hung from the bare, brown
branches of the trees. If the sun shines on them long enough,
they will weep, too, thought Barbara. We shall send out the
notes today, said her grandmother, staring up at the sky. In
the spring, she said, staring just as intently at Barbara's face,
you could hold a memorial service for him. In London. Yes,
Barbara said, her face changing slightly, becoming more alive.
So I could. I want a marble bust and a memorial tablet and—
she stared at her grandmother. I miss Harry, she said, her face
changing again. He was with me in Paris, Grandmama, when
Roger left before— Her grandmother patted her hand. It must
be a fine service, she said. One befitting his station. You must
plan it carefully. Yes, said Barbara. Yes, I must.

Montrose burst into the small room at Devane House which
White was using as a bedchamber. His face was red from the
cold outside, and he still wore a cloak and gloves.

"Is there a letter for me?"

Without waiting for an answer, he shuffled through the
papers and notes on White's table, found what he was looking
for and ripped past the seal.

"Oh, God," he said. "Oh, God, it is true—"

"What is true? Francis, what is wrong?" White got up from
his comfortable chair by the fire.

"Lord Devane is dead."

"I do not believe you!" White strode over and snatched the
letter from him, as Montrose sat down on the bed, the expression on his face dazed.

"I heard it in White's," he said. "Someone was speaking of
it, and I said, repeat yourself, sir, and then when he did, I
threw a cup of coffee in his face, Caesar. I did. And I ran all

the way here, and I said to myself over and over as I ran, It is not true, it is not true. . . . Oh, God . . ." He looked up at White. "I may have to fight a duel."

In spite of his shock, White laughed, which made Montrose laugh also.

"Lord Devane will be so amused—" Montrose broke off. Suddenly, without warning, he began to sob.

White stared past him, past the letter with its words which must be true since they were written by Lady Devane herself, to the windows misted with cold, misted the way a memory is around the edges. Many brave men lived before Agamemnon, but all unwept and unknown they sleep in endless night, for they had no poets to sound their praises, Lord Devane had said. Clerk away in my library, such as it is. Knowing he had no funds, knowing his pride. Write your poems. And I will be your patron. I have an urge to be someone's patron, and it may as well be you, and he had laughed, throwing back his head. The handsomest man White had ever seen, charmed by the sight of him, his laughter, his warmth, his compliments. And his kindness. Kindness to a stiff-necked young poet with a crippled arm and a soul burning to write. I never once told him how much he meant to me, thought White, staring once more at the words of the letter. And now it is too late. He is dead.

Carefully, black brows pulled together in heavy concentration, Walpole poured more brandy into the three glasses on the table. Across from him sat the Duke of Montagu, glassy-eyed. And to his left was Carlyle, without his wig; it hung from the tip of a drapery rod. The four brandy bottles they had finished were arranged in the center of the table, candles burning in their narrow necks. A memorial, Carlyle had said, when he fixed in the first candle, to an absent friend. The waiters at White's were under strict orders to look in on Robert Walpole and his party of two every fifteen minutes, so that they did not burn down the house in their drunken grief.

"To—to the finest . . . friend a man ever had," Walpole said, slurring only a few of the words, his mind on the difficult act of holding his glass and raising it to his lips. "I owed him five thousand . . . and he . . . never asked for—for a penny. . . . Not that I could have paid it."

Montagu made a sound, and the other two turned to him.

"Speak, great duke," bellowed Walpole in his best House of Commons voice.

Montagu opened his mouth. He belched. A long, loud, rumbling belch. Then, without warning, he fell over, his head dropping to the table before him like a cannonball, knocking over the empty brandy bottles with their burning candles, knocking over the half-full brandy bottle from which they had been drinking, knocking over their glasses. Immediately, two waiters entered and stamped out those candles that had not burned out upon impact with the floor. In seconds, they were extinguished, spilled brandy mopped, broken glass swept, a fresh bottle and glasses upon the table. They glanced at the Duke of Montagu lying across the table, his wig tipped over his nose, but Carlyle waved them out.

"Be gone," he said grandly. He stood up, and to the background of Montagu, who had begun to snore, he recited, one hand over his heart, as he swayed dangerously:

"Was this the face that launched a thousand ships?
And burnt the topless towers of Ilium?
Sweet Helen, make me immortal with a kiss.
Her lips suck forth my soul; see, where it flies!
Oh, thou art fairer than the evening air
Clad in the beauty of a thousand stars . . ."

He waited.

Walpole stopped humming the popular ballad he had begun to hum, in time to Carlyle's recitation and said, irritably, "Helen who?"

"Helen of Troy."

"Helen of . . . what has that to do with Roger! Good God, man, my dearest friend has just died, and you stand around reciting some nonsense about Helen of Troy!" He blew his nose on the lace of his sleeve and glared up at Carlyle.

" 'Fairer than the evening air,' " repeated Carlyle. "That was the point." He began to weep, his tears making little paths through the rouge and powder of his face.

"Helen, Helen, Helen," sang Walpole softly, rocking back in his chair. "Helen, Helen, Helen . . ."

* * *

Outside, sleet beat against the windowpanes. Abigail listened to it. Sleet tapping against her window, beating down the branches of the trees, covering the flower beds with another layer of frost. Tony was out in it, riding to Tamworth, to Barbara. She stared down at her hands, puffy around her diamond rings. Roger Montgeoffry, so ageless, so impervious to time, dead. Even though she had seen him at Devane House, seen the seriousness of the attack, she read the words of the letter from Tamworth with a sense of unbelief. Dead. The poisonous tendrils of the South Sea Company had fastened about him and killed him. Walpole had burst into tears upon hearing the news, it was said. The king, in a council meeting, had walked away from his ministers to spend an hour alone in his chapel. Well, Roger was free from South Sea now. He would never stand before the House of Lords and answer their angry questions. He would never be fined or imprisoned, as some in the Commons had demanded. Forbid the directors to leave the kingdom. Inventory their estates. Appoint a committee of secrecy to investigate. Others would bear the burdens he left behind him. Barbara . . . and Tony . . . and others. What shall I do? Mary had sobbed to her yesterday. She will take him back now. One death, and all plans, her children, lay vulnerable. She closed her eyes. The crackling of one of the logs in the fireplace made her open them again. She must write to Philippe. He would want to know. She put her hand to her breast, well exposed in the deep black velvet gown she wore. There was an ache there. He would want to know.

"Jane," said Gussy, coming into her darkened bedchamber. "I have some sad news."

Sad news, thought Jane. Her mind felt dull, wrapped in flannel, like a shroud, like the white flannel shroud one wrapped a dead child in. Jeremy lay outside under the white snow. She had dressed him in his warmest clothes, tenderly wrapping a muffler about his neck and down his chest, so that he should not be cold in his coffin. It was foolish, but it gave her a small comfort, to know he would be warm. His body had been so thin, so frail under her hands as she washed him

that final time. Her mother had helped her. And her Aunt
Maude. And her sisters. Her friends. All soft and murmuring.
Quietly talking as they washed and dressed Jeremy, and
watched her comb his wayward hair. Sharing her grief.
Knowing. Many of them having done the same as she now
did, having bathed and dressed a beloved child for burial.
Where is Jeremy? Amelia had demanded, her tiny hands on
her hips. When will he come back? Never, never, never,
never. I want Bab, Amelia had screamed, and her father had
picked the child up and hushed her. Bab was nursing her husband at Tamworth. He lay dying, said her father. Dying, Jane
had thought dully. This is the winter of death.

"Barbara's husband has died," Gussy said.

He held her hand and began to say prayers. She did not
even know if Barbara loved her husband anymore. Once she
had. She knew she should feel sad for her, but she felt nothing. The hurt for Jeremy took all. Green pastures, thought
Jane. Still waters. Surely the Lord had green pastures and still
waters for her Jeremy. It was the only way she could bear his
death. To believe so. . . .

Barbara lay back against one of the walls encasing a window
seat, the beginnings of a list of those she would invite to a
memorial service thrown to one side, the dogs huddled in her
lap as she scratched their necks and backs over and over. They
said New Year's Day had come and gone, but she had no memory of it. Twelfth Night was around the corner. Cook would
bake the special plum cakes, two of them holding hard black
beans, and those who found them in their cakes would be king
and queen . . . for a night. She closed her eyes. She could not
sleep. She could not eat. She could not think for any length of
time. A feeling of loss came upon her and took her in its jaws
and shook her, leaving her stunned and bewildered. She had
begun the list for the memorial service. Yet she found each name
more difficult than the last to write because each name reminded
her that he was dead. Tears rolled down her cheeks and fell
silently into the fabric of her gown.

Outside, Hyacinthe and two stableboys built a snowman for
her. But she was not watching. When a man rode into view,
his horse tiredly picking its way through white drifts of snow
that covered the avenue of limes, they stopped what they were
doing and ran to him, slipping and falling on the ice. The

man sat straight and slim in his saddle, and he wore a great sloping hat that partially covered his face. As Barbara opened her eyes she saw him dismount and disappear from her sight as he walked into the small stone porch at the front entrance. Charles, she thought for the briefest of seconds, remembering even as his name flashed quicksilver in her mind that now he was married, no longer free to make the impulsive, generous gestures he could sometimes so unexpectedly make. How tired I am, she thought. I do nothing all day, but I am more tired than I have ever been in my life.

The dogs ran to the door, their paws skittering on the floor, whining, each lifting a front paw. They barked as the door opened, and a tall man took off his great hat and smiled slowly, shyly, at her. Tony. He had ridden all this way, through snow and sleet, for her.

She ran across the room to him, stumbling against her long skirts and her dogs, and he caught her in his arms and lifted her off the floor and held her tightly against him, one hand in her hair, so that her cheek was hard against his. His cheek was so cold, so firm, so alive. Roger, she thought. It should be Roger holding me so, and she curled her fingers into the wet folds of his cloak and began to cry again. He carried her across the room to the window seat and sat with her in his lap, and she shivered and trembled and sniffled with her tears, and he untied his cloak and wrenched it off and wrapped it around her, tying it neatly at her neck as if she were a child. She laughed, and hiccuped and then cried even harder. Gravely, he gave her his handkerchief, and she sobbed into it, deep, rasping sobs that shook her body, that felt as if they were tearing out pieces of her heart, clotted pieces of heart. Roger, Roger, Roger. He held her and rocked her, and his love was warm around her like a woolen, fur-lined cloak and it was good, it was kind, it was gentle, it was Tony . . . but it should have been Roger.

"How do you think she does?" Tony asked.

"As well as can be expected." The Duchess's answer was short.

"I brought her letters. From the solicitors, from Montrose. She has many decisions to make, for I am almost certain Roger will have left her executor of his estate, and the Commons are after that estate. Walpole's engraftment is a side issue now. They have selected a committee to investigate wrongdoing, and many want reparations from the directors."

"Roger's death is not enough?"

"Not nearly enough."

Startled, upset by this unexpected visit of Tony's, the Duchess stroked Dulcinea. Tony sat before her rubbing his eyes, slimmer than ever, a dimple having appeared in one cheek from further loss of weight, quite a handsome dimple. His face needed shaving, and somehow that fact made it more masculine, stronger, and she was frightened by it. There was an air of suppressed exictement about him. Of purpose. How he had gotten though the snow she did not know. His horse must be half dead. But Barbara was a widow now, and something lay behind those blue-gray eyes, eyes that reminded her more and more of Richard's in their calmness. He had been with Barbara for hours. She knew. There was nothing that happened in her household that she did not know, if she had a mind to know it. In his lap, Annie had said grimly, her news coming from the housemaid sent to rekindle the fire in Barbara's bedchamber. Barbara slept now like a baby, said Annie, her first long sleep since Roger's death. She slept curled up in her cousin's cloak on the duke's great bed. In his lap. The Duchess had a memory of sitting in Richard's lap long ago. Much could happen in a man's lap, especially a determined man's. Too much.

She watched Tony rubbing his face, stretching. She pretended to half doze, as her cat did. He would break his heart loving Barbara. He would. He frightened her. His growing strength. His young maleness. His determination. Never had she imagined that he would be stronger than she, and yet she lay old and frail and tired in her bed, and he had ridden through miles of snow and bone-chilling cold to see his heart's desire. It was a mistake to show himself so clearly . . . it also showed his youth. . . . He would be formidable with more years on him, far more formidable than she could ever have imagined. She shivered, and Tony, seeing it, leaned forward to pull up her bed covers, and she shrank back from him, forgetting why she was frightened, but feeling frightened just the same.

"Grandmama, are you cold?" He smiled, that sweet, grave smile. A woman could grow to love that smile.

"Go away!" she said harshly in her confusion. "Leave me be!"

Her anger rolled off his back as water did a duck's. He leaned over and kissed her cheek, and she smelled him, leather and horse and sweat and young man. She touched his unshaven face with her gnarled hand—she could not help it—and smiled at him.

"Rest," he said to her. "I will take care of Barbara now."

She snatched her hand away. Frightened again, but not remembering quite why. Something about Barbara. Something about the way she could feel the young, male impatience of him straining against the leash with which he held it. He left the room.

"Annie," she called weakly, her legs paining her, and when Annie did not come, she reached for the small silver bell on her bedside table and in her reaching—the pain had suddenly doubled—she knocked over a vase of winter holly and ivy leaves, and water drenched the books and papers littering her table.

She pushed Dulcinea to one side, and stiffly hoisted herself to rescue her papers . . . too many of them . . . no telling what they were . . . letters months old . . . a deed. A deed?

She waved it to and fro, and then opened it, blowing on the smeared ink. "I, Harry Christopher Alderley, do deed the following to Alice Margaret Constance Saylor, Duchess of Tamworth, if I should not pay her the loan of June 6th, the year of Our Lord 1720, within sixty days . . ."

Well. It was long past sixty days. . . . She struggled to remember . . . something about Harry looking at her with those violet eyes, serious for once . . . leave me some dignity . . . yes, he had said that . . . and she had signed his paper. Carelessly, never intending to keep it. In fact, forgetting it until this moment. She read the deed, squinting. She was mistress of some two or three thousand acres in Henrico County, Virginia, wherever that was. What on earth would she do with this? Add it to Diana's legacy. Or to Tony's. Perhaps leave it to Barbara. The thought struck her then, a bolt of lightning flashing across a dark summer's sky. A wild, foolish, mad thought.

"Richard," she said out loud.

She stared at his portrait above the fireplace. I am stronger than Tony, she thought, remembering now the reason for her fears. But only just. He will be angry. Richard looked at her from the portrait, strong, young, calm, forever gone from her. He will not forgive me. She closed her eyes. She was old. She was foolish. But their times were not right . . . his and Barbara's . . . and it was not her doing, it was life's.

"I will have to bear the consequences," she said to Richard. "He will hate me. And I love him. I do."

Her lower lip trembled. She looked down at the deed. The decision would not be hers . . . only the offering of the opportunity. . . . She felt old and frail.

She rang the silver bell impatiently.

"Pen and paper!" she snapped when Annie finally ran into her bedchamber.

"The way you were ringing that bell, I thought your legs—"

"My legs be hanged. They hurt. They always hurt. I am old. Bring the pen and paper, Annie. Now." And then, to the portrait, "Watch over me. I depend on your care."

A sleigh, pulled by two horses, whose leather bridles were adorned with jingling bells, crept down the avenue of limes, the driver and his two passengers bundled up into anonymous lumps against the cold. When it pulled up before the porch, one of the lumps descended imperiously, knocked impatiently on the front door, swept past Perryman when he opened it, and said in an unmistakable voice—a low, throaty voice that might have been Barbara's, but was not—"Pay the driver and help Clemmie down. She is too fat to move."

Unwrapping layers of shawls and mufflers and scarves and cloaks, Diana walked through the house. Before the door of her father's apartments, she smoothed back the wings of striking gray in her dark hair and smoothed her cold cheeks, nervous gestures, uncharacteristic. She took a deep breath and opened the door. A scene of quiet domesticity met her eyes. Barbara sat before a table writing, Hyacinthe and the two dogs stretched out at her feet under the table, and Tony lounged long and lean in a window seat, reading a book.

Startled at the sight of Tony, who rose as he saw her, she swept forward to Barbara, who put down her pen.

"Mother."

The dogs barked and came out from under the table to leap up on Diana's skirts. She kicked at them, and Hyacinthe called them softly and held them.

"I came as soon as I could," she said. "I have been a week traveling. The weather."

"That was kind of you, but you did not have to come. He is—he is buried. Some two weeks ago. Tony and I are working on the guest list for his memorial service. I intend to hold it in London, as soon as I go there, in a month or so. He—he died quietly, Mother. In his sleep—" Her voice broke, and she stood up abruptly and walked to the window, her back to Diana. Diana frowned at Tony, her expression telling him to go away, but he stayed where he was. His eyes met hers, levelly.

Diana made an impatient movement. She walked forward and put her hand on Barbara's shoulder.

"Barbara," she said, and her voice was soft, none of the hard undertone of which she was such a master. "I am sorry. Truly."

Barbara whipped around. "You never wanted us to be together, not when you saw this South Sea thing! I know that. Well, you have your wish!"

Diana bowed her head and began to cry. Barbara stared at her, her eyes narrowed.

"Why do you cry? You did not love him!"

"But you did!" Diana said, her face contorted, ugly with its weeping. "And you are all I have left! And if I lose you I will have no one. I cry for you." She put her face in her hands, her shoulders heaving. "I loved Harry. And I love you."

Hesitantly, Barbara took one of Diana's hands, and Diana cried even harder. Gently, she helped her to the window seat and sat beside her and patted her hand. Poor Mother, she thought. It is too late, too late for you and me. But she continued to hold her hand. What had her grandmother once told her . . . compassion comes from great pain . . . and so it did.

"I have brought you l-letters," wept Diana. "Letters of condolence. The prince has written one, he was m-most upset. And others were, too. Many cared for him, Barbara."

But I loved him, thought Barbara. And I always will.

* * *

"What the devil is this memorial service?" Diana blew her nose. Her face and eyes were puffy. Swollen. In her bed, the Duchess regarded her through half-closed eyes, as did Dulcinea.

"Something to occupy her mind. In these first months. The death was a shock. She needs the comfort of a ceremony to get her past it."

"Well, she picked a fine time is all I can say."

The hand that stroked Dulcinea never paused, but the Duchess's eyes closed a fraction. She was tired. The composing of the letters about the plantation had left her exhausted, and excited. And she was too old for excitement. And here was Diana, unexpected . . . plowing her way to Tamworth as determinedly as Tony, but not with his quickness. Both of them were concentrated on Barbara.

"A fine time?"

"The Commons is in an uproar. They are in the midst of drafting a bill that forbids the directors to leave the kingdom for one year—"

"Roger can comply with that."

"This is no time for your morbid humor. They want recognizance of a hundred thousand pounds from each director, and do not think they will overlook Roger, dead or not, and two sureties of twenty-five thousand pounds. And they want an inventory of each estate. They are going to assess fines. Perhaps sequester some of the estates. She ought to lie low."

"A simple memorial service—"

"Will remind them not to overlook the Devane estate. They may even try him in absentia."

"They are going to try the directors?"

"Yes."

"Sweet Jesus."

"Yes. I know for a fact that Roger softened the king's mistress for passage of the South Sea Act with some discreet bribery, a chance to obtain stock at no cost. And some of the other ministers. He was in a position to negotiate between the directors and those far higher."

"Bah. It is done all the time. Why is it your concern?"

"Well, for God's sake, Mother, who will marry her if she has no estate? What will she do?"

"Marry? You have someone in mind already? Diana, you shock even me." For a moment the Duchess was breathless, feeling as if she had been carried back five years. As if Diana, and not she, suffered from lapse of memory. Had they not once had the same conversation about Roger?

"Of course I do not. I have only her welfare at heart. I am looking ahead. Planning. Remember how Father believed in foreseeing all difficulties. The only way to truly defeat your enemy, he said. That is all I do. Foresee difficulties."

The Duchess closed her eyes. The irony was that it was true. Diana did have her daughter's welfare at heart. And her concern was good. But her resultant actions . . . well, now . . . that was something else again. Diana would bear watching but then when had she not?

"They will be reading *Robinson Crusoe* downstairs, ma'am," said Annie, coming into the room with Tim behind her.

The Duchess pushed Dulcinea, who rose languorously, stretched even more so, hissed at Diana and flounced off the bed.

"Call Tim! Call Tim! I will not miss it." And then, when she saw Tim, "Where have you been?"

"It is only a book—" began Diana.

"It is not a book!" flashed the Duchess from Tim's arms. "It is an adventure!"

Plow Monday passed, the first farming feast after Twelfth Night. Young plowmen blacked their faces and turned their coats inside out and dressed their plows with ribbons and danced from house to house demanding largess, which they would spend to drink and eat supper at a tavern. Tamworth gave its largess.

St. Agnes's Eve came. Barbara cried at the memory of her wedding, and Tony walked with her through the fresh snow to the chapel so that she could pray near Roger. Now and again, letters came through, welcomed and read aloud before the fire. London was aflame, wrote Abigail. In the night the cashier of the South Sea Company, after hours of grueling testimony before each house, had packed up the company books and fled across the sea. The ports were closed. A reward was offered. There was a riot in front of Westminster. The bill, fining directors, curtailing their actions, flew through both houses and was approved. Several directors were arrested. One, who was a minister to the king, chancellor of the exchequer, resigned. Those that were members of the House of Commons were expelled.

She does not know it, thought the Duchess, watching Barbara's face as she read the letter, but she is fortunate not to have to witness such disgrace happening to Roger. But, then, Roger might have calmed the waters, might have handled the nervousness of the directors. He had a way about him. It might never have gotten this far. . . . She sighed. In another month, Barbara would leave for London. Montrose wrote her. The solicitors. She must come to London. She worked feverishly on the memorial service, and the Duchess was glad to see her mind thus occupied. Idle hands were the Devil's plaything. Less time for brooding. She would do the brooding. As she watched Tony watch Barbara, she would do the brooding.

Philippe sat before the fire in the green-and-gold salon of his Paris town house, reading English poetry. It was a habit he could not seem to shake.

Death be not proud, though some have called thee
Mighty and dreadful, for, thou art not so,
For those whom thou think'st thou dost overthrow,
Die not, poor death, nor yet canst thou kill me.
From rest and sleep, which but thy pictures be,
Much pleasure, then from thee, much more must flow.

He stopped and shivered and leaned forward to stoke the fire. John Donne, as Roger had so often pointed out, was a remarkable man, but not so remarkable that he should make him feel, as the peasants put it, as if someone had walked over his grave.

His footman entered, the small silver tray he carried piled with letters and notes and invitations. Philippe put aside the book and sifted through them, stopping with a frown at Abigail's letter, ripping past the seal, thinking as he did so that this was unexpected; he had thought Abigail far too well bred to write him.

"My dear Philippe, it is with deep regret that I write to inform you that Roger has died at Tamworth from the attack he suffered at Devane House in November—" He stopped.

He reread those lines, feeling shock course through his body at the words "has died." Carlyle had written of an attack, and he had written that letter to the Duchess of Tamworth and heard nothing in reply. Roger will be well again, he had reasoned, angry at the silence, the lack of news. His luck will cover him. He slammed his fist into a nearby table, and a bowl of camellias tipped over, as well as a candlestick. The water from the camellias dripped over the book, and the candle smoked as it burned itself out against the floor, but he made no movement. He sat still. Pain filling him, swelling in him, as completely as the pain from the splinters of the cannonball that had maimed him or the sword that had cut his face open to the dawn. But Roger had been there then, to hold his bleeding face together. Roger. He crumpled Abigail's letter into a ball, and threw it, and it landed in a corner of the room. Waiting for him to retrieve it, and smooth it out and reread it. Death be not proud; on the contrary, he thought, be proud, for you have taken the finest of men, the handsomest man I ever saw. And he remembered, through pain, the first time he had ever seen Roger, walking beside the great Duke of Tamworth, in love with him, but not yet knowing, innocent still, a young soldier whose face glowed with the joy and laughter of love. Who lay now in the arms of that lover whose embrace would suck the flesh from his bones and leave only dust. Death. Roger. He put his hands to his eyes to blot out the sight.

Candlemas, the second day of February, the day to take down Tamworth Christmas greenery, brown and dry, crumbling in one's hands. Yesterday the yule log had been lit once more, to burn until sunset, when what remained was quenched and cooled to put away to light next year's log. The season of Lent was just ahead. Repenting. Meditation. Prayer. Fasting.

" 'But all these things, with an Account how three-hundred Caribbees came and invaded them, and ruin'd their Plantations, and how they fought with that Number twice,' " read

Hyacinthe to those gathered about him in the great hall, " 'and were at first defeated, and three of them kill'd but at last a Storm destroying their Enemies Canoes, they famish'd or destroy'd almost all the rest, and renew'd and recover'd the Possession of their Plantation, and still liv'd upon the Island.

" 'All these things, with some very surprizing Incidents in some new Adventures of my own, for ten Years more, I may perhaps give a farther Account of hereafter.' " Hyacinthe looked up at all the pairs of eyes regarding him. " 'Finis,' " he read and closed the book. Thérèse looked up from her mending; Perryman sighed; two or three of the grooms blinked their eyes; Annie sniffed.

"Brandy!" said the Duchess, striking her cane against the floor. "The finish calls for a drop of brandy—a drop, Perryman—to each and every one here."

Lambing. Wet. Snow. Chill. A few snowdrops unfurling their green heads tipped with white between patches of snow. The news from London. The Earl of Stanhope dead after a heated exchange with the Duke of Wharton in the House of Lords, over South Sea. A letter from Montrose. He must send an inventory of the estate to Parliament. Barbara must come to London. Wind, and rain. A crocus found among the brown flower beds. And there a hyacinth. Hyacinthe laughing over his valentine. Blackbirds sighted, a robin singing.

The Duchess received a large folded packet from London. My legs, she moaned to her household, and then she lay in bed for three days, seeing only Annie, reading through the maps and letters and pages copied from books that Caesar White had sent to her.

"Alexander Spotswood, who served under your husband, is the current governor of Virginia, but the gossip in the coffee-houses frequented by colonials is that he will soon be replaced. He has built a handsome governor's mansion in the town of Williamsburg.

"Not many works exist on the colony. Three which I was able to locate are: Captain John Smith's *General Historie of Virginia*, Robert Beverley's *The History and Present State of Virginia*, in four parts, and Robert Sherrod's *The Royal Dominion of Virginia, a True and Vivid Accounting*. I have copied certain pages from all three works as well as included a map so that you may see where it is located.

"The plantation, small by colonial standards, is off the James River, a large river which goes far inland. It was owned by a distant cousin of one Robert Carter, called 'King,' who owns many plantations there. His son studies at the Inns of Court in London.

"The main crop grown is tobacco, which tires land easily, which is why the most prosperous planters have several plantations and large holdings. The fields are worked by negro slaves captured from the coasts of Africa.

"I have done as you asked me and told no one of your commission to me, and I thank you for the generous money you included in your letter. I will be sending more to you, including the books mentioned when I find them. I burn with curiosity to know why you have a sudden interest in a colony so far from these shores."

Barbara dreamed she lay against Roger, naked. She kissed his throat, and he made a sound and leaned back against the pillows, pulling her with him, his hands caressing her bare back, her buttocks, the tops of her thighs. She pulled his head to her breast and shivered as his hands touched her, as his mouth sought her.

"I want your child," she said, and his tongue flicked against her breast before he raised his head, and then he put his mouth on hers, and their tongues twined and she desired him, aching, and his hands were in her hair and around her neck and across her breasts and sides, and she murmured his name over and over.

Barbara woke, hearing the strong, pulsing rhythm of her heart, her quickened breathing. The only sounds in the silence.

"A dream," she said out loud.

She sat up in the darkness and touched her breasts. The tips were hard. She put her hands to her face. He was dead. He would never hold her in her arms again.

Primrose time, that time in late February, when yellow primroses grew beside the lanes and hedges and promised spring, and sometimes there was warmth amid the cold, and roads and ditches began to thaw, to turn to mud. The colts-foot weed bloomed in the meadows; the new lambs sheltered from the wind beside their mothers; on the bare branches of trees were tiny, green dots, the beginnings of a leaf, a bud, a blossom.

Face and hands red with cold, Barbara carried an armful of primroses into Tamworth chapel and put them into the basalt vases. Carefully, she laid some across the reclining marble statue of her grandfather.

"From Grandmama," she said, "who will come when the weather is warmer."

Just as carefully she laid some on the floor, above where Harry and Roger lay in the vault. She sat down on the marble bench and rubbed her hands together, putting them inside her cloak to warm them.

"I am going to London," she said. "I will give you a fine service there, Roger. I promise."

In London, she said goodbye to her mother outside Diana's town house on Haymarket Street, leaning out the window of her carriage, watching as her mother and Clemmie climbed up the steps; Diana climbed, Clemmie waddled.

Tony leaned down from his horse. "Shall I come on with you?"

She shook her head no. He straightened and turned his horse away. He must go to Saylor House and she must go to Devane House. Inside the carriage, they were all silent, she and Thérèse and Hyacinthe and Justin; even the dogs were quiet. Homecoming, thought Barbara, only there is no longer a master of that home.

Daffodils were blooming in the garden of Devane Square, their yellow trumpets open to the cold air. There was an abandoned, neglected look to the square and garden and houses. The wooden frames of houses never finished stood bare, weathered now, open to the sky. The carriage lumbered past Wren's church, its doors and windows boarded over, its grounds raw and muddy, never landscaped. There was no gatekeeper at the gates, and Hyacinthe jumped down to open them. The coach lumbered past the fountain, empty, lichen and moss growing upon the stone body of the nymph: they drove through the gardens, which were full of coltsfoot and wild field flowers, creeping slowly in to claim their territory once more. They went around the curving driveway to the house, massive and unfinished. Like my life with Roger, thought Barbara, as she stepped down from the carriage, the dogs leaping around her, and Cradock came running down the steps to shake her hand, tears in his eyes, as if she were his master.

"Lady Devane," he said over and over, following her up the great sweep of steps into the huge, cold hall. Montrose and White waited there for her. Both bowed over her hands; there were tears in Montrose's eyes. I represent him, she thought. To them, I represent Roger. She pulled off her long gloves and walked through the rooms to the gallery, the furniture covered in dust sheets, the rooms with that sleepy, neglected air rooms possess when no one lives in them. Montrose followed her, talking all the while.

"The solicitors want to see you at your earliest convenience to read the will. I have reserved St. James's Church as you requested. There are three dates you may choose from. The bust has arrived—"

Indeed it had. It stood on a table near the windows, and she walked to it. Roger. His shoulders and head rising up abruptly out of nothing. She touched the marble cheeks. So cold. The marble could not capture the blue of his eyes, the warm color of his skin. Only angles and planes. Not the man. Not the man at all.

"—and I must tell you that this first report to the Commons from the committee of secrecy has been a bad one. London has talked of nothing else. Roger has been named among many others for wrongdoing. There is a resolution now in the Commons to sequester the estate."

"Sequester?"

"Hold it as security against debt."

"Meaning?"

"It will no longer be yours. It will be theirs."

"Ah . . ."

"The second report is going to be presented tomorrow." Montrose coughed. Barbara knew that cough. She turned to face him.

He tugged on his cravat. "Have you considered a more select service? Quieter. They are trying Aislabee now for corrupt practices. The rumor is they will try Charles Stanhope."

"And do you think my holding a memorial service will make them try Roger? He is dead."

"They could . . . ah . . . try him in absentia."

"He died alone, Montrose. I want him remembered. When can I order the invitations?"

There was a short silence. "The engraver will wait on you tomorrow."

The list of names in her trunk had been carefully selected over these last months at Tamworth. She had planned the music, the flowers, written to ask Walpole to give the eulogy. All her time and care had gone into this service so that, at last, he could be properly mourned. No one would take this from her. No one. She would not allow it. Everything else was gone. She wanted this.

"How is she?" White asked, strolling with Thérèse through the house.

Thérèse shrugged, a lithe, little movement with her shoulders. "It takes time to heal from the death of a loved one." Her hand went to her neck, to the small lump beneath the fabric of her gown, the mourning ring suspended from its gold chain, intertwined with her crucifix.

Barbara kept her widow's veil lowered. She did not wish anyone to see her face as Mr. Craven of Roger's firm of solicitors read the will aloud to the those assembled to hear it— she and her mother and Tony and the servants, Cradock and Justin and Montrose.

It was much as she had expected. Roger left the estate to her entirely if there should be no children. The customary one third to her if there should be. But—of course—there were not. Unexpectedly, he requested that the estate be entailed to her firstborn son, should he die without children and should she remarry and have children. And if she should die without issue, he left the estate to the second Duke of Tamworth "in memory of his grandfather, and my friend, Richard Saylor."

There were bequests to the faithful: Cradock, Montrose, Justin; to friends, Walpole, Carlyle, Montagu; to the Prince de Soissons. Barbara's fingers curled into claws. She was glad of the widow's veil.

Craven coughed. Cradock and Justin were bowing over her hand, leaving the room, while Craven shifted the papers before him.

"Now," he said, "there are certain matters which you must consider, Lady Devane. First, the estate is sequestered. We have had the letter from Parliament. That means that you cannot sell anything toward Lord Devane's private debt without their permission. We already have a petition before Parliament to waive the fines of January, and I recommend another petition stating the extent of Lord Devane's personal debt and asking a lifting of the sequestration and an allowance for you. . . ."

Bankrupt, Barbara thought. What it truly means is I am bankrupt. Now I begin to understand why Harry slit his throat.

"The land itself," Tony said, "came as Lady Devane's dower. Could that not be exempt from the sequestration, from the debts?"

Diana turned to stare at Tony in surprise.

"There is precedent," Craven said excitedly. "The widow's right. Yes. Yes, Lord Tamworth! An excellent point."

Later, when they were gone, and Barbara sat in her bedchamber, staring silently at the sea-foam damask on the walls, Diana said, "I think a private audience with the Prince of Wales would be a good idea. He will have influence in Parliament's decisions."

"Yes," said Barbara absently. She unfastened a diamond brooch. "Where ought I to go to pawn this?"

"Whatever for? You can live for years on credit."

"I need to honor the bequests to Montrose and Justin and Cradock—"

"Nonsense! Let them put liens against the estate. They will get the money eventually."

Barbara did not say anything. Diana watched her profile, which was not angry or stubborn or anything but serene.

"You are going to pawn it anyway, are you not?"

"Yes."

Diana sighed and held out her hand. "Give it to me. If there is one thing I know, it is how to pawn jewels."

* * *

She waited with her mother in the drawing room at St. James's Palace, once more using her widow's veil as her shield. No one would recognize her under it, and if they should, they would respect her grief and leave her alone. Her mother had come to Devane House this morning to oversee her dressing. Barbara had let her have her way over her rouge and powder and patches and jewelry, knowing her mother still treasured hopes that a frog, the Frog, might hop into her bed.

A footman opened the door to the private apartments and nodded to them. Barbara walked past clusters of those she had known so well this summer, Hervey and Campbell and their wives, the former Mistresses Lepell and Bellenden, Mrs. Howard, Mrs. Clayton. She kept her veil down. These people were nothing. It was the Frog she must capture. If she captured him, the toads would follow.

The Princess of Wales came to her, plump, blond, highly rouged, blue eyes assessing, wishing, as Barbara well knew, to see past her veil. We were so sorry, she murmured as Barbara curtsied to her. Roger was such a favorite of ours. And there at last was the Frog. Eyes as buggy as ever, pale blue and cold; he was old enough to be her father. He wore one of his military uniforms; he loved to wear military uniforms. He bowed over her hand, excited by the secrecy of her widow's veil. He led her to a window; her mother, thinking herself clever, engaged the princess in conversation. The Frog pressed her hand to his mouth. He trembled. His complexion was pale, pasty in the sunlight from the window. Near Roger's age, but the difference! My dear one, my poor Barbara, we share your grief, he was our friend, we miss your presence at court. She allowed him to continue holding her hand. Will you be coming to the memorial service? she asked. He was silent. She bent her head. It would mean so much, your highness. She raised her veil and allowed him a glimpse of her face, of her large tear-filled eyes, so much larger now that she had lost weight. I would never forget your kindness, she said. She dropped the veil and went to her mother, as the prince stared after her. There were more murmurs, whispers of condolence, pressed hands.

Barbara smiled under her veil as she walked away with her mother. How did one catch a Frog? Easily. I think I have him. For you, Roger.

"Did you mention the sequestration?" asked Diana.

"Yes, I did."

"But you did not say too much."

"No. I said just enough." She was thinking of her interview tomorrow with the king. It would be so much easier. They could be honest together, for Roger had been his friend, and she knew he would come to the service because of that.

She stood in the front entrance of St. James's Church to receive the guests. Can you make me beautiful? she had asked Thérèse anxiously that morning, as she stared in the mirror at her gauntness. Please make me beautiful for the memory of him, and Thérèse had, weaving magic with powder and patches and rouge and lead combs and discreet padding and diamonds glittering against her mourning black. The rising notes of Handel's "Chandos Anthems" rose through the vaulting ceiling of the church and swelled outward toward the door. Roger's bust stood by the font, draped in ivy and white roses. Tony and her mother stood on each side of her. Hyacinthe held her black fan and a basket of black mourning gloves to give each guest. The guests had begun to arrive, and Barbara kept track of each one, the guest list written in her mind. The Duke and Duchess of Montagu; Tommy Carlyle; the Dukes of Chandos, Newcastle, Leeds, Devonshire; Lords Townshend and Kent and Scarborough and Pembroke; Wart, bowing over her hand, winking at her (she knew he held Roger responsible for Harry's death, and yet he had come); the South Sea directors, Blunt, Chapman, Chester, Child, Eyles, Gibbon, Janssen; Robert Walpole and his wife, Catherine, and his brother Horatio. Sir John Ashford, from home, in London to attend Parliament, to see the creators of the South Sea Company punished, bowed to her. He came out of respect to her grandmother. She smiled at him. The Prince and Princess of Wales and their entourage were arriving.

"You have done it," her mother said, squeezing her arm. "They came in spite of the scandal. I never thought they would."

There came Alexander Pope and Lady Mary Wortley Montagu, the Earl of Burlington, Godfrey Kneller, William Campbell, Sir Christopher Wren, Sir Hans Sloan and an old man whom her mother seemed to know, whom she had not invited.

"Mr. Pendarves." Her mother smiled, while the old man bowed over her hand, ancient liver spots on his face and hands, dirt under his fingernails, missing teeth, snuff stains in the corners of his mouth, pressed into wrinkles. "My guest. Mr. Pendarves has never married," said Diana, watching him fondly as he walked past her into the church, with the look of a cat who has just drunk a bowl of cream.

Her Aunt Shrewsborough was arriving, walking between Charles and Mary. Charles bowed over her hand, and his eyes glowed down at her like two dark sapphires. She stared after him.

"Philippe. This way, Philippe."

She turned to stone. Before her unbelieving eyes, her Aunt Abigail was entering the gates, holding them open for Philippe de Soissons, who was limping more slowly than usual. How can he be here? she thought wildly; but the King of England was entering the churchyard behind them, his entourage surrounding him, Melusine von Schulenburg, now the Duchess of Kendall, on his arm, and Barbara swept into a low curtsy, rising as the king lifted her up and leaned forward and kissed her cheeks, and Diana smiled beside her. She lowered her widow's veil with trembling fingers. Philippe! But she must put him to one side, for her guests waited, Roger's memorial service waited, and she must do it justice to the last.

All stood as the king walked to the front pew, and remained standing as Barbara followed, on Tony's arm. Handel's anthems came to a swelling end that filled the church to its curving ceiling, and the rector, solemn in his white robes, bowed his head to lead a prayer.

There was a silence afterward, broken by the rustle of gowns, as Robert Walpole walked heavily to the intricately carved pulpit.

"We gather today, in a time of crisis, of accusations, of moral and spiritual malaise, to honor the memory of a man who was friend to all of us here. A man much maligned. A man much blamed. And yet a man I cannot praise too highly, a man who was the height and depth and breadth of grace and dignity. . . ."

It is going to be all right, Barbara thought, glancing at the faces to each side of her. Walpole was skillful, recalling Roger's years as a soldier, his service under the great Duke of Tamworth in Queen Anne's wars, his service to the House of Hanover, recalling his generosity and kindnesses. The committee's report linked him with bribes of stock to the Duchess of Kendall and other Hanoverians, but Walpole was reminding those gathered of his life before South Sea. The faces of those about her were softening in memory, and some were weeping. Walpole's voice rose and fell, carrying the guests with him.

"I close with the lines from a poet who was also a churchman. 'No man is an island, entire of itself; every man is a piece of the continent, a part of the main; if a clod be washed away by the sea, Europe is the less, as well as if a promontory were, as well as if a manor of thy friends or of thine own were; any man's death diminishes me, because I am involved in mankind; and therefore never send to know for whom the bell tolls; it tolls for thee.' The bell tolls for Roger Montgeoffry, who was my friend, and yours, who gave of himself in some way to each of us here. We are the lesser for his death."

And above them, the voices of the choir rose in the Twenty-third Psalm, the Lord is my Shepherd, as Walpole stepped down from the pulpit, and stopped in front of Barbara, and gave her his arm, and she stood and walked with him down the aisle, thinking, You have had a fitting goodbye, my love. And the bell of St. James's pealed its solemn, single toll of death.

She waited by herself in a corner of the tiny church garden, under a tree, for her carriage. At the sound of an uneven step, she turned, for all the guests were gone, and Philippe stood not far from her, leaning on his cane, his face thinner and more bitter. He has lost weight, she thought, as have I. Grief. Grief has done that to us. She felt as if she had been waiting forever for this moment.

"It was a fine service. You did justice to his memory."

"I did not invite you." And then she could not help herself. Something surged in her. "Did he love you?" She had to understand. She had to know. For certain. The words seemed to echo and swell and fill the church garden; she knew they filled her head. "Did he?"

His face had become still, as if he struggled with the answer, and she hated him at that moment, more than she had ever hated him.

"It does not matter now—"

"Tell me!"

She heard the cutting arrogance in her voice, but she could not stop it.

An eyebrow raised, that familiar ironic expression came to his face. "Always the headstrong fool. . . . Yes. Love. It was love. Before you and after you. Do you feel better, or worse? Does any of it matter now?"

She felt a roaring begin in her ears, and when it had quieted, he was gone. Inside, she was dazed, as if she had fallen from a great height, and lay crushed and mangled, but no one knew. No one saw. You are a fool, she said to herself. It was better as it was.

"It does me good," said Walpole, waving a chicken leg to those about him, at the reception at Saylor House, Tony's contribution to the memorial service, "to see us gathered as friends together once more. This South Sea disaster has torn us apart."

Barbara was standing in the great parlor, greeting guests, listening to their compliments about the memorial service, to their condolences, to a memory here and there of Roger. Carlyle stood by her, rocking back and forth on high red heels, surveying the guests, feeling free to comment on them and their style, or lack of style.

Diana came into the room, gracious in her black gown, on the arm of Mr. Pendarves. Carlyle raised his eyepiece, a magnifying glass attached by a red ribbon to his yellow and white vest.

"What is it?" he said.

"Barbara," said her mother, smiling, pulling Pendarves along with her, "Mr. Pendarves was just telling me how touched he was by the service, by your dignity—"

"Lumpy!"

Carlyle jumped, and Diana and Pendarves both turned as Aunt Shrewsborough sashayed forward, skirts swaying, for all the world as if she were sixteen instead of seventy. She pushed

Diana to one side, and stood before Pendarves, waving her fan back and forth flirtatiously.

"Lumpy Pendarves, is that you? I saw you in church, and I could not believe my eyes. How many years has it been—"

"At least a hundred," said Carlyle, but Aunt Shrewsborough swept right past him.

"It is me. Lou. Your Lou. Remember?" And she cackled, and the powder and rouge caked in her wrinkles fell in little flakes onto her gown.

Pendarves made a smacking sound with his mouth. "Lou?" he said hesitantly. Aunt Shrewsborough pinched a fold in his cheeks.

"Yes, Lou! Lumpy was a beau of mine," she said to Barbara. "Years ago. He swore he would never marry when he could not have me. I understand you are as rich as Midas now. Give me your arm, and we will drink a glass of wine to Roger Montgeoffry. That rogue. I lost fifteen thousand pounds because of him, but you would never know it to hear Robert Walpole. It was a pretty service, Bab. Diana, move out of the way."

Diana watched her drag him away.

"Incredible," said Carlyle, watching them through his eyepiece.

"I will never marry him, you know," Barbara said.

Diana and Carlyle both looked at Barbara.

"And he will never marry me. The debt, Mother. Mr. Pendarves does not look much like a man to take on so much debt. And then, I am more used to a handsomer man. He does not favor Roger, does he?"

Carlyle broke into laughter.

"Barbara—"

But she was walking away.

"She has grown up," said Carlyle. "You have your hands full."

Across another room, Barbara watched Charles and Mary as they stood at the buffet table, Charles filling Mary's plate. She was fashionable in black and pearls, lead now darkening her brows and lashes, like Barbara's. But she was young, and looking up at her husband with eyes that loved him. Charles lifted his head and stared at Barbara. She read his eyes clearly. A mistake. I married out of anger and pride. I love you still. But the Prince and Princess of Wales were arriving, and she went to greet them, and then she had to stroll through the rooms of Saylor House on the prince's arm, listening to his compliments whispered amid his loud public greetings. The somberness of the memorial service was wearing off, as Tony's wine and punch and brandy began to take effect. People spoke in louder tones, laughed, flirted, drank to Roger's memory, more than once, more than twice.

Toward evening, she found herself in the hall, dark with the landing above it, the black and white squares of marble on the floor. The servants had not yet lit candles. I want to go home, she thought, and home was not Devane House, it was Tamworth. Love. It was love. Before you and after you. She found that tears were rolling down her cheeks.

"Barbara."

Charles took her hand, and led her to the shadows under the stairs, the shadows made by the way the stairs swept upward on each side to the landing above. And he dried her cheeks with a handkerchief, and he held her.

"My love," he said. "My dear, sweet love. We have been fools. But we are going to begin again, and I promise it will be better between us. I promise." It felt good to be in his arms. It felt good to be held by a man who knew how to dry her tears and who held her so firmly, as if they belonged together, and she wished that he had not married, and that Roger had not died, and that she had not asked Philippe that question. Charles was kissing her palm, his mouth becoming more searching, and she shivered with the hunger, the loneliness that rose in her. Change is an easy thing to decide and a difficult thing to do, her grandmother said in her mind. It is the day-to-day struggle of it that defeats people. If she were to take Charles back—it would be so easy—she would be the same as Philippe.

"Come to my rooms in the city," he was saying, and his voice was like silk against her bare skin. "Tonight. I want to comfort you. I want you—"

"Barbara."

She stepped out of the shadows into the hall. Tony stood framed in the doorway. Charles stepped out behind Barbara, and Tony's face changed.

"Guests are beginning to leave," he said abruptly.

And so they were gone, the last of the guests. Her mother was getting drunk. Aunt Shrewsborough had left early with Mr. Pendarves. Walpole had gone back to St. James's Palace with the king.

Over, thought Barbara, looking around at the dirty plates, the wilting flowers, the guttering candles, the smudged glasses. All over.

She gathered her hat and veil and gloves and cloak. Thérèse and Hyacinthe were gone, back to Devane House with Montrose and White.

"Shall I escort you home?"

Tony was abrupt, and she knew why. She shook her head, and outside she shivered in the cold, dark air and raised her face to the night.

"To Devane House?" asked her coachman. She hesitated. Come to my rooms tonight, Charles said. And if she did, if she knocked on that door, what lay behind it for her?

"Drive me . . . wherever you wish. Just drive until I tell you to stop."

The carriage lumbered through the streets, some of them lit by lanterns attached to the houses, others of them dark. Down Cockspur Street to Charing Cross with its bronze statue of Charles I, down the Strand to the large gate of Temple Bar, on to Fleet Street and Ludgate Hill, St. Paul's Cathedral rising in all its glory. She had the carriage stop so that she could stand and look at it. This is my favorite building in London, Roger had said. She ordered the coachman to take her to London Bridge, easily crossed now, its daylight traffic of carriages and carts and wagons and pedestrians gone with the night. Houses and buildings towered on both sides of the bridge, some of them leaning out at their back over the water and shored up with long poles. The upper front stories of the houses and buildings were joined across the middle of the bridge by iron tie bars so that they would not topple backward into the Thames, roaring down between the stone arches.

Barbara leaned over the stone railing and listened to the water rushing below her. Boat-shaped outworks of piles in the riverbed protected each pier of the arches of the bridge, but they also forced the river water into dangerously narrow and fast-moving channels between the arches. Watermen who made their living carrying passengers up and down the Thames in small boats regularly shot the bridge, which meant going through those arches in the river's dangerous, rushing current in their small boats, but most passengers disembarked on one side and walked around. If boat and waterman made it through the arches of the bridge without sinking, the journey continued. Every year, someone died who attempted to shoot the bridge. Barbara remembered a drunken summer night with Harry and Charles when she had wanted to do it, had bet with Harry that she could and she would have, if Charles had not picked her up bodily and carried her out of the boat, Harry laughing like a wild man at her. She smiled and shook her head at the memory. Before her were ships, many ships, at anchor, their sails furled shut against their wooden masts. They reminded her of birds, ducks and geese sleeping in a pond, heads tucked into their wings. She could see the lantern lights burning on their decks and below. This was the Pool of London, on the east side of the bridge, the side closest to the sea, and ships from other lands anchored alongside British ones.

She stepped back from the railing, the sound of the river rushing through the arches, the great water wheel that turned at one end to supply the city with water, in her ears. Charles's rooms were near here. So he kept them still. For the occasional actress or opera dancer—or widow—that took his eye. It had hurt when she first knew him, and it hurt now. Nothing changed and everything changed. Her thoughts were clear, like the March night. She would not begin again. The woman of the summer was gone, and she would not allow even Philippe's words, which still echoed at the back of her mind, to bring her back again.

"Home?" asked her coachman, anxious for her to be back in the coach, disliking the streets at night.

"Home," she said.

Cradock sat dozing in the hall, starting awake as she shook him by the shoulder.

"You did not have to sit up—"

"Lord Tamworth is here, ma'am, and has been for some time."

He stood against the windows of the gallery, his face shadowed, for only a single branch of the candelabrum was lit.

She walked toward him, thinking how glad she was that he was here.

"Where have you been?"

She stopped short.

He crossed the space between them, surprising her, and he grabbed her by the shoulders, hurting her, shaking her, his face hard and furious.

"Where were you? By God, Barbara, if you were with Charles, I swear I will kill him!"

She pulled out of his hands tiredly. "I was not with Charles."

He stared at her, his head lowered, like a bull still on the verge of charging.

"Not at his rooms, perhaps, but somewhere else with him, Bab? Where? Where else with him?"

"How do you know I was not at his lodgings?"

"Because I waited there."

She stared at him. He looked away, a muscle clenching in his jaw.

Her head hurt. She felt like crying. And she was tired of crying. Of feeling like crying. When did one get over grief and go on with the business of life? Love. It was love. Well, she had asked for it, and she had gotten it, and it was going to take her more than a while to recover. More than a while. She sat down in the window seat.

He knelt before her, his young face earnest and surprisingly handsome. It was odd how she could be with Tony for weeks and never notice how he looked, and then look up and think, He is growing handsome. The clean planes and angles of his face. The nose. The mouth, the clear eyes. No regrets in them yet. As she had. . . . It was love.

"Marry me, Barbara. Let me take care of you."

She could only stare at him. He opened his mouth and she put her hand on it quickly. "Hush, Tony. If you say one more word, I will begin crying, and if I begin crying tonight, I will not stop. You had too much wine at the reception—"

He kissed the palm of her hand.

"No!" she said sharply.

The word reverberated between them, splintering something; she saw its damage, saw the bones of the relationship changing with it, and she felt a terrible swell of sorrow. I have lost my dearest friend, she thought. He stood up and walked away from her. With his back to her, he said, "What will you do?"

"I have signed the petitions for my allowance, for the dower lands. Cradock and Justin are provided for. They will seek new positions. Montrose will continue to work on clearing the estate. I am closing the house and going back to Tamworth."

"Such clear-eyed purpose."

She flinched at the sarcasm in his voice.

"Good night, Barbara."

She watched him walk away.

Outside, in the cold dark, he took the reins of his horse from the coachman, but he did not mount. The coachman, holding a lantern, waited.

"Leave me."

The man hesitated, but seeing the young duke's face in the lantern light, did as he was told.

Tony stood at the side of his horse. He raised his fist and slammed it down into the leather of the saddle. The horse shied and neighed and pulled against the reins.

"I new it was too soon," he said into the dark. "I knew it!"

Thérèse was not in the bedchamber, and Barbara did not search for her. Instead, she picked up a candlestick and walked into the smaller adjoining room, where, in Roger's dreams, she was to have planned her household and written her letters and embroidered her cloths. And played with their children. She sat down on the floor, her knees drawn in tightly to her chest. Still in its corner sat the cradle. Gently, with a fingertip, she touched the edge of the cradle, and it rocked. She put her head on her knees.

"Why do you cry?"

Thérèse was kneeling beside her.

"You know," Barbara said.

CHAPTER TWENTY-NINE

The Duchess floundered through layers of sleep and opened her eyes. Annie, thin, brown, grim, leaned over her.

"Lady Devane is here."

"Here? Here? Where did she go?" And then, as Annie opened her mouth, "I know! Never mind your lectures. I forgot. I am old. Do not stand there staring at me! Send her to me! Go on!"

She pushed herself up against her pillows and straightened her huge lace cap, which had slipped to the side of her head during her nap. She retied the bows crisscrossing the front of her velvet bed jacket and noticed that *The History and Present State of Virginia* lay open at her side for all the world to see. She shoved it under a pillow. The sound of barking dogs, shrill, high, yapping, came to her ears. Dulcinea, who had been dozing beside her, lifted her head at that sound and twitched her ears. The barking grew louder, and Dulcinea mewed and jumped off the bed and ran out the door. The Duchess did not mind her fickleness. She smoothed the folds of her bed jacket and waited . . . and waited. . . . Barbara did not come to her.

She frowned; she fidgeted; she pursed her lips. Finally, she rang her silver bell, inordinately pleased with its demanding, high, continuous clang. Breathless, Annie ran into the room, and the Duchess glared at her.

"Call Tim for me."

"Let it lie—"

"Very well. I will call him myself. Tim! Tim! Come here, Tim!"

"She needs to be alone—"

"Do not tell me what she needs!" She had hoisted herself to the edge of the bed, and her legs hung over it, thin and spindly. She kicked her feet in their embroidered slippers out defiantly. "There you are, Tim. Where have you been? Take me to Lady Devane." And as Tim picked her up and carried her from the room, she looked back at Annie, who stood with her hands on her hips, frowning at her.

"Bossy old stick. Telling me how to run my family. I will dismiss her," she said to Tim. "I will. The older she becomes, the more impossible she is." Tim was too wise to answer.

She knocked on the door of Barbara's bedchamber, and even though there was no reply, she had Tim open the door and carry her in and set her in a chair and then she dismissed him with a wave of her hand, her eyes darting about the room, weighing, assessing. Barbara stood at the window, staring out, and she was still dressed in her traveling gown. She had not even taken off her hat, and it was a dashing hat. Black silk with black and white trailing feathers, the Duchess noticed. She also noticed a certain set to Barbara's profile, and she glanced over at Thérèse, who was unpacking a trunk, and Thérèse looked away from her quickly. The Duchess's eyes narrowed. She cleared her throat.

"Grandmama," Barbara said from the window, and the Duchess heard the tiredness in her voice. And something more. Something she did not understand . . . yet. She retied a bow on her bed jacket, glancing up at Barbara as she did so. Barbara said nothing, not one word of the memorial service, of London, of the will, of all the things the Duchess had expected her to bubble over with. If the enemy seems hesitant, attack him, Richard always said. Hit him strong and hard with your foot troops. She had always found it a good principle in many things besides warfare.

"You heard the will?" Her voice was precise and hard, no sentiment in it.

"Ah, yes."

"And . . . ?"

"I am inheritor of the estate. An estate that is two hundred fifty thousand pounds in debt."

The Duchess's mouth fell open.

Barbara smiled at the expression on her grandmother's face and looked back out the window. Spring at Tamworth almost made her forget the problems left in London. It was a lovely, gently greening time. Young lambs raced in the meadows. Peas and early spinach were tender green shoots in the gardens. Willows along pond and river edges stood peeled white, the rich smell of their bark following you, as the women and children dried them in strips by the riversides to weave them later into the sturdiest of baskets, willow baskets. Spring baskets.

"The estate," she said, not looking away from the green view of the window, "is entangled almost beyond fixing. It is a certain thing that Parliament will take a portion of it toward the relief of South Sea sufferers. What portion I do not know, and I may not sell a thing or take a penny from it until they decide. I pawned jewels in London to have some ready coins. I may emerge with Bentwoodes mine though, when all is said and done. Because Tony reminded the solicitors that it was my dower."

The Duchess's ears pricked up the way Dulcinea's had at the first sound of barking. Tony. Something had happened. With Tony.

"He chose not to come with you?"

"He chose not to come with me."

The Duchess did not like the way she said that. Follow up with cavalry, said Richard. Riding in hard and fast. "The memorial service . . . it went well? Everyone was there?"

Barbara laughed, and the Duchess's eyes went quickly to Thérèse, who, once more, looked away from her. Ride in hard and fast.

"Lord Russel was there?"

"You need not worry about Lord Russel!" Barbara said sharply. "He and I have quarreled. And Mother and I have quarreled. And Tony and I—" She stopped. "I am tired from the journey, Grandmama. You must forgive my bad manners. I stopped to see Jane in Petersham, and the stopping delayed us a day, and I was already tired."

"Jane does well?"

Barbara sighed. "We saw Jeremy's grave. It is . . . so small."

"The death of one's child is a hard thing to get past."

"I would not know."

Barbara unpinned her hat and took it off and jabbed a long hatpin tipped with onyx into the soft silk.

"I showed her Harry's memorial tablet."

"Did she approve?"

"Yes." And the Duchess heard the catch in her voice.

"What else did you bring from London with you?"

Grief, thought Barbara. Bitter, hard grief. And regret. And a half-dozen paths suddenly open before me, none of them good.

Montrose had found the plans for Devane House. Sketches by Roger, some by Wren, some even—impossibly—by herself. Found them in a small box Roger kept locked, along with a pair of her gloves, leather gloves she had worn in Paris. What shall I do with them? Montrose asked her. She took them. Dreams, she thought, that had turned to dust in both our hands. He would never live in his Devane House now, the great lord, surrounded by beauty, by his children. And neither would she. The words "burn them" came to her lips but she could not say them. She put them back in their wooden box, and brought them to Tamworth. Parliament could have the rest. But not this.

"I brought the marble bust of Roger."

"Ah. And does it look like him?"

Barbara turned away at last from the view of the window and looked at her grandmother. She shook her head, and her eyes were full of tears, which she did not shed. "No."

Thérèse and Hyacinthe stood at the edge of the Duchess's high bedside, while she took a moment from her questioning to throw a pillow at Dulcinea and the dogs, who wrestled and growled together at the foot of the bed. The high bed gave her an advantage. She towered over them, like a queen.

"So," she said, looking at the two of them once more, "there was no one unexpected at the memorial service. Nothing unusual happened." She slapped her hand hard on the bedside table, and it trembled, and a sheaf of papers slid to the floor. "I think you lie!" she said harshly.

Thérèse and Hyacinthe looked at each other and then away. Hyacinthe's lower lip trembled. Thérèse looked down at her shoes.

"Yes, lie," said the Duchess. "Do you know what I do to liars?"

"The Prince de Soissons," said Hyacinthe in a gulp. "He was there. He was not invited. I heard Lord Tamworth saying to Madame Barbara that his mother had invited him, and Lord Tamworth asked Madame Barbara what was wrong and later—ouch!"

Hyacinthe glared at Thérèse.

The Duchess concentrated on him, the weak link broken to her will.

"Did they speak? Did they?"

"I did not see it," answered Thérèse swiftly, looking down at Hyacinthe with a glance that told him to be quiet or else. "There were so many people there, you understand—"

The Duchess kept her eyes on Hyacinthe. He shrank before her.

"The truth."

"I saw them. They spoke."

"And did you hear what they said?"

"No. But I heard what Lord Russel said."

"Lord Russ— What did he say? What? And when?"

"He came to see Madame Barbara just before we left for here. She and Lady Alderley had had a quarrel. Such shouting, heard all over the house, your grace. Lady Alderley did not want Madame Barbara to come here—"

"Never mind Lady Alderley. There is always shouting when Lady Alderley is about. Tell me of Lord Russel."

"Well, he came to see Madame Barbara. And I go to the gallery, and they do not see me, and they are kissing. For a long time. And I try to go before they see me, but Madame Barbara, she sees me, and she tells me not to leave her. To stay. And Lord Russel is angry. At me. At her. I see his face. And he tells her she can run away, but that when he chooses, he will come and get her—Thérèse! Stop! Ouch! Stop!"

"Big mouth," Thérèse hissed in French. "Traitor."

Hyacinthe stared up at the Duchess. She shook her head. "You did the right thing. Go and tell Annie to give you a licorice. Tell her I said so." The Duchess watched him run from the room. She looked at Thérèse, who was staring once more down at her shoes, frowning.

"You have nothing more to add?"

Thérèse shook her head emphatically.

"You keep your mouth closed. I like that. It is a rare and valuable trait in a lady's maid."

Thérèse looked up at her, and her dark eyes were flashing.

"I love her, too," the Duchess said. "Even more than you. Go away, now. I want to be alone."

Lent was sliding into Easter, the ceremony, the rite of resurrection and rebirth. First came Mothering Sunday, when the servants left to visit their mothers, carrying small presents they had made, as well as gifts of food from the Duchess. Sir John Ashford rode over from Ladybeth to tell them Jane had been safely delivered of a boy, which they were naming Harry Augustus. Damned if I understand Gussy, said Sir John, for it is his idea. Damned if I would do it. But Barbara and her grandmother smiled at each other. Harry Augustus. Gussy had not feared the man, and he did not fear the memory. It was a kind thing. We shall send apostle spoons (spoons with the heads of the apostles carved on the handles), to his christening even though we are not his godparents, said the Duchess to Barbara. Palm Sunday came, and Hyacinthe worked into the night fashioning tiny willow crosses for each person to carry into church, and then Good Friday, when Cook baked hot-cross buns, and the Duchess sat in the churchyard watching the villagers and neighbors and servants tending the graves in the graveyard of Tamworth church. All must be free of weeds, and the crosses whitewashed, and the gravestones limed and straightened, for Easter. The church altar must be decorated with flowers, as well as Richard's chapel, and the large, white Pascal tapers lit to signal the Easter vigil. The news from London was that Sunderland had been acquitted, and the city was near riot. South Sea director Caswell had been found guilty, and postmaster-general Craggs had died, of suicide, it was whispered, rather than face questioning about his own part in the South Sea downfall. It goes on and on, thought the Duchess, watching Barbara pull weeds from a grave, touching all our lives. Barbara, she had noticed, received letters from Montrose about the estate. None from her mother, and none from Tony. And a letter had come in a bold handwriting which the Duchess did not recognize, but Annie had happened to see a signature. Charles . . . Lord Russel, who had said he would come after Barbara when he chose. . . . Mary's husband now. . . . Abigail must grieve Roger's passing as deeply as Barbara. She stood up, leaning on her cane, and Tim came to help her to chapel. She sat on her marble bench and conferred with Richard, who had no answers for her. She stared at the flower-bedecked bust of Roger Montgeoffry, stared at it for such a long time, without moving, that Tim shook her roughly by the shoulders, and when she tried to hit him with her cane for it, stammered that he thought she had died.

She and Barbara sat under the shady oaks on the small hillock, enjoying the smell of the wood violets, and the sight of the daisies' white, pert faces growing wild at their feet. Above them, blackbirds and thrushes sang.

"What do you hear from Montrose, Bab?"

"No decision yet on the estate. It will be May or June before it is decided. Robert delays it in Parliament, thinking time will cool tempers and leave more for me. Dear Robert. Montrose thinks they will sequester only that acquired after December 1, 1719, but the committee haggles with Roger's solicitors over how to separate the buildings from the property. Mr. Jacombe, with his banker's heart, has suggested Devane House be torn down, dismantled and sold piece by piece, leaving the property free and Parliament's fines paid."

"Barbara," said the Duchess quickly, squeezing her shoulder.

Barbara pulled away from her. "It was never mine. It was Roger's." She plucked a daisy fiercely from the grass, staring at its yellow center, its clean white petals. "It was such a lovely thing," she said softly.

The Duchess bit her lip and watched a blackbird fly to his nest with a piece of dangling straw in his mouth. His mate greeted him cheerfully, and they began to work the straw into the nest.

"Estates," the Duchess said vaguely, "can be such a bother. I, too, have decisions to make about my estate."

Barbara looked up from the daisy whose petals she had been shredding. "About Tamworth? What decision do you need to make about Tamworth?" The Duchess sighed, a large, heaving sigh. "My other estate." She let the words drift off.

"What other estate? I thought Tony inherited all the Tamworth property."

"Not this. This came later. Much later. It is not part of the entail."

Intrigued, Barbara waited.

"Decisions . . ." said the Duchess, drifting.

"Grandmama!"

"What? What? Did I doze off again? My mind—"

"What estate do you need to make a decision about?"

"Oh! Oh, yes. I must make a decision whether or not to sell a plantation in Virginia."

Barbara stared at her, her mouth open. The Duchess smoothed back a wisp of hair which had come loose from her lace cap.

"Harry left it to me. When I lent him money in the summer, he deeded it to me as collateral. I forgot all about it— you know my mind these days, Barbara—and now it seems the cousins of the original owner are interested in buying it back. I do not know, I have not seen it. I do not like to sell something sight unseen. That is bad business."

"Where on earth is Virginia? And what is a plantation?"

"A farm. They grow hemp— No! Tobacco. Yes, they grow tobacco. It is across the sea, a colony in the North Americas. I have a map." She saw the interest and curiosity in Barbara's face and went on as if she had not seen, "I do not know whom to send. I cannot go myself. There is no one—" She stopped and clapped a hand to her breast and looked at Barbara, amazement crossing her face. "Bab! You could go for me! You have no ties. You could go and act as my agent and look at it and tell me what to do—" She stopped at the expression on Barbara's face.

"Go across the sea to some place called Virginia and inspect a plantation for you?" Barbara repeated slowly.

"I thought . . . I thought it might be worth keeping. It might be well to acquire other properties there. I have funds made from South Sea, and they sit idle at Hoare's bank, drawing interest. And you might like it there well enough to oversee it for me—"

"You are jesting!"

"Am I?" snapped the Duchess, suddenly sitting up straight, while a butterfly perched on her cap. "And have you any better offers?"

"Indeed I do!" Barbara snapped back. "I can become Charles's mistress, or the Frog's. And there is always Mr. Pendarves, if Aunt Shrewsborough does not scratch my eyes out first. Have I told you of Pendarves? He is Mother's latest candidate for my husband, and a far cry from Roger Montgeoffry, let me tell you. As far as one can go."

"Never mind," said the Duchess, slumping down, looking tiny and frail again. "It was a madness on my part. I am old, after all. At times, I do not think properly. I can send someone else. Or simply sell it."

"It was a madness," said Barbara firmly.

Barbara laid a bouquet of meadow daisies and bluebells at the base of Roger's bust and sat down on the marble bench, her hands twisted together in her lap, as she remembered, not only Philippe's words, but many other things. I loved you so, she thought, looking at the bust. Since I was fifteen, my life revolved around you, hating you, trying to hurt you, hurting only myself, nursing you, burying you, planning your memorial, and now it all is done. You are gone from me, and the core of me is empty. Unfilled. I love you, Charles writes to me, and his letter is ardent, but never as beautiful as yours were. I could love him, Roger, but I do not want to be his mistress again for reasons other than Mary, yet Mary is reason enough, and I know if I see him again what will happen. We will quarrel, and we will kiss, and we will bed. It is inevitable. The desire between us is so strong. Was it that way between you and Philippe? Love, Philippe said. It was love. I knew it, and yet I had never heard the words from your lips. Remember in Paris how you refused to speak to me of him, and so there was always the faintest of doubts to hold on to, to cherish. It hurts me, Roger. It takes my grief for you and makes it harder to bear. There is so much of you that I did not know, I cannot now understand.

She waited, almost as if the bust would open its cold lips and reply, and after a moment, when she realized what she was doing, she shook her head. I am too young to ape my grandmama, she thought, talking to a tomb's statue, loving a portrait. Standing up, she walked restlessly about the chapel, stopping before each tablet, reading the names, touching some of them with her fingertips, as if she could touch the person they spelled out, but she touched only cold. She leaned her cheek against the bronze of Harry's tablet. I miss you so, she thought. The silence of the chapel answered her. I am alone, she thought. Truly alone.

A few days later, she strode into the Duchess's bedchamber, the dogs swirling and barking at her feet. Dulcinea leapt from the bed to attack the dogs and the three animals went whirling under the bed, snapping and growling at one another.

"How much do you know of this Virginia?" Barbara said abruptly.

The Duchess tried to think above the sudden roaring in her ears.

"I have books and maps—"

"May I see them?"

She managed to wave casually toward her crowded bedside table. "Look there. Or there. They are here somewhere. Perhaps there."

"Have you ever heard of a place called Virginia?" Barbara asked Thérèse as she brushed out her hair. The windows were open to the night, and Tamworth's night sounds came in through the window, crickets' cries and gate creaks and branches rubbing together, as did its smells: fresh dirt plowed up in the fields, dung from the stable horses, perfume from the flowering vines.

Thérèse's brushing stopped. Harry had won a plantation in Virginia. In the early summer, after three days and nights of card playing in a back room at Young Man's tavern, and the loser had gone back to his lodgings and blown out his brains with a pistol. Or so Harry had said. She had not known whether to believe him or not, his eyes were so teasing. Come with me to Virginia, he had said, taking her by the waist and holding her close. Come live with me and be my love. And for a moment, they had laughed and dreamed a little, of the journey, of how they would live. But Harry went on to another day, and it was not mentioned again, and she forgot it easily, never taking him seriously.

"I have heard of it."

"Well, grandmama has asked me to go there. Harry left her a plantation, which is a—"

"Farm—"

"Yes, a farm, and she wants me to go over and see it to decide if she should sell it or not."

Thérèse heard the underlying excitement in her voice, but she did not quite comprehend all the words yet. The Lord moved in mysterious ways. . . . Virginia yet again. . . . Barbara stood up and ran to the window, her body rail-thin in her nightgown. She sat in the open window like a gypsy.

"At first, I said no. I thought the idea mad. And then, the more I have thought about it, the more I think, Why not? There is nothing here for me, Thérèse. I have no ties. Montrose can handle the details of the estate, and there are people I do not want to see. And it might do me good too"—she paused and smiled—"to have an adventure."

Thérèse held her hands together so that Barbara should not see their trembling. "It is across the sea."

"Yes. Six weeks' journey, I understand." She stared out the window into the night. "What would you do if I went?"

"I . . . I could find another position. Or stay and work here, perhaps. Or go back to France."

"Would you come with me?"

Thérèse stared at her. Barbara smiled, and she reminded Thérèse of a little girl, a bad little girl up to mischief. Jane's Amelia had nothing on Barbara at this moment.

"It is craziness," said Thérèse.

"It is madness," agreed Barbara.

"We might die in a shipwreck."

"There are savages there. They might eat us."

"What would we do with Hyacinthe and the dogs?"

"Take them, of course. More for the savages to eat."

Thérèse began to smile. "You are mad," she said to Barbara.

Barbara jumped down from the windowsill and ran across the room and whirled around and around in its center, making Thérèse laugh.

"I am mad. And I need an adventure that hurts no one. Just one tiny adventure," she sang. "Then I will be good. I promise."

She sat on her grandmother's bed, Dulcinea and the dogs wedged between them, while she and her grandmother whispered together like conspirators.

"I will want to know everything," said the Duchess. "What the property yields, how fertile its fields are, the crops grown, the profits, the losses. If I should buy other properties. What I should pay for them. You may hate it once you are there, but I expect you to do your work before you come home to me. You see if that property is worth keeping. Visit the other landowners. Look at their fields. Ask their yields. Their problems. Find out where they are buying land. There might be money to be made, and part of whatever I make will be yours. If you are careful, Bab, you could build up another estate."

Barbara's eyes shone suddenly.

"Caesar will handle the travel arrangements for us," the Duchess continued. "You should leave from Gravesend and not London." Barbara did not ask why. She knew. Gravesend was farther from London, closer to the sea. There were those in London who must not know.

"Montrose will need to know," she whispered back. "As my agent of business."

"Can he keep a secret?"

She nodded, beginning to feel greatly excited. She and Harry and Thérèse and Hyacinthe and the dogs had journeyed across France to Italy, and she had loved it, the exhilaration of travel, of motion, of new sights, overcoming even the discomfort.

"Are you certain?" whispered her grandmother.

She nodded her head and then shook it.

"Good," said the Duchess. "At least I am not sending a fool to tend my business."

"A cow!"

Barbara stared at her grandmother. "I am to take a cow?" The Duchess's lips worked stubbornly. "And chickens."

"Surely those things are already there."

"It is my plantation, and you are acting as my agent, and I wish it stocked with Tamworth's finest."

Barbara stared at the stubborn set of her grandmother's face. "But what if I decide the plantation should be sold?"

"It will fetch an even greater price with Tamworth stock on it. And if we do not sell it, we have eliminated the need of your sending for stock."

Barbara stared at her grandmother, wondering for a moment what was in her mind, truly.

"Richard," said the Duchess. She gasped and closed her eyes, and her voice was quavering. "Is that you?"

Barbara turned away. "That will do you no good. I will take the chickens but not the cow."

"You will take the cow. She has mated with my best bull, and if she calves, you will have the best stock in Virginia. Why, we could make a fortune off mating fees alone. You will take the cow."

"Richard," said Barbara, imitating her grandmother down to the quaver in her voice, "she will not take the cow."

Someone burst out laughing. The Duchess turned swiftly in her chair to glare at Tim. He sobered at once.

"Another sound out of you, and I will send you across the sea with her."

"Oh, no, ma'am. Not me. I leave adventure to Lady Devane and Robinson Crusoe."

"You will take the cow," said the Duchess, turning back around.

"Annie," she said later, when Tim had carried her to her room, and Annie was rubbing liniment into her legs. "She looks better. I see it. I do. She always was ripe for an adventure. Do you remember when she made Harry run away with her to Maidstone—"

"Hush," said Annie. "You need to rest."

"Is Thérèse copying the recipes? There are so many. How will we know what she will need over there? There is a great wood of trees there, endless, Annie, and a river as wide as the sea—"

"Hush now."

"Bah!"

"Bah, yourself."

"I will send you to Virginia with Bab if you are rude to me!"

"Bah!"

"Oh, bah, yourself. Bossy old stick."

The letter came from London informing her that Parliament had found Roger guilty of breach of trust as a South Sea director and was fining him a portion of his estate and earnings. There was no cash with which to pay the fines, wrote Montrose, and she must seriously consider Jacombe's recommendation to dismantle Devane House and sell it piece by piece. Part could go toward Parliament and part toward Lord Devane's creditors, who were becoming increasingly insistent. Enclosed were papers that would begin the process of dismantling.

Barbara looked up from the letter. She sat on an old stone wall that separated the woods from the orchards. The apple and plum and cherry trees were full of blossoms, lacy white, edged with pink, their fragrance the sweetest of smells. Bees dove among them drunkenly, so swollen with the nectar of their flowers that they could scarcely fly. She stared once more at the papers she must sign. The dismantling of Devane House—necessary, or she would live under a burden of debt which would crush her forever. Roger. . . . Only the plans would be left, the dead dreams in a wooden box.

On the way back to the house, she gathered all the bluebells she could hold in her arms, and walked into the great hall with them, past her grandmother, who sat by a window in the sun, reading her letters.

The Duchess looked up at her, at her straight back and rigid profile, as she began to arrange bluebells in a bowl.

"Abigail writes me the news. I am sorry."

Barbara was silent, and the Duchess said no more. Abigail had written, in addition to the news about Roger's estate, that Robert had been made first lord of the treasury and chancellor, a victory indeed for a man who had been outside the king's cabinet for three years. A victory that would keep Diana in London, sharing the triumph. Another month, and she would send her granddaughter to Gravesend with Perryman to board a ship sailing to the Americas. Another month, and she would buy her granddaughter time. The only thing that healed one completely . . . time.

May Day, and Tamworth village held its May feast in the churchyard. The young men of the village competed against one another in leaping and vaulting and archery, and they raised a maypole, though Vicar frowned, not quite sure of the church's position on such pagan rites. The girls danced around it, flowers in their hair. Barbara, sitting beside her grandmother—both of them in black—was a severe contrast to the white and scarlet and green of the village maidens' gowns, to the pastels of the flowers woven in their hair. The Duchess had hired a troupe of Morris dancers, and everyone watched, enthralled, as they acted out a garbled version of the legend of Robin Hood, entwined with dancing and singing and the sound of pipes and tabor, and the children cheered for Fool and Hobby Horse, while the maidservants sighed at Maid Marion and dashing Robin Hood.

"I have had a letter from Caesar," said the Duchess.

Barbara looked at her.

"Three weeks," said the Duchess, and Barbara turned back to watch the Morris dancers.

Tony guided his horse through the gates of Devane House and trotted up the circular drive, which did not have its usual allotment of carriages and bystanders assembled to watch the dismantling. I would have fought, Abigail had said. I would have kept them in court for years. The directors were not even allowed counsel, Tony had replied. Bab is fortunate to be given the allowance and dower land and such furnishings and personal items as they are permitting. Is it not strange to you, Abigail had said, how little we hear these days from Tamworth? Is it not strange to you that Barbara does not come to London to oversee? Abigail tapped a finger against her lip. It is not like the Duchess, she said.

He passed men uprooting trees and shrubs in the gardens, and dismounted and walked past workmen going up and down the front stairs, carrying elaborate chimney-pieces and mirrors and marble floor tiles from the house. Inside, workmen were everywhere, some on ladders, carefully prying intricate ceiling moldings from their place, others loosening the expensive, embroidered damask from the walls. Montrose stood in the gallery with a pencil behind each ear, and his wig pushed back, arguing with a foreman.

"No," he was saying. "The chimneypieces in this room were purchased in Italy in 1716. I have the receipts here. You are not to have them."

"I was told to take all the chimneypieces—"

"Well, you were told wrong! Five of them belong to the estate prior to 1719, and I have an order from Parliament in my hand allowing them to Lady Devane—"

"Montrose!"

Tony and Montrose both turned. Diana, looking sleekly plump again in a black gown and a glittering new necklace of rubies, walked in from the bedchamber.

"They are trying to dismantle and take away the bed in there," she said.

"It is on my list! It is on my list. These people. They are like locusts!" And Montrose ran past Diana into the bedchamber.

She looked Tony up and down, and he smiled slowly, shyly, and bowed over her hand. She stared at the top of his blond head.

"Why will you never wear a wig?"

"They are hot."

"Nonsense. Though I must say, your hair becomes you. Where have you been? They are trying to pick this place clean. I swear I should take the time to drag Barbara up here by her hair. Why she is not here, I do not know! It is ridiculous to leave this all to Montrose, though he does his job. He thinks there will be enough to make a good sale, once Parliament takes its part. He thinks we may whittle the debt down to a manageable size within three years, if we do not sell too quickly." Tony smiled at her use of the word "we" but she did not notice. She sighed and walked over to a window. "Look," she said. "They are even digging up the trees."

"So you hear nothing from her?"

"Not one word. Not that I expected to. Well, I can do more without her than I can with her. I leave her to her grief. A year or so at Tamworth will make her easier to manage in the long run." Diana shuddered. "I never could abide Tamworth."

"And do you hear from Grandmama?"

"Yes, but such short letters. Look, Tony, they are taking away the French cabinets."

He came to stand by her, and they watched a crew of workmen staggering under the burden of heavy cabinets, intricate in their layering of different woods, in their delicate carving. A pensive look crossed Diana's face. "This was a beautiful house," she said.

Tony looked around him. Paneling lay stacked in a corner, and all the furniture and paintings were gone, as were the draperies and wall fabric. Workmen were gathered by the fireplace ready to pull away its marble surround, yet still the room retained the outline of something once fine and gracious.

"Yes," he said. "It was beautiful."

"She ought not to have allowed it dismantled!"

"How else will she satisfy Parliament's fines and pay off Roger's debt?"

"I do not know!" Diana said irritably. "But if she had stayed in London as she ought, someone would have helped. The prince. Someone." She glanced up at Tony in a half-challenging way. "She did not even bother to explore all the avenues open to her."

"The avenue of Charles Russel is closed."

Diana stared at him, interested, mocking. "Oh?"

"I will not allow him to hurt my sister."

"And how will you stop him? Or her?"

Tony was silent.

"I want to see her married again," Diana said. "Secure. Name someone who will marry a penniless widow!"

Tony smiled, a slow, shy, unexpectedly attractive smile. "I will."

Diana stared at him, as he walked away, over to Montrose, who was arguing once more with the foreman; he had set a crew of workmen to pull out the marble chimneypieces from the wall.

"I told you that this belongs to the pre-1719 grouping—"

"Montrose," said Tony, "what do you hear from Lady Devane?"

"Nothing," Montrose said, harassed, distracted, looking through his sheaf of papers for the necessary receipt. "She will be at Gravesend most likely—" He broke off.

"Gravesend? Why would she go to Gravesend?"

"Gravesend? Who is in Gravesend?" Diana asked, walking up behind Tony.

"Did I say Gravesend?" said Montrose, his cheeks scarlet; then he laughed nervously. "My mind is on so much. There is an offer for sale of a chimneypiece from a man living in Gravesend. Yes. That is what I was thinking of."

Barbara stood in the courtyard, waiting for her grandmother, who was still in her chamber, resting. Thérèse and Hyacinthe and the dogs were already in the carriage, and Perryman sat beside the coachman. Behind the carriage was a wagon full of the items her grandmother insisted she take to Virginia: spinach seeds, Duke of Tamworth rose cuttings, jars of jam, books on husbandry and farming, the Duchess's only copy of Thomas Tusser's almanac, a miniature of the duke, herb seedlings, bolts of fabric, a small barrel of nails and two hammers, a French table and armchairs, many of Barbara's gowns (a decision the Duchess and Thérèse had made independently, reasoning that once her year of mourning was over, she would have need of them, to impress the colonials if nothing else). There was also a small wooden box packed away, a box filled with sketches and a pair of leather gloves. A widow must be allowed her whims, thought Barbara, as it was placed in the wagon. Her dreams. Even dead dreams were better than no dreams. Thérèse had half of Barbara's jewels sewn in the hem of her gown, and Barbara had the deed to the plantation and her grandmother's letter appointing her agent tucked inside her corset. A cow was tied to the wagon, and from several closed baskets came the nervous, continuous clucking of chickens.

Inside the house, Annie tried to shake the Duchess awake.

"She is leaving. Wake up, your grace. she is leaving. For Virginia."

"Who?" said the Duchess irritably, trying to sit up, trying to see through her lace cap, which had slipped over her eyes. "Who is going to Virginia?"

Annie and Tim exchanged a glance.

"Mistress Barbara—" began Annie, but the Duchess interrupted.

"Mistress Barbara! Why would she do a fool thing like go to—" She stopped. She pulled her lace cap back out of her eyes. "I am old," she said with great dignity. "I forget."

"What you are," said Annie, "is an old pain. If you do not really mean her to go, after all the fuss and secrecy—"

"I mean it! I mean it. I forget why, but I mean it. Move, you old stick, and give me my cane."

"You cannot walk two steps without falling. Tim is here."

"Tim is here," muttered the Duchess. "They treat me like an invalid."

"She is upset by the leaving," Annie whispered to Tim. "She will be impossible."

Tim nodded and leaned down and smiled and gathered the Duchess in his arms.

"Wipe that smile from your face," the Duchess said savagely. "I will not have it."

Downstairs, in the courtyard, Barbara was going from servant to servant; they had gathered to say goodbye to her, not only because she was their favorite but also because they wanted to see with their own eyes someone who was actually crossing the great sea and going to Virginia, wherever that was. It was like an adventure, they whispered among themselves. Like *Robinson Crusoe*.

Tim carried the Duchess outside. She blinked at the sun and motioned for him to put her down, and leaned against her cane, watching Barbara, who was hugging a kitchenmaid. Barbara walked over to her, and the two of them stared at each other.

"You have the miniature?" the Duchess asked.

"Yes."

"See you hang on to it. If you decide on any wildness, you just look at that miniature, and remember who your grandfather was. The finest man I ever knew."

"Yes."

"You have a Bible?"

"Yes."

"Tusser's almanac?"

"Yes. And the seeds and nails and rose cuttings and the hundred-and-one other things you wished me to take. I can always send for whatever I need once I am there."

But it will take weeks and weeks and weeks, months, thought the Duchess, for your letters to arrive. We will be separated by such distance. You are going a world away. Oh, Richard, what have I done? . . .

From the top of the carriage, Perryman said, "It is getting late, ma'am. We must leave."

Barbara smiled suddenly at her grandmother, her grandfather's smile. "Come with me," she said.

For a moment, the Duchess's eyes sparkled. "If I could, I swear I would! If I were ten—no, five—years younger, maybe I would." She swallowed and said, "You just remember who you are."

"I know who I am." Barbara took her in her arms and hugged her. "The granddaughter of the Duchess of Tamworth." Then, to Annie, fiercely, "You better keep her well."

"She is too mean to die," Annie replied.

Barbara stepped back from her grandmother. "I must go." She got into the carriage and shut the door, and the carriage lumbered off, with Barbara and Thérèse and Hyacinthe leaning out the windows, waving. The servants gave a cheer; some of them were crying. The stableboys ran after the carriage, escorting it out. Annie blew her nose fiercely.

"Half-gypsy, that is what she is," she said to herself. "Always was. Always will be."

"I want to go to chapel." The Duchess's voice broke on the word "chapel."

Tim picked her up at once. She was crying. Tears streamed down her face, down its wrinkles, and lost themselves in the lace ruffles of the neck of her bedjacket.

"Never you mind," Tim said to her gently. "I will take you to chapel. Yes, I will. Right now."

Inside the carriage, Barbara wiped her eyes with a handkerchief and blew her nose. "What are we doing?" she said to Thérèse, who laughed and shrugged her shoulders. Barbara leaned out the window. "Stop at Tamworth church," she told the coachman.

At the church, she leapt out and ran quickly through to the chapel. She stood a moment before each memorial tablet, touching the names of her brothers and sisters, standing the longest at Harry's. Then she went to Roger's bust. The wildflowers she had brought yesterday were faded; wildflowers never lasted long. She touched a marble cheek.

"Goodbye," she said. And then she went out of the chapel and down the aisle of the church and out into the waiting carriage.

White was at the appointed place in Gravesend, and he straightened up as the carriage lurched down the cobbled main street, a cow tied to the wagon following behind. He waved his arm. The coachman pulled the carriage up short, and Barbara leaned her head out the window as White walked up to her. From the wagon came a clamorous clucking of chickens. White smiled at the sound of it.

"What have you brought with you?" he said to Barbara. Thérèse leaned out the other window, and the dogs began to bark.

"You would never believe it," she said.

"Well, the ship is delayed, but only for a few days. I have reserved rooms for you at a tavern. Did you know Pocahontas is buried in the parish church here?"

"Who?" Thérèse asked.

"An Indian princess," said Barbara. "From Virginia." She leaned farther out the window and pressed White's hand. "You have been a good friend."

"A well-paid one."

"No one knows?"

"Only Montrose. Speaking of which, I have at least ten papers he insists you must sign before you leave. You have made him a happy man, you know. The settling of Lord Devane's estate will take at least four years, and he is inundated with paper and legal documents and schedules he must keep, and he complains all day and makes lists and has never been more satisfied with himself."

Barbara laughed, and called up to Perryman, "We are going to a tavern. The ship is delayed. You take the wagon onto the ship. It is the *Brinton* under Captain Smith."

While she was talking, White smiled at Thérèse.

"You have made your choice, have you?" he said, the edges of his smile sad.

She nodded and touched the mourning ring suspended on the gold necklace she always wore.

"We are on an adventure," Hyacinthe said behind her.

"Indeed you are," White said.

Two days later, a carriage, driven hard, pulled into the courtyard of the tavern, and the coachman jumped down and opened its door, while the horses stood heaving, spittle at their mouths. Diana, her face grim, stepped down into the courtyard and strode into the tavern. Local men, tradesmen, merchants, a few sailors, stared at her—her beautiful set face, her rubies, her sweeping black gown, her hat with its trailing feathers. The tavernkeeper hurried to her, bowing and smiling.

"Have you a Lady Devane here?" she snapped, before he could open his mouth.

"Why, yes, your ladyship. She leaves today on the—"

Diana seemed to swell in her clothes. "Where is she?"

"In the room just down that corridor, ma'am. May I announce you?"

Diana pushed past him. "I will announce myself."

The door slammed open with such force that it bounced back from the wall, but Diana caught it with one gloved hand. She stared at Barbara, obviously dressed for travel, who was looking at her with a face that held surprise and chagrin and the beginnings of anger. But Diana was past anger. Thérèse, playing solitaire, sat looking at Diana with her hand suspended in midair, and Hyacinthe, sitting beside her, said, "Oh, no."

"Oh, yes," said Diana, closing the door behind her. The dogs, at Hyacinthe's feet, jumped into his lap at the sound of her voice. It was cold and determined and clearly furious. She walked slowly into the middle of the room. No one moved.

"I hear that you are going on a journey." Her voice was like the lash of a whip. Barbara had a sudden memory of the same tone in her mother's voice when she had talked to Harry about Jane, so many years ago. Well, I am not Harry, she thought, and she met her mother's eyes. Thérèse made a sound, but there was a knock on the door, and the tavern-keeper put his head in.

"A message from the *Brinton.* The captain says come. They sail this afternoon—"

"Get out!" Diana shrieked, and the tavernkeeper pulled his head back like a turtle darting back into his shell and shut the door. Hyacinthe's lower lip began to quiver, and the dogs trembled under his hands.

"Thérèse," Barbara said calmly, "take Hyacinthe and the dogs and wait in the carriage."

"You are not going to leave," Diana said, walking toward Barbara. "I am not going to allow it."

"How will you stop me?"

Diana hesitated at the simplicity of her question. Barbara stood up and stepped around her and began to walk toward the door. Diana grabbed her arm, hard, and Barbara pulled away, just as hard, turning quickly, her skirts swirling.

"Fight me," she said. "Because that is what you will have to do to stop me."

Diana was frozen, staring at her. Barbara's hand touched the door handle. Diana ran forward, words tumbling from her mouth.

"You must listen to me. Stop and listen! You are doing a mad thing. You could die in a shipwreck—"

"Or in an overturned carriage, or from smallpox, or I could cut my throat with a razor."

She opened the door. Diana grabbed her arm again.

"You can stay at Tamworth. Forever. I will not interfere in your life. Ever. I swear it. Do not leave. It is the grief. You were besotted about Roger, out of all proportion. It has made you temporarily mad. Wait, Barbara, I beg you. If you still want to go in six months, I will help you. I swear it."

Barbara pulled her arm away. "Goodbye, Mother." She began to walk across the public room of the tavern.

"No!" Diana screamed, running after her, to the interest of those drinking ale in the public room, who had heard most of the quarrel, at least Diana's part.

"No! No! No! Barbara, wait! I beg you."

But Barbara was outside. Diana stood at the entrance to the tavern, and she began to sob. "I cannot believe this," she said, over and over. Barbara walked back to her from the carriage. Thérèse and Hyacinthe hung out the window, their faces taut. And Perryman, atop the carriage, pulled his hat down so that Diana should not recognize him.

"Thank God," Diana said, trying to stop crying, trying to wipe her face, which was a mixture of tears and lead and powder and rouge running down her cheeks and onto her gown.

"A goodbye kiss," Barbara said.

"No," Diana whispered, but Barbara leaned forward and kissed her as Diana grabbed her and held her.

"Do not leave me," Diana begged. "You are all I have! Do not—" But, once more, Barbara pulled away, walked back to the carriage and climbed inside.

"No!" Diana screamed, stamping her feet, the veins standing out in her neck, several of the tavern customers spilling their ale at the loudness and ferocity of her scream. The carriage lurched away. Diana bent over with sobs, and the tavernkeeper helper her to a chair.

"My daughter," she wept into a napkin. She could not stop crying. "Fool!" she screamed, slamming her fist into the table. People were paying now, leaving as fast as they could. She broke into fresh sobs. "She is a fool!" she screamed to the room at large. "I do not even know where Virginia is."

Aboard the ship, they made their way to the small quarterdeck reserved for the ship's passengers and for the livestock. Above them, the first mate was shouting orders, as the captain stood by the great wheel, his arms folded. The cow, tied down, lowed at the sight of them, and Thérèse petted her nose. Hyacinthe stared at the sailors, his eyes shining, as they climbed the masts and rigging in their bare feet, as nimble as if they were climbing stairs. He ran over to the side and pointed down, and Barbara joined him. Small boats on each side of the ship, connected to it with great lengths of thick rope, were preparing to row the ship out into the river's tide. Other passengers, two men and a woman, sat on crates and talked among themselves. The ship began to move, almost imperceptibly, as the men in the small boats bent and heaved, their arms moving back and forth in time with the oars. On the shore, Perryman waved his hat, and they waved back to him. They moved out into the river, and as if by magic, at a shout from the first mate, the sails came rumbling down, with creaks and groans and loud hisses, as the sailors scurried to tie them down, and then suddenly, they filled with wind, and the ship gave a great heave, as it caught in the tide, and Barbara staggered and fell back against the cow, who lowed again, and Thérèse laughed, and Hyacinthe grabbed the basket which held the dogs and said, "We are at sea!"

"We are at river," Thérèse corrected. Then she crossed herself.

"Harry would have loved this," Barbara said, her eyes shining as bright as Hyacinthe's. She stared at the shore of England, of all she knew and was familiar with. Goodbye, Grandmama. Goodbye, Roger. Keep thy heart with all diligence, she thought, for out of it are the issues of life.

Several hours later, a solitary horseman rode into the tavern courtyard and dismounted. He handed his tired horse to a groom, walked inside and spoke a few moments with the tavernkeeper, who told him that yes, a Lady Devane had been staying here, but that she had sailed early this afternoon. For Virginia, on a ship called the *Brinton*, under Captain Smith. The man, who was tall and wore his blond hair long and pulled back, and tied with a ribbon, rubbed his eyes a moment at the tavernkeeper's news. Another lady came looking for the same person, the tavernkeeper informed him, and she raised quite a rumpus. She was resting now in a private room.

Tony knocked on the door, entered, and pulled a chair to the bed where Diana lay, one arm over her face. She pulled her arm back long enough to see who it was, and long enough for Tony to take in her red, swollen face, without its rouge now.

"Why did you not tell me?"

Diana gave a mocking laugh. "What could you have done?" She began to cry.

"I could have stopped her."

Diana wiped her eyes. "I tried. God knows I tried. She would not listen. Now, I am all alone." She sobbed into her hands. "Tell the tavernkeeper I will pay for the glasses I broke. And the chair."

"I will take you to Tamworth," Tony said. He rubbed his eyes with his hand again, his face suddenly tired, and older looking.

"Tamworth!"

Diana sat up straight in the bed, her hair falling all about her shoulders. "You know whose idea this is, do you not!"

Tony stared at her, his face taut and disbelieving.

"Yes! No one else's. I know her." Her face crumpled again. "My daughter. She has sent my daughter away from me. You just take me to Tamworth, Tony Saylor. I have a thing or two I wish to say to my mother. That old witch. I hate her!" Diana kicked her feet against the bed and screamed. "I hate her!"

At the bar, the tavernkeeper heard her cries, and he crossed himself quickly. "Not again," he said, and sure enough, there came to his ears the sound of something thudding, like a chair being thrown against a wall. He picked up the stub of a pencil and added another sum to those already listed.

Diana muttered and cried and swore against her mother throughout the journey to Tamworth. Tony, on the other hand, was almost completely silent, but his face grew steadily more grim and hard. When the carriage drove down the avenue of the limes, the sun was shining in dapples through their spread of leaves, and the corn was young and green in the fields, and the long grass was being scythed for hay. The carriage lurched to a stop, and Diana stepped down into the gravel of the courtyard, Tony following. She pulled hard, furiously, on the door pull, and the two of them could hear the bells jangling in the house. Perryman opened the door, and Diana swept past him.

"Where is my mother?"

"Lady Diana," stammered Perryman.

"Where is she, Perryman? It will do you no good to lie. I know she is here. Tell me, now, or I will scream this house down—"

The Duchess sat on the terrace, in the June sun, where she could see and smell her roses, glorious in their fat, lush blooming. She felt old and tired, and she missed Barbara, so that now there was a new constant ache added to all her other aches. And even though she continued to pray hard, she was not sure that she had done the right thing. Richard gave her no answers; neither did God. Dulcinea lay sluggishly in her lap; she carried kittens, her first. I, however, thought the Duchess, stroking her cat's back, have no kittens.

"You interfering, self-righteous old witch."

The Duchess started and turned. Diana stood in the door way that opened to the terrace from the library. Tim, sitting on the terrace wall, stood up at Diana's words and stepped forward, but the Duchess motioned him still with a wave of her hand. She faced Diana, waiting, as she had been waiting since Barbara left, for the inevitable.

"You sent her away! I know you did! You thought of no one but yourself. You are self-righteous and meddling, and wrong! Do you hear me, Mother? Wrong!"

The Duchess flinched.

"She could *die*," Diana was saying, her words flying like arrows from her mouth, across the terrace, into the Duchess's heart. All words she had thought herself. "Either on the way, or once there. It is across the sea! How could you do it!" Tim stood still, blinking rapidly, uncertain of what to do.

Behind Diana, the Duchess saw Tony, tall in the shadow of the doorway. She made a sudden, agitated movement at the expression on his face. She turned around to face her roses again, and her hands held on tightly to Dulcinea's fur, so tightly that Dulcinea mewed in complaint and leapt lithely from her lap to the terrace wall and down into the gardens.

The Duchess's mouth worked. Deserted by all. Annie was at Ladybeth. Perryman was a weak fool. "I did what I thought best—" she began stubbornly.

"What you thought best!" Diana spat. "You are mad! A candidate for Bedlam! I will have you committed! I swear I will! She has not gone across to the next county. She is cross- ing the sea in a tiny, wooden ship!" Diana's face was ugly, contorted, beyond anger. "I will never forgive you for this! Not for as long as I live!"

The Duchess kept her back turned. Her daughter's skirts hissed as she walked away from her. Out of the corner of her eye, the Duchess saw Tony, who had not walked away with Diana, who had stayed. He stood next to her chair now, and she glanced up at his face quickly, and then away just as quickly, her heart beating so fast that she thought it would kill her. Richard, thought the Duchess, over the hurting of her heart. Richard.

Tony knelt down beside her. His blue-gray eyes looked at her, angry, amazed, and she thought, I do not know him now. The boy is gone. He has become a man, and I do not know this man.

"I love her," he said deliberately, his words striking her like blows.

Tim's hands clenched and unclenched as he watched the Duchess's face, and he wiped his sweating face with his hand.

"All Aunt Diana said is true. You are a meddling, self-righteous, interfering old woman—"

A sob broke from the Duchess. She put her hands up to her eyes.

"William," she said. "Please."

"No," said Tony, standing up, towering over her, his face hard and contemptuous. "Not William, but Tony. Your bumbling, stupid Tony. You thought I was not good enough for her. But I am."

Tears rolled down the Duchess's cheeks. "I want to go to chapel," she said in a faint voice. Tim took a step toward her, but Tony stopped him with a look.

"Yes," he said. "You go to chapel, and you pray for forgiveness. I hope you receive it from God, Grandmama, because you will never receive it from me."

"Ah-h-h-h," the Duchess cried, leaning over and bowing her head, rocking with grief, as Tony walked away. Tim picked her up, his own chin trembling. She was tiny in his arms, like a child.

"I-I did it for the best," she whispered. "I did. I did."

"Hush, now," Tim said, crying a little himself, walking down the terrace steps with her, determined to get her away from these people; but then someone touched his shoulder. He turned, and the young Duke of Tamworth stood before him, his face still angry, but there was something else in it, too. Compassion? Love? Tim did not know.

"Give her to me."

Tim did not move.

"For God's sake! She is my grandmother! Give her to me!" Gingerly, Tim did so. The Duchess was sobbing so hard that her body was shaking. She clutched the lapels of Tony's coat. "T-Tony," she sobbed. "Oh, T-Tony. Do not h-hate me."

"Hush," Tony said, and though his face was still hard, Tim let out the breath he had been holding.

"Hush, Grandmama. You are going to make yourself ill. I will take you to chapel."

Tim watched the young duke carry his grandmother down the rest of the steps. He found that he was weak in the knees and that he had to sit down. She was still crying, but not as hard. Tim wiped his own eyes and blew his nose. The young duke carried her down the gravel path, his heels crunching against the stones, but as he passed the rose garden, he stopped, and, shifting his grandmother's weight, picked a rose from the garden, a dark, lush, red rose with many petals, and gave it to her, and the Duchess held it to her breast and cried as if her heart were broken. It was a Duke of Tamworth rose. But Tim could not know that. Only Tony and the Duchess did.

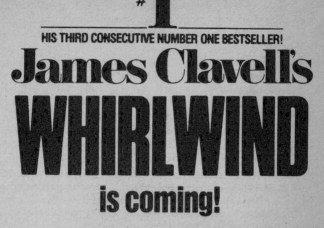